King Alejandro

THE RETURN OF HER COLD-HEARTED ALPHA

Book 5 of The Alpha Series

MOONLIGHT MUSE

King Alejandro

THE RETURN OF HER COLD-HEARTED ALPHA

To my amazing readers:

Thank you for sticking by me, through the cliff-hangers, the pain, and the sorrow. I won't apologise for the enjoyment I get when I play with those emotions! I hope this book brings you plenty of joy, happiness and of course tears!

A Message

KIARA

The smell of sizzling barbeque food mixed with the fresh earth and flowers from outside the open window swirled around me and intertwined with the scents of my loved ones. Upbeat music was playing, and the warmth of the summer sun bathed my holiday bedroom in a pleasant glow.

"Skyla, stop it!" My son, Dante's, frustrated voice reached me.

"Make me, dumb dumb!" His younger sister, Skyla, snarkily replied.

I smiled. The two often clashed.

I shook my head, turning back to the mirror and adjusting the top of my dress over my boobs. *I swear this dress wasn't this tight when I bought it... or was it?* I wasn't sure, but with Alejandro, my deliciously, dangerously, sexy and hot mate, telling me it had looked perfect on me, no wonder I didn't pay attention. I smoothed the creases in the satin dress, doing a slow turn and examining my reflection. The fuchsia pink satin of my mini dress hugged my figure like a glove, emphasising my ample breasts, narrow waist, curvy hips, and large, perky ass. I smiled in satisfaction, adding a few delicate pieces of jewellery to finish my look.

I ruffled my light sandy brown hair that I had curled loosely, just as a familiar scent hit me; a deep, seductive, woody scent with the intoxicating underlayer of fragranced musk. My heart raced as I turned to look at the man who had entered; my king, my mate, my Alejandro...

His dark piercing eyes ran over me, flashing a blazing red as they lingered on my boobs, making my core clench as it always did whenever his gaze fell upon me.

He wore a white shirt that strained over his muscular body so tightly that the outlines of his nipple piercings were visible, with the sleeves rolled up. He had it paired with black pants and boots. Tattoos covered his arms, neck, and parts of his hands and peeked out on his chest from the open buttons of his shirt. His regular chains around his neck remained, and his dangly earring in his right ear flashed as the light caught it. His black hair, which was short on the back and sides with the top styled back, only added to how lethally good he looked right then.

"If beauty could fucking kill, I'd be dead right now," his deep, seductive voice drawled, making a whisper of pleasure wash over me as he made his way towards me. The power and arrogance in his every step exuded dominance and his rank. His hands grabbed my hips, pulling me against his firm body, making me gasp as the intense sparks sizzled through me. "It's been nine fucking years we've been together, but every fucking time I see you, it feels like it's for the first fucking time…" I raised an eyebrow.

"Then kiss me like it's the first damn time," I whispered seductively, locking my arms around his neck as my long nails scraped down his skin.

"With fucking pleasure…"

In a flash, I was slammed against the wall next to the vanity table, making me gasp. His body was moulded against mine. His lips came crashing against mine in a hot, sizzling kiss that sent sparks exploding within me and pleasure straight to my core, making me clench my thighs together as I kissed him back with equal pleasure and passion. His hand ran up my thigh, the other squeezing my ass, and I felt him throb against me, groaning into my mouth as he dominated me completely.

No matter how strong I was, in his arms, I was helpless, and I loved it. I loved the way he conquered me, the way he consumed me, the way he kissed me… I moaned helplessly, unable to fight the pleasure that threatened to drown me.

"Fuck, Amore Mio…" he growled, pulling away and breathing hard. His eyes flickered from red to black as he tried to control his emotions.

"We should go outside before the kids and everyone else realise that we are taking far too long…" I whispered, running my hand down his chiselled abs, loving the way they felt through the fabric of his shirt, before playing with his belt.

"Oh, yeah? Keep at that, and I'm tearing this fucking dress right off you and fucking you right here. I won't care who fucking hears or not."

My stomach fluttered, and as much as that sounded appealing, I knew we had to head outside. Today was our twin baby girls' sixth birthday party. Some of our closest family and friends were waiting right outside, too.

"I better stop then, but tonight I think I want you to do just that," I murmured sensually, tiptoeing and kissing his jaw. At five-feet-five-inches, even in heels, I didn't quite match his six-foot-four frame.

"Without a fucking doubt."

He squeezed my ass, his other hand wrapping around my neck as he kissed me once more, squeezing my throat slightly and cutting off my air supply for a moment. Goddess, I loved this man...

We stepped out into the sun, and I scanned the beautiful set-up in bright pink, white and gold. We were at a family-owned villa not far from both our pack territory and Alejandro's nephew, Rayhan's, pack territory. Alejandro was the King and the Alpha of the Night Walkers Pack, whilst his nephew was the Alpha of the Black Storm Pack.

Unlike the rest of us, Alejandro was a Lycan, the only one of his kind. He had created a council and brought all the packs under him, creating peace and law. He had been thirty-four when I found out he was my mate. I had been only eighteen myself. Despite our sixteen-year age gap, we were perfect for one another.

Back then, he had been consumed by his darkness, considering himself nothing more than a monster whose only job was to protect our kind. But now... nine years later, we were together with a family of our own. Our eldest, Dante, was eight years old. Two years later, we had Skyla and Kataleya. It was their sixth birthday, and both of my princesses were dressed in matching white lace dresses with a bright pink sash, with pink bows in their hair.

"Mama, Skyla was being annoying, as usual," Dante stated, frowning as he came over to me, shoving his hands into the pockets of his black jeans. Like his father, he was wearing a white shirt with his sleeves rolled up. His black hair was styled messily, and his eyes, which were as red as the day he was born, were filled with annoyance.

"What the fuck did she do?" Alejandro asked.

"She keeps sprinkling the stupid glitter poppers on me," he almost growled.

"I'll tell her off, but it is her birthday. Won't you let her have a little fun?" I proposed gently, crouching down and brushing a strand of his hair from his face. He rolled his eyes in frustration.

"Girls." I chuckled lightly as he ran off towards one of the other children.

"Well, that fucking worked," Alejandro remarked as we walked over to the other adults.

We had kept it small, only inviting our close friends and family, but even then, there were plenty of little ones running around. My brother, Liam Westwood, the Alpha of the Blood Moon, had quintuplets; five boys: Jayce, Theo, Ares, Carter, and Renji, who were two and a half years old. Then, there was my sister, Azura, who was eight years old, like Dante, and she was the leader of the Westwood Quintuplets. She was fiercely protective of them and would let them get up to whatever they wanted. There was also Artemis, my friend, Alpha Damon's, daughter, who was two and a half years old, and their one-year-old son, Asher, Rayhan's son, Ahren, who was almost two, and his one-year-old daughter, Sienna, and finally, Raihana's son, Tatum, who had turned two a few weeks ago. Raihana was Alejandro's niece.

Plenty of kids, but I loved it.

"Baby, no!" Raihana scolded Tatum as he almost put his hand into the cake. "I swear, these kids."

"You were a fucking handful, too," Alejandro drawled mockingly.

"Uncle! Seriously, all I seem to do is run after him."

"Good exercise."

"I'm sure she gets enough of a workout," Chris, her mate, remarked with a cocky smirk.

"I'll pretend I didn't fucking hear that," Alejandro replied coldly.

"Pups don't just get made by themselves," Chris shot back.

"Okay, put aside the male testosterone," Raihana warned them, kissing Chris on the cheek before pouting at Alejandro. "I'm not a baby, Uncle."

"I didn't say you fucking were."

"Food's done!" Dad called.

I smiled warmly at him. Although he was just six years older than my mate, at forty-eight, he looked no older than his mid-thirties. I guess, being a werewolf, our genes help in many ways.

"Kiara, where are the sauces?" Mom asked me, drawing me out of my thoughts.

"Oh, I think I left them inside." I brushed my hair back.

"Shall I grab them?" Delsanra, Rayhan's mate, asked me. I shook my head.

"I'll go get them. Just keep an eye on the kiddies!"

I ran towards the lodge, feeling Alejandro's intense gaze on me. I turned, looking at him over my shoulder, and he winked at me from where he stood with Rayhan and Damon.

I love how that ass of yours jiggles, but I love it even more when I'm the one who's working it.

My heart skipped a beat, and I teasingly licked my lips before disappearing inside, unable to wipe the smile from my lips. *Goddess, I can never get enough of him.* I hurried to the kitchen, about to grab the tray of sauces I had prepared earlier when I froze. An uneasy feeling suddenly filled me, and I felt the hair at the back of my neck stand on edge. My heart thundered as I spun around, looking through the archway that led back into the hallway. Leaving the tray, I walked out, my eyes blazing a dazzling purple as I scanned the hall.

Silence.

The only sound I could hear was laughter and the hustle and bustle of the party outside. My wolf was restless, and the urge to follow my instincts overtook me, leading me down the hall and up the stairs to the first floor. The wooden floorboards creaked under my heels. I walked down the hall, paying attention to everything, including the dust particles that hung in the air, the rays of light that shone through the windows, and the sound of my heart beating like the drums of war as I walked down towards the twins' bedroom. I pushed the door open slowly and scanned the room sharply.

The sun had lit the room aglow. The pale blue walls, bright white curtains, and bedding were all in pristine condition. Nothing.

I exhaled, that dark feeling of foreboding vanishing, and I shook my head. That was weird.

I was about to leave the room when I saw it: a black piece of paper lying in the centre of the double bed. Frowning, I crossed the room and stared down at it. I couldn't smell anything strange about it, yet the moment my fingers touched it, I felt a burst of power swirl around me. Whatever the paper was, it contained powerful magic. My eyes fell on the words that were written in the centre of the paper. They seemed to almost burn orange against the black paper.

PAY THE DEBT BY THE BLOOD OF THE BEAST AND YIELD TO THE CRIMSON KING.

What did that even mean? Suddenly the paper caught fire, and I gasped, letting go of it and stepping back as it turned to ash before vanishing completely, leaving me completely derailed.

Someone had placed that there… but how? With so many Alphas and even witches gathered outside, how had no one sensed it? I looked out at the clouds that were gathering in the skies, and that unsettling feeling that had settled within me returned with a vengeance. I turned to hurry downstairs when, suddenly, flames sprang up all around me, making my heart thunder.

"Alejandro!" I shouted, panic filling me as the heat of the fire began to lick at my skin. "Alejandro!"

Nothing.

I tried to mind-link him, but it only made me dizzy.

The screams of the children filled the air, and I spun around, trying to run to the window when another blast of flames made the floor give way. I stumbled back, trying to find a way out. Which way was the door?

I couldn't breathe. The smoke was becoming suffocating, and the lack of oxygen was weakening me. I ran blindly, screaming as the fire burned my skin before I finally burst through the door and into the hall. Even here, everything was on fire. A part of the ceiling caved in, and I jumped out of the way just in time.

"Dante! Kat! Sky! Mom!"

No one was answering!

What was going on?

I needed to find Alejandro! Or anyone!

"Alejandro! Liam! Delsanra!"

I stumbled, realising I was near the stairs and ran down them as fast as I could, trying to summon my aura to shield me, but it wasn't working. I was far too weak.

My eyes were on the front door, and the fear of where everyone was consumed me. I stumbled through the doors and froze as I stared at the blood bath before me. The entire forest surrounding the villa was on fire, destroyed as if the fire had been ongoing for hours, yet the most horrifying thing was the bodies of my loved ones that were strewn across the grounds; charred, lifeless, but still clearly recognisable as to whom was who. My heart stopped for a moment as the sheer terror of what had happened consumed me.

No... My entire body shook as I looked around in horror at the bodies of all the pups.

No... Alejandro, please, this can't be happening.

My eyes stung with tears as I searched for him, panicking. I spotted him lying not far from where I stood and ran down the stone steps, falling to my knees near him and turning his burnt body onto his back. Summoning my healing, I tried to heal the burns that covered him.

There was no heartbeat...

No! Fuck!

"Alejandro!"

Nothing.

He was... dead...

His Concern

ALEJANDRO

"KATALEYA, HOW OLD ARE you now?" Azura questioned Kataleya, hands on her hips as she did.

I knew that the little devil was trying to test her. She fucking acted like she was eighteen or some shit like that. She was a dangerous one. Kataleya blinked and held up six fingers.

That's my fucking pup.

"Good girl," Azura replied with an approving nod and went off to fuss over one of those Westwood pups. I may see them often enough, but they all fucking looked the same. Well, maybe they didn't, but to me, they did. Not my fault that there was an entire fucking army of them.

"Kia's taking her time," Liam remarked, glancing towards the villa as he picked up one of his little fuckers.

"I'll go fucking take a look."

I took a final drag on my cigarette before tossing it to the ground and making sure I snuffed it out with my boot. I walked towards the house, almost fucking stepping on one of those roach-sized pups. *How the fuck are they all over the place?*

I followed her scent, frowning as I realised she was upstairs, but what got me worried was the speed of her heartbeat. It was far too fast for my liking. In a flash, I was up the stairs. My heart was racing with worry the moment I saw her on the floor in the girl's bedroom.

"Kiara! Kiara!" I lifted her into my arms, tapping her face. Fuck, what the hell happened? "Come on, wake up!" Her eyes flew open, blazing purple, and she sucked in a breath as if she had been deprived of oxygen.

"Fuck, Amore Mio…" I hugged her tightly, my voice hoarse and my heart thudding with relief as I held her close, stroking her back. "I got you."

"Al…" she whispered, grabbing my shirt, her heart beating erratically as she looked around and then up at me. The sound of the kids screaming and laughing from outside reached us, and she exhaled, slumping in my arms with clear relief. "Thank the goddess… you're all okay," she murmured, her lips brushing my neck before she showered my neck with quick kisses, sending rivets of sparks through me.

"Yeah, we're fucking okay, but what about you? What happened?" She looked around the room and the ground as if searching for something.

"I… there was a… a note."

Her eyes looked haunted as she looked around the room. I kissed her lips softly, my hand twisting in her hair and stroking her waist, wanting her to know she was going to be fucking okay.

"It's okay, everything is fucking all right. Relax." I reassured her before looking around to see what note she meant. "Where's the note?" She shook her head, looking confused, and I wondered if last night's fucking sexathon had fucking drained her out.

"I…" She placed a hand on her glossy hair and sighed, biting those luscious lips of hers before she shook her head in defeat.

"Never mind. We'll deal with this shit later; shall we go outside?" I asked, stroking her thigh.

She nodded, looking into my eyes, and I felt my stomach twist. The look of fear that filled her soft blue-rimmed soft green eyes was one I hadn't seen in years…

Whatever the fuck happened was serious, and I was definitely going to ask her later. For the moment, I'd get the men to scour the area. I stood up, lifting her to her feet, and wrapped my arms around her tightly, never wanting to let her go. If there was one thing I fucking hated above everything else, it was seeing my queen in any kind of pain. I kissed her neck and shoulder sensually, my hand massaging her back comfortingly until her heartbeat steadied.

"I love you, my sexy beast." She looked up at me, her eyes holding so many emotions, and I frowned. Whatever the fuck happened had shaken her.

"And I fucking love you, Amore Mio," I replied, gripping her chin before kissing her passionately, only breaking away when she gasped for air. "We'll talk later, all right?" She nodded, exhaling and giving me a tight hug before we returned to the garden after grabbing the sauces.

"Are you okay, Kiara?" Scarlett, Kiara's mother, asked her.

"Yeah, perfectly," Kiara replied, blushing lightly under everyone's gaze. My nympho always looked fucking hot, but I fucking swear, with each passing year, she seemed to somehow become even fucking hotter…

"Right, everyone, sit down!" Raven, Kiara's brother's mate and also Kiara's best friend, called out. She was probably the smallest one there; I was sure Dante was her fucking height already. No idea how the fuck she'd had five pups at once. She had looked a fucking sight.

"Is the Alpha council still on next month despite Elder Allen's health?" Rayhan asked me as he took the seat opposite.

"Yeah, we can't really delay it. The winds are changing. It's fucking needed."

I glanced over at Elijah and saw his frown deepening. There was something afoot. After years of living in fucking peace, I could feel it in the air. Something was coming… but I didn't know what…

"Do you boys really need to discuss work?" Maria, Rayhan's mother, scolded.

"Blame him, I didn't do anything," I replied coldly.

My brother, Rafael Rossi, died five years ago protecting Maria, his mate, and Delsanra… it was a death I wouldn't ever get over. It was taking its toll on Maria, too. With each passing year, she got weaker, slimmer, and more exhausted, as if simply living was becoming harder for her. Although she had kept her sanity, with our kids serving as a fucking distraction for her, it still wasn't enough. I didn't want her to lose herself, but when you were mated to a powerful Alpha, the parting was even fucking harder…

"Alejandro?" Maria's voice brought me out of my fucking thoughts, and I raised an eyebrow.

"Yeah?"

"Are you okay?" She asked, concern clear in her grey eyes. I smirked.

"One hundred fucking percent," I replied. She smiled slightly, giving me a nod. Once upon a time, we couldn't stand each other. *I'm sure Raf's fucking proud of our bond now.*

"Daddy, may I sit next to you?" Kataleya asked softly. Her large dark eyes were the same colour as mine yet were filled with a warmth mine lacked.

"Sure thing."

My youngest pup, I swear, despite how fucking crude my language was, that angel was the politest, fucking sweetest thing on the damn planet, and sometimes I felt she was far too pure for this fucking world. Unlike her elder twin and brother, her special ability was completely different from theirs. She smelled of something soft and sweet, yet you could only smell it when you were around her. You wouldn't sense her coming or be able to track her scent, which could become fucking worrying at times in case she wandered off.

Kiara sat down on my other side, kissing my lips softly, and I was fucking relieved. She seemed a little better again.

"After eating, I can't wait to cut the cake," Skyla stated. She was the elder of the twins and I swore she was fucking Lucifer incarnate at times.

"Once you finish your food properly," Scarlett told her granddaughter.

Scarlett was only three years older than me, yet her daughter was my mate. It was fucking fun when that shit came out in the open. Who would have thought…

Skyla's sharp green eyes turned to Kiara.

"Can I use the big knife to cut the cake?" She asked, her eyes sparkling.

"Not the big one. Now, eat your food," Kiara replied, shaking her head. Skyla pouted with displeasure, and I smirked.

You ain't getting away with shit when your mama's around, pup.

Kiara's hand found mine, and she gave it a squeeze, almost as if she was reassuring herself.

We'll figure out the note later, but whatever it was, don't worry about it. I will always fucking protect you and the kids, I said through the link, letting my confidence and reassurance flow through the bond.

She gave me one of those beautiful smiles of hers and nodded, and I knew she was going to be okay. I just hoped that whatever it was, it was no big deal…

Cake & Flirting

KIARA

"TIME TO CUT THE cake!" Mom called, making both Skyla and Kataleya turn in excitement. I smiled. The kids had just spent the last hour playing games, and I thought they were ready for some dessert.

"Oh, I can't wait!" Skyla exclaimed, skipping over to the cake and pulling her sister along with her. Alejandro picked both up, making them giggle when he kissed their cheeks.

"Daddy's beard is poky," Kataleya giggled cutely, patting her dad's cheek before kissing him.

"Yeah, well, I ain't going to have a fucking babyface, now, am I?" Alejandro smirked, nudging his cheek against her own, making her giggle.

"Where's the knife?" Skyla asked. That girl and her love for weapons!

"Here. Now be careful, okay?" I warned her, passing her the knife and placing Kataleya's hand on top of her sister's as everyone began singing happy birthday. I kept my hand on top of the girls, guiding it to the cake and helping them slice it before I took the cake and fed them both a piece each, kissing them after I did so. "Happy birthday, my angels," I whispered, before my eyes met Alejandro's. He leaned forward, kissing me softly before he turned to the girls in his arms.

"Now, how about you two feed me some cake? Let's see if it at least tastes any better than it fucking looks."

"Daddy! It's pretty! It's a unicorn cake!" Skyla scolded.

"Yeah, we're fucking werewolves. Why would you want a cake of an animal that doesn't exist and one that looks weird as fuck?" Alejandro remarked, allowing them to feed him cake.

"All children would want that cake," Delsanra added.

"Guys, I wouldn't mind a cake like that!" Raihana added.

"Actually, I wouldn't want a cake like that, but then again, I'm not a kid. Right, Del?" Dante asked Delsanra, giving her a charming smirk.

I shook my head. Ever since the first time he saw the white-haired beauty, he had developed an infatuation with her, and despite getting older, that didn't seem to have vanished - much to the irritation of his cousin Rayhan.

Delsanra was a hybrid witch-demon, and, unlike the rest of us who saw her in her human form, Dante saw her demon form continuously; a form that was so dangerously beautiful, that any unmated wolf wouldn't be able to deny her beauty when she shifted.

"Right, my churro," Delsanra replied, squeezing his cheeks.

He pouted, tugging away, despite the blush on his cheek. Rayhan frowned, pulling Delsanra into his arms and making a few of the others chuckle. It was an ongoing thing with them, but I did hope Dante got over it.

I sliced the rest of the cake, passing everyone a plate, and was just about to put a slice of the chocolate cake onto one more plate for Alejandro when his strong arms wrapped around me from behind.

"Not going to feed me, Amore Mio?" His deep seductive voice sent shivers of pleasure through me as his hand caressed my stomach, making a jolt of pleasure go through me.

"Won't you feed me?" I countered with a pout as I broke a piece of the cake with my fingers, turning in his arms and resisting the urge to sigh as I brushed against the bulge in his pants.

"No, I'd rather fill you up later with something else..." He winked at me before taking hold of my hand and taking the cake from my fingertips.

Dad cleared his throat, shooting him a glare, and I giggled. Nine years together and despite Dad himself being open with PDA, Alejandro's no filter mouth was a bit too much for him. I loved it. I liked how dirty my man got. I bit my lip, my stomach knotting as he slowly licked my fingers, not giving a care for Dad's intense glare of disapproval.

You really do like to tease him, I mind-linked him with amusement.

I fucking do, I won't deny that, he replied. **But I also want to fuck you day in and day fucking out. Not my fault he has an issue with that.**

I kissed his lips. The taste of chocolate cake lingered in his mouth, and I sighed. Perhaps that letter was just… I didn't know, but whatever it was, everything seemed okay. Everyone was happy…

I pushed the feeling of unease away, but even then, I knew I couldn't ignore that someone had placed it there… or it had been done by magic. Either way, I needed to tell Alejandro. I opened my mouth, but once again I felt blank, unable to form the letters. The more I thought about it, the more the words became jumbled. Just then, Dad and Mom came over, making me give up on my futile attempt.

"So, Marcel didn't come again?" Dad asked quietly, his eyes on Mom before he looked at us.

I frowned slightly, looking up at Alejandro with concern. Marcel was Alejandro's other brother; however, due to a complicated past, his son, Leo, who had turned seventeen, had begun to hate the rest of the family. Especially his cousin Rayhan…

"No. I don't think we'll be seeing him on any future occasion," Alejandro said coldly, and although his face was emotionless, it was something that caused him enough worry and concern. Despite how cold and uncaring he often looked or may appear, he was one of the most attentive and loving people I knew. I placed a hand on his chest, and he looked down at me, giving me a cold smirk that told me he was fine.

"He'll come around," Dad said quietly.

"I'm not going to fucking count on it, but I'll keep trying," Alejandro replied, taking out a cigarette and lighting it.

❦

Night blanketed the woods, and everyone had left. I had just put the girls to bed and walked over to the window, satisfied to see that patrol was posted right outside.

Breathe, Kia, it's nothing… But then why couldn't I even speak about the letter? Something was up…

I glanced at the sleeping girls on the bed before I left the room, closing the door silently behind me when someone suddenly grabbed my arms and spun me around, my back slamming against a hard chest. It took me a fraction of a second before the sparks that coursed through me gave away who my attacker was.

"It's rude to manhandle people, Mr Rossi," I scolded with a pout.

"It's a fucking crime to look so fucking sexy, too, Mrs Rossi," he growled back, making me giggle breathlessly.

"Oh yeah? How will you punish me for my crime then?" I challenged him seductively, turning my head to stare up at him. I didn't miss how his eyes flashed as he dragged his gaze away from my breasts.

"How about I fucking show you?" I smiled. The letter flashed in my mind, and I glanced back at the girls' bedroom. "You're still worried... I've had the men do a thorough search of the area. You need to relax." He kissed my neck softly, and I closed my eyes, leaning into his hold.

"Maybe..." I breathed. My core clenched in anticipation.

"Allow me to help..." he whispered huskily.

His hands grabbed my boobs as he squeezed them, his lips attacking my neck with sensual, illicit kisses that sent sparks of pleasure erupting through me. He lifted me up bridal style and carried me swiftly down the hall to our room, kicking the door shut behind us and locking it before he walked over to the bed and dropped me onto it unceremoniously.

I gasped, my breasts bouncing. That sexy, cocky smirk on his lips told me he was about to fuck me the way I liked best: Alejandro style. I bit my lip, the burning desire of want pooling in my core. I could smell my arousal perfuming the air, and from the way his eyes glowed red, I knew it was getting to him, too.

"You are already wet, and I haven't even punished you," he remarked arrogantly as he leaned over me, pinning my wrists to the bed.

I let my mental barrier down, letting him know exactly how much I wanted him. How I wanted to take his cock in my mouth and milk him until he had nothing left to offer.

"Keep going with those fucking dirty thoughts, and I'll be fucking you until you black out, Amore Mio," he growled threateningly, gazing down at my body. The look of pure animalistic hunger on his handsome face only made me crave him even more.

"Punish me, Alpha," I moaned, reaching up to kiss him. One of his hands wrapped around my throat, pinning me to the bed, and he smirked.

"Not so fast."

His tongue traced my lips, making my core throb, but he didn't kiss me, simply moving away and placing rough, sensual kisses down my jaw before he sat back, releasing my hands and yanking my dress down from my breasts. His eyes darkened with approval as he admired my boobs.

"Fuck, you're divine..." he growled before ripping my dress off completely. The fabric chafed my skin as he left me in nothing but my tiny nude thong. He delivered a sharp tap to my breasts, pinching my nipple and making me whimper.

"Fuck, Al..." I whimpered. He squeezed my breast, his mouth taking the other nipple into his mouth and sucking hard. "Goddess..."

Pleasure coursed through me, accompanied by that sting of pain that only added to how good it felt. He went lower, his tongue running along my under-boob tattoo before he bit into my waist, sucking hard. His other hand continued to play with my nipple, twisting it and making me whimper. The closer he got to my lower regions the wetter I became, yet he took his time devouring every inch of my body, save my pussy.

"Fuck, don't tease me, Alejandro," I moaned as he ran his tongue sensually along my inner thighs.

"This is a punishment, remember?" He mocked huskily.

Fuck... I moaned, parting my legs only for him to run his finger along the centre of my damp panties. I cried out at the light touch that was only making my body scream for more.

"Look how fucking wet you are..." he growled, tugging on my thong.

"I'm wet for you, baby. Fuck me," I whimpered.

But he wouldn't. Not until my body came to the brink. I reached down, stroking his hard shaft, but he didn't let me for long. Flipping me over onto my stomach, he delivered a sharp tap to my ass, making me whimper.

"Fuck, Amore," he groaned, rubbing my ass. I wriggled my ass a little, but that only resulted in another pussy-dripping tap as he grabbed my breasts from behind and attacked my neck with rough, passionate kisses.

"Oh, fuck, Alejandro," I moaned wantonly.

"That's it, baby girl, beg to be fucked."

"Please fuck me..."

"A king can never disobey his queen," he whispered huskily, pinning my arms behind me with one hand. I heard him unzip his pants before I gasped in pain and pleasure when he thrust into me with one brutal thrust...

A Typical Rossi Family Morning

KIARA

*T*HE SUN SHONE THROUGH the curtains, and I could still feel the after-effects of last night. The ache between my legs was a pleasant reminder of what had happened. Goddess, the man had incredible stamina, but I wouldn't change it for anything. I turned in bed, missing the feel of his arms around me, and touched the other side of the bed. Although his scent lingered in the room, his side of the bed was cold. I sat up, glancing towards the bathroom door, brushing my hair back from my face.

Alejandro? I mind-linked.

Morning… I hope you slept well.

Perfectly. Why didn't you wake me up? What about breakfast? I asked. We didn't bring any Omegas along for the cooking, so it was just the five of us.

You were spent after last night. As much as you love spreading those legs for me, you fucking push your limits. I smiled, rolling my eyes.

As if you're not to blame for me wanting you.

Good, because I intend to fuck you like that every fucking day. I shook my head.

Good.

And, yeah, about breakfast, kinda not fucking managing.

I'll be there in twenty.

I got out of bed, wincing at how sore I felt, and made my way to the bathroom. Goddess, that man was a beast, but I knew that already. I turned the shower on and leaned against the cool tiles, allowing the warm water to wash over me before I quickly soaped my body and washed my hair. Those kiddies wouldn't wait for long.

Once showered, I pulled on a pair of white shorts and a floral print chiffon blouse before leaving our bedroom and heading downstairs. I could hear Skyla talking to Alejandro about something, and it made me smile. I stopped at the archway that looked into the kitchen area, tilting my head as I watched Alejandro leaning against the counter and drinking coffee whilst Dante buttered some toast.

"Are you making Dante make the breakfast?" I asked, amused.

"No, but I had to since Dad here isn't able to." Dante frowned as he took the toast he had just buttered and gave his sisters two slices each.

"It's called fucking survival skills," Alejandro replied, smirking as Dante frowned, displeased, before he turned his burning gaze on me.

"Oops, one pound, Daddy," Skyla exclaimed, holding her hand out.

That one was thrifty. She made an agreement with Alejandro that every time she heard him say 'fuck' or 'fucking', she would ask for a pound. The only thing is, it didn't make Alejandro stop, and he never carried a pound around…

"This goes for the next fucking five," Alejandro said, handing her a five-pound note.

"Three pounds left."

I sighed as I walked over to the counter and kissed both girls on the cheek.

"Good morning, Mama." Kataleya smiled at me. Her hair was just like mine in colour, with eyes as dark as Alejandro's whilst Skyla had black hair and green eyes.

"Good morning, my angel," I replied, ruffling her hair.

"Morning," Skyla said, tucking the note into her pocket carefully.

"Good morning, and thank you, Dante, for making your sisters toast. Now, who wants eggs or bacon?" I asked, going over to the fridge after kissing Dante's forehead.

"Can I have you?" Alejandro asked, making my eyes fly open in shock.

"Al! Food."

"What do you mean you want Mama? You're mated, let her breathe," Skyla added, dramatically shaking her head as if she wasn't six but sixteen.

"Eat your damn food," Alejandro growled, only for her to give him a challenging look before smoothly returning to her toast. I placed the egg carton on the worktop just as Alejandro's strong arms wrapped around me, and he kissed my neck. "You look fucking fine…" I smiled, closing my eyes at his touch. Goddess…

"Daddy swore again," Skyla's voice came, bringing us out of our moment.

"Yeah, I fucking know," Alejandro growled, kissing my lips before walking over to Skyla and prodding her forehead.

"Ouch, Daddy!"

"Why are girls so loud?" Dante asked, taking his bowl of cereal to the counter.

"Not all girls," Kataleya replied as I cracked two eggs into the sizzling pan. "If you find girls annoying, then why do you like Delsanra?" She giggled.

I looked over my shoulder as Dante's brow furrowed, pouting. He had so many young pups wanting his attention, yet his infatuation with Delsanra remained.

"I told you to tone that shit down," Alejandro added disapprovingly.

"I didn't do anything." Dante frowned. His eyes seemed to turn a brighter red.

"Guys…" I said, making both father and son turn their attention to me.

"I behaved, Mama," Dante added coldly. He was about to get off his seat, ready to walk out.

"Stay. It's fine, you were okay. Just eat. Let's not argue this early," I said, giving him a warm smile.

Baby, don't bother him. It's not his fault, I added through the mind link.

He's getting older, he can't continue this shit.

I know, but not today, I sighed.

Fine, Alejandro agreed, coming over and kissing my lips. I kissed him back, smiling up at him when Skyla gasped.

"Oo, I got an idea. Can I get fifty pence every time Daddy says shit?"

"Fuck, this girl's greedy as fuck. No, you can't, " Alejandro growled.

"But, Daddy, you say it a lot!"

"And you said it too, Skyla. We aren't allowed to," Kataleya whispered.

"I know. I guess Daddy just gets away with S H I T," she said, making Alejandro frown at her. The two were the most similar, and that banter was the norm for a Rossi family breakfast.

"Thank you for our birthday party yesterday, Mama and Daddy," Kataleya piped in softly when I placed their plates in front of them.

"You are most welcome, darling," I replied, kissing her forehead from across the counter.

"Any fucking time, princess," Alejandro added, pouring two glasses of orange juice and walking off to the far counter.

"That's another pound…" Skyla chimed in.

"It fucking ain't," Alejandro replied, bringing over the hot chocolate that he had made for me.

"And another. Daddy, you owe me!"

"Skyla, you have five pounds already."

"I need more. When I grow up, I'm going to travel the world."

"You're fucking six, and you ain't going anywhere until you're twenty-five," Alejandro added, taking a seat next to me.

"I can too."

"Can fucking not."

And that is exactly how our mornings went, and you know what? I wouldn't change a thing.

❧

Once breakfast was over, I washed up and prepared them a lunch hamper, yesterday's events returning to my mind.

Pay the debt by the blood of the beast and yield to the Crimson King.

Those words screamed in my head, but I couldn't voice them. It involved magic; I was sure of that. I just needed to find a way to relay the message to Alejandro. It gave me an ominous feeling, and I knew there was more to it.

"Amore Mio." I turned when Alejandro walked in, wrapping his arms around me. "I'm taking the pups down by the river."

"Alejandro, I don't know. I just… after yesterday, I feel worried."

"I'm going to be with them. We won't go far. You get some rest. I'll make sure we have dinner delivered tonight, alright?" I looked up at him and nodded. I didn't feel any unease today, it should be okay.

"Okay, I'll get a lie-in." I smiled.

We had decided a few days ago that he would mind the kids for the day, and I could sleep in. I needed it. The last week had been crazy and all I wanted was to get back into bed and get some good rest.

"Promise to behave for your daddy, okay?" My eyes fixed on Skyla as I hugged and kissed Kataleya before meeting the other two. "And don't go too far," I added, looking at Alejandro.

"We won't," he said, pulling me into his arms. "Get some rest."

"Oh, I will…" I replied, gazing into those gorgeous dark eyes of his. Goddess, he was far too handsome. "I'm going to miss you in bed."

"Oh yeah? We both know you don't get much sleep when I'm in bed with you." His hands squeezed my ass, and I raised an eyebrow.

"True, but I wouldn't have it any other way," I replied softly, locking my arms around his neck and pulling him down to kiss his luscious lips. He pulled me against him, and our bodies moulded as one as he kissed me back harder. His lips dominated mine as he plunged his tongue into my mouth, making my core clench.

"Daddy, I'm going to die of old age, you're making us wait so long!" Skyla's voice came. Alejandro growled, tugging away and glaring at his little girl.

"This one's a fucking nightmare."

"She's annoying," Dante agreed. "All girls are, but can we go now?"

"Patience is a virtue, guys." I smiled in amusement as they all headed out, and I watched them walk down the path.

Kataleya gave me a wave and blew me a kiss before she skipped off. Alejandro turned, giving me one of his sexy smirks before they vanished from view, and I shut the door. *I guess I'll text the girls a little and then get some rest.*

◈◈◈

I awoke suddenly. The sun was still in the sky, albeit lower, and I stretched. Had my phone rang or something? But there was only silence. I reached over and unlocked it and smiled, seeing Alejandro had sent some pictures. In a few photos, Dante was in the river, clearly enjoying himself, and Kataleya was making something out of branches whilst Skyla was throwing rocks into the water.

They look so cute and clearly having fun. Did you have lunch? I tried to mind-link, but it seemed he was a little out of range, so I texted him instead.

'All finished. They ate well. Did you get some rest?' He texted back.

'Yes. I can't mind-link, how far out are you?' I frowned. I had told them not to go too far, but maybe I was just being paranoid.

'We went towards the waterfall; we will head back in an hour or two.'

'Perfect, but please be safe, Alejandro, I'm still worried… and have fun.'

'Don't worry, I had the men do a thorough check.'

I read his message and nodded to myself. Maybe I needed to calm down. I put my phone down and yawned, stretching as I stood up. Maybe I could have a bubble -

My heart thumped when my gaze fell on the black paper on the bedside drawer. My stomach was twisting as I reached for it before I froze. No, I needed to take a picture of it this time. I grabbed my phone, my heart thumping as I clicked the camera on and looked at the paper, unable to make out the letters. I gingerly reached for it, my camera at the ready. Yet the moment my hand made contact with it, I felt a strong surge of power. My phone slipped from my hand, clattering to the floor, and my eyes were stuck to the paper.

The orange words glowed on the paper, searing like embers.

A DEBT MUST ALWAYS BE REPAID BY BLOOD OR BY LIFE.

I dropped the paper as it caught flames and turned to ash. I stepped back, my heart thundering as I grabbed my phone, not caring about the cracked screen, and unlocked it, needing to call Alejandro. But just then, I felt something weigh over me. My vision blurred, and then there was darkness…

The Wolves

ALEJANDRO

T HE KIDS WERE HAVING a fucking blast, and as much as I wanted Kiara to have been there, I knew yesterday that whatever happened was on her mind, and she needed rest. I made sure the villa was surrounded by guards. The kids were safe with me, but I was not going to fucking risk leaving her alone.

This place was pretty fucking neat, with the mountain backdrop, the waterfall, and the clear river. The greenery and the trees were in full bloom, and the sound of birds chirping in the trees rang in the clear blue sky. I frowned, watching Dante take his shirt off, seemingly irritated, and I realised what he was about to do.

"Dante, don't," I warned, closing the gap between us and grabbing his hand as he was about to yank the necklace of concealment off.

"Dad, I just want to go in the water without this. I feel stronger without it." He frowned.

A sliver of guilt rushed through me, knowing we were practically subduing him as a person, but without it, he had the aura of a full-fledged Alpha… that was something I couldn't risk anyone finding out. He had worn that necklace since birth; it had been given to us as a repayment gift by a witch when Kiara healed her.

"Dante, listen to me, son." I crouched down, placing my hands on his shoulders. "I know you don't want to keep it on, but it's for your safety." I hoped he understood. The annoyance in his eyes told me he did, but he didn't like it.

"When I grow up, I'm never hiding who I am," he said defiantly. I nodded, brushing his wet hair off his forehead.

"Got it, I just need you strong enough to protect your -"

Something was wrong. I could feel it, like a wave of darkness and unease washing over me. My heart thundered as I stood up, scanning the area - Sky and Kat. Where were they? Skyla's heartbeat reached my ears.

"Girls!"

I turned sharply, seeing the tops of both their heads behind a large rock. Thank the fucking goddess they were together. Kat's ability to hide her heartbeat fucking messed with me. I grabbed Dante, despite his protests, and rushed over to the girls. Something was off, and I wasn't going to stay in that opening when –

Suddenly, wolves burst from the trees from every fucking direction. There were far too many to count, their fur all similar shades of auburn and brown and their eyes burned a shade of crimson-orange that I had never seen before. But the thing that fucking threw me was that I hadn't sensed, smelled, or heard them. At all.

"Stay with your sisters," I told Dante as I shifted.

In a flash, I ripped the first wolf that reached us to shreds, turning my head to swipe another one away from my pups. Fuck, I couldn't even mind-link anyone; I was out of range...

I heard Kat whimper and felt Skyla's aura. We didn't know what her ability was, but when emotional, she had an aura, although it was faint. I slammed another one away from them. One fucking wolf or a hundred, I would handle them all. The smell of blood, the menacing growls of the burning-eyed wolves and the beating hearts of my pups were filling my senses. My only thought was to protect them by all fucking means.

"Dad!" Dante shouted.

I turned, ripping the heart of one of the wolves right out of his chest before it could attack the girls. Blood sprayed over them, making Skyla shriek, her arms tightly around Kataleya whilst Dante stood there defensively.

I hissed as I felt the claws of another wolf dig deep into my back. I growled, throwing him off and allowing my aura to roll off me in waves, but it did nothing to stop the wolves from advancing. I turned, ripping through two more. If I was alone, I'd be fine, but this was a fucking nightmare...

"Dad's phone," I heard Dante mutter. I knew he was planning to call for help. *Fuck no!*

I growled, but he didn't even pay attention, darting out from behind the rock and aiming for my phone that lay on the rock a few metres away. Several wolves hissed, turning their gaze on Dante. *Over my dead fucking body.*

I growled, launching myself at the back of the closest one. Another barrelled into my back, and I was thrown to the rocky ground. A wolf ripped into my leg, and another four jumped at me.

"Dad!" Dante's voice came.

Fuck.

I turned, killing two instantly, my blazing red eyes filled with rage. The darkness of my aura enveloped the area, yet even then, the flame-eyed wolves refused to back away, almost as if they didn't feel pain, relentlessly attacking until they faced fucking death. I ripped another two hearts out, the taste of my own blood in my mouth. I lunged forward, blocking the girls from being attacked. I never ran... but for their safety, I needed to. I wasn't going to win without them getting hurt.

I grabbed the girls, rushing for Dante, who was fighting a wolf off with a stick. He may have only been eight, but he was already an impressive fighter. Yet, he was still just a pup; he was no match for them. Growling menacingly, I ripped the attacker off him. I was about to grab Dante when I was thrown to the ground. The girls slipped out of my arms, but I just about managed to cushion Skyla's head from hitting the ground.

"Kataleya!" Skyla sobbed. I turned, seeing one of the wolfs grabbing her and running.

No.

Fear consumed me like never before, digging its claws into me as I growled, running after the wolf only for another six to jump on my back. I stared at her, seeing the wolf run further and further away, her body being flung around like a rag doll as he ran with her.

Please, no.

I growled murderously, the ground vibrating at the sheer force as I ripped them off when I saw Dante fall to the ground, his entire body shuddering. Torn.

The choice before me was fucking me up. There was no way I could choose between my pups.

Kataleya was getting further and further away, and Dante was about to get killed, blood dripping down his chest from where he had been slashed. In a flash, I was before him, killing the attacking wolf before I grabbed him and Skyla, running after Kataleya, the wolves doing their best to stop me.

Their heartbeats were thundering like roaring storms, and I knew the fact that they had gotten so close without me sensing them meant there was magic involved. Their scents were exactly the same... fire and ash. Whatever they were, it wasn't normal.

I tried to push at the limitations of my mind link, but I had really gone too far out... this wasn't the plan...

Fuck, I should have listened to Kiara.

Kataleya... I could no longer see the wolf that had taken her. My heart was thudding as I pushed myself. My baby girl, I couldn't allow anything to happen to her...

Suddenly, the entire forest around us erupted in flames. Kataleya's distant cry reached my ears, but I could no longer make sense of direction. The flames rose higher and higher, and Skyla began coughing, struggling to breathe. Dante was pale, his entire body still convulsing, and I saw the trickle of blood from his nose. I kept running, but it was only getting harder to breathe. I needed to get these two to safety before I went after Kataleya.

The painful decision before me ripped my heart into two. It clenched painfully in my chest as I forced myself to turn, knowing I was turning my back on my pup for the two in my arms. Fear that something might happen to her or that she may die consumed me, but I had to hold onto hope that she'd be okay because if I went after her, the two in my arms surely wouldn't.

I promise you, baby girl, Daddy will come for you, and when I find the one behind this... I'll fucking kill them in the most painful possible fucking way.

My Worst Nightmare

KIARA

"I'M OKAY," I SAID, looking up at Julio, who had found me. My body was aching, and I could barely think straight.

"What happened?" He asked, frowning. "Should I call the Alpha?"

"I don't know, there was a paper… I… I'll call him just to see how they are," I murmured, looking at my shattered phone.

Worry, pain, and fear were swirling inside of me, but they weren't my emotions - Alejandro. What was happening?

"Contact Alejandro!" I exclaimed suddenly, making Julio grab his phone, but just then, the sound of running reached my ears, and Alejandro appeared at the door, blood and dirt covering his body. He was clad in only torn sweatpants which told me he had shifted. My eyes snapped to the limp bodies of Dante and Skyla in his arms, and I sprang up.

"What happened?" I cried, my powers surging around me.

Panic and worry consumed me as I took in their state. Skyla's heartbeat was steady yet weak, but she seemed to simply be unconscious, whilst Dante's heartbeat was racing, his skin was clammy, and he was shaking. He placed the kids on the bed, and I quickly placed my hands on both of them, my purple aura blazing around me. As a blessed wolf from the Asheton bloodline, I had the gift of healing. Skyla began to heal, yet I could feel the pain Dante was in, even when the injury on his chest healed. What was this? Goddess, help me!

I removed my hand from Skyla, caressing her hair when I froze. My heart thundered as I realised Kataleya wasn't there. I snapped my gaze to Alejandro, trying not to let the fear of the worst consume me.

"Where's Kataleya?" I asked, unable to stop the distress and worry from seeping into my voice.

"She's…"

Please, baby, tell me she's okay. I stared into his eyes, which were wracked with guilt and sorrow, still pouring my healing into Dante, trying to focus with everything I had.

"Alejandro! Answer me!"

"They took her," his pained reply answered, placing his hand on my arm.

My breath hitched as I jerked away from him, my entire body shaking. *No. No. Goddess no.*

"Kiara… I'll get her back, I promise yo-"

"Go. Please, go find her," I said, my voice harsh and shaky, unable to even look at him, trying not to break down. It wasn't his fault, but I needed my baby.

He didn't speak, and I felt a surge of guilt, my own at my behaviour, but most of it was his before he put his walls up. I looked at him as he turned to leave the room, and I placed my hand on his arm.

"Wait," I whispered. I let my healing pour into him before tugging him close and reaching up to caress his jaw. Our eyes met, and the pain suddenly became unbearable. "You got this," I whispered, trying to control the storm of tears that were threatening to fall.

He turned, wrapping his arms around me tightly, his heart thudding as much as mine. Although I didn't stop trying to heal Dante, I closed my eyes, unable to stop the tears from spilling down my cheek.

"Please bring her back," I whispered pleadingly as he kissed my cheek.

"I will," he promised, letting go of me and the loss of his touch hurt.

Do I tell him I can't heal Dante?

No… I needed him to go find Kataleya. Just the thought of her being taken terrified me. *I will deal with this. Please, Goddess, protect our babies.*

His lips met mine for a fleeting moment before he left the room swiftly. I took a deep breath and looked at Julio, who was standing in the hall.

"Give me a phone," I said, trying to control my emotions.

"Here." He handed me his phone, unlocked, and I quickly dialled Delsanra's number, my hand shaking as I stared down at Dante. His heartbeat was still racing, and nothing I did was helping him. He wasn't injured. Whatever it was, it was something else.

"Hey, Kia," Delsanra answered.

"Del, is it possible for you to come to the villa?" I asked, trying to keep my voice strong, but even then, it trembled.

"Of course I can, Kiara… is everything okay?"

"No… nothing is. There's something going on, and I wish I…" Once again, I wasn't able to utter anything about the letters. "Dante. There's something wrong with him, and Kataleya's been taken, and you know we can't track her," I whispered. I heard her take a sharp intake of breath.

"We are coming," she said. Her voice was strong and comforting. I closed my eyes, praying she could help. Julio took the phone from me, his eyes full of concern.

"It's magic, isn't it?" He asked, looking at Dante.

"I think so," I whispered, dropping to my knees as I stroked his hair. His trousers were torn where he had been bitten. I had healed that, too, but there was something else going on inside of him. I kissed his forehead, trying to fight my tears.

"Mama…" Skyla stirred before she opened her eyes and jumped up, looking around, terror clear in her eyes.

"I got you, baby," I whispered as she launched herself into my arms, breaking into tears.

"Mama, Kat!"

"Daddy will bring Kat home. I promise," I whispered as she began sobbing in my arms. I cried silently, rocking her, one arm tightly around her and the other holding Dante's trembling one.

I felt the surge of magic from outside, and my heart leapt, knowing that Delsanra was here. Within seconds, she and Rayhan were running up the stairs, their scent hitting my nose before they stepped into the room.

"Kiara," Delsanra said, her eyes burning red. She was currently in her demon form. I stood up, and she hugged me tightly, Skyla crushed between us both. Only then did I realise that I was shaking, too. "We are going to fix this," she promised, softly kissing Skyla on the head as she continued to sob into my shoulder.

Rayhan was by Dante's side, placing the large bag he was carrying down before checking his pulse and forehead. A deep frown set on his face with his shoulder-length black hair falling in his face before he turned to us frowning.

"He's in pain, but it's not physical," he murmured softly.

"Let me see what I can do." Delsanra let go of me, determination clear on her face.

"I'm going to head out to help Uncle. It's going to be okay. We will find her," Rayhan reassured me, placing his hand on Skyla's head for a moment before he left the room, pulling his leather jacket off as he did so. Rayhan was the finest tracker that I knew, and I was confident that his help could prove vital. It just terrified me that Kataleya's special ability would deter them immensely. Of all three, her being taken was my worst nightmare.

"It's magic, but there's something else, too, and it's powerful," Delsanra murmured as she stepped back from Dante and unzipped the bag that Rayhan had placed down.

"Will you be able to fix it?" I asked.

All I could think of was how he had given me that smile before leaving this morning. Who would have thought this was how he'd come home to me?

"I don't know, but I intend to try." Determination was clear in her voice as she planted a kiss on Dante's forehead before she gave me a smile. "Don't worry. Our little Churro isn't so easy to take down." I nodded, watching her begin to draw symbols on the floor before she lifted Dante, placed him in the centre, and began to light some candles. "I think it's a curse," she whispered.

"What?"

"I don't know for sure, but there's something that's happened. I'll do my best," she murmured, placing a few crystals down.

She stepped back as she began whispering a spell. Her power surged around her. The flames burned high, and I saw red veins spread from Dante's chest where his injuries had once been. The candles flickered, and Delsanra's brow was furrowed with concentration as her voice got louder. The veins began seeping from Dante's chest, spreading across the symbols on the floor and towards Delsanra.

"Del, be careful," I warned.

Something was off.

The air seemed to become colder, and I could feel something else in the room. I stepped back, cradling Skyla tightly. My heart thudded when suddenly Delsanra was cut off. Blood sprayed from her neck as she choked before she was thrown against the far wall. A sickening crunch filled the room before she crumbled to the floor. The candles were blown out, and a sharp wind rushed through the room ominously, shattering the windows.

"Del!" I screamed, rushing to her side. I placed my hand on her neck, healing her as her heartbeat faded. Her heartbeat steadied, yet I could sense the same thing from her that I did from Dante. *Oh, please, no.* "Del?"

She didn't reply, her body as lifeless as my son's that laid not far from her.

Goddess, why is this happening? And who is responsible for this?

The Unravelling of Hope

ALEJANDRO

FEAR RAN THROUGH MY veins, and although I may have been the strongest shifter out there, I felt helpless.

Kataleya. She was all I could fucking think of. Remembering the way the wolf's teeth were clamped around her tiny body, the blood dripping from his mouth, her blood... and the terror in her eyes as they got further and further away. I'd give my fucking life for her safety.

Then Kiara's pain, the way she pushed me away, ripped at my heart. I knew she was in pain; it was a natural mother's reaction, after all. She was the perfect mother to our children, not like my own fucking mother, who had played dead for years and then came back with her psychotic plans to destroy the world over eight years ago. She sure fucking didn't care if any of us went down with her. But Kiara, she was firm, fair, and affectionate. She loved her pups unconditionally and, even then, made time for me, her family, our pack, and her friends, as well as for a certain fucker I couldn't stand. She cared for everyone and did her best to be there for us all.

I sped up, the wind rushing through my fur. There was no way I was going to be able to track Kataleya, so instead, we were trying to follow the tracks of the wolves, hoping for any speck of blood that left a trail. Many of my men were somewhere assisting, but it was fucking futile. The ground near the river where the fight had occurred was just a field of ash. Not even a body or a drop of blood remained. That just made things fucking harder.

Alpha, Alpha Rayhan is here to help.

Rayhan? Kiara must have told them, and I guessed his spitfire of a mate must have teleported them here. A reminder that I wasn't alone. *We will find her…*

Fill him in on everything. I'm still trying to scour the entire north side. There are no fucking paw prints or anything.

Understood, Alpha.

✺⊙᷈᷉✺

Fourteen hours had passed, but there was still no answer or clue.

I was not going to fucking let them get away with it. The fear that so many fucking hours had passed and what may have happened to her consumed me like fucking poison. I didn't feel the link break, so she was still alive… that was all I had to fucking hold on to.

The exhaustion was catching up to me, but there was still no sign of her, so I couldn't stop. I had alerted the Alphas of the packs that I truly trusted to send their men out, but at the same time, I also didn't want to put Kataleya in more harm than she already was by telling everyone that my daughter was taken.

Alpha… there's nothing. They are gone without a trace, Darien, my Beta's, voice came through the link.

I can't stop looking, I whispered back, trying to control the agony in my voice.

Alejandro… look, let's let everyone know – put a prize out there for her. Let the word out that you're willing to give anything to the kidnappers. Surely there must be a reason for this, and they must want something. We can contact our business partners in the human world, too, and make it clear that your daughter was taken. Someone may have seen her. We will find her. The voice of reason that stuck by me even on my darkest days long ago… he was a friend that had been by my side from the fucking start.

But I can't stop searching when she's out there.

Not yet.

Al… please. Kiara needs you; Dante and Luna Delsanra are still unconscious.

I froze in my tracks, my heart thundering. What?

What the fuck do you mean? Kiara wasn't able to heal Dante?

The Hybrid Luna tried to cast a spell to fix whatever was ailing Dante, but whatever it was has spread to her. We told Alpha Rayhan, and he did return to check on her before continuing to look for Kataleya. We need to regroup; I'll have new men out here scouring the woods. Alpha Liam also wishes to speak to you. He is currently with his sister at the villa.

Turn my back on her again... fuck. I tried not to imagine the worst as I closed my eyes. Darien was right. I needed to reach out and have another plan in place rather than just searching blindly.

I'm coming back.

❧☙

I reached the villa, my heart sinking with every step. I was returning to my queen without our pup. How was I going to face her? Darien gave me a bottle of water and some pants, but I refused the water, simply taking the pants. I didn't think I fucking deserved water... I should have fucking listened. I should never have gone so fucking far out. I should have paid attention to what Kia was saying, but it was a tad too fucking late right then.

Her scent enveloped me. I closed my eyes, grasping onto it. I would never fucking let on, but I was doing my best not to unravel completely. I needed her; her comfort, her embrace, her fucking presence. Rayhan's and Liam's scents came from the room upstairs, along with Scarlett's. I adjusted my pants that I had just pulled on before I pushed open the door to the room, seeing Kiara sitting on the bed whilst Delsanra and Dante lay upon it.

Both looked as grey as death, red veins creeping along their entire bodies. Rayhan sat on the opposite side, holding Delsanra's hand, his hair shielding his face, and I felt another storm of guilt. Because of my fucking mistake, there was another casualty.

Scarlett was rocking a sleeping Skyla in her arms gently whilst Liam stood behind Kiara, arms crossed and a deep frown on his face. They all turned to me when I stepped inside, but my eyes were on Kiara's red puffy ones. She had cried a lot...

I'm fucking sorry, Amore...

"Alejandro," Liam said, frowning as he gave me a small nod. Kiara stood up, her eyes filled with fresh tears as she looked at me before closing them.

I had failed her.

"Nothing?" She whispered, her voice trembling. I shook my head as Darien stepped into the room.

She came towards me, her hand pressed to her chest. I pulled her against my chest, wrapping my arms around her tightly as she broke into stifled sobs. I rested my head on top of hers, closing my eyes as I inhaled her hazelnut chocolate scent that calmed me. Scarlett sighed, frowning as she looked at me.

"We will find her. Elijah is out there, and we will continue to search, but we need to let every pack know. If this is the doing of another pack or some sort of uprising, then we will surely find an answer."

"I'm going to do that. I'll be putting the word out to the humans, too. Even if they just see her, I'll put out a reward," I said, my voice hoarse due to the lack of fucking water.

"Offer them a reward they can't refuse. The Rossi Empire has funds that you are welcome to take," Rayhan replied quietly as he looked up at me. Being the son of the eldest Rossi, he held the majority of the empire, not to mention he was the main heir to his mother's entire side of wealth as well. I refused to take more than needed. Our eyes met, and I saw the pain in his stormy grey ones.

"I'm sorry that Del got caught up in this shit," I murmured quietly. He gave a small shake of his head, kissing his mate's hand.

"We are family, and I don't think she'd have been able to sit back and do nothing," he replied, trying to hide the emotions in his voice. "Don't beat yourself up over it."

But it was my fucking fault.

Kiara pulled away, taking the water bottle from Darien, unscrewing it, and holding it out to me.

"You need to drink something, and, Darien, get him some food," she said quietly, her lips trembling.

"Forget food. Set up the video call with all members of the council. I'm going to do this shit now."

"Ale-"

"Not now, Amore Mio. I'm not wasting any more time. It's been fucking hours since she was taken, I can't afford to lose any more," I said quietly.

Darien hesitated, looking between Kiara and me. "That was a fucking order from your damn king. Move," I growled viciously, my aura rolling off me and forcing Darien to submit. I saw Kiara frown, but she said nothing. I walked over to the bed, looking down at the two on it. "What's wrong with them?"

"Some sort of curse," Liam replied quietly.

"I felt something else in the room when she was thrown against the wall. Those vein-like things travelled from Dante to her. I think anyone who tries to sabotage it will get affected," Kiara whispered. So not only did I need to find Kataleya, I needed to find a cure.

"Raihana, I don't want her to attempt the same shit, but do you think she'd be able to find some answers?" I asked quietly. "Or the witches? They fucking owe us anyway. Tell her to contact them." Rayhan nodded, taking his phone out, and I turned to Liam.

"Anything? Does your intuition tell you anything?" I asked. He and Kiara both had the gift of knowing things. One I had blatantly ignored from Kiara…

"Nothing," he replied, frowning. His eyes, which were always blazing the colour of his wolf, met mine. "But I'm going to go back out there and keep looking for her."

"The letters," Kiara whispered. "There were two."

"What did they say?" I asked her sharply.

She opened her mouth, frowning as she struggled. A few moments passed, and she looked at us hopelessly.

"Kiara… don't tell me you're unable to voice it," Liam replied, his eyes narrowing. Kiara nodded, her eyes pooling with tears.

I closed my eyes. *Fuck.*

I stepped closer to her, cupping her face. The sparks of the bond rippled through us as I caressed her cheeks with the pads of my thumbs, brushing away the tears that streamed down her cheeks.

"We are going to figure this shit out, okay?" I promised with determination. I fucking swore, anyone fucking involved was going to burn.

She nodded and I pulled her close, my lips crashing against hers in a deep, passionate kiss. My arms tightened around her, one hand tangling into her hair as I held her close, needing her, needing this.

I will bring her back to you.

I kissed her cheeks, the taste of her salty tears mixing with the sweet taste of her mouth that lingered in mine.

Alpha, everything is ready for you, Darien's voice came through the link.

I turned away, not saying anything, and left the room, unable to ignore the pain I felt from Kiara but I had to do this. For Kiara, for Kataleya, for Dante, and for Delsanra.

I washed my face before grabbing a shirt and walked into the living room, where Darien had set the laptop up for me. The Alphas and elders who were part of the council were on the screen, as were two of the high witches of the fucking coven. It may be some shit they could help with.

"King Alejandro," Allen, the eldest member of the council, greeted.

"I won't fucking waste time with greetings. Kataleya, my youngest pup, was taken today, precisely fifteen hours ago. My queen has received two letters, yet she is unable to speak of what she's fucking read. My son has some sort of curse that even Delsanra Silver, the Luna of the Black Storm Pack, was unable to counter. I'm calling a fucking code red. I want every single pack searching for her. Those that are in your area, I expect you to pass the message to those packs as well. I want everyone to find my daughter. I will send an outline of what exactly went down as soon as this call is fucking over. Put the word out that if my daughter is found, the pack responsible will be given a huge fucking reward. As for the coven, I would hope that someone can come to the location we are at to see if they can give any more insight on what is happening." The Alphas nodded. I could see they knew the seriousness of the situation.

"Very well. I personally will come, and I will get in touch with Janaina," Magdalene, the high witch of the coven, said emotionlessly.

I gave a curt nod. It wasn't like me to ask for help, but right then, I needed to pull out all the fucking stops I had at my disposal. The witches and werewolves were at peace. We did not like each other much, but as the years passed, we began to blend and tolerate one another.

I ended the video call and began typing the email, pulling up an image of Kataleya. I had always kept my pups out of the public eye… this was the first time the entire fucking country was going to see Kataleya Tamia Rossi…

I looked at her picture. It had been taken a few weeks ago. Her large innocent eyes stared back at me, and I felt that suffocating guilt crush me once again. I should have been able to protect her... did I do the wrong thing by not going after her? Did I fucking lose the only chance I had? Fuck.

"That notice is good. Get some rest. I'll attach her picture and send it off," Darien said softly.

"I'm fucking doing it," I replied icily.

"Al..."

"Go make yourself fucking useful and leave me the fuck alone," I growled dangerously, my eyes flashing red.

He simply sighed and nodded, leaving the room and shutting the door behind him. I was not going to fucking rest until I found her, and I would, even if I had to fucking destroy the entire fucking planet in the process, I would.

Their Pain

KIARA

"Leave him." I glanced at Rayhan as I was about to lift Dante from the bed.

"You need to sleep, too." He shook his head.

"I can't sleep anyway. Leave him here. I'll watch over them both." Our eyes met, and I nodded, feeling terrible.

"I'm so sorry, Ray," I whispered. He shook his head, giving me a small smile that didn't take away the emotions in his eyes that were riddled with worry and pain.

"We're family, and we stick together. You need to stop apologising," he said, caressing Delsanra's snowy white hair. "She's a fighter. They both are…"

I nodded as I kissed Dante's forehead. How much pain was he in? Was he going to be okay? I looked over at Delsanra, caressing her hair for a moment. She had two little pups, Ahren and Sienna. Goddess, they needed their mother.

"Kiara?" Rayhan's voice snapped me out of my thoughts, and he raised an eyebrow. "They'll be okay."

I nodded, unable to say anything, feeling absolutely devastated. I had to fix this. I had to get Kataleya back…

Liam had gone to see if he could track anything whilst Darien and Alejandro were working on putting the word out. Mom was with Skyla and Dad was out there doing what he could too. Only I was doing nothing…

Kataleya…

I stepped into the room, placing the suitcase I had brought from the other room onto the floor of the one that Dante had once occupied. I switched the light on and walked to the adjoining bathroom whilst trying to control the tears from spilling down my cheeks. I looked in the mirror, the words on the letters screaming in my head. I had to get them on paper somehow. What if I tried to write them?

I splashed water on my face before returning to the bedroom and rummaging in Dante's things until I finally found his sketchbook and his pencil case. Taking it over to the bed, I sat down, opened it up to a blank page, and took a deep breath.

Pay the debt…

I placed the pencil on the paper, my heart beating as I used all my willpower to try to write the words. Jarring pain rushed up my arm, but I didn't stop. I was a blessed wolf, and I was not going to let anything hinder me. I looked out at the glowing moon and let my aura surge around me, drawing power from the moon itself. *I am not weak. I will not bend to whatever this was.*

P… a… y…

I gritted my teeth as I continued. Splintering pain tore up my arm, but I needed to get it on paper.

The… debt…

I could taste coppery blood in my mouth as I continued. My entire body was shaking by the time I managed the message from the first letter, my vision darkening as I wiped the blood that trickled out of the corner of my mouth. My hand was stinging, and it looked raw, my skin peeling as if it had been scraped against a grater. *Goddess, what is this?*

The next line…

A… debt…

The pen fell from my hand, searing pain making my vision darken, just as the door burst open.

"Kiara!"

I looked up as Alejandro caught me before I almost tumbled to the ground, the sparks from his touch were all that I could focus on, the pain began to dissipate a little.

"Read it," I whispered, staring into his blazing red orbs. He didn't let go of me, holding me close as he grabbed the book.

"Pay the debt by the blood of the beast and yield to the crimson king?" He tossed the book down, grabbing my hand as my vision darkened. "Hold on, Amore Mio. Fuck, I need you." His words made my heart pound, and I clutched onto his shirt.

"I'm okay," I whispered, despite how exhausted I felt.

"You're fucking bleeding," he growled, lifting me up.

He carried me to the bathroom and placed me in the shower as he began to undress me gently yet swiftly. I watched him through my blurry vision. Even then, he kept his walls up, blocking off his emotions from me, something we rarely ever did. It hurt knowing he was hiding his pain from me, but I had pushed him to that…

"Have you eaten?" I whispered. He didn't reply, just simply nodded.

He hadn't.

"I know you well enough to know when you're lying," I scolded him lightly, staring at him under the spotlights of the bathroom.

"I don't have an appetite," he responded, examining my hand before he ran his tongue along it, sending my stomach into knots.

Alpha saliva had healing properties that increased the rate of healing. He placed a gentle kiss on my palm before letting go of me carefully as if worried I'd fall. I stepped back, leaning against the wall as he undressed and stepped into the shower with me, switching it on. A downfall of cold water hit me, and I gasped, clinging to him. He wrapped his arms around me, shielding me from the cold water before it warmed up. I didn't move away; my heart was aching and his embrace was comforting.

"We will find her, right?" I whispered, staring up into his eyes.

He nodded, his wet black locks falling in front of his forehead. I reached up with my raw-looking hand that was slowly healing and brushed the strands back.

"I can't live without her." I knew I was putting pressure on him, but it was all I had. I needed her, and he was my only hope.

"I know, Amore Mio,,, and I will fucking make sure we find her," he murmured, kissing me deeply.

Sparks coursed through me, yet there was nothing sensual about the kiss. It was deep, raw, and a silent promise that he'd do his best. I just hoped it was enough…

Once we had showered, I mind-linked Darien to get someone to bring food upstairs. Alejandro was sitting on the bed in nothing but sweatpants, looking as handsome as ever. He was smoking a cigarette as he looked at the message in the book. Just when I had put on a nightgown, I was mind-linked by one of our men.

Luna, the food.

Coming.

I pulled open the door and reached for the tray. My hand was pretty much healed but just looked very raw and was tender to touch. He lowered his head to me, and I thanked him before he closed the door for me. Alejandro looked up, frowning when he saw the tray. He stood up and came over, taking it from me.

"I told you I wasn't hungry. Have you eaten yourself?"

"Mom made me," I replied, taking a seat opposite him as he placed the tray down, clenching his jaw. We both fell silent, and I knew he was thinking about our little princess. "Do you think they'll hurt her?" I whispered, my chest tightening.

"If they want something, I would hope not," he replied, his hand balling into a fist.

"I pray to Selene that you are correct." I looked down, forking up some pasta and raising it to his lips. "Eat. We need you to keep your strength up to find her," I encouraged softly.

His brows furrowed as he took the bite, and I scooped some more up. We didn't need to speak but the pain that weighed down upon us was only getting stronger, with each passing minute it became harder. I knew my baby girl was out there. Alone. Had she eaten? Was she alone? Were they treating her humanely?

"I've issued out a search for her as well as reaching out to the human world. You never know where she may show up," he said as he drank some water. I could tell eating was hard for him, and I didn't blame him. "I'm also going to make a video to put out there on the dark web and let it circulate. If they want me, then I'm willing to trade places." As much as that hurt to know, for our baby girl, I knew we were both ready to make any sacrifice necessary. He picked up the notepad again and frowned. "I'm sure I'm the fucking beast they're speaking of... but who the fuck is the crimson king? That's who I need to find," he murmured. I nodded.

"What about the attacks that have been occurring? Could it be linked?" He shook his head, placing the notepad down, and looked at me thoughtfully.

"I doubt it. These wolves that ambushed us were not normal, or nothing I've seen before anyway. Whatever they are… it's something we've never encountered before."

His words left an ominous feeling in the air and we both fell silent. Putting aside the tray, he pulled me into his arms. Neither of us would be able to sleep tonight, not when we knew our daughter was out there… facing goddess knows what, utterly alone.

KATALEYA

I'm scared. I want Mama and Daddy.

I looked around the dark room. It was cold, and it smelled horrible. *I'm so scared.* My stomach was bleeding, too, and it hurt. The bad wolf had bit into me.

Why wasn't Daddy coming? Why was I here alone?

I wrapped my arms around my legs, crying softly into my knees.

Mama… please come, Mama… I don't want to be here…

The sound of the key scraping in the lock made my heart thunder with fear.

Please go away.

The screech of the metal door swinging open followed. I clamped my hands over my mouth, trying my best not to cry. I didn't want them to get angry like earlier when I started crying. Tears blurred my vision as a tall man with a dangerous feeling coming from him, stepped into view.

I'm scared, Mama… Daddy…

His footsteps echoed on the metal steps, ringing in the room as I began to tremble. This man was more bad than the other one from earlier, I could sense it from him. He was very tall, maybe taller than Daddy… he was really big, too. He fixed his suit jacket, and just that move made me whimper. He was going to hurt me…

I quickly got to my feet, looking up at him. His cold reddish-brown eyes stared down at me as if he was looking at something filthy. I pressed my lips together, being brave just like Skyla and Dante. His face was scary;

more than half of it was burned. *I'm scared...* The man was important, I knew that much.

"Sir, may I go home?" I whispered, my voice shaking despite trying my best to speak politely. He tilted his head, looking me over.

"They got the wrong fucking one..." he hissed. His voice was scary, too, and I whimpered in fear, backing away.

He walked towards me, and I flinched the moment his gloved hand twisted into my hair. It was hurting. Tears began tumbling down my cheeks as he scoffed.

"A fucking useless pup," he hissed. He talked a bit differently, too. Was he from somewhere far away?

"I'm sorry," I whispered as he pushed me to the ground.

"Fuck this! I don't need this! She doesn't even have anything special!"

I rolled up into a ball, protecting my head as he kicked me once more before he turned and stormed up the stairs, leaving me alone in the dark room. I sobbed quietly, daring not to move from my position.

Will you find me, Daddy?

The Witches

KIARA

I HADN'T BEEN ABLE TO sleep properly. Both Alejandro and I had tossed and turned. The sun hadn't even risen, but I sat up, picking up the pad and forcing myself to write the second message. I was halfway through it when Alejandro woke up. We had barely slept, although we had been trying to for the last four hours. How could we sleep when our baby girl was somewhere? All alone. I knew he wanted to get back out there to look for our pup.

His arm was around me, his hand over mine as I wrote the words, painstakingly slow. The sparks of his touch were like the comfort of warmth on a winter day. He didn't speak, simply placing a few comforting kisses on my neck and shoulder.

A debt must always be repaid by blood or by life. I had done it!

I gasped, dropping the pen. Alejandro instantly grabbed some napkins from the tray of left-over food from last night and dabbed them gently over my bleeding hand, then over the paper that was smeared with blood.

"This person's got some fucking problem with me."

"A debt? What are they going on about?" I closed my eyes, leaning against his shoulder. My intuition was doing nothing to help. I hated this.

"I don't know, but it could be fucking decades old. The witches should be here soon, and I need to make the recording to put out there for the kidnappers' demands before they get here," he said quietly.

I nodded and he gave me a deep kiss before we both got up, ready to face the day and find answers. He left first after washing and dressing. I washed my face and brushed my teeth before rummaging through the suitcase I had grabbed from the other room last night and pulled on some shorts and an oversized top. I didn't want to wear any of that colourful crap, but it was all I had brought along. Who would have thought our family trip for the girls' birthday would end like this?

How had Kataleya spent the night? My stomach twisted and I felt sick with worry. She was out there...

I had just left the room, carrying the tray of leftovers from last night, when Mom stepped out of Skyla's room, although it wasn't even dawn yet. It seemed I wasn't the only one who couldn't sleep.

"Kia." She smiled softly at me and came over, running her fingers through my hair. Oh, yeah... I hadn't combed it... "We are going to find her," she said, determination blazing in her sage green eyes. I nodded as she took the tray from me.

"I know."

"Sky is asleep. I'll keep an eye on her."

"Thank you... I'm just going to go check on Dante and Del."

She nodded, and we both went our separate ways. I knocked lightly on the door but heard no reply. I slowly opened the door to see the bathroom door was shut and the shower was on. Both Delsanra and Dante lay there in the same state as yesterday. I sat on the bed, placing my hands on their chests as I poured my healing into them. Still nothing... I sighed, staring down at Dante with sadness in my eyes.

The bathroom door opened, and Rayhan stepped out, wearing only his pants and a towel around his shoulders.

"Seems like everyone's up early," he said, pulling on his shirt. I nodded and pointed to the wardrobe.

"Alejandro has some clothes in there if you need anything." I stood up, looking down at the two. "Was there any change at night?"

"Nothing at all." I sighed heavily, feeling restless. I needed to make myself useful.

"Have you asked Maria about the kids?" I asked, feeling another flash of guilt rush through me. He nodded.

"They're fine. Ri's gone down. They'll be alright."

"Thanks," I sighed. "I'll leave you to it. Have breakfast before you head out."

He nodded and I left the room, heading downstairs. I paused at the open archway to the sitting area. Alejandro was seated there, his face emotionless and cold as he looked directly at the laptop screen. Darien was standing to the side, out of view of the camera.

"… all means. If it's revenge or a debt, then I'm who you want. Whatever your fucking demand is, I'm ready to accept it. Just make sure the child is unharmed. Money, power, or if I'm your fucking goal, say the word and I'm yours."

His face was emotionless, his eyes hard and cold. If I didn't know him better, one would think he wasn't really bothered about the loss of his child, or that he didn't have a heart. Despite the fact that his words said otherwise, his cold and uncaring demeanour remained.

"I'll await your demand."

He switched it off and ran a hand through his hair before taking out a cigarette and lighting it. His eyes met mine, and I forced a small smile before heading to the kitchen where Mom and Serena, Darien's mate who must have come sometime last night, were making breakfast.

"Kia," she said, brushing back a strand of her blonde hair and hugging me tightly.

"Serena…" I hugged her back, not saying anything, before pulling away and began helping.

I knew the men were leaving soon. Liam had already gone, and I wanted to go too… I couldn't just sit back and do nothing. I took a plate to the lounge, where Alejandro was at the open patio doors, smoking and using a phone with the other hand, a frown on his face.

"Baby." He glanced at me, and I raised the plate in a gesture for him to eat.

"I'm not hung-"

"For Kataleya." That stopped him, and he took a slice of toast, biting into it. "I want to come with you. I want to search for her, too."

"No. We can't risk it. If something happens to you -"

"Al, she's my daughter, too. I can't just sit by when I'm worried for you, for everyone, and above all, for my baby girl."

"No. I'm not risking it."

"Al… I want to go," I pleaded, feeling a sting of pain at his blatant refusal.

"And I fucking said no. I'm not having someone else I love out there."

"Excuse me? Rayhan is out there! Is this because I'm a woman, so I should stay holed up inside?" I exclaimed. Didn't he get that I couldn't just stay still and do nothing?

"Think of it however the fuck you want. You are not leaving this villa." His tone was cold and final, and when his piercing black eyes met mine, I knew he wasn't going to budge. His words stung, and I pressed my lips together.

"I am strong and I am not going to sit by and let my daughter suffer whilst I play the helpless, worried, mother!" I snapped, my irritation brimming over the surface.

"Kiara. This is about fucking playing safe," he said quietly, glancing at the open archway, but I didn't care who heard.

"I am not going to play safe when my daughter is out there!" My voice shook and my vision blurred.

"You will." My eyes flashed as I glared at him through my tears. I was a queen, and I was not going to back down. "Kia…" He put his phone away, reaching for me, but I stepped out of his reach, shaking my head.

"What about you? Don't you think that it hurts me, too, knowing that you might be sacrificing yourself? Do you see me complaining?"

"I'm her father -"

"And I'm her mother!" I cried as he grabbed hold of my arms.

"I know, Amore Mio, and you always fucking will be, but I need to do this for my family. For me to be fucking sane out there, I need to know that the rest of you are safe," he said coldly, despite his voice remaining quiet. One hand forced my chin up to look at him. I refused to, staring past his head.

"We aren't safe here either. For Goddess's sake, Alejandro, they were here! They placed those letters! I am a blessed wolf, I'm the queen, and, above all, I'm her mother! I can't just sit back and do nothing!" His eyes flashed red, his brows furrowing.

"I fucking know, but it's safer here than out there. Besides, the witches are coming, and I need you here."

"They won't be here forever," I replied.

"We are not doing this, you ain't fucking going." I ripped free from his hold, glaring at him. "Kia…"

"Whatever."

I shook my head, turning and storming out of the room, not caring about the men and few women who were ready to leave with Alejandro. *I am not going to just sit here and do absolutely fuck all!*

"Kiara." Mom's voice broke me out of my rage, and I knew she had heard the argument. "I don't agree with him, but he has a point. He won't be able to focus knowing you are out there."

"That's not my problem," I whispered, brushing past her. My heart clenched with pain at my harsh words.

"Kiara!" Mom called, but I refused to look at or listen to anyone when Skyla's little voice called me.

"Mama?" I turned, my heart breaking at the sight of her sorrow-filled face.

"Darling," I whispered. Rushing up the stairs, I hugged her tightly.

"Mama, Kataleya..." she whispered.

"We are going to find her," I reassured her, trying to hide my own tears.

"And bring her home. I fucking promise." Alejandro's voice came from behind me.

I tensed, feeling guilt fill me as he crouched down, placing a hand on my back. His other arm wrapped around Skyla and my shoulder. He kissed her forehead before looking at me.

"Forgive me, Amore Mio…" He leaned over, claiming my lips in a deep, passionate kiss. I kissed him back slowly, looking up at him as he moved away, brushing away a stray tear from my cheek before he stood up and took the steps down three at a time.

I would give them three hours. If there was nothing, then I was going to go, and no one was going to stop me from looking for my daughter. He stopped at the door and turned, so his gaze met mine.

I love you, Amore Mio.

I love you too.

He gave me one of his sexy smirks before he disappeared just as the sun began to rise outside.

"Sky, Kia, how about some breakfast?" Mom asked. I nodded, lifting Skyla up.

"Mama, I'm not a baby," she whispered, and I frowned, concerned at her words.

"I know, baby, but can't I carry you?" I asked her as she led the way down the stairs.

"No. I'm a big girl. I'm going to be strong, like Kataleya," she whispered, her eyes saddening.

"You are both strong." I gave her hand a gentle squeeze, following Mom into the kitchen.

"Will Dante wake up? I promise I won't call him a dumb dumb again." Skyla asked, climbing onto one of the bar stools as Serena placed a plate of food in front of her.

"He will," I said, smiling gently at her. I took a seat but refused the plate of breakfast Serena offered me, instead just picking up the mug of mocha Mom had passed me. "Now, eat up so you can get dressed and watch some TV."

I was very aware of Julio and several guards situated inside of the house, all on alert. Once Serena took Skyla to get her dressed, Mom turned to me, concern clear on her gorgeous face.

"You know Alejandro will do his best."

"I know, Mom, but I can use my abilities, too."

"Liam's there. He is intuitive, too. Keep faith, Kia, and trust in them."

"Mom, if it were you, would you just sit at home?" I asked, frowning. The sunlight bathed the counter, and if one didn't know better, they would never think there was so much conflict and trouble within the walls of this villa. She looked down before giving me a small, faint smile and shaking her head.

"No, but from a wiser person's point of view, don't be reckless."

"You're contradicting yourself, Mom."

"But please, listen to him," she persisted.

"I'm giving him time," I said quietly. I turned towards the window, feeling the witches' approach. Mom hadn't sensed them. "They're here."

Mom looked up sharply, her heart skipping a beat, and I knew she was hoping that the witches had some answers to what was happening to Dante and Delsanra. I left the kitchen, hurrying to the front door and pulling it open, looking at the two older women who stood before me.

"High Witch Magdalene, High Witch Janaina." I lowered my head slightly in respect and both women did the same to me.

Janaina had once been a lone witch; it was when Rayhan found his mate Delsanra that we ended up being at peace with the witches. Janaina was Delsanra's paternal aunt, although she didn't really like to talk about it. She was also the one who gave me the necklace that Dante wore to conceal his aura.

"Would you like a drink, or shall we head upstairs?" I asked.

"Let's not waste time," Magdalene said, waving her hand and the door shut behind them. She observed the guards around the hall as I led the way upstairs.

"What exactly happened?" Janaina asked, and I swiftly filled them in on what I knew; how Delsanra's spell seemed to backfire and the ominous feeling I had felt in the room. "A presence?" She asked sharply as I opened the door to the bedroom.

"Yes, I definitely felt like there was something here," I admitted.

My eyes fell to the two on the bed, the red veins still covering their entire skin. Magdalene sucked in a breath whilst Janaina frowned deeply.

"They are cursed," Magdalene stated the moment she looked down at the sleeping duo. "It was a natural mistake for Delsanra Silver to make… her ability of darkness and fire… if you use the wrong magic against a curse, it only strengthens it. Neither she nor Serafina would be able to break this curse, for it is only fuelled by the element of fire."

"Then, can you help?" I asked.

She paused and sighed, "We need the talisman where the curse was cast upon. In this case, it may have been a weapon or something, whatever made contact with the prince."

"Alejandro said a wolf attacked him, and he killed that wolf," I added, looking down at Dante, whose skin looked grey.

"Then, it's a loss… the only one who can break it is the caster," Janaina murmured.

"So, until then, what can we do?"

"We could try to see if we can at least ease the effect of it, maybe to the point of bringing them to consciousness," Magdalene muttered, placing a finger on Delsanra's forehead. She frowned, and I felt power emanate from her. She jerked back suddenly, almost as if she had been burned, clutching her hand. "Odd…"

"What is it?"

"This is not the doing of any witch or necromancer," Magdalene said in a hushed tone.

"Then, what is it?" I asked, fear filling me.

"A demon."

From the look on both their almost emotionless faces, I knew there was a lot more to it than that, and something told me it was not going to be good…

Her Decision

KIARA

"*T*HIS IS WORSE THAN we thought, isn't it?"

"Demons are rare, and if this was cast by a demon, and I'm sure it was, then finding the one behind it is going to be rather difficult, even for us." I closed my eyes, wishing that was not the case.

"Is there no other way?"

"Of course there is, finding the one who summoned the demon. If we find him, then we find the rest of the answers," Magdalene stated, smoothing out the sleeve of her dress. The two women exchanged looks. I knew they were keeping something from me.

"There's more to it, isn't there? Tell me," I demanded sharply, just as Mom entered. Janaina sighed heavily.

"If anyone else had performed this spell, or any spell for that matter, trying to lift the curse…. they would have died instantly. The only reason Delsanra survived is because of her demon side." Her words made my blood run cold. I felt as if I had been slapped across the face. Goddess.

My heart was thundering erratically, thinking of the consequences of what could have happened. I had called her here; she could have died…

Mom placed her arm around me, and, for a moment, I took comfort in her touch before I walked over to Delsanra, thinking of what could have happened.

"What do you propose?" Mom asked them.

"We shall perform a spell to simply bring them to consciousness, however, they will remain cursed. That means hallucinations, weakness, and whatever other side effects there may be. I can't be fully sure," Magdalene said quietly.

"Are they not better off staying unconscious, then?" Mom asked.

"No, there is a chance they will begin to lose their minds if this continues. Time will run out. We need to make sure the curse is broken before then, but how long that may take, I am not sure. Whoever is behind this planned it very carefully," Magdalene continued.

Janaina sighed, "Someone strong enough to summon demons and to have them do their bidding... that's a first."

"We all know what happened the one time our kind tried that; male demons are extremely hard to capture... to think they made a deal with them. It has to be a Djinn. Normal demons are more... childlike, you could say; they don't think like humans. Then, there are the Djinn. How they managed to get a hold of one, however... is beyond me. He must have paid an extremely high price..." Magdalene murmured.

"So, is the enemy a witch?" I asked, frowning.

"We cannot say for sure, but if it is, it is not anyone we know of. Someone of this calibre... is definitely not from our coven," she replied.

I listened to them, my mind made up. I was going to have to find this person.

"They left a message." I reached into my pocket, grabbing my shattered phone, and held up the picture of the notepad where I had written the two sentences. Janaina took the phone from me, and they both read it, looking thoughtful.

"The Crimson King, I haven't heard of anyone by that name. We can check if there's anything we can find on him via magic. For now, let's perform the spell," Janaina remarked when Magdalene raised her hand.

"Wait... I feel like I may have heard the term somewhere... I will look into it," she mused.

I nodded, watching both women get to work. Individually they may not be as powerful as Delsanra, who was at a calibre beyond even the most powerful witches, yet it was clear they had experience on their side.

With each passing moment, as I looked upon the two forms on the bed, their hearts beating fast and those dark, angry veins lining their skin, I knew that I had to do something. I couldn't just sit there and allow everyone else to be out there...

The two high witches had been at the spell for a while. It took them almost an hour to steady Dante and Delsanra's heartbeats. I left for a short while to check on Skyla whilst Mom got the witches some refreshments, despite both being in full concentration mode.

When Delsanra and Dante's eyes flew open simultaneously, they blazed red as they looked around. The veins still remained on their bodies, and their skin remained ashy, yet their heartbeats were level.

"Mom?" Dante croaked as I rushed to the edge of the magic trigram that was surrounding them.

"Baby, you're going to be okay," I whispered, relief flooding me. I fought back my tears. His eyes met mine, confusion clear in them as he looked around, tensing.

"They're coming," he croaked.

"Who is?" Magdalene asked sharply.

"The wolves of fire," he murmured.

I exchanged looks with Mom, turning back to him. His eyes closed, and he took a deep breath. Anything Dante said that wasn't in normal conversation was not something to sideline. His intuition was far stronger than mine or Liam's.

"I see the boy is special," Magdalene said keenly.

I did trust her, but I wasn't completely comfortable with them knowing about my son's ability. Dante knew I was having twin baby girls when I had first found out I was pregnant. Janaina had given me the amulet that Dante always wore, and she must have seen it. I was sure she had her assumptions.

"Delsanra," I called, turning towards the white-haired beauty. She looked at me and gave me a small, weak smile.

"Sorry, I just caused you more work. I messed up, and I wasn't able to help him." She looked at Dante, reaching over and stroking his hair. For once, he didn't blush or pout. Instead, he just stared ahead, his face deathly and his eyes dark with thought.

"They won't be able to do much, but at least they are conscious for now. You are on a short time leash, Queen Kiara." Magdalene's words held the weight of reality in them. If I'd had any doubt, it was gone. I had to do something. "As the Lycan king asked, he wished for some protective spells to be placed around the Night Walker Pack. So, without further ado, we should head there. I'm sure it will be safer for you all as well," she continued.

I nodded. They were right. Returning to the pack would mean better security, and from there, I would decide what to do. I kissed Dante's cheek before giving Delsanra a hug.

"Want to talk to Ahren and Sienna?" I asked her softly. Concern filled her eyes, and she nodded.

"How long have we been out?"

"A day," I replied, taking the water bottle from Mom and holding it to her lips as Mom helped Dante drink.

"Not too long." She seemed relieved. She was a mother, too, and her pups were still so young.

"I will pass the message to Alejandro," I said, deciding to reach out to the nearest of our men who formed a chain of communication that reached each wolf that was out there searching.

Let Alejandro know we are returning home with the witches. Julio and Phillip will remain to keep an eye on the villa in case something else odd shows up. Also, let him and Rayhan know that Dante and Delsanra are now conscious.

Understood, Luna. That is great news.

෨෧෧෨

Night had fallen, and I had just put Skyla and Dante to bed. Mom would watch them; as much as I didn't want to leave them, I had to. I had made my decision. Delsanra was still there; however, Raihana had brought her pups to see her and to check on Skyla and Dante.

I felt better being at home in the comfort and safety of our mansion. Alejandro had called at one point to speak to Dante, and I had filled him in on everything the witches had said. They had put some protective spells in place before they'd left with a promise to look into the Crimson King.

It was silent, with everyone having settled down for the night. Mom would sleep in Dante's room. I was meant to be sleeping with Skyla, however, I would tell Serena before I left and order her to stay with Skyla. I brushed my fingers through Dante's hair, having slipped a small note under his pillow, letting him know I'd be back soon. I was about to leave the room when Mom stepped out of the adjoining bathroom.

"Kia." I turned as she towelled her vibrant red hair with a navy towel.

"Hmm?" She didn't speak. Her eyes were locked with mine as if she was peering into my soul. *You can't hide things from your mother, right?*

"Are you heading to bed?" She asked after a moment. That was not what she was about to say...

"Yeah, I'm just going to shower and then get some rest." I turned the door handle.

"Kia..."

I looked at her, and I knew at that moment that she knew I was going to go. I didn't reply as we stared at each other. I saw her concern and worry, too, but mixed in with it was the conflict of letting it slide.

"I am not a child, nor am I just a trophy on my king's arm... I am a fighter, a queen, and, above all, a mother," I replied quietly, staring at the handle that I was still holding onto.

"I know. Take care of yourself," she replied quietly.

I didn't reply, casting her a small smile and leaving the room. I returned to my own, where Skyla was fast asleep. I sat down on my bed, brushed my fingers through her long hair, and sighed heavily.

I will be back soon. I didn't want her to get scared, but I needed Kataleya home.

"Mama?" She asked sleepily, her eyes fluttering open.

"Darling, I'm here, but I'm going to go find Kat, okay?" I whispered, bending down and kissing her forehead. She looked at me, frowning as she took in what I had just said, and the sleep vanished from her eyes before she nodded determinedly.

"Okay, Mama," she replied.

"Be a good girl for Mama Red, okay?" That's what they called Mom. Skyla had started it off, and even Dante, who used to call her grandma, called her Mama Red.

"I will, Mama. I love you." She sat up, hugging me tightly as I wrapped my arms around her.

"I love you, too, baby; you, Kat, Dante, Daddy." I kissed her cheek before she lay back down.

"I know, Mama... will you come home tomorrow?"

"I'll come home when I find Kat, okay?"

"Okay! Mama is strong." I hoped so. I just needed to find my baby.

"Sleep. I will stay here until you fall asleep, okay? Want me to sing to you?"

"Yes, Mama, a Disney song, please! Savages! From Pocahontas!"

I laughed lightly. Only Skyla would choose such a song. I began singing the song, and she joined in with the chorus.

"Savages! Savages!"

I didn't think it was the best choice to make someone go to sleep, but if that was what she wanted, then so be it. She soon settled down as I sang softly despite her choice.

"Mama... those wolves were savages..." she murmured drowsily. I frowned. Yeah... they were inhumane... *I will do what I can, and I will bring her back.*

"I know, my love. Now, sleep..."

"Night, Mama..."

She fell asleep. I stood up, ready to pack myself a bag and get out of there. I grabbed two outfits, a wireless charging pad, and my phone. I slid my wedding and engagement rings off, placing them on the chest of drawers. Gazing down at them, I felt a pang of pain. *Forgive me, Alejandro...*

I mind-linked Serena, asking her to come to my bedroom.

"Everything okay, Kiara?" She asked when she walked in after a light knock.

"I need you to stay with Skyla." She raised her eyebrows questioningly before her eyes widened in shock as realisation sunk in.

"Kiara, you aren't -"

"Just do as I say, please. Good night, Serena," I cut her off. I didn't want Al to take his anger out on her when he found out.

I gave her a small smile, hoping she understood, before I left the room and headed to Alejandro's office. I needed to grab my staff, some poisons, and antidotes. I walked down the quiet halls, memories of Alejandro chasing the girls down this very hall when they wanted him to play the wolf, and they were the little red riding hood twins, made me smile. I remembered he had actually shifted just to make them happy when they had begged him to. Their shrieks of fear and excitement as he chased them ever so slowly, although they had run as fast as their little feet could take them, their little red capes flying behind them. It had made them super happy. Soon I hoped we had that back in this home… all five of us together again, safe and happy.

I keyed in Alejandro's office code; the beep sounded extremely loud in the silent hall. I glanced down the hall, knowing that the guards were posted everywhere; sure enough, one of them appeared instantly. Seeing me, he relaxed, and I gave a smooth smile. I knew I was going to have to knock one or two out on my way because there was no way Alejandro didn't tell them to keep an eye on me. I was not going to be a prisoner in my own home.

I shut the door behind me, glancing around the office. It was decorated in browns and blacks with a large desk and a chair. Sofas stood to the side, and shelves lined one wall. His scent lingered, and my heart clenched, knowing I was going to hurt him by doing this. I just hoped he understood when he calmed down that I had to do this.

I walked to the far wall where the huge shelves lined the wall and moved aside a few items, then pressed a certain area of the wall. It popped open, revealing a keypad. Keying in the code, I stepped back as the wall on the left moved slightly. I walked over to it, pushing it wider and stepping inside. The automatic lights came on, and I deactivated the alarm system and then scanned my fingerprint before the red sensors vanished.

I stepped forward, sparing the door to the vault that was on one side a glance, but then I walked down the left side to the room that contained poisons, weapons, and antidotes. Although most of this stuff was kept under security at the pack headquarters, we had some at home. I took my metal staff that would become triple its size with a sharp tip on each side if I pressed the button in the middle and grabbed some antidotes and poisons, along with a few anti-scent sprays and several magic talismans that Delsanra and Raihana had made for us. *Okay, I think I'm sorted.*

I filled my bag and returned to his office. Placing the bag down, I sank into his leather chair, picked up a pen, and rummaged around for some paper, ready to pen him a note and promise to stay in touch via phone. I wasn't sure he'd even see the note, considering he said he wouldn't be back, but still, just in case…

I had snuck away from the mansion with the help of an anti-scent spray after grabbing some food from the kitchen. I only had to knock one guard unconscious before I shifted, holding my bag in my mouth as I ran into the dark, the urge to find my little princess rushing through my veins.

I'm coming, Kataleya…

I relaxed my mind, letting the glow of the shining moon sink into my white fur, praying that Selene guided me to her. I had nothing in mind, no destination, but to follow my instincts. My wolf was on edge, reeling to go, and I knew she wanted to find our pup just as much as I did. I was heading south, and I sped up, not stopping. If that was where I was being guided, that's where I'd go. It was all I could really follow anyway, and I just prayed it was the right way…

I will find you, my baby. I promise.

His Irritation

UNKNOWN

I FROWNED, WATCHING MY FATHER pace the room in anger as I stood against the wall; chin up, shoulders back, hands crossed behind my back, ready and paying attention to whatever he might say.

He took his jacket and gloves off, revealing his burnt skin. The side of his face was burned, too, but it wasn't as bad as the rest of his body. People found him quite scary, with his skin all raw and burnt. The burns didn't look normal either; they had an angry red shade to them despite them being there since before I was even born. But Father was still the best, the strongest, and the most powerful.

"I asked you, men, to bring me the boy," Father hissed, staring at the four men who looked almost identical to each other, with their flaming red hair and pale orangey eyes. Power exuded from them, but it didn't match Father's; nowhere near close.

"Alpha… we tried, but he wasn't making it easy. The boy or this girl -"

"Did I ask you to talk back, *hijo de puta*?" Father spat, his powerful aura blanketing the room.

I looked down. No matter how angry he was, he wouldn't hurt me… I kept my gaze straight ahead when Dad ripped through one of their necks. The gargling sound of choking and the strong smell of metallic blood filled the room, and I swallowed, trying not to gag. Father wanted me there so I learned exactly how to keep order within our people. Father was strict and dangerous; he was the perfect Alpha, one I wanted to become just like when I was old enough. He was my role model. A true king.

I glanced at the body of the man he had killed emotionlessly.

"Tell me, mijo, if an order is given, what do we do?" Father's cold glare was on me, and I smiled confidently, making sure no emotion reached my eyes.

"We complete it by all means necessary. There is no such thing as failure," I replied emotionlessly.

"That's my son." Father's glare returned to the other three men. "The girl is useless, without even an ounce of power or aura within her. The Lycan won't care if she's collateral damage. She's not his heir!"

"King… forgive me for speaking up, but from what we have been told, the Lycan actually loves his children. I think he will want her back," one of the men replied quietly. Father's lips curled in disgust, his burned skin stretching as he did so.

"She's a girl! I don't think anyone will come for her! She is useless to me!"

I frowned, tilting my head. A girl? I didn't know that they had managed to bring one of the Lycan's children… albeit the wrong one. I had heard of his abilities even from across the ocean. He was said to be a force to be reckoned with. *Well, I guess he hasn't met Father.*

"Padre… it's worth a try. If it doesn't work, just kill her and send him the video," I shrugged. Father smirked coldly, his eyes full of burning rage and pride.

"That's an idea." He turned his gaze on the other three, his hatred and anger growing tenfold.

I frowned. I wanted to see the girl… the child of a Lycan. Was she powerful? People said they could already sense my aura, although I was only ten.

"May I see her?" Father looked at me, frowning as if he had not expected that request.

"Very well. You may." He said, "Take him!"

One of the men nodded, bowing his head to Father before I made my way out of the room, pausing for him to walk ahead and lead the way. I had no idea where she was kept, after all. I wouldn't deny that I was curious to see her.

"Alpha Prince, she's in the basement."

I raised an eyebrow with curiosity. A basement in this place? I didn't even know there was one. We had been away from our home for the last year… but Father had important work here, more so with this Lycan.

We walked through the pantry, and Rodrigo unlocked the huge padlock. I was a little curious. If she was nothing special, then why was she kept under such security? The metal door screeched open.

"I'll manage alone from here, Rodrigo. Wait upstairs," I said emotionlessly.

I wasn't sure how old she was, but I was sure even if she was older than me, I could take her if she tried anything funny. Clearly, Rodrigo thought the same as he didn't argue. I walked down the stairs, and the scent of cherry blossoms and a soft cotton breeze filled my nose. I frowned. That wasn't exactly what I was expecting a Lycan's hybrid to smell like. I scanned the darkness down below. There was a small arch that led to the toilet and sink, but then the rest of the room was empty.

I heard a gasp and a cut-off whimper, so I raised my eyebrow. Where was she?

I paused when I saw her huddled in the corner, her hands clamped over her mouth and wide, doe eyes staring back at me with fear. I barely hid my surprise. She was young, really young...

She seemed to be confused as she looked me over, and it was then I realised I hadn't even been able to sense her until I spotted her. Strange. Her long, light brown hair was a mess, but I could tell she was a pampered little princess from her dress.

"Please don't hurt me," she whispered; her voice was soft, too, like her scent. Gentle and full of emotions. I didn't really hear it often. It was... strange. Who would have thought the Lycan's daughter would be so much of a disappointment? I was expecting someone brave, strong, and unyielding. How pathetic... at that age, I had already killed.

"I don't hit girls," I stated arrogantly, crossing my arms as I walked over to her. "Stand up," I commanded coldly.

Her eyes widened, impossibly large, her heart thumping. I realised when I entered that I hadn't heard it either. So, she wasn't completely ordinary. Wait... was it possible she was hiding her abilities?

She obeyed, standing up quickly. To my surprise, she held my gaze. Hmm... so she was indeed the Lycan's child. Usually, people would look away. She looked around seven, I thought. She was cute, I had to admit, pretty even, not like the picture I saw of the Lycan... was she really his daughter?

"Is your father the Lycan king?" I asked. She nodded.

"Yes."

"You don't look like him." She blinked, and I shook my head. Of course, she doesn't look like a grown man. I sounded foolish. "Have you been given food?" I changed the subject, hiding my blunder.

I wasn't sure why I had even asked… I remembered what I told Father about killing her, but at the time, I didn't think she would be so little… and innocent.. but Father would kill her if he deemed it was best.

"No," she replied.

I didn't reply. It wasn't my business. I was about to leave when she spoke.

"Umm, will they let me go?" She asked softly.

"No," I stated emotionlessly.

"Oh." Her voice trembled, and I walked to the stairs swiftly. *I shouldn't stay here any longer than necessary.*

"I will see if you are allowed food," I said simply before exiting and slamming the door behind me.

"Young master, I doubt she is permitted to have food," Rodrigo said, bowing his head.

"I didn't ask you for your opinion," I replied coldly, walking off.

If she isn't allowed food, then she isn't. I didn't care.

Then why couldn't I shake the thought out of my head?

ALEJANDRO

Another day had fucking gone by, but nothing. I was not far from Marcel's pack and decided to stop by. He had joined in on the search and had told me I needed a break. As much as I fucking didn't want to stop for the night, I knew I had to keep my fucking energy up. The search for Kataleya was not going to stop; when we stopped, others took our place. There wasn't anything solid yet, but we did get some information on some odd events over the last few months, and it was down south, so we'd fucking see.

I walked through the huge silver gates of the Sangue pack with Marcel at my side, everyone bowing their heads to us as we passed. They had come a long fucking way since they first became a proper pack. They were like any other pack, despite being rogues to start with. Marcel had done a good job and had managed to bring the unruly wolves under his control. Despite being manipulated by our mother and under her control, he had been strong enough not to let it get to his fucking head.

This pack was seen as outcasts by many. Over the years, that image faded, and people weren't treating them as badly or coldly as they once were, but, despite that, the seed of hatred lingered in the form of none other than my nephew... Leo Rossi. Even when we entered Marcel's mansion, he was coming down the staircase and paused in the process of pushing up his sleeves. Like me, he was fucking tatted all over. His pale blue eyes only seemed to get paler and colder as the years passed. He was seventeen, but he was almost as fucking tall as I was. His chocolate brown hair only added a few fucking inches, too...

"Alejandro," his icy voice came.

"Leo. Good to fucking see you. You've grown a few inches," I replied, giving him a smirk despite how fucking worried I was about Kataleya. His face didn't change, but he gave me a curt nod.

"I'm out," he told his father.

"Leo, stay for dinner. Your cousin Kataleya's still not found. Perhaps you can give some insight," Marcel suggested quietly. He raised his eyebrow.

"And that's my issue, why?"

I frowned, my anger flaring up, but I wasn't going to lash out when that was what he fucking wanted. I saw myself in him, and it wasn't a pretty sight. Rafael had been there for me when I let the darkness consume me, and I intended to be there for Leo continuously, even if he was a fucker that I wanted to smack over the head most of the fucking time. *Fucking pups.*

"Leo!" Marcel growled.

"What? Will eating together solve the fucking issue? I don't think so," he scoffed before pushing past his dad and walking out. The door slammed shut behind him.

"He's getting worse... the only thing I can pride him on is that he is fair when it comes to the pack, and he's studying hard," Marcel growled.

"It's that age. I'm sure he'll come around, that, or he'll get a mate who will fucking whip his ass into shape."

"I want to see what girl can do that... she's going to have to be extremely strong-willed," Marcel sighed.

"Yeah, someone like Kiara. I don't know how the fuck she fixed me up," I agreed coldly, needing a fucking cigarette. Marcel chuckled dryly.

"Well, the Westwood women are something else."

Yeah, they fucking are. Scarlett is even more fucking feisty and equally head-strong as her daughter.

I glanced over at him. Despite only being six years older than me, he looked aged. He had lost his mate. There were signs that were bound to catch up. Second-chance mates existed, but not everyone got one. Life fucking sucked. If he took a chosen one, maybe things would get fucking easier? But I also knew he was Marcel; he wasn't over her... many Alphas took chosen mates just to keep their sanity.

"Come, I'll show you to a room where you can shower, and then dinner will be ready." I nodded, allowing him to lead the way.

Once I was left alone in a guest room, I took my phone out of my oversized shorts pocket. First, I checked for updates from the other men and filled them in on where I was and the plans for tomorrow. I sat down on the bed, lying back and feeling the tiredness in my bones.

I needed to talk to my nympho. How was she coping? Were the kids and Del doing okay? I called her, frowning when it went straight to the answering machine. Why the fuck was it turned off? I tried again, but nothing. The fuck?

I sat up, dialling Darien. He should be there. His phone rang, but he didn't answer. Worry began consuming me, and a thousand fucking scenarios rushed through my head. Did something fucking happen? The only thing fucking keeping me from losing my shit was that I hadn't felt anything through the link. *Fuck.*

I rang Scarlett next, my heart racing as I tried to tell myself they were okay. The witches did a fucking spell, right? Nothing should have fucking happened...

"Hello." I closed my eyes. Never had I been fucking happier to hear her voice.

"Why the fuck is Kia's phone off?" I growled.

"Hello to you, too, Alejandro." The woman was so fucking antagonising at times.

"Pass it to Kiara." Silence followed, and I clenched my jaw. Was she really fucking doing this? "For fuck's sake, please?" I added coldly.

"I'm not asking you to be nice, Alejandro. It's just that Kiara isn't available right now," she replied calmly. *The fuck she means unavailable?*

"Scarlett… where is Kiara?" My stomach twisted, my heart thumping with unease. *Don't fucking tell me she left…*

"She went after Kataleya."

I closed my eyes, my aura flaring around me as her words sank in. Fuck. Kiara was out there alone… phone off… with no one…

"She'll be okay, Alejan-"

"Do not fucking tell me she'll be okay when my daughter is out there alone, and now Kiara? Fuck, why did you let her go?" I hissed, standing up. I couldn't stay here when she was out there alone.

"She's a mother -"

"Who clearly had no faith in her mate," I said icily.

I didn't care if those words were harsh because what I felt inside… was fucking worse. I was doing my best… I fucked up… Kat was gone because of me, and now, Kiara decided to go look for her herself? I really wasn't fucking enough, and it was clear she had no faith in me.

"Alejandro, please don't think like that, she's only -"

I cut the call. I did not need Scarlett talking shit to me. I needed to find Kiara now, too.

Fuck this.

My phone rang as I stood up, and I answered it after glancing at the name Elijah. I had half a fucking mind to let him know what his daughter had just done. *Actually, I think I fucking will.*

"What is it?" I asked coldly.

"I'm in Oxford, and there's been a sighting that may or may not help. Someone said they saw a mass of reddish-coloured wolves, although the old man seemed to be a little lost in the head. I think it's all we got to go on."

"Perfect. I'll head there now…" I closed my eyes, feeling some fucking hope… "By the way… Kiara left, and your mate allowed it. You know it's not fucking safe out there," I growled.

"What?" Elijah's voice was sharp, and I could hear the irritation in it. I smirked coldly.

"Yeah, exactly. She doesn't fucking listen. I'm going to send a team out to find her, and I'm coming down to Oxford. If we have a lead, I'm not wasting more time allowing my baby girl to be out there alone for longer than necessary." Elijah sighed heavily.

"That makes sense… when you get here, you, Liam, and Rayhan can head forward. I'll find Kiara."

"Yeah, and let her know when I find her, she's in fucking trouble," I growled, hanging up.

My eyes blazed red. *I swear if anything happens to her….* I closed my eyes, running a hand through my hair and trying to control my anger. I told her I couldn't fucking focus if she was out there… I told her to stay…

I dialled Darien. That fucker didn't answer because he was fucking scared, I knew that much…

"Hi, Alpha."

"Hey, fucker. You couldn't keep Kiara there?"

"Listen, she snuck out. No one realised…"

"Oh, yeah? I'll be fucking sorting this shit out when I get home. For now, anything with my demand on the net?"

"Nothing, maybe he hasn't seen it yet," Darien said, clearly nervous.

"Push for it to get more fucking exposure. I want my girl back by all fucking means." I ripped open the door to the bedroom and stormed downstairs.

"Al… didn't you shower or -"

"I need to go. Kiara left to look for her, too, and Elijah may or may not have found a lead. You don't come, you need your fucking rest."

Not waiting for a reply, I shifted and rushed from the house. I spotted Leo sitting high up in a tree, smoking a cigarette as I ran past. My only aim was to get to Oxford and pray that my baby girl was somewhere there. As for Kiara… I frowned deeply. No matter how fucking pissed I was at her, the worry for her safety clawed at my mind and chest. Fuck, why was she so damn reckless?

The trees were a blur as I zoomed through them as fast as I could. The moon was hidden mostly by clouds, and the night was still, yet that burden that hung above my head was fucking looming heavily. I needed to fix this shit.

An Act of Kindness

UNKNOWN

I COULD HEAR THE SOUNDS of night animals outside my bedroom window hooting, howling, and crying out extremely loudly as I stared at the ceiling, lying on the hard plank of wood that was my bed. My room was luxurious enough, but, as future Alpha, there were certain things I didn't need and shouldn't get used to, like soft beds, for one, or blankets. As a werewolf, my body kept itself warm, and it was better to get used to things than to be spoiled with useless, unnecessary items.

It had been a while since I talked to the Lycan's daughter, but I couldn't brush off how innocent she seemed. I knew her father was a horrible person who owed my family a lot, and I knew that inevitably she might die, but whilst she was alive, perhaps I could offer her some sympathy or something of the sort. I sat up, remembering how her dress was torn at her waist and covered in bloodstains. She had lost a lot of blood, too…

I ran my hand through my black hair, sighing. It wasn't like me to show compassion. It was a weakness, after all. *Is this why Father says women are nothing more than something to bear pups? Regardless of that, perhaps I should ask Mother.*

I got out of bed and exited my room. Father stayed on a separate floor from my mother and me. I guess that was convenient right then. I didn't like going behind his back, but something about the girl in the basement didn't sit right with me. I walked down the carpeted halls and knocked lightly on mother's door. It was past two a.m.; she was probably asleep.

The door opened, and I looked up at her. Although Father said I shouldn't care for anyone, I dared not tell him that I did care for Mother.

I loved her dearly, just as much as I loved him. She had black hair with large hazel eyes that were similar to mine.

"Mi Vida, what a surprise," Mother said softly. She wore a good mask, too; she knew Father's rules.

"Yes. I wanted to ask you something, if I'm not intruding," I stated. I wasn't allowed to visit her too often as Father said it made me weak, and it was a waste of time.

"Of course not," she replied, smiling slightly. I walked into her room, and she closed the door.

"There's a girl in the basement, the Lycan's daughter. I went to visit her earlier. I know we shouldn't trust anyone or anything, no matter how helpless and innocent they may look, but I was wondering, how bad would it be to give her food?" I asked. Mother's smile vanished, and I could hear her racing heartbeat.

"Mi Vida... don't do it," she whispered. "The Alpha will not forgive you." I tilted my head. He wouldn't need to know, and it was clear, despite Mother's refusal, that I still wanted to.

"I understand. Good night." I turned and left the room swiftly.

"Mi Vida…"

I ignored her and walked towards my room, hearing Mother sigh and close the door to her room. I glanced back at it before changing direction and heading downstairs instead, making my way to the kitchen. I needed to take something that I could carry discreetly. We'd had ribs for dinner, perhaps there were some left…

I entered the large kitchen. The silence was deafening. I began opening the drawers, knowing I would have to hide the food when I went down. I took a plate and went to the fridge. As I assumed, there were some left-over ribs and roast potatoes. I put them on the plate along with some spicy rice and placed it in the microwave. *I've never really used this before…*

After pressing around on the random buttons, I finally got it figured out. The sound seemed to be blaring loudly, and I hoped no one would come to check. I frowned, wondering if Father would hear me. He usually liked to have adult time at night, whatever that meant. Hopefully, he didn't hear me. Whilst the food was being heated, I busied myself with finding something to place the food in. I rummaged around in the drawers until I found some kitchen foil and a freezer bag. That should do. I glanced towards the hallway before I spread two layers on the worktop and got the plate from the microwave. Placing the ribs, potatoes, and rice on the foil, I wrapped it up. She would have to make do without a spoon.

I placed the foil into the freezer bag, hoping it wouldn't smell too strongly. Going to the fridge, I grabbed a bottle of orange juice before sliding the hot food bag under my baggy top and leaving the kitchen. I headed towards the basement and saw only Ronaldo, one of the four brothers, standing there. Well, one of three brothers now.

"Open the door. I want to see the foolish thing," I stated emotionlessly. His gaze dipped to the bottle of orange juice in my hand, and I smoothly unscrewed the cap, taking a gulp. "I just stopped by the kitchen for some food as I felt peckish, and now I can't sleep. I need to vent some of this anger. I'm sure Padre wouldn't care if she gets a little injured," I smirked coldly, and he lowered his head.

"Yes, of course." The moment the door opened, I glanced at Ronaldo.

"Keep the door shut. I will knock when I'm done. I don't want anyone to get disturbed."

He nodded, bowing his head to me, and the door shut behind me. I didn't hear her this time. I scanned the dark room below and saw her body on the floor near the sink. Had she tried to drink water? The tap was on, but it was obvious it didn't really work. A dirty trickle of water was coming out of it. I took the food parcel out from under my shirt and placed it on the floor along with the juice bottle before walking over to her. I switched the tap off, frowning when she didn't even stir. It seemed she had fallen unconscious.

How weak… I'd been without food for two weeks several times, Father made sure I learned how to cope, yet here was this little weak thing, unable to even keep awake after a few days. I crouched down, and I suddenly realised her body was bruised. *Those weren't there earlier…* My heart began to race… she had been beaten. Had Father done this? My stomach twisted. I wasn't sure, but this wasn't right… even if he was to kill her, why prolong the suffering?

No, I shouldn't question Father.

"Oye, chica, get up," I said, shaking her slightly.

She whimpered, my eyes falling on the large bruise on her face. Had Father actually beaten a child? Sure, my training consisted of beatings, but that was for me to get stronger…

"I have brought you food, but if you do not get up, then I can't help you."

Still, she didn't get up. I frowned, lifting her body and carrying her to where I had left the food. How troublesome. I propped the life-size rag doll against the wall, prodding her head that lolled to the side. Actually, she looked a lot like a China doll. Creepily cute with too much hair…

I don't have time for random thoughts. I tapped her cheek lightly, and this time her eyes fluttered open.

"Wake up, chica," I whispered. Her eyes flew open, her heartbeat thundering as she flinched as if ready to be hit again. "I don't hit girls." I rolled my eyes and held the orange juice bottle to her; confusion filled those dark eyes of hers before she took it.

"Thank you." Her soft reply was rather pitiful as she sipped some of the juice with trembling hands, supporting the bottle. I quickly opened the plastic bag and unwrapped the foil. I prayed that by tomorrow the smell would vanish or Father may do worse.

"Is that for me?" She asked.

"No, it's for me. I decided to come and eat down here because it's much more appealing than the dining room." I frowned. "Of course it's for you, but be quick." She was hesitant, almost as if wondering if it was a trick question.

"Thank you…"

"Is that all you can say, chica?"

"My name is not chica. It's Kataleya," she said, giving me a smile that lit up her bruised face. My eyes widened in shock. Did she not realise I was the enemy?

She slowly reached over, moving the foil closer to herself, flinching with pain that clearly shot up her arm. *Girls are so useless.* I shook my head, pushing the foil paper towards her.

"Be quick, chica."

Kataleya… it was an interesting name.

She reached for a potato first and looked at me as if waiting for me to beat her, but once she realised I wasn't going to do anything, she bit into it. We stayed silent as she dug in. Even though I knew she was starved, either she was far too weak to eat faster, or, from what I could tell, she was eating with manners. Tears streamed down her cheeks silently as she ate, and they were beginning to irk me.

"I'm sorry I couldn't bring a spoon or fork," I stated when the silence and awkwardness became too much, thinking I had forgotten tissue as well. Instead, I tore off a square of my pyjama sleeves and gave it to her.

"It's okay, this is more than enough. I really am grateful for it. What is your name?" She asked, taking the square of fabric and patting her lips. I frowned. Was it important? Well, she was probably not going to live long…

"Enrique. Enrique Ignacio Escarra, future Alpha of the Fuego de Ceniza Pack," I claimed proudly. Her eyes widened as she looked me over before fear flooded her eyes, and she shrunk into the wall.

"That man… was he your papa?" She whispered, utterly terrified, visibly beginning to tremble. I looked over the bruises on her tiny body and frowned.

"Yes." She nodded, gulping, but I could tell she was tense; her heartbeat was erratic, and she was shaking. "Finish the food, I don't have all day," I added coldly, getting up and turning away from her.

"I-I'm done. Thank you," she whispered.

How foolish… did she not realise that she wouldn't get any more food here? Well, that was her loss. Silently, I wrapped the remaining food back up with the foil and shoved it into the plastic bag.

"Drink the juice," I commanded, glaring at her. She quickly obliged, fat tears rolling down her cheeks, but they only annoyed me even more. "Padre is right. Girls are useless."

I pushed the empty orange juice bottle into the plastic bag and stood up, shoving it under my top, and made my way up the stairs without even looking back. I had just about reached the door when it was pulled open before I even managed to knock, revealing none other than Father himself. His nostrils flared, and his eyes blazed goldish brown.

Oh, damn…

"Did you give the girl food, mijo?" He asked me. His voice was scary, and I knew I would be punished.

"Yes, I did, Padre," I admitted, lowering my head to him in submission.

He scoffed before he backhanded me across the face, sending me reeling into the door to the basement. The food packet slipped from under my top, falling to the ground as my vision spun from the sheer force of Father's hit. My head pounded.

"Well… well… well… Enrique… what have I told you about rules and law?"

"I must always abide by yours, Padre…"

"And yet you didn't."

I heard a quiet sob from down below and the sound of scurrying footsteps. Realising what was about to happen, I frowned. The foolish chica was going to help me? She really had a death wish!

Father smirked as Kataleya appeared behind me.

"P-please don't hurt him, I promise I won't -"

"Bitch!" He growled, suddenly lurching forward and kicking her square in the chest and back down the stairs. I heard her tiny body tumble down the stairs, but no sound escaped her. My heart thumped in my throat; I shouldn't have given her food! This was my fault!

Father was about to go down the stairs when I stepped in his way.

"Padre, I disobeyed and commanded her to eat. It is I who needs to be punished for defying you," I stated, praying the silly girl stayed down. Father frowned before smirking coldly.

"Indeed, mijo, indeed…" He grabbed me by my hair painfully, pulling me away from the door. "Lock the fucking door and make sure no one sees her!" Father hissed, and I knew what was to come when he dragged me outside. Lashing or a beating.

The moment Father took his belt in his hand, I raised my head, prepared for what was to come. After all, I had learned how to take this…

I closed my eyes when the first hit connected to my back. Father would unleash all his anger upon me, but it was the right of the Alpha…

That was how I would learn to be the best kind of Alpha…

Just don't feel…

The House in the Countryside

KIARA

W HEN THE FIRST RAYS of dawn began to appear, that instinct that
I had been following through the night suddenly vanished. My
wolf fell silent, and I suddenly felt all alone. I was exhausted from the
running as well. Should I stop and take a small break? Maybe it would be
better if I did, but I wouldn't stop for long. Kataleya was out there, and I
needed to find her.

I wondered if Alejandro had found out that I had left already... I was
sure he had probably tried calling at some point.

I shifted and dropped to my knees in exhaustion. I opened my bag, pulling out some sweatpants and a crop top, putting them on quickly before
sitting back, feeling the pain in my legs and arms. Goddess...

Kataleya. I hoped she was okay, wherever she was... I would never be
able to forgive myself if something happened to her. *Please let her be safe...*

I stared at the sky, my heart clenching with worry as I tried to compose
myself. The distant whimper of my wolf in my head told me she was still
upset.

We are going to find her, okay? I told my wolf, although I knew I wouldn't
get an answer.

I ripped open a granola bar and bit into it as I took out my phone and
switched it on. The shattered screen was still working for now. I hoped it
would make do for a while. I sighed, seeing the thirty-seven missed calls.

Oh, fuck.

Three from Alejandro… twenty from Dad… *Goddess, Dad, relax…* four from Raven, two from Rayhan, three from Darien, and five from Liam. I sighed, so the entire population knew I had vanished…

I looked at my messages, my heart thudding at the single message from Alejandro.

'I asked you for one thing. One fucking thing. To stay the fuck safe. Seriously, Kia? Just up and leaving like that? I had half a mind to ask Ri to fucking find you, call me when you see this. ASAFP.'

I closed my eyes. He was pissed, as I expected him to be… I needed to call him.

I skimmed through the other messages. Dad and Liam were stressing out like it was the end of the world. Dad was incredibly pissed off as well, also warning me that Alejandro was furious, and he fucking should be. Was I sixteen or something? These men were being ridiculous. I understood their point, but I was not an incapable woman who was going to sit at home whilst my daughter was out there. I was sure I could help find her. The more of us looking, the better.

My own irritation and restlessness were flaring up, and before I could even do anything else, Dad's incoming call came again, and I sighed, answering it.

"Hel-"

"Kiara, why did you leave? Why was your phone off all night? What if something happened? You and your mother do not fucking listen -"

"Dad!" I cut him off. "Calm down! I'm fine, and I can't really answer in wolf form, can I? I think you and Alejandro forget that I am not a child anymore. I'm capable enough to help look for Kataleya, and I'm sure the more people looking, the better. Please understand that."

"We know that, but we also know that even Alejandro wasn't able to deter these wolves when he has taken down hundreds of wolves single-handedly in his teens! These wolves are something else, Kiara, and nothing to be taken lightly!" Dad growled. I frowned. I knew that…

"Dad, I'm not stupid."

"Kiara, you were the one who found these notes. Don't you think Alejandro is worried that, just like Dante is cursed, something may happen to you?"

Okay, I didn't think of that… but I was fine.

"Dad, she's my daughter! I am not going to sleep on a bed, not knowing how she is doing! She must be terrified; how do you expect me to just sit at home? Please, Dad, let's not do this," I almost pleaded, unable to hide the pain in my voice. He sighed heavily in defeat.

"I understand, but we were on it. We are going to get our Kataleya back. Where are you?"

"I was following my instincts. You know how I've always been able to sense this stuff, what if I am able to find her? I'm not that far out from your pack. Just south," I said quietly.

"That in itself makes me think we all may be on to something. We got news that there were some odd occurrences near Oxford. If you're heading south, stay that way. Maybe we are close." My heart leapt at his word, any clue or sighting was hope.

"Understood."

"Kiara. Wait for Alejandro though."

My heart was pounding with hope, and when I cut the call, I quickly dialled Alejandro's. His phone rang, and after a few moments, he answered.

"Let me speak," I said before he could even answer. "Please."

"Do I have a fucking choice? You'll just hang up and continue doing whatever the fuck you want if I don't."

I winced at the anger in his voice. It hurt having that rage directed at me, I couldn't deny that, but we weren't going to agree, and I didn't want to argue. This was about our daughter, and I was going to help find her.

"So then just listen," I said stubbornly, resulting in a murderous growl ripping through the phone. I exhaled slowly, trying to stay calm. "I am not far from Oxford. I'll join you there, but if you even think about sending me home… I won't listen, Alejandro." I heard him sigh in irritation, and when he spoke, frustration was clear in his tone.

"Fine," he replied through gritted teeth.

"I'm heading towards Oxford now. I'll meet you there," I replied quietly.

It hurt so much. I realised how angry he was at me, but I couldn't voice what I was feeling inside. The pain of having her away from me was killing me. I just wished he could understand how hard it was being a mother and unable to do anything for our daughter and not even knowing how she was. Was she fed? Was she safe?

"How far are you?" He asked me, his voice as cold and emotionless as it was when he spoke to others.

"Not too far. I should be there in a few hours."

"Hmm."

The silence between us was so tense and painful, it wasn't like us. But right then, we had different mindsets, and there was nothing that I could say would change his anger or make him realise how I felt.

"I'll see you soon," I whispered softly.

I hung up. My heart was aching as I stared down at my shattered phone screen, sighing heavily. *I better get up and head out. Alejandro's waiting for me.* Replacing everything in my bag, I shifted and began running once again, not caring about the pain in my body as I ran. Determination fuelled me as I made my way through the forest and towards Oxford.

Kataleya, I'm coming for you, my angel.

An hour had passed since I had been travelling, and then suddenly, that instinct that had filled me returned. I tensed. Could something be here? I looked around, scanning the area. On one side, there were hills and bushes, along with many trees, scattered to one side. We were in the countryside. To the right were some fields of farms. My wolf was restless after being silent for so long, telling me to go forward, and I did, my heart thrumming with panic and anticipation. Was Kataleya close?

After a good fifteen minutes, I became confused. There was nothing out of the ordinary. I slowly continued on my way, my eyes darting around, my senses on alert. I sniffed the air, my ears perking as they tried to pick up on anything that was out of the ordinary. Was there perhaps a cavern or something?

Slowly observing the ground, I tried to pick up any footprints, any track marks that would give me a clue as to what was around here. It was after a good fifteen minutes that I saw the paw prints on the ground. Faint, but they were there. My heart began beating erratically. Was I onto something? I padded along slowly. Taking note of every inch, every millimetre of the ground.

My heart began thumping fast as I realised that they were becoming more and more frequent, clear signs that wolves had definitely been here. The size of the paw prints belonged to no ordinary wolf but werewolves with big paws and claws. From what I knew, there was no pack around here, and it was clear these paw prints had tried to be covered up; if I hadn't been observing carefully, I would have missed them.

After another twenty minutes, there was still nothing, but my intuition was becoming stronger. I paused, wondering if I should call Alejandro, but what if I wasn't onto something? What if it was just a false alarm, and I called him away from somewhere closer to Kataleya? *I'll keep searching for a bit longer and take it from there.*

I was about to lose hope as I was taken out of the forest and towards open countryside, feeling unsure if I should continue or not, and was about to turn away when I saw it. It was nothing out of the ordinary, just one of several similar places I had just passed, but something about it gave me the chills.

It was a large country home with grey walls, and it was huge. Many trees surrounded the actual building beyond the black iron gates with sharp spears and barbed wire at the top that was clearly made to keep trespassers out. The entire property was surrounded by those metal fences. I couldn't sense anything or anyone around. However, my wolf kept telling me to go forward, urging me to, and so I listened. Could this actually be where she was being kept?

Just the thought that I may be close made my heart leap in excitement. I looked beyond the gates, and in the distance, past the bushes and trees, I could see the huge house, or should I say manor. There was no life or light in the windows, not an animal or person in the surrounding gardens, but still, I felt like I should go check it out. *How do I get in? Do I just see if there's any broken part in it and just sneak in?* Sounded like a plan. *Let's do this!*

Something at the back of my mind told me that I should stop, shift, and let Alejandro know where I was first, but the stronger part of me that was telling me to keep on going forward, something that told me that my daughter was there, and I couldn't ignore that voice. Still… for Kataleya, just in case she was there, I should tell Alejandro. I quickly shifted, took the phone out and sent a quick message.

'I'm at this location. I feel as if there's something here, I thought I'd let you know before I check it out. I don't know if I'm even on to something, but I have this feeling that she's here.' I texted before sharing my location.

Putting the phone on silent, I slipped it back into my bag and shifted into my wolf once more. I broke into a run, rushing around the premises, keeping alert just in case there was anyone out there because if they were even there, there would be some security. My eyes darted around, searching for a way in, but there wasn't any. I frowned, and then I knew what I was going to do: jump the wall…

I looked up at the huge iron fences. They were at least twenty feet high. If I got caught on one, it wouldn't be pretty…

Then, Kia, you just got to make sure you aren't impaled on it.

I began to back away, putting space between me and the deadly wall that promised to kill me. With my bag in my mouth, I took a deep breath of determination and broke into a run, heading towards the huge metal wall of spears before I leapt into the air, my purple aura blazing around me as I launched myself over the wall. *Fuck!*

I reigned my aura in, my heart thumping, knowing anyone could have sensed my ability. I felt the spears graze the underside of my belly, making me growl internally. Agonising pain tore through me, and I bit back a whimper. It was more than what a normal cut should have been. The agony was far more than a normal wound. For a second, I couldn't breathe, and I grunted. There had to be some sort of poison on those spears. I landed on the other side on my feet, hissing slightly as I dropped my bag. Fuck, that hurt.

I glanced around quickly, hoping that nobody saw me, before I quickly shifted back. I took out an oversize hoodie and the second pair of sweatpants that I had, examining my stomach before I pulled them on. The cuts were quite bad, but I couldn't smell any poison or anything. Fuck. What was that?

I quickly rummaged in my bag and took out one of the antidote vials. I wasn't sure if the spikes contained silver or wolfsbane, but I was not going to risk it. *Goddess.* I downed the vial quickly and put the empty bottle back in my bag before picking it up and walking towards the country house silently. I made sure to stick to the sides, keeping hidden by the bushes and trees that lined the property.

There was still no one coming for me… maybe I had been wrong. Otherwise, I should have been attacked by then. My wolf was calm again, too. Too calm… I couldn't even sense her emotions. How strange.

I took my phone out, wondering if Alejandro had seen my message.

'That's risky, Kia, wait for us. I'll be there in fifteen.' I frowned but nodded. He wasn't wrong. I needed to be careful.

'Okay. I'm on the property, though, I'll hide.' I texted back.

By the looks of it, the property was lived in. I could see that clearly from the way the house was well kept and clear marks of footprints covered the ground.

I kept to the shadows, trying to find the best place to lay low, when I felt that same ominous aura behind me that I had felt when Delsanra had performed that spell on Dante. My heart thumped in my chest, and I spun around quickly, tossing my phone into the bushes.

Before I could even see or take in anything else, something grabbed my throat. Pain seared through me as if I was being burned to death. A shriek left my lips at the pain that hammered my entire body. Pure agony was ripping through me. It was an excruciating pain that made my head, and my body scream for reprieve. What… I could handle pain usually… this…

Whatever was holding onto me was like poison and death itself. I felt my energy being drained from me as I struggled to free myself with everything I had, but it was futile. My attacker was unseen as it slammed me against a tree, but it was there, and I could feel its darkness and power.

I couldn't breathe. I couldn't….

I clawed at the invisible hands that squeezed my neck. I could see the blood that was dripping down my neck and smell it in the air. Goddess… Kataleya.

Fuck, no. I couldn't let this happen. I had to be strong for her. Summoning everything I had with a burst of energy, my eyes blazed purple. I was not weak! I was not going to succumb to this. With strength that I did not even know I still had, I pushed whatever was holding me away from me, my aura swirling around me like a shield.

"Do not mess with me," I growled venomously.

The dark entity that I couldn't see pressed against my barriers, and I heard it hiss as it moved away. So, whatever it was, it couldn't go against my barrier. Good, because I was not there to lose. Not when my daughter was close.

Just when I thought that I might win this round, loud growls erupted in the air, and I spun around just as six blazing, urban, reddish-brown wolves lunged at me with their eyes glowing like burning embers. I couldn't even move out of the way. The impact knocked me to the ground, and two of them began biting into me viciously. I kicked them off, my anger flaring up.

"I demand to speak to the Crimson King!" I growled ferociously. The command in my voice emanated throughout the area, and I saw the hesitation in the wolves as they exchanged looks.

So, I was correct. It was the home of the Crimson King. Which meant Kataleya was there. She was there, and I was going to find her. *Mama's coming, baby girl, just hold out till we got you.*

The wolves watched me carefully as I got to my feet, my aura still swirling around me. As much as I wanted to rip them all to pieces for everything they had done, I knew I wouldn't win. The bites on my thigh and hip were painful, but nothing was as bad as the aftereffect of the unseen entity. I didn't move, hoping they understood I was waiting for their reply. I had a feeling they were conversing with one another from the way they were looking at each other until one of them shifted into a man with pale skin and flaming red hair. His eyes held such a coldness that they didn't seem... human.

"So, the queen has come to get her pup all alone." His voice was as bitter and cold as the rest of him, filled with disgust and hatred towards me. He had an accent... Spanish? Well, the feeling was mutual.

"Yes. I'm here for my pup, and I will not leave without her. As for anyone who has hurt her, I will unleash hell. Now, show me to your king, who seems to want something from us. Let's see what this debt is regarding."

One of the other men who had shifted had my bag, and even though I tried to reach out through the link, either Alejandro was too far out, or something was blocking me from communicating with him because all I could feel was the block. I just prayed he got my location notification and that my phone didn't break completely.

It was obvious whatever that thing earlier was didn't care about the phone. Was it the Djinn? I shuddered inwardly at the very thought.

I had to play it safe, even if it meant stalling for time. We just needed to get Kataleya out. I just needed my baby girl safe...

His Hatred & Darkness

KIARA

"VERY WELL, IF YOU so wish to see him. Cover her eyes!" He finally commanded, his cold eyes almost biting into my skin. I would obey. The main thing was that I needed to buy Alejandro time. Was Kataleya okay?

"I will allow you to blindfold my eyes, but first, can I see my daughter?" I asked, trying my best to sound emotionless, despite the worry that was eating me up inside. He smirked,

"You don't make the rules here."

"I'm only asking to see my daughter first," I growled venomously. "Just one look to make sure she's okay."

He fell silent, mind-linking someone before his sharp gaze turned to me. My aura was still around me, but I couldn't keep it up. If I was to save Kataleya, I needed all my energy, which was already dropping.

"You are in no position to ask for anything. Remember that," he spat icily.

"Fine."

I clenched my jaw, but I didn't want to do something so reckless that they did something to Kataleya. I just hoped Alejandro would get there soon. I would just need to buy enough time until then. *Goddess, please give me strength.*

I stayed silent, allowing them to blindfold my eyes. I felt a sharp object push against the barrier between my shoulder blades, prodding me forward.

"Walk."

I didn't reply, thinking I had spent years of my life fighting with a blindfold on, years of fighting blindly in the dark. Despite how strong I was, I lacked night vision, which was the price for my healing. What many didn't know was that I actually couldn't see in the dark at all, but it became my advantage over many others. The rest of my senses were heightened, advanced, so I was able to walk and manoeuvre efficiently.

These wolves thought I was just going to listen to everything they said and follow them silently, and yes, I would for now. However, if things went south, I would need to find Kataleya and run. The house was not that big; I'd be able to locate her. If worst came to worse, I would do what I could, even if I could just get her out…

I felt the warmth of the sun vanish from my back and the dirt of the ground become hard beneath my feet the moment we stepped inside. It was cold, and something told me despite the house smelling of expensive wood and a spiced scent, it was a house with a dark interior. The dark windows had given that away to start with. We walked along the hall. The floors were paved, maybe marble…. or stone. Our footsteps echoed off the walls.

We slowed down, and suddenly all my sense of scent vanished. Even the ashy, smoky smell of the wolves around me just disappeared. Anti-scent spray? Were they being careful? Probably so I didn't pick up the scent of the Crimson King, or whatever he called himself. What exactly was his link to us? What did he want from Alejandro? I was sure that was who he meant by beast.

"Sit." I was told. They pushed me forward until my leg hit a chair. I reached out, feeling the item against my back prod harder before I sat down, keeping my aura around me as a shield.

The room fell silent. I was about to speak when I heard the echoing sound of footsteps approaching. I kept my heartbeat steady, feeling the aura of the man approaching. He was indeed powerful, maybe not on par with Alejandro or Liam, but powerful enough to be on par with Dad.

"So, we have the queen here," he hissed venomously, and even though his voice was emotionless, it was cold and full of hatred. I heard him take a seat. The chair creaked a little under his weight. The urge to rip off the blindfold and take a look at the man was strong, but I remained unmoving. Buying time was the main goal.

"And we have someone who kidnaps children," I replied calmly.

"Women should know when to hold their tongue."

"Well, I am not one of your women for you to command as you wish." My voice was calm despite how much hatred I felt for him. A sadistic chuckle left his lips, and I frowned.

"A woman of strong will. I'm surprised the Lycan allows you to be so disrespectful. If you were mine, I would break you into submission." I clenched my jaw, feeling his gaze roam over me. My stomach twisted with disgust.

I'm not yours. I didn't say it out loud, not wanting to trigger him.

"You said there was a debt owed to you. What exactly do you want from us?"

"The debt must be paid in full, but I won't talk business with a woman." His arrogant, disgusting attitude was irking me, but right then, I was in his hold. It was clear his opinion of women was that they were nothing more than the dirt beneath his feet.

"Then, whilst you do your business, allow me to see my daughter." He scoffed maliciously.

"And you think I will just bend to your wishes?" He mocked in his accented voice.

"We will give you what you want, but I have come here –"

"And you won't be leaving," he cut in. "You will be leaving this property with the dead body of that pup."

My eyes flashed as anger flared through me. I ripped the bandage off before any of the men could move, my aura spreading around me and my eyes meeting the ones of the man before me. He was not what I was expecting. He looked far more unhinged than I could have imagined, and something told me he really wasn't someone I could ever reason with. His reddish-brown eyes burned into mine as his dark hair fell over one eye. His skin from the side of his face to his cheek, neck, hands, and arms was all melted and burned, a burn that stretched every time he moved.

He raised his hand ever so slightly, barely lifting his fingertips from the table, warning the men to let me be.

"You have a problem with us, take it out on us! When Alejandro comes for you, and he will, you will regret this," I hissed coldly.

"Oh? Who says he will manage to find this place?" He smirked, making my stomach twist.

"What do you mean?"

"We saw you approaching hours ago. We allowed you to enter this place. Do you really think that 'feeling' you had was purely your intuition, dear blessed wolf?" His sneer grew, stretching the burnt skin in the process, making him look even more sinister. I frowned, praying that Alejandro at least got the signal… "I have far more power than you can ever imagine. It seems like the beautiful Luna didn't expect that." His gaze trailed over me, and I clenched my jaw.

"Fine, you got me as you wanted. Where's my daughter?" I asked.

He ignored me and stood up, striding towards me. He was tall, and his aura surrounded him like a sickening plague. The closer he got, the stronger it seemed to grow. He tilted his head, his leering gaze falling to my lips.

"The Lycan's mate is indeed beautiful. No wonder he treats you ever so highly. It's either that or he is just far more pathetic than I'd heard."

There were five of us in this room… should I risk it? I wasn't sure I'd be able to if that other entity returned…

"He's a man you can only ever wish to be," I replied, smirking coldly. His gaze snapped up, leering at me.

"Don't think that pretty Moonfire aura will protect you." He suddenly grabbed my neck. My eyes widened in shock as he didn't seem to have any issue penetrating my aura. The darkness I felt earlier was wrapped around him as he squeezed my neck. "No one is more powerful than I. Not you, and not your Lycan."

I grabbed his hand, trying to loosen his hold, but the force behind it was suffocating me. The same pain erupted through me, and it felt as if my entire body was on fire.

"What would you give to have your useless pup back in your arms?" I would have her back in my arms soon. *I promise you, my angel, I am coming.* He was grinning sadistically as if seeing me in pain was entertaining.

I guess for him, it was, but if he thought I'd go down without a fight, he sure had another thing coming. Summoning all the energy I had, I grabbed his hand again, gritting my teeth as my hand burned from the touch, and lifted my leg, kneeing him straight in the crotch. His grip loosened. He had not been expecting that.

"Alpha!"

"What's the matter? Need your men to help you fight against a woman?" I hissed, aiming another swing at him.

He blocked, spinning around, and in a flash, twisted my arm behind my back. There was a sickening crunch as he broke my arm and dislocated my shoulder, sending another searing spasm of pain through me.

"I don't need anyone to help me to defeat the likes of you," his venomous voice answered, his men hesitating from helping. This was about his ego, and I knew he wouldn't allow them to help, just as I wanted.

"But you use your Djinn, though, despite thinking you're all-powerful without it?" I taunted as I made use of my already broken shoulder to rip free from his hold and aimed a kick to his flank, putting all my force into it, followed by a blast of my aura.

Despite the fact I was managing, everywhere that his hand had touched me burned as if hot oil had been poured onto me, searing my skin almost as if it was peeling the top layer off. I continued attacking him, throwing kicks and punches as I tried to get the opening that I needed to rip his head right off, but he was guarded and I saw no weak points.

"I am no fool to fall for your words in rage. I have power, but I paid a price for that power! I gained that power! No one can do as I did! I attained what I wanted!" He hissed. "You disrespected me, and so you shall pay!"

This was not how I wanted this to go. I needed to find Kataleya!

"Alpha! The Lycan is approaching with a powerful witch and an army!"

I felt him tense, but it was not fear that was in him, it was just as if he was simply calculating the best course of action to take. My heart was pounding at the thought that Alejandro was close. Kataleya would be saved.

"We won't face them now!" I heard him thunder just as that ominous aura filled the room. My head felt like it was being split open as if claws were being dug into my head.

Alejandro... I knew he couldn't hear me, but would he feel this pain? Would he know that something was wrong? My aura was depleting fast. I was barely managing to hold him at bay as I stared blurrily at the man before me. I fell to my knees as blood dripped down my face. I didn't know how long I could hold on... I did my best to stop him from ripping my head open...

"Leave..." he growled to his men.

The claws sank deeper into my skull, and a scream ripped from my lips as that dark, ominous aura grew. For a second, I felt as if there was something else before me, something made of pure fire, the body doubling around the Alpha before me. Burning red… crimson…

He looked like he was on fire… the power and darkness oozing from him…

I felt something inside my head. Something was wrong.

"She has been touched…" This time when he spoke, the voice wasn't his own. This voice alone made me feel worse, dark, sickening, and evil. Something that was not for the mortal ear to hear.

Just when I felt like I wouldn't be able to hold on any longer, he stepped away, smirking as if he had gained a victory. Glancing towards the window, he left the room swiftly, leaving me in the middle of the office, bleeding onto the woven rug on the ground.

I kept my aura up just in case he came back and tried to kill me completely, knowing I needed to find Kataleya before they took her. I couldn't get up, but I crawled to the door. Using all my strength, I snapped my shoulder back into place, groaning due to the pain. My head was burning with agony. Blood coated my light brown locks.

I needed to find my baby girl.

The smell of fire filled my nose, and I froze. The vision that I had after I had found the first letter returned to me in full force. Had that been a premonition?

Goddess, please, no!

Kataleya!

I grabbed the door handle, pushing my body to my feet. I didn't know how I managed, but my only thought was of my baby girl. *Where do I look?* The fire was enveloping the entire building.

Think, Kia… where would you keep a prisoner…

The basement or attic!

I looked up at the ceiling that was completely on fire, I wasn't sure if the fire was real or if this was an illusion, but either way, it was hot and it was destroying the house.

"Kataleya…" I staggered through the burning flames. *I'll take a look in the basement first, then I'll head upstairs.*

I rounded a corner when suddenly a sob reached my ears. A voice that I yearned to hear. My heart leapt like an eagle taking to the sky, relief and happiness flooding me.

"Mama?"

"Baby!" I looked around frantically, spotting her standing at the far end of the hall.

Tears streamed down her cheeks, her large eyes full of sadness and fear, eyes that lit up when they saw me. I could see a few bruises on her face, which only made my anger rise. Her dress was a mess, torn and bloody as the flames were beginning to touch her, yet when she didn't even flinch, I realised that they were created by magic. My angel was immune to magic.

"Kataleya…" I stumbled over to her, pulling her into my arms and swatting away the fire that had caught her dress. I began kissing her on her head, shoulders, and face. "Baby, are you okay?" I cupped her face, looking at the bruises on her body. How could they…

"I'm okay, Mama! Let's go, you're hurt," she whimpered, looking at me.

I didn't care if I was hurt. Seeing her safe filled me with relief. With renewed energy, I wrapped my hand around her small one, kissing it as tears filled my eyes. My baby was okay.

"I'm okay, Mama," she whispered, brushing blood and tears from my cheek.

I nodded, holding her hand firmly, turned, and hurried down the hall. I just needed to get her out of there. The windows were all barred from the inside, and I didn't think I'd be able to break them.

We were almost at the door when the roof caved. I wrapped my arms around Kataleya. She may be immune to magic, but she was not immune to a tonne of wood falling on her. Her scream pierced the air as one of the wooden beams fell on top of us. I kept my back arched, shielding her beneath me.

"Go outside, Kataleya," I whispered, feeling my vision darken.

"No, Mama!"

"Baby… now," I commanded, praying she listened.

She looked down at me. I could see the tears streaming down her dirty face before I was pulled into the abyss of darkness, and my world went dark…

The Second Clash

ALEJANDRO

I WAS WAITING FOR KIARA to show up when I heard my phone beep and knew it was her by the notification tone. I looked down at my phone, frowning when I clicked on the message. Reading her message, I opened the map, zooming in on her shared location. I texted her quickly, waiting for her reply before I mind-linked the others. I needed to get to her location now.

'Get everyone close enough to the location I'm forwarding now. Head here and wait for my arrival.'

I forwarded the message before shifting and running off towards the location. I hadn't gotten far before pain wrapped around me, and I gripped my throat. My eyes blazed red as my aura raged around me. Kiara was hurt!

Kiara's in danger! Eight miles northeast of Oxford! Move! I growled through the link.

Hold on, Amore Mio... I'm coming.

I had a fucking thousand questions running through my mind? The pain in my body lingered, meaning she was injured. Fuck. Did she find something? The guilt that the last time we talked, we had argued rushed through me. I fucking regretted it.

I'm coming, Amore Mio... and I'm fucking going to kill the one who hurt you...

Drake, I need a witch. Can you find out if Raihana can portal over to me? I just need her for barriers. I'm not risking her like Del.

Understood, Alpha. Silence fell before Drake mind-linked me again after a short while. **Alpha, Luna Raihana said she didn't need the disclaimer, and she'll see you in a few...**

I was sure Raihana probably said that in a much more fucking colourful manner. I came to a stop. Looking around, it was just open fields for miles. Where the fuck was Kiara?

I shifted back, scanning the ground as I tried to keep my aura suppressed, not wanting to be discovered. I knew many of my men were approaching; those who were in the area would be there soon. I kept to the trees, despite them being pretty scarce. I could see some country homes, so I walked forward, trying to find the exact location. We were close... but where was she?

I felt the presence of a witch behind me. Her scent hit me, and I knew before I even turned that Raihana had teleported. She was dressed in a mini dress that I wouldn't actually call a fucking dress and ridiculously high heels.

"I'm here."

"Yeah, looking like a fucking flamingo. What are you, a neon light to give away our location?"

"Oh, I know I'm glowing, thanks. But, I mean, I really think everyone will notice a pink flamingo compared to the terrifying furry beast standing by her side, right?" She smirked at me, twirling a strand of her hair. I gave her a withering glare.

"I'm not even in fucking Lycan form."

"You were. Anyway, I can lower the illusion."

"Don't push against it. I don't want you messing with a fucking Djinn's power," I warned. I knew what the witches had said would happen if it was anyone other than Del that had tried that spell. They would have been fucking dead.

"Don't worry. Del used a spell to withdraw the poison from Dante's body... I won't be doing that. I'll just be breaking something," she said quietly as if she knew what was on my mind. I gave a curt nod, just as more of our men reached us, including Elijah and Damon. Raihana took a deep breath, ready to cast the spell.

"Just... take it easy," I warned her. "Just make it visible. I'll break through myself." She gave me a small smile.

"Relax, I'll be fine."

I didn't reply, but I wouldn't risk her life. I was fucking worried enough about the two who were inside this place. I really hoped that Kataleya was there... fuck, I needed them safe.

She chanted a spell, and after a few moments, it was as if an entire veil was being lifted from our eyes. A huge country house surrounded by tall black gates topped with spikes appeared. I could see the haze-like shield around it, but it didn't feel like normal magic...

"Uncle... be careful... whatever that is... it's dark..."

"I've got this." Liam's voice came from behind us.

I turned as Liam and Rayhan appeared, both in sweatpants, and clearly, they had run fast. Raihana crossed her arms and I glared at a few male wolves, daring them to look at her. Fucking idiots.

I glanced ahead, hoping Kiara was okay. The pain I had felt was still there, and the worry that gnawed inside of me was keeping me on edge.

Liam's aura surged around him as he strode towards the barrier. Similar to Kiara's purple one, his was blue, like flames reaching high into the sky. His magnetic blue eyes looked almost shimmery. The moment he barrelled into the wall, Raihana whispered a spell, a dazzling bolt of fire heading straight above Liam's head and hitting the shield. The impact of both forces made the barrier flash and tremble. I glared at her for disobeying me. Did these fucking women not know how to obey orders?

"Once more, Raihana," Rayhan commanded, his sharp eyes on the barrier.

"And this time, we just fucking push through," I said, shifting and letting out a menacing growl as Raihana and Liam struck the barrier once more.

I saw the thin crack appear, and I charged forward, ramming straight into the wall.

Burning heat. That's what it felt like. My entire fucking body was on fire.

I pushed through, exhaling when we penetrated through, followed by Liam, Rayhan, and the rest as the barrier disappeared.

"Raihana, stay with me," was the last thing I heard Elijah say before the growls of wolves filled the air from both sides, but theirs were running away, save a few who came to meet us head-on. It was odd seeing every wolf the exact same colour, as if they were all exactly the same, from their scent to their size and the colour of their eyes, too. I frowned, seeing the haze that surrounded the far side of the house as if masking something ahead. Was that fucker here?

Suddenly, the entire house went up in fucking flames.

Kiara and Kat!

Follow the wolves, I'm going to go find Kiara! I shouted through the link to my men and to the Alphas present. Hopefully, my baby girl was there. I just fucking hoped so.

I ran ahead. As much as I wanted to fucking rip the bastard behind this to shreds, I needed to find my girls first. I just prayed that this time no one slipped out of my hold.

Ask Raihana if there's anything she can do to make sure that they don't take Kat or Kiara, I told my men, hoping whoever was closest to her would pass the message.

She's casting a blood cage; anyone from the Rossi bloodline won't be able to leave the premises… just in case they try to take Kataleya. There's nothing she can do about Kiara.

That's fine.

I'd find them.

Kiara! I called through the link.

I ripped the front doors off the hinges, walking straight into the blazing fire.

"Daddy!"

My heart skipped a fucking beat as my eyes fell on my little girl, my emotions overwhelming me for a second. Thank fuck she was alive. Despite the bruises on her face, she was alive. What had she been through? Despite that thought eating up at me, I was so fucking relieved to have finally found her.

I frowned, realising she was trying to tug something from the ground. My stomach twisted as I realised it was Kiara's arm. She was stuck under a beam that was on fire.

I was in front of them in a flash, pulling the beam off of her, but the sight before me was not one I was expecting, nor one I ever wanted to see. Her forehead along her hairline was cut, blood seeping out of it. Her entire head of hair was full of blood, as if someone had tried to carve the top of her skull right off. Fuck…

"Mama's hurt," Kat whimpered as I wrapped my arm around her, unable to reply in Lycan form.

I lifted Kiara tenderly into my arms. My queen… fuck…

Slowly, I wrapped my arm around her tightly as I didn't want to shake her too much. She was clearly in bad fucking shape. Her heartbeat was faint, too. With the other, I lifted Kataleya, tucking her against my chest and shielding her from the flames.

Safe. They were going to be okay. I was never going to let this happen again… and whoever was behind this would surely pay. I jumped back as a huge chunk of the house caved before climbing over it and getting out of this fucking place. Once upon a time, I would have had the enemy in my hands right then, but now I had a family that came first, one I needed to make sure would be safe.

I looked around, scanning the grounds. There weren't many of the enemy wolves left. I saw Liam tear the head of one right off before his gaze snapped to me, falling on his sister. He'd have my back. His grey wolf lowered his head to me, and I ran through the remainder of the enemies and the fire that had spread out into the grounds. I spotted Raihana easily in her disturbingly pink clothes as she blasted wolves away, killing a few as she stood there, her power rising behind her. I shifted the moment I was close to her, looking for a place where I could place Kiara down safely.

"Raihana!"

She turned, her black hair blowing in her face. She ran over as I placed Kiara gently on the floor behind a tree away from the chaos. My gaze fell to the side of her neck. Fuck, it looked like someone really had tried to cut open her fucking skull.

I didn't let go of Kataleya, making sure she didn't look at Kiara as Raihana crouched down by Kiara.

"Goddess…" she murmured in horror. "Move away."

Despite not wanting to let go of Kiara, I knew I had to. I crouched down, my arms around our little girl, and pressed my lips to Kiara's softly. Strong sparks coursed through me, reassuring me that she was okay, and I forced myself away. We couldn't waste time.

"Is Mama going to be okay?" Kataleya whimpered. I nodded, kissing her forehead.

"She is going to be just fine. You all are."

I looked down at her, brushing her hair off her face. I was so fucking glad she was okay. We just needed to find the answers for Dante and Del… I knew we were on a short time schedule, but at least we were fucking together. I hugged her tightly, and she wrapped her arms around me tightly as she began sobbing into my shoulder. I caressed her hair, inhaling her soft scent. My anger grew when I saw the bruises on her arms.

"I got you, angel. No one's going to fucking touch you again," I growled venomously.

Keep one or two of those fuckers alive, knock them unconscious. I want them for questioning, I commanded through the link.

I watched Raihana heal Kiara. It was clear it was taking longer than normal. Raihana was brushing the sweat from her brow, and I could see the wound along Kiara's neck was healing extremely slowly. I frowned, taking in the rest of her injuries. There were marks around her neck, a clear handprint with long fingers literally imprinted around her neck. I clenched my jaw.

Oh, when I find you all, even hell will seem like fucking heaven when I'm done…

"Daddy, will Enrique be okay?" Kataleya brought me out of my thoughts, and I furrowed my brow.

"Enrique?" She looked up at me, and I brushed her tears away. I fucking hated my baby girl crying, and I didn't even know the extent of what she had been through yet.

"Yes, the horrible Alpha's son. Enrique was nice to me," she whispered, staring at the burning house. I looked at her sharply. She had seen the fucking shit head…

"His father probably took him," I said coldly. He had a fucking son, yet he could harm other pups…

"But Daddy, he hurt him, too," she whispered. The anguish in her eyes and the way she said 'he hurt him too'…

What had that thing done to my daughter? And his own son? He was a fucking sick bastard who needed to be fucking castrated and fucking skinned alive, then doused in wolfsbane.

"I'm sure he'll be okay," I said quietly. Seeing the sadness in Kataleya's eyes, I sighed. "When I find him, I'll make sure the kid is okay. How old was he?"

"I don't know, Daddy. He looked a little older than Dante," she said sadly, resting her head on my shoulder. Who the fuck was this guy, and where did he come from?

The fight was over. We had two enemy wolves in our hold, and a few of my men had gone to see if they could find out where the rest had escaped to, but it seemed magic, or whatever you call the shit that Djinn could fucking do, was at work. They had simply vanished.

I turned my attention back to Kiara, wanting to go over to her but staying fucking patient as Raihana did what she needed to. When she finally sat back, the blood was slowing down, yet the cut remained.

"Sorry, Uncle, it's the best I can do," Raihana whispered, and I realised she was shaking.

"We'll get her home. You fucking okay?" I asked.

She nodded as Rayhan came over to support his sister whilst I looked down at my mate. *Fuck, Amore Mio... you should have waited outside of the territory for me...*

I placed Kataleya down, lifting my mate into my arms before scooping Kataleya back up. Elijah was by my side, adjusting some basketball shorts as he looked at his daughter and granddaughter.

"Come on, Kataleya. I'll carry you, okay?"

"Ok, Grandpapa," she whispered, holding her arms out to him.

He smiled, taking her from me, and although I didn't want to let her go, I knew she was safe with him. He kissed her forehead and cheek, giving her a small smile. Despite his gaze flickering to Kiara, he kept his emotions under control. I knew he wanted to ask about her, to know what happened, but even I fucking didn't know, and I didn't think stressing Kataleya out with all the fucking questions was going to be a wise move.

"I want squad seven and eleven of my pack to stay behind and scour this fucking area. See if there's anything you can find here and put that fucking fire out. There might be some clues inside. As for the rest of the Alphas who have helped, I'm grateful for it. Let's move out."

The rest obeyed my command. I looked down at the woman in my arms. Her heart was steady and I could tell she was simply asleep, but I couldn't wait for her to be fully healed and back to her usual self.

The so-called fucking Crimson King clearly had issues with me, yet it felt like he was playing a game, one that he was drawing out purposely. I was not going to let him pull me into this fucking cat-and-mouse game of his. If he wanted to play a proper game, then it was high fucking time he learned how it felt to be the hunted.

Back Home

ALEJANDRO

THE SUN WAS SETTING through the window, casting red and orange hues around the room. As much as I wanted to be by Kiara's side, I was doing what I knew she'd want me to. Be there for our pups.

"How you feeling?" I asked, sitting down on the sofa in the living room next to Dante, who was leaning back against the cushions, clearly exhausted.

"I'm completely fine, Dad," he replied, despite the red pulsing veins that covered his body.

"Yeah? Glad to hear you're not a fucking wuss, but you know it's okay to fucking say if shit hurts," I remarked lightly, reaching over and ruffling his hair. He gave me a cocky smirk.

"Obviously, but I'm completely fine. I'm glad Kat's back," he added, frowning slightly as he looked at Skyla, who was setting up the dollhouse for when Kataleya returned from her bath.

Scarlett was showering her. We had been back for an hour or so. After the doctor had checked her over, taking note of her injuries, she had fallen asleep and had only woken up a short while ago. I still had to look at those reports, knowing they weren't going to be easy to see. I knew I was delaying it, trying to build the courage I needed to face them.

Skyla had been on edge wanting to see her twin. From the moment we had entered, she had been beyond fucking ecstatic.

Currently, Elijah was there, as was their pup, Azura. Rayhan had taken Delsanra and headed home. I was fucking grateful for all his help.

Everyone else had also returned home, apart from those working on finding that fucker.

I knew Kiara had seen him, and Kat, but I was not going to question her, not when I knew that experience was fucking traumatic for her. Raihana did say she'd stop by if I needed her to so we could probe Kat's mind, but I wasn't sure yet. She had managed to heal the most severe of her injuries before leaving.

Guilt still fucking consumed me; I was the reason this shit happened. On top of that, Kiara had been the one to find her at the expense of her own safety. I fucking hated that I had failed my pups and queen.

"So, Dad, we are getting pizza, right?" Azura's voice broke me out of my thoughts, and I removed my hand that was resting on Dante's head.

"Are we?" Elijah asked her, raising one of his brows from where he was standing by the window, busy on his phone. I knew he was handling the search for now, telling me to take a break, not that the fucker took a break himself.

"Aren't we?"

I glanced at her, her eyes a little too suspiciously wide as she stared at her dad, looking like a fucking puppy. Azura Rayne Westwood; she may be known to the world as Elijah and Scarlett's daughter, but she was really the daughter of Indigo, Scarlett's biological sister, who died eight years ago. The pup had almost died, too. If one of their relatives with witch heritage hadn't performed a spell, sacrificing her own life to place the unborn pup into Scarlett's womb, she would have.

Indigo had been mated to a man from my pack... one who was fiercely loyal and efficient, yet he had been abusive. Right under my nose, and I had missed it. Yeah, I knew he was a fucking shit show, but Indigo still refused to leave him, but I had missed all the abuse. It had reduced Indigo to a shell of the woman she had once been. Looking at her daughter, I saw the same fire in her that the young Indigo once had, and I hoped it remained. Indigo had always had Elijah wrapped around her finger from when she was a fucking pup, and her daughter sure was the same.

"I'll order it," he finished.

I didn't miss her victorious smile as she winked at Skyla. *Right, so Lucifer incarnate had a say.* Speaking of, she turned to me, giving me a devilish smile.

"Is everything okay, Daddy?"

"Yeah, sure is."

Scarlett entered with my little girl looking normal, not a bruise or a speck of dirt on her, but we all fucking knew the unseen effects remained.

"Kataleya! Look what I set up." Skyla pointed to the dollhouse, brushing her hair back from her face. She usually didn't play with dolls often. Everyone fucking knew it was an act of kindness towards her sister. Kataleya smiled as Azura jumped up.

"Come on, Kat, let's play," she stated, walking over to my pup and taking her hand confidently.

"Girls are so loud," Dante added, shaking his head.

"Dante, be nice because I'm trying to be nice," Skyla shot back, narrowing her eyes.

"Play nice, children. So, I heard we are having pizza?" Scarlett raised an eyebrow, walking over to Elijah and tugging him down for a kiss. I stood up.

"Mind staying with the pups? I'm going to go have a smoke," I remarked.

She nodded, although the look in her fucking eyes was almost as if she knew where I wanted to go, or more like needed to. Kiara was my real addiction, and I needed her to feel fucking sane. The guilt inside of me was only growing, and I needed a dose of Kiara before I saw my princess' medical report.

I walked through the hall and up the stairs, heading to my bedroom. I opened the door, her scent hitting me like a strong dose of nicotine. Serena and Kevin were both in the room.

"Alpha," Kevin said, politely lowering his head. I gave a curt nod before looking at Kiara.

"Excuse us," Serena murmured as they left the room. The door shut behind them with a click.

I looked down at Kiara, the clear cut along her head still vivid, although the blood had stopped flowing. The blanket was draped over her, pulled up to her chest, and her plump, kissable lips were slightly parted. I walked over to her and sat down on the bed.

"Fuck, Amore Mio…"

I ran my hand tenderly through her hair, making sure not to pull at it. Despite it being cleaned up, there were still traces of dry blood that remained, making her hair stick together. The sparks of the bond danced along my hand and arm. I closed my eyes, inhaling her intoxicating scent that overpowered the distinct scent of whatever the doctor had used to clean her wounds.

"You found her… protected her, and I didn't even get there in time to protect you," I murmured quietly.

I knew she wouldn't blame me, and I was still fucking pissed that she went alone, but I also knew she was the one who had found her, the reason our angel was back with us, and that she was capable… but still.

Pretty fucking useless; that was how I fucking felt… I couldn't even protect my family.

On top of that, times had fucking changed. There was a time I would have found the bastard behind this and killed him slowly and fucking painfully. I would have kept going, not caring for anything but to reach my goal. But now, I had priorities and responsibilities, to make sure my family was safe, and as much as I wanted to get the fuck out there and find the fucker, I couldn't go and leave any of them behind. Kiara in this state, although the doctor said she'd be awake soon, Dante… Kat… even Sky, who, although she was acting like she was okay, was fucking affected by everything that had happened.

I leaned down, a few strands of my hair brushing her face as I touched my forehead to hers ever so lightly, not wanting to hurt her. The sparks between us danced across my skin.

I fucking love you, Amore Mio… so fucking much. I moved back slightly, my nose brushing hers before I kissed her deeply.

"Wake up, so I can fucking punish you in the best fucking way for running off," I smirked, running my fingers through my hair, pushing it back, and standing up.

Time to go see my girl's reports… I walked past the dresser, spotting Kiara's wedding rings. I picked them up, and glanced towards the bed, my chest constricting at the memory of how we had parted that day. I placed them down before I left the room, glancing at Kevin and Serena.

"Keep an eye on her."

"Yes, Alpha," Kevin replied with a nod.

I left the mansion, heading towards headquarters.

Callum, meet me at my office, I said through the link to the head doctor.

I entered the silent building, although I knew there were people around in the many different departments doing their duties. I glanced at the guards who stood in position, attentive, alert and doing their job.

Order. It was something I tried to keep, but when something came, it tore apart everything I had put in place. No matter how much you try, you can never be prepared for everything. A question from earlier replayed in my mind as I thumbed in my passcode and entered my office, leaving the door open.

Was Kiara safe, or had she perhaps been cursed? It was a question that Elijah had asked, and it made me think that, just like Dante, she had been injured. Raihana had said she wasn't sure, she didn't sense anything from her, but I had also refused to allow her to probe too far. That was the fucking problem. I couldn't risk hurting more people no matter how desperately I wanted answers and wanted Kiara safe. *Fuck, Amore Mio…*

I took out a cigarette and lit it just as I heard Callum coming. Fucker was slow.

"Alpha," he said gravely when he appeared at the door, bowing his head.

"Skip that shit. Show me the report," I cut in, taking a drag on my cigarette. He hesitated before approaching.

"Alpha, both Doctor Jemimah and I were the ones to perform the examinations. The good news is, there were no signs of sexual abuse, and Doctor Jemimah confirmed that." A wave of relief washed over me, but from the look on his face, I knew there was still more.

"Pass me the file."

"Do you mind if I explain it to -"

"Take a fucking seat, and I don't want or need shit sugar-coated." I reached over, snatching the file from him, and sat, backflipping it open…

Several fractures in the ribs, a fractured collar bone, a fracture in her left leg, and both forearms… her pinkie on the right hand had been broken. Bruised spine… some had been partially healed… it seemed she had used her arms to protect herself whilst being kicked repeatedly… there was a hairline fracture to her skull.

It felt like someone was punching me repeatedly in the gut, cutting off my fucking windpipe… I swallowed hard.

"Leave."

"Alpha, she will heal. Her regeneration gene -"

"I said. Leave," I growled, trying to control my emotions.

"Alpha." I didn't look up, clenching my jaw and focusing on regulating my erratic heartbeat.

The door shut with a click, and I closed my eyes, lowering my head.

My daughter had gone through this... all of this...

The file felt heavy in my limp hold. No parent would ever want their child to be treated like this. Well, no fucking sane one...

My angel had gone through so much at the hands of that fucking bastard. I was going to rip him apart. But it wouldn't change the past... it won't turn back time. It wouldn't take away the pain she had experienced... I had turned my back on her that day. If I hadn't, perhaps this wouldn't have happened. Had I made a mistake?

I dropped the file, placing my head in my hands. *How do I fix this? Werewolf or not, no child deserves this.*

I get it now... what a father feels when his child is hurt... or if anyone tries to hurt them... The unfamiliar sting in my eyes made me take a deep, shuddering breath. *Fuck, Al...*

A light knock on the door made me quickly wipe my eyes roughly. *Fuck this shit.*

"What do you want?" I growled, knowing exactly who was on the other side of the door. He opened the fucking door like he owned the damn place.

"Did I give you permission to enter?"

"Did I say I needed your permission?" I glared coldly at the dickhead, who gave me a smirk that held no humour, his cerulean eyes as shadowed as my own.

"What do you want, Elijah?"

"To see the report," he replied as if that was fucking obvious. Coming over and crouching down, he picked it up off the floor.

I stood up, taking a long drag on my cigarette, trying to fight the agony that was ripping through me. I walked to the window, staring out at the shadows that had settled over the pack grounds. The sun was gone from the sky. *Will my family ever be fucking safe?*

"Don't blame yourself for this."

"Fuck off. I left her that day..." He sighed, and I could sense his irritation.

"Alejandro, you didn't have much of a choice. You made the right choice. Now, Kataleya is safe and back with us."

"Yeah, but the mental damage of being fucking tortured and abused doesn't go, does it?" I could hear the pain in my voice no matter how much I tried to conceal it.

"No, it doesn't, but with love and care, she will be okay. She's a Rossi as well as of Westwood blood. All we can do is stay strong and continue to be that wall of strength and support for the ones we love. No matter how hard it gets, or how hard that wall is battered on… if we stay strong, then so will they."

What do you say to that? He was right; I knew he was, but what happened when that shield had failed? I allowed her to be taken…

"You will need to ask her what happened, but perhaps it's better to do that when Kiara is awake. Do it together," he added quietly.

"Yeah."

"Well, pizza should be here soon. Get back home. I'm sure if Kiara wakes up soon, she will want to see that ugly mug of yours."

"Yeah? Well, she fucking loves this mug," I shot back cockily.

"No fucking idea why," he replied, equally fucking arrogant.

"I could list a few things if you're ready to hear exactly what she loves about it."

"No thanks," he growled as he held onto the file, opening the office door. I was sure he got the fucking hint. I pushed past him, smirking slightly. Yeah, if only he knew what his daughter liked about this face, or better, where.

My smile faded as I smoked my cigarette. Sometimes you became friends with the most unexpected of people. Although I was closer to Elijah's age than Kiara's, he was her fucking dad, but he was still my closest confidant after Kiara, the only one who saw the demons I tried to hide…

We walked in silence through the pack grounds, heading towards my mansion. One day soon, I hoped everything was back to normal.

"Any updates?" After a moment, he spoke,

"They are looking for leads on the curse, along with the witches, too. The only problem is that Delsanra is affected. She could have proved vital in finding answers." I frowned. That was fucking true…

"Yeah? Well, we are going to have to find a way to fix that shit without her, and we will."

Over a Slice of Pizza

ALEJANDRO

WE RETURNED TO THE mansion and entered the living room. I looked around at all the kids playing. The three girls were sitting on the carpet with Kataleya in the centre. I could tell by the way that the girls were fawning over her that she was being taken good care of by them. Goddess, even the fucking pups knew when something wasn't right. I sat down next to Dante, running my fingers through his hair and ruffling it up.

"So, not getting fucking bored, are you?"

"Nope. Besides, I get to watch TV, and there're so many episodes I've been wanting to catch up on, so why not do that now? I haven't got anything better to do anyway. No schoolwork, no training, just chilling."

He gave me a grin, but I could tell from his eyes that he wasn't okay. For me, he was fucking trying. That was what I had done. Now my fucking pup, who was only eight years old, had to pretend that things were okay when they fucking weren't.

"Yeah. Make the most of it for now, because once you're better, you'll be catching up double time." He nodded. The spark in his red eyes returned for a moment, and I fucking promised that I'd make sure he was back to normal soon enough. Whatever the curse was, we would find a way to break it.

The doorbell rang, and I knew it was probably one of my men with the pizza.

"Daddy, it's the pizza," exclaimed Azura.

Those pups sure could eat, and they definitely enjoyed their food. Well, whatever fucking made them happy with the mood being so fucking down, I was all for it.

I had Clara, one of the two Omega housekeepers, answer the door. Moments later, she came to the living room. She knocked lightly on the door before stepping inside.

"The food is here. Would you like me to serve you here or in the dining room?" She asked politely.

"I think the kids will enjoy eating in the living room for today. What do you guys think?" Scarlett asked with a smile as she looked at the girls and Dante.

"Who can say no? I would love that!" Skyla replied dramatically, tossing her hair over her shoulder. I was sure she fucking would. That girl loved to chill. She even said when she grew up, all she was going to do was relax. When I asked her how she was going to survive or how she was going to end up providing for herself, she said that that was what I was there for.

She wasn't fucking wrong. As long as I was alive, that girl could do whatever the fuck she wanted.

Clara placed the pizza boxes on the coffee table, and soon Claire, her twin sister, the other housekeeper, entered, placing some plates down. "Should I get squash or juices?" Claire asked politely.

"Get a mix of fizzy drinks and juices. I think the kids can have some fun today in celebration of Kataleya's return. It's only right," Scarlett replied with a small smile.

"Yes, of course, Luna," Claire replied before she quickly left the room. I leaned over, grabbed one of the plates and opened the pizza boxes one at a time.

"So, tell me, kid, which one do you want?" I asked Dante.

"I'll have two slices of the cheese and tomato pizza, please, Dad."

I looked across at him with his head leaning against the sofa. He wasn't his usual self. Seeing that straight-up fucking hurt. The boy could usually have had like five to six pizza slices, and now what? He was going to stick to two.

"Do you want some fries or chicken strips?" I asked. He shook his head as I placed the plate in his lap. He picked up his pizza slice slowly, and it was clear that he didn't have much of an appetite.

"Okay, girls, be careful," Scarlett was saying.

I glanced at the girls and saw Kataleya watching me. I motioned for her to come over, holding my hands out to her. She gave me a beautiful smile before she rushed over and climbed into my lap, hugging me tightly.

"I'm so happy to be home, Daddy," she whispered, looking into my eyes. I kissed her cheek softly, her soft, pure scent soothing as ever mixed with her shampoo.

"Yeah. I'm fucking happy that you're home as well, baby girl." She smiled at me. Her dark eyes, which were the same colour as mine yet were the entire fucking opposite, were full of warmth and innocence. "Do you want your usual? Or do you want to be a little more adventurous and have some chicken and jalapeno topped pizza?" I asked.

"Oh, no, Daddy! I want my usual. I want one huge slice of cheese and tomato pizza with lots and lots of fries, and I want to have chicken wings." She gave me a huge smile that lit up her face. *How the hell do people hurt children?*

"Do you think this tiny tummy can handle that many fries?" I asked, tickling her. She giggled, writhing in my hold. I pulled her close, kissing the top of her head.

"I sure can," she replied breathlessly. It was good to see her fucking smile.

"Kataleya is really a food monster who can eat lots and lots. Instead of making her tummy big and round, her food vanishes into space!" Skyla added as she bit into her pizza, topped with a mix of vegetables and chicken.

"Or what your Aunty Raven used to think was that she had tiny alien-like insects inside of her tummy that ate all her food and didn't allow her to grow," Scarlett added.

"Oh, that's because Raven is short," Azura giggled. I smirked.

"Yeah, you got that right," I agreed.

"Mama Red is small, too," Dante added, smiling slightly.

"I'm two inches taller than Raven, though," Scarlett replied, giving Dante a smile as she finally finished tending to the other two girls and took her large plate over to Elijah. She sat down next to him, placing the plate on his thigh.

"I think when I'm older, I'm going to be the tallest," Skyla finalised with a nod.

"I think I will be," Azura added with a thoughtful expression. "You're quite small, Sky."

"I am not."

"You kind of are, but it doesn't matter. I'll be the tallest of you all since girls are always much smaller," Dante added, mustering up a half-assed smirk.

"He's right," Elijah added.

"But we all know that height doesn't matter," Scarlett interceded.

"But, Mama, I heard Raven talking to Taylor, and they said size matters," Azura added.

I almost choked on my fucking drink, clearing my throat and smirking as I looked at the couple across from me. Both exchanged looks.

"Guess size matters, huh?" I mocked. Scarlett, who looked a little shocked, smoothly covered up her surprise and took a bite of her pizza.

"Well, I'm sure they were talking about something else," Scarlett tried to cover up as Elijah simply shook his head, a small smirk on his face.

"No, they were talking about Liam and Zack," Azura frowned. "It's okay. I'll ask them when I go back."

"I don't think Aunty Raven should say size matters when she's so tiny herself," Skyla giggled.

"Okay, let's change this topic," Scarlett stated. *Yeah, I'm sure no one wants to fucking imagine their son's dick size.*

I kept my hand on Kataleya's plate as she ate, and I noticed something sticking out of her pyjama pocket. It was a dark piece of fabric. I reached for it, but to my surprise, she quickly grabbed my hand.

"That's mine, Daddy!" She exclaimed, fear filling her eyes. Instantly, I felt like there was something wrong. Did it have some magic on it or something that she was told to keep close to her?

"Let me just have a look at it, angel," I replied quietly.

"Can I have it back after?" She asked hesitantly, fat tears beginning to spill down her face.

"Yeah, I fucking promise." *If it's safe.*

She slowly took it out and clutched it tightly, still unwilling to give it up.

"Please save him, Daddy. His papa hurt him," she began to sob as Scarlett rushed over, taking the plate from us and crouching down next to me as she stroked Kataleya's hair.

"It's okay, baby, you can keep it. Who is he?" She asked soothingly. That kid she mentioned outside that fucking place…

"Enrique. He was the bad Alpha's son. He gave me food." She began crying uncontrollably, and I hugged her tight as Scarlett rubbed her back, looking upset despite masking it well. There were similarities between her and Kiara, but Scarlett definitely hid her emotions better.

"Okay, I won't take it from you. It's going to be okay," I murmured as the two young girls opposite exchanged looks, worry and concern replacing the amusement from earlier.

"Why would he help you?" Dante asked, despite his state. His eyes were sharp as he questioned her.

"He didn't say," Kataleya sobbed.

"She said earlier when we were there that he was around Dante's age or a bit older," I said quietly to Elijah and Scarlett. Scarlett's eyes were filled with concern and worry. I knew it was for the pup. Kataleya may have some answers, but I couldn't ask her.

"You can't trust the enemy, Kat," Dante said firmly, his eyes cold.

"But when there was shouting, he's the one who hurried to unlock the basement door. He didn't know the fire couldn't hurt me… he said to me my family had come for me and to go outside quickly…" she whimpered.

So… this fucker had helped her…

"The day he gave me food, his papa found out, and Enrique told him to punish him. The guard at the door said if the young alpha prince died, it would be my fault. Then, when he unlocked the basement door, he was still unable to walk properly. I saw the marks on his neck…" Dante scoffed.

"Alpha prince. His father is no king, and nor is he a prince."

"Dante…" I warned.

Arrogance and pride were two traits that Dante definitely had, but as much as I agreed with him that the man was no fucking king, I would not allow him to upset Kataleya, who clearly had been treated with some humanity by the fucker's pup. Although I didn't like any boy being nice to my girl… I was glad she hadn't been fucking alone. That kid had done more for her than I ever could have within those walls…

"Okay, let's finish our pizza and not argue," Elijah said, glancing at the irritated Dante.

"Dad, we are not arguing," Azura stated with a pout. "We are discussing…"

"Don't worry, Kat. We will find your prince, okay?" Skyla smirked, winking at her sister, making both Dante and me frown at her. To my fucking surprise, Kataleya blushed as she wiped her tears, making Azura giggle.

"He isn't her fucking prince," I growled. Skyla cocked her eyebrow.

"You can't decide that, Daddy. Besides, now that Kat's home, you owe me…. three hundred pounds."

"For?"

"For swearing."

Okay, I do fucking swear, but I have not said the fucking word around her three hundred times… I hadn't even been around for that fucking long since we got back.

"Thrifty," Elijah smirked.

"Nah, just a fucking thief," I growled as she stuck her tongue out at me cheekily. "You ain't getting any money for that." She looked away sullenly after giving me a dirty look as she bit into her pizza viciously.

Once dinner was over, the girls played for a while, or tried to, but it was clear Kataleya was not ready to cheer up, still holding onto the torn piece of fabric.

"Okay, you two girls need to shower and start getting ready for bed," Scarlett ordered. "Azura, I am going to check your hair. Make sure you wash it properly, okay?"

"Okay, Mama," she replied with a pout.

"Daddy, will you tell me a bedtime story?" Kataleya asked.

"About a certain prince charming?" Skyla teased before she burst into a fit of giggles.

"No fucking prince charmings," I frowned.

Why the fuck was this girl even talking about boys? They were not to even go there. Like fucking ever. I glared at her and spotted Elijah fucking smirking.

"What do you want?"

"Just thinking of you in my position… karma."

"Don't speak too soon; you have one left," I reminded him.

"Well, at least there're no more Rossis," Elijah smirked.

"There is one…" Scarlett added with an amused smirk before her smile vanished, and she shook her head, frowning. "Far too old."

The three of us exchanged looks, clearly fucking disturbed by the direction that went. Yeah, too old... but then again... I was sixteen years older than Kiara.

Leo... nah, the goddess isn't that fucking sadistic to play that shit all over.

I glanced at Dante, who was falling asleep holding his can of drink. I took it from him and picked him up.

"Dad, I can walk." I didn't argue, knowing it was his pride, and placed him down as I helped him out of the room, pausing at the door.

"I'm getting Dante to bed. Have your teeth brushed, and then I'll tell you a damn story."

"Ooo, Daddy is telling a story for once!" Skyla giggled.

Yeah, fucking torture, but just seeing them all together was enough. Once Dante had changed and brushed his teeth, I helped him to bed. Elijah would be staying with him for the night.

"The pillows okay?"

"Yeah, Dad, I'm fine. A curse can't do anything to me," he said, quietly staring at the stars that were projected on his ceiling.

"But you're still worried about something," I pushed quietly.

"Well... Delsanra's also like this because of me. So, does Ray hate me?" He asked so quietly that I barely heard. He was clenching his jaw as he tried to remain emotionless. I smirked slightly.

"Rayhan? Far from it. For a moment, I thought you were worried about Del."

"I am... but we are both going to be okay," he replied with such conviction that something told me he knew more than he could say, but those words gave me hope.

"Yeah?"

"Yeah. There's something we need to do." He gave me a smile, looking far older than his years. I frowned, nodding.

There were things he said that we didn't understand. Both Kia and I decided it was for the best not to push it and just accept what he said, take note, but still treat him like he was just a normal pup. Although he was a fucking mature one.

"Good," I replied, kissing his forehead. "So, want to talk to Rayhan?"

"Umm... not now..." he mumbled, looking down at his duvet.

"Alright. When you want to, just say the word, okay?"

"Okay." I tucked him in before I stood up.

"Night, son."

"Night, fucker," he replied. I smirked. Yeah, that's what I would have usually said.

"Don't let your mom catch you saying that."

"I won't."

I left the bedroom door open a crack, heading to the twin's room. The door was open, and the sound of the three giggling could be heard down the fucking hall. What the hell was with girls? Did they need to giggle twenty-four-fucking-seven? I knocked lightly on the door.

"You can come in, you know," Azura's voice called, her sharp blue eyes peering at me through the gap in the door. "Don't worry. Mama is dressed."

I raised an eyebrow. She fucking knew I knocked because of Scarlett. I pushed the door open, entering the pale pink, extra girly room that really confused the hell out of me. I couldn't say only girls love pink but… yeah, not my fucking colour. Unless, of course, it was on Kiara.

"I'm beginning to wonder between Skyla and you which is the bigger devil."

"Oh, but I'm so innocent," Azura replied, pulling the hood of her unicorn onesie up and blinking those large eyes at me.

"Yeah, I can see…"

I don't trust this girl, and unlike Liam, I won't fall for her tricks.

Scarlett came out from the arch that led off to the girls' dressing room, play area, and bathroom, holding two pink bath towels.

"Bedtime storytime, huh?"

"Yeah." I looked at the three girls who had settled into one bed, looking at me with anticipation.

"Daddy, you really look good in a pink room. Maybe you should wear pink at times," Skyla added.

I narrowed my eyes, hearing Scarlett chuckle as she left the room, leaving me with the three girls, two of who were as fucking devious as devils…

You can handle anything, Alejandro. I'm sure one extra child wasn't going to be an issue. The only problem was that she was a fucking Westwood, and I knew that she was not going to make this easy…

His Inner Turmoil

ALEJANDRO

*A*PART FROM KATALEYA, THE other two were clearly finding this amusing. I sat on the other bed, and Skyla giggled when the mattress creaked a little. The fuck was it creaking for? I was sure these things were fucking expensive.

"You are too big for that bed," Little Miss Obvious stated, tucking her black hair behind her ear. "You men really need to learn to sit on the floor when telling stories."

"Yeah? Is that where you get El and Liam sitting?" She smiled innocently.

"Oh no, us Westwoods don't really sit on the floor." Skyla cackled like a witch.

"Burn, Daddy! She's saying Westwoods are better than Rossis!"

"Yeah, well, I don't think so. Now, zip those mouths or no story," I growled. *I am not going to argue with an eight-year-old brat.*

"Oh… so are you better than Kiara?" The sassy little devil pushed. I narrowed my eyes.

"She's a Rossi now."

"Not by blood," she smirked.

"Daddy, you are amazing. You don't need anyone telling you that," Kataleya piped in gently. *Okay, fuck, now my daughter was trying to make me feel better?*

"Nothing this little thing says bothers me," I growled. Azura simply blinked back as if she had no fucking clue what I meant and shrugged.

"Oops, sorry, Alejandro," she said, blinking. I exhaled, running a hand down my face.

"Alright, what kind of story do you want to hear?"

"How you and Mama met!" Skyla piped in.

I was sure they had heard this shit a thousand times, and because I had to fucking censor it, I didn't even remember what the fuck Kiara or I had told them before...

"Right... so, I was chasing this monster, and it led me towards the Blood Moon Pack territory. Then I saw your mother, who was this amazing white wolf with burning purple eyes. So, I killed the fucker and saved Kiara from being killed."

"Or she could have protected herself," Skyla added. I narrowed my eyes at her as all three girls stared at me, waiting for me to continue.

"Maybe. So, anyway, she couldn't see me, but I remember looking into her gorgeous blue-green eyes as she asked me who I fucking was."

"So, she shifted back?" Azura asked.

"Yeah, because she was hurt."

"So, she was naked. Oh, my goddess, you saw her naked?" She gasped. Skyla giggled.

"Doesn't fucking matter. Anyway, Liam, Raven, and some other fucker came, so I left. The next day, I was at Elijah's, and she entered the room, and well, let's just say she couldn't keep her eyes off me," I smirked.

"Dad, it's you who can't keep your eyes off Mom," Skyla remarked, rolling her eyes. "Why do men think it's all about them?"

"Trust me, you have no idea how egotistical these Alphas are," Azura replied. I exhaled, thinking I needed a fucking drink after this, or maybe fucking ten.

"I think Mama and Daddy both couldn't keep their eyes off each other," Kataleya added softly, hugging the plushie she was holding tightly. I didn't miss the fabric she held tightly in her grip and frowned slightly but said nothing.

"Hmm, maybe. Then what happened?" Azura asked.

"Then, she got angry because I told her dad that she was attacked, and so she was pissed off and came up to my room and just barged in."

"Ooo," Skyla smirked. "Then what happened, Daddy?"

"Then I told her I'm the fucking king, and I do as I fucking want," I smirked, remembering how I pinned her to the bed that day... "and she obviously wasn't having it. Then she came over to my pack..."

I continued telling the very PG-rated version of the story, with Azura sometimes chipping in and Skyla having her fits of laughter whilst Kataleya listened with a gentle smile on her face. It felt good knowing she was home. Now to break the curse on Dante and Delsanra. I prayed we would have a fucking solution soon. I kept going until the twins fell asleep, but the Westwood devil remained awake, her creepily unblinking eyes staring at me.

"And then?"

"There's nothing more to tell," I said, running a hand through my hair.

"Hmm. Well, you aren't very good at telling stories. Dad is far better," she stated, snuggling down into the sheets.

"Yeah, well, he can tell stories next time. Unlike him, I'm not so old that I've got nothing better to do," I replied, standing up and pulling the duvet over all three. I noticed how Skyla and Kataleya held each other's hands in their sleep. This incident would always remain with both of them…

"Well, you aren't much younger… but don't worry, Kataleya is going to be fine. You can go now. With me here, even the devil himself won't approach," she said, yawning. I frowned. If only she realised we were up against some kind of devil…

"Well, night, little brat."

"That's what they all call me when they have no better comebacks…" she murmured, turning over. I frowned as I looked at her back. Sassy little brat.

Shaking my head, I left the room and saw El and Scarlett outside of Dante's room. Their arms were wrapped around one another as they looked into his room. I guessed they were going through shit, too, no matter how much they tried to hide it. These kids were their grandkids, and they were Kiara's parents…

I walked down the hall, lighting a cigarette.

"The girls are asleep. That pup of yours is fucking draining. No wonder you look so fucking old. She sucks the fucking life out of you," I remarked.

"She is a notch above Kiara as a kid, for sure," Elijah smirked. It was then that I realised Scarlett's eyes were slightly red. She looked away, smiling faintly, always acting fucking tough.

"She's entertaining," she replied smoothly as Elijah kissed her, running his fingers through her hair. I could tell they were mind-linking, and Scarlett nodded.

"I can get someone else to sit with Kiara... if you two want to stay together, I can watch the girls," I said quietly. Although I wanted to be by her side, I was willing to sacrifice my own needs to do what I knew Kiara would want... be there for our pups and for her parents.

Scarlett shook her head, looking up at me.

"No, you need to be by her side. I'm completely fine," she whispered, despite her eyes glistening with unshed tears. She reached up, placing a hand on my shoulder. "You need the rest too."

"I'll fix this shit," I promised quietly.

"We will, together," she replied, tiptoeing as she yanked my head down and kissed my cheek.

Scarlett and I didn't really have a mother-and-son relationship considering she was far too fucking close to my age, but despite the fact that there was no name to our relationship, she was Kiara's mother, and that was the most important thing. The frown on Elijah's face told me how fucking jealous he got of anyone Scarlett gave attention to, and I smirked, wrapping my arms around Scarlett. Who doesn't like to add a little spice to Elijah's irritation?

He frowned when Scarlett hugged me back. I gave her a quick squeeze, thinking I fucking knew how she was feeling.

"Your man's fucking jealous," I remarked, letting go of her. She rolled her eyes.

"Seriously, of your daughter's mate?" She asked him sceptically.

"I wasn't jealous," he growled, pulling her into his arms and kissing her neck. *Fucking possessive.*

"Yeah?" I smirked, glancing into Dante's room.

He was fast asleep, the red veins looking even more prominent as he slept. I re-entered the room, going over to the sleeping boy, and slowly took off the necklace that suppressed his powers. His strong aura filled the room, promising a truly powerful Alpha when the time came.

"What are you doing?" Elijah asked from behind me.

"He once said he feels like it weighs him down. I know it won't do anything, but at least he can feel a little lighter." I glanced at him, and he nodded, moving back the blanket that lay on the mattress onto the floor before he dropped onto it.

"Makes sense."

I gave a nod, leaving the room and shutting the door behind me quietly before returning to my own room. Kevin and Serena both looked tired yet alert. The empty pizza box on the side told me they had at least had food.

"Anything?" I asked

"No," Serena sighed. I nodded emotionlessly.

"Head home. Get some rest."

She nodded, casting a final glance at Kiara before picking up the empty pizza boxes and the two cans.

"Night, beautiful," Kevin murmured, picking up Kiara's hand and giving it a soft kiss before laying it back on top of the duvet. He lowered his head to me before he left the room, shutting the door behind him.

I locked it before going over to the bed. The cut along her forehead was almost gone. Her long lashes touched her face lightly, her plump lips looking as fucking kissable as ever. I took hold of her chin, rubbing my thumb along them whilst taking a long drag on my cigarette with the other.

I missed her. Despite her being right there, I fucking missed her voice, her touch, her embrace... just her.

I turned away from her, trying to calm the overwhelming emotions that threatened to take over, the guilt returning with a vengeance. I stubbed the cigarette out, leaving it in the little ashtray, and headed to the bathroom, placing Dante's necklace on the drawer next to Kiara's rings. Maybe a shower would relieve some of the fucking tension I was feeling. Who was I fucking kidding? Until I found that bastard, killed him, and fixed all this, I couldn't relax.

I stripped, getting into the shower and letting the water run down my tattooed body. I closed my eyes, bracing my hand on the wall, and rested my forehead against the cool tiles.

It had been years since that feeling of uselessness and being a fucking failure had returned to me... ever since Raf's death... and it was fucking back. Maybe I had gotten too soft. Sure, I trained a little less now that I had a family, but if I was going to be at my best, then I needed to become stronger, needed to fucking do better... I had slipped and gotten far too relaxed.

I almost punched the wall, barely controlling myself as I grabbed the shampoo bottle instead. Twenty minutes later, I stepped out of the shower, grabbed a towel, and wrapped it around my waist as I returned to the bedroom after brushing my teeth. I walked over to the curtains, shutting them completely before I grabbed some sweatpants and pulled them on, towelling my hair. I tossed the towel to the ground and walked over to the bed. Moving the duvet back, my eyes raked over her luscious curves that made my dick twitch. Fuck, she was out cold, or as Raihana insisted - simply asleep, and I was still fucking unable to stop myself from checking her out. I got into the bed, and, gently lifting her head, I slid my arm under it and tugged her close.

A soft sigh escaped her, and I smirked, pulling her against me. Her body moulded against mine perfectly as I kissed her neck softly. The smell of blood and smoke lingered, yet it was overpowered by her intoxicating scent. I squeezed her ass before hugging her tightly.

Wake up, Amore Mio…

I couldn't sleep, my mind a storm of emotions and thoughts, wondering if there was any progress about the so-called Crimson King. My only grasp on serenity was the woman in my arms. I wasn't sure when sleep finally came over me, but the first rays of dawn had begun to seep through the crack in the curtain…

His Punishment

KIARA

"**K**ATALEYA!" I JOLTED UPRIGHT, looking around in the darkness, panic and fear consuming me. Was she okay? Did she get out safely? Where-

Sparks tingled through me when an arm wrapped around me.

"She's safe." Alejandro's soothing voice made my eyes shut in relief. "We're back home, Amore Mio."

I let out a shuddering breath of relief, slumping against his chest, my heart pounding rapidly as I clutched onto his arm. Thank the goddess for that... I needed to see her. I looked around, wondering what time it was. It was still dark, which meant it was still the middle of the night.

Alejandro rubbed my back soothingly, and I turned in his hold, feeling so protected in his strong arms. I kissed his chest softly, my lips brushing one of his pierced nipples making his heart rate spike. I looked up at him.

"I'm glad you got there in time," I whispered, gazing into his glowing red eyes. In the dark room, they were all I could see.

"You fucking scared me, Amore Mio," his husky voice admitted.

"I know..." I reached up, cupping his face, the bristles of his stubble prickling my fingertips, a feeling I so loved... "I'm sorry," I whispered, knowing I worried him.

"Yeah? Well, I'm not letting you off the hook so fucking quickly," he replied huskily.

Then he was kissing me passionately, deeply, hungrily...

My entire body hummed at his touch, rivets of pleasure rushing straight to my core. His firm yet soft lips dominated mine completely, his hand gripping the back of my neck as his heart thudded as one with mine. I could barely breathe with the overwhelming emotions and love that I was feeling, his and mine intertwined as one. He was here, Kataleya was safe, we were together...

The moment he squeezed my ass, I broke away, gasping. As much as I wanted him, and that ache in my core was strong, I needed to see my babies first...

"I want to see the kids," I whispered, cupping his face...

"Sure." I knew he was smirking from the tone in his voice. I could smell my arousal clinging in the air. "Light," he said clearly. The lights came on, and I looked into the handsome face of my king. I hugged him tightly, and he stood up, his hands cupping my thighs. "How do you feel?"

"Completely okay, just like I've had a good training session," I replied, frowning as I tried to remember what had happened. All I remembered was pain and fire... then the burning house... Kataleya... I shook my head as he quietly opened the door. "What time is it?" I asked, making him glance over at the clock.

"Near three in the morning."

"I'll be quick," I whispered. He followed as I first went to the girl's room.

"Scarlett's with them."

I nodded, slowly opening the door. Instantly I heard Mom wake up, her heart rate quickening.

"Kia?" She whispered.

"Mom." She switched the lamp on, and I saw that Kataleya was sleeping in her arms whilst two heads of black hair were on the other bed. I smiled at Mom; she looked so relieved to see me awake. I quickly hurried over to her and hugged her tightly.

"Thank the goddess," her hushed voice whispered, kissing my cheek.

I moved back, looking at Kataleya. Clean, no bruises and seemingly at peace... I crouched down by the bed, running my hand through her hair and kissing her forehead softly. I closed my eyes as I rested my head against hers. She was safe. She was home... *Goddess, thank you...*

"How has she been?"

"She woke up crying a short while ago, so I brought her to my bed," Mom replied, running her hand through my hair.

I looked into her soft sage green eyes, knowing she was doing her best to control her emotions. Growing up, I often felt like Dad was too protective and, don't get me wrong, he was very overbearing, but when I became a mother... I realised why; the fear of losing a child or of them getting hurt was terrifying... just the way Mom was relieved that I was okay. I totally understood that.

"I'm fine," I said softly. She nodded, cupping my face, and I placed my hand over her pale one. "Thank you for letting me go. I know it was hard for you, too." She didn't reply, nodding. I knew she was trying to control her tears. "I love you, Mom."

"I love you too, baby," she whispered, wrapping her arms around me once again as a very quiet shuddering sob escaped her. I closed my eyes, my arms around my baby girl and my mother. For a few moments, we remained like that until Mom moved back, wiping her tears. "Goddess, Kia, I don't cry," she sniffed lightly.

"It's okay to at times." I smiled softly before kissing Kataleya gently. "I want to take her to my room."

Mom nodded. I walked over to the other bed kissing Skyla and Azura tenderly. Azura was a messy sleeper, just like Aunty Indigo. Her arms and legs were sprawled all over the place. I tucked her in slowly, careful not to disturb her, and caressed Skyla's hair. She wasn't the type to speak up about things that troubled her. I just hoped she'd be okay. We all would need time to heal from this. I stood up.

Baby, take Kataleya to our room? I mind-linked Alejandro, who was at the door. His sharp piercing eyes met mine, that sexy, arrogant pout on his face, and his clenched jaw only added to how handsome he looked. I knew he wanted me, but he was going to have to wait for tomorrow...

I made my way down the hall to Dante's room whilst Alejandro took Kataleya to our room. I opened the door slowly, and, as expected, Dad was up in a flash, his eyes blazing in the dark.

"Kiara."

"Dad," I replied, walking over to him. I left the hallway door open to cast some light in the dark room. He hugged me tightly, and I smiled up at him.

"How are you feeling?"

"I'm perfectly fine," I answered, pulling away after a moment and going over to Dante. His aura filled the room. Seems like his necklace was removed. His eyes fluttered open, frowning as he looked around before realising it was me, and a small smile graced his lips.

"Mama."

"Baby." I pulled him into my arms, wishing I could do something about those veins that covered his body. *We'll find a way.* He hugged me tightly before I moved back and cupped his face, planting a kiss on his forehead. "I missed you," I whispered.

"Me too… I'm glad you woke up." I nodded.

"Me too."

I sat with him for a few moments, settling him back down and promising that we'd talk more in the morning before bidding both him and Dad goodnight. I returned to our bedroom, where Kataleya was fast asleep in our bed. The lights were on dimly, and Alejandro was standing near the window, which was slightly open, smoking a cigarette.

My eyes ran over his body, my heart skipping a beat when he glanced at me as I entered, closing the door quietly behind me. I walked over to him, wrapping my arms around his waist, very aware of his manhood against my stomach. Goddess…

"Did you see him?" He asked, his eyes hard and cold. I frowned.

"Yeah… I did…" I remembered asking to see the Crimson King… wasn't I shown into an office? Then what? I placed a hand on my neck and shook my head. "I can't remember," I whispered. His frown deepened, his eyes flashing as he squeezed my ass.

"He probably made sure you didn't remember… do you remember anything?" I pondered over what happened, but it was just… empty.

"I remember demanding to see him… then walking along the hall… and then I was in a fight…or something happened because I was hurt…"

I unwrapped my arms from around his waist, pushing my hair back as I turned away. Why the hell couldn't I remember? It was frustrating. They must have done something.

"So, they've made sure you forgot everything that you saw or some shit like that. When I saw you, you were a fucking mess. They did a number on you and looked like they were going to fucking carve your head open." His voice held venom, and I placed my hand on his bicep.

"I'm fine. Did you come inside, or did Kataleya go out?" I asked, glancing towards our angel, who was sleeping peacefully.

"I came in. She was trying to pull you out from under a beam." His arms locked around me from behind, pushing my breasts up as he kissed my neck. I closed my eyes, leaning into him.

"Hmm… I'm glad you came."

"Yeah? Care to explain why you didn't leave it to me? You snuck out, Kiara, and it fucking worried me." His voice was quiet, but I could sense his anger and irritation.

"I couldn't just sit and do nothing, and you didn't allow me to go. Look, Alejandro, she's home, she's safe. Let's not think about it," I pleaded, tilting my head back to look up at him.

"I saw you fucking near death, Amore Mio... I can't just not think about that shit. We can't just fucking pretend it never happened."

He frowned, but I didn't reply, not wanting to argue. There was nothing I could do about it, and something told me this conversation wasn't over. I understood his concern, but he clearly didn't want to see my point of view. I knew we were going to have to talk about it, but not when Kataleya was around. The last thing we needed was for her to see us argue.

Despite his anger, his arms remained around me tightly while he placed kisses along my neck, but I could sense his emotions...

"Let's get to bed," I said, softly pulling out of his arms.

I walked over to the bed and slipped between the sheets, pulling Kataleya onto my arm and holding her tightly. I felt the bed dip when he got in. His intoxicating scent made me feel safe, and when he pulled me against him, I closed my eyes, wishing that we managed to sort our issue out soon.

I love you, I murmured through the mind link.

That shit ain't ever-changing. I love you, too.

A small smile graced my lips before I fell asleep, once more holding my baby girl close.

I won't ever let you go again...

ENRIQUE

I stood silently before my father's desk. My face was emotionless, my chin tilted up, and my shoulders back despite the pain that filled my body. He had summoned me, but I wasn't sure why. It couldn't be good; he was still angry at me for giving the chica food.

My punishment was carried out daily, and I wasn't healing as well anymore. The lack of food and water was slowing me down, but I wouldn't let it show. I was strong, an Alpha who could handle anything.

I looked at Father's back. He was standing behind his chair, taking something off the shelf. I could feel his anger, his irritation, and the darkness of his immense power surrounding him.

"Padre, you called for me?" I asked after a few minutes. Standing there was unbearable. Pain was spreading through my calves and back. Today's punishment had been hard.

"How are you finding the new location, mijo?"

I looked around his office. The house was darker than the previous one. When we had gone earlier, all I could think about was if the chica got out…

"It's good, Padre."

"Is it? What of the other one that burned down to a crisp?" He spun around, his hatred burning in his eyes as he glared at me. I lowered my head.

"It was also befitting, Padre," I replied, keeping my head bowed in respect.

"You know that girl would have died… but I heard that somehow… the door was unlocked. Do you know who unlocked the door?"

Danger.

His voice was so scary I couldn't help but flinch. I saw the warning signs in his burning eyes as I stayed rooted in my spot. If I lied, I was dead. If I told the truth, then what would happen to me?

"Yes, Padre, I do," I replied quietly.

"And who unlocked the door? Was it Ronaldo? Maybe I should kill him for disobeying me… I gave no order to anyone to unlock that door." He dropped into his seat, and I could see the small, thin blade in his hand.

"No, Padre. it was me." I swallowed, trying not to show how scared I was

"Then do we kill you, Enrique?"

I struggled to voice my thoughts, feeling a strange emotion overcome me. It felt like there was something stuck in my throat, and I couldn't speak.

"I…I'm sorry, Padre, she was only a chil-"

A menacing growl echoed around the room, and he lunged across the table, grabbing me by my neck.

"Who was meant to die!" He growled. "What magic has she done upon you that you have disobeyed me not once but twice?"

I couldn't breathe. His grip around my neck was painful. He dragged me across the table, slamming me face forward onto it.

"Was this the hand that you used to free her?"

He grabbed my right hand, pinning it to the table as I gasped for air, relieved he had let go of my neck.

"Padre, please! I'm sorry! I'm sorry! She was only little- AHHH!" I screamed in agony and fear. The smell of blood filled the air as I stared in complete horror at my hand, or where my hand once used to be.

Father had cut it off completely.

"No, Padre!" A strangled sob left my lips as I begged him, but it was no use, as my entire hand went up in flames.

I stared at my bloody stump numb. My entire life flashed before me; I'd never be able to run in wolf form… I'd never be the best I could be…

"Reap the repercussion of your actions," Father hissed before he walked out of the office, leaving me behind.

I couldn't stop the tears. It was strange to cry. It hurt so much. It hurt physically, but it also hurt inside…

I stared at the ashy pile, all that was left of my hand as I fell to my knees, sobbing silently. I felt so… broken. Was this the price of kindness?

A Hot Punishment

KIARA

THE NEXT MORNING, DESPITE waking up early thanks to a certain something that I loved poking my ass, I didn't move. Although I needed a good shower, I wanted to be here when Kataleya woke up.

Goddess, this man…

I pouted when he throbbed against my ass. His hand that rested on my hip already made my stomach all fluttery. It travelled up my waist before he squeezed my breast, making my eyes fly open, and I swatted it away, turning my head to look into his eyes and give him a small frown. Kataleya was right there!

The strands of his black hair were falling over his eyes. I reached behind, brushing them back and letting my hands run down the side of his head where his hair was kept short, enjoying the feeling beneath my fingers.

"Morning, Amore Mio," he murmured huskily, his morning voice making my stomach knot.

"Morning, my sexy beast," I replied softly. I closed my eyes when his lips met mine, igniting the sparks of pleasure within me. I could never get enough of this…

We broke away, both of us breathing hard as we tried to control the emotions that enveloped us.

"She slept alright…" he remarked quietly, his arm wrapping around my waist tightly. I nodded, looking down at my little angel. I knew there were going to be days she'd wake up traumatised by everything. I just needed to make sure I was always close. "She's a strong one."

"She is," I whispered.

Her eyelids fluttered open, and Alejandro propped himself up on his elbow behind me. Her eyes met mine, and they flew wide open as a huge smile crossed her face.

"Mama! You're awake!"

"I am, baby girl." I smiled softly, hugging her tightly. She giggled happily.

"I'm so happy, Mama!"

"So am I, angel." I kissed her. "We are all together again." She nodded before I sat up, hugging her tightly.

"How did I get here in your room?" She asked, confusion clear on her cute little face as she looked around my bedroom.

"I brought you here. I thought it would be a nice surprise when you woke up and saw that I'm awake, too." I smiled, brushing her hair back. She nodded happily.

"I am very happy, Mama," she agreed, turning to her father.

"Morning."

"Morning, Daddy." Suddenly her smile vanished, and she began to look around the bed frantically. "Where is it?"

"Where's what, baby?" I asked, concerned.

"My cloth!" I frowned, seeing her jump away as she frantically searched the bed. I glanced at Alejandro, concerned, and noticed he was frowning deep in thought.

"It's in your bedroom. Come on, we'll go get it," Alejandro said quietly. She didn't wait, sliding off the bed and rushing to the door. What on earth was going on?

Alejandro ran his hand through his hair, getting out of bed.

"What is she looking for?" I asked standing up.

"A piece of torn fabric…" he said quietly, despite the look of seriousness on his face. He left the room, leaving me concerned and confused as I followed them out.

❦

Two hours had passed since then. After Kataleya had found her little torn fabric, she had calmed down. Alejandro quickly told me about the cloth before we all got dressed for the day and had breakfast. The kids decided to play in the mansion garden whilst Alejandro and I had returned to our bedroom to talk. Despite the protection spells and guards, we were still being very careful.

Alejandro had filled me in on everything properly; Enrique, how he had helped Kat, what happened when he came after me… and ended with Kat's medical report. I stared down at the file, biting into my bottom lip as I tried to control my emotions. Whilst I was sitting at home, she had been subjected to so much…

I closed the file, dropped it onto the bed, and placed my head in my hands. My hair curtained my face before Alejandro wrapped his arms around me tightly. We remained silent, simply holding each other in silent comfort.

We needed to question Kataleya. I really didn't want to upset her, but it was something we were going to have to do. Even if we got someone to do a spell to probe her mind, it wouldn't work. She was completely immune to magic.

"Shall I go get her?" Alejandro asked.

"No, let's get some ice cream and some treats out in the garden. We'll ask her when the time feels right. She's been through a lot, and Enrique, he's a child, for Goddess's sake. Kat isn't wrong, we need to get him away from that monster." Alejandro nodded, despite the frown on his face.

"Yeah, although I wouldn't trust him to be completely innocent. If he's been drilled with bile since childhood, then he may not be someone we can trust."

"Alejandro, he's a child."

"Who may also be a killing machine, one who may be a risk."

"But we can't leave him to suffer!"

"We also can't just remove him. He may have other family."

"Who clearly don't seem to care about him! Kat said he was beaten for helping her." I shook my head; I didn't know how people could be so twisted and treat children like this.

"I know, but he's the child of the enemy. We will need to tread carefully," he replied with finality. I stood up, letting out a breath of frustration. I understood his point, but I also couldn't allow a child to be treated like that and do nothing.

"I wish I remembered something, something that could give us some answers."

"I wonder if the only reason Kataleya remembers stuff is either because they wanted her dead or they didn't realise magic doesn't work on her. That's assuming that they did use magic or whatever shit that Djinn uses," he added coldly, frustration and anger clear in his voice.

"I'm assuming it could have been the second, but who knows," I sighed, standing up and fixing the strap of my sage green dress. I could feel his intense gaze on me.

I walked to the door, but before I could open it, he was behind me in a flash, his arm shooting out and bracing his hand on the door as he looked down at me. I made the mistake of looking up, only for my blue-rimmed green eyes to meet his piercing dark ones. My heart skipped a beat, and I knew that the conversation from last night was not over...

"We aren't done," he replied huskily.

I crossed my arms and turned to face him, making his gaze dip to my boobs. His Adam's apple moved as he swallowed hard. He may be the Lycan king, but I was still the one who had the power to affect him strongly. Pressing my back against the door, I tilted my head upwards to him.

"Hmm?"

"You disobeyed me, Amore Mio. I'm still pissed."

"I know... but I'm not a baby, Alejandro. My instincts led me, and I followed. I did find her, and you saved her. We work better as a team. I'm your queen. I'm one of the strongest fighters in this pack. I'm capable of being on the front line," I reasoned softly, placing my hand on the crisp fabric of his white shirt.

"I never said you weren't fucking capable, but it meant you put yourself in danger." He closed the remaining gap between us, his hand still on the door beside my head. I knew he was angry, and unless I apologised for acting like any mother would have, he would snap, but I wasn't sure I'd mind that.

"I don't regret going after her. Maybe I did do it in the wrong way, but I wouldn't change it." I pouted slightly, fiddling with the button of his shirt. I couldn't apologise for doing what I felt was the right thing to do.

"So, you're going to act fucking stubborn?" He frowned, his eyes flashing.

"Maybe?" I snaked my arms around his neck, pressing my body against his. "Al... listen to me. I know I worried you, but I truly was losing my mind sitting at home. Forgive me?" I whispered coquettishly.

"I almost lost you." I sighed; he was not buying it. *Please understand me, Alejandro...*

"You risk your life for us all the time. This wasn't any different," I explained softly.

"It's fucking different," he growled, gripping my hips as he yanked me against him, making me gasp as rivets of pleasure rushed through me.

"Oh? How?" I challenged, raising an arched brow. He narrowed his eyes, one hand wrapping around my neck.

"Because your life is fucking worth more," he growled, his anger flaring.

It was my turn to frown at him. He was damn wrong. My eyes burned brilliant purple as I glared up at him.

"How can you even say that? You mean the world to me. Do you think we can just carry on if something was to happen to you? I worry every time you have to leave. I'm scared of losing you, too, but I deal with it. We are equal, Alejandro; you can't be selfish and put a higher value on me over your own worth."

"I've lived far longer than you, and if I had to choose between you or myself, I'd choose you every fucking time." His hold on my neck tightened, his eyes blazing as they flickered to my lips.

"Oh, for fuck's sake. That means nothing because I choose you and my children over myself. I'd do anything for the lot of you!" I shot back.

We never agreed on this, and it annoyed me. He quirked an eyebrow, licking his lips, trailing his gaze over me slowly.

"You're fucking stubborn, Amore Mio… too fucking stubborn. It's fucking infuriating, but it's also fucking hot…" My breath hitched when he pressed himself against me, feeling the hard shaft in his pants.

"I won't apologise for going after her, but I'm sorry for worrying you." I pouted, hoping he'd let it go. The moment he was about to frown, I wrapped my hand around his wrist, which still held my neck. "Then how about I make it up to you in another way?" I murmured suggestively, running my hands down his abs and sliding my fingers into his pants.

My sexy man, one who I knew thousands of women wanted… but he was mine alone. An arrogant smirk crossed his lips, but just as he was about to speak, I grabbed his hard shaft over his pants, cutting off whatever he had been about to say as his eyes flashed red.

"Fuck, Amore…" he growled as I stroked his dick.

"So, tell me… how about you vent all your anger out on fucking me senseless?" I whispered, tiptoeing as I kissed his lips ever so lightly. His hand tightened around my throat, sending another spark of pleasure to my core.

"You don't want me to fuck you right now because you won't be able to walk when I'm done."

"Try me," I challenged, my entire body rippling with anticipation.

I wanted him… needed him… and there was just something so incredible about the way that Alejandro fucked me…

His lips crashed against mine in a rough, hungry kiss. His other hand yanked my dress up, exposing my bare ass and delivering a sharp tap to it, making me moan wantonly as I kissed him back with equal passion and desire. *Oh, fuck, that's it…*

I undid his pants quickly; he didn't waste time, ripping my thong off. I gasped as the fabric rubbed against my pussy. He removed his hand from my neck, grabbing my breast.

"Fuck, Alejandro…" I moaned, lost in pleasure.

While his one hand groped my breast, the other tapped my inner thigh sharply, making me part my legs. The cool air hit my dripping core, making it clench. It felt so fucking good…. He kissed and sucked on my neck, and I knew when he was done, I'd be littered with marks.

"Promise not to disobey me again," he growled. At the same time, he parted my pussy, his finger finding my clit. Instantly, immense pleasure ripped through me. I barely managed to yank his pants down a little, freeing his thick, hard dick completely.

"I can't promise that," I murmured, gasping when he brushed my clit roughly.

"You're so fucking stubborn."

"Not that you mind it," I whispered before our lips crashed against one another's again.

Our hands moved fast, with a desire and need that could never be satiated. I could never have enough. He left me desperately wanting more every single time…

He reached behind me, locking the door before turning me and pushing my face up against it. He ripped my dress off in one go, making me gasp.

"I want to taste you," I whimpered as his hands squeezed my breasts, kissing me down my neck. I wanted to have his cock down my throat and watch his face fill with pleasure as he fucked my mouth hard.

"Not sure if that's punishment enough…" he growled, his hand squeezing around my throat. He yanked me up and back against him, the other hand running down my stomach before he massaged my pussy for one delicious moment, sending incredible pleasure rushing through me. "Unless this pretty throat is ready to take it all."

Fuck, yes, I want it, I want it all.

"Yes, baby, fuck my mouth. I'll take it like a good girl," I whined hornily, unable to stop myself from begging. I wanted him.

He didn't reply. His hand tangled in my hair as he turned me around and pushed me down onto my knees. I only managed to rip open his shirt before I was level with his large, pulsing cock. My pussy clenched at the thought of what was to come. I pulled his pants down completely, his hand twisted into my hair, and I wrapped my hand around his dick. Sticking my tongue out, I ran it over his tip, moaning at the salty taste of precum that filled my mouth.

"Fuck, baby," I whimpered, running my tongue along the base right down to the hilt, making sure to lick every inch of it before I took his tip into my mouth, taking a moment to breathe as he stretched me out. I began sucking on his dick, my tongue twirling around his length, going faster.

He took control, ramming into my mouth harder and faster. My eyes started stinging as he hit the back of my throat, making me gag, but it only fuelled the desire within me. My moans grew louder as he assaulted my mouth hard and rough. I grabbed his thigh with one hand while the other played with his balls. Goddess, he was perfection. His sexy groans and that look of pleasure on his face made my heart beat faster. He was all mine.

"Fuck, that's it," he groaned, slamming into my mouth with a few brutal thrusts as his orgasm neared before he pulled out just as he shot his load, coating my face, neck, and breasts in his milky goodness "Fuck, you're so good at this."

I stuck my tongue out as he delivered a few rough strokes to his dick, letting the last few droplets coat my tongue. My throat was burning from his assault, my pussy begging to be fucked, and I cupped my breasts, leaning down and licking his cum from my left boob. My eyes locked with his. The pleasure that I had inflicted on him was clear on his face. His eyes blazed red as he watched me lick my nipple.

"Fuck…"

His hand that was twisted in my hair tightened, and I stroked his muscled thighs, leaning forward and licking the tip of his cock one final time before I stood up, staring into his eyes as he breathed hard. His hand wrapped around my throat as he yanked me close, his lips crashing against mine. I plunged my tongue into his mouth, letting him taste himself on me as I tore his shirt off completely. Running my hands down the planes of his chest, my thumbs rubbed his pierced nipples.

"Fuck…" he growled, pulling away, and tugged me towards the bed.

He pushed me onto it, face down, and grabbed my hips. He lifted me onto my knees, and before I could even get my bearings, his mouth was on my pussy, licking and sucking my dripping core, making my eyes roll back in pleasure. I braced my weight on my hands, rolling my hips and rubbing my pussy against his face. I gasped when I felt him part shift, a low growl ripping from his throat as his long tongue plunged straight into my pussy. Oh, fuck! There was something about that... the way his tongue hit my g-spot in an entirely different way.

"Fuck, baby, that's it, fuck!" I yelped when he suddenly flipped me onto my back, his tongue still fucking me.

Touch yourself, Amore Mio, he commanded through the link.

My cheeks burned as I obeyed. Reaching down, I placed my finger on my clit, increasing the pleasure that he was already drowning me in. My moans became louder, my core knotting as I felt myself nearing. I gasped when his finger probed my back entrance before he slipped two fingers inside, making me whimper. I felt full, not to the extreme as I had been many times, but enough to make me groan in pure ecstasy as he began fucking me with his fingers and tongue faster.

"Fuck, I'm going to come!" I whimpered, my head lifting off the bed as I felt my walls tighten before a huge wave of pleasure ripped through me, making me cry out.

The height of my orgasm consumed me when he suddenly pulled out and positioned himself at my entrance, thrusting in with one hard push as my orgasm still spasmed through me. I bit my lip, moaning with pleasure as he filled me. I loved how stretched out I felt…

"Fuck me, baby," I breathed, clenching the sheets as my king began fucking me hard and fast, setting off a second orgasm that jarred through me. Each thrust hit my G-spot, sending me into a high of pure bliss. My moans filled the room, and I had to do my best to keep my volume down as Alejandro pounded into me. This… this was euphoria… being fucked by my king was something incomparable.

His lips crashed against mine in a rough, brutal kiss that was full of emotions and dominance, but he had won. I was a mess beneath him, unable to stop the scream that left my lips when he sank his teeth into my neck, triggering another incredible orgasm to rip through my body like a tidal wave. His own release followed soon after, and I felt it fill me up. He pulled out, and I could feel his seed leaking out of me, mixed with my own juices. He dropped onto the bed next to me and pulled me into his arms.

"You're fucking perfect even if you are fucking stubborn, Amore Mio."

"Hmm," I managed to reply, kissing his neck. We remained silent, catching our breath and relishing in our post-sex state.

"How long were we up here?" I asked after a moment. He smirked as I glanced around. Grabbing his wrist, I stared at the time and blushed deeply.

"Who the fuck cares?" He shrugged. "Let's shower and then head the fuck back out." I bit my lip when he rubbed my pussy whilst kissing my lips.

"Sounds like a plan… fuck, Alejandro…" I whimpered, forcing myself back.

"We'll continue tonight…"

He delivered a sharp tap to my ass before standing up and carrying me to the bathroom. I rested my head on his shoulder, feeling content. The pleasant ache between my legs felt good, a feeling I relished in.

He placed me down in the shower and turned it on. I watched him, admiring every angle of his sexy god-like body. Goddess, I could never stop admiring him. It was like it was the first I was seeing him…

I tilted my head, frowning. The first time I saw him… how did we first meet anyway? My heart thumped as he began to soap my body as I stood there frozen. Why couldn't I remember? I racked my brain, trying to remember the oldest memory of Alejandro I had, but there was nothing. I was drawing a hazy blank…

There were no memories of our first kiss… our first conversation…

What on earth was going on?

Her Concern

ALEJANDRO

*E*VER SINCE THE SHOWER, Kiara seemed quieter. I had let out all my fucking pent-up emotions, fucking that pussy of hers with everything I had and fucking enjoying every moment, but then I didn't know what the fuck happened. We were okay up until we showered. She had selected a white high-neck dress to cover all the marks I had left on her neck and pulled her wet hair into a messy bun, but I could tell she was completely preoccupied.

We headed downstairs and entered the kitchen as she began to take the ice cream stuff out.

"You fucking okay?" I asked, trying not to look at her ass in that dress.

She looked over her shoulder at me, a natural pout on those plump lips of hers that looked a tad fucking sore, and she gave me a smile, nodding. *Yeah... there's something bothering her...*

"Babe, could you grab me a tray?"

"Which cabinet?"

"I'll get it, Luna," Claire said as she entered the kitchen with a tray of glasses and an empty jug. My eyes didn't leave Kiara's as she gathered several things onto the tray before she picked it up and smiled as her eyes met mine.

"Shall we?"

I held the door open for her, kissing her lips as she passed me before we both walked to the garden. Questioning Kat... I didn't think I'd ever be fucking ready for something like this, and I'd questioned adults and kids countless fucking times in my life.

The twins were on the swings, whilst the Westwood devil was hanging upside down in one of the trees, her arms crossed over her chest, her eyes staring blankly ahead, and a creepy as fuck smile on her face as Dante sat on the bench with Scarlett and Elijah. Scarlett glanced up when we approached, a smirk crossing her lips as she looked at her daughter knowingly whilst I walked over to the swings. Kataleya looked a little distracted, and once again, I saw that same piece of fabric in her hands.

"Daddy, push me!" Skyla asked. I obliged, pushing both girls slowly.

"Faster, Daddy, we aren't scared," Skyla complained.

"I got ice cream, kids!" Kiara called.

"I'm a bat. I can't come down," Azura whispered. I glanced at her, and she smiled, looking even creepier than before. Kiara smiled back at her.

"Okay, then tell me what you want, and I'll put it on your cone or in a bowl for you."

"A cone will do for a bat," Azura replied.

"You are so weird," Dante remarked.

"That's no way to speak to your aunt," Azura retorted, glaring at her nephew.

"You are not my aunt."

"Am too, pup," she retorted. Dante glared at her with pure irritation.

"Azura, behave," Elijah warned.

"I didn't say anything wrong," she remarked, shrugging. She sure had fucking good balance. Skyla jumped off the swing, rushing over to Kiara, and I looked down at Kat.

"So, what do you want? Ice cream in a cone or bowl, and which flavour?" She shook her head.

"I don't want any, thank you," she replied, shaking her head. I frowned and gave a small nod.

"Why not?"

She simply shook her head but didn't answer. That was a first for her, not sharing what was on her mind. I glanced up, exchanging a look of concern with Kiara, who was passing everyone ice cream before she began topping a new cone up.

"Azura, come down now if you want ice cream. You are going to feel sick like that," Scarlett called. Azura pouted before she jumped down.

"I wouldn't be sick," she mumbled before going to the table and taking her cone.

"What's on your mind, Angel?" I asked Kat, pushing her sandy brown hair off her face and crouching down by the swing. She looked at me with sadness in her eyes.

"Please help him, Daddy," she begged softly, her eyes filling with tears.

I sighed heavily; she was really fucking hung up on this little fucker. But what exactly had she seen or experienced? That was something we didn't know yet. I glanced at the cloth. That had been a part of his clothes… something that belonged to him.

"His name was Enrique, right?"

She nodded just as Kiara came over, passing Kataleya the cone of ice cream, her thick sexy thighs coming into view. I wouldn't deny that I took a moment to appreciate how fucking good she looked.

"Yes, Enrique Ignacio Escarra, the future Alpha of the Fuego de Ceniza Pack," she stated it carefully, as if she had repeated it and memorised it thoroughly with effort until she had burned it into her memory. Kiara and I exchanged looks; this was more than I was fucking expecting. We had a name and a pack…

"What did he look like?" Kiara asked, crouching down next to me as she cupped Kataleya's hand, brought the ice cream cone towards her own mouth, and took a lick.

"He had dark curly hair and very pretty green eyes with yellow in them and long lashes." Wasn't that a tad too many fucking details about his eyes? I frowned, and Kiara placed a hand on my thigh knowingly.

"What about the horrible Alpha?" Kiara probed gently. Her face instantly fell, fear filling her eyes, and Kiara wrapped her hands over her small ones.

"He was scary. His face was burned, and it was all red and looked painful. He was horrible, Daddy." She looked at us, clearly terrified.

"He can never hurt you again, my angel." Kiara frowned, her eyes flashing purple.

"He was mean and said I wasn't good enough, that I'm better off dead, and that you wouldn't come for me, Daddy, because I'm not Dante." She broke into tears. I took the cone from her loose grip as Kiara wrapped her arms around her tightly.

So, the fucker had wanted Dante…

"Oh, baby, he's just a horrible person. You, Dante, and Skyla, you are all equal to us," Kiara whispered, soothingly caressing her hair. I frowned, pondering over what she said.

Darien, see what you can find on an Enrique Ignacio Escarra and a Fuego De Ceniza Pack right now.

On it, Alpha, he replied swiftly. I stood up. Didn't that stand for Ash fire or some shit?

With a name and pack, we could even find the boy, Kiara's voice came.

Hm, or better - the father...

Alejandro... what do you plan to do? Her voice was full of concern.

If this boy is his heir... then I'm sure he's fucking worth something. I felt her shock through the bond, but I thought it was high fucking time this man had a taste of his own medicine...

I crouched down next to Kataleya again.

"Do you want me to take that so I can use it to find him?" I asked her. She frowned slightly, staring at her piece of cloth.

Alejandro, we are not kidnapping children, Kiara's stunned voice came into my head. I looked into her gorgeous eyes, which were wide with shock and disapproval.

Yeah? You aren't.

But I fucking am.

"Promise you will protect him, Daddy?" Kataleya asked me, her eyes filling with fresh tears.

"I'll make sure his father doesn't find him," I promised as she finally let go of the piece of fabric.

Perfect.

I stood up, feeling Kiara's gaze still on me. I walked towards the house, needing to do some of my own research. It wasn't like I was going to fucking beat his pup how this fucker beat mine. There was a difference

I heard the sound of her heels as she grabbed my arm, stopping me just when I was halfway through the house.

"Al! You can't possibly be thinking of kidnapping him!" She whispered in shock, clearly not wanting anyone to hear her.

"I'll do what I need to."

"Alejandro..."

We weren't going to agree on this shit, I knew that much.

"Look, Amore Mio… I realised that I was far too soft and relaxed to start with. I let myself fall into failure. Over the years, I've clearly let things go… it almost lost Kataleya, and she went through more than she ever should have. Dante is fucking cursed, and Skyla won't ever forget this shit, either. It's high time I remembered I'm the Lycan king, and there are things I need to do, regardless of if they are the fucking right thing but rather the shit that needs to be done." My voice was cold, and it held a finality that I was not going to change my mind, letting my alpha aura roll off me. It didn't affect her as much as others, but I wanted her to get my fucking point.

"Alejandro, you can't say that. You have done so much, you need to stop blaming yourself for this, but kidnapping a child? You will ask Raihana to do this, won't you?"

"Whoever I ask is my decision. I'm not going to change my mind." Our gaze met, and I could see the hurt in her eyes.

"Can't you just see if he's safe or just try to find his father and portal? Don't kidnap a child. If you want to help him, that's different… but your intentions…" she trailed off pleadingly.

"Yeah, we all know an entire fucking army can't portal. Secondly, with the Djinn, I'm sure it's not that fucking easy. A summoning spell is the only damn way."

"Two wrongs don't make a right," she whispered, cupping my face. I gripped her wrists, inhaling her scent.

"No, they don't, but sometimes we need to do shit to get the answers we need," I replied, removing her hands from my face. It fucking hurt doing that, but I wasn't going to change my mind.

"There's a way to do things, baby," she pleaded desperately. I caressed her face, pulling her into my arms. She was far too pure to ever agree. This time we just weren't going to.

"I know, but sometimes we have to choose the fucking hard path. That fucker touched my family… so he's going to pay." My eyes were burning red, and when she looked up, I felt a wave of guilt wash through me. She sighed in defeat, resting her head against my chest for a moment.

"Alejandro, listen to me; I don't want you to get angry, but I think there's somethin-"

"Amore Mio, I'm not going to fucking change my mind."

I pulled her close, kissing her plush lips deeply and ending the fucking conversation. I was going to get that pup, and I would hold him as bait, and if the fucker behind this didn't care about the pup, I'd put him somewhere safe.

"Alejandro, listen, I wanted to -"

"I'm going to go meet Darien. I'll be back later." She looked down but simply nodded in defeat. "I love you," I said quietly, taking hold of her chin and tilting her face up.

"I love you, too," she whispered.

I frowned, quite surprised that she was actually near tears over this shit. Neither of us exchanged any more words before I left the house, heading towards the pack headquarters. I hated when I disagreed with her over anything.

Searching For Answers

ALEJANDRO

I ENTERED THE BUILDING AND followed my nose until I found Darien and Dustin, one of my two Deltas, in one of the tech rooms. Having two Deltas really fucking helped, knowing that there were more commanders to take control when needed.

"Alpha," Dustin greeted, lowering his head as Darien looked up from the computer he was working at.

"Right on time, Al. I think we found something," he remarked seriously. I cocked my brow.

"Already?"

"You gave us a pack and a name. I don't think that was information this guy planned on letting out," Darien remarked, pushing his seat out. "It's not much, but there's a pack in Puerto Rico with that exact name."

"The Caribbean…" I tilted my head. "I don't get what fucking debt I have to pay to someone from so far fucking out…"

"Yeah, but it could be a century-old debt or something like that. You never know, it doesn't need to be directly you," Dustin added thoughtfully.

"Hmm, anything on the name?"

"The Escarras. There's a wealthy family who owns a shitload of stuff in the States, but they are private people. I'm not sure if it's the same, and nothing on an Enrique Ignacio Escarra," Darien said, scratching his short beard thoughtfully.

"Hmm, we'll relay what we learned to Janaina. They were from the States, they might know something. There's also Alpha Kenneth of the

Shadow Wolves Pack, his mate's from the States. See if you can organise a meeting with them."

"That pack…" Darien raised an eyebrow.

Yeah, okay, the guy was a fucking Ken doll and spoke like he was the fucking King of England with an accent and mannerisms of the royal family. Let's just say he and I did not go well at one fucking table.

"Yeah… I'm sure his woman's from Florida…" I frowned. Darien smirked slightly.

"Well, I better get on a call to Buckingham palace then," he joked with a mock accent. I gave him a small smirk as I turned away, shoving my hands into my pockets as I pondered on the new information.

"Dustin… also, there are the old archives of packs from around the world. I doubt we'll have them all or if they are even up to date, but if our families have crossed paths with this fucker's, then maybe there's something in the old archives…"

"The ones that were originally from the Black Storm Pack?"

"Yeah, I think some may still be there. Not all of them were brought here. I'll contact Rayhan myself." I needed to check out how Del was coping, too.

I left the room, taking my phone out as I walked to my office, unlocking the door with my fingerprint. The lights came on automatically when I entered and walked over to my desk, dropping into my seat as I video-called Rayhan. Taking out a cigarette, I lit it as I waited for him to answer.

Moments later, he answered the call, clearly having just stepped out of the shower, wearing nothing but some jeans and a towel in hand.

"Eager to answer my call?" I remarked, taking a drag of my cigarette as he sat down on his bed,

"You wish, but I did think it may be important," he replied, towelling his hair. The fuck did he keep his hair so fucking long for? The amount of care that shit needed made no fucking sense.

"Hmm. So, how's Spitfire doing?" I asked. He looked at the screen, and I didn't miss the anguish that flickered in his eyes before he masked it, looking off to the side.

"Handling well… but she's exhausted. It's fucking draining her," he replied. I felt fucking guilty. I really needed to sort this shit out as soon as fucking possible.

"Is she awake?" He nodded, and for a moment, I was looking at the luxurious ceilings of the Rossi Mansion, or the fucking palace if you wanted to call it that. "Kitten... I got you." His quiet words came along with a whimper and a whisper.

"I'm okay."

The camera was back on them, and I looked at Delsanra, who, like Dante, was covered in those veins. Her skin looked almost as white as her hair, and her blue eyes looked pale.

"Hey, Spitfire, still holding up?"

"Obviously," she replied, giving me a small smile as she leaned against Rayhan's chest, his arm around her tightly as he cradled her in his lap.

"Good to fucking hear. We got a pack name and the fucker's son's name. The pack originates from Puerto Rico, and it's called the Fuego De Ceniza Pack. The Alpha family's called the Escarras." Rayhan frowned, running his fingers through his wet locks.

"Doesn't sound familiar..."

"Yeah, I know. Just check the old archives of packs that we do fucking know of. See if you can bring them down."

"I'll do that. Mom wanted to speak to you, but she's been holding off, knowing you're busy. Could you give her a call when you have a moment?"

"I will." I gave a curt nod, looking at Del once more. "We will get this shit sorted. How are the pups?"

"Both are doing great; Lola and Rose have taken them for the day," Rayhan replied, kissing Delsanra's lips, referring to his Beta couple. I could tell from the way she could barely keep her head up that she was suffering more than Dante.

"I think we need to fucking regroup... can Lola hold down your pack if you five come down here? It might just be easier to deal with stuff if we're together." *Fuck, those words sounded cheesy as fuck...* That annoying smirk of his crossed his lips, but before he could speak, I spoke up, "Don't go getting fucking ideas, but the pups might just be a little more occupied if they're together." Yeah, Lola and Rose had a pup, but still, there were four here...

"I think that would be nice," Delsanra added, smiling gently. I knew Raihana had cast spells around their pack, but still being in one place may fucking help.

"Well, you can ask Mom what she thinks, too."

I nodded. I knew Scarlett and Elijah would need to also go back at some point. Liam was working on the case, and although Raven and Damon covered for him, they had six pups between them.

"I'm going to call her now," I said before ending the call and scrolling to Maria's number. She answered soon after, seemingly in the kitchen, a place Maria didn't often go.

"How the fuck did anyone manage to get you into the kitchen?" She smiled slightly, raising an eyebrow.

"Hello to you, too, Alejandro, and no one at all. It's my personal choice. I was making Delsanra some of her favourite dishes... there isn't much I can do for her," she explained as she began to slice some peppers.

"Ah, makes fucking sense... so that pretty son of yours said you wanted to call. You know I'd always have time for you. You should call if you want to." She smiled and nodded.

"I know you do, but still. I know you are busy... I rang Kiara to ask how you were all doing."

She looked down at the chopping board, and I took a moment to look her over. In her long-sleeved, high-neck, deep green dress, I could tell she was as skinny as ever. She was getting fucking thinner every time I saw her. I knew the signs of someone losing it all once their mate was gone... and she was getting there. Slowly but surely.

I wished I could tell her to take a chosen mate, although it fucking hurt to even think of that. I knew she was Rafael's mate, but I also knew he wouldn't want her to lose herself over him...

"About that, I was thinking you and the kids should come down for a bit. Think you all could use the change of space, and Rayhan's Beta can hold down the fort there for a bit. I was thinking of asking Raihana, too. I think it would be fucking ideal for everyone." I smoked my cigarette, waiting for her answer. She nodded her head slowly.

"That's going to be a lot of children in one place," she replied with a smile.

"Yeah, well, seems like everyone around is fucking having kids. Besides, they prove for good distraction or entertainment," I replied, smirking before I frowned. Maria was quite smart and had studied abroad for a few years...

"That is true."

"Mari... ever heard of a Feugo De Ceniza Pack?" She frowned, tapping her chin.

"No, not that I recall... why?"

"It's most likely the pack the fucker behind all this shit is from."

"If I remember anything, I'll let you know," she mused thoughtfully. I nodded and sat up.

"Well, I'll let you go. I need to get some shit sorted. I'll be expecting you and the kids soon." She gave me a nod.

"Of course."

I ended the call and sat back, just as Darien mind-linked me.

I've made an appointment with Alpha Kenneth three days from now. Good luck. He's expecting accommodations.

Ever heard of suggesting a fucking video call?

He said sometimes discussions are better in person, and he has desired to talk to you in person for a while now. I resisted the urge to roll my fucking eyes. He was such a prick.

Did you tell him I desire to fucking kick him in the fucking balls? Darien's snicker came through the link, and I ran my hand down my face. **Yeah, we'll give them one of the villas. Make sure security is in place. Did he say how long he'll be around?**

Two days and nights.

I hope he had fucking answers… or I was just putting up with his tailored ass for no fucking reason.

Her Dark Hair

KIARA

*L*ATER IN THE EVENING, Alejandro had told me about the Alpha of the Shadow Wolves Pack coming down in three days' time. I had been about to tell him something earlier, but he had cut me off… and I couldn't even remember what it was.

What was it? Something told me it had been important…

I shook my head to clear my mind as I looked at the grocery list that Claire had prepared.

Maria, Rayhan, Del, and the kids would be coming tomorrow, including Raihana and Chris, so it was going to be a full house. I was looking forward to it, knowing the merriment of more of our family together would help everyone.

"Perfect, I think you have everything covered," I commented, glancing over at Claire. Even after a long day, her white hair was in perfect position, all neatly tucked up into a bun.

"The desserts for when the Alpha of the Shadow Wolves Pack comes are still undecided, Luna,"

"Hmm, let's go for -"

"Victoria sponge, Crème Brulé and of course Trifle." I turned as Azura walked into the room, a few stray leaves stuck in her hair.

"Oh, yummy." I smiled.

"Can we get a chocolate gateau, too?" She added, looking up at me as she strode over to us, hands locked behind her back. I chuckled, picking out the dried leaves from her hair.

"Of course we can, Madam Azura Rayne. Now tell me, why does my little sister have leaves in her hair?"

"Oh, I was climbing on the roof, and I fell into the tree." Concern flooded me. As much as I knew those children were tough as cookies, it still worried me.

"You need to be careful, Azura."

"Don't worry, Dad and Alejandro were nearby, and Dad caught me!" I smiled in amusement, removing the last of the leaves.

"Well, since you are here, is there anything you fancy for tomorrow's dinner?" She tilted her head.

"Let's make sure Dante's and Kat's favourites are on the menu," she said with a nod.

"And what of yours?" I asked.

"Well, me and Sky are okay without. We just want them to get better soon…" She furrowed her brow, and I stroked her head.

"You are such a sweetie, Zuzu," I whispered, hugging her tightly.

"Oh, Goddess, please don't call me that! I'm not a baby anymore," she groaned.

"You still call Liam, Wiyam." I smiled, tugging her cheek.

"I do, but it's cute." She shrugged.

"Just like you," I replied with an amused smile.

I wondered who she got her hair from. Neither Mom nor Dad had dark hair… odd. I shook my head at the random thought, turning back to the list and adding a few more items to it.

"I'll add the desserts and their favourites down, Luna," Claire reassured me. I nodded before motioning to Azura to follow me back to the lounge.

"It's nice to see my two girls hanging," Dad said. I smiled at him as Azura ran over and hugged him. He kissed her forehead, giving her a small smirk.

"Of course, we hang out often, Daddy. You just never pay attention to it. You're busy looking at Mama," she stated, sitting down next to him.

"Oh, really? I can multitask pretty well. Mind games won't work on me."

"Who's playing mind games?" She asked innocently.

Dad motioned me over, and I smiled, walking over and taking the seat on his other side. He wrapped his arm around me, kissing my forehead gently. I leaned my head on his shoulder, a strong wave of nostalgia washing over me.

I glanced around the room. Dante was lying down, his head on Mom's lap, fast asleep. Kat was watching TV with Sky, but she looked lost in thought as she leaned against Alejandro, who was sitting on the floor next to them. His eyes met mine, and I smiled at him, wondering what he was thinking.

You look fucking beautiful, Amore Mio, he said through the link.

Thanks, I replied, crossing my legs smoothly and giving him a good view of my thigh.

The ache between my legs had faded earlier, and I was ready for another round all over again. I was satisfied when his gaze fell on my legs. I hid my smirk, leaning my head on Dad's shoulder whilst giving my man a good view.

Keep teasing, and I'm fucking taking you out of here right fucking now. His eyes met mine, and my core knotted in pleasure.

It sounds tempting…

"What time is Maria getting here tomorrow?" Mom asked, bringing us both out of our conversation.

"Afternoon," Alejandro replied, his arms around Kataleya, who fiddled with the hem of her dress.

"How is Delsanra doing?" Dad asked.

"Not as good as Dante," Alejandro replied quietly, making my heart thunder.

"What?"

"I saw her earlier on the video call," he said. His eyes met mine, and I knew he could feel my guilt. Goddess…

"Don't blame yourself," Mom said quietly.

"Things will get fixed," Dad added confidently, glancing at Azura, who was listening with enrapt attention. She gave us a cute smile, and I chuckled.

"Goddess, you are such a little minx," I teased. "You know, I was thinking in the kitchen, who does Zuzu look like? Her hair is so dark compared to the rest of us, it's just like how Grandma's used to be."

Dad tensed and looked at me, confusion and shock clear in his eyes. I raised my eyebrows, realising the tension that had fallen in the room. I glanced at Mom, who looked slightly pale. What did I say? Azura tilted her head.

"That's true… Liam's hair is like Mama's real hair, Kiara's is like Daddy's, then whose is mine like?"

Amore Mio... I glanced at Alejandro, who was frowning with concern.

"Like grandma Jessica's," Mom said with a smile. "Like, look at Skyla's eyes. They aren't like her Mom or Dad's." I nodded.

"Yeah, her eyes are a lot greener than ours," I replied, glancing at Mom. Azura nodded in agreement before she got up and hurried over to Skyla.

"Let's watch something different."

Amore Mio, that question was a bit fucking odd, don't you think? Alejandro's voice asked through the link.

What do you mean? It wasn't odd. I was just wondering where Azura got her dark hair from...

He looked at me but didn't say anything more. Strange. I glanced at Mom and Dad, who were clearly conversing through the mind link. Did I say something wrong? I was about to ask Alejandro when Claire mind-linked me.

Luna, dinner is ready. I will feed Dante whilst the rest of you can eat at the table.

Okay, thank you, Claire.

"Dinner's ready," I said out loud.

"Are you okay, Kiara?" Dad asked when we stood up. I smiled warmly and nodded.

"Of course."

He gave a small nod, yet I didn't miss the concern in his eyes...

⚮

Night had fallen, and I had just gotten the kids to bed. Alejandro had gone out to deal with some stuff and returned when Kataleya had asked for her cloth back for bedtime. She had begun to get very worked up without it. Alejandro had given it back, despite feeling quite concerned about her getting so attached to it.

"She's only a child, baby," I reasoned as I let my hair down. The bathroom door was open.

"I know she is, but her being a little too fucking attached to another pup is not healthy." I chuckled.

"Are you worried she's crushing on him?" I teased, squeezing some toothpaste onto the brush and began brushing my teeth.

"Kind of," he almost growled, making me giggle.

"There's nothing wrong with it if she is," I replied, finishing off and adjusting the strap to my burgundy silk nightdress.

I stepped out of the bathroom, my gaze instantly falling to Alejandro's ass. He had just stripped and was holding a pair of sweatpants, wearing nothing but his black boxers. Goddess, the man was utterly fine…

I walked over to him, wrapping my arms around him from behind, my hand cupping his bulge and making my core throb.

"Fuck, Amore…" He placed his hand over mine and when I felt him throb, I moved my hand away, resting it on his chiselled abdomen.

"Hmm… you need to stop being so worried about Kataleya's concern with this little boy. Remember, he helped her escape and gave her food. You know how loving she is," I murmured, kissing his upper back. He turned his head, looking down at me.

"Maybe. What was that about Azura's hair colour earlier?" He asked. I raised an eyebrow.

"You're asking me? Even Mom and Dad got weird about it," I replied, amused. He unhooked my arms from around him and turned around, cupping my face.

"Amore Mio… you know she looks just like Indigo. Why would you even ask that?" Aunty?

"That's true. She does, now that you mention it. I was just wondering because she doesn't look like Mom or Dad." His heart was racing, and I could feel a sliver of worry through the bond.

"Kiara… why… I mean, who is Azura's biological mother?"

It was as if he had just slapped me.

"What does that even mean? Of course Mom is." Was he insinuating that Dad had an affair or something? Confusion flitted through me, and my head felt heavy, and with it, my irritation grew. "What are you trying to say?"

"Kiara, you're worrying me… Indigo is Azura's biological mother."

"What? Alejandro, I remember Mom pregnant. I remember her birth…" It was hazy… I placed a hand on my head, confusion and fear settling into me.

"The child was transferred into Scarlett when Indigo was killed, remember?"

I looked up at him. I knew he was telling the truth thanks to my ability of being able to sense if a person is lying or not, but...

"No. I don't remember."

Moments of Doubts

ALEJANDRO

"NO. I DON'T REMEMBER."

Her words rang in my head as she stared up at me, fear clear in her gorgeous eyes. I wouldn't fucking lie, my heart was pounding as I pulled her into my arms, inhaling her intoxicating scent of hazelnut chocolate. I held her close, trying to control my own fucking storm of emotions. *Doesn't remember...*

What the fuck did that even mean? How could she fucking forget that Azura was not Scarlett and Elijah's biological daughter? That was not something fucking small.

"Alejandro, is something wrong?" She asked. I knew she'd be able to tell if I was lying...

"Don't worry too much. Let's head to bed. I need to leave early, but I should be back by tomorrow evening," I said quietly.

"You didn't answer the question," she replied, her heart thundering as she pulled away from me.

"Amore Mio, things will be okay. Maybe it's just a side effect of him making you forget whatever the fuck happened when you went to the country house," I replied, trying to figure this shit out.

"I don't want to forget important things," she whispered, her hand on my chest.

"You won't," I replied. Taking hold of her wrist, I kissed her knuckles softly. "You won't."

I could hear the conviction in my voice as I reassured her, but the fear that I might be fucking wrong was beginning to eat up at me inside. The cut along her head came back to me, and I knew something was really fucking wrong…

She nodded, despite her thumping heart still racing.

"Let's get to bed," I said quietly. Cupping her face, I kissed her hard.

Deep down, a niggling thought came to me that what if… what if she forgot me? Just the thought of that happening made me pull her close, crushing her body against mine as I kissed her harder.

An hour later, after a round of hot passionate sex, she had fallen asleep in my arms, yet I couldn't fucking sleep. I was a fucking mess of worry. I needed her to be fucking okay…

Maybe I was fucking overthinking it. Maybe nothing like that was going to happen, and maybe I just needed to chill the fuck out.

I slowly untangled my arms from around the gorgeous bombshell in my arms and got out of bed slowly, pulling on my discarded boxers and sweatpants. Grabbing my lighter and a cigarette packet, I left the room. I needed to talk to Elijah. Even if I fucking smelled of sex, I didn't really care.

Meet me on the back patio, I mind-linked him.

Despite being able to mind-link other Alphas, it still fucking gave me a slight headache. Moments later, Elijah stepped out, and I smirked, not missing the hickeys around his neck that peeped out from his T-shirt. His wet hair fell in his eyes. It seemed like I wasn't the only one who had just had sex. He frowned, and I knew he probably could smell the sex on me.

"What do you want that couldn't wait until you had showered?" He growled. I smirked at him, lighting my cigarette as I cocked my brow.

"What's wrong? Does it fucking still piss you off knowing I just fucked your girl?" I taunted. Despite being in no fucking mood to mock him, I couldn't help it. Sometimes shit just came out. His eyes flashed a cobalt blue, and I rolled my own. "Seriously, are you still doing this shit nine years on? I'm sure I've fucked her more times than I can even cou-"

"What the fuck do you want? Did you call me out here for this?" He growled murderously. I smirked humourlessly.

"Actually, no…" My smirk faded, and I looked at him seriously. "You know about earlier… when she asked about Azura… I asked her, and she…" I ran my hand through my hair, staring up at the cloudy night sky.

"And?" He asked, his anger dissipating, replaced with seriousness.

"She couldn't remember anything more than you and Scarlett being her parents. Indigo… what happened, nothing," I said, the fear settling into the pit of my stomach again. His heartbeat quickened, and he looked pale.

"But Raihana checked her... she wasn't cursed..."

"No, she wasn't... but they did something. She's forgotten some parts of her past. I'm guessing it's when they made her forget whatever happened in there. But I'm just a tad fucking worried that she may begin to forget more..." I swallowed hard, trying not to think of the worst fucking case scenario.

"She won't forget you," he replied quietly, placing a hand on my shoulder before removing it incredibly fast. I smirked before glancing at him.

"I fucking hope not because she's my fucking lifeline," I said quietly. She was. Without her, I would fucking lose my mind...

Our eyes met, and he looked at the sky, shoving his hands into the pockets of his pants.

"I know... but I'm sure she's fine. Get Raihana to check her over tomorrow," he suggested quietly. I nodded. Yeah, I really fucking needed to.

"Don't you often feel like the fucking moon goddess does not want to leave us in peace?" I asked, sitting down on the steps and taking a drag on my cigarette. He sighed heavily.

"Yeah..."

He walked off, and I heard the door open and shut behind him, leaving me alone in the garden. I stared up at the sky, wondering what was to come. Something told me that Kataleya's kidnapping had just been the fucking start of all this shit...

I ran my hand through my hair when I heard the door reopen, and Elijah stepped out again. He sat down, leaving a metre gap between us, and placed down a case of six beers.

"Sometimes a fucking drink helps," he said, taking a can out and opening it with one hand before passing it to me.

"Yeah, guess you're fucking right. The only problem is a hundred of these don't fucking help," I sighed, taking a gulp as he opened another can for himself.

"Yeah, true."

We fell silent again, just sitting there in silence, drinking the beer. The smell of fresh earth and grass mixed with the cool breeze was refreshing. The promise of approaching rain clung in the air. I tossed my cigarette stub onto the ground and took another one out.

"Want one?" I asked, holding out the packet.

"Why the fuck not?" He shrugged, taking one and placing it between his lips. I smirked. That was a fucking first. I took the lighter out, lighting it for him before lighting a second for myself.

"I'm guessing Scarlett would fucking blow if she knew I got you hooked."

"I won't get hooked. Besides, she won't know unless you fucking snitch," he remarked, taking a drag on his cigarette.

"Is she with the girls again?"

"Yeah, and Clara is currently with Dante. I'll be going back, though," he remarked.

"I appreciate you two being here and shit, but with Liam working over-time, you would need to go back." I blew out the smoke, slowly staring out at the swaying short grass.

"We'll go back when we need to. Right now, they have it covered, but if what you're saying about Kiara is true... I don't want to leave yet," he replied quietly.

I didn't reply.

Kiara... fuck, I really hoped she was going to be okay...

We sat there silently, going through three cans of beer each, making small jokes, or in my case, annoying the fuck out of him, but when the first drops of rain began to fall, we decided to head inside.

Sometimes you just needed that moment to sit back with someone who got you.

❧

The following day, I tried not to think about what she had said about Azura. It was maybe just a fucking one-off, and she was going to be completely fucking fine. Elijah said he'd let Scarlett know to keep an eye on her whilst the both of us were out.

The day fucking flew by. Research after research got us fucking nowhere. It was late afternoon, and I really fucking hoped Kenneth, the fucker, had some answers in two days' time - because I had fucking nothing.

"Alpha, high witch Janaina is on the phone," Drake, my other Delta, held the phone out to me. Was it weird that I just realised that both my Deltas names and my Betas started with a fucking D? Maybe that's why they were all dickheads at times. "Alpha?" He snapped my attention out of my thoughts, and I gave him a scathing glare, taking the offered phone from him.

"Yeah?"

"Hello to you, King Alejandro."

"We can skip pleasantries." This woman was fucking antagonising.

"Well, I have checked on our side. There is nothing that we have discovered that linked Endora to the Feugo De Ceniza pack, so you can rest assured that it isn't something she has done. It may be something from the Rossi side, perhaps from your father's past."

I frowned. So for once, that bitch Endora was not fucking behind this. Then again, I couldn't fucking rule her out entirely. She had fucking messed up shit for us more than once.

"How fucking sure can you be?"

"Very sure. I would not have called you if I wasn't. However, if anything happened after she was mated to your father, then I cannot speak for her. I am speaking of what she did before she found him. We looked into her parents' pack and everything else, but there was nothing. Whatever this Alpha wants, it's not because of Endora, I can assure you of that." Her voice was firm and cold, like always.

"Fine. Thanks for looking into it. If you do find anything else, let me know."

"I will. We will continue to look into any way to locate the Djinn, but currently, I don't think we will find a solution. It will be extremely difficult, and I fear that it is something you will have to figure out yourself."

"Yeah. I fucking guess so." I hung up, rubbing my jaw as I frowned. The silence in my room was fucking loud.

My current plan of action was to find the pup and see if the fucker came for him. In that time, question the kid and grill him for any fucking information possible, then find the one behind it, his father, and somehow get everything fucking undone. A sudden thought occurred to me; I looked down at the phone and rang Janaina back.

"Hello."

"One more thing… does killing a Djinn undo his magic?" I asked. Silence ensued, but I didn't miss her small intake of breath.

"King Alejandro… you may be a Lycan… but you are treading an extremely dangerous path of thought. To kill a Djinn means suffering the consequences. There is always a price to pay to kill an immortal."

"You didn't answer my fucking question. Will killing him undo the curse?" She huffed with irritation.

"Yes, because Djinns are immortal. As long as they live, their magic is intact. If they are killed, then, yes, with it all, their magic unravels, too," she replied in a clipped tone. I sat back in my chair, placing my legs on the table and crossing my legs at my ankles.

"Then you know my next question, right? How the fuck do you kill a Djinn?"

Brothers

ALEJANDRO

"How the fuck do you kill one?" I repeated, my voice cold and emotionless yet laced with authority that she dared not defy, even if she wasn't a werewolf.

"I… I do not know." I didn't know if I should fucking believe her or not.

"Then how about you try to find out."

"It could cost you your life," she replied quietly. Something told me she knew more than she was fucking letting on.

"Well, I'll be waiting for the answer… I'm sure you wouldn't care what the fuck happens to me."

"Not at all, but you are also vital for the balance," her clipped voice countered.

"I don't plan to die. Get me the answers I want, or I'll get them myself. This involves your niece, too, remember?" Although she didn't go around stating it, Janaina was Delsanra's paternal aunt.

"She is your family, and I'm sure you will find a solution," she replied dismissively.

"Yeah, I fucking will, with or without you. So just do as I'm fucking asking. All I need is the answer. I'll do the rest."

"Very well," she said reluctantly after a moment of silence. "If anything happens to you, I will not be responsible to answer to your queen."

"It won't come to that." I hung up, my brows furrowed deeply.

Killing the Alpha behind this was not going to be enough. I knew that I needed to kill the Djinn, too. I threaded my hands together, dropping my legs to the ground and leaning forward. How to kill a Djinn…

I wouldn't just rely on Janaina to find that answer. I'd look for my own, too.

❧❦❧

I returned home when night had fallen whilst Elijah instantly pulled Scarlett aside, kissing her like he had fucking been away for years. Well, I was just being a fucking hypocrite because when I found my mate, I planned to kiss her until she begged for air.

She had mind-linked earlier to ask if I'd be back by dinner, and I told her we would. The house was a fucking storm of sound, but one that I didn't really hate. I could hear the girls laughing and shouting in excitement whilst Ahren and Tatum were fighting over a toy. Sienna was toddling along, trying to escape from the room. While Delsanra lay on the sofa with a blanket over her. Raihana was sitting next to her, using her magic to make Sienna do a 180-degree turn. The poor kid looked fucking confused as she kept her balance, blinking those dark grey doe eyes of hers as she realised she was no longer facing the door.

Why the fuck did kids look so fucking deceiving? They were not innocent…

Kiara was trying to soothe the boys, looking fucking smoking hot in that tiny dress of hers. Her sandy brown hair cascaded over her shoulder as she broke up the fight. Tatum ran off with the toy whilst Ahren glared after him angrily. Maria was braiding Skyla's hair; Azura and Kataleya had similar braids in their hair as they ran circles around Maria and Skyla.

"Whose fucking annoying you?" I asked Sienna, picking her up as all eyes turned to me. Kiara stood up, coming over as Sienna looked near tears. Yeah, she was at that stage where she got fucking tearful if I picked her up.

"Uncle, hey." Raihana gave a small wave.

"Hey."

I pulled Kiara close, kissing her lips hard. Fuck, I missed her. I tried not to pay attention to how fucking good her body felt pressed against mine and those tits… let's just say I'll be admiring them later.

"You look fucking divine," I murmured, slowly kissing her neck over her mate mark. Satisfied with the soft sigh that escaped her, I let go of her, and she took Sienna from me just as she burst into tears. "Pups."

Raihana stood up, and I walked over to her, giving her a tight hug. She was a decent height, and with her heels, she was nearly six feet.

"What happened? Did you empty the entire pot of glitter on your face or some shit?" I asked, looking at her bronzed face. She rolled her eyes.

"Oh, Uncle, are you jealous that I look so fine?" She asked. Clearly, she was not bothered about what I had just said.

"Well, I'm afraid if I kiss you, I'm going to have that crap all over me," I mocked, placing a kiss on top of her black locks.

"You always do look more than fine, Princess," her mate, Chris, remarked upon entering the room. Those two were fucking made for each other. If their pup was half as fucking conceited as them, then I felt fucking sorry for his mate…

Well, the moment they began sucking and eating each other's faces off, I walked over to Delsanra. Her eyes were open, but she looked exhausted.

"Hey, King Burrito," she whispered.

"Hey, Spitfire." I crouched down by the sofa, placing a hand around the back of her head before I kissed her forehead. Her pale eyes met mine, and I silently promised that she was going to be fucking okay… "Where's pretty boy?"

"Rayhan? Dante wanted to talk to him." She sounded amused, and I frowned slightly, nodding.

"Guess the cousins are fucking bonding."

She gave a weak nod, and I stood up, going over to Maria, who stood up. She looked a bit better than she did on the video call. I didn't say anything, hugging her tightly. Every time I saw her, I remembered Raf. No matter how much time fucking went by, I couldn't forget him or get over his loss. I had lost many in life, and I just dealt with that shit… but Raf… there was something entirely different about losing him. You didn't get over it, you just learned to deal with it. I let go of her, and she smiled slightly.

"It's good to have you here," I said before turning to the girls. "Nice hair."

"Thank you, Daddy," Kataleya replied. Her eyes bore into mine. I knew she wanted to ask me if I had done anything about finding the pup. Even if I brought him here, I did not plan on allowing her to meet him…

I glanced at Raihana. That was a spell we were going to do later, one I knew Kiara was not going to fucking approve of.

"I'm going to go change," I informed Kiara, leaving the room.

"Don't take long, dinner will be ready soon," she replied as I gave her a quick kiss and a nod.

I had smoked countless fucking cigarettes and needed a fucking shower. I headed upstairs, taking two at a time, and slowed down when I heard the sound of Rayhan and Dante talking...

❦

RAYHAN

We had gotten there a short while ago, and I had gone up to check on Dante. It was weird not seeing him downstairs, annoying the hell out of me as he talked to Delsanra and complimented her on how she looked. I would tolerate all of that happily if they could just both be okay again.

I reached his bedroom and knocked lightly on the open door. One of Uncle's most trusted guards was sitting on the sofa in his room. He stood up and lowered his head to me before he left the room, leaving us alone.

"Ray..." Dante said, frowning slightly as he sat up. His aura filled the room, and I knew that when he did shift, he was going to be truly strong.

"Hey, kiddo," I replied, walking over and ruffling his hair. He raised an eyebrow, pushing my hand away weakly.

"Don't touch the hair," he warned, trying his best to sound like his usual self. He looked like hell, but it was clear he was coping better than Delsanra was.

"Mind if I sit?" I asked, motioning to the edge of the bed.

He shook his head, and I sat down, looking at him. He had some music playing in the background, but it was faint. Apart from that, there didn't seem to be anything that he had to keep himself occupied.

"How's Delsanra?" He asked with a small pout on his lips. I raised an eyebrow.

"I'm surprised you weren't downstairs to greet her, considering you are usually always the first at the door." I smiled slightly. "What's wrong? Not up to it or just don't want to see her anymore?" I asked lightly. He frowned, his eyes flashing with irritation.

"Don't say I don't want to see her, I do... I just..." He glared at me, crossing his arms as he sat up straighter. He stared down at the striped bedding, and I could sense his uncertainty.

"What's up?" I asked, leaning forward and running my fingers through my long hair.

"Do you hate me?" He murmured hesitantly, shocking me as he looked up at me with those ruby-red eyes of his.

"Why would I hate you?" I questioned, confused. I heard Uncle silently come up the stairs, but I knew Dante hadn't sensed his father yet.

"Because what happened to Delsanra was because of me. I'm always a nuisance to you, right?" He asked nonchalantly, despite the fact that I could tell this was weighing on his mind.

Seeing your mate like that… it fucking hurt. It tore me up inside, and I wished that I could take away that pain, that it was me in her place. I'd give anything to see her happy, smiling, and laughing… yet I couldn't do anything but watch her go through this with nothing I could do and feel absolutely useless. It was killing me, but was I going to blame a child? No. He wasn't even conscious when Kiara called us over. If it was anyone else, maybe I would have been pissed that Delsanra had risked herself, but Dante was a kid. He was eight, and no matter how irritating the asshat could be, I loved him.

"Want the truth?" I asked him. He swallowed and nodded with defiance.

"Obviously." *Now that's more like the kid I know.*

"I don't hate you, but I am pissed at you for even thinking that I could hate you. Am I that bad?" I raised an eyebrow, and I almost smiled as I saw the flicker of relief in his eyes.

"Sorry…" He looked down, clenching his fists.

"You and my kitten are going to be okay because you are both fighters," I said quietly. Reaching over, I gave his shoulder a gentle squeeze. "I'm glad you asked me, but seriously, I can't hate you." He nodded, giving me a small, cocky smirk.

"Yeah, and I guess Delsanra can never hate me, either." I raised an eyebrow, this -

"Fucker," Uncle's voice came, and we both turned to see him standing there, arms crossed.

"I was thinking more along the lines of asshat…" I countered with an amused smile.

"Fucker does the job," Uncle remarked coldly. Coming over and taking a seat next to Dante, he placed an arm around his shoulders, "Right, fucker?"

"Yeah. I guess us Rossis suit the name fucker. Right, Dad?" He replied cockily. Like father, like son…

I smiled slightly, remembering my own father. To be the Alpha, son, and mate he'd want me to be… was I making him proud? I could feel Uncle's sharp eyes on me, but I didn't look at him, keeping my mask in place.

"Yeah, we do. Especially you two," Uncle said mockingly. "Or more like you three. Your last brother is an equal dick."

The three sons of three brothers… I just wished we could have a strong bond, something I doubted would ever happen with the hatred that Leo felt towards me.

"Right, I'm off to shower. Think dinner is almost fucking done, too," Uncle said. Standing up, he slapped my back before he left us alone once more. Dante pushed the bedding off and got up. I could tell it took a lot out of him.

"Need help?"

"No, I'm just going to go get ready, too."

I smirked. Okay, Dante was still perfectly able. If he was ready to get all dressed up, then he was definitely doing okay.

"For whom, may I ask?"

"Who do you think?" He replied arrogantly, giving me a cocky, annoying smirk before sauntering off the best he could despite his exhaustion.

I chuckled, lightly shaking my head. They were both definitely going to be alright.

Her Strong Belief

KIARA

*D*INNER HAD BEEN PLEASANT. It felt nice to have a full house, and for fleeting moments, we were able to forget the weight of everything going on around us. I healed Delsanra, and although it did nothing to the curse, it did give her a little energy, another reason I was glad they were here.

I had just tucked the girls into the bed, Raihana was making Tatum and Ahren sleep, and the rest of the adults were downstairs. Mom was making hot drinks for us all whilst I made sure Dante was settled. He never used to want me to put him to bed, but he didn't argue over it since the turn of events. I ran my hand through Dante's hair, kissing his forehead gently as I poured my healing into him, but it did nothing for him. I sighed heavily, looking at my sleeping baby boy and fought back my tears. *You are going to get better.*

I wished there was more that I could do for him. For Delsanra…

My phone beeped. I picked it up from the bedside drawer and smiled, seeing it was a message from Raven. I unlocked my phone and clicked on it.

'Call me if you have a moment,' it read, followed by a purple and black heart emoji. I hit the call button, and she answered almost instantly.

"Hey, Kia, how are you?"

"Hey, hun. I'm okay. Just getting by, I guess. How are the kiddies?"

"They are all fine, I just got them to bed and thought I'd call. How are you and the family today?" I smiled. Having five toddlers to handle was no small feat.

"We are all doing okay. We have some answers. I'm not sure if Liam's told you, but Kat had a name and a pack name, so we are getting somewhere."

"I'm glad. No, Liam didn't mention that. He should be coming back tomorrow. I'm thinking of you. You know, if there's anything you need me to do, I'm here, or if you just need to vent." I knew she was; Liam was still at the burnt-down country home, trying to scavenge for any hint or anything that could help.

"You two are already doing so much, I mean, you have the kids and the pack, Mom and Dad have been here, and Liam's not home."

"I can handle the kids with ease! Besides, I do have help, but they miss Zuzu. She's the ringleader, and without her, I think they feel it. I'm just hoping things are sorted soon." Her tone was softer towards the end, her worry and concern for us clear in her voice.

"I'm sure it will be," I replied. "Thank you, Raven, for everything."

"Nothing to thank me for. That's what I'm here for."

We ended the call shortly after, and I smiled down at the phone. She was such a good friend. Goddess, I'm grateful that she came into my life. I tilted my head; I couldn't remember how we became friends… did we become friends after she was mated to my brother? Or did I know her from before? I brushed my hair back, frowning, and pondered over it for a moment.

I shook my head and stood up, being extremely careful not to disturb Dante, and silently left the room, heading back downstairs. The sound of my heels echoed in the silence. My mind wandered to what Alejandro was planning on doing. I didn't agree with it, but I also knew he was not going to listen.

I turned the corner when suddenly someone grabbed my elbow, spinning me around and straight into their strong arms. I smiled as the intense sparks coursed through me, his intoxicating scent hitting me hard. I closed my eyes for a moment, enjoying it as I wrapped my arms around his neck. I looked up at him slowly, my heart thumping. His body moulded against mine oh so perfectly.

"Can I help you, my love?" I asked, kissing his neck.

We had been fine during dinner and everything, but that disagreement between us still remained, and I just felt recently we were having far too many of them. He didn't reply for a moment, his cold eyes staring down at me.

"Do I need a reason to hold you?" I bit my lip as his hand travelled down my back.

"Not at all," I replied, feeling giddy.

"Good."

And then his lips were on mine, one hand tangling in my hair as he yanked my head back and kissed me roughly. We broke apart after a few moments, the intensity of the kiss leaving me lightheaded.

"You know, if you two are done, the drinks are getting cold!" Raihana's voice came from the living room. I heard a light chuckle, and I blushed, realising the door was open.

"Babe, you can just keep the drinks hot," Chris's drawl came. "That's not hard for a smoking hot bombshell."

I pulled away, and Alejandro wrapped his arm around my waist as we both entered the living room. Rayhan was seated in the corner with Delsanra in his lap, a blanket over her shoulders as he cradled her body, running his fingers through her hair. Maria was next to them, carrying little Sienna, who was the only one awake from the kids, with Mom on the other end of the sofa, her leg draped over Dad's.

Chris and Raihana were on the other sofa, their arms around one another. Alejandro took a seat in the armchair, and I picked up the remaining two mugs, which were steaming hot - something I knew was courtesy of Raihana and her magic. I walked over to Alejandro, and he pulled me slowly into his lap before taking his mug. With the kids all in bed, it was a lot quieter. Even Sienna was falling asleep in her grandmother's arms.

I took a sip of my hot chocolate while resting my head on Alejandro's shoulder as Mom and Maria made small talk. When silence fell, Chris spoke up.

"So, when are you planning on doing that spell?" He asked, his eyes fixed on Raihana. She looked at Alejandro, and I looked up at him, hoping he'd reconsider.

"Soon. Let me just finish this drink," Alejandro replied, glancing at me for a split moment. I sat up straight, looking at Mom and Dad. Everyone in the room knew the plan.

"Do you guys actually agree with this?" I asked, keeping my gaze on Dad.

"He isn't planning to torture the child," Dad said quietly. I pursed my lips.

"But it's a child."

"Who is in a bad position. This may be better for him, Kiara," Mom reasoned quietly. Okay, even she was okay with it… I looked at my nude acrylic nails and then up at Raihana and Maria.

"Am I the only one who isn't okay with this?"

"Is it a feeling you have, or you just generally don't think it's right?" Rayhan asked, raising an eyebrow.

"I generally don't think this is right," I murmured, gripping my mug tightly. Delsanra looked at me, too, and I realised that we needed answers. She and Dante couldn't carry on like this, but I wished it wasn't the way to go about it.

"Sometimes a decision isn't easy, but we have to get it done," Maria sighed softly. "Where do you plan to keep the child?"

"In a room, safe," Alejandro's reply was curt and cold.

"You mean as a prisoner. If he's a little older than Dante, say nine or ten, even then, that means he'll remember this," I debated. "Look, I didn't want to bring this up, but sometimes we think we do the right thing, but it can have lasting consequences… we've seen it happen before." I glanced at Rayhan, who frowned, looking down.

"But I wouldn't have done anything any differently, even if I could go back," he replied, his eyes flashing green. Delsanra placed a hand on his cheek, soothing him. I didn't say anything else; I was outnumbered on this one…

The urge to tell them to carry on and that I would not be a part of this was on the tip of my lips, but if they were going to bring a child here, then I wanted to reassure him that he was going to be okay. That we were not going to hurt him. I remained silent after that. Getting up from Alejandro's lap, I placed my mug down, but I didn't return to his side. I was trying to control the emotions that were whirling around inside of me.

Amore Mio. I glanced at him, trying to mask my emotions as I picked up the tray of empty mugs.

I'm just going to put these in the kitchen.

I turned away feeling upset. I heard Raihana follow me out, but she didn't speak until we entered the kitchen.

"Kiara, I'm sorry," she said, coming over as I placed the mugs in the sink and began washing them.

"You don't think there's anything wrong with it, so why are you apologising?" I questioned quietly.

"Because I know I'm upsetting you by doing this, but we aren't going to hurt the boy. He may be better in our care."

"There's a difference between being in our care and using him as bait, but I know we won't agree, so let's forget it. When are you doing the spell?" I asked, my irritation seeping into my voice. She crossed her arms and shook her head.

"I don't get why you are making this sentimental, Kiara."

"As a mother, I don't think it's right."

"This involves our loved ones. It's not so easy to make these decisions."

"Can we just end the conversation?" I replied, my eyes flashing. Raihana frowned.

"Fine, we won't discuss it then. I really don't think you should be there when the spell happens if you are just going to get hurt over it. This is war; that monster has resigned Delsanra to the state she is currently in, and she's in pain, as well as Dante. I think getting back at him is perfectly fine," she replied, her own eyes blazing.

"Exactly. That monster is responsible, not his son. Not a child who helped Kataleya! Even if he didn't help her, we shouldn't be targeting him," I shot back.

"Girls. Calm down," Maria's voice ordered. We both turned to see our mothers standing there. Raihana was only two years younger than I was, and I didn't think we'd ever argued before.

"Kiara, I think it's better if you head to bed," Mom said quietly. I clenched my jaw, feeling my aura surge around me as I tried to control my emotions.

"No, I'm coming along because this is a child who clearly has no one on his side," I growled, and I didn't wait for an answer, brushing past both older women and knocking straight into Chris in the hall. He didn't say anything as he steadied me by the elbows, a frown of concern on his face. I walked back to the lounge and crossed my arms, looking at Alejandro, my eyes icy. "Let's get to this spell. Where do you plan to do it?" Alejandro stood up, frowning.

"At headquarters. I'd appreciate it if you stayed here."

"I'm going to be there," I replied firmly, my eyes flashing.

"You fucking ain't. Elijah, make sure she stays here." His aura rolled off him in waves and I could feel the command in it.

Alejandro strode over to me, his power and dominance rolling off him in waves. He reached for my face, but I stepped out of his hold. I shook my head, not masking my utter disappointment. I could never get my head around using a child for any purpose. I… it was wrong.

"I hope you're happy," I whispered before I turned. I was about to leave the room, only for Alejandro to grab my arm and yank me into his arms. Sparks rushed through me, and my chest squeezed painfully.

Let go of me, I commanded through the link, not wanting to cause a scene with Dad right there. He frowned but did as I said. I knew he could see the fire in my eyes.

I hope that in time you fucking see that I did the right thing, he replied.

I didn't answer, running upstairs and walking down the hall. I entered the girl's bedroom, messaging Mom that I'd sleep there tonight. I did not want to see him. My phone beeped, and I looked down at Dad's message.

'Kiara, can we talk?'

'No, I'm going to bed,' I texted back, tossing my phone onto the small sofa in the girl's room and running my fingers through my hair.

I walked to the window and stared out into the night sky. I saw Alejandro, Raihana, Chris, and Mom head out and clenched my jaw, feeling helpless.

This was wrong. This child was going to feel as if he was a prisoner. He was a child, not a monster.

I closed my eyes, leaning against the wall, turning away from the window.

Goddess, protect all our children…

The Enemy's Heir

ALEJANDRO

I HATED HURTING HER, BUT she was stubborn. I would listen to her, too… but I needed to do what was best for my family and me. If that meant taking this pup, then so be it. Scarlett wasn't meant to come, but I knew she came to fucking make sure the child was okay, probably to reassure her daughter.

The silence was deafening. Raihana was frowning, and I knew her disagreement with Kiara in the kitchen was playing on her mind. As much as I loved others to get at each other's fucking throats, when it came to two women I loved, it wasn't as fucking fun.

"Kiara is right in one aspect of what she said," Scarlett stated, falling in step with me. I didn't bother looking at her. I got her point, but I needed to do this shit.

"Yeah? Well, if you don't want to be here, don't," I replied coldly.

"I didn't say that. Don't twist my words," she growled, her eyes flashing silver. *Fucking Alpha female…*

"I'm not, I'm just not in the fucking mood to hear shit when I know I have to make some fucking decisions that aren't fucking easy," I shot back, my voice harsh and cold, but I didn't really care. I hated it when Kiara was angry at me.

"I get that. Just remember, he *is* a child," she replied quietly.

We didn't speak again until we entered the pack headquarters and went up to my office.

"Babe, can you clear the floor?" Raihana asked Chris, who gave her a nod and moved the chairs back whilst I pushed my table aside. "I'll set some barriers just in case they try to locate him when we pull him through. I don't know how strong they will be, but I'll try."

"Is doing this on pack territory wise?" Chris asked, glancing out the window.

"It's safest since the grounds have been spelled, too," I replied as Raihana opened the bag Chris had been holding that contained her supplies.

She began to draw symbols on the ground with one of her jars of ash. I never got this mojo shit, or how the fuck it worked, but it sure was fucking useful to have at hand. Scarlett stood there, arms crossed, a frown on her face as she watched her intently.

"Aunty Red, if you keep staring, I can't focus…" Raihana remarked.

"Don't mind me," Scarlett replied with a small smirk, but she did turn her back on Raihana and instead turned her attention to me. "Where are you keeping him?"

"I'm not fucking answering to you," I replied, leaning against my desk and taking out a cigarette.

"Uncle, no smoking. I don't need anything messing with the spell," Raihana warned, and I fucking pocketed it. Today was not my fucking day…

Kiara? I called through the link, but she had put her block up.

I frowned deeply, taking my phone out of my pocket instead. The urge to message her was strong, but… I needed to do it in person. I shoved it back into my pocket just as Chris spoke.

"If this kid is raised to be anything like his father, he may not give us the answers we need. Then what's the plan?" He asked.

"Then I'll have to probe his mind," Raihana replied, taking the cloth I had taken from Kataleya before she went to bed.

"I'm not risking you doing that. If the Djinn had anything in place, I don't want you hurt," he remarked, but despite his level tone, his cocky smirk that was always on his face was gone.

"I'll be fin-"

"No. I'm fine with you doing this stuff, but I do not want you risking yourself. We can all see the state Del's in," Chris replied firmly.

"You're right. We won't risk shit like that… especially since he seems to be fucking careful," I added.

Raihana nodded in defeat as she lit the candles and stood up, fanning her face for a moment before she took a deep breath.

"Okay, I'm doing this… if anything feels odd, just break the circle."

Chris walked over to her, pulling her close and kissing her lips. She locked her arms around his neck and kissed him back. They exchanged something through the link, and she nodded slightly, smiling whilst he held her chin for a moment before moving back. Scarlett stepped forward, and I saw her pointed stiletto an inch from the edge of the circle, ready to break it if needed.

Raihana's powers surged around us, her eyes burning bright. Her thick, dark hair defied gravity as it floated around her as she started chanting the spell. I could feel the intensity of the spell as she whispered his name. A portal would open, and then I was going to reach in and pull the pup through. I was guessing there would be guards around him. We couldn't leave a note in case it was used in a similar manner to get back to us, so if a guard was there, I was ready to pass a fucking message if need be.

Soon a shimmery transparent wall appeared, and I readied for the moment. Chris had his eyes on Raihana, his eyes shimmering the pale gold of his wolf, ready to protect her if the need arose. My gaze snapped to the room that appeared just on the other side of that translucent veil. My frown deepened as I took in the dark room. Thick velvet curtains covered the windows, but save from that, the room was almost empty with only a rectangular wooden box in the centre of the room, which had a boy lying on top of it, without a blanket or pillow…

Was this really his son? It didn't seem like the room for the son of an Alpha. Did Kataleya get it wrong?

Raihana and Scarlett exchanged looks, and I stepped forward, knowing I had to be fast. I jumped in, but before I even reached the boy, his eyes flew open. He was about to jump up, but I was faster. Putting a hand over his mouth and lifting him up, I was back through the veil.

Raihana whispered something, and the portal slammed shut. She broke the circle at the same time as Chris and Scarlett did. Everyone knew how fucking risky that had been. Raihana stumbled, and Chris caught her, scooping her up bridal style and carrying her to the two-seater near the window. We didn't know how far out they had been located or how much it would take out of her, and by the fucking looks of it, it had taken a lot.

All eyes turned to the pup in my arms, and I knew he was indeed an Alpha pup. He looked older than he probably was. Maybe he was about ten or eleven. His dark hair fell across his forehead, but the hatred in those hazel eyes of his looked far too intense for a pup.

"Calm down, and I will let you go," I spoke quietly, yet my alpha aura rolled off me.

His eyes burned with anger, and he didn't obey. It was then that I realised he only had one hand that was clawing at my arm. His other arm, which had been covered by the sleeve of his long black shirt, peeped out, and it looked like something had recently happened to it. All I could see was that it looked like his hand had been sliced off.

I released his mouth, feeling a sliver of guilt go through me when I saw the bruises that covered his neck and jaw.

"So, the Lycan decided to kidnap me. You made a mistake. There is nothing you do that can make padre bend to your will," he spat coldly, his eyes glaring into mine. His voice was cold and accented. It confirmed we had the correct pack. I was sure this kid was from Puerto Rico.

He held my gaze. I was doing my best to fucking control my alpha aura, but even then, he was forced to look away after a moment.

"Enrique, isn't it?" Scarlett asked, placing a hand on my arm she tried to move me away.

We exchanged glares before I stepped back and crossed my arms, taking the time to scrutinise the boy before me. His hair was slightly wavy with a square jaw, high cheekbones, and a strong, straight nose. He had a few small, faded scars across his jaw and one on his lip that never healed properly. Another two were along his forehead and across his left eyebrow, leaving a small gap where the hair would never regrow. His arched brows were furrowed together. The only soft thing on the boy's face was perhaps his eyes; deep hazel green rimmed with dark black and those flecks of yellow with thick lashes, but even then, there was still a hardness in them.

"We aren't going to hurt you," Scarlett continued, placing her hands on her thighs as she bent over to look him in the eye as he looked down. I didn't think she fucking realised he was her damn height... *Midget*. I smirked at that. The boy simply turned away from her.

"Okay, look, pup, it's your choice. We do it the easy way or the hard way," I said coldly.

"You should speak before he follows up on that," Chris added quietly as he crouched next to Raihana, who had her head on his shoulder, clearly drained.

"Do your worst," came his fearless reply. Scarlett frowned at me, standing straight.

"We do apologise for -"

"Nothing. Your father took my daughter and hurt her. He attacked my mate and has a grudge against me. When I have tried to reach out to him to deal with this man-to-man, he's refused, so I had to stoop to his level. Or almost, because unlike him, I'm not a fucking loser. Clearly, he beats you too -"

"Padre punishes me when I disobey him. Do not try to manipulate his teachings into anything more." His face was emotionless as he stared ahead. His voice was cold and empty. I frowned; didn't he realise he was already manipulated? I shook my head at his words.

"So, the more recent bruises on you... are these the results of disobeying him by freeing Kataleya?" I asked quietly, my Alpha command rolling off me. "Answer me." I saw the dimples in his cheeks twitch as he tried not to answer, gritting his teeth, but his head bowed in submission within seconds.

"Yes."

Raihana's breath hitched, clearly shocked. Scarlett ran her hand through her hair, and Chris was frowning in concern. I wasn't going to deny that I fucking wanted to beat the shit out of this pup's father. I placed my hand on his shoulder and crouched down before him.

"Thank you," I said quietly, surprising even myself. "For giving her food and for helping her." His face didn't change but I saw the haunted look in his eyes as he glanced down at his right arm.

"It wasn't worth it," he replied blankly.

I swallowed hard, staring at his arm. A sickening thought came to me, but I pushed it away. No, that wasn't possible...

"It's late. You can go to bed for now. We will talk in the morning," I stated before mind-linking two of my men to come and take him to the room that was set up for him.

It was down near the cells, but it would be in one of the lesser interrogation rooms. I had asked them to put a more comfortable bed in there, some books, and a laptop with no internet, but giving him access to some movies, as well as a mini-fridge with snacks. I knew I was still holding him fucking hostage, but I couldn't trust him.

He didn't reply, simply turning his back on me. There was a knock on the door, and I told my men to enter, thinking I needed to get Kiara to take a look at his injuries tomorrow...

A Reunion

ALEJANDRO

"ALEJANDRO," SCARLETT SAID AS we entered the mansion. I paused, glancing over my shoulder at her as she shut the front door. "Kiara is with the girls today." The sting in my chest was like a fucking punch, but I kept my face passive and nodded. She didn't want to see me…

"Then you and Elijah should take a guest room for the night. I'll stay with Dante." Concern and something else that I couldn't make out, crossed her face, but she was good at masking her emotions and I couldn't really read her. She nodded.

"Goodnight."

"Night," I replied as she walked past me and up the stairs. I looked at the time on my watch; it was late…

Kiara? I called through the link, but I reached a wall. Again.

I walked down the hall and down the stairs to the wine cellar, then took a bottle. *I guess this is going to be my company tonight…* I grabbed a glass and some ice from the kitchen before I headed upstairs to Dante's room just as Elijah and Scarlett stepped out of his room.

"… a hand, I think it's been removed recently," Scarlett was saying.

Elijah was frowning deeply, giving me a nod before I entered my bedroom and grabbed my laptop. Kiara's scent lingered, and I found momentary calmness before I left the room, going to Dante's. Settling down on the couch, I poured myself a glass and began to do some research instead. With Kiara fucking pissed at me, I wouldn't be able to sleep. I glanced at the sleeping boy before I got to work…

"Daddy! Daddy!"

I woke with a start, realising I had fallen asleep on the couch. My laptop sat on my legs, and I could feel the kink in my neck. Dante sat up slowly as Kataleya rushed into the room, her eyes wide and her heart beating erratically.

"What is it, princess?" I asked, catching her and placing the laptop aside with one hand.

"Raihana said Enrique is here!" The happiness in her voice was fucking making it hard for me to tell her that I didn't want her seeing him…

"He is… but Kat listen, you can't see him."

"Why not? Daddy, he'll be scared," she worried, her lips trembling. That pup was definitely not scared… or he was just good at masking his emotions.

"Look… he's in a room, just in case, for safety measures. His father isn't a good man, and we can't trust him…" Her happiness faded as she let my words sink in, and she quickly got off my lap.

"But, Daddy, Enrique is a nice boy. May I see him?"

I sighed inwardly. She was not going to drop it. I just didn't want her seeing him there…

"Yeah, we'll go after breakfast. I wanted your Mom to go see him, too. He has a few bruises," I replied, ruffling her hair. Her smile returned and she rushed from the room, calling for Kiara. I turned to Dante, who was sitting there, arms crossed, a frown on his face.

"You okay?"

"She need not get too attached," he remarked coldly before turning his back and pulling the blanket back over him. I ran my hand through my hair. *I fucking do not get kids.*

A while later, I had just gotten dressed in a black shirt and pants with a leather belt. Kiara had expertly been able to avoid me, first showering and then getting the girls ready, but when I stepped out, fully dressed, she was finishing off doing her hair.

She was wearing a pale pink halter top that left her entire back on view paired with fitted black jeans. Her hair was pulled up into a bun on top of her head, and a few strands framed her face. She slid a final pin into her hair and picked up her mascara. Usually, she would put on a lot more make-up and jewellery, but since everything had happened, she had stopped. I knew she was just trying to appear normal for the kids when she was worried.

I leaned against the door as she stood up, hearing her heart skip a beat as I walked over to her. I wrapped my arms around her from behind and buried my head into her neck, inhaling her intoxicating scent, relishing in the sparks of our touch. Fuck...

She relaxed into my arms. I knew she couldn't resist me, even if she was fucking upset with me.

"Did Kataleya tell you about going to see the kid after breakfast?" I asked quietly.

"She did. She went to ask Claire to prepare a meal for him, too. She said she'll eat with him," she replied, her voice soft, yet I could sense her disappointment in it. Because of me...

"Yeah? And what about you? Still not going to look me in the eye?" I asked, looking down at her as she stared ahead.

She turned her head and looked at me. For the first time, I realised her eyes looked tired and maybe a tad fucking red. I hated her upset. I bent down and pressed my lips to her plush ones, kissing her slowly and snaking one hand around her throat as I deepened the kiss. She kissed me back, our bodies reacting to one another, the pleasure coursing through us both as her ass brushed against my crotch.

I pulled away, my eyes flashing red as I did my best not to let my emotions loose. There was something about Kiara that messed with my head. I could be angry with her, but I still needed her, like a fucking drug to survive. She was my lifeline, and as much as she fucked with my sanity, at the same time, she was what kept me fucking grounded and rational.

"You could burn down the world, and I'd still love you," she whispered like a promise in the stars, tilting her chin up as she stared into my eyes. The single light in my dark ones...

"But you won't stand by my side and support me," I replied quietly. If she didn't approve... she wasn't going to be there... just last night when she had shut me out. A flash of hurt filled her eyes before she looked away.

"I'm sorry, but there are things I don't approve of," she whispered.

"When you see him, I'm sure you'll believe it was better for him. He's missing a hand, and I don't think he was born that way. Besides, he refuses to speak." She frowned, her heart skipping a beat.

"I will take a look at him. Maybe he'll talk to me," she replied, concerned.

"Yeah, probably," I replied. She was the fucking light to my darkness and the one who had a better heart.

"Don't do that."

"What?"

"You're thinking negatively about yourself again."

Our eyes met, and the urge to fucking kiss her all over again was threatening to break through, but at the same time, I was trying to fucking keep myself in control so we could talk.

"Hard not to when I'm obviously not making the 'good' fucking choice," I replied coldly, knowing that came out harsher than it should have. I let go of her and turned away. I hated arguing with her, I hated when we didn't agree. Her silence was painful, but she didn't reply. "Let's head down to breakfast."

There it was again. Another conversation that fucking ended in disagreement. We left our room, side by side, yet the conflict between us was fucking suffocating. The smell of several dishes being cooked promised a big breakfast full of variety, but I didn't have a fucking appetite.

⁓ ⁓ ⁓

Breakfast was over. Kiara, Kataleya, and I were heading to headquarters. Kataleya was holding the basket with the food in it. She had refused to have breakfast, saying she was going to eat with Enrique. I wasn't happy with that, but Kiara had said she could. Her excitement was palpable; she was two steps ahead of us, her feet barely hitting the ground as she tried to contain her happiness as she reached the doors of the building first. My men opened them when I gave them a small nod and we all stepped inside.

It wasn't the first time Kataleya had been here, but she hadn't seen the cells. Luckily, the room I was keeping the pup in was more of a questioning room that had been transformed into a bedroom for him, and it wasn't too far down. We walked through the corridors, stopping at a metal door. Kataleya frowned.

"Daddy, why is he here?" She asked. Kiara crossed her arms and looked at me questioningly, too.

"To keep him safe," I responded curtly, unlocking the door.

We stepped into the darker corridor, and I went to the door where two guards stood outside.

"How is he?"

"He didn't sleep, nor did he touch anything. He's been standing all night," one of the men, Arnold, said emotionlessly. The second one, Milo, shook his head sympathetically.

"I tried to talk to him, but he ignored me."

"Open the door," Kiara commanded coldly, her eyes flashing. The mother in her was not going to let this slide. The men obliged, and Kiara was the first to enter, with Kataleya hurrying behind her.

I looked at the boy who was standing, arms crossed in the middle of the room, a frown on his face as his cold eyes met mine.

"Enrique!" Kataleya exclaimed, rushing passed Kiara and over to the boy. He looked at her indifferently, and if I didn't know better, one would fucking think he didn't even know her. "Look, Enrique, I brought breakfast. You gave me food, so I give you food now," she said, placing the basket on the bed that had not been slept in or even touched.

"I don't need it. Leave," he spat coldly, making my eyes flash.

No one talks to my daughter like that. I stepped forward, but Kiara blocked my way, stepping in front of me as she gently placed her hands on Kataleya's shoulders. I didn't miss the flash of surprise in the child's eyes at Kiara's move when she blocked me.

"Enrique, it's nice to meet you. Kataleya has spoken a lot about you," she said, her voice soft and soothing.

"The chica has some misconception; I don't want to talk to her," he stated, looking directly at Kiara. Kataleya's heart was beating faster than it fucking should have, and this kid was fucking pissing me off.

"Enrique…" she whispered before gasping and jumping toward him. "What happened to your hand?" He stepped back harshly, glaring at her.

"It's not your business," he spat.

"Did your papa do that?" She asked, horrified. I glanced up sharply, hearing the skip of his heartbeat.

"It's none of your business."

He turned his back on us and Kiara looked at me, her gorgeous face pale, and she let go of Kataleya. Reaching for the boy, she placed her hand on his shoulder. He was about to push her away, but she knocked his hand aside, keeping her grip firm on his arm as her aura grew around her. He struggled violently as she tried to heal him.

"Calm down. Please let me heal you," Kiara said softly yet firmly.

He was doing well trying to get free, but she was far stronger. Soon, he stopped struggling as Kataleya stood a few feet away, watching with her eyes wide with concern and fear.

"What the... let go of me!" He hissed.

"All done," Kiara replied, letting go of him and moving back.

He had many broken bones, Alejandro.

Well, just imagine if he was left there, I added, raising an eyebrow at her. She frowned slightly but I had a feeling she was glad he was removed from that fucked up situation.

"Enrique, we aren't here to hurt you. Kataleya was worried about -"

"So, this is her fault?" He turned his gaze on her, and I strode over, picked her up, and gave him a warning glare. "I did not ask for help, nor did I need it!"

"Your father hurt her enough. I will not tolerate you speaking to her like that," I growled, holding Kataleya close.

"Don't, Daddy... he took care of me," she whispered, cupping my face.

Yeah, well, he's a little fucker.

"It wasn't worth it. I should have left you in that basement," he replied coldly, his eyes haunted with anguish. His gaze fell to his right arm once again and I saw him clench his left fist.

Kiara, take Kat, I said through the link, hoping she just listened. But her eyes were on the boy.

Al... you take Kat. I'll question him. I will be able to find out if he's lying or telling the truth. She had a point, and so I looked down at my little angel.

"Come on, Kataleya. He's just a little upset. Let's go outside?"

She nodded, her lips quivering as she stared at the pup, but being the ass he was, he didn't even look at her. I glanced at his hand, feeling my stomach fucking twist. Something told me my assumption might be fucking correct. If this pup lost his hand because he helped Kat... then I was fucking indebted to him for life...

I turned around and walked out, leaving Kiara with the pup.

One Who is Innocent

KIARA

I LOOKED AT THE YOUNG boy, feeling his pain despite the mask of indifference he wore.

"Enrique, please take a seat and have some food. Can we talk?"

"It's odd that the Lycan is allowing you to interrogate your prisoner."

"You aren't our prisoner," I refuted, smiling warmly and raising my hand in surrender. "But I also know that we brought you here by kidnapping you." I frowned in disapproval at this, and he raised an eyebrow.

"You are the Queen Luna," he stated after a moment, observing me. "The chica looks like you." I smiled and nodded.

"Yes, she does," I replied, taking a seat on the bed and opening the basket that Kataleya had so excitedly brought along. "Do you feel better?"

"You healed me," he stated, sounding almost bitter.

"You were in a lot of pain, Enrique. How did you get hurt?" I asked, unwrapping the turkey sandwich and the pastries. The smell wafted into the air, and I hoped he would soon be tempted, or I at least wished he would be.

"I didn't get hurt." He meant that. I could sense that.

"Did your father do that?" I rephrased. He stayed silent. I looked into his hazel eyes.

"This is the price of disobedience," he replied quietly, turning away from me. He believed what he said, too...

My heart squeezed as I gazed at his back, noticing the scars on his neck. This boy had been through more than anyone of his age.

"Enrique, do you wish to return to your father, or would you like to start a new life somewhere safe?" I asked gently. He turned back to me sharply, his brow furrowed.

"I am the future Alpha of the pack! I will return home. My padre is only doing the best for me. He only teaches me… how to be the best of Alphas…"

He looked down at his hand, and he blinked furiously. I stood up, not caring about the consequences and pulled the child into my arms, hugging him tightly as I tried to control my own emotions. He lost his hand for disobeying his father… for Kataleya. I knew that even if he didn't say it out loud.

"You will be the best Alpha. Not because of your father, but because you are a good person," I whispered as he struggled to push me away, but at the same time, it was clear he didn't want to attack me. His heart was racing, and I could sense his sadness.

"I don't think so… I won't even be able to run in wolf form," he whispered bitterly, yanking free from my hold. I looked at him with sadness and gave him a gentle smile.

"You know, when I was two years old, we were attacked by a rogue attack and my ankle was crushed. For years I had a limp, and I was in constant pain, but I learned to fight in wolf form and in human form. I used a staff for support, too," I confessed. Looking at the food and picking up a sandwich, I offered it to him. He shook his head, refusing the food, yet his eyes were on me, clearly listening to the story.

"Where there is a will, there is always a way," I continued softly. I was sure there was something else I was lacking… but I couldn't remember. It was just there niggling at the back of my mind. I brushed it away as the boy shook his head.

"Then how are you cured? You have no limp now."

"No… I think…" How was it cured? The blanks in my memories were worrying me.

"It doesn't matter. Hand or not… I will do my best." His words were full of sadness even though he was trying to mask his emotions.

"You know… you could stay here until you are of age to lead your pack. We can take care of you," I offered, gently taking hold of his right wrist and tugging him towards the bed. I knew it wasn't that easy, but I was ready to legally fight the council or whoever I needed to if he so wanted it.

"No thanks, but I am in your hold until you free me," he refused coldly. I placed the sandwich in his hand.

"I am sorry, but Alejandro means well. I'm just sorry you were brought into it." He stayed silent, refusing to eat, and I knew I had to give up before he got angry. "Kataleya was worried for you; she was concerned about your safety, too."

"She cost me more than she is worth. I don't want to see her as long as I'm here," he hissed resentfully.

I nodded, feeling a pang of hurt. I understood Kataleya's concern... but at the same time, I understood the little boy before me. He had lost his hand because he protected her.

"I will explain that to her," I promised, standing up. It hurt knowing how much he had gone through and how his act of goodness had cost him so much... I wished there was a way I could help him, but even I couldn't regenerate limbs. "Please, eat and watch some movies to pass the time. If you need anything, let the guards know. I will have some clothes sent to you later. Is there anything else you would like? Games? A Play Station? Books?"

"Nothing." His reply was icy and flat. I nodded and gestured to the food.

"Try to eat, and if you need to go to the bathroom or would like to shower, you can ask the guards," I told him before taking my leave. The moment the door shut behind me, I looked at one of the men.

"Milo, please keep an eye on him."

"I will. Don't worry, Luna."

I nodded and walked down the hall, following Alejandro's scent until I found him in the main hall, where Kevin was playing with Kataleya, trying to cheer her up. Alejandro looked up when I approached.

"How did it go?" I shook my head.

"He's hurting, but he'll be okay," I replied, looking over at Kataleya, who was listening. It stung seeing her sadness. She had been so excited to see him...

He lost his hand because he helped her, I whispered through the link. He frowned. I sensed his anger and sadness through the link before he blocked his emotions off.

That fucker hurt his own pup. He's a fucking sicko.

He is... but, Alejandro, we cannot keep him locked up. Let's bring him home.

I can't risk that.

We can always have someone around him, but I don't think this is good for him.

"Let's head home," Alejandro spoke out loud, his voice cold, looking at Kevin and Kataleya.

I knew the conversation was over. Again.

The next day dawned cold and cloudy, and although Alejandro and I were speaking, he refused to budge from his decision on Enrique.

It took a lot of time to reassure Kataleya that he was just a little upset and that he'd get better. I knew he was just a child who tried to do the right thing, yet when he did, he was punished for it in such a way there was no recovering what he had lost.

I really wanted to bring him home, but Alejandro was not agreeing, so I had gone to visit twice yesterday. I wanted to help, and I intended to. I wished there was a way to restore his hands, but I couldn't recreate limbs. I planned on going to visit him again. This time, I'd take Azura; maybe she would have a better way of getting him to talk.

Although Alejandro wanted to question him, I was adamant about giving him at least a day or two.

Today Alpha Kenneth Arden of the Shadow Wolves Pack was arriving, and perhaps he'd have some answers for us rather than us having to interrogate Enrique.

After breakfast and spending a little time with the rest, I told Azura to come with me. Mom and Dad would be leaving before Alpha Kenneth even got here. Apparently, he and Dad did not see eye-to-eye. They had attended Alpha training together, and something had happened. Whatever it was, Dad refused to talk about it, but he also didn't want to be here to see him, saying he would break his fucking teeth. I was surprised to learn it was Dad's hatred towards him that was the reason Kenneth was not on the council despite being one of the strongest Alphas in the country.

"We'll be back soon," I promised Mom before Azura and I left the mansion.

"So, this is the boy that helped Kataleya?"

"Yes, and I think you might be able to get him to talk," I replied.

"Dante could have." She crossed her arms, looking thoughtful.

"He isn't really well enough, and he gets quite angry when I talk about Enrique…" I frowned. I needed to ask him about that. Nothing ever had no reason when it came to Dante.

"Hmm, that's true. Besides, I'm older than him, I'm probably much more useful." She did a cartwheel before spinning around and slipping her hands into the back pockets of her denim jeans. "What exactly do you want me to do?"

"Just talk to him. He's not very open. I brought these chocolates and snacks, perhaps you can offer them to him?" I suggested, passing her the bag. Her eyebrow shot up, and she looked at me sceptically.

"You actually want me to give a boy chocolates? I don't think so."

"Zuzu!" I pouted.

"Kia! I steal chocolates from boys, I do not give them," she pouted back, and I sighed.

"Fine. I'll give the chocolate…"

She nodded as if this was the right choice as we entered the building. I hid a smile as Azura stared every guard in the eye and gave a curt nod. My little Alpha princess. We reached the room, and I glanced over at the two guards.

"How was he during the night?"

"He ate a little. Once again, he refused to use the bed and slept on the floor. He only called when he wanted to go to the bathroom, and he took a shower." I frowned; he was being treated like a prisoner. A sudden idea came to me as the door opened, and I smiled faintly. Perfect.

"Good morning, Enrique," I greeted as Azura tilted her head, looking the taller boy over as he stood there, arms crossed. He frowned coldly at her, and she smirked.

"Don't frown at me. I bite." She planted her hands on her hips. "This is the boy you wanted me to see? He's cute but a bit young for me." I almost chuckled as his glare grew.

"Young? You're just a child," he growled back.

"Oh? Well, mentally, I'm so much more smarter."

I watched them glare at each other and knew that Enrique was definitely the one who had seen more than he should have at his age. I raised an eyebrow.

"What do you mean, too young? Azura, you are eight."

"Yes, but my mate is going to be an older boy. You know, Kia, boys grow up slowly, so that's why." She shrugged, and I almost laughed at that confidence.

"Noted," I replied, amused. She reached into the bag I was carrying, pulling out a few bars of chocolate.

"Want some?" *This is why I brought her; my sister is a queen in the making.*

"No thanks," he hissed. "I don't eat junk."

"Oh? What a shame." Azura shrugged nonchalantly, ripped open the packet with her teeth, and bit into the Aero chocolate bar, then dropped onto the bed. "So, what's your name?"

"None of your business." He turned his back on her, and Azura frowned, jumping off the bed and walking over to him.

"It's rude to turn your back on people," she stated.

"Don't talk to me," he growled, shrugging her off. It was then that Azura noticed his arm. Her eyes widened before she tossed the empty wrapper aside and reached over, grabbing his wrist.

"Oh, my goddess, you don't have a hand!"

"Azura!" My smile vanished, and I stepped forward, seeing Enrique's anger rise, but she didn't care.

"That's so cool! You can wear a hook! And when people don't listen to you, you can wrap it around their necks and yank them forward like this!" She grabbed his neck, only for him to push her away, staring at her as if she had lost it.

"You're weird. Take her away from here," he almost growled as he turned his attention to me. Okay, so that didn't go as I wanted…

"I'm not weird! You can become Captain Hook! The Pirate Alpha! Wait! Wait! The Alpha of the seven seas!" She jumped onto the bed, looking around as if she had just hit the jackpot. "The seas are unclaimed by any pack! You can claim them all!" I looked at Enrique, and for a moment, there was a glimmer of life in them, almost as if he saw hope, but then he scoffed and shook his head.

"Let's hope I am even fit to be called an Alpha… that is, if I make it out of here alive."

The Queen Luna

ENRIQUE

I SAW THE WAY THE Queen's smile vanished at my words. She genuinely looked shocked at what I had just said, and that look of sadness that followed… I hated it.

"Why wouldn't you?" The annoying girl remarked. She was nothing like the chica… I hated loud, annoying girls.

"I'm a prisoner who will never speak or give this pack any information about my padre or pack. No matter how much I'm tortured."

"Oh, it's okay. We won't torture you, silly. We have witches. They can read your mind," she smirked.

"Then I'll kill myself before they can do so," I replied coldly. Her smile vanished, and she took a confused step back, looking at the queen.

"We won't force you to tell us anything. You have my word," the queen promised, her eyes flashing a beautiful purple. I almost believed her. Almost.

I didn't understand her. She was caring as a Luna should be… but she was also strong… and it was clear the Lycan didn't treat her like she was beneath him. It was weird seeing an Alpha and Luna so different from how Father was towards Mother.

"Would you like to go for some fresh air, Enrique?" The queen asked, giving me another smile.

How strange… but I think I like it better like this. Yes, they kidnapped me, but at least they're being hospitable, even if it was probably to get me to talk and spill our pack secrets.

I wonder how long she'll continue to be nice to me before her mask falls away.

"That would be nice," I remarked, deciding to take her up on her offer.

I was sure the Lycan wouldn't like it, and then I'd be dragged back in here. She smiled and took a few bars of chocolate from the bag, placing the rest down. I actually wouldn't mind trying them… I had eaten chocolate, but it was very rare as it was unnecessary to eat such food. If she offered me again, I would take it.

"Let's get going then," the queen said, motioning to the door. I raised an eyebrow.

"Won't you blindfold me?"

"Of course not."

"You will let me walk through your pack and assess the layout?" To my surprise, she laughed.

"It doesn't matter. I am not blindfolding a child unless we are playing pin the tail, and we clearly aren't." Pin the tail? What was that? She was weird, just like the girl next to her.

"Come on, slowpoke," the girl piped in, jerking her head towards the door.

Was it a trap to get me to walk out, and then I'd be attacked? I began walking towards the door, and the girl skipped out first. I tensed when the queen's arm went around my shoulders just before we reached the door.

"Luna," one of the guards murmured, surprise clear in his eyes.

"Not now. We are just going for a walk," she replied firmly, her voice ten times icier than what it was when she spoke to me.

"I don't think the Alpha would approve…" the other man interjected.

Her aura surged immensely, and she looked over her shoulder. They didn't say anything else, but I knew they were mind-linking. I remained quiet until the two men lowered their heads in submission to her.

I let my mind wander. Father wanted the Lycan's son... since I was here if I killed him, I was sure father would be happy. Maybe I'd be able to regain some approval. I didn't even bother looking around as I walked alongside the queen. She opened a chocolate bar and held it out to me, and I felt a flash of irritation. Even if I only had one hand, I was capable.

I'll show Father I am still capable… Since he cut my hand off, he had looked at me like I was a piece of dirt. I knocked it out of her hand, my anger raging inside of me. I readied for the impact of a hit or something, but instead, she simply bent down, picked it up and tossed it to the girl.

"Can you put that in the bin, Azura?" She nodded and ran off ahead, leaving us alone. "I'm sorry, here. Which one would you like?"

I clenched my jaw and picked a random one without giving it a thought. Ripping open the wrapper with my teeth, I took a bite, trying to quell my anger. The queen opened a second wrapper as we strolled along, biting into it.

I had to think. What should I do? Should I try to win her over? I looked at her, and she was looking ahead. The chica was indeed like her mother. Calm, kind, and maybe too innocent. Why trust the son of your enemy? I wouldn't. I frowned. What do I do? Use her kindness to get close to her family? I was sure Father would approve. Currently, there wasn't much else that I could do, but if they somehow welcomed me into their home or even in the proximity of the Lycan's heir... maybe, just maybe, Father would be happy.

The annoying girl, Azura, returned and fell in step with me. See? They weren't even being careful, or they really did think I was completely useless. I'd just use that to bide my time...

"What does the Lycan want from me?" I asked, staring ahead. "I will not tell him any secrets." I kept my gaze trained far ahead, sensing she was watching me.

"He is trying to rile your father up to make him come forward to claim you. He still has not told us what debt we owe him," she confessed, almost as if she didn't want to burden me with the truth. That sounded far too innocent on their part. They had no compassion. They were monsters, just as my father said. We are all monsters, and only the strongest survived...

"Hmm. Father won't fall for it," I replied confidently.

"He won't leave you here," the queen's reply sounded almost as if that wasn't a possibility. She sure didn't know my padre...

We reached an open grassy area. There were swings and benches, with some pups and adults around. It was slightly cloudy, but it seemed everyone was still having fun. They smiled at their Luna yet carried on with their conversations after bowing their heads respectfully. They didn't stay silent in her presence. How weird.

I ate my chocolate slowly, savouring the taste.

"Do you want to walk around?"

"Is that not what we are doing?"

"I meant alone if you want some space," she replied with a smile. There was a trick to it, but if it was a test, I'd behave.

"Sure."

She nodded and motioned for me to go ahead. I began walking, and I felt her presence behind me. Glancing back, I saw she had left a five-metre gap between us and was looking up at the sky. Hmm, so she planned to follow… I took the time to observe the area without her having her eyes on me and making sure I kept my head straight ahead, not wanting her to know what I was doing.

The girl, Azura, had gone off and was currently trying to climb a tree. She should have been born a monkey. Weird girl.

I finished my chocolate. It had begun to melt a little, leaving the wrapper slightly covered with melted chocolate. I looked around, spotted a bin, and walked over, tossing it in. I was about to push my sleeve up with my other hand when the reminder that I had no hand to do that with returned. I froze as I stood there, staring at my stump. The memory of the agonising pain I had felt when my father cut it off returned. He had left me there… and I don't know what was on the knife, but it hadn't healed. I had been in agony for so long… but then again, I didn't have the capability to heal such a big injury. I didn't have my wolf yet.

The queen had taken away the pain that wracked my body constantly. She had made me feel better than I had ever felt in my life. My body wasn't hurting anymore. I could breathe without that constant pain from the brutal training that I hadn't even realised was always present.

I once heard my father's old Beta say that he needed to let me heal before pushing me so hard, or I'd be damaged for life. Father had killed him for that. I think he was right… I felt so much stronger now.

"Here," the queen's voice came, and I turned as she held out a hand wipe. I hesitated, taking it and rubbing it in my hand, trying to get the chocolate off with just the one. I was not going to let having one hand deter me. *I'll be the strongest…* "Are you okay, Enrique? Do you want to talk? I promise I won't tell anyone anything you say." She seemed to mean it, too, or she was an incredible liar.

"No, thanks. I'm fine."

She nodded, and we continued walking. I glanced over at her. I remembered something my mother told me once about the beast that the Lycan truly was.

"Is it true the Lycan kidnapped you and forced you to be his mate? That he killed his Padre and Madre, too?" Her face filled with concern, but she shook her head.

"No, he didn't. In fact, he tried to let me go, although he knew I was his mate because he thought he didn't deserve me." She smiled when she spoke, "He…" I glanced at her, seeing confusion flit across her face before she shook her head as if pushing the thought away. "He loved me. He still does and treats me well. As for his parents… I don't… remember." She frowned, placing a hand on her forehead and massaging her temples. Her heart was racing. I looked away, not bothered to hear any more excuses about the Lycan.

"I wish to return to my cell," I stated suddenly.

"I'm sorry you are being kept there," she replied softly before she turned. "Zuzu! Come on!"

"Don't call me that, Kia," the girl grumbled as she jumped down from the tree.

Kia. It was strange not having someone call the Luna by her title, no matter how they were related. Strange. The entire pack was strange. And above all, I was surprised I was still alive.

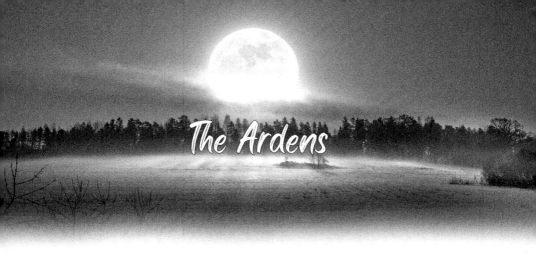

The Ardens

KIARA

*M*OM, DAD, AND AZURA had left just after food, whilst Kataleya had been very quiet. When Azura had said the boy was annoying, she asked if Azura had visited. She became upset but said nothing. She had silently gone and sat with Ahren and Tatum but refused to play with Skyla or Azura. Kataleya was a sweet girl who could be just as stubborn as Mom when she wanted to be. Alejandro hadn't said anything when he found out I took Enrique out. I just hoped it was because he realised that he needed some space to breathe and that he was, after all, just a child.

I had just gotten changed for the evening in a strapless black satin dress paired with red heels, nails, and lips. It was hard to dress up and act like everything was okay when it wasn't. Delsanra and Dante were still suffering. That monster was still out there. I ran the straightener through my hair until it fell sleekly over my shoulder. Once I had finished, I tied it up in a high pony and pinned it into place.

"Ready?" Alejandro asked, stepping into the bedroom, fully dressed and looking incredible in a white shirt and black pants.

"Yes," I answered, standing up.

His eyes raked over me, shimmering red with approval, as he closed the gap between us and grabbed my hips, pulling me against him. I gasped, my hands splayed on his chest, and looked up at him as my entire body reacted to his touch. His eyes burned into mine, igniting that molten pleasure deep within my core.

"We have guests awaiting us," I reminded him breathlessly, despite my pounding heart.

"They are five minutes from pack territory," he murmured, "and I just want to ruin you in every fucking way…." He ran his fingers through my hair, and I knew that he wanted to yank it free from the perfect pony I had created.

"It's going to take us five minutes to get to the packhouse," I replied pointedly, reaching up and kissing him softly. I pulled away before he could deepen it and turned to grab my bag when he took hold of my wrist, yanking me back into his arms.

"Are you angry?"

"A little," I admitted. Reaching up, I cupped his face. "No matter who his father is, he is no monster." He frowned and gave a small nod.

"I know that. I'm just being careful because I can't fucking risk anything happening to anyone who is under my care again."

"He's currently under your care, too," I countered softly. His eyes flashed, and I felt his aura surge around him, blanketing the room with a heavy darkness.

"Look. I don't want to fucking argue with you but push me one more fucking time, and I swear I won't let you see that pup ever again."

His words cut me like a knife, and, for a moment, it felt like someone had cut off my supply of air. The anger in his eyes was unmasked, and from the way his fists were clenched, I knew he was trying not to break something.

There was no point in arguing. We were never going to agree.

"The Ardens are waiting," I replied, walking past him and to the door.

I opened it and headed to the stairs, not waiting for him, although he caught up pretty fast. The house was silent, and the children were in the living room with the rest of the family. I popped my head in and blew them a kiss.

"We're off." I gave a small smile, masking how I truly felt.

"I'll have the kids in bed," Maria promised.

"Thank you."

I shut the door again, glancing at Alejandro, who was already at the front door, holding it open with his foot as he lit a cigarette. A cold wind was blowing, and the chill from that morning seemed to have gotten worse. I stepped out into the night. The paths were very well lit, considering werewolves could see in the dark. We walked in silence. I knew he was still angry, taking long drags on that cigarette of his.

Al, Kia, they have entered the pack premises and are heading to the packhouse now, Darien called through the link.

We're there, Alejandro replied as we reached the packhouse. Serena was already waiting, dressed in a knee-length, deep forest green dress. I greeted her with a small wave, having seen her earlier.

"We'll head inside. Bring them in," Alejandro commanded coldly, not even sparing her a second glance. She quirked an eyebrow questioningly at me, and I shook my head.

It's nothing, I replied through the link, but she gave me a sympathetic smile. She knew it was something. After all, she knew us both well enough.

I followed Alejandro inside to the formal living room, which was not used by the pack members. I looked at him sitting on the two-seater, his arm stretched over the top of the sofa, the other holding his cigarette, his left ankle resting on his right knee, and his eyes as cold as could be. My sexy king. Often it felt like he wasn't even human... his every angle and feature were perfection.

A tray of refreshments was already sitting on the table, ready for our guests.

"Take your seat, Amore Mio, or are you going to stand there and throw a fucking tantrum?" His eyes met mine. His voice was cold and mocking.

I exhaled in frustration. I knew I was going to end up flipping out soon. He was pushing me to my limits. I walked over, having half an urge to whack him over the head with my clutch bag. I stood next to the sofa, knowing that once the Alpha and Luna came, I would have to meet them anyway.

"I don't bite. Do sit," he remarked mockingly.

"No thanks." I knew if I did, he'd do something, and I'd forgive him.

Are they alone? I asked Alejandro emotionlessly through the link.

They're bringing their sons, he replied, just when we heard the front door and the sound of talking.

I knew the Alpha of the Shadow Wolves Pack had two sons, twins born a day apart, as well as a daughter who was much younger. The sound of footsteps approaching came, and the door was opened by Darien, who was dressed smartly in a grey suit. He stepped aside, and Alpha Kenneth entered.

He looked no older than his late thirties, but that was the werewolf genes. He was just a year or two younger than Dad. His golden blond hair was styled sleekly, and he was completely clean-shaven, with eyes that were such a pale blue they looked almost silver. He wore a navy suit with a silver tie, and not even one crease seemed to ruffle his appearance. He was tall and well-built, and his strong aura surrounded him.

Next to him was a woman who was model-like, tall and slim, towering over six feet with her designer heels. She had light brown hair that was styled elegantly into a bun, and grey eyes, with classy yet subtle make-up. She was wearing a two-piece outfit with a large diamond brooch on her breast. A pearl necklace hung around her throat with matching earrings and a few rings. Her nails were short, painted a soft nude.

"Alpha Kenneth, Luna Catherine. Welcome to the Nightwalkers Pack." I smiled gracefully and walked over to them. I met Catherine with a handshake and two kisses.

"Thank you, Queen Luna," Kenneth replied, taking my hand and placing a soft kiss on it.

"Take a seat." I motioned, knowing that Alejandro was not going to get up. No matter how many years had passed, his manners as a host didn't improve.

"King Alejandro, it's an honour to finally be asked to visit," Kenneth remarked with a hint of haughtiness in his tone.

"Asked? You fucking weren't ready to talk over a video call. What was it? Too much screen time might damage your eyes?" Alejandro smirked coldly. Catherine's eyes widened slightly, and I knew it was because of Alejandro's language.

"Well, I am an old-fashioned man. I prefer face-to-face," Kenneth replied, taking a seat.

Serena entered along with two blond-haired boys. They looked similar yet different; both had blond hair, slightly different shades, and were rather tall.

"My sons, Aleric and Royce." Catherine smiled as she motioned to each boy in turn.

"I didn't know you were okay with your sons being part of serious conversations?" Alejandro asked, his eyes on Kenneth as both boys gave me a polite nod and took a seat after lowering their heads to Alejandro.

"They are thirteen, not children. I believe, as Alphas, we should start young to teach our legacy how to be the very best."

Both boys were as smartly dressed as their father; one in a black suit, the other in navy. They almost mirrored each other in their posture. It was rather strange to see them so in sync, from their behaviour to their passive faces. I couldn't tell which one was older; both had strong auras, not giving away who was the firstborn.

Darien and Serena took a seat, and I did the same, settling into my place beside Alejandro. Home. No matter how angry I was at him, his closeness and warmth were my havens.

"That's true," Alejandro remarked. "Luna Catherine, you're from the States, correct?"

"Yes," she replied as she sat by her mate's side, her legs tucked to the side, back straight, chin out. Their reputation didn't fail them, known for being a wealthy, strong, rather posh pack who kept to themselves.

"Ever heard of the Fuego de Ceniza Pack from Puerto Rico?" Catherine's brow furrowed ever so slightly as she thought over what the king had asked.

"Help yourselves to something," I offered the boys.

"No, thank you, My Queen," Royce replied whilst Aleric took a glass of iced juice.

"I have, yes. I am not a hundred percent sure, however, there was a woman who I went to Luna training with. It's something we have over in the States for Alpha's daughters or if you know you are mated to an Alpha," she explained. "This woman, Esmerelda, she may have ended up mated to someone from that pack. I vaguely remember it, but we are not in touch or anything."

"Esmerelda… any surname?"

"Martinez. Esmerelda Martinez." She nodded with confidence. "Yes, that was her name." Alejandro glanced at Darien, and I knew someone was going to be looking into it already.

"I'm assuming this pack is heavily involved with the recent threat," Kenneth remarked as Catherine helped herself to a drink.

"Yeah, it is, and I intend to fucking find them soon," Alejandro replied coldly.

"Will you go to the States?" Kenneth's voice was calm, yet he was watching Alejandro sharply, and the glimmer of curiosity in his eyes didn't go unnoticed.

"If need be. Do you know anything about that pack?" Alejandro's eyes were fixed on him even when his hand snaked around my waist, caressing my side.

"No, I do not. However, I have heard from my patrol of some strange wolves on my northern borders. When you were in search of the Alpha princess, we were on holiday abroad. However, I have some images which I will forward to you via email."

Then he fucking didn't need to come here, Alejandro growled through the link.

He looks like he wants something, Darien replied.

"So, you came all this way to hit send whilst you were here. What is it? Was Ken-fucking-gham Palace out of fucking Wi-Fi?" My eyes flew open at Alejandro's comment, and even Catherina looked shocked as Darien hid his smirk. Alejandro sat forward. I could sense the irritation rolling off of him. "If you had any proof, your men should have given it to me when I asked for fucking information," he said coldly.

"I am still the Alpha of my pack, Alpha King Alejandro, and they answer to me. I didn't need to mention these images, but I did."

"A tad fucking late."

I glanced at the two boys; this was not the place for children, no matter what age they were. Both were watching Alejandro, and I could tell they were paying attention.

"Luna Catherine, would it be alright if you, myself, and Serena went for a walk with the boys in the garden? I think the men can do the talking." Usually, I wouldn't say it was a man's place, but I'd rather protect the children from the conversation turning ugly.

"I think it's a lovely idea," she replied, glancing between Alejandro and Kenneth. Neither spoke and so she stood up, motioning to the boys to follow.

"We wouldn't mind staying, Mother," Aleric commented, curiosity in his eyes as he watched Alejandro.

"The Luna Queen has offered to show us the gardens," Catherine replied. Her voice was calm, but her command was clear, and so the five of us left the room.

"I don't trust you, and I never will..."

That was the last thing I heard Alejandro say. I knew he had no reason not to trust him, but Dad's opinion of Kenneth had left a lasting impression on Alejandro.

"This way." I gestured as I walked down the hall. Reaching the back entrance, I stared at the keypad, trying to remember the key code...

"Luna Kiara?" Serena called. She only addressed me as Luna in front of guests. I frowned, stepping back.

I can't remember the code, I admitted through the link.

I'll do it, she offered.

I stepped back, allowing her to step forward and key it in, unlocking the back door. She glanced at me. The confusion in her eyes when they met mine mirrored exactly how I felt inside. How could I have forgotten it? I had unlocked this door many times.

I needed to talk to Alejandro about this, and it had to be tonight.

His Ridiculous Request

ALEJANDRO

THE WOMEN AND THE twins left. I looked at Kenneth, a small annoying smirk playing on his fucking face.

"Relax, King Alejandro. There's no need to be so uptight." My phone beeped, and I knew I had just received an email by the tone. "My men have just forwarded the email to you."

I took my phone out and went into my email, frowning as I looked at the first few pictures – the very same wolves that we had seen when we were attacked and at the country house.

"Where is this?"

"Just on the edge of my pack territories. We saw them a few times. The same sighting always happened there, yet there were no tracks onwards from this part. They just vanished."

"No tracks at all?"

"None at all. Of course, I have men doing a little more research... as you know, my pack is powerful."

"Or you fucking think it is," I remarked, taking a drag on my cigarette. He smiled pleasantly, but there was nothing fucking pleasant about the look in his eyes.

"Not everything is as it appears. You should really think of the future and ways that can benefit the King's Royal Nightwalkers pack."

"Is that a threat?" I asked, my eyes flashing.

"Not at all. I'm offering a proposal." I cocked a brow.

"Yeah, and what proposal is that?"

"I have two sons, one who will become the Alpha of my pack and the other who may become the Alpha of Catherine's birth pack in the States."

"And I give a fuck why?" He smiled and sat back, crossing his legs arrogantly.

"You have two daughters. An alliance -"

I felt a flare of anger. I was up in a flash, grabbing the bastard by his fucking throat as a menacing growl ripped from my chest. Did this fucking dickhead think he could just parade in here and actually think he could even fucking ask for my daughters like that?

"Al!" Darien's voice was in the distance as I glared at the cunt in my hold.

"No one is touching my daughters; they are fucking six, and you're trying to fucking have me sign away their fucking choice? When, and if, the time comes and they want to choose a mate or fucking accept their fated mates, that's on them. But no one, and I mean fucking no one, is going to take their choice from them. That's not how we do shit around here." I slammed him back into the couch roughly, doing my best not to punch him as Darien pulled me back, his face pale.

Al, calm down.

"It was but a suggestion," Kenneth replied, his voice harsh as he fixed his suit jacket.

I zoned him out, trying to control my anger. My own words rang in my head, and I realised I was doing just that. I refused to allow Kiara to do what she wanted... *Yeah, well, I'm a fucking hypocrite.*

"Dinner's ready," Darien said, but neither I nor the fucker cared. Our eyes were trained on one another, and the hostility between us had just risen by another fucking one hundred percent...

❧❦❧

After spending the evening with Ken-fucking-Arden, I was done. The man was shrewd. He knew how to fucking twist words and act fucking innocent. I didn't like it. Past that façade, there was more to that shit than what showed on that flawless fucking face of his.

Darien had told Kiara what had happened, and she had kept her hand on my leg through fucking dinner, calming me down every fucking time I wanted to shred that fucker to pieces.

I pulled my shirt off the moment I entered our bedroom, tossing it aside as I rolled my neck, getting the kinks out. He had fucking stressed me out, and I really wanted to go for a run or beat the shit out of someone. Preferably him. Speaking of the fucker, he had a few guards who had come with him, but I had my own placed around his given quarters.

Kiara and I had been fine over dinner, but that issue with the pup still fucking lingered. She was sitting on the bed, lost in thought, as she took her earrings off.

"Are we just going to stay angry at each other?" I asked, my voice sounding dangerously cold.

"I don't want to... just let me bring the boy home," she pleaded, standing up. That dress of hers wrapped around her curves like it was fucking made for her, emphasising her waist, curvy hips, and those fucking tits that I loved so fucking much.

I raked a hand through my hair, wanting to ignore her, but wasn't she the voice of reason in my life? If she was being so stubborn about something...

Compassionate and loving. That was what Kiara was. Her heart was equally as pure as her thoughts were dirty in bed.

I glanced back at her as she walked over to me, and to my fucking surprise, she joined her hands together in front of me, making my heart thud with a fucking storm of emotions. Was this that fucking important to her?

"I'm begging you. Please show him that humanity exists. Don't let the darkness cloud his heart. For me, for Kat, and for Rafael. Show him that kindness exists. He is only a child. Mine or someone else's, I can't let this happen. It's killing me inside, Alejandro." Her voice cracked as she swallowed hard, staring at me.

No. I'd never understand that level of love. Yeah, I cared for my own... for my race... but... for the child of an enemy? I wouldn't hurt him. I wasn't hurting him. I didn't like the fact that his father had hurt him... but he was being taken care of, so why should I bring him into my home?

The powers of a Djinn were immeasurable. What if he used the boy as a fucking medium or some shit? They were capable of far more than we knew.

It was my suspicion and protectiveness of my family on the one hand, with Kiara's heart, happiness, and conscience on the other. I exhaled in frustration, placing my hands over hers and lowering them.

"The only time I like you begging is when you're dripping wet and begging for me to fuck you, one way or another. Why is this affecting you so fucking deeply, Amore Mio?" I asked quietly, kissing her hands as I pulled her close.

"He's been through so much, and he doesn't deserve this," she whispered, trying to blink back her tears. I frowned but nodded in fucking defeat, exhaling in frustration.

"Fine. If this is what you want. First thing in the mornin-"

"Now?" She asked, tilting her head, a pout on those gorgeous lips. I clenched my jaw.

"Who's the fucking king?"

"You are." She smiled.

"Who fucking bows to his queen," I growled in annoyance as she quickly put the heels that she had kicked off back on.

Bring the boy to the mansion, I commanded the guards on duty outside his room through the link.

Yes, Alpha, came the prompt reply.

She smiled at me as she walked back into my arms and hugged me tightly. Just the way I liked it. Mine for fucking forever.

"I'm sorry for being stubborn," she whispered, kissing my neck over my mark.

"Yeah? No point in fucking apologising after you got what you wanted," I replied, scowling. I squeezed her ass and pressed her straight into me. She fitted so fucking perfectly…

"You only agreed because you know it's the right thing to do," she replied softly.

"Yeah, maybe." I pulled two pins from her hair and slid the hair tie out, letting her hair cascade down around her shoulders. "You looked beautiful tonight."

"Thanks," she replied, trailing her fingers down my chest. It took my all not to fucking react to her touch. "Shall we go get him?"

"He's on his way," I replied, frowning slightly, only for her to yank me down by the neck and kiss me hard.

Had I ever mentioned I fucking love it when she gets like this? There was not a sexier woman on the fucking planet, and she was mine.

I gripped her hips tighter, kissing her back harder, dominating the kiss. Her sweet minty breath and the taste of her mouth were fucking perfect.

A soft moan escaped her, and I turned us, slamming her up against the wall. I wanted to fucking yank her dress up and devour every fucking inch of her. Why fucking not?

Kissing her hard, I wrenched her dress up, making her whimper.

"Alejandro... we..."

She moaned when I kissed her neck, sucking hard over her mate mark as she writhed with pleasure in my arms, her arousal perfuming the air. Placing a kiss on her cleavage, I bent down and spread her legs, lifted one over my shoulder, and pushed aside her tiny panties, inhaling the intoxicating scent of her arousal deeply.

"Oh, fuck!" She gasped the moment my tongue flicked along her smooth pussy.

Her hand tangled into my hair, tilting her head back against the wall as I devoured her. Her moans became louder as my tongue flicked her clit. I knew my men would be there soon with the boy. We had a matter of minutes.

I liked the challenge. I looked up at her, the curve of her breasts blocking my view of her face as I ate her out, licking, sucking, and flicking her clit as she moaned, her entire body reacting to me. Her sighs and moans became louder, driving me fucking crazy. This was my fucking addiction. She was my fucking drug. My lethal pleasure that I couldn't live without.

"I'm going to come... fuck, Al... nh..."

She moaned in pure pleasure. She grinded against my face as she neared. I slipped two fingers into her and began fucking her hard and fast, my tongue moving fast along her clit. Her juices coated my fingers, her walls clamping around them as she neared her release. My dick was hard, straining against my pants. She was fucking heaven and more. No woman compared with the nympho above me and never could.

She cried out as her orgasm tore through her, her walls clamping around me as her juices trickled out of her. I didn't stop, not until she had ridden out her orgasm, whimpering breathlessly above me as she struggled to move back. I growled, lifting her other leg onto my other shoulder and plunging my tongue into her dripping core. She tasted fucking heavenly. I licked up every drop of her sweet juices as she trembled, trying to move back.

"Alejandro..."

"Now that was dessert," I murmured, moving back slightly and running my tongue along her inner thigh, licking up her sweet juice and admiring her smooth pussy once more.

A soft moan left her before she slid her legs off my shoulders, and I stood up, kissing her again.

"See how fucking good you taste?" I growled when I pulled away, admiring the slight blush that crossed her face. My fucking sexy nympho.

Just then, Julio mind-linked to say they were outside.

Right on fucking time.

For Forever

ALEJANDRO

IARA WIPED HERSELF CLEAN with some wipes, and I splashed my face with water before we both headed downstairs. She cast me a warm smile before she hurried to the door and pulled it open.

Julio gave us a nod, and I didn't miss his gaze flickering to Kiara's neck, one that still contained a few marks. I was sure we both still smelled of her arousal, and a flare of possessiveness shot through me. I gave him a cold glare, and he looked away, looking slightly embarrassed as he realised I was fucking shirtless, too.

Fucker. If he didn't have a mate, I'd have fucking ripped him apart, but I knew he was just a nosy dickhead.

"Hey, Enrique. I'm sorry if we disturbed you from sleep." Kiara's voice brought me back to reality, and I dismissed Julio with a jerk of my head. He gave a nod and placed the bag he was carrying down before taking his leave.

"I wasn't sleeping, Queen Luna," he replied. I cocked a brow. So he called her Queen and called me Lycan. I hid a smirk. The fucker had gall, I'd give him that.

"Then let's get you set up in a bedroom where you can get a good night's sleep." He frowned and looked at me suspiciously.

"Giving me a place in your home won't get me to talk," he remarked.

"I know," Kiara said, ruffling his hair. He jerked away from her, and she turned, about to pick up the bag, when both the boy and I reached for it simultaneously. I raised an eyebrow, allowing him to pick it up.

"I'll carry it," he muttered, frowning as he stared ahead. Either he was smart and knew I was watching him, or maybe I was being too paranoid. Not once did he look around, scanning the place.

I was allowing him to stay, yet there were going to be guards outside his windows as well as his bedroom door. I wasn't going to allow him a free pass to do whatever the fuck he wanted.

He followed Kiara up the stairs, and I followed, trying not to look at her sexy ass. She walked down the hall as the few men who were standing around nodded at us as we passed. I didn't like my men in our home, but with everything going on, we needed to be careful, and someone needed to be observing the kids constantly. Kiara stopped outside one of the unoccupied guest rooms and opened the door, flipping the switch on.

"I hope it's okay?" Kiara asked him. He didn't reply. Placing the bag down, he gave her a nod as an answer.

"I will sleep now."

Kiara nodded. Going over to the bed, she pulled the bedding back, and I leaned against the doorframe. She was too fucking good to everyone…

"I don't sleep on beds. As werewolves, we don't need blankets, nor do we need a comfortable resting area. That only makes us lazy," he replied curtly, walking over towards the window. Well, he had a fucking point… I hated getting out of bed when I was in it with my doll.

"Have you tried it?" Kiara asked.

"I don't want to." And with that, he lay down and closed his eyes.

Stubborn fucker.

I frowned slightly, remembering the wooden plank he was sleeping on when I had brought him here. How much had he fucking been through? Whether I trusted him or not, this shit was fucking messed up.

"You're sleeping on the fucking bed. Now," I growled, my command rolling off me. Kiara turned, frowning slightly.

Want him to get a fucking good night's sleep? I asked her.

Not by forcing him, she replied pointedly as the boy struggled for a fraction of a second against my command, yet frowned as he was forced to obey.

Yeah, well, I'm not in his good books. Today, he's fucking forced. Tomorrow, he'll sleep there of his own fucking choice. I don't give a fuck about being the bad guy. I turned away as the boy got into bed, glaring at me.

"Thank me tomorrow," I replied with a cold smirk, glancing at him over my shoulder.

"Goodnight, Enrique. The bathroom is through there," Kiara murmured before she dimmed the lights and followed me out. "You have a good heart; you just do things a bit crazily," she added once the door clicked shut.

"Yeah? Well, we aren't all fucking angels." I pulled her close, kissing her lips hard.

I apologise for being fucking stubborn over this shit.

Apology accepted, her soft, seductive reply came as she locked her arms around my neck and kissed me.

Have you sent a message out to him?

Yeah, on the dark web. Let's see if he responds or not.

She nodded, pondering over what I said as we returned to our bedroom. Kiara turned to me, her smile vanishing as I unbuckled my pants.

"That's not usually the face I see when I'm stripping," I remarked. She gave a small smile and shook her head.

"There was something I wanted to tell you earlier, but then I got side-tracked," she sighed, brushing her fingers through her hair.

"Oh, yeah?" I took hold of her elbows, making her eyes flutter shut for a moment as I drew her close. Sparks rippled through us as I looked down at her in concern. My breath fanned her face, and her heart skipped a beat. She opened her eyes after a moment and gazed up into mine.

"Earlier, when we were leaving the packhouse to go for a walk, I... I couldn't remember the passcode for the back door," she whispered, her heart thundering.

My stomach plunged, twisting inside of me. With the shit going on, I had almost hoped it had just been a few small things she had forgotten...

"I can't remember how we first met either... or how Raven and I became friends..."

With each word she said, she stared at my chest, tracing my tattoo with a single finger, unable to hold my gaze but sending pleasure coursing through me. She was also making my heart fucking squeeze in fear.

Didn't remember how we first fucking met.

Didn't remember Raven.

The key code hasn't been changed in the last eight months.

"I'm forgetting more and more, and I'm scared," she whispered, forcing a smile before she began chewing her bottom lip as she tried to control the emotions that were seeping through the bond.

"We are going to figure this shit out. I fucking assure you," I replied huskily, tilting her chin up and running my thumb over her lips. I gently tugged her bottom one free from between her teeth as I looked into those gorgeous eyes of hers before I claimed her lips in a silent promise. There was no fucking way that she was going to forget me.

She couldn't.

❦

I had just finished my morning training and showered when I stepped into the bedroom wearing a pair of blue jeans to see Kiara applying some makeup, dressed in a sky-blue, chiffon, floral halter dress that showed off her gorgeous breasts from what I could see in the mirror. Her back was on show with a criss-cross string detailing holding the fabric in place. I walked over to the drawer and picked up her wedding rings, which she hadn't put back on since our return. We'd had enough shit going on, but it was the longest she had been without them, and, as much as I wasn't fucking sentimental, after last night, I was fucking worried.

I walked over to her, and she smiled up at me. Looking fucking gorgeous. Damn, the goddess had exceeded herself when she made her....

"Do I look okay?" Raihana had wanted a garden party before she, Chris, and her pup left, so we were fucking spending the day out back.

"More than fucking okay," I replied, going down on one knee next to her as she turned towards me.

I kissed her breasts before trailing kisses up her neck. She let out a breathless laugh, wrapping her arms around my neck. When I teasingly ran my fingers over the strings of her dress, she wriggled in my hold, especially when my fingers brushed her waist, tickling her.

"Alejandro!" I smirked, moved back, and held the rings out to her.

"Want to wear these?" I asked. She smiled as she looked at them.

"Those are so pretty. Sure, why not, if you want me to wear them," she replied with a stunning smile, taking them from me.

My smile faded as I watched her try one of the rings on her middle finger. My heart clenched as I reached out, taking the rings from her and sliding both onto her ring finger as I tried not to let my emotions show on my face. She was forgetting. Fuck she had forgotten they were her wedding rings…

Fuck.

"Thanks… it looks like we're married now," she remarked teasingly, moving her hand and allowing the light to reflect on the diamonds, making them sparkle brightly.

"We are," I responded ever so quietly, not wanting to ruin her fucking day.

"Hmm?"

She turned back to me, and I cupped her neck, kissing her hard before she could reply. It felt like another one of my fucking nightmares was coming true. I couldn't bear to hear her say she couldn't remember our marriage… fuck. I kissed her with a desperation I couldn't control, and I could hear her heart thundering as she tried to keep up. She parted her legs, and I pulled her against me as I knelt between them.

Would she forget the way this felt? The way my lips felt against hers? The taste of my mouth? The way we were meant to be.

Alejandro, are you okay? She whispered through the link, a soft sigh escaping her lips. I didn't know what to say. *How do I explain my fear to her?* I couldn't lie to her without her realising either.

We broke apart, and I brushed my finger over her lips, pressing my forehead to hers.

"I fucking love you more than life itself, Amore Mio," I murmured, inhaling her scent.

"I love you, too," she replied, cupping my face and claiming my lips in a softer, slower, yet equally sensual kiss. "And everything about you." She smiled softly, and those gorgeous blue-rimmed green eyes looked directly into mine. Her thick lashes caressed her cheek when she blinked.

"Likewise, my sexy nympho queen," I smirked as she blushed lightly.

"Yours."

"Mine."

For fucking forever.

Family

ALEJANDRO

USIC WAS BLASTING LOUDLY in the back garden of the mansion, but it felt like I was just watching it all happen like an outsider looking in. Kiara's issue was echoing in my mind, but I was trying to act like nothing was fucking wrong. Although, aside from Kiara, I didn't think anyone would notice anyway. I had my walls up so she didn't get fucking worried as I smoked a cigarette.

Kiara had invited the fucking Ardens, although I wanted to rip that fucker to shreds after his comment about my girls, but, for the sake of being the fucking king, I was being hospitable. I wondered if I could get the fuckers face tipped into the barbeque grill. Might improve his fucking pretty boy looks…

Rayhan, Delsanra, and Dante were sitting on the balcony on the first floor, where Raihana had created an illusion so the fucker and his family couldn't see them. I glanced up at him, and I smirked humourlessly. He was doing the exact fucking thing I was, acting like shit was okay as he showed Dante something on his phone. We were both worried for our mates yet trying to act fucking normal…

I saw Rayhan take on the same exterior as when Raf died, remaining strong despite the pain inside. His mate was so weak she could barely sit up alone. The effect of the curse was making her health deteriorate fast. Obviously, it was probably fucking with him like crazy. I just needed to break the fucking curse.

It was probably the longest I'd seen him and Dante get on without Dante pissing him the fuck off. I had heard their conversation that night, and I had to admit the fuckers had their own kind of bond. *I guess all brothers fight, it's just who we are.* Didn't mean they didn't care for each other. At least I knew if I was gone, he'd have Rayhan.

I looked around the garden, taking a moment to observe everyone. Kiara had tried to get Enrique to join, but he had refused. I wasn't going to complain; I didn't need the visiting Alpha Ken-fucking-doll knowing more shit than he already did

His boys were currently talking to Chris whilst Maria was talking to Catherine and Kenneth. Thank the fucking goddess for her, or more so to Raf. She was raised in a wealthy home and was a proper lady, or whatever you wanted to call it. It fucking showed in the way she was handling the Ardens. My gaze wandered over to Kiara, who was next to Darien and Serena near the grill, whilst the children played to the side with Raihana watching them, or more like taking selfies of herself while allowing her magic to watch the children. She stopped the toddlers from venturing too far off.

Sienna was fucking looking confused as always. I swore she was going to fuck up the kids if she kept using her magic and confusing her like that.

If she stopped looking at herself... she sure didn't get bored of seeing herself. If there was a way to be mated to yourself, it would be fucking perfect for her. She loved herself far too much.

"Jealous of how amazing I look, Uncle?" She asked, flicking her hair.

"Nah, I was just wondering why the fuck you look like the fucking Tin-Man from The Wizard of Oz," I smirked coldly. Skyla cackled as Raihana pouted.

"Not funny, you little devil," she said to Skyla before turning to me. "You know, Uncle, let me just give you a facial and fix up those brows and stuff. I swear you would look so much better."

"You got your mate for that. I'll pass."

I watched Kataleya, who was more distracted, looking into the distance towards the bedroom windows on the first floor. None of the rooms belonged to Enrique, but she knew he was there... and she wanted to see him again. The thing was, he refused to be around Kat, so even though he came here, he was still happy to stay confined in his room.

I didn't trust that boy. He was still his father's blood, and I was sure that Djinn had the fucking power to locate him. Even his father hadn't bothered to reach out to my message.

How to kill a Djinn… that was an answer I still needed.

I crouched down in front of Kataleya.

"Hey, angel. Want to play on the swings?" She shook her head, glancing toward the grilled food.

"Can we take Enrique food?" She whispered.

I didn't miss Kenneth's attention perking at what she said, and I cast him a cold glare. I knew he had probably done his own fucking research on my pack thoroughly. I couldn't stand him, and it was obvious he didn't like me. I really needed to get Elijah to share the reason he didn't like this dipshit.

"I'm sure someone will. Your mama won't forget," I replied, pinching her cheek lightly.

She looked at me sadly, a small pout on her face. I thought she needed therapy. Fuck, if Del wasn't in the state she was in, she would have been the perfect person for Kataleya to talk to, having studied to go into this very field. The trauma of the events still haunted Kataleya, and it fucking killed me to see her smile was gone. She had gone from the happiest child around, one who would constantly smile, to the quietest…

Sparks rippled through me, and I looked up, greeted by the view of the underside of Kiara's breasts. Well, that was one fucking view I loved. She crouched down next to us, a gorgeous smile on her face as she held her arms out to Kat.

"Come, let's take some food."

You know he said he doesn't want to see her; this shit will only hurt her.

I will explain it to her and make her remain in the hallway. She only wants to see him, she replied, turning and gazing into my eyes with those gorgeous ones of hers.

Always got a plan, huh?

Always.

I reached over, gripping the back of her hair as I kissed her hard. *Don't fucking forget me, Amore Mio…* I squashed the thought away. *Don't think it, and it won't happen…*

"Will you take the food upstairs to them?" Kiara asked me. I knew she meant the trio on the balcony, and I nodded.

"I never knew I was a fucking waiter. I don't serve." *Unless of course, it meant her….*

"You are everything and more. A tray or two will do no harm," Kiara replied with a small amused smile, taking hold of Kataleya's hand, and they both went over to the grill.

"Why are you two exactly the same?" I turned, seeing Skyla questioning the Arden twins.

"How so?" One of the fuckers replied.

"Well, you both look exactly the same. Were you cloned?"

"No, and we are not exactly alike," the other one replied with a small smile.

"Well, I have a twin, and we are both very different, you know," Skyla remarked.

"I can tell."

This girl had a fucking reason to talk to anyone. The two Ken dolls in the fucking making exchanged looks. Skyla hurried off to play with Sienna, who was currently playing in the ball pit, with Raihana crouching down next to them and talking to her. She wasn't the type to be so hands-on usually, but with Delsanra in her current state, I knew she was trying her best to do what she could.

I went over to Darien and Serena, picking up the tongs and flipping the meat patties.

How is she today? Darien asked through the link, and I knew he had opened the link to both Serena and me. I didn't need to ask who he fucking meant. Serena had been there when Kiara forgot the passcode.

She's forgotten we're married, I remarked coldly, doing my fucking all not to let my emotions show. I flipped another patty over, remaining emotionless. Serena's heart was thudding.

She'll…. will it… I mean, will she be okay? She asked.

I don't know, but it makes the incentive to find this fucker fast even more vital. We have Dante and Del being run down with this curse, Kiara's losing her memory, and the fucker's son is on our pack grounds, who he doesn't seem to care for. Time's running the fuck out, and I need to fix this shit.

We need to fix this. We are a pack, a family, and we do this stuff together, Darien added, looking me in the eye. I gave a small nod. *Yeah, we will…* **Drake checked the name of the woman Luna Catherine mentioned yesterday. He said her files are coming up classified. I think**

if we want answers, someone's going to have to fly out there… Darien explained.

I frowned. I couldn't rely on anyone else to do this… but I also couldn't leave everyone here alone. Fuck, this was messed up…

I'll figure some shit out. Pack meeting tonight at ten. I let everyone who I needed there know through the pack link. I took off the five of the patties, lost in thought.

☙❦❧

"Anything?" I asked Raihana as she entered my home office, her face serious.

They were to leave soon, and she had just checked on Kiara's memory. Although I hadn't asked in front of Kiara, I was fucking worried to hear if Raihana managed to find something. She had just told Kiara she wanted to check her over, which wasn't exactly a lie, and so Kiara hadn't picked up on it.

"No. I can't seem to see anything blocking her mind or any sort of spell. This is something I feel totally at a loss with. I was thinking if I did some research, maybe I could find something about Djinn and their magic. What if I called on my witch ancestors -"

"Del cut that link you had to them, we all know they are no longer bound to you. If you summon any for answers, it's going to be a fucking risk, and we are in no way in fucking hell risking Endora to come back in any form. I've made it clear I am not risking anyone else."

"Uncle, this is my family, too. I'm a Rossi. I'm capable of so much more than this." She came over to the desk, and, for a moment, it was like the sixteen-year-old girl I first began to get to know was before me as she glared down at me, displeased.

"You are doing enough, but I need you at your best and fucking safe." I frowned. "When we brought Enrique here, how far out do you think he was? Any idea? You were clearly fucking exhausted after."

"I've tried to open a portal across the oceans, and I'm unable to. My limit is 400 miles, give or take, if I go by what I have tried to pinpoint. I think we are looking at some location under 300 miles." So she had been trying to figure this shit out already…

"Yeah? How can you be so sure?"

"I've been trying to figure it out, and don't worry, I'm being careful," she added with an eye roll.

"Yeah, good," I replied coldly.

"Honestly, I'm not a child," she growled, frowning at me. "Anyway, I think I opened a portal up north… I wanted to use the piece of fabric to see if I could find anything else, but Kat didn't want to let me look at it again." I frowned. She had that shit? But the fucker was here… "Hey, don't tell her you know. She asked for it back and said not to tell you or Kia…" Raihana replied, looking concerned. "I did mention it to Kia, of course."

I felt my stomach twist. So my own daughter didn't want to share shit with me? Fucking great. This was the same girl who would talk to me day in and day fucking out.

"I won't mention it. I don't get her fucking infatuation with him, but the kid lost a hand for helping her… do you think there's any way we could fix that shit?" I asked her. I didn't think I'd be the one to ask that. She looked defeated and shook her head.

"I don't think there is, but I will look into it. Once I get back, I'll look in the grimoires or see if I can find anything about cell regeneration." I nodded.

"Yeah, let me know if you see anything. I've still not heard from his father."

"Well, shall I just check his mind before we go? See if we can learn anything?" I shook my head.

"As much as I fucking want to, Kiara refused to allow me to use the child like that."

"We can do it without her knowing," Raihana offered hesitantly. I sighed. I was tempted. I needed answers… and if that boy had some…

"Give me a little time. I'll try to question him today. If he doesn't spill, then we'll work on something."

We exchanged looks, and she nodded. I was about to say something when I thought I heard something. I leaned forward, honing in on everything around me. What was that…? Beyond the beating of our hearts… there it was… a tiny beat. I looked up at Raihana sharply. She was watching me curiously.

"Yeah, I was right, you need to take it fucking easy, and this time, I mean for fucking real."

"What are you going on about?" I sat back, taking a cigarette and my lighter out of my pocket. I glanced up at her as I lit it and took a drag.

"You're carrying a fucking pup."

A King's Promise

ALEJANDRO

RAIHANA HADN'T BEEN EXPECTING that. She had paled and asked me not to tell anyone, that it wasn't the time for such news. I got where the fuck she was coming from and agreed, but it put the decision down in fucking stone. I was not risking her in any fucking way. She was totally out of the picture. Although I knew she wouldn't just sit back, she had helped enough. Fuck, we needed answers and fast…

"Take care on the way back," Maria was saying, kissing the little fucker, Tatum. Had to admit that the pup was cute. I went over, taking him from her.

"Of course, Mom, we are going by teleportation," Raihana replied, kissing Chris before she pulled away.

Tatum looked up at me with his large green eyes, and I narrowed mine. I swore these little devils were embedded with some sort of power or shit. Something told me that if any of these pups asked for something, I'd fucking give it to them. Nah, can't let that shit happen…

He reached up, giving me a smile. Fuck it, I'd give him whatever he wanted. He rested his head against my shoulder, and I snuck in a quick peck when no one was watching, narrowing my eyes when I saw Kiara smile knowingly. She wasn't even looking in my direction.

You are so cute, my sexy beast.

I fucking ain't. I'm just doing what Raf probably would have on his behalf.

You don't need to explain it to me. I glared at her as she looked as if she was about to burst out laughing. *I'll spank that ass tonight.*

Raihana crouched down next to Dante.

"My handsome prince, get better soon. This visit hasn't been the same without you at your loudest. You know you are the male version of me."

"I am not," Dante retorted, wrinkling his nose. "I'm Dante Rossi, there's no one like me." The women laughed, and I smirked.

"Exactly what I mean," Raihana smirked, ruffling his hair and making him glare at her as she turned to Rayhan. "Take care of her."

"Obviously," he replied as Raihana hugged Delsanra tightly. They exchanged a quiet word before nodding at each other, and Raihana kissed Delsanra's hands.

"Well, see you all soon. Come on, Tatum," Chris said, coming over and taking his pup from me. He went willingly; we exchanged a firm handshake, and then they took their leave, so I decided to get some stuff done.

"I hope things are sorted soon," was the last thing I heard when I left the room.

I needed to question Enrique, so I made my way upstairs and looked at Milo.

"Has he said or done anything weird?" I asked quietly.

Unknown to Kiara, I'd had a camera installed that morning when the boy was in the bathroom having a shower, taking the chance to get someone from the tech team to sneak in and set that shit up.

"Nothing, Alpha. He just stands there or sits, staring at his right arm," Milo replied, frowning slightly.

I nodded curtly, knocking on the door before I opened it. Sure enough, he was standing there, emotionlessly staring out the window. He turned upon seeing me, and I sighed inwardly. I did not want to have a fucking prisoner, especially a damn child…

"Hey, kid."

He didn't respond, and I left the door open, not wanting to make him worry. I walked over to the bed and took a seat, knowing my large frame was intimidating.

"Can I ask you a few questions?" I asked, deciding on a different approach.

Silence.

"Your father has cursed my son. My nephew's mate is also suffering because of this curse when she tried to lift it. I'm trying to reach out to him… but he isn't responding. I won't be punishing you, nor will I hold it against you if you don't reply, but if you can, from the bottom of your heart, give us some answers as to why we are being dealt this shit, I'd fucking appreciate it." He remained silent, but I didn't miss the small frown on his face.

"I won't answer. The Lycan King may punish me or kill me… it doesn't matter anyway." The last part of his words was so silent I knew he didn't think I'd hear.

"I'm not punishing you, kid, and I'm not asking you as the fucking Lycan King. I'm asking you as the father of a child who is suffering. I'm pleading for his sake to repay the debt we owe, a debt I just wish your father told me about. How can I fix shit when I don't even know what the fuck it is?" I asked.

He looked at me, and, for a moment, I felt as if that cold front had dropped a little. He looked down at his hand again, and, fuck, I wished I could do something to help him.

"Padre never mentioned what debt it is. Only that you will pay for everything he has suffered for," he finally spoke, not even looking me in the eye. "I don't know about the curse. He never said anything about it."

Oh, he knew more than he had just said, but it seemed he wasn't going to tell me. I nodded.

"I appreciate your help. How about you come downstairs and join the family for pizza and a movie later?" His eyes snapped to me, and his heart thudded as he stepped back.

"I… no, I don't…"

"It's a movie. You're going to go fucking crazy in this room, and until your father contacts me, I don't know what the fuck I'm going to do with you. You're stuck here, so get the hell downstairs in an hour." He frowned and simply nodded.

"If that is what the Lycan King wants."

I raised an eyebrow. That was twice he'd said 'Lycan King', and I sure as hell didn't think he was fucking softening. The pup was smarter than the average ten-year-old, and whatever shit was going on in his mind was not so fucking simple. *I'll keep an eye on him…*

"What do you do for pastime? Any hobbies? Football? Gaming?"

"I don't waste time, or as you call it, pastime. I train, I study, and I work hard… to be the best alpha I can be." His words were monotonous, as if they had been drilled into him repeatedly.

"Yeah? Well, you're still a pup, kid. You need to live a little. I grew up thinking I was a fucking monster, that my purpose was to protect this race, and that was it. That I was far too fucking messed up to have what I have now." Curiosity filled his eyes, and he looked at me.

"Did the Queen Luna change you?" I raised an eyebrow, not expecting that question.

"Yeah, she did. She somehow loved me for whoever the fuck I was and showed me that I was worth more than I thought. My parents always expected so much from me, although my father was under my so-called mother's influence. I was always told I wasn't what I should be. I ended up killing my father when I first shifted, and I thought I killed my mother, too. That was it; then I began to shut everyone out... but you know it was her ploy, all part of her plan to take control of me and rule the fucking world. Look, kid, what I'm trying to say is you are not, nor do you need to be, what your parents expect you to be. You are fucking allowed to do whatever shit you want. Think from the heart and do what feels right..." I trailed off, seeing his gaze fall to his arm.

I got off the bed and walked over to him. Crouching down before him, I took hold of his arm when he was about to step back. It was healed fully, the edge a smooth stump. No kid should have fucking gone through this... *I swear... when I find that fucker, I will kill him slowly...*

"This might just piss you off, but what you did for Kataleya, I won't forget it, and neither will she. No matter whatever the fuck the future brings, just remember that the Lycan King owes you."

I wanted to fix it, but I couldn't give him false hopes as I had nothing to fucking go on. He looked into my eyes, and I knew he didn't believe me.

"There is no future."

ꝘꞒꝹꝒ

"What you did tonight... thank you," Kiara whispered, wrapping her arms around my neck.

Pizza and movie time was over, and the kids were all tucked into bed.

"I questioned him, too," I remarked.

"I was outside. You did it nicely. Thank you, my sexy beast." She tugged me down, claiming my lips in a passionate kiss.

Well, as long as I got to fucking kiss her senseless or fuck her brains out, I didn't need to explain shit. If she was happy, that was all I fucking needed. I squeezed her ass and kissed her back.

Throughout the evening, Kataleya's eyes had been fixed on the pup, but he had refused to acknowledge her. That fucking pissed me off, but I couldn't blame him either.

"I'll try not to be too long," I whispered huskily when we broke apart, trying not to focus on how hard my dick had gotten.

"I'll be waiting," she replied, her gaze dipping to my package. Biting her lip and leaning up, she placed those hands of hers on my shoulders and stuck her tongue out, flicking my ear sensually and making me growl. My eyes flashed before she laughed and pulled away. "See you later, my love."

Blowing me a kiss, she walked off up the stairs, giving me a good view of her ass in that tiny dress of hers. As much as I wanted to fuck her right then, I needed to head to this meeting.

It was twenty minutes later, and my Beta, Deltas, and I were all seated around the table, including my head warrior, Carmen, Rayhan, and Maria. There were also a few of my other pack members, all of whom were in top positions in my pack. We had just gone over everything again, including what Kenneth had told us, the images, and everything else we managed to dig up. Liam hadn't managed to find much at the burned-down country house, but there had been blueprints of our pack, something I was not fucking pleased about.

"Raihana said we teleported the boy here from under 300 miles, that could be in any direction although she thinks it's north. I need someone to fly to Puerto Rico. We need to see what we can find from there," I said, tapping the island on the map.

My phone beeped, and I picked it up, knowing it was from Kia, but realising it was a voice message with a message underneath it, I didn't click on it and read the message.

'That message isnt something important but listen to it when you have a moment alone, tomorrow will do. Now get back to the meeting.' I smirked, texting her a quick reply.

'I will, and I'll see you soon.'

"I'll go," Maria spoke suddenly, making my eyes snap towards her.
"You? No."

"I'm not asking you, Alejandro, I'm stating it. I have a way with people, whether you believe that or not. Besides, with the correct magic, I can appear as an ordinary human who is going on holiday. I will find out what I can. You need people you can trust and who will blend in. I'm that person."

"It's dangerous, Mom," Rayhan added.

"Ya hayati... right now, everywhere is dangerous. The Alpha isn't in Puerto Rico, so I will be alright." Rayhan frowned, and I massaged my temples.

"I can go with Ms Maria," Carmen offered.

"And I'll take my guards. I think you need your men here, Alejandro," Maria replied firmly.

"I could go, too," Darien added. Darien was of Alpha blood, and I knew he was stronger than many Alphas out there.

I glanced at Maria. What the fuck was with the women of my family... but this was Maria. She needed something to keep busy. She needed to know we still needed her because I knew the moment she felt she was no longer vital to our lives, she'd let herself go...

Rayhan frowned, and I knew they were mind-linking. By the way his frown was deepening, his eyes flashing green constantly, I knew he wasn't impressed.

If it was Kiara, I wouldn't want her to go... just being away from her and worrying about her. Things were different with Maria, and as much as I wanted to keep her protected, she needed this.

"If Rayhan's cool with it, I'm fine with it," I said finally, still feeling hesitant. Rayhan's blazing green eyes snapped towards me, and he clenched his jaw.

"Mom is not going. I think the women of my family have suffered enough. I'm not risking another." With that he stood up and stormed out, leaving me feeling like fucking crap.

Our family. They were my family, too... but he wasn't wrong either. He was holding his shit together, despite the state his mate was in... I didn't mean to send Maria just like that... *Fuck this.*

"I'll talk to him." Maria arose from her seat gracefully, giving the table a small nod, her face as passive as ever. Everyone remained silent, the sound of her heels echoing in the room as she left.

I ran my hand through my hair. I didn't address the shit that just went down. We went on to the next state of matters and planned some scouting to see if we could find any new leads. A good three hours later, we decided to call it a night, and I headed back home. Maria had sent a text saying she would be going, that she talked to Rayhan, and he understood. I fucking hoped she wasn't going against him.

I would make sure she had some protection. I did not want shit to go down or anything to happen to her. She needed this. If I didn't see her deteriorating before my eyes, I wouldn't have agreed. I would talk to Rayhan tomorrow.

I returned home and entered my bedroom to see Kiara was fast asleep already. I smirked wryly. I took too fucking long...

I walked over to her, the duvet was pulled up to her chest, showing off the tip of her lacy bodysuit, and I slowly pulled the blanket back, drinking up her sexy-as-hell body. She was so fuckable right then, and I throbbed hard in my pants.

I stopped, staring at her pussy clad in that tiny piece of lace and looked into her content, peaceful face. She hadn't slept so easily for a while... I wasn't going to disturb her. She needed all the fucking rest she could get.

Silently, I entered the bathroom and decided to wash up. Not to mention, get rid of my fucking hard-on before calling it a night myself.

Was He a God

KIARA

I FELT SO COMFORTABLE SNUGGLED against the hard, firm body next to me. A deep, seductive scent filled my nose, and I inhaled deeply. A strong pair of arms were wrapped around me tightly, and, to my utter surprise, one hand was firmly on my ass, his fingers between my cheeks, making my face heat up. My eyes flew open, and I found myself staring at a tattooed chest.

Fuck, fuck, fuck! What happened? How did I get here?

Slowly, I pried his arms off me, trying to ignore the tingles that coursed through me and the way my body seemed to enjoy his touch, and moved back. The lamps were on, but I could see the sun rising outside. I stared at the man lying there, and my breath caught in my throat.

He was, simply put, a complete and utter sex god. From his tanned skin, refined jaw and black hair to the tattoos that covered his entire body, save some parts of his abs. He was hot as fuck. His nipples were pierced; his chest rose and fell deeply as he slept. For a moment, I didn't think I minded if he had his hands on me again...

He was ht as hell. He was built with muscles and ridges that any man would die for, right down to his bulging biceps, to his abs, and that V...

He wore a pair of sweatpants, and I almost gasped, noticing the long rod in his pants. Goddess.

Did we fuck? Maybe. I was sure I would be feeling it if we had... I looked down at myself, realising I was wearing a lacy black bodysuit. I slipped out of bed, my heart hammering. Where were my clothes?

"Kiara?"

A deep, husky, dangerously sexy voice came from behind me, making me jump as I spun around to see the god had risen. He was sitting up, and I found myself staring into a pair of dark, dangerous eyes, eyes that seemed to peer into my soul. My heart raced even faster when I saw his gaze rake over me, his eyes flashing red and making me nervous. I could tell from his aura he was someone strong. Dad was going to kill me.

"Hi," I said, inching away. He frowned, watching me warily as he got out of bed.

"Kiara, are you alright?"

How the hell does this god know my name? Did I die? Am I in heaven? Am I dreaming? No, I don't think so... Did I get drunk last night?

He was inching towards me. He was tall... maybe a foot taller than me... or more... I backed away slowly, raising my hand.

"Can you talk from a little away?" I said, my voice sounding shriller than it was meant to.

"Amore Mio..." He seemed serious and concerned, watching me sharply.

"I don't know how I ended up here... but I should go. Um, where are my clothes?" I asked, realising I was practically naked and flaunting my assets in front of this god.

"Go?" His face seemed to pale slightly. His heart was thudding, and I tensed, ready to jump if he tried anything funny.

"Home?" I replied softly.

"Kia... do you recognise me?" He asked, his voice so quiet and strained that it confused me. He sounded like he was in pain...

"Nope... should I?" I replied, backing away until my back hit the wall. "If we, uh, met at a party or something... then, I'm sorry, I should really get going. My dad will kill me." I scanned the room, assessing if the window or the door would be better. I glanced back at the handsome god, who seemed frozen despite the heaving of his chest.

"Do you remember anything?" *Why does he keep asking me that?*

"Excuse me? About last night? Nothing.... um, can I go now?" I asked in a hurry. I was sure if I'd had sex with that thing, I would have felt it. Goddess, it looked big...

"I think you should sit down; we need to talk."

"No thanks, I'd rather go home," I repeated.

"Kiara, this is your home."

"No, it isn't." What did he want? Was he trying to keep me here?

"It is. If you have any doubts, you can take a look at the pictures around this room or on our phones. You'll see there are plenty of photographs of us together. That ring on your finger? We're married, Amore Mio."

I glanced at my finger; indeed, I was wearing two rings. No, that wasn't possible, though...

This was a trick; I didn't need to see any pictures. I nodded, glancing at the phones he had gestured to. *Walk past him, then bolt for the doors...*

My heart thundered as I slowly edged past him, acting as if I was about to go for the phone, and instead, I darted towards the door. Before I even reached it, he was in front of me, his eyes blazing red. A rumbling growl reverberated through his chest and before I even realised what was happening, he had me on my back on the bed, straddling my hips.

"Let go of me!" I shouted, my heart pounding when I felt an intense surge of sparks ripple through me, sending pleasure straight to my core.

"Calm the fuck down. Listen to me, Amore Mio. We need to talk. You're my fucking mate. You know I'm not lying," he growled.

I stared up at him. I couldn't deny the pain in his eyes that he was trying to hide, the concern that was enveloping him, and the sparks of his touch. But how? How was this possible? I didn't remember him or anything. The last thing I remembered was... *What is the last thing I remember?*

I shook my head, trying to push away the throbbing headache that was beginning to form. I knew he wasn't lying. I could sense that...

"I don't know you. Get off me," I said quietly as he slowly got off of me but refused to let go of my wrists. He knelt down in front of me on the ground, pulling me upright until I was sitting on the bed instead of lying down.

I was terrified. What did this mean? What kind of trick was this? Was I dreaming? I needed to call Mom or Dad. Or Liam... surely, they must have been worried about me...

He caressed my wrists, and I felt a surge of fear rush through me. He was dangerous... I could sense the power from him. I was about to pull away, but to my surprise, he raised my hands to his lips and placed a chaste kiss on my knuckles before looking up into my eyes.

"Do you remember anything?" He asked quietly. I was not going to sit there, naked, and tell a stranger what I remembered or not, whatever he meant by that.

"Just what I needed to remember," I replied, pulling free and covering myself with my arms. "Can I get some clothes?" His heart was racing. I suddenly felt fear... and then it was gone. I shivered for a moment. It felt like it had been my emotion ... but it hadn't been. Strange.

"Okay... let me grab you something to wear," he said quietly.

He raised his hand to my face, and I moved back, turning my face away. I didn't know this man, and I was not happy with him trying to get into my personal space. He didn't say anything else, standing up and walking off through the archway. I looked down at my thighs, realising I had a garter belt tattoo around one thigh. I didn't remember that either... what on earth was going on?

As much as I wanted to run for the door, I didn't even get to ponder over it before he returned with a black t-shirt in his hand. Seriously? Did he bring me one of his shirts?

"Where are my clothes?"

"In your wardrobe, but I thought this was easier to grab," he said. His eyes looked hard, and his voice was dangerous and cold. Deep down, something told me he wasn't an enemy... my wolf wasn't panicked. Surely that was a sign?

I took the shirt and pulled it on quickly, watching him warily as he picked up the two phones from the bedside drawer. He unlocked the first and held it out.

"That's your phone," he said quietly.

If you say so. I didn't recognise it. I looked down at the image on the screen wallpaper, frowning slightly. It was of me and the god. His arms were around my waist, one hand on my breast, his nose buried in my neck as I smiled for the selfie. What the...

I began scrolling. There were lots, some with some young women I didn't recognise... I even looked a little older in these images. Did I somehow jump into the future? Was that possible?

My head began throbbing. Each picture I looked at made my mind reel. There were too many for me to think they were fake. There was even an image of Dad and the guy in front of me, although it looked like whoever took the picture did it sneakily... I stopped scrolling, staring at an image of me, the god, and three children. My heart thundered as I stared at it...

This looked...

"Our kids. Our son, Dante, Skyla is the one with black hair, and mini-you, Kataleya," his deep voice explained.

My ears rang with his voice, a sudden squeezing pressure wrapping around my head. This… this wasn't possible. What was going on? The ringing only grew louder, and I gripped my head. Why did it feel like the truth, but it didn't add up?

"Kia… Kia, baby look at me…"

His voice was distant, and suddenly I felt a surge of emotions the moment his hands gripped my arms. I looked up into his eyes, my vision blurring as tears threatened to fall.

I didn't know him. I didn't know how to digest his words, and above all, I couldn't remember much.

"I want to talk to my dad or mom. Now."

A flicker of hurt flashed in his eyes, but it was gone as fast as it had come and he nodded.

"I'll call them. Can I ask for one favour?" He asked quietly.

"What is it?" I asked, shuffling away from him on the bed.

"Our son is currently sick. Our youngest daughter, Kataleya, was kidnapped. Around the time you found her, that's when they did something to your memory, but I'm not trying to justify anything. I just… at least treat them as your own. You've always loved everyone… but I don't think Kat could cope if she knew you have forgotten her."

My heart clenched at his words. Our son? It sounded foreign, but a child who was sick? I nodded. He didn't need to ask that of me. I wouldn't do anything to harm a child in any way.

I pulled my legs to my chin, wrapping my arms around them as I sat there, trying to comprehend what was going on. After a moment, I looked up sharply.

"Wait, if we're from the same pack, we should be able to mind-link," I said suddenly.

We sure fucking can, his reply came into my head, making my heart thump.

Unless he forcefully marked me… But that didn't explain why I couldn't remember anything much. I needed Mom or Dad…

"Call my parents. I want to talk to them," I whispered. I couldn't remember anyone but my family…

He took the phone from my hand, his hand brushing mine, and a surge of sparks rippled up my. I jerked away. Our eyes met but he didn't say anything, and instead dialled a number. If he really wasn't a kidnapper or something, Dad or Mom would pick up the call.

"Hello?" My heart leapt when I heard Dad's voice, and I jumped from the bed, snatching the phone from his hand.

"Dad!"

"Kia, are you alright?" He sounded sleepy. I guess it was still quite early.

"Dad, please come get me," I whispered, my heart thundering as I felt the god's energy fill the room.

"Kia, what happened?" Dad sounded concerned and fully alert.

"I don't remember what I'm doing here... do you know where I am?" I asked him.

Silence.

"Fuck... Kia, it's alright. Alejandro won't hurt you. You had an injury and you hurt your head. I'll be there in an hour's time, okay? Just relax."

"But, Dad, I don't know him," I whispered, knowing he could hear me.

"He's your mate, and I assure you he cares for you. Just hold on for me, I'm coming."

My mate? Why was Dad saying the same thing? Was it really the truth? Nothing made sense.

"Okay... please come soon."

"I will, don't worry, princess... can you pass the phone to Alejandro?"

Alejandro... The god, or should I call him Alejandro, was watching me, his face cold and unreadable as I slowly held the phone out. *He's my mate...*

"I'll be there soon. We'll figure this out..." I heard Dad say.

Alejandro didn't reply before hanging up. He tossed the phone onto the bed as he advanced towards me. I moved away, making him stop, his eyes blazing red with anger.

"You're mine. I'll fucking tear this world apart until I find the one responsible for fucking with your mind and make sure this shit is fixed," his cold, threatening voice promised. He reached out for me, and I flinched, making him pause.

He clenched his jaw before looking away. I couldn't remember him, but I could tell beyond that calm, cold exterior there was a man who was in pain and raging with immeasurable anger...

Not Letting Her Go

ALEJANDRO

*C*RUSHING, AGONISING PAIN. THAT was how it fucking felt. I hated to admit it, but I felt like I couldn't breathe. She was my fucking world, but she had forgotten me. Deep down, I had hoped she wouldn't forget me, but she had. Fuck, she had.

From the corner of my eyes, I could see the way she was hugging herself, her eyes watching me warily. Had she forgotten my touch? Nine years… nine years of being together and she had forgotten it all.

The anger and hatred I felt for this so-called fucking Crimson King and his Djinn was growing. I was ready to pay the price to kill them both as long as it didn't affect my queen. She stood by the window, her heart racing, my shirt draping off her shoulder. Amore Mio…

Focus, Alejandro.

I was trying, fucking trying to keep myself in control but the urge to go on a fucking rampage was growing.

"You're bleeding," she said softly making me snap out of my thoughts. I looked down realising blood was spilling onto the floor where I had dug my claws into my palms.

"It'll heal," I replied, my voice sounding cold but seeing her flinch hurt fucking more. I had a feeling she had forgotten her abilities, too…

"Is this your pack?" She asked looking out of the window.

"Yeah, it's our pack," I corrected. "The Night Walkers Pack."

"Night Walkers…. isn't that the name of the Lycan King's pack?" She asked thoughtfully. My heart thudded. So there were things she still remembered.

"Yeah, you're fucking looking at him," I remarked, crossing my arms as I walked over to her. Instinctively, she stepped back until her ass touched the wall behind her.

"You're the Lycan King?" She looked confused, and I raised an eyebrow.

"Yeah, I fucking am," I replied.

Would she remember me if I kissed her? I wasn't sure, but I was not going to fucking risk it and end up pushing her away. No matter how much I wanted to express my love to her and show her that she was my fucking lifeline, I couldn't. Not until she was ready...

Raihana hadn't been able to pick anything up, so whatever this was... it should be able to be undone by killing the Djinn.

"I'm going to use the bathroom..." she said, smoothly moving away from me.

"Through there."

I jerked my head towards the dressing room and bathroom, and she all but ran. I heard her shut and bolt the door, something she would never usually do, leaving me alone in our bedroom. I looked at the ground feeling tiredness settle over me. Life...

I walked over to the bed, dropping onto it, and picked up my phone. I stared at the image on my lock screen... me, Kiara and the kids. I unlocked it and stared at my wallpaper. Her and I... the smile that lit up her face... fuck.

I swallowed, clicked on her number, and skimmed through the messages.

'Love you more.... Can't fucking wait to see you when I'm back... Want me to make you brownies tonight?... One hundred fucking percent, do I get to smear them over your tits and lick them off?... I like the idea...'

I kept scrolling, each one making the pain in my chest grow. How did it come to this? I frowned, remembering her voice message from last night. I scrolled down until I reached it and clicked on it.

"Alejandro... I know I can say this in person, but I just wanted to tell you... I love you; I will always love you... no matter what." Her voice became a whisper, and I could tell she was fighting back her tears. "I thought I'd message, instead, because tonight we might get a little busy and I... I might forget to tell you... I love you; I love you, Alejandro. No matter what the future holds, you're mine and I'm yours."

The message ended and I closed my eyes, hanging my head. This was a fucking nightmare... a fucking nightmare that I wasn't able to wake up from...

What did the fucker want? Did he not give a fuck that his son was here? Was this all a fucking game? What was he waiting for?

Two hours later, I was pacing the hall. Elijah had shown up, having run in wolf form, and Kiara had been fucking ecstatic to see him. In a way, I was glad she remembered someone, at least someone who could guide her, but it still fucking killed me that she had forgotten me. I was half of her soul… so why had she forgotten me?

She had been uncomfortable with me in the room, so I had stepped out. They were in our bedroom, still talking. Although I was out here, I could still pick up what they were discussing despite the soundproof walls. I guess having far better hearing than the rest was fucking ideal. Some of her questions made my heart fucking clench though.

"How long have I and Alejandro been together?"

"How did we meet?"

"I'm scared."

Elijah had explained everything that happened with this fucking Crimson King, and, from what I could tell, even showed her some videos of our wedding and shit. For the last half an hour she had been asking about the children, their favourite foods, their likes, dislikes, personalities… it was obvious she was going to give it her all for them. You could take away her memories, but you could not fucking take away her personality, good heart, or what she believed in. I hoped deep down… the memory of her love for us all remained…

Because I fucking felt empty…

"What about Alejandro? He seems… cold," Kiara's hesitant soft voice asked.

Had I been cold? Didn't fucking mean to. What the fuck was I meant to do? Be gentle? I didn't even know the meaning of that shit. I couldn't act like a fucking pussy now, could I?

Elijah chuckled.

"Coming from you that's a first. His cold exterior has never bothered you."

"So this was our wedding…" I heard the faint music as she replayed the video. "We look happy…"

I stopped pacing, leaning against the wall near the door as I lit a cigarette.

"You two are happy together and I'm positive that things will return to you," Elijah's firm reply came. "Your memory may have gone, but you are still the woman that I'm proud to call my daughter. The Lycan King's queen and the best of mothers. I would love to take you home to give you time to heal but the kids need you, Alejandro needs you here. Just follow your heart, Kiara, and I'm sure you'll be okay."

"Yeah… I can't believe I'm twenty-six… I was somehow imagining myself so much younger." She laughed, sounding embarrassed. "When I woke up, I was thinking you would kill me."

"Nine years too late. He's sixteen years older than you, imagine how I felt when I found out you and he were mated when you were only eighteen…"

She giggled and I couldn't resist the twitch at the corner of my lips. Elijah was right; she could forget me, but not the bond or the love that remained subconsciously. So, all I had to do was win her over. It wasn't that fucking hard the first time, and that time I tried to push her away. This time I wasn't going to let her go, no matter what.

With renewed resolve, I took a long drag on my cigarette. Call it corny or shit, but what we had between us was far too strong for any power in the heavens or earth to destroy, and I was ready to prove that to the fucking world.

❧❧❧

It was a few hours later, and Kiara had asked Elijah to stay for a while longer. He agreed and said as long as he didn't have to see the dickhead, Kenneth, whilst he was there. Well, we were on the same fucking page. I had gotten Darien to entertain the fucker because I was done with that dickhead.

I had gotten ready, waiting for Kiara to come out of the dressing room. When she did, she was dressed in a black strapless corset and some wet-look pants with heels. Her hair was open, and her face was free of makeup. For a moment, she reminded me of the young woman I had met at the Blood Moon Pack.

She was still wary of me. All I wanted to do was pull her close and kiss her until she fucking begged me to take her. Instead, I had to be the fucking gentlemen, and so I tried not to stare at her boobs all pushed up in that corset and swallowed instead.

Down boy.

"Let's get going," I said, sounding as cold as ever.

Yeah, I couldn't do nice, but it didn't matter. She'd fall for me because this was what she fucking fell in love with. She was no fucking angel, so we were going to be fine. We had to be.

She nodded, strands of her sandy brown hair falling in front of her eyes, I shoved my hands into my pockets although all I wanted was to reach out and brush them back. We entered the lounge where Rayhan, Delsanra, and Dante were having breakfast already.

"Dante," Kiara murmured. Dante looked at her sharply as Kiara inched forward before she crouched down before him. Reaching over hesitantly, she cupped his face.

"It's okay, Mom… you don't need to pretend," he said quietly, making me glance up. Rayhan and Delsanra turned too as Kiara shook her head.

"I'm not pretending," she whispered, sounding genuinely upset before wrapping her arms around him tightly. He hugged her back, his eyes trained on me.

"Your memory…" he mumbled.

"I'm sorry," Kiara whispered, moving back as she took his hands, kissing them gently.

"Don't be. It's not in your control."

Rayhan looked at me with concern in his eyes, and I remembered I still needed to talk to him about Maria.

"Kiara, Alejandro, are you eating in the lounge or dining room?" Maria asked from behind.

"Dining room is fine," I said, wrapping my arm around her shoulders and kissing her forehead.

"Yes, I'm watching television, can I not be disturbed?" Dante remarked.

"I don't think I've watched this much TV since I first had the leisure to," Delsanra added, looking up at Rayhan with a smile on her lips. He kissed her passionately before smirking slightly.

"Yeah, I guess there's a lot more we prefer to do in our free time," he whispered, although we all heard.

"We don't want to know," Dante retorted with a small pout as Maria smiled.

"Go eat," Maria told the two of us, and Kiara slowly stood up before smiling at Rayhan and Delsanra. We left the room and she looked at me.

"The man with the long hair, he looks a little like you."

"He fucking doesn't," I growled. She blinked but didn't speak, and I sighed. "He's my brother's kid. Maria. The woman at the door is his mom," I explained.

Don't go comparing that fucker to me, why the fuck did she think that? I knew it was just my ego and the memory of that one night that didn't want me to be compared to him. Even if there were some similarities, which I doubted, I didn't want my woman pointing that shit out.

"You don't like him?" She asked curiously. I gave her a cold glare.

"Nah, we're cool." She didn't speak after that, and I felt fucking guilty. *I swear, this is fucking rough.* We entered the dining room, and Kataleya smiled seeing us.

"Mama, look! We having pancakes," Skyla said, stabbing a pancake viciously.

"Oh, they look lovely," Kiara said, walking over to her and giving her a peck on the forehead. "Hey, Kat." Kataleya smiled. Kiara gave her a hug and kiss before taking a seat next to her.

"Good morning, Mama, good morning, Daddy," Kataleya greeted, smiling at us both.

"Morning angel," I said, ruffling their hair before I sat down opposite my three girls.

"Mama, I put Nutella on my pancake and Skyla had maple syrup," Kat explained quietly.

"Oh, they look so yummy," Kiara smiled, looking much more relaxed than she did when we were alone.

"I love syrup. Shall I tell you what syrup is made out of?" Skyla smirked, her green eyes glinting, and I knew for a fact that whatever she was going to say was going to be fucking twisted.

"Sure, enlighten us," I said, taking a gulp of my coffee.

"It's the blood of aliens," she whispered loudly, holding a square of pancake up and letting the maple drip onto her plate.

"Eeee!" Kataleya shuddered, giggling a little.

"I think it's more like melted gold," Kiara added. Skyla shook her head.

"No, no, it's blood," she said in a hushed sinister voice. The kid was fucking psychotic but guess so was I. Kiara smiled, and our eyes met. Her heart skipped a beat before she looked away.

Yeah, it still hurt like a bitch.

❧❧❧

A short while later, Elijah was about to leave. Kiara was in the living room playing a game of monopoly with Del, Maria, and the kids. I had filled Maria in about Kiara's situation along with Darien and Serena.

"What's the issue between you and Ken-fucking-Arden?" I asked glancing at the dickhead. Elijah frowned.

"It doesn't matter."

"I want to know," I said as Rayhan tilted his head looking at us.

We were all standing near the car Elijah would drive back. Darien had been the one to bring the car. He, too, remained silent, watching Elijah. We all wanted to know, and Elijah's reaction was only making me more intrigued.

"It's in the past," Elijah replied, irritation clear in his tone.

"Not if you can't get over it," I remarked, smoking my cigarette as Elijah got into the driver's seat of the Range Rover. I had lost count of how many cigarettes I'd been through since morning. Elijah gave me a scathing glare as he shoved his hands into his pockets.

"No."

"The fucker tried to get me to agree to tie my girls with his fuckers. In a fucking alliance. I don't need him or that fucking alliance, not sure what the fuck he considers himself. So, for him to have the fucking cheek makes me wonder what he did to piss the shit out of you," I growled, my hand on the car door. Elijah's eyes flashed, and he shook his head before exhaling.

"That's crazy…" he sighed. "You're fucking pushy."

"I fucking know." I retorted knowing I had won.

"I don't know if you remember, but I once saved Raf's life…"

A silence fell over us as both Rayhan and I nodded. Raf had mentioned it many times but never told the story behind it. I never asked because I was never fucking interested.

"It was thanks to that fucking dickhead that he almost died."

A Grudge

ALEJANDRO

M Y EYES WIDENED IN shock; I wasn't expecting that.

"Was it an accident?" Rayhan asked, his eyes burning green.

Elijah scoffed, "Accidents are forgivable. I'm not discussing this out here."

"Then we'll get in the fucking car. I want to know," I growled. That fucker hurt Raf, and I actually dined with him? Hell fucking no.

"Yeah, sounds like a plan," Rayhan added, his voice dangerously low. I knew he was angry but was trying to remain calm, ever the perfect one. I walked around and got into the front whilst the other two got in the back. "Dad said it was a training accident or something." Rayhan mused.

"I heard a few different stories, but never fucking bothered about some fucker's heroic tactics," I remarked mockingly as Elijah scowled.

"Well, the Shadow Wolves Pack are powerful yet private. Rumour has it they excel in experiments and such. Healing remedies, poisons, energy vials."

"We all know that shit, it's baseless research and they ain't gotten far. We had some dealings with them, there's nothing special," I remarked, taking a drag on my cigarette.

"Oh, they definitely got farther than we think. You may not know, but Kenneth has a lot of links abroad. Not only will his mate's pack become his, but he has several research labs here and abroad." I knew that.

"Yeah, I don't get what this shit has got to do with Raf and you being a blue-eyed dick-faced hero?" I hated when people took time to get to the damn point.

"Can you ever keep that fucking mouth shut and listen? Or shall I drive off?" Elijah replied, smirking coldly. My eyes flashed as Darien sighed.

"Can we hear the story? If anyone sees the four of us sitting in a car they will be damn confused."

"We were on a camping break after our exams. When it came to tactical and strategy, there were three of us who were chosen to go forward for the annual recognition award." He smiled humourlessly, looking into the distance, and I wondered what he was thinking. "Me, Arden, and Rafael. Ultimately, Rafael took the award. Unlike me, who was happy with being known for my combat skills, Arden had an issue… one he didn't forget."

"What did he do?" I asked coldly. "Cut to it."

"He gave Rafael a drink, told him to drink to his victory. Not even a few minutes after he drank it, he began convulsing and bleeding from his mouth, nose, and ears. There were only a few of us, but no one seemed to move. I remember making him puke it up and cutting him in several places to bleed it out. Grandma Amelia taught me that. She said a wolf can die of poison, but we won't die from heavy blood loss. It slowed it down and I managed to get him back to camp as he bled out. We found that the drink had contained a high level of silver and wolfsbane, and it was so strong it could have killed him, if I hadn't done what I did."

"Didn't Dad smell it, that it contained something?" Rayhan asked.

"Strangely no. The rest of it was spilt and there was no proof, but even when I smelled the remnant of it, I didn't pick up on anything either," Elijah replied.

"And if that's the case, why is he still a fucking Alpha?" I growled.

"It was my word against the other seven. Arden was adamant he didn't know how it was poisoned and said perhaps someone was trying to poison him. Rafael said he had a drink, but he didn't want it to cause trouble with other packs. He was a young Alpha with no father behind him and the Arden's had a lot of influence, so Raf told me to drop it. He made me promise to drop it, although we both knew that bastard was behind it," Elijah sighed.

"I don't get it; didn't they even look into it?" Darien asked as I sat back, taking in what he had said. I hated that man a thousand fucking times more.

"They did. There was no proof, but I'm sure with their research they could have made very concentrated pills or something to transport with ease. Either way, Rafael and I knew what happened, but the Shadow

Wolves Pack is one of the richest packs in the country and, unlike the Rossis, whose wealth may be higher, the Shadow Wolves Pack has ties to allies across the borders. They may not be the pack of the Lycan King, but they do hold power. Rafael was a peacemaker and said let it be when that fucker apologised, saying to forgive him if he had done anything wrong, but he stuck by his word that he didn't poison the drink…" Elijah scoffed bitterly. "I swear, if Rafael didn't make me promise to keep my mouth shut about it, I'd have fucking destroyed him."

"So, he basically got away with attempted murder? Because Rafael had no one…"

"Yeah. At the time he wasn't mated to Maria, so he didn't even have the support of her pack. I told him my dad would help but he refused. So, I've told you, now I don't want to talk about that bastard again," Elijah said coldly.

"And now you're going to say to honour Raf, I can't fucking do shit?" I growled.

"Yeah, but kick him off your pack grounds," he replied.

Yeah… I would… and although Elijah made a promise to Raf, I didn't. The moment I found some dirt on this fucker, I was going to fucking destroy him. I just needed some proof.

⚴⚬⚴

Elijah had left, and Rayhan and I had gone for training as I knew Kiara needed some space. She got all tense around me and seemed to enjoy spending time with the kids and women.

Maria had told her about her healing, and she had used it on Delsanra. I knew Kiara's healing was the only thing keeping her able to stay upright. The spitfire I knew was weakening, and we needed to move fast.

I had told Kiara about Enrique because I knew she'd want me to tell her, and as expected, she had brought him down to join the family. Although he sat silently ignoring everyone.

It was late in the afternoon, and Rayhan, Darien, and I were in my office. There had been a lead up north, and we were hoping for some answers. The fucker still didn't seem to give a shit about his son.

"Is Tia down?" I asked Darien, as I knew his daughter was meant to come. She had found her mate in a neighbouring pack not long back.

"Yes, she and Serena are catching up. She isn't here for long," Darien remarked. I nodded.

"Then you should go spend some time with her." He looked surprised.

"You sure?"

"Do I fucking look unsure?"

"Alright, I'll go." He nodded, closing the file he was looking at.

Life was short and family was important. Although at one point I never thought I'd say that shit...

Once he left, I looked at Rayhan, who was making some marks on one of the maps, frowning in concentration as he scanned some images. When we had some clues, both of us were meant to go. We were both excellent trackers... but with the state Delsanra was in, and if shit got worse, I couldn't let him. It had to be me. When the time came, I wasn't going to let him risk his life. If something happened to me... he needed to be here.

"Maria said you were okay with her going?" I asked, taking out a cigarette. He paused, his brows furrowing as he looked at me.

"She didn't really give me an option," he replied icily.

"I know it's not what you want... but she's a Rossi."

"We aren't invincible," he replied with a bitter smile.

Yeah, I know... Raf, Kiara, Del... they were all proof of that...

"She'll be safe. I'm sending my best with her. Plus she'll be spelled to appear human. They all will."

"There's always a risk, Uncle. I've lost Dad already. I don't want to lose Mom," he said quietly, trying to mask the pain from his voice. He was a strong fucker, I'd give him that.

"I know, but imagine being told you can't fucking do anything. It's driving her crazy. She needs this," I said quietly. I didn't want to say I was seeing her spiralling... I hoped it wasn't true, I fucking did, but I had seen the signs many times.

He didn't reply for a moment before he nodded.

"Neither of you will listen to me, so I'm not having this conversation," he said curtly, his eyes flashing green when he looked at me. I took a long drag on my cigarette.

"I'm sorry for all the shit you're going through. I'm going to fix this. I promise," I replied, standing up. He nodded, looking down at the map once more, his hair curtaining his face.

"We will."

"Yeah."

No. I would.

Because he was right, no one was fucking invincible, and I was going to protect my family with everything I had until my last fucking breath.

⁓⊙⊙⁓

KATALEYA

He didn't even look at me. It was all my fault. His papa hurt him because of me and now he hated me, too…

I didn't want to cry, but it hurt inside. He was sitting there just staring at the TV, but I knew he wasn't watching. He was angry.

"Kataleya, are you alright?" Mama asked me. She smiled at me, I tried to smile back and nodded.

"Go play with Sky, Kat…" Dante said coldly. He was angry at me, too. I didn't know what I did wrong to upset him.

"Dante, be gentle," Mama scolded gently before she came over and put her arm around me.

"I'm okay," I whispered, forcing a smile.

"Queen Luna, may I go to my room?" Enrique asked Mama suddenly. He wanted to go already? He didn't talk unless someone talked to him…

"Yes, of course," Mama smiled.

"I'll take you," Aunty Mari offered.

He stood up silently. I hoped he'd turn and look at me, but he didn't. Not even once…

"Don't bother trying." Dante's angry voice came. I blinked and looked at him.

"Dante…" Delsanra said gently, shaking her head at him.

"No. She needs to realise he is the enemy."

"He isn't," I said feeling sad and upset. Why didn't Dante get it? Enrique wasn't bad.

"Dante, please," Mama murmured.

"Heed my warning, Kat, stay away from him. Remember, he is not a friend."

"Stop it! Stop saying that! Enrique hasn't done anything for you to hate him! Stop being nasty!" I cried, jumping up from Mama's hold. Tears filled my eyes as I stared at Dante.

"Dante, don't. Please, for me," Delsanra said weakly.

"She's going to do something stupid and regret it. Trust me. I don't trust him," Dante shot back; his red eyes full of anger.

I didn't understand why he hated Enrique, why Daddy had Enrique watched like a prisoner. Enrique didn't do anything wrong. What Daddy and his papa were doing to him was wrong!

"Baby, don't cry," Mama whispered, trying to hug me, but I pulled away.

"I hate you!" I cried at Dante, casting him a final glance before I ran from the room.

I didn't like being mean, but Dante was making me sad. I felt miserable inside. I was always scared, and I knew Mama wasn't well. Dante wasn't well either, and I was horrible for being mean to him, too.

"Kat!" Mama called.

I ran faster. I wanted to hide. I needed to get away. Turning a corner, I quickly hid behind one of the large vases, wrapping my arms around my knees as I breathed steadily. I didn't want anyone to find me…

"Kataleya…"

I jumped to see Mama kneeling on the ground in front of me. How did she find me? I looked down, realising she must have seen my dress. I broke into tears, feeling awful for behaving like that, but she simply pulled me into her arms and hugged me tightly.

"Things are going to be okay. I promise" she whispered as I cried into her chest.

"I'm sad, Mama, it's hurting here," I sobbed, patting my heart.

"Oh, baby, I'm so sorry," Mama whispered. There were tears in her eyes, too.

She held me tightly, rocking me as we sat on the floor in the hallway. The beating of her heart and her smell soothed me. We stayed sitting there until I heard Daddy approach. I kept my eyes closed. I didn't want to talk to anyone…

"Why are my girls sitting on the floor out here?" Daddy's deep voice asked.

"She had a small argument with Dante," Mama replied, kissing my forehead. Daddy sighed, and I heard him bend down. He kissed my forehead, his beard tickling me.

"It's going to be alright," he promised.

I wanted to believe him. I wanted to hope that everything was going to be okay. I wanted Dante to be okay, I wanted Enrique to be okay... Mama to be okay... I wanted the bad man to go away... Delsanra to be okay...

"Promise?" I whispered, opening my eyes. Daddy smiled, his dark eyes glittering, and he nodded.

"I fucking promise," he said, making Mama gasp for some reason. I simply smiled and nodded.

My daddy never broke a promise.

Night Time Ride

KIARA

*A*LEJANDRO HAD SAID HE would put Kataleya to bed, and I had agreed. It was strange to explain, but when I saw those children, I didn't need a DNA test or anything to tell me they were mine. I felt it. Which would also mean the king was my mate, right?

That one was a little harder. I could hug children and make them feel better, but a man who looked as dangerous as he did handsome was an entirely different story. I wouldn't deny that his every glance made me feel all giddy, but at the same time, I was wary of him.

I took a shower before I rummaged in the drawers. The clothes were all my size and this place smelled of me. I sighed. I knew it all pointed to their words being the truth, but it was still odd. Mom had called earlier, and I had ended up talking to her on video call for nearly an hour. She had tried to ease my mind, but the terrifying reality was that I only had their word to go on. Raven, Liam's mate and my apparent friend, had called, too. It was hard knowing I had forgotten everything. It was strange. I felt tired by the end of the day.

Everyone was trying to help, giving me small tips and reminders, but each thing I was told made the reality that I had forgotten most of my life sink deeper and deeper into me. Would I ever recover my memories? Was what they said really true?

I put on a black thong and some black loungewear before I brushed my hair. I heard the bedroom door open, and I froze, my heart thundering. Wait, were we going to share a room? All day I hadn't been anywhere alone with him. Although his eyes were on me whenever he was around, this was the first time we were completely alone again.

I placed the hairbrush down and slowly edged towards the bedroom. Peering inside, I froze, realising he was taking his shirt off. My eyes widened as my gaze fell on his abs and I became distracted. That was until he tossed his shirt to the side, brushing the long hair on top of his head back.

"Like what you see?" He asked with an arrogant smirk on that sexy face of his. I crossed my arms.

"I'm sure you already know the answer to that, considering we were mates." His eyes flashed red, a deep frown crossing his face.

"We *are* mates. That doesn't fucking change."

My heart thudded, and I nodded, suddenly feeling cold. He sighed and was about to approach me when I quickly walked over to the bed, but before I even got there, he grabbed my elbow, spinning me around to face him.

"What do you want?" I asked, trying to calm my emotions.

"I didn't mean to scare you."

"I don't get scared," I replied defensively, pulling away slowly.

"I just don't like you talking about us in fucking past tense. You may have forgotten me, but you're mine, Amore Mio, and if I have to fucking win you over all over again, then I'm ready for that shit."

He didn't need to tell me that. I could see it in his eyes, that he wouldn't let me go. I didn't know if that should terrify me or make me as lightheaded as I felt. Unable to come up with a comeback, I simply stared at him. His eyes dipped to my lips, his hand threading into my wet locks as he leaned forward. My heart thumped, and for a moment I thought he was about to kiss me only for his lips to touch my forehead.

"You're my fucking world," he whispered, his large hand cupping my face as he stared into my eyes. A wave of guilt washed over me. If it was all true, how could I have forgotten him? I slowly stepped away and turned my back to him.

"Good night," I said, feeling as if I had failed in something.

"Night," answered his deep reply.

I walked over to the bed and got in. I might have forgotten everything, but I felt a deep sense of disappointment in myself. I could sense his pain even though he was trying to block it off. I closed my eyes, hoping to sleep before he came back, but that didn't happen. He was back pretty quickly, his intoxicating scent filling my nose. My heart skipped a beat when I felt the bed dip as he got in on the other side.

"Relax. I won't do anything unless you want me to," his deep, rough voice promised, laced with a mocking tone. My eyes flew open when his hand landed on my hip and he kissed my shoulder from behind, sending a thrill of pleasure through me.

Unless I wanted him to…

My cheeks burned at the very thought. It was weird knowing he knew things about me that I seemed to have forgotten. It all made sense, but deep down, there was a sliver of doubt that maybe, just maybe, something else was at work. I couldn't just blindly trust their words. I had to tread carefully…

❧❧

"My Queen…"

I frowned, looking around the dark hallway of what looked like a stone castle.

"Who's there?" I called out, my voice echoing.

"Your king." My heart skipped a beat as I turned, trying to look into the darkness.

"King?"

Alejandro?

It didn't sound like him…

"I'll find you, I promise. Don't trust them," his whispered voice came before I was suddenly plunged into darkness. A shriek left my lips as I felt myself falling at a terrifyingly fast pace.

"Help!" I screamed.

"I'll find you," the voice promised again.

"Kiara!"

I felt a sharp slap on my face. My eyes flew open, and I found myself staring into two red glowing orbs.

Why was it dark? I couldn't see anything! Why was it dark?

I pushed him away, my aura raging around me as I jumped from the bed.

Why couldn't I see?

"Kiara, calm down. It's me," Alejandro's deep voice came before the lights came on.

"Why couldn't I see?" I whispered, fear and panic beginning to surge within me.

"You can't see in the dark, Kiara. You were born like that. A price for your gift of healing," he said, walking towards me.

The words from my dream returned to me. *"Don't trust them."* I stepped back, nodding.

"Isn't that one of the first things you should have told me?" I asked quietly. He didn't move towards me as if worried I would run away. I had half a mind to.

"I'm sorry; it's something that we're so used to, and the mansion is equipped to be bathed in light. I didn't think to remind you. Come to bed." I shook my head, running my fingers through my hair.

"I'm not really tired. I'll just take a seat on the couch."

He closed the gap between us, reaching for me. I tensed, but he only ran his fingers through my hair. The sparks of his touch along my head soothed my thumping heart. I just needed space; the room felt too tight.

"Are you okay? You screamed."

"Yeah, perfectly, I just need air."

"Want to go for a ride?" He asked softly, making me look up at him.

"Uhh…" I glanced around the large room; the car would be tight, too… "I just need some air…"

"I have a bike," he said with a small sexy smirk. I nodded after a moment, knowing he wouldn't give up. "Then give me a minute. I'll go get dressed," he said, walking off.

I looked around, thinking about my dream. It had felt so real…

"Here." Alejandro's voice came as he held out a jacket and heeled boots to me.

"Thanks…"

I took them from him, slipping them on as I watched him pull on his own leather jacket. His shirt rode up a little, showing off the band of his boxers and his sexy back. I looked away quickly.

"Come on. We haven't done this in a while."

He held his hand out to me, but I looked away, following him to the bedroom door. I gave him a small smile, not wanting to appear rude, but I wasn't just going to hold his hand.

Ten minutes later, we were sitting on a gorgeous black motorbike with red accents. I may not know the make or anything about bikes, but I knew this one was a beast even before it roared to life.

"Hold on, Amore Mio," he said, looking at me over his shoulder.

I nodded, slowly wrapping my arms around his strong waist. My core knotted, and I resisted the urge to run my hand over his abs. I held on tight as we rode out of the garage and down the path.

I stared at the sky. It was pitch black, and as we left the light of the pack living area, I was enveloped by darkness. My only source of light was that of the moon shining through the trees. I clung to him, knowing that if he wanted, he could just drop me in the middle of nowhere or kill me.

Everything I had been told yesterday, from Dad, Mom… Alejandro… the children I spent time with, the way they all treated me… wasn't it too perfect? I didn't know… the dream was odd. Maybe I was just being paranoid.

I inhaled the smell of the leather mixed with his seductive masculine scent, and I closed my eyes, enjoying the wind that rushed through my hair. After a good while, I felt we were travelling a little slower and I opened my eyes, realising we were in a city. The streetlights glittered and I looked around, unable to see much despite the dim lighting, but I could still make out some things as we passed.

"Want something hot or cold?"

"Hmm?" I asked, looking at the back of his neck and noticing his tattoos disappeared into his hair. I felt a little hot with my arms around him like this…

"Ice cream? Beer? Pizza or some shit?" Why did that all sound good…

"Ice cream," I decided after a moment. It was a little hot being so close to him so something cold was better.

"Perfect."

We drove for a few more minutes before we stopped outside a brightly lit dessert shop. He parked up and got off the bike with ease, his long legs catching my attention. I had to admit he was really hot everywhere…

I gasped when he lifted me off the bike, his hands on my waist, and our eyes met for a moment. I gave a small smile, looking away. He let go of me, and I let out a breath I didn't even know I was holding as we walked to the shop entrance. He took my hand as he pushed open the door, and my heart skipped a beat as I stared at our combined hands.

"Hey, what can I get you guys?" The man behind the counter asked, looking cheerful despite the late hour in his pink and white striped shirt.

"Anything in specific or want me to order?" He asked me.

"You order," I said. If I liked it, it meant he knew me as he said.

"We'll get two of the ice cream roll pots, one in Oreo Blast the other in Nutty Dream. Weird fucking names."

The man chuckled nervously, and I could tell he looked a bit scared of Alejandro. I didn't blame him. Even though he was masking his aura, he still had a very powerful energy around him.

"Ah, yes… anything else aside from that?"

"Nah."

The man got to work, and I watched with interest as he began to create the ice cream rolls. So fascinating. Once he was done, he sprinkled some Oreo biscuits on top before starting on the second one and drizzled some melted chocolate on top. Alejandro took out his wallet, and I frowned, seeing a picture of me in it. I only caught a glimpse as it was at an angle, and he flipped it shut, sliding his wallet back into his pocket.

Hmm… he didn't even open it in a way for me to see it… maybe I was being paranoid.

He picked up the pots and we stepped back into the cool night. Passing me the Oreo pot, he took my hand as we walked back over to the bike.

"Thank you," I said, tugging my hand free from his and slowly began eating. It was so yummy. I glanced at his pot. So he liked nuts….

"Hazelnut chocolate. You smell just like it but better," he smirked. My eyes widened in surprise.

"I don't think I smell like chocolate." I sniffed my jacket, and he smirked.

"Trust me, Amore Mio, you do. Hazelnut chocolate had always been my favourite until you came into my life. Want to try?" He held his spoon out to me, and I tasted it slowly. It was nice, but I preferred the Oreo. "Fucking small spoons." I smirked.

"Don't you complain about everything?" I asked before realising what I said.

"Maybe." Our eyes met, my heart racing under the intensity of the emotions in his eyes. "Guess you're the only one who can put up with me.

You came into my life and fucking turned it upside down. Not only did you become my favourite dessert you also became my all… you are and always will be the only one I will love." I swallowed, my stomach a mess of nerves at his words.

"I…" He placed the back of his finger against my lips.

"You don't need to say shit. I waited years for you to find me…. I can wait for however long I need to, as long as, in the end, you return to me," he said quietly. The emotions in his husky voice made my heart thunder.

"Alejandro…"

I didn't know what to say. He wasn't lying, I felt like I could sense that. His emotions were so intense that I couldn't breathe properly, but he was right. I didn't need to say anything, so instead, I simply raised my cup of ice cream.

"Thank you."

A small smirk crossed his lips, and he nodded as we stood there, gazing into each other's eyes, and something told me that maybe, just maybe, things would be okay…

For Him

ALEJANDRO

*S*HE HAD RELAXED, I could sense that much as she ate her ice cream, licking her spoon slowly as if savouring every little drop. Her eyelids fluttered shut and I leaned against my bike, tugging her gently by her hips in front of me. Her heart hammered as her eyes flew open, staring down at me.

"I won't bite, Amore Mio." I leaned over, brushing a strand of her hair aside.

Unless, of course, you fucking want me to, then I'm ready to mark every inch of this divine body and make you fucking see stars.

She nodded, giving me a small hesitant smile. She was the most beautiful woman I had ever laid eyes on, from her unique blue-green eyes to her plump lips... my fucking goddess...

"Is it... does it hurt that I've forgotten you?" She asked quietly. She was watching me sharply despite asking that, and I wondered what was going through her mind. I smirked,

"I won't lie, because you can fucking tell if I do, right?" She nodded, and I placed my empty cup down on the bike next to me and caressed her hips. "Yeah, it does, a whole fucking lot, because the thing is, you are my fucking lifeline, the light that kept me focused. My reason to live and my reason to be the best I fucking can be."

Her cheeks turned a gorgeous hue of pink as she nodded, her gaze falling to my neck before she looked up at me, her eyes sharp as if a sudden thought came to her.

"We are mated and marked?" I nodded.

"I'm sure these sparks are proof of that," I whispered huskily, slipping my hands under her top and caressing her smooth skin. The sparks between us surged through us, and her breath hitched.

"So, how did we first meet?" She asked me, her heart pounding as she placed her hand on my shoulder. I knew her enough to know the effect I was having on her. This was going to be pretty fucking simple. All I needed to do was take advantage of the attraction she felt towards me.

"The story isn't pretty. Let's just say first we fucked. I still remember that day in my office. Since the first time I saw you, there was just something about you... you felt the same, and one thing led to another..." The urge to kiss her right then was getting the better of me, so I broke our eye contact. She let out a breathy laugh, and I smirked.

"That actually sounds believable. Even if I couldn't sense if you're telling the truth, it sounds like something that could happen between us," she said, turning and tossing her ice cream pot in the trash can not far from the bike. She smiled when it went right in.

"Yeah?" I asked.

"Yeah..." Her eyes dipped to my lips before she looked away, seeming to be very aware of our position.

"What is it? Want me to fuck you all over again?"

"No! I meant, I just..."

"You know, Amore Mio, if you want me to revive that memory, I'd be more than willing," I added huskily, yanking her close, her chest against mine. Her heart was pounding wildly as she stared into my eyes.

"No thanks... so, umm, what happened next?" She asked, trying to change the topic.

"I tried to push you away. I knew you were too fucking good for me. I was in a dark place and didn't think anyone needed that shit in their life, but you remained stubborn. I chose someone else to be my Luna... but when it came to marking her, I couldn't do it. All I could think of was the fact that I wanted my nympho, even if it was selfish of me. The rest is history. Found out I had put a fucking pup in you, too." I placed my hand on her stomach, and, fuck, it took my all not to kiss her. I didn't sugarcoat shit because there was no point in lying or hiding it. I hated what I did back then, but we got passed it.

"You sure are to the point," she replied, amused.

"Yeah, I am."

"I kinda like it." She whispered hesitatingly.

"Yeah?"

Yes, but don't let it get to your head, she replied through the mind link, rolling her eyes.

"Now, let's go home. I want to sleep." As much as I would have preferred to just talk to her all night long, I knew I had to take this at her pace.

"Sure thing."

I moved back on the bike, tossing my pot in the trash can and flipping my leg over before I motioned for her to get on in front of me.

"A little keen to have your arms around me?" She replied, and I smirked. She may have forgotten most of her memories, but she hadn't lost that spark.

"No. I rather have you bouncing on my dick if we're being honest."

And that is how it's played.

She blushed, and I motioned for her to get on. It felt good to have her in front of me. I inhaled her scent before revving the engine and driving towards home.

"Alejandro…"

"Yeah?"

She leaned back, but I could sense her unease. She may know certain things, like mind-linking, but she didn't know how to block her emotions off, and I was not about to point that shit out, either.

"I had a dream."

"A dream?" I asked, the wind rushing through my hair as I looked ahead, frowning deeply. Did she mean today? Is that why she panicked, and I had to give her a slight slap to wake her?

"Tonight… I was in a castle. It was dark, but I knew it was some sort of stone castle, and someone called me. He said, 'my queen'. I asked who was there, and he replied, 'your king', but it wasn't you. It didn't sound like you."

My heart rate quickened, and a thought crossed my mind, was that fucker somehow getting into her head?

"Anything else?"

"He said he'll find me and not to trust anyone… and I know that I can't get my head around everything, but I can't deny that we have a connection." As much as that made me smirk cockily, now was not the fucking time. This was not fucking good.

"I won't lie to you. No matter how fucking hard this shit is, I won't. Don't trust him. It's probably the one responsible for your memory loss."

"I thought that too. It made me doubtful… but after what Dad and you both told me about this Crimson King… I didn't want to just stay quiet about it."

"Smart move. We can't trust him, and from what I know, to break this curse on Dante and Delsanra, we need to find him."

"How can I help?" She asked, her voice full of sadness and concern.

"Just take care of yourself, and if anything else weird happens, make sure to tell me."

"I will… I promise."

"I'm liking that one ice cream bought your trust pretty fast, huh," I teased, nudging her shoulders. She smiled slightly, glancing up at me.

"Don't get too cocky. It was not the ice cream."

"Then what was it? My fucking charm?"

"As much as I find you rather… appealing, no. It was your honesty," she said. "Thank you for not treating me like something fragile or broken."

"You've never been fucking fragile or broken. Trust me, I know." I winked at her, and she turned away, her eyes wide and her heart thudding.

Neither of us spoke, a comfortable silence falling between us, and when I bent down to kiss her neck, she didn't jerk away. A soft gasp escaped those plush lips of hers, her heartbeat picking up, and she simply turned her face away.

Yeah, that's my girl.

ENRIQUE

They had installed cameras in my room. I wasn't stupid. But I planned to use them to my advantage. I had pretended to be asleep and set the bed to look like I was sleeping when the guards changed spots. It was risky because if they had a recording, they could turn it back and see what I had done, but as long as I got to do what I needed to do, then I didn't mind what they did to me. At least I could make Padre happy.

I had been pressed against the outside of the window, making sure to stay against the wall when the patrol passed. I stood there for long enough that I knew the exact timing. There were two standing at the bottom, but they took a ten-minute break twice every night. I had my window open, so my heartbeat was the same as if I was in the room. *Now I just need them to go…*

"Let's go grab some coffee, bro," one of them murmured.

"Yeah."

They walked off, and I quickly looked to the adjoining balcony. I had less than ten minutes. I needed to get to the Lycan's son's room. Padre wanted him. *I'll make him proud.*

I stepped back, ready to jump, and broke into a run, flipping in the air for leverage and grabbing onto the wall of the balcony next to mine. I winced, wishing I had my right hand; it was always my better one. I struggled, pulling myself over the ledge and looked at the window. I had to be careful about passing the next window because it was in use. The Lycan prince's room was the one after.

I glanced at my pocket, where I had my weapon ready. I had broken a mirror earlier today but pretended I was just angry and upset. I took the chance to hide a piece, and that piece would kill the Lycan's son.

I jumped onto the other balcony, praying no one heard me, but the windows were shut. The next room was my destination, and even if I had to break the window, it was okay as long as I killed him in time. My heart was thumping, the fear of being caught and failing Padre growing with each passing moment, but there was something else too…

The chica's face.

I didn't understand her. She kept defending me, kept worrying for me. It must be because she knew I had lost my hand because of her. Well, it wasn't worth it. She was just a spoiled princess who didn't understand anything about life. She made me angry.

I kept down and, with ease, climbed onto the small balcony outside his room. To my surprise, his balcony doors were wide open. I frowned, peering inside. There he was, sleeping on the large bed, his heartbeat steady. The lights were off, but the star ceiling above his head moved peacefully. I slowly padded into the room, taking my weapon out.

Plunge it into his heart and then tear it out.

It was simple. Just like padre had taught me.

Kill or be killed.

My heart was thundering, and I wondered if the boy in the bed would feel it. If I made it fast, it wouldn't hurt, right? He was young, but he already had such a strong aura…

I raised the piece of glass, clutching it so tightly that it cut into my hand.

Do it, Enrique.

Only a coward would attack someone who was sleeping…

No. Padre said it didn't matter… But then why, deep down, did it feel wrong?

Kill him and make Padre happy…

"Do it."

My eyes flew wide open, and I found myself staring into a pair of deep red ones…

My Actions

ENRIQUE

"*D*O IT," DANTE REPEATED. "What are you waiting for? Kill me. That's why you are here, aren't you? I even left the window open for you."

He wasn't afraid or even alarmed. He was simply watching me calculatingly. How did he know that?

"You knew I was going to come?" I asked sharply. How?

"This isn't what I saw, though…" he murmured, a flicker of curiosity in his eyes. He closed his eyes, and I frowned. Wasn't he going to shout for help? "Kill me and get it over with. My parents are out as it is. Now is your best chance," he added arrogantly.

My anger flared through me as he turned onto his side, his back to me. I raised the piece of glass, but once again, the image of the chica's face filled my mind. *If I kill him… she'll…* Her tear-filled eyes flashed in my head, and I stared at the glass.

What the Queen Luna and the Lycan King themselves said… the fact that they didn't need to keep me here in their home. They didn't need to treat me nicely, but they did. If the Lycan wanted, he could have beaten me as Padre beat the chica.

I looked at the prince, no… the boy before me. I then looked at my right arm, staring at the place where my hand should have been. That wasn't love. That extreme punishment was wrong…

I watched how they treated their children here. How the Lycan treated his Queen. The Lycan… maybe he was telling the truth… perhaps he didn't know what the debt was or why Padre was angry. Even I didn't know the reason. Padre just wanted revenge… maybe Padre was wrong.

"I'm getting bored, are you going to kill me or not?" The annoying boy asked, sitting up. The veins on his body looked painful, and his skin looked pale despite how confident and defiant his eyes were.

I felt a surge of hatred for him. He and the chica, they had a life of luxury. He would grow up and become the Alpha he was born to be… and me… I stared at my bloody hand that still clutched the shard of glass and then at my other arm. I would be useless…

"By now, you should know your father is responsible for causing you pain. No one but him," the boy on the bed stated.

"Aren't you scared that I could kill you? You are currently very weak." He smirked.

"I won't die. You made that clear the moment you hesitated… why did you hesitate?"

He watched me curiously. He knew I was going to come here. What powers did he hold? There was something about the boy on the bed. His aura in itself was immense, like an Alpha's… but how was it possible he hadn't even shifted?

"You seem to be all-knowing," I retorted coldly. He raised an eyebrow.

"Not all-knowing…" He looked out of the open balcony, staring at the sky. "Was it because of Kataleya?" I frowned.

"No!" How dare he think I hesitated over a girl. I felt my irritation growing, feeling embarrassed.

"I hear you lost your hand for giving her food."

"What are you, my interrogator?" I glared at him.

"I thought we were having a conversation, future Alpha to future Alpha," he remarked, leaning back against his cushions and crossing his arms. I didn't understand him… I didn't understand his calmness or his words. Why was he so calm?

"Alpha. I'm not worthy of being Alpha anymore," I spat, holding up my right arm. He smirked.

"You're right, but it's not your missing hand that is at fault. It's your attitude. You better fix how you think and become a better person, or I will never allow it to happen."

"Allow what?"

"Fate," he muttered, closing his eyes. "Now, go. I'm tired, thanks to your dad."

"What do you mean, fate?" Why wasn't he answering me properly?

He opened his eyes, and for a moment, it felt like I was looking at someone who was a lot older than me.

"The future isn't set in stone... tonight you shifted it."

This boy was annoying, but his words remained in my head. Become better, the future wasn't set in stone... for some reason, I felt like I had a sliver of hope. I turned away, ready to leave the room, when he called me.

"Oh, and one more thing."

"What?" I glared at him.

"When she came home, she was worried about you. She kept that ripped piece of fabric by her side and begged everyone to find and protect you from your father. Don't be so mean to her." I felt my cheeks burn with embarrassment. What a silly chica. That was so awkward! What would everyone be thinking?

"I don't want to talk to her," I scoffed. "She needs to stay away from me." He simply chuckled, much to my annoyance. I stormed to the door when he turned sharply.

"Where are you going?"

"Yes, you are right. It's clear you are not all-knowing," I replied mockingly and left the room, slamming the door behind me.

I wanted to see what they would do to me. In a flash, there were two guards before me.

"The boy's escaped!" One of them shouted, and just like that, the Lycan's nephew, Rayhan, came out of his room, his eyes flashing green. One glance at the bloody glass in my hand, and he rushed into the room behind me. One of the guards disarmed me in a flash, pinning me to the wall.

"What did you do?" He growled as the other one followed Rayhan into the prince's room.

"What's going on?" The Lycan's cold voice asked.

I turned to see him and the Queen Luna coming up the stairs. My heart began racing, no matter how calm I tried to act. *Now we'll see what they do. Their true colours.*

His eyes flashed when he saw the glass in my hand and was that fear in his eyes? The Queen Luna paled as she hurried past us to check up on their precious son.

"Dante, are you okay?" The queen whispered, worry clear in her voice.

"Yes, perfectly fine. May I sleep now?" His haughty reply came. I frowned as the king muttered something in relief from the doorway.

"You've done it, kid," The guard muttered, his face pale.

"Scared you didn't do your job properly?" I scoffed fearlessly. What was the most they would do? Hurt me? I didn't care. Padre had done much worse. I was used to it.

"Watch it," he growled.

"Go question him. I'm tired, I want to rest."

"You really are a little prince," the queen's relieved voice came.

The Lycan King stepped in front of me. His face was unreadable, his eyes sharp as he stared at my bloody hand.

"How the fuck did you get in there?" I raised an eyebrow.

"I've done far more complicated things with broken bones. What is one balcony away?" I replied rudely. *Go on, show me your true colours...*

The queen and Rayhan stepped out of the room and shut the door behind them.

"Let's take this somewhere else," the Queen suggested softly.

"I'll head back," Rayhan replied with a nod before casting me a final glance and returning to his room.

To my surprise, the Queen put her hand on my shoulder, and I felt the pain in my hand vanishing. I pulled away from her, confused. Why heal me?

"How about we go downstairs to the kitchen?" She suggested, motioning the guards away. The king smirked slightly.

"Still the queen you were born to be," he remarked as he led the way down the stairs.

Five minutes had passed, and the Queen Luna had put a glass of milk and some warm chocolate cake with ice cream in front of me as I sat there on the bar stool. How strange. I tried to kill her son, and she was giving me a treat? I wanted to think it was poisoned, but I knew her enough to know it wasn't. She was a strange one.

"Where's mine?" The king asked.

"You had ice cream already..."

"Well, since I can't have my favourite dessert, I need to settle for what I can get, and I still crave more dessert," he replied, his cold eyes fixed on her.

She smiled and, turning away, began to fix him a plate. I didn't touch mine, staying silent. What was going on?

"What were you trying to achieve?" He asked me suddenly.

"Padre wanted him, so I wanted to kill him. For Padre," I replied monotonously. Even to me, my reason sounded empty. Why did I want to do it for padre?

The queen turned, her eyes full of sadness and worry. *Yes, now you know that I'm not someone you should be worrying or caring about.*

"But you didn't do it," she said softly, coming over and placing the second plate in front of the king, who was leaning against the worktop. He ran his hand through her hair before picking up his spoon.

"Eat," he commanded. His powerful aura rolled off him, and I was forced to pick up my spoon. I didn't like being told what to do.

"I might have done it. I had every intention of doing it. So will you kill me now?" I asked, eating some of the cake. It was really tasty…

"Why would we kill you?" The Queen Luna asked.

She was very beautiful. Her large eyes seemed to contain so many emotions. No wonder the Lycan said she had helped him see the light. If Madre had treated Padre like this… or more like if Padre let Madre be by his side, would he have been different? I pushed the thoughts away angrily.

"For trying to kill your son?" I raised my eyebrow as if this was obvious.

"That was a shit move, kid," the Lycan added.

"So, kill me."

"You didn't kill him. You yourself hesitated. You did the right thing, and I'm proud of you." The Queen Luna smiled. "Why did you want to hurt him?"

"To do something for Padre… because…"

"Because he doesn't fucking need you anymore?" The king's cold voice asked. I looked up at him, trying to hide the pain inside of me.

It hurt.

I clenched my jaw and nodded, trying to act like I didn't care.

"You're the one who doesn't need that fucking bastard. Listen to me, kid, when I find him, I am going to rip him to fucking shreds. He's fucking abused all your damn life, and you think this shit is okay? It fucking ain't -"

"Alejandro…" The queen placed her hand on his shoulder.

I felt the anger, the sadness, and the pain in my chest. It was true. Padre wasn't fair… it wasn't fair at all.

He growled, slamming his fist on the table and denting the worktop, making me look up into his glowing red eyes.

"Listen to me, pup. You don't need to go back there. When I find him, I will be fucking ripping his throat out, but it's up to you if you want to return to your pack or not."

He wasn't lying… he was going to kill Padre… or Padre would kill him. One or the other had to die because it was clear neither would stop until the other was dead. But which one's death would ultimately be better? Padre, who always seemed to hurt people? Or the Lycan, who Padre said was a monster? Why did Padre seem like the monster? Was I being blinded, or was I seeing things properly?

"I will be going back, if you let me. Even if Padre is killed, the pack needs me."

Did they need me? I was useless. I stared at my stump, feeling bitter.

"Then, I think it's high fucking time we find his ass," the king replied coldly.

I knew where Padre might be… but should I tell them? I looked up, catching the queen's concern as she watched me. A small smile crossed her face, and for a moment, she reminded me of the chica.

At that moment, I made my decision. I thought it was time I told them, so I could get away from her and this family. I didn't like how they made me feel…

"I know a few names of locations where Padre has houses in the United Kingdom," I stated, placing my spoon down. "But in return for the information, I want something."

Rossis & Westwoods

ALEJANDRO

*E*NRIQUE HAD GIVEN US seventeen fucking locations. As shocked as I fucking was that the fucker knew that shit and we had to wait for him to tell us, I was grateful he told us of his own accord. I wasn't happy with his request...

Kiara had become silent, and I understood her concern. His words rang in my mind once again. I paused as I looked at my reflection, the conversation replaying in my mind.

"Fine, what do you want in return, pup?" I asked.

"I want you to let me go. I don't want your help, I don't want to have anything to do with you. I just want to return to my home," he said emotionlessly.

I heard the sharp intake from Kiara. She knew the shit that kid had gone through, we hadn't hidden anything from her, and I knew hearing him wanting to go back there... she would always worry about him.

"But... of course, you can go back there, but will you be okay? I mean, do you have family who can take care of you and protect you from your father?"

"Yes."

He's lying, he doesn't believe that, *her fearful voice came.*

It doesn't matter. He won't have a fucking father to fear when I'm done.

"Deal," I said out loud.

"Then, after I give you the location, I want you to let me go."

"Do you want us to take you somewhere?" Kiara asked him softly. He shook his head.

"No, Padre will think you let me go to lure him out. I will stay hidden for a bit and make my own way home."

"You're only a child." Kiara's voice was full of sadness.

Chances were his father would have considered that he knew the locations and may not even be there. It was obvious he didn't care for his son. I hadn't heard one fucking response from him.

"I know how to survive," he replied emotionlessly.

"Does your father know you're aware of these locations?"

"I don't think so. I used to try to learn as much as I could, so if he ever asked me anything, he'd be proud."

He's telling the truth.

Yeah? Well, the bastard had a son who seemed to want to make him proud, and he actually went and fucking amputated his hand. He's fucking psychotic.

I know, and it's heartbreaking. Our eyes met, and I reached over, giving her hand a small squeeze.

"Enrique, are you sure you want to go back? We can help –"

"No. I want to go far away from all of you. I hate being here. I want to return to where I belong," he cut Kiara off, the anger and pain in his eyes fucking clear.

"Fine. I'll make some provisions, and you can go." Kiara's eyes widened as she looked at me, clearly not happy with my agreement.

"And you promise not to send guards after me to watch me?"

"I promise," I said, and I meant it.

The pup had been fucked around all his life, and if he needed someone to show him that they believed in him, then I would do it. Even if he fucking thought it was because I didn't care, it didn't matter as long as he was happy. He was a survivor, and I knew that he'd make it.

"So when I tell you the locations, will you let me go straight away?" He repeated it as if he didn't believe that I had agreed.

"No. I need three days."

"Why?" Kiara looked at me curiously, too.

"Because I'm not setting you loose in England. You're from Puerto Rico, right? I'm having you flown there."

Both looked at me, surprised, before a ghost of a smile crossed the boy's lips, and he nodded.

"Deal."

I sleeked my hair back, put the comb down, and left the bathroom, only to see Kiara in the dressing room, slipping some sheer black tights on. Her back was to me, and my eyes fell on her ass clad in a thong. Fuck…

She tensed. I knew she could sense me watching her… but, fuck, did I want to bend her over and fuck her senseless.

"It's rude to stare," she said softly, not even turning as she picked up a hot pink cami, slipping it on over her bra. I was sure she was doing that on fucking purpose. If only she knew how much I loved that ass of hers…

I walked towards her, and just as she reached for her skirt, I gripped her hips. Her racing heart only fucking turned me on even more.

"Well, since I don't have any fucking manners anyway, can I just say I want to bend you over and fucking fill up both your ass and pussy, then watch my seed dripping out of you as you fucking lay there, unable to move from exhaustion?" I growled huskily, running my hand down her stomach.

She gasped, her heart pounding, but to my satisfaction, she leaned into me, a soft moan leaving her lips when she felt my dick hard against her back.

"Alejandro… we…"

I know. She was not fucking ready… but fuck did I need her.

I kissed her neck, right on top of her mate mark, as my hand cupped her perfect pussy, massaging it for a few seconds and making her moan softly. The smell of her arousal filled the air, and, feeling fucking satisfied at her reaction, I pulled away.

"See you downstairs," I remarked huskily with an arrogant smirk. I tapped her ass before I turned and left the dressing room, leaving her struggling with her emotions. I was sure sooner or later, memory or not, she'd want me. Just like I craved her, I was her fucking drug, too.

My smirk faded away, remembering that our enemy was powerful and there was always a price… I pushed the thought away.

❧❀☙

A while later, Liam had just arrived as we had some important things to deal with. Plus, he had wanted to see Kiara. Watching Kiara meet him was interesting, to say the least.

"You look so… different."

"Do I?" He grinned, raising an eyebrow.

"You have a scar… you look so big and older." She looked him up and down.

"Care to share what age you think I am?"

"I don't really know, just older." She smiled sheepishly before hugging him tightly. He hugged her back, kissing the top of her head. "So, tell me, what brings you here?" She asked.

"Well, I wanted to see my sister, but it's regarding work as well." He kissed her forehead, and she nodded, resting her head against his chest. I wouldn't deny that I felt a tad fucking jealous that she remembered him. Fucking Westwoods…

"Well, if you two are done with the fucking reunion and shit, shall we get to my office? Then you can spend the entire fucking afternoon together after." Kiara smiled, amused, and cocked a brow at me.

"Are you jealous?"

"No," I growled. She giggled.

You are.

I turned, walking down the hallway to my fucking office. *I am not doing this shit with her.* I heard them both laugh quietly as they followed me. Ten minutes later, Maria, Darien, and Rayhan were in my office as well.

"So… that was your plan?" Rayhan asked me, looking surprised. I raised an eyebrow.

"No, I was planning to send Maria abroad without any protection," I replied sarcastically. "I knew you couldn't go because of Delsanra. I fucking can't either. After the Rossis, I'm sure the Westwoods are the next best thing." Darien chuckled as both siblings glared at me, and Liam raised an eyebrow as Kiara pouted.

"That's not nice to say," she stated.

"I told you I'm not nice." I shrugged, looking at Liam.

He was probably the biggest Alpha in size and aura I knew after me, the closest thing to the original Deimos. A little like how my being a Lycan was fucking rare, he and Kiara were powerful, too.

"We Westwoods are powerful, too," Kiara replied as Maria smiled at her.

"Too bad you're a Rossi now."

"Oh…" She paused, realising what I had said, and I saw her glance at her ring.

"Well, Rossi or Westwood, we kinda just blend into one. Both are pretty capable, and I won't deny I feel a whole lot more relaxed knowing Mom will have Liam with her," Rayhan added, running his fingers through his hair.

"Not only Liam," I said with a smirk.

Maria was my brother's queen, and there was no fucking way I was about to risk her life. I heard the footsteps in the hallway and smirked, taking a cigarette and lighter. *Right on fucking time.*

Come in, I said, through the link.

"Then who else?" Rayhan asked, frowning slightly, just as the door opened, and everyone turned to look at the two men standing there.

"As I said, the Westwoods are the next best thing after the Rossis, so who else but a Rossi to go, too? Marcel, welcome," I smirked.

"Alejandro," Marcel said, giving everyone a small nod.

Sitting back, I lit my cigarette as everyone in the room looked at each other in surprise, but my attention was on both my nephews. Leo and Rayhan looked at each other, the hatred in Leo's eyes was unmasked, and the hostility between them was fucking obvious…

"Leo," Rayhan said, his eyes sharp, his voice level. I knew it had been ages since those two saw each other, and although Rayhan tried to get through to the younger boy, Leo had refused to allow him in, and with time Rayhan had backed off.

"Bastard." Came Leo's cold, arrogant reply. I frowned, taking a long drag on my cigarette. I may be one to revel in others' problems, but I didn't like that shit one bit. Not when it involved my own fucking nephews…

"Cut it out," I growled.

Leo raised an eyebrow, crossing his muscular arms over his chest. Dressed all in black, it only made his light blue eyes look even icier. He scanned the room, taking a drag on the cigarette in his hand, before turning his gaze on me. When he spoke, his voice dripped with sarcasm and pure, unfiltered hatred.

"Well, it sure is a fucking honour to be in a room full of the so-called elite. To what do I owe the fucking pleasure?"

Glitter & a Promise

RAYHAN

THE TENSION IN THE room grew to the point that it felt suffocating. I knew he hated how I handled things years ago, but like I'd said, I wouldn't do anything differently. All I could do in return was be patient with him.

I hadn't seen him in a while, and he looked older, bigger, and bulkier, but the hatred in those eyes of his only seemed to have grown. He held my gaze, and although I didn't submit, for the sake of peace, I broke our eye contact, turning back to Uncle Al. The rest greeted one another, and I gave Marcel a nod before glancing at uncle.

"So, Marcel and Liam will go with Mom?" I asked, crossing my arms.

"Yes, they will. They'll be leaving tomorrow morning."

Uncle sat forward, his eyes on Kiara, who was standing next to Liam a lot more comfortably than she had been around any of us lately. The entire situation messed everything up for us all. We just needed to have this all sorted out. It was fucking with me seeing Delsanra in that state...

"Now, Enrique has given us some locations. I'm planning on having all the ones up north tracked to see if we can find anything. This fucking dickhead doesn't seem to give a shit for the boy either, so that's a damn dead end," Uncle growled, frowning as he smoked his cigarette.

"I'll go," I said quietly. The closer we got to finding him, the closer we got to fixing everything. I heard a 'hmph' from Leo but ignored it.

"I wanted you to go. You are the best." Uncle nodded.

"But can we defeat him without knowing how to kill a Djinn?" Mom asked.

"We'll find that shit out, but we do need to find his location first, hence why I want it done on the low, so we can prepare."

"So why the fuck did you call me?" Leo asked as if he was bored just being there. I glanced at him. It was weird seeing him and Uncle together. It was almost like a mirror image with the cigarettes, the tattoos, piercings, and the coldness in their eyes. But they were different.

"I actually didn't think you would fucking come, but I wanted to see if you could hack into a certain system for me. You're pretty good when it comes to computers, right?" Uncle said with a smirk.

"I could do that if I want," Leo replied, taking a drag on his cigarette.

"Is that legal?" Kiara asked, her eyes wide as she stared at Uncle.

"Amore Mio, I don't think anything we do is really legal. Kidnapping a pup, killing people, the usual shit we do out here? We're supernatural beings. We don't fucking go by the damn law." He smirked arrogantly, and she nodded slowly as if she had just realised that now.

"That's true…"

"In your defence, you didn't want him to kidnap the boy," Liam added, wrapping his arms around her shoulders, making me smirk as Uncle glared at him.

"I didn't?" She actually sounded relieved.

"Didn't fucking matter, I was still going to do it," Uncle shot back, glaring at Liam. Loved the guy, but he did have a knack for putting his foot into things without meaning to. He gave Uncle a small sheepish smirk as he ran his hand through his hair.

"So, if that's sorted, shall we go through the details?" Mom asked, waving her hand. I knew the smoke was annoying her. She would probably go shower after this.

"That would be a good idea," Marcel added, stepping forward. Mom gave a small smile before looking back at Uncle. I knew she found it hard looking at Marcel, considering he looked almost identical to dad.

"Well, the main thing you lot need to do is gather intel and see what we learn by just being there. There has to be something about this fucking debt that will help us get the answers that this so-called king is refusing to fucking share…"

A while later, I entered our bedroom silently, not wanting to disturb Del in case she was asleep. My eyes fell on her. She hadn't realised I had entered, and it fucking tore at my heart to hear her whimper as she hugged her body, taking deep breaths to try to control the pain she tried to hide from me…

I walked to the bed, sat down, and scooped her into my lap. She gasped, tensing as she stared at me. Her tear-filled eyes only made the pain in my chest far worse. I knew she was trying to downplay how she felt for me and everyone else.

"It's going to get better," I whispered, brushing her hair back. It had lost its lustre.

I could tell she was in so much pain. She had lost weight. She was beginning to look a lot like she had when I first met her, and it brought back memories of the pain and suffering that she had experienced. I pressed my lips to hers deeply, trying my fucking best to be gentle despite the emotions that were coursing through me.

"I love you, Kitten. We are getting closer to fixing this," I whispered tenderly, placing another kiss on her forehead. The veins beneath her skin pulsed, and she nodded, her lips quivering. She pressed them together, nodding again as she curled into me, running her hand weakly down my chest.

"I love you, my yum yum." She smiled up at me weakly, and I smirked.

"Just the way it should be," I whispered as she threaded her fingers into my thick locks and gently pulled my forehead to hers.

She really was the sexiest, most beautiful woman to ever exist, and one that meant the fucking world to me. Goddess, was I lucky that she was mine.

KIARA

"Mama, is it true Enrique is leaving?" Kataleya asked, sadness and worry in her eyes.

"Oh, baby, who said that?" I scooped her into my arms.

I didn't know she knew that. I glanced at Liam, who was letting Skyla do face painting on him, or so he thought. She was doing a full face of make-up. I may have lost my memory, but in the short time I'd spent with her, I realised she was not to be trusted. Strangely, when she had asked him if she could do a Spiderman face painting on him, he agreed and sat on the floor… but he was currently turning out to look more like a clown with garish make-up.

I looked back at the girl in my lap, brushing my fingers through her hair. They were my children. No matter what else was true or not, I could feel it. I kissed her forehead softly.

"Tell me who told you that?" I repeated.

"Enrique said it this morning before he left the table at breakfast, that he's happy he's leaving in three days," she whispered. I looked into her worry-filled eyes and sighed.

"Yes, we are sending him somewhere safe though. He's going to be okay."

"But his papa will hurt him."

I could sense that she was getting really worked up. The pain in her eyes for the boy was breaking my heart. She had suffered, too, but she was still worried about another.

"We won't let his father hurt him anymore. I promise," I said confidently, and I meant it. She seemed a little at ease at that and nodded.

"Promise?"

"Pinkie promise," I vowed, raising my pinkie finger. She giggled as we sealed our pinkie promise.

"I trust Mama and Daddy."

"Uncle, stop scrunching your eye!" Skyla scolded.

"Princess, you poked me twice," he replied.

"Oh, don't be a baby, you're such a scaredy puppy!"

I felt sorry for him, but he seemed to be used to the treatment, trying not to flinch as Skyla dabbed bright purple to his lids and then added some glitter. My eyes widened as I realised it was nail polish!

"Skyla, that's not for eyes!" I exclaimed, startled.

"But it's more glittery," she responded, glancing at me.

"But it's not good for eyes," I repeated.

"He'll heal if it gets in his eyes. Don't worry, Mama," she reassured me with a sly smile. Well, if I had any doubt that Alejandro wasn't my mate, it was gone. She had the same wicked smile as her father.

Father… my stomach fluttered, remembering our moment earlier on. Goddess, he was a dangerous temptation…

"Glitter? But Spiderman has no glitter... what are you doing, Sky?" Liam asked, opening his eyes suspiciously.

"Just trust me." He wasn't going to fall for that, was he?

"Okay..."

He did. Wow.

Dante snickered, and I looked over to where he was sitting with Ahren, who was watching something on the tablet.

"Uncle, I would think you would have learned from living with Azura that you should not trust girls."

"I'm trusting you, Skyla. Go less on the glitter..." Liam warned, opening his eyes a little.

I felt sorry for him when he was going to have to remove that nail varnish from his eyes. Didn't he realise by the smell what it was, or wasn't he worried? My poor, simple brother.

"Uncle, you look pretty," Kataleya added before she patted my arm. "Mama... before Enrique leaves, will you ask him to talk to me? Please?"

My stomach twisted; I didn't miss how he seemed to get angry when he saw her or how he ignored her, and it broke my heart. I understood she wanted to see him, but would he just be hurtful to her? Looking into those dark eyes full of sadness, I knew I had to try. I cupped her face and nodded.

"Okay, my little angel, I will try," I promised, placing a soft kiss on her forehead.

"Can you ask him soon?" The need to talk to him, the desperation in her eyes, was so obvious that I nodded.

"Okay. I'll go ask him now."

"Thank you, Mama!"

The sound of crying came from the hallway. Sienna!

I stood up, rushing out, only to see the boy, Leo, or more like Mini-Alejandro, crouch down as he picked up the one-year-old who had tumbled over. It seemed all the Rossis were easily noticeable; they had their similarities.

"You should be watching her," he said coldly, glancing at Claire, who had hurried out of the playroom after the little girl.

"I'm so sorry."

"It's okay, Claire." I smiled gently, knowing she looked terrified. Leo looked at the little girl who watched him, her eyes wide with terror.

"Who is she?" He asked me, flicking a strand of her curls out of her face and raising his eyebrows questioningly at her, only making her lips quiver.

"She's my daughter."

Leo and I both turned, seeing Rayhan standing on the stairs. His eyes were sharp as he stared at his cousin…

His Hatred

KIARA

*L*EO'S EYES SEEMED TO turn even colder as he glanced at the girl in his arms.

"Your daughter…" A dangerous smirk crossed his face, making my heart race.

"Come here, Si," Rayhan came down the stairs, walking towards Leo, only for the younger man to step back and hold up a finger warningly.

"What's the rush? Scared I'll hurt her? I guess she is in my hold…"

"Leo." Rayhan's voice was menacing and cold, his eyes flashing green as he glared at his cousin in a clear warning. What was wrong with them? The thick tension in the air was scaring me. *What do I do?*

Suddenly, Leo threw the girl in the air, making me gasp. Although it was only a foot in the air, it was obvious he was trying to rile Rayhan up. Rayhan lunged to catch her, but Leo pushed him back, catching the girl, who burst into tears. It hadn't been a high throw, but it was obvious she was terrified and that Leo was taunting Rayhan.

Alejandro! We need you at the mansion! Now! I called through the link, unsure of what else to do.

"Bastard!" Rayhan hissed, grabbing his daughter from Leo's arms and shoving the younger man back roughly. "This is not a fucking joke!"

Coming. I was relieved Alejandro didn't question me and was coming. I heard footsteps behind me, only to see Liam, Kataleya, and Skyla approaching.

"Go inside, girls," I commanded, wondering if I should take the crying child from Rayhan as Leo laughed sadistically. Both girls hesitated before Skyla nodded and pulled Kataleya away.

"Don't worry. Unlike you, I don't target the innocent," Leo replied coldly, his laughter vanishing as he stared at Rayhan with pure hatred.

"Don't ever fucking think you can do that again. Touch my kids one more time, and I will fuckin-"

"And you will what? If you want to kill me, you need to do it now whilst I'm still wolf-less, 'cos once I shift..." He left his threat hanging, raising his arms as if inviting Rayhan to attack him.

Mustering my courage together, I hurried over, hoping Rayhan trusted me, and took the crying child from his arms. To my surprise, he let her go, and I stroked her hair, backing away from the two men.

"There, there, princess. It's going to be okay," I whispered, hurrying back to where Liam stood with a face full of make-up as he watched the two men sharply. Come to think of it, his eyes weren't the shade I remembered. Weren't they meant to be cerulean blue? Why were they that dark, magnetic blue? And that scar...

Just a fake. He isn't the real Liam, a voice whispered in my head, making my heart thunder as I pushed the terrifying thought away.

"Don't try me, Leo -"

The front door slammed open.

"What the fuck is going on?" Alejandro's cold voice asked, and I had never been more relieved to see him. He stood at the front door, his large frame filling it with his Beta, Darien, just behind him.

"Nothing at all," Leo smirked.

"Either he leaves from here, or I do. I'm not keeping my family here unless he's fucking gone." Rayhan's voice was calm, yet the anger in it sent a chill down my spine.

"What's this, making Alejandro choose between blood? Well, that's not a hard choice. Of course he'll choose the son of the oh-so-perfect Rafael Rossi," Leo taunted.

"What happened?" Alejandro repeated, his eyes simmering red as he ignored Leo's remark.

"Your favourite will fill you the fuck in whilst I'll make it easier for you and leave. You don't need to pretend to care," Leo replied, ignoring Alejandro.

I rocked the girl in my arm, relieved she had calmed down, her tiny heartbeat still rapid.

"Leo." Marcel's voice came from behind Alejandro and Darien.

"Come, Dad, grovel at their feet," Leo shot back before pushing past Alejandro roughly. "I won't be joining you."

I looked at Liam, who, if the situation hadn't been so dire, would have made me giggle. He looked concerned, and when I turned to Alejandro, I didn't miss the look of pain and torment in his eyes. The urge to go over to him almost took over, but what was I meant to say?

"How about we sit down and talk this shit out?" He suggested, turning to glance at his nephew, who was almost out the door.

"How about you deal with that?" Leo countered, cocking a brow towards the ceiling.

He turned, throwing something incredibly fast and aiming it at the lighting fixture on the ceiling. I saw the flash of silver, and I quickly turned my back, my every instinct telling me to protect the child in my arms just as the entire thing came crashing down with a huge clang, the glass shattering. I felt a surge of aura surround me and looked up to see Liam had raised some sort of blue force field, stopping any of the glass from touching me. Once again, that sliver of doubt flittered through me.

Was that Liam?

I looked around at the hall; the anger in Rayhan's eyes, the way Alejandro was frowning, the look on Marcel's face... the family had appeared so perfect... but it was clear it wasn't. Again, the terrifying doubt that it was all an illusion overcame me. I didn't realise I had stepped back until Alejandro called me.

"Amore Mio, are you okay?" My eyes snapped up to him, and I nodded. Just then, Rayhan came over, taking his daughter from me.

"Ray, a word?" Alejandro called after him as he made to go upstairs.

"Not right now," answered his quiet yet dangerous reply. Alejandro ran his hand through his hair and looked at Liam, sighing in frustration.

"The fuck you meant to be?" He asked, and I wasn't able to stop the giggle.

"Spiderman," Liam replied with a small sheepish smile.

"You mean Glitterman or some shit?" Alejandro raised an eyebrow whilst Darien hid a smirk.

"Yeah, Sky got a little carried away." Liam bunched his shirt up and began wiping his face, flinching when he saw the purple and pink makeup transferred onto it. Oh, if only he saw the nail polish… some was in his eyebrows, too. Alejandro shook his head.

"I will never get how the fuck you let these girls walk all over you."

"I think you do, too…" Darien remarked, earning a glare from Alejandro, who turned to Marcel.

"Don't let it bother you. They're just kids. They'll argue and shit all the time. Come on, I'll get Claire to bring us something to drink," he said, slapping his brother's shoulder.

"It's not a light matter, Alejandro. He must have done something to trigger Rayhan like that," Marcel mused gravely.

"Yeah…" Alejandro agreed.

All eyes turned on me, and I felt a rush of nervousness as Alejandro approached me, reminding me of a predator advancing on his prey…

"Care to share what exactly went down, Amore Mio?"

I looked at the other three men. Liam gave me a small encouraging smile. Pushing that niggling doubt regarding him away, I turned to Alejandro, taking a deep breath, ready to tell them what had happened.

❧

Later in the day, I finally managed to get a moment alone, and I was planning on speaking to Enrique as I had promised Kataleya. Alejandro's mood had darkened when he learned that Leo had taunted Rayhan by throwing his daughter up in the air, even though it was clear he had no intention of harming her. He had scared her and succeeded in riling Rayhan up.

Marcel had been apologetic, but Alejandro had told him not to blame himself. Maria had tried to smooth things over. I felt dreadful for saying what happened in front of him; I didn't know he'd feel so guilty. Rayhan had avoided everyone, and his mother said to give him some space.

My doubt had eased; I could sense when someone lied, and I had to remember Alejandro had not lied to me. Not once had he hidden anything from me, nor had I sensed him lying. I decided I would tell him about the voice I had heard in my head later.

I knocked on the door to Enrique's bedroom before opening it and stepping inside. The boy was standing by the window, his arms behind his back, head straight up and shoulders squared. My heart ached for him. When his hazel eyes met mine, all I could see was a child who had suffered so much.

"Hey," I said, smiling softly as I entered, leaving the door slightly ajar.

"Can I help you, Queen Luna?" He asked, his voice sounding dead. Must he leave? Couldn't I keep him and take care of him? He needed to be loved and nurtured. I smiled, not wanting him to notice how I was feeling, knowing he hated pity.

"I have actually come with a request today," I explained gently, taking a seat at the edge of the bed. He waited for me to speak. I looked up at him. "It's about Kataleya." Instantly a frown flashed on his face.

"What now?"

"Before you leave, will you talk to her?" His anger seemed to rise, and he turned away from me, his heart beating fast as he glared out of the window.

"No. I never want to see her or speak to her ever again."

"Please? Enrique, she really just wants to speak to you, just once?" I pleaded.

"Will you force me to speak to her?" He asked icily. I shook my head.

"No, but I'm begging you, as a mother. Please, just speak to her once. You won't see each other again. Do you think you could find it inside of you to fulfil her one wish?" I whispered, joining my hands together in front of me. A sudden, overwhelming sense of Deja Vu filled me, and I brushed it away.

"I hate her," he hissed. "If she comes before me, I won't be nice to her, so it's your choice." I felt a sharp pang of pain, but I nodded. I couldn't force him to.

"Okay… could you at least be patient with her?" I asked gently.

"I can't promise anything. The chica should realise we are not friends. I don't even want to see her. She's just a useless chica, one who annoys me!"

Luna, Princess Kataleya, is outside. My heart thudded as I closed my eyes. I hadn't sensed her…

Okay…

"Okay. I will let her make the decision," I replied, defeated, standing up. "Thank you."

I left the room, shutting the door after me just in time to see her little head of sandy brown hair vanish around the corner. I closed my eyes, leaning against the wall, not even noticing the guards who stood there. The only thought in my head was that she had heard his every word… knowing that it only broke her pure little heart a little more.

A Goodbye

KATALEYA

I RAN DOWN THE STAIRS quickly before Mama caught me listening, my tears spilling down my cheeks. Why did Enrique hate me so much? Was it because his papa took his hand off because of me?

I clamped my hand over my mouth, rounding the corner as I stifled a sob, only to knock into Daddy and almost fall back. I got to my feet, ready to run away when he caught hold of my arms and knelt down in front of me.

"What's wrong, princess?"

I shook my head, flinging my arms around his neck and sobbing into his arms. He picked me up, and I clung to him. I knew Dante called me a baby when Daddy carried me, but I was sad.

"It's going to be fucking okay." He stroked my hair, and I closed my eyes, inhaling his smell. "Tell me what happened?"

Safe. I was safe with Daddy. I slowly moved back, staring at him. I needed to be brave and strong.

"Nothing, Daddy. I'm a brave girl," I whispered, brushing away my tears with one hand.

"My girl is fucking brave. Always remember that." I nodded, playing with the chains around his neck.

"Yes. I will."

And I will talk to Enrique, even if he doesn't want to talk to me. I will make him see me because this is my last chance to thank him and say goodbye. Forever.

Dinner was over. Everyone usually went to the living room, and Enrique would go to his room, not wanting to spend time with us.

Rayhan was still angry over what happened earlier with Leo, I thought, so everyone was very quiet. I pretended to play in the playroom with Sky, Sienna, and Ahren, but I could hear Uncle Marcel asking Enrique about Puerto Rico in the entrance hall. That was where Enrique was from.

I took the chance to sneak away when Clara wasn't looking. They never noticed when I snuck away because they couldn't hear me. I needed to go before Enrique. I quietly made my way upstairs and hurried to my room to grab the present I had made him; I then ran down the hall and slipped into Enrique's room before he came up. Otherwise, the guards would find out I was there. They only guarded the room when Enrique was in it.

I looked around the room, panicking. *Where do I hide?* I didn't ask Mama about talking to him because I had heard what he said earlier. If I was stubborn and said I wanted to talk to him, it would only hurt Mama even more because she would stay with me, and I knew Enrique was going to be angry.

I heard the door handle turn and hurried into the bathroom, clutching my present to my heart. I heard him shut the door and sigh. Should I go out? I peeped through the gap, watching Enrique walk over to the window and stare out at the moon. He looked sad. The angry face he usually made wasn't there. It made me unhappy that he looked so lonely and sad...

He turned, glancing towards the bathroom door. I quickly hid behind it, my heart racing. I heard him approaching, and then he pushed the door open, roughly stepping into the bathroom and looking around. This was my chance.

Taking a deep breath, I pushed the door shut just when he turned to look behind the door. He became so angry when he saw me and was about to grab the door handle, but I stood in front of it, blocking his way.

"Please don't ignore me," I pleaded softly. *Please.*

"What do you want?" He frowned, crossing his arms. My heart ached as I looked at my shoes.

"I wanted to say I'm happy you are going to be safe. I-"

"Hurry up!" He snapped, making me jump.

Don't cry.

"O-okay. I... I'm sorry you suffered because of me. If I could turn back time, I wouldn't have allowed you to bring me food. I wouldn't have let you get hurt. I wish-"

"If I could turn back time, I wish I had never met you!" He hissed, his anger burning in his eyes. I nodded.

"I know," I whispered. It hurt.

"The thing is, we can't change the past, but I can look to the future. Stay away from me. I hate you; I hate the fact that I ever met you. You were nothing but a bad mistake. You cost me my entire future; I hate you! I should have left you to die!" He shouted. My lips quivered, but I simply nodded, agreeing to his every word.

He was right. It should have been me who lost my hand, not him. It was my fault. If I could give my hand, I would.

"I'm sorry... I'm so sorry," I whispered. "I wish I could make it up to you."

"If you want to make it up to me, don't ever talk to me again because talking to you makes it hurt even more! You destroyed everything; don't you get it? Seeing you hurts me! I hate remembering what happened because of you!" I flinched, brushing my tears away as I stared at him. If that was what he wanted, then I would do that.

The little pouch with the crystal necklace I had made almost slipped from my fingertips.

"Okay. I promise that I will never speak to you again," I whispered.

"Then leave me alone now!" He hissed. I swallowed, staring at my little pouch, but I wasn't brave enough to give it to him. *"Get out!"*

I jumped, dropping the pouch and pulling open the door. I fled before my tears fell. I rushed from the room, ignoring the guards who called out to me. I just wanted to be alone. I reached my bedroom and rushed inside, curling up on my bed and sobbing quietly.

I'm so sorry, Enrique, for ruining your life...

I wasn't sure when Skyla came and saw me crying or when Mama came and held me. All I remembered was Enrique screaming at me to get out. All I had to remember him by was that little piece of torn fabric. I would always keep that.

The pain had become stronger. I felt strange. It was hard to breathe... it hurt, but I also couldn't feel anything else either. What was happening to me?

ALEJANDRO

I had not been fucking expecting Kat to sneak into the fucker's room and try to talk to him. Whatever he said to her had made her cry for hours. Only about ten minutes ago did Kiara say she had calmed down and fallen asleep.

As much as I wanted to sort the pup out for upsetting her, it was fucking complicated. Her infatuation with him fucking worried me, too. Once he was gone, it was going to be fucking easier. She needed to get over her guilt, and the best way was for her to forget him. They both needed to heal, and time would do that. More like I fucking hoped it would.

I looked at the fucker in front of me. He was smart, that was for sure, despite being a mouthy dickhead.

"Want to say something?" Leo asked as he clicked away at the keyboard.

He had spent the last two hours hooking up several screens to his laptop, which he had brought along. I raised an eyebrow at the image of the busty woman in a barely-there bikini that was covering his entire screen.

"Sexy, isn't she?" He asked.

"Far from it," I replied. The fuck was hot about her? She was a fake as fuck, silicon, walking plastic doll.

"I'm sure you wouldn't say that if you were single." He gave me a humourless smirk before he pulled up some windows.

Fucking kids.

"I do want to say something, actually. What you did to Sienna... you don't mess with kids. Do that shit again, and I won't just stand by," I growled, resisting the urge to smack his head.

"I tossed her up just like I'd do any of the kids back home. I wasn't going to fucking hurt her." He cast me a scathing look, his icy blue eyes rolling irritatingly.

"Yeah? But you did it to piss Rayhan off. It was fucking wrong to use a pup like that. She's fucking one."

"Yeah, I did, and?"

"You need to allow him to explain his reasons, Leo."

"I don't need to allow him shit. The wanker fucking thinks he's some sort of big shot," he sneered, sitting back as he carried on working. "If you want me to do this, I need you to stop fucking bothering me." He glanced up at me, and I knew he was at the edge of snapping.

"Hatred and bitterness won't get you far. We all make mistakes... but sometimes, try to understand what the cause behind those actions is."

"I could say the same." His voice was quiet and dangerously level, and I could feel the anger rising from him.

I ran my hand through my hair. How did I tell him what Delsanra had fucking been through? I had seen some of her memories, and they fucking made me sick. The thing was, Leo refused to fucking listen.

"One day, you'll realise what he did. When you find your mate and realise that you'd destroy the world for her, that's when you'll realise that he didn't do anything wrong. I saw some of her memories... what she suffered... I wouldn't wish it on anyone," I explained quietly.

He didn't react, and I didn't wait for a reply, knowing I wouldn't get one, leaving him to do his job but mind-linking two of my men to keep an eye on him. I was not having him walk around the pack alone, not after that fucking stunt he had pulled with Sienna.

I returned to the mansion that was silent. The hallway had been cleaned up, and someone would fix the light tomorrow. I had examined the weapon he had used, which was very thin and extremely sharp. Something like that could slice through someone's neck if thrown with enough force. Leo would shift soon when he turned eighteen, and I didn't want to think of the chances that the darkness within him might grow...

I headed to my room, needing Kiara. I just wanted to fucking hold her and kiss her senseless. She was the only thing that kept me fucking sane. The anger I was feeling inside towards the Crimson King and Djinn was only growing with every passing day.

I entered our bedroom, but she wasn't there. I glanced around before deciding to take a shower first. I entered the bathroom, the smell of her shampoo and body wash lingering. I stripped, stepping into the shower that was still wet.

Where are you? I asked her. Since she had showered, it meant that she had been in here not long ago.

I was making us some hot chocolate... came her hesitant reply. I smirked.

Sounds fucking good.

Although the only thing that smelt of chocolate that I wanted was her. My dick twitched and the urge to wank off to her was fucking tempting. The only problem was that she had ruined that for me. She was all that I fucking wanted to get me off…

I heard the bedroom door open, and the key turned in the lock. I smirked, a thought coming to me. I finished showering quickly, grabbing a towel, but instead of wrapping it around me, I quickly wiped myself down, glancing down at my fucking hard-on. I was probably going to scare the fuck out of her… but who fucking cared?

I left the bathroom, towel in hand. It just about covered my dick, and I smirked, spotting her bent over as she plugged her phone into the charger. To my surprise, she was clad in a black silk nightgown, and from the way she was bent over, I could see she was only wearing a thong underneath. The fuck was she trying to do to me?

"Nice view."

She turned, startled, and tugged at the hem of her gown, which only resulted in making the fabric strain against her nipples. Fuck, she looked too fucking hot. Her eyes flew open when they landed on my body. I tilted my head, smirking as I stood in front of her naked, the towel in my hand only covering my raging cock. I heard her breath hitch as her gaze skimmed my body. She swallowed, biting her lip as her gaze lingered on my towel.

"What's wrong, Amore Mio?" I asked, walking towards her.

"Nothing at all," she replied defiantly, despite her pounding heart and the tell-tale sign that I was getting to her when she pressed her thighs together.

"Really? Because seeing you like this is fucking turning me on…" I murmured huskily, taking hold of her chin just as I let down the barrier on my emotions, letting her feel exactly how I was feeling. How much I wanted to fuck her and how much she fucking meant to me. She gasped, almost stumbling backwards if I didn't catch her.

"Al… Alejandro…" she whispered shakily, her eyes widening when she felt my cock press against her through the towel between us. "Fuck…"

Yeah, fuck is the right term, baby.

Her heart was pounding, so I reigned in my storm of emotions, not wanting them to influence her. If she wanted me, I wanted it to be of her own accord. I looked into the beautiful eyes of my fucking queen and just then the scent of her arousal filled the air, making my eyes simmer red. The hunger and desire within me threatened to unleash themselves.

"Wait... I... there's something I need to tell you first," she whispered, her hand going to my shoulder. Her heart thundered as she looked up into my eyes. It was taking my fucking all not to kiss her right now.

"What the fuck is it?"

"Earlier, I heard a voice in my head."

And just like that, my mood changed. The harsh reality of what she had just said hit me like a fucking freight train...

This Fire Between Us

KIARA

*W*E HAD BEEN TALKING for the last twenty minutes. He had explained everything about Liam to me, and I felt stupid for even assuming that it wasn't him.

However, the most distracting thing was that he was sitting on the bed with the towel loosely draped over his manhood. It was so distracting, and I was doing my best not to stare. He was a work of art, one covered with so many tattoos that I wanted to trace my finger over every single one. How low did they go?

My cheeks flushed, and I didn't miss the smirk on his face, almost as if he knew what I was thinking. He raised one leg slightly, resting his arm on it, making my attention instantly go to his muscular thigh. *Goddess, this man was made to sin…*

I scanned the room instead, brushing my fingers through my hair, feeling a little jittery.

"Any more questions, Amore Mio?" He asked. I looked into his dark eyes and shook my head before staring at his chest, where I realised my name was tattooed on his left breast.

"When did you get that?" I asked, staring at the words,

My Nympho Queen Kiara, ruler of my heart, body and soul.

"When Dante was just a pup. I got his name on my wrist and the girls' names on the other."

He held his arms out, and I leaned forward, taking a look. Indeed, on one wrist, it read *Dante* alongside numerous other tattoos, and on the other arm, he had both girls, with Skyla's name just above Kataleya's. He had been nothing but truthful, and I believed him. I nodded, reaching over and tracing my finger over my name on his chest, trying to ignore the incredible sparks that rushed through me at our touch.

"What worries me is the strong doubt that fills me so quickly that all logic seems to fly out the window," I mused, glancing up at his glowing red eyes staring back at me.

"Then next time when that shit happens, mind-link me straight up," he said, stretching his muscled arm and running his fingers through his hair. My gaze fell to the towel. Goddess… "So… how about you give in to your temptation and remove this fucking towel? We both know you want to."

My eyes widened, and if I wasn't red before, my face was absolutely heated up now. I tossed my hair, swallowing hard.

"I do not," I lied.

"I don't need your fucking ability to know you're lying. So, how about you come here, and I'll give you a taster of exactly how we fucked?"

He didn't wait for a reply. Reaching over, he grabbed me by my elbows and yanked me into his lap. I gasped, feeling his hard cock beneath the towel press against my pussy.

"Aren't you getting a little ahead?" I asked, although my entire body and my mind were saying to just kiss him.

"Who the fuck cares?" He murmured, his hand threading into my hair and yanking me close. His other arm snaked around my waist, his face inches from mine, making my heart thump wildly. Did I care?

I looked into that handsome face. No one looked as sexy as the man before me. To hell with the consequences.

"Not me," I whispered, locking my arms around his neck. We both leaned in, and our lips met in a sizzling kiss that made my core throb with intense pleasure.

Fuck, I should have kissed him the moment I woke up and saw him. This felt so… there were no words to describe the intense pleasure that consumed me. I whimpered, my entire body aching for more. His kiss was rough, passionate, and fuelled with hunger, dominating me entirely. I kissed him back with equal passion and desire, not holding back the moan that left my lips and arched my back as I pressed myself against his chest, twisting one hand into his hair.

Fuck, Alejandro, I whimpered through the link as his tongue plunged into my mouth.

It felt… natural. Our bodies moved together as one. He let go of my hair and my stomach knotted as he began to undo the belt on my gown. I knew we had been together… but this…

I gasped for air, trying to avoid the hammering in my chest when he yanked me close and kissed me in the crook of my neck. My eyes flew open, and I felt a flare of heat rush through me. He ripped the gown off me, his fingers digging into my back as he ran them up and down my back, leaving sparks of pleasure in his wake.

Suddenly the urge to pull away ripped through me, but instead, I dug my nails into Alejandro's shoulders, breathing hard. What was going on?

Don't trust him.

I gasped, ripping away from him as if I had been burnt.

"Amore Mio…"

"The voice," I whispered, my heart thundering as I stared at him. His eyes narrowed, and I could feel his anger.

"It's trying to keep us apart…" His anger was palpable, and I could feel it through the bond, too. He wasn't wrong. My instincts were telling me one thing, and that voice was telling me another…

"Then how about we ignore it, and you fuck me so hard I can't focus on anything but you?" I whispered, getting onto my knees. I reached behind me and unhooked my bra, slowly letting it slide off my boobs before I tossed it to the floor. His eyes darkened with lust, his gaze on my breasts as I ran my hand through my hair, enjoying his attention on me.

"Sounds like a fucking good plan," he growled sexily, making my core knot with anticipation.

"Then drop the towel, my sexy king, and show me exactly what I'm missing," I whispered, crawling towards him just as he picked up the towel and tossed it to the ground right next to my discarded gown. "Goddess…"

My core knotted as I stared at his huge cock. I licked my lips, desire enveloping me as it throbbed, its thick long length making me moan. I wrapped my hand around it just as he yanked me forward, kissing me hard once more. Passion and fire consumed me. His kisses were fuelled with so much passion that I soon became dizzy in the throes of pleasure that made me feel like I was in heaven. How did one forget something like this?

I pumped his dick in my hand, rubbing my thumb over his tip and spreading the beads of pre-cum that had already escaped. I wanted to taste him, but he was in control. Yanking my hand away, he pushed me back on the bed, his hand around my throat whilst his other one squeezed my breast and pinched my nipple painfully. I whimpered, the mix of pain and pleasure only making me wetter. Fuck, he was good.

He kissed me down my neck, his hands running down my waist, placing kisses down my breast, sucking hard in between. Those would leave a mark. He ran his tongue down the centre of my stomach, making me gasp when his fingers slid my thong down, and he began placing kisses along my pubic bone.

"Fuck, I missed this pussy."

I blushed, but, despite his crude words, it only made me hornier. Tangling my hand into his hair, I closed my eyes as he pushed my legs apart and ran his tongue along my entrance.

"Fuck!" I groaned, arching my back. His hands squeezed my ass as he continued to lick my pussy, flicking my clit. Just when I didn't think he could make me feel any better, he thrust two fingers into me.

"That's it, baby girl, enjoy it."

He looked up at me, his gaze roaming over my breasts before I pulled him up and kissed him hungrily. Scraping my fingers down his chest, I rubbed my thumb over his nipple. He grabbed my hand, kissing my wrist before pinning it to the bed.

"Hands to yourself, Amore Mio," he smirked, kissing me roughly on the lips just as he slipped a finger into my ass.

"Alejandro!"

"Relax... you've had a lot more than a finger up there," he whispered in my ear.

"I... fuck!"

Goddess, it felt so good... I didn't hold back the cries of pleasure as I dropped back onto the bed and Alejandro went down on me, flicking and sucking on my clit as his fingers penetrated me hard and fast. My orgasm was building, the pleasure ready to explode.

"That's it, fuck, Alejandro! Faster! Ouch, fuck!" I cried out. The delicious sensation of my release coursed through me. I screamed as my entire body trembled. He didn't let up, licking my clit as he thrust his fingers harder, hitting my G-spot as my juices leaked out. "Goddess..." I gasped, dropping back onto the bed as Alejandro slipped his fingers out, delivering a sharp tap to my ass.

"Fuck, you are one hot nympho." He murmured huskily, grabbing me by the neck and kissing me hard. I could taste myself on his lips, and it only made me want more.

Fuck me, I whispered through the bond. His reply was to grab me by the ass, lifting me off the bed, and instead pinned me up against the wall beside it.

"Now I'll fuck you so hard you'll be begging me to stop."

"Then fuck me," I murmured sensually, claiming his lips once more in a sizzling kiss. I gasped as he rammed into me without warning. For a moment, I couldn't breathe, feeling the pressure in my lower back as I accommodated him.

"What are you, a beast?" I giggled breathlessly, kissing his neck.

"Yeah, your fucking beast," he replied, kissing my neck as he began fucking me.

He was right, he fucked like a beast, and I loved it. My entire body rippled with pleasure. Each thrust hit my G-spot and knocked the breath from me.

When a quiet moan escaped his lips, I bit my lip. Fuck, it sounded so good to know he was enjoying this just as much. The sounds of skin against skin and our breathless sounds of pleasure filled the room. Just when I felt myself nearing once more, he sped up, chasing his own release.

I felt something in my mind once more, but it seemed to be struggling to make its presence known.

"What is it?" Alejandro breathed, fucking me harder.

"Mark me," I commanded, my heart pounding as I felt a searing pain in my head. The urge to rip away from Alejandro was consuming me, and the moment I spoke those words, it only grew. "Now!" I whimpered.

He didn't argue, biting into my neck right on top of the mark that already adorned it. I screamed as a storm of sensations filled me. His release matched mine as our orgasms tore through us, but alongside it, I felt the pleasure from my neck wash through me like a wave of pure water, bathing my mind in a coolness. With it, I felt as if something inside of me snapped. My eyes flew open, my head feeling lighter as I stared at him the moment he moved back, breathing hard.

"What the fuck happened?" He asked. He was still inside of me. Even when he wasn't hard, he was an incredible size, and I could feel him getting hard again.

"I... I think you marking me shut that voice out... but time will tell..."
I whispered. He frowned before exhaling and pressing his forehead against
mine.

"Fuck, Amore Mio..."

"Mmm... well... I was thinking... since I've forgotten a lot..." I pouted,
caressing the back of his neck.

"Yeah?"

"Why don't you show me what else you can do?" I blinked coquettishly,
running my fingers through his hair as I bit my lip.

"That's my girl," he growled, grabbing my neck as his lips claimed mine
again...

A Past Forgotten

ALEJANDRO

"*H*ARDER, BABY!" SHE MOANED.

The shower water poured down on us as I had her pushed up against the tiled walls. One hand tangled in her hair, the other hooked around her lush thigh as I fucked her ass hard from behind. The pleasure that I had been deprived of was rushing through me as I stared at her ass, which was covered in welts and bruises from our night of sex.

We had crashed at one point, but I had woken up to Kiara on top of me, my cock in her mouth, looking so fucking sexy, and that had awoken the beast within me all over again. We had gone to shower, but seeing that ass of hers sticking up so fucking sexily had fucked me over completely, and that was how we ended up banging against the shower wall.

"Fuck!" She screamed, and I could feel my orgasm close. I reached around, shoving two fingers into her pussy as I continued to fuck her in the ass. "I'm going to come, ah!" She moaned hornily.

"Then come for me," I growled, yanking her back and biting into her neck as she cried out in pleasure, triggering my own release as I shot my load into that ass of hers, catching her body against my chest as she caught her breath.

Her neck was a mess of bites, so I slowly ran my tongue along the latest bite. Fuck, she looked a mess, but I fucking loved it. There was not a part of her that I hadn't left my mark on. Even then, exhausted as she clung to me, the fire in her eyes remained.

"Seems like I've reawakened the goddess within you," I murmured, kissing those sore lips of hers. She kissed me back, staring up at me with lust-coated eyes.

"One that can't resist you," she whispered, placing a kiss on my neck.

"Just as I can't fucking resist you, but if I fuck you one more time, I don't think you'll be able to hold up," I murmured, squeezing her breasts. She smiled, closing her eyes and resting her head back against me.

"I will get my memories back, won't I?" She asked after a moment.

"Yeah, you will."

And I fucking meant it.

༄

I had left her to sleep whilst I went to train. Darien had taken photos of the pup for a fake passport. I was currently with Leo, who had spent the night at headquarters.

"So, got anything?"

"Maybe," he said, dropping his legs to the floor and clicking something on his laptop. "As far as it goes with the Escarra name, there's plenty of shit. They aren't a pack with the cleanest record in businesses, it may involve drugs and shit. Anyhow, something else interesting did actually come up, but I don't know if it is of any use." He threw a knife up in the air, catching it between his teeth before sitting forward and pulling up a few files.

"What is that?" He placed the knife into the side of his boot. How many weapons did he carry?

"The Escarras had dealings with a certain company called Lupo XII Rossi over a hundred years ago. Not sure if it rings any bells, but it's a coincidence, ain't it?" I frowned, bending down. I had not heard of any such company... but it was too much to be a coincidence.

"Lupo. That's not a coincidence. "

"Yeah, the Rossis are originally from Italy, correct?"

"Yeah, obviously. It was our great-great-grandfather who moved here after his pack was destroyed or some shit."

"So how many years ago on estimate would you say?"

"Over a hundred and fifty. Would you be able to find anything about that company?"

"Already did. There's nothing on the public domain, but if you dig further and get past some security systems, you will find that it was an arms company that was actually funding the Italian Mafia or some shit. Then, enter the Escarra Enterprise; apparently, there was a 'dealing', and the Escarras bought out the Lupo XII Rossi. Then, listen to this; this all happened around one hundred and forty years back."

Around the time the Rossi's moved to England… the fucker was smart, got to give him that. I scanned the documents, frowning.

"So something had gone down between our ancestors and the Escarras…"

"Something that made the Rossis leave Italy and set up here. I don't get why they're saying there's a debt… unless…" Leo ran his fingers through his hair, sitting forward and picking up a pack of cigarettes and a lighter. "Want one?"

"Sure. Ain't you a tad fucking young for this shit?" I asked allowing him to light my cigarette.

"Ain't you a few years fucking late to comment on this shit?" He countered, copying my tone but sounding ten fucking times worse. Fucker.

"Bastard." He smirked, and I narrowed my eyes. He sure fucking knew what I was thinking. He lit his own cigarette while staring at the screen. "Unless what?" I asked, glancing back at the screen.

"Unless the Rossis did something to the Escarras regarding that takeover…" He had a point. Why else would they run?

"You may be onto something. Well, your dad and Maria are going, we'll see if they find anything from there. If this is the case, then the Rossis must have done something to have made the family remember it forever, but what exactly? Pay the debt… by the blood of the beast…"

"What else is new? The Rossis just take whatever the fuck they want, right?" His voice was cold and bitter. I sighed.

"Look, kid. I know the Rossis have done shit. The past is gone, but we can pave the future." He shook his head.

"Nothing can change because no matter how much time passes, there's still discrimination in every fucking aspect of life. We say we want to be open-minded, but isn't it the same? Racism, homophobia, and prejudice still exist. We are no different. We are still ranked, not only by blood but by packs. We have the elite packs at the top, such as the Black Storm, the Nightwalkers, and the Blood Moon, then we have the influential packs, the standard packs, the weak packs, and then right at the bottom, we have the Sangue Pack. Rogues. I'm right, aren't I?"

"That's not true, Leo. The Sangue Pack is not at -"

"It is, not because we haven't progressed, or the fact that we aren't strong enough, but because we are rogues."

"Were rogues," I corrected.

"We still are. A rogue pack, a pack of outcasts among regular packs." He stood up and looked me in the eye. "We won't ever fucking agree on this, and I don't give a shit. Whilst you were enjoying your long night…" He glanced at my neck pointedly, before smirking humourlessly. "I pulled up anything I could on the Escarra and Rossi interactions. It's all there, plus some addresses Dad can use in Puerto Rico. So, whether the king loves it or not, I'm fucking out."

He tossed the memory stick he removed from his laptop at me and, snapping the laptop shut, walked out the door, smoking his cigarette. I sighed heavily. He was a smart kid… I just hated seeing the resentment within him. My phone rang, and I pulled it out of my pocket.

"Yeah?" I answered, seeing whose number it was. "I hope you have a fucking answer."

"Oh, I do. I don't think you will like it."

"Try me." Janaina sighed heavily.

"Well, to kill a Djinn… you need the blood of six hundred and sixty-six virgins coating a blade made of pure iron." I scoffed. Was she for fucking real?

"Virgins?"

"Yes, if even one isn't a virgin, it can ruin the entire thing. We just need about a syringe worth from each, combine them, and then dip the iron blade into it."

"That's it?"

"It's not so easy."

"Sounds pretty easy to me. Now we just find virgins willing to give fucking blood."

"They must all have hit puberty. It won't be easy."

"No shit, Sherlock. Finding ten virgins is fucking hard, and you're asking me to find over six hundred."

"You wanted answers, I found you the answers. Now listen carefully. There's more. The price."

"You mean the consequences of killing a Djinn…"

"Yes. The cost is…" She hesitated, and I couldn't deny I waited with bated breath for her next words…

The Lupo Nero Pack

ALEJANDRO

THE WEIGHT OF JANAINA's words lingered in my mind.

The price to pay… well, obviously, it wasn't going to be a fucking walk in the park, but I did hope it wouldn't come to this shit.

Well, I'll deal with that when the time comes. But for now, how the fuck do I find six hundred and sixty-six fucking virgins? Do I go round asking all the damn teens in the pack? Nah, I'll come off like a fucking creep. This was fucking messed up.

I took a drag on the cigarette as I walked out of headquarters, spotting Leo leaning against the wall as two young she-wolves talked to him. He didn't seem to mind the attention, although he wasn't giving them his full attention, but I guess girls loved bad boys.

What are the chances he was a virgin? I could ask him, though, wouldn't be too fucking odd. Right?

The girls saw me approaching and, bowing their heads, left quickly. Pups…

"So, are you a virgin?" The girls gasped from behind me as I looked at Leo, waiting for a reply. He gave me a withering glare, clearly pissed that I asked that. Shame, I didn't really fucking care. That got his attention, glancing at me sharply and raising an eyebrow.

"Do I look like a virgin to you?" He asked coldly.

"Don't know, you might be all talk or some shit. Putting on a bad boy front or something." He looked at me as if I had grown an extra fucking head, and I didn't fucking blame him. The conversation was weird as fuck.

"Although it's none of your damn business, no, I'm not a virgin, but at least now I know that you were at my age."

"I sure as fuck wasn't."

"Really? You seem to have been the most insecure dipshit around. Full of self-loathing?" He mocked. Fucker.

"Not that my sex life is your business -" He scoffed.

"But mine is yours? Ah, yeah, the double standards, right?" I sighed. Why did he have to do this every fucking time?

"No, actually it's regarding the situation." I glanced around, making sure we were actually alone this time. I wasn't going to let him just carry on with that assumption. "I need the blood of six hundred and sixty-six virgins who have hit puberty to defeat the fucker." Leo raised an eyebrow, before snickering.

"That's fucking crazy. Where will you find that shit? I mean, if it was just blood, you could have gone around and taken it from all the pups. But resorting to asking an almost eighteen-year-old? Yeah, you won't have any luck."

"I know, but I still wanted to try my luck. I had hope that one Rossi had kept it in his pants," I grumbled. This was going to be fucking hard.

"Well, do what you're best at, commanding others. Use your Alpha command on your pack to have all virgins step forward." Not waiting for a reply, he walked off.

I frowned. I knew he meant it in a mocking way, but if done properly, I could use the command to make sure that they were indeed virgins... or I could ask Raihana for help. That might actually work.

I guess I needed to hit the archives and see if I could find anything about the history of when the Black Storm pack was formed. Rafael had given me most of the archives, along with old history books and stuff. I had just stored them. If not here, then the ones that remained at Black Storm, may have something.

⁋⁌⁍

Much later, I was in the archive vault. Lola, Rayhan's Beta, was searching the archives over at his pack, but, so far, neither of us had found shit.

The sound of heels reached my ears. I didn't need to turn or smell who it was to know it was my nympho. Her scent was strongly mixed with mine thanks to the intense night of sex. I turned as she knocked on the open door.

"Hey." She smiled, her cheeks flushed a gorgeous pink.

"Hey."

She was dressed in a long-sleeved fitted black dress and sheer black tights. I knew it was to hide the mess I had made. Her hair was left open, and she was wearing make-up. On her feet, she wore red heels that matched the red on her lips.

"Can I come in?"

"You don't need to ask for permission, Amore Mio." She smiled and walked over, holding out the large mug of coffee.

"I thought you might want a drink?" She offered with a pout, her heart racing as she looked away from my intense gaze. I smirked.

"The only thing I want is you."

I placed the book down, snaking an arm around her waist and bending down to kiss her deeply. Her breath hitched before she kissed me back slowly, whimpering slightly. Fuck, I could do her all over again, but I had to give her a break and find fucking answers too. Forcing myself back, I looked her over, my eyes lingering on her tits.

"Thanks for the fucking coffee." I took it from her grip, amused that she was blushing despite being naughty as fuck all night long.

"What are we looking for? I could help," she suggested, ruffling her long locks.

"We're looking for when the Black Storm Pack was founded and anything to do with events that took place around one hundred and fifty years ago," I replied.

Nodding, she turned to the shelves, walked to the end, and began looking at the book names. *Damn, I'm glad to have her back.* Even if she didn't have her memory of us, at least we had come together again. Another half an hour passed, and the dust was fucking pissing me off. We still hadn't found any fucking answers.

"Uncle, it's Ri." I turned to see Rayhan holding his phone out. There was no connection in here, so I strode over to him.

"Nothing from Lola?"

"Not yet, but Ri was adamant about talking to you," Rayhan replied, but it was obvious he wasn't impressed.

"Oh, stop acting like I'm wasting your time. I'm offended." Raihana's voice came. I took the phone from Rayhan, looking at the screen where Raihana was seated on a sofa, giving me a small wave.

"What do you want?"

"That's not a nice way to greet me, Uncle, especially when I'm here with information," she replied, rolling her eyes as she admired her nails. "But if you don't want to know… fine. I have better things to do with my time."

"Alright, don't be a damn diva. What the fuck do you know?"

"Ask nicely," she replied, smirking. *This woman…*

Chris appeared from behind, placing his hands on her shoulders, and she tilted her head back to kiss him.

"I'm covered in fucking dust, and I'm pissed as fuck. Spill," I growled.

"Please?" Ri persisted.

"Be nice," Kiara whispered.

Her words made my heart fucking race. Be nice. Something she always fucking said to me. Turning back to the screen, I gave Raihana a cold glare.

"Please," I growled, making Rayhan smirk.

"Well, that wasn't so hard, was it."

Damn, that woman was fucking hard work. Kiara's presence next to me was fucking calming.

"What do you know, Raihana?" Rayhan asked.

"I heard from Chris, who heard from Lola, that you were looking for the founding history of Black Storm. Well, you are in luck. Dad made me study it all."

"You know the history of the Rossis settling in England?"

"Yes, as well as the controversial reasoning. Although I don't know how true it is," she replied. "The Rossis' origins are from Italy. Alfonso Rossi was the bastard son of DeAngelo Rossi, the Alpha of the Lupo Nero Pack, a pack that was massacred by an enemy pack." I frowned. I knew we didn't have any other family out there, but I didn't really care to research either.

"What enemy pack?"

"It didn't actually say, just that DeAngelo Rossi had taken the Alpha's daughter and claimed her as his own, making their enmity grow. She was one of the five women he had claimed over time. His original mate gave birth to a son and daughter, then the next two women he ended up killing in anger within months of taking them as his mistresses. His mate committed suicide, and he then took another chosen mate. This woman was Alfonso's mother. However, he also ended up taking her life. It's said that with each passing woman, he became more and more insane. DeAngelo then saw a woman at a pack meeting and, taking an interest in her, took her by force, making her his fifth woman, hence starting a war between the two packs. The Lupo Nero Pack managed to win the battle and destroy the other pack, but it cost them far too much. Alfonso was one of the rare survivors, along with his half-brother, the new alpha." I frowned, as Raihana took a deep breath, fanning her face. "I need a drink, my throat is dry."

Seriously, this woman. Did she take anything seriously? Remembering her pregnancy, I decided not to say anything. Fuck, I was becoming soft. How the fuck did that happen?

She smiled, holding an iced drink in her hand that she had picked up from the table, and took a sip.

"Anyway, the woman DeAngelo had taken as a mate, her brother's mate was from abroad, and he had killed her in that battle, too. So, her family came for revenge. They were powerful and bought out all the Rossi business shares. By hook or crook, they relentlessly began to isolate the Rossis from the other packs and the world. Then, when they were at their weakest, they killed them."

It still wasn't making sense.

"Alfonso barely escaped with his newfound mate. He came to England and set up here."

"Then?" Rayhan asked.

"That's it." Raihana shrugged.

"There's got to be more. Let's say this pack was the Escarras, who came and sought revenge. Then what debt are they on about?" I shook my head.

"Unless, of course, the last of the Rossis, Alfonso Rossi, did something before he escaped? Or they wanted all the Rossis dead?" Kiara murmured thoughtfully. We fell silent, pondering over her words. It did seem like they were the only viable answers…

"So, we need to find out exactly what happened before Alfonso Rossi left for England," Rayhan added.

"Yes. Although DeAngelo was an insane man, from the books and journals I did read, he was loved by Alfonso," Raihana added.

"So now we find out exactly what happened then, and there's only one way to do that shit," I said, frowning deeply. "We go to Italy."

More Than He Seemed

KIARA

It was the day Enrique was leaving. The weather was cool, and although the sun was shining, it didn't match the mood of the Rossi Mansion. Looking at him standing there with nothing but a small cross-body bag with some cash and a passport broke my heart. He was a child with his life ahead of him, but, seeing the empty look in his eyes, it was like he had given up on his life.

Kataleya stood hidden behind the front door. She didn't say anything to him or try to meet him again, and he had said nothing to her. I could hear her stifled sobs as she peeped out through the crack, knowing that it was the last time she'd see him. I hated seeing her in pain too…

"Are you sure you don't want the phone?" I asked, holding up the phone he had passed back to me.

"No, thank you, Queen Luna," he replied, his eyes cold.

"He doesn't fucking trust it," Alejandro said, crouching down before the boy. "So, one of my men will take you to the airport, you get on the flight, and you're in Puerto Rico. Are you sure you'll be okay once you're there?" I knew he wasn't keen on sending a ten-year-old alone, but everything was prepared, and he'd be allowed onto the flight.

"Yes." Alejandro exhaled in defeat and nodded.

"You're a stubborn little fucker. Here's my number, if ever you need it." He handed him a black card and then held up a small velvet pouch. I heard Kataleya gasp from behind me and I wondered what happened. I was about to go check on her when Alejandro stood up. "Now, I don't want to force you or anything, but if my girl gives you a damn gift, you keep it." I looked at the small pouch in his hand, realising what he meant.

"I don't want it," Enrique replied coldly.

"You haven't got a fucking choice, kid," Alejandro growled, opening the boy's bag and placing it inside. "Keep it." I heard Kataleya's footsteps retreating and looked at Enrique, who was frowning coldly at it.

"I will throw it away when I get to Puerto Rico," he spat, turning away from us.

"Goodbye," I said quietly, walking towards him. I placed my hand on his shoulder, but he pushed it off and hurried towards the waiting car, getting in and slamming the car door shut after him. "Enrique…"

"Let him go," Alejandro said, quietly taking hold of my wrist. I looked up into his eyes before nodding as I watched the car drive off.

"I'll go to Kataleya," I replied softly, pulling away. My daughter was in pain. I hated how things had ended.

Hurrying inside, I went to find her, only to spot her in the lounge. Delsanra had her arms around her, stroking her head soothingly.

"It's going to be okay, my little pot of cotton candy," she comforted her.

I could tell she was barely able to sit up by herself. We needed to figure everything out fast. I walked over to them, and sat on the other side of Kataleya, who was crying into Delsanra's lap.

"I'm sorry," I whispered to her. I knew she was hurting, but I didn't know what more to say…

"Kataleya, boys are dumb. Come on! Do you want to go play?" Skyla tried, coming over to her sister.

"No, Sky, I don't want to play," Kataleya whispered, trying to stifle her sobs. Delsanra and I exchanged looks. I stroked Kataleya's hair and at the same time placed my hand on Delsanra's, allowing myself to heal her a little.

"Don't cry over him, Kat," Dante added from the sofa, where he was lying down.

"Don't be mean, Dante," Skyla scolded. Dante sighed heavily.

"I'm not being mean." He opened his eyes and looked at me with a thoughtful expression on his face. It unnerved me. I wasn't sure why but it…

My heart began racing and I felt an odd surge of fear rush through me. Why though?

I stared back into his red eyes, unable to hear Kataleya crying any longer. It was as if I was being sucked into a burning abyss of power. He didn't blink, just holding my gaze. My head felt like it was being crushed, the fear within me growing, but why? He was only looking at me.

"Mama? Mama!" Skyla shouted, making me gasp. My eye contact with Dante broke, and it felt like I could breathe once more.

"Y-yeah?" I asked, my heart still racing wildly. From the corner of my eye, I saw him smirk slightly, making me nervous once again.

"I was saying we should have a girls' sleepover; me, you, Aunty Mari, Delsanra, and Sienna. Oh, and Ahren can come too because he's a baby. All us girls."

"I don't know... I mean, sure, if Delsanra is up to it." I didn't want to agree, especially if she wanted the comfort of her mate at such a trying time.

"I don't mind, it sounds fun!" She replied, smiling happily despite the tiredness on her face.

"Then I think we should get some midnight snacks ready and a movie," Maria said, entering the room, a small smile on her face. "Dante will be the only child left out then. Shall we invite him?"

"No thanks," Dante added. At the same time, Skyla shook her head vigorously.

"See? Dante doesn't want to come."

"Delsanra and Mom need to stay with their mates," Dante added, staring at the ceiling.

"That's a first," Delsanra replied with a giggle. Dante tilted his head and looked at her, pouting slightly, and to my surprise, a little blush coated his cheeks.

"I'm just saying…" he mumbled. Maria frowned thoughtfully and nodded.

"Well, I'm sure we can have a girls' night, then Delsanra and Kiara can go to their own rooms, and the five of us can stay together," she suggested.

"Okay! Pyjama party!" Skyla jumped excitedly.

Kataleya had become silent, her sobs becoming tiny sniffles, but I could tell she was in pain. I lifted her from Delsanra's lap. The woman looked like she was going to faint at any moment.

"Come on, my little angel, things will get better," I whispered, kissing the top of her head. I just hoped they would get better soon.

Night had fallen, and somehow the girls' time had become a family night. Everyone was in the cinema room with blankets, pizzas, desserts, and snacks. Rayhan was holding Sienna in his lap with his arm around Delsanra, who was leaning against him. Maria was sitting with Ahren and Dante. Skyla was right at the front with Marcel, whilst Kataleya was between Alejandro and me. We were watching a live-action movie.

"This is the life," Skyla stated, taking another pizza slice. I was quite surprised at the amount she could eat.

"Eating pizza and watching a movie is life?" Dante asked sceptically.

"Yes," Skyla replied confidently. «It's fun.»

«Fun,» Dante scoffed.

"Alright, no arguing," Maria intervened lightly, and I was glad she spoke; from what I saw, those two did get a bit temperamental.

I still worried about speaking up as I had forgotten everything. What if I said something that upset them? Remembering what had happened earlier with Dante, I glanced over at Alejandro.

He was breathtakingly hot, a beast in all aspects and one that I craved. There was just something about him devouring me that made my core knot.

Keep thinking like that, and I will fuck you all over again. I blushed when his voice came in my head. I knew there was a way to block your mate out, but I wasn't used to it and often forgot.

I wouldn't mind reliving that night all over again, I replied back in a flirty tone, keeping my gaze fixed on the screen ahead.

Fuck, Amore Mio, he growled back. I almost giggled when he readjusted his position, grabbing a share-pack of Doritos and putting it on his lap. I smirked before glancing down at Kataleya, who was staring at a chocolate bar in her hand.

"Want to eat it?" I asked her gently. She shook her head, and I didn't push it, although I was sure it would melt soon enough if she kept a hold on it.

Alejandro. Dante, he's special, isn't he?

Aren't all these fuckers?

They are… but I mean there's something different about him. Earlier, we had a moment where our eyes locked, and I felt as if he was looking

into my soul. It scared me, and I don't know why, I explained through the link, knowing I sounded stupid. Alejandro frowned thoughtfully.

That's strange, but with Dante, it's best not to ignore shit. I'll talk to him, he replied, making me feel a little relieved.

Thanks.

You can make it up to me after. Our eyes met, and his eyes dipped to his crotch pointedly, making my cheeks burn.

With pleasure, I responded, tossing my hair. He smirked, but before he could respond, our attention fell to Kataleya, and what I saw made my heart break.

She was fiddling with the chocolate, trying to open the wrapper, but what devastated me was that she was trying to do it with one hand, using her mouth to help her. Her other hand rested on her lap, clenched in a ball, silent tears streaming down her cheeks. I was unable to hold back my own, pulling her into my lap and hugging my daughter tightly.

The painful truth was that it was going to take a lot for her to get over the trauma that she was suffering or to come to terms with it to some extent. This enemy had committed the worst crime by targeting children, and I would never forgive him.

⁂

ALEJANDRO

Much later, Kiara was helping Maria get the children in bed, although Ray's pups had fallen asleep whilst watching the movie. Sienna was with her parents for the night. Seeing Delsanra's state getting worse was making me fucking uneasy.

Maria, Marcel, and Liam would leave tomorrow, and I hoped they found the answers we needed. Liam had gone back to his pack to spend some time with his mate and pups before their trip, which hopefully wouldn't last too fucking long. He would be back in the morning. Raihana was going to come down in the morning to spell them so they appeared human.

As for our other lead, I was going to go to Italy myself. I didn't want to leave the rest behind, but I didn't really have a fucking choice. Scarlett was going to stay at the Blood Moon Pack and Elijah would come here. I hated that I had to leave the kids and Kiara, but Rayhan and Elijah would be there, which gave me a little fucking reassurance.

I had just settled my damn debt with Skyla, who said I apparently owed her a hundred pounds for using the fuck word. I swear the little devil was robbing me. She had walked off smug as fuck, leaving me irritated as fuck, and I had gone to Dante's bedroom to help him settle into bed. Although the fucker acted like he didn't need any help. The fuck was wrong with these kids? What Kiara had said earlier was still on my mind, and I planned to ask him about it.

"Wanna share what happened earlier? Between you and your mama?" He looked at me, his red eyes calculating. It was kinda hard to explain, but it felt like he was fucking looking into my head. "Stop with the staring shit. Answer me, pup."

"What did she say?" He asked after a moment, lying back and placing his hands behind his head. The dark veins moved slightly under his skin as he stared at his overhead ceiling of the galaxy.

"She said she felt scared." He smirked.

"Why would Mama feel scared of me?" His eyes snapped to me, raising an eyebrow pointedly. I frowned, my stomach sinking as a thought occurred to me.

"What are you fucking saying?"

"I'm not saying anything. I'm just asking, why would Mama fear me?"

"Are you trying to say something else is in her head?" He shrugged but didn't say anything, but I got the fucking answer that I so fucking did not need…

"You should take Mama to Italy with you," he added, closing his eyes.

I frowned, leaning over and brushing his hair back. I hated how he had the weight of the fucking world on his shoulders. I hadn't told him about Italy, but he knew… I often wondered how much he knew. Could he see the future? The outcome? Did he know what was going to happen? We had asked him once, and he had replied, "*I can't say too much, or the balance will be destroyed.*" The haunted look in his eyes at that moment had made me promise myself never to question him about it again.

"I'll take her with me," I promised, standing up. "Must be fucking hard to have to deal with all that shit. You must feel fucking tired." He smirked slightly, his eyes remaining shut.

"Or I feel like the game master, watching all the pieces move on the chessboard," countered his arrogant reply. I glanced back at him sharply.

"Fucker," we both said at the same time. I smirked, shaking my head.

"Night."

"Goodnight, Dad."

I dimmed the lights, leaving his projector on to illuminate his room. I left the door open a crack so Milo could keep an eye on him through the night and made my way down the hallway.

Drake. Kiara will be going with me to Italy. We leave in two days. Make sure her papers are ready as well, I said through the link.

Got it, Alpha.

Dante's words replayed in my mind as I returned to my bedroom, seeing my nympho removing her earrings, a beautiful smile on her face. It fucking killed me to know she was still in the grasp of the enemy. Did they know exactly what was going on? Did I have to start hiding the truth from her?

I knew the answer to that, and it fucking killed me with guilt. I had just won her trust. By hiding certain things from her, would it affect her faith in me? Closing the gap between us, I kissed her with everything I fucking had…

Puerto Rico

MARIA

$\mathscr{J}$ UST OVER AN EIGHT-HOUR flight later, we landed in Puerto Rico. The moment we stepped out onto the steps, I was hit by how humid it was. The weather was rather warm, and I waved my hand, fanning my face.

"It is really hot," Liam murmured. Dressed in three-quarter pants and a white short-sleeved shirt with sunglasses, he was prepared for the weather. I was, too, wearing tan pants and a white chiffon blouse with a large tan-coloured sun hat and sunglasses.

"It is. It's nice," Marcel replied. He was dressed the most casually in a t-shirt and jeans, unlike both Liam and I, who looked like tourists. His similarities to Rafael were always a painful reminder of the man I had lost, but they were moons apart. My Rafael was one of a kind, no matter how similar one looked.

We made our way down the steps. I could hear music in the distance, and as we made our way through the airport to collect our luggage, I could tell that the locals all seemed rather friendly, smiling as they walked past or from behind the counters.

"Would you like a drink?" Marcel asked me. Once again, the similarity to Rafael caused a stinging pain in my chest.

"Yes, I wouldn't mind one," I replied smoothly with a small smile.

"Are you okay?" Liam asked, taking off his glasses to reveal his dark magnetic blue eyes. I nodded.

"Of course. You should let them know that we have landed," I advised.

We were posing as a family; Marcel and I were meant to be married, and Liam was meant to be my stepson. I glanced at his dyed dark brown hair. Although it was strange to see Liam with anything but strawberry blond hair, it did suit him and tied him in a little with Marcel, who had his hair pulled back in a bun and had trimmed his beard, which made him look a little neater. He had also donned some glasses to make him look older. Being werewolves, we looked to be in our thirties, not our forties. My fake passport age was thirty-five, whilst Marcel's was his real age.

"I've texted her."

He smiled, and I knew he was referring to Raven. He grabbed one of our suitcases from the luggage belt. I looked down at my plain black suitcase. It was a shame I couldn't bring my designer luggage set, but we were meant to blend in. I wasn't sure we were doing a good job, as several young women and a few older women admired Liam. It was obvious he didn't realise that half of the looks he was getting were suggestive smiles as he innocently smiled back. He was very different from his parents.

I remembered when I found out Kiara was mated to Alejandro and not Rayhan. I had been very disappointed. I was glad later because they each had the perfect mates; I could not imagine anyone but Delsanra for Rayhan. However, after that time, I remembered hoping Liam and Raihana would be mated, but it wouldn't have worked. They are far too different, and Raihana would have transformed poor Liam into a slave.

If reincarnation is real, I was sure Raihana was an empress in a past life. I shuddered at the thought. The moon goddess always knew what she was doing and created us in pairs that worked well together. Most of the time, she was right. There were cases where things were far from perfect.

"Here you go," Marcel said, holding out a cold bottle of juice.

"Oh, thank you." I took it gratefully, unscrewing it and taking a few sips.

"This is the last one. Are we getting a taxi, Dad?" Liam grinned, grabbing the last suitcase.

We had to be careful. Puerto Rico wasn't big, and only one pack ruled over it. The fact that we were actually going to be digging up information about the pack was bound to get people's attention, so we needed to stay low for as long as possible. It was a short visit to try to find out what exactly the history of the Escarra family was.

"Alright, let's check in to our hotel, it's not far from here. Then we get something to eat before we begin exploring," Marcel said, picking up two suitcases whilst Liam grabbed the other two.

Exploring meaning get to work.

I nodded. I was fluent in the language, and I would be the one doing most of the digging, with both men acting more as bodyguards. Their huge sizes weren't easy to miss, and as I walked between the two men, it was obvious they were drawing attention.

It felt like a long time since I was of some use to my family and our packs. I didn't like to fail. I hoped we found the answers we needed, and I would do my best, I thought as we stepped out into the sun…

❧

A while later, we checked into our hotel suite, which had two rooms. I had my own, and the men were sharing the other. We showered and headed out to find something to eat. We were down by the beach, where there were a variety of restaurants and kiosks. Marcel and Liam were happily trying out several different dishes.

I had settled on a deep-fried dish called Alcapurrias. It was made up of a plantain-based dough roll filled with crab. I had to admit it was rather tasty.

Despite the warm weather, I was enjoying sitting out here in the sun. Music was playing loudly, and the atmosphere around us was a very happy one. It was hard to believe that this was the home of the Crimson King.

"You can tell you are Ri's mother right now," Marcel remarked quietly, making me look at him sharply.

"What do you mean?" He smirked slightly.

"Nothing at all."

I frowned slightly. I had a good idea of what he meant, but I was not complaining despite how hot I was feeling. I bit into my roll, looking around. From behind my glasses, I could see there were a few werewolves among the humans. Seeing one who looked just a little younger than me at a kiosk, I decided to make myself busy.

"I'll be back, I'm going to go get myself something else," I said, removing my sunglasses and motioning with my eyes.

"Sure, love," Marcel replied, trying to play the part. I turned, walking away.

Even with the sun shining, the gloomy weight of sadness washed over me, threatening to pull me into the abyss of darkness once more. I took a deep breath, trying to focus on the present.

"Can I get an iced lemonade, please?" I asked the man behind the counter.

"Right away!" I fanned my face, and, as expected, the werewolf glanced at me, his eyes skimming over me.

"New here?" He asked in accented English. I smiled charmingly, taking a seat on the stool and crossing my legs.

"Yes, just having a small family holiday," I said, making sure to look tired, and sighed softly.

"Oh? It doesn't seem like you are as happy as one should be when visiting here." The man behind the counter placed my iced drink before me, and I smiled slightly, running my finger along the rim of my glass. As expected, his gaze fell to my perfectly manicured long nails.

"Trying to be," I replied, looking him over and hoping it worked.

The only man I ever tried to seduce was Rafael, and it didn't require much work. In fact, he had been the shameless one, trying to sneak into my bedroom when he wasn't meant to until we were married. I blushed, remembering his shameless tactics. One wouldn't think that Rafael Rossi, who was always so charming, had another incredibly sexy side to him. One that was reserved for me. My king. How I yearned to be with him…

"You know, if you want, and of course, if you can get away from your family, I could show you the true magic of Puerto Rico," he suggested, ordering himself a drink.

"That actually sounds great… but I don't know, I don't even know you," I said hesitantly. I couldn't pretend to be that easy. I knew the men could hear me, but we didn't really have time to waste, and if flirting was the way to go, then so be it. Even if it left a sour taste in my mouth.

"Don't worry, I'm not going to abduct you and take you far away." He chuckled. "We'll remain in public places if that's what you prefer."

"Well…" I hesitated until he reached over, picked up a napkin, and grabbed a pen behind the vendor.

"If you change your mind, senorita." He held the napkin out, and I took it smoothly.

"Thank you." I smiled, letting him notice me looking him over. He smirked, flashing me a wink before walking off. Werewolves.

Humans would fall for them with ease, so he probably thought I was up for it. I resisted the urge to run my fingers over my mark that was hidden by a layer of makeup and Raihana's spell. We were taking extra precautions just in case.

"She's sexy," I heard another man say quietly to the man who had spoken to me.

"She is. I think if I'm lucky, I'll have some fun," the man chuckled, speaking Spanish. "You know, I like foreign women."

I took out some money to pay for my drink, not even turning toward them. After all, they didn't know I could understand and hear every single word. The man behind the counter smiled.

"It's paid for by the kind sir," he replied sunnily.

"Oh, thank you," I replied, turning to see if he was still around, but he had vanished. Taking out my new phone, I quickly typed in his number and sent the message,

'Thank you for the drink.'

Hitting send, I walked over to the table and sat down.

"That was smooth," Liam complimented quietly.

"Hmm," I responded, looking up at the sky.

I just hoped I got some answers out of him. I had a few things in my possession that would get him to speak, and if not him, then I'd find someone who would give me the answers that we needed.

A Dark Truth

MARIA

"So, we'll follow secretly and keep hidden away," Marcel said.

The bedroom door was open as I finished getting ready for the evening. I had chosen a strapless beige lace dress that reached just below my knees, curled my hair, and slipped on a pair of matching beige heels. I wasn't wearing any jewellery, and as I applied my makeup, making sure to cover up my mate mark, my mind once again went to my love.

My wolf's whimper in my mind squeezed at my heart, but what could I do? There was nothing that could take away the pain of the fact that he had died protecting me. I should have died that day, not him. I closed my eyes, holding the lipstick in my fingers tightly. It took me a moment for that anguish to calm within me, and, exhaling softly, I continued to apply my make-up.

"Yeah, we have a locator on Aunty; we just need to be careful," Liam agreed with Marcel.

I had messaged the man, who I learned was named Carlos, and he was going to meet me at the corner. I had told him that my 'husband and stepson' were going to be going out for the night, and I wouldn't mind him showing me around. Of course, he had jumped at the offer. I just hoped we got answers.

I was carrying my bag with a few items that may come in use. However, I also had some weapons on me. Down the back of my dress, I had hidden two thin blades, and the few pins I had used in my hair to hold my curls to the side were dipped in poison.

I walked out into the sitting room of our suite, only for Marcel and Liam to stop talking.

"Wow, you look gorgeous, Aunty." Liam smiled.

"And very young," Marcel added, scratching his beard. "I hope this man behaves."

"I assure you, you don't need to worry. No one gets to misbehave with me," I replied with a small smile.

"Passive-aggressive, I like it." Liam winked at me.

"Not at all, just stating facts. I'll be reporting to Raven on your behaviour," I threatened jokingly, making him grin. Well, if anyone did cross the line, I didn't forgive easily.

"Does Alejandro know what you're doing?" Marcel asked.

"I'm not a child. Now you two should get going." I glanced at the clock on the wall, and they both stood up.

✁✁✁

An hour later, I was laughing along with Carlos. It wasn't hard to pretend; I had been raised to be a good host and play the part. Those teachings came into use many times over the years. I poured him another glass of wine that was set on the table before us. I had been able to slip in the extra drug to get him to open up when he had gone to get us some food.

We were outside at a restaurant. Music was playing loudly, and I was relieved that I couldn't sense any other werewolves around. I had a feeling Carlos brought me here on purpose so none of his pack would see us. Well, that worked for me. I rested my elbow on the table, reaching over and smiling sweetly as I brushed back one of his brown curls.

"You have beautiful eyes," I commented, knowing Liam and Marcel were close by somewhere hidden away, listening and probably watching.

"You think so? I don't think they are anything compared to yours," he said huskily, sitting forward. He was a handsome man and much younger than me, which was horrifying.

"Thank you." I smiled seductively, brushing my fingers through my thick curls.

"So, Malika… isn't it? That's a beautiful name…" The drug was taking effect… perfect.

"Do you think so?" I asked, placing my hand on his thigh. He tensed, his eyes blazing blue, and I almost smirked. He was so far gone he didn't even have control over his wolf. Forcing myself to run my hand up his thigh, I leaned closer. "So, tell me, what is your rank in the Fuego De Ceniza Pack?" I whispered. His eyes widened, a flicker of confusion crossing his face.

"What? How do you..." I ran my hand closer up his thigh, and he blinked his eyes, becoming slightly hooded again.

"Shush... now tell me, what are you? A warrior? Maybe a Delta?" I whispered.

"Uh... I'm a guard, you know... I'm, like, meant to be a guard for the Alpha's family, but, you know, most of them are abroad. So it's kind of been quiet," he sighed. "I don't know how this pack is going to survive if our Alpha doesn't come back."

"Where has he gone?" I asked, removing my hand from his thigh and instead running it up and down his arm slowly.

"To get revenge. You know, we have been wronged."

"Oh no... How?"

He frowned, peering at me. I took his hand and placed a kiss on his knuckles. I needed to wash my mouth out after this... He relaxed and shook his head, grabbing his glass.

"You know, years ago, our Alpha had just one daughter. We are a small island, yet when a powerful pack's Alpha claimed her as his fated mate, we were ecstatic. She would go abroad and live a life of happiness as the Luna of the Luna Morte Pack. But no, no, her life was going to be cut short. You know, she was going give birth, but she was murdered by an enemy pack due to the two packs having conflict..."

I frowned. So this woman from the Escarra pack was mated to the brother of the woman stolen and claimed by DeAngelo. Why did it feel like the Rossi family, or more so DeAngelo Rossi, may be in the wrong and the cause of all of this?

"Then what happened?"

"Our Alpha lost it. He was hellbent on revenge. His daughter was the jewel of his eye. How can we let her death go? He went to Italy. They say he made a deal with the devil for power... and you know... he won. He wiped out the entire Rossi line, save one. The one he couldn't kill. They say the devil tricked him... he didn't give him the full revenge he wanted. He could not kill one of the Rossis until the time was right. You know...

that's where our Alpha has gone. They say… I shouldn't be saying this… I don't even…"

"You can trust me. All I want is to hear you talk. Your voice is so charming…" I ran my finger up his arm, and he shuddered, making me internally cringe. *Gods and goddesses, do forgive me.*

"Even we aren't meant to speak of it, I heard by mistake, but they say…" He looked around as if checking if we were alone or not. "They say Santiago Escarra made a deal with the actual devil himself. A Djinn. That he managed to summon one, and the Djinn asked for a price in return for granting him power… If the price is not paid, the Escarra line will die. Time is running out. Our Alpha is dying. They say the devil has possessed him, that he is paying for his ancestor's crimes. Alpha Sebastian once said he would break the curse for his son, but now, now they say he has lost his mind. He is unrecognisable. The Djinn's powers have burned him from inside, that even his face is unrecognisable."

My stomach twisted as I listened to what the man before me was saying. If this was true… this Crimson King was a puppet for the Djinn, who was hell-bent on getting what he wanted.

"What is it that the Djinn wants?" I asked, my heart pounding as I stared into his eyes.

"The blood of the beast," he whispered, so low I could barely hear. I leaned in. His eyes looked haunted, sending chills down my own spine despite the warm weather.

"The Lycan King," I murmured. Carlos chuckled.

"The Lycan? No, what will he do with his blood? It's the blood of the most powerful being on this… earth…"

He slumped forward onto the table, knocking over the glasses of wine and spilling my untouched one. I stood up quickly, not wanting the liquid to spill onto me. My heart thudded as the words he spoke echoed in my mind. Deep down, I had a feeling I knew whom he meant…

Glancing around, I quickly snuck away, seeing Marcel and Liam step out of the shadows.

"That was… interesting," Marcel muttered. "Well played. You really can pull the charm."

"Don't ever mention this to anyone. Ever," I said, casting him a cold warning look. Maybe I needed to get Raihana to remove the memory from their mind. Goddess, I never wanted anyone to see me doing that.

"Noted." Liam smiled slightly. "I'm sure Rayhan wouldn't want to know his mom was flirti-" I glanced at him sharply, and he shut up.

"What did he say at the end?" Marcel remarked, frowning.

"You didn't hear?" I asked sharply. They shook their heads, and I frowned.

"Let's get out of here. I'll fill you in," I replied.

I was sure I knew who it was, and if I was right, then Dante was the one in danger. Right then, Kiara and Alejandro were in Italy. I needed to let Rayhan know. Immediately.

Italy

KIARA

W E HAD REACHED ITALY, landing at the airport in Milan late in the afternoon. After doing a little more digging, thanks to Raihana, we found that this was roughly the area where the Lupo Nero Pack once resided, an area now under the hold of a new pack and Alpha.

I was standing on the balcony and looking out at the scenery before me. We were in a small town on the outskirts of the city, in a small hotel that we were only stopping at for a few hours to rest and freshen up before we headed on to our destination. It was haunting to know that powerful packs could be wiped out and forgotten, just like nations, empires, and tribes of long ago. Imagine diving into the past and learning about all this stuff. Would we one day be forgotten as well?

"Care to share what's on your mind?" Alejandro asked, wrapping his strong arms around me from behind. I closed my eyes, relishing in the sparks of his touch. He had just showered and was only wearing pants as he held me against his bare chest. Goddess, he was so fuckable. All I wanted to do was turn around and drop to my knees...

I quickly pushed the thought away, making sure he couldn't hear my thoughts. I was learning to put up my wall, but it was hard at times.

"I was just thinking, who would have thought that your ancestor's pack once ruled here?" I murmured as his lips touched my neck.

"Mmm, guess so. Things are always fucking changing, though."

"Yeah... one day... would we be forgotten?" I asked softly, a wave of sadness washing over me.

"Maybe? With time, I guess, yeah. Weird shit this conversation is."

"Hmm, maybe one day, someday, someone will write our story, and we will live on in the pages of our love story," I said before shaking my head sheepishly. "Sorry, I just had this sudden moment of sadness."

"I have a way of making you forget about that shit," he murmured huskily, kissing my neck harder. I sighed softly, my heart beating as his teeth grazed my neck, sucking on it. His hand squeezed my breasts.

"Fuck, Alejandro…"

"I would like to do just that," he growled, making me whimper as his hand slipped under my skirt and massaged my pussy. I moaned, feeling my core ache.

"But we have somewhere to be," I whispered, forcing myself to pull away from him.

"Yeah? Who fucking says?" He raised an eyebrow as he advanced toward me. My eyes widened as a smirk crossed his lips.

"Umm, don't we need to get back on the road? To do some digging? You had the name of someone who might have some information…" I backed away, only for my legs to hit the bed. Alejandro smirked, his hand closing around my throat as he pushed me back onto the bed and straddled me, making my core knot in anticipation.

"Yeah, but we both know it doesn't take long for this pussy to be dripping wet."

I didn't get a chance to reply before his lips were on mine, dominating me completely. I kissed him back with passion, the hunger for him settling deep in my core, making my pussy clench. His hands tore off my top and bra, letting my breasts bounce free. His eyes blazed red as he admired them.

"You're fucking perfect," he growled, squeezing my breasts as he ran his tongue along my under-boob tattoo, making me sigh softly.

Fuck… I want you to fuck me hard, Alejandro, I whimpered through the bond

With fucking pleasure, he growled, attacking my neck with rough kisses. He twisted my nipples before he went down, licking and flicking them, making me cry out in pleasure. He pushed my skirt up and ripped off my panties, slamming his fingers into me before I could even get my bearings, making me moan loudly.

In the back of my mind, I knew that the walls of the room weren't that thick, but I was unable to stop myself from crying out as he finger fucked me hard and fast. Pulling out, he was about to flip me over when I sat up, unzipping his pants and pulling them down to free his thick hard cock. Goddess, this man was so huge…

I wrapped my hand around it, licking the tip and enjoying his groan of pleasure as I pumped it with my hands while I sucked his tip. He yanked me back, flipping me over onto my stomach and lifting me up on my knees so my ass was up in the air. He delivered a sharp tap to it, and I blushed despite how horny I felt.

"Want me to fuck you, baby?"

"Yes, fuck me hard, Alejandro," I moaned.

"That's my girl. Now… tell me, how do you want it?"

"Fuck me like the beast you are," I replied breathlessly, reaching behind me and stroking his cock for a second.

"Oh, yeah."

And with that, he rammed into me, making me scream. For a moment, I couldn't breathe as he began fucking me relentlessly. His hands gripped my hips, our skin slapping against each other as pleasure consumed us. How was it possible that someone could make me feel so good and had me turned on so fast that all I wanted was for him to fuck me day and night, and, even then, I just wanted more.

"That's it, baby," I whimpered hornily, my orgasm building.

He moved back slightly, still half-buried in me, before he lifted my leg and yanked me onto my side. As he draped my leg over his shoulder, he placed one of his knees on either side of my other thigh as he began fucking me fast once more. The new angle only allowed him to bury himself deeper into me, making me cry out in pleasure…

❧❦❧

Two hours later we were on the way to our destination. Freshly bathed and aching down below, I felt refreshed. Dressed in tiny white shorts and a neon pink crop top, I was basking in having Alejandro's eyes rake over me. There was something empowering knowing that someone craved me and desired me the way Alejandro did. Even as we sat in the back of the car, his hand on my thigh sent pleasure to my core, and I felt at ease.

"So where are we going exactly?" I asked, tilting my head up towards him. Alejandro hadn't actually told me the details of our trip.

"To see someone who might have some answers about the history of the packs." He leaned over, placing a kiss on my forehead, making my stomach flutter.

"I see. How did you find this person?"

"Through some connections. Although we don't really talk to packs abroad much, I know a few, and with the recent mating balls spreading worldwide, I was lucky enough to make some neutral ties with a few people."

I nodded, leaning against his arm. After another half an hour the driver stopped, and we got out.

"Wait for us here," Alejandro ordered.

We walked for a few minutes on foot. The area was greener and soon we stopped, spotting two men dressed casually, sunglasses on, and as if waiting for someone. Us. I could smell that they were werewolves.

"Alpha King Alejandro Rossi. It is an honour," one of them said in accented English.

"In the flesh. I appreciate the fucking welcome," Alejandro replied arrogantly, his alpha aura rolling off him in waves. His voice was serious, level yet exuding so much power that it was obvious he was silently showing his status. And it was not missable.

"Blessed Luna Kiara, it is an honour. We have heard of your powers." I smiled graciously as they lowered their head to me.

"It's a pleasure to be here too," I replied warmly.

"Our Alpha is awaiting you. Follow me," the second man said, motioning for Alejandro to step forward, respectfully taking their place a half step behind Alejandro, whose arm was around me tightly as he led the way into the trees.

We didn't need to walk far until we reached a wall surrounding some premises. It was silent, especially if it was their pack grounds. The gates opened and we were led to one of the buildings. It became obvious that it was not the living area, but more just a work area of a pack.

"Please take a seat," one of the men said when they led us to a formal-looking lounge. Alejandro took a seat, and I followed suit.

"Our Alpha is on his way." The man bowed, motioning to the array of refreshments that were on the table. "Please, help yourselves." They left us alone, and I glanced around.

Don't eat anything, Alejandro commanded through the link, just when I was about to reach for one of the yummy-looking pastries.

But they look so good, I pouted.

I'll take you to some bakery or some shit when we're done with this crap, so just wait. We can't trust anyone, even if they are willing to help. His words were weighed down with seriousness and I didn't argue. I'd hold him to that. I would make sure he got me some fresh Italian pastries.

A man who looked a lot older than Alejandro entered, a metal cane in hand. Despite his limp he held himself with arrogance.

"To have the Lycan King himself visit our pack is a great honour," he said, his deep voice resonating in the room. The two men that had accompanied us here stood in the doorway.

"Alpha Matteo Bianchi, I appreciate the welcome," Alejandro said, standing up. The men hugged as if they had met before, but I knew that wasn't the case.

"Queen Luna." He bowed his head slightly, and I bowed mine. He held his hand out and I took it. He gave it a firm shake before taking the seat opposite. The curiosity to know what was wrong with his leg intrigued me and I was tempted to ask.

"I didn't know you were bringing the queen, or I would have had my daughters be here."

"It's fine, it was short notice for the both of us. I just appreciate the fact that you took time from your schedule for this," Alejandro replied, his eyes cold. Watching him, it was like he was a completely different person than the one I knew. Cold, aloof, powerful…

"Then let's get down to business. Shut the door," he commanded his men, motioning them to leave. They bowed their heads and backed out of the room, shutting the door behind them. "So, you want to know about the Lupo Nero Pack."

"Yes," Alejandro responded with a nod as he took out a packet of cigarettes and, placing one between his lips, flicked his lighter on.

My heart thudded as I watched him. His eyes flicked to mine and my core knotted. Goddess, why did he have to look so handsome doing something so bad like smoking? I pouted slightly and he smirked, looking back at the other Alpha as he took a drag on his cigarette.

"I'm all fucking ears," Alejandro said, leaning back on the sofa.

"Then let me tell you. I don't know too much, but what DeAngelo Rossi did was a heinous crime that none have forgotten. His barbaric ways shaped the future of the Packs of Italy."

Unexpected Events

ALEJANDRO

Kiara frowned as she listened to him. Matteo was straight to the point, and it was clear he didn't have any hidden agenda. Well, so far, he hadn't displayed anything strange, but I'd withhold judgement until the end of the meeting.

"DeAngelo Rossi was the most powerful Alpha around, and he proclaimed himself a king of Alphas, a title he took by his own means, forcing the other packs to bend to him or they would be slain. At first, many packs refused to obey, and he followed up on his threat." Matteo frowned slightly, shaking his head. "But that was not enough. He began to interfere in other packs' internal affairs and take women of choice for his entertainment. Many women were stolen away and never seen again."

"He had five women over the course of time, correct?" I asked sharply. Matteo shrugged.

"He took many women, but only a few of those who he took were recorded or given any importance. Those are the ones you are most likely referring to. The fear of our women being taken, tortured, and abused the way he did, made each pack isolate themselves from other packs, not wanting anyone to see their women. Other Alphas began copying the path DeAngelo had set, seeing it as a display of power."

"That's fucked up. The fourth woman that he took as his chosen mate, she was from a prestigious pack, correct?" I asked.

"Yes, I don't know the name. It's a pack that was completely wiped out. In fact, everyone thought the Lupo Nero Pack was completely annihilated in that clash as well. If you yourself hadn't told us about the link, I would never have made the connection. In fact, when I mentioned it to someone who I thought may know of this matter, it turned out you were correct. Alfonso Rossi made the wise choice to leave, or he would have been killed by the many enemies that his father had created." Matteo motioned to the snacks as he poured three glasses of wine. Kiara leaned over, taking one, despite the fact that I had told her not to. Although I knew she could sense a person's intentions, I still didn't take anything.

"Yeah, so you don't know anything about the pack that went to war with the Lupo Nero Pack, but do you know about the link they had to a pack from abroad?" Matteo shook his head.

"No, but I do know someone who has more information, the one I mentioned earlier. I wouldn't have wasted your time to call you all the way here. However, to protect them, I couldn't mention them over the phone. I hope you understand." *Well, what do we have here, a fucker I actually don't fucking mind.*

"I appreciate that. Is there anything you want in return?" I asked. He smiled slightly, and it was the first time he had.

"I would only hope that the Lycan King considers the Zanna Di Diamante Mortale Pack as its ally."

"Consider it done, especially if you have the information of someone who knows more."

"I do, and as asked, I have written the address -" I gave a curt nod, not wanting Kiara to think anything of it.

"That's great. We should head out then," I said, standing up swiftly. He looked surprised but said nothing and nodded as he, too, rose from his seat.

"May I ask what's wrong with your leg?" Kiara asked, smiling warmly at him. He looked down at his leg and gave a wry grin.

"This is the battle injury I gained when I saved my little petal from a rabid wolf." Rabid? Did he mean rogue?

"Oh, and it didn't heal?" Kiara questioned.

"No, due to the poisoning. I can, in fact, no longer shift. The poison from his fangs made me lose my wolf. I don't sense his emotions in my head. My mind link and my ability to heal have all gone." He smiled gravely. I frowned. How the fuck was that possible?

"How the fuck did that happen?"

"That is a problem we are handling. You should focus on your own troubles, Alpha King Alejandro. Come, I will show you out."

I frowned. That sounded fucking crazy. I guess everyone had their own shit going on. He led us through the building. Despite holding his back straight with pride and arrogance, it was obvious he was in pain and no more than a human, but he was still the Alpha...

The fucker remained stubborn, leading the way to the gates.

"Thank you for gracing us with your presence," he said politely.

"No, thank you for having us," Kiara replied, taking the older man's hand. I felt her aura surge around her. His eyes widened, but Kiara didn't let go, her purple aura becoming visible as she fuelled her power into him, a deep frown creasing her gorgeous face. "You... you're in a lot more pain than you are letting on," she murmured.

Matteo smiled slightly, trying to remove his hand from Kiara's but without a wolf to help him, he had no fucking chance. She was way fucking stronger.

"I do not want the Queen Luna to heal me. It is not why I called you here," he replied, and I could sense the pride he had.

"I know that you are telling the truth, but it's not something I can do, to walk away from healing someone when I know I can help them."

Without another word, she continued to heal him, whilst the elder Alpha could do nothing but watch. My attention was on Kiara; memories or not, she was a fucking queen at heart. Born to be one and fucking full of compassion for all...

❧❦❧

That night we stopped in Verona. Our next location was not far from there.

Matteo had been beyond grateful; the image of him placing his cane aside and taking a few steps stayed in my mind. It wasn't his ability to walk now that he was healed that stuck, it was the look of pure happiness on my nympho's face. I didn't know how I got so fucking lucky to have her as mine, but I was not fucking complaining. My fucking perfect queen...

It was morning, and we had left the hotel before the crack of dawn. We had gotten a few hours of sleep after a round of hot sex, which I was sure several people heard because the staff that was around in the morning were unable to look at us and had red faces when we had checked out. Not that I fucking cared.

Kiara was dressed in a white halter top which just about covered half her tits, leaving her stomach and the middle of her breasts uncovered, showing off her underboob chandelier tattoo and her entire back. I was going to fucking enjoy the view all fucking day. She had paired it with cropped khaki cargo pants and a pair of block heels. Her hair was up in a messy, stylish bun.

Our designated driver had been waiting outside by the sleek black car, and we were on our way to see a man by the name of Antonino Venturi. Kiara hadn't asked me for any details, and I was relieved. I didn't want to hide anything from her, but if the Djinn still had some sort of hold over her, I couldn't risk giving her all the details. I hated that, knowing that I was keeping secrets, but I hoped she understood. If worst came to worst, I would just tell her why. She'd understand, but it would also give the Djinn a heads-up that we knew.

After a while, we finally made it to our location, and following the instructions Matteo had given me, I found the vineyard with a moderate-sized house belonging to this Venturi guy.

"Welcome, Alpha, Luna," a young woman at the door said, clearly expecting us.

"Is Antonino Venturi here?"

"Yes, he's waiting for you."

I gave a curt nod as we both stepped inside. I just hoped he had some fucking answers…

⚜

Half an hour later, after pleasantries, we had gotten down to business. It was obvious Antonino wanted a price for his knowledge, saying it could put him in danger. I was willing to pay that price, and the fucker knew it. After coming to an agreement of fifty thousand pounds, he was finally sitting back, ready to speak. I had gotten half wired over to him, and he would get the other half after we got our damn information.

"Yes, it has come through," he replied, smirking slightly.

I could rip the fucker to shreds if I fucking wanted, dickhead. Kiara placed her hand on my thigh, and I slung my arm around her slender shoulders, casting Antonino a warning glare as his eyes roamed over Kiara.

He looked away swiftly. At least he was smart enough to know not to fucking mess with me.

"The pack in question is from Puerto Rico, run by the Escarra family, one of the oldest packs to hold the Alpha title in their family. They indeed started buying out all the shares to the Rossi businesses, selling them off at very low prices, and even framing them for illegal arms distribution. I'm not saying the Rossis were innocent, after all, they funded many illegal avenues. Also, I know Matteo has already told you about what your ancestor DeAngelo did."

"Yeah, he did, and regarding illegal avenues, you're talking about the Lupo XII Rossi, right?" I cut in. I didn't have time to waste here.

"Ah, so you know that already."

"A little, yeah. Carry the fuck on."

"I will, I will. Anyway, this company was the main source of income for the Rossis, the only holdings they had left, but the Escarras were not finished. When the Rossis were financially weakened, they then began isolating them from other packs, destroying their trust by truth or by lies. Who knows? But the Lupo Nero Pack was falling apart. DeAngelo's son even tried to get his father to step down. He refused, and then there was open war. The Escarras gathered their allies, and they ambushed the pack, killing DeAngelo. It's said that Cortez Escarra was so consumed by his daughter's loss he made a deal for power. He even called upon the help of witches to assist him, and he succeeded. He gained such power that he was a beast that could not be slain." Antonino paused as if waiting for a reaction.

"We know all that already," I stated. If he was thinking he could ask for more money, I didn't think so. We got a name, Cortez Escarra, but it still didn't answer the questions we needed. "I heard there's some debt that was left."

"Well, I guess the fact your line has lived on. I am assuming Sebastian Escarra now wants you all dead as it was meant to be." I frowned.

"Do you know anything of use? Because if that's all you fucking had, it's no damn use," I growled. He raised his hand and looked thoughtful, as if he was actually trying to remember.

"Well, if memory serves, Cortez knew one of DeAngelo's bastards got away, but he said he couldn't do anything about it - that when the time came, they would both get the revenge they wanted."

"They?" Kiara asked curiously.

"Well, rumours, it is, but apparently, it means he and the demon that possessed him. The demon that witches helped him summon. A devil that he struck a deal with. A deal that meant he couldn't kill the Rossi bastard. Not yet anyway."

I frowned. So he was waiting for something. Pay the debt by the blood of the beast... did he want my blood? Did they know a Lycan would be born? And waited? What was with this blood and shit? There was this fucking Djinn after my blood, and then there was me, who needs the blood of six hundred and sixty-six fucking virgins.... *Yeah, I hope my Deltas and Rayhan are enjoying handling that shit.*

"And how do you know all this?" I asked sharply. He was a lone wolf, so although he had a pack, he didn't live with them. Matteo had said he was not from their pack.

"Knowledge is power, King Alejandro. Power."

Memories of Brownies

ALEJANDRO

"Yeah? Well, I hope it does you fucking good. Let's just hope you're not killed for power," I smirked sardonically, standing up.

"Ah no, that is your forte." He tensed as if scared of my response, but I didn't have time for this shit. I looked down at him.

"When I return home, I will transfer the rest of the money. If anything else comes to mind, you will let me know," I commanded coldly, my aura rolling off me. His heart began racing, and I saw the panic that flitted across his face. "What do you know?" I growled, grabbing him by the collar and slamming him up against the wall.

"I…I… I can't say," he choked,

"You can. What. Do. You. *Know?*" I thundered, releasing my aura. I heard Kiara gasp as the man struggled to breathe.

"King Alejandro, you are a fool… your son… we all know he appears like a normal boy, but the eyes of the world are on him. We know you have witches on your side. It's easy to mask his abilities but tell me, how long will you hide what he is?"

"What do you mean?" I asked, my heart racing. Why was this fucking pointing at Dante? Was the 'beast' they talked about Dante? And if so, did that mean he was a Lycan?

"It means your family will always be in danger." He chuckled coldly, and my anger flared through me. I was about to rip his fucking throat out when Kiara pulled me back.

"Alejandro!" Her eyes were wide with concern as my chest heaved with rage.

"My family will deal with whatever shit is thrown at us," I hissed.

"Even if it's forces beyond this world?" He muttered, massaging his throat.

"Explain what the fuck you mean," I commanded coldly.

"There's a prophecy... I can't say!"

"I don't care, you will tell me!" I growled, lifting him up and slamming him against the wall. The smell of blood filled the air as I hit his head hard against the wall.

"Alejandro, maybe he can't -"

Answer me! I thundered, ignoring Kiara.

"Al..." I needed answers, and I wanted them now.

"Answer me," I commanded, my eyes blazing red. Unable to resist my command, his gaze fell to the floor.

"When the blessed wolf gives birth to a..." he trailed off, his entire body tensing, and then, to my shock, he stilled. I let go of him, realising his heartbeat had vanished as he tumbled face-first onto the luxurious woven rug.

"He's..." Kiara gasped, stepping away, her heart beating erratically. I looked down at the body, the cold reality of what had happened settling in. I didn't know how, but he was fucking dead.

৩৩৩

We had left Antonino's place and were heading back; my mind was still reeling with everything that had happened. I had straight away told Matteo what happened. He had said he would deal with it and to leave it to him. I knew they had been friends as he had protected Antonino's identity.

We were a few hours' drive from Verona, and the weather was scorching hot, although it wasn't even midday yet, and I could tell even in the air-conditioned car that Kiara was going to fucking feel it when we stepped out. She had asked if we could stop an hour ago before she had fallen asleep. The driver had said he knew of a good place where we could stop on our way back.

I glanced over at her. What with the fact that we had been out and about since yesterday, I could see she was fucking exhausted. Her eyes were shut, and her breasts rose and fell with every deep breath she took as she caught up on some sleep. Fuck did she look good in that sexy outfit of hers, although I knew she'd look far fucking better naked. Or even better, wrapping those tits around my dick so I could fuck them until I came over that gorgeous face of hers.

"Where would you like me to stop, sir?" I pushed the thoughts away, trying not to get hard right there.

"You can stop here," I told the driver in Italian.

We had just gotten into the middle of a town, not far from Antonino's place. Looking out, I spotted a bakery and remembered the promise I had made to her yesterday. Despite the weather, the place was packed. Even though I had my aura reined in, people could still sense it.

"Ah, of course, sir. Will you be okay from here?" The driver asked in Italian.

"Yeah, we will. We won't be long," I replied, unsure if I had said that correctly. Kiara smirked, and I knew it was because my Italian wasn't the fucking best. What was she expecting? Raf was the only one from us who spoke fluently, and I thought Rayhan could. Fuckers.

You sound sexy speaking in Italian.

Yeah, we both know I fucking don't.

You do when you call me Amore Mio, she responded teasingly.

You're mocking me. I gave her a cold glare. **I'll be punishing you later.**

Can't wait, same her seductive reply.

Kiara thanked him for the ride, telling him to take a break and go for a stretch before I opened the door and stepped out into the open, holding the door for her. She got out gracefully, adjusting her top over her breasts, making my attention fall to them. Fuck, was she hotter than fire. The urge to take her down a deserted street and bury my dick between her breasts sounded like a good fucking idea.

We were in a cobbled town centre, with a variety of shops and shit all around. There was a fountain in the centre and as much as I wanted to just go to the bakery and leave, seeing Kiara's eyes widen as she looked around with curiosity made me fucking hesitate. We had been in Italy twice since we'd been together, but this wasn't a place we had come to, and by the looks of it, her eyes had fallen on that small bakery.

"Want to stop over to grab something to eat?" I asked.

"Can we?" She asked, her eyes sparkling.

"Guess so."

"Great! Raven texted, and she said I needed to try this certain pastry, which apparently, I loved on our last visit…" she trailed off and looked up at me with a wave of sadness filling her eyes.

"Maritozzi or some shit like that. It's sweetened bread with cream inside of it," I replied, remembering how things had gotten a little messy with those in a fucking good way.

"Yeah, those are the ones Raven mentioned." She smiled, grabbing my hand as she hurried towards the bakery. Seemed like Liam had gotten them two talking again. I was glad, not wanting her to feel any further doubt, especially with the fact that the Djinn still had some level of hold over her.

I pushed the door to the bakery open. The smell of dozens of freshly baked treats was actually fucking appealing, but the place was too fucking packed, although Kiara didn't seem to fucking mind.

We walked over to the counter, waiting until the few people ahead of us were served. Kiara scanned the display of treats, and I felt my heart squeeze, remembering how she loved to bake.

"You loved to bake," I remarked, placing my hand on her ass.

"I did?"

"Yeah." I cupped her neck with my free hand, pulling her close and kissing her passionately as I squeezed her ass.

"What did you like the most? From what I baked I mean?" She asked me when we broke apart, her cheeks coated a pretty shade of pink as she tried to ignore the stares we were getting.

"Your brownies," I said when we finally got to the counter to be served. She chooses some pastries and gets the one she wants before we step out.

It was good to see her so fucking happy. I just hoped, with all the shit that went down earlier, that things didn't get any worse. "So, we head home now?" She asked me, biting into one of the cream-filled pastries.

"Yeah. We got the answers we needed, so we head back."

Sinful Magic

RAIHANA

I HAD TOLD CHRIS ABOUT the pregnancy the same day we had returned from Uncle's pack. He had been concerned with everything going on but super happy, pampering me even more than normal, if that was even possible, and although I wanted to share the news with everyone else, it was not the time.

With Mom in Puerto Rico and Uncle gone to Italy, I felt even more restless. I had initially suggested to Chris we should go to Uncle's pack, but he refused, saying they'd call if they needed us. I knew he was just being protective of me and our unborn pup. I had gotten a scan done, and our little baby was healthy and growing well, although it was still early days.

"You need to relax, ma chérie," Chris whispered, walking around the sofa as he placed his hands on my shoulders and began massaging them, making sparks dance through me. I moaned softly, loving the feel of his hands my skin. It was past midnight. Chris had been finishing off some pack work in the living room, and I had stayed with him.

"You know, baby, there's one way that really relaxes me…" I placed my hand over his and looked up at him.

"Oh, I know exactly what you mean," he smirked, running his hand down my neck and over one of my breasts. "I actually had an idea…"

"Care to share what that idea is?" I asked, scraping one acrylic nail down his jaw. Goddess, he was so handsome. I was proud to call him mine. His lips touched my neck, making me sigh softly as he squeezed my breasts sensually, and I moaned.

"I was thinking, since you did that spell last time making a double of yourself... how about you use it on me so I can see exactly how you look taking two dicks?" His words sent a spark of excitement through me, and I smirked slightly, tilting my head up.

"Oh, that's a fantasy that has crossed my mind," I replied, twisting my hand into his lush blond locks as I stared up into his sharp green eyes.

"Then let's make it a reality," he smirked, winking at me before he stepped away and peeled off his t-shirt.

He walked around the sofa, tossing his shirt to the ground. He held a hand out to me, one I took willingly, allowing him to pull me up and into his arms. I instantly hooked my legs around his waist and allowed him to carry me out of the room as he kissed me passionately.

A spell that created a body double. The one it was used on could see through both pairs of eyes and feel what the body double could. Although it was a spell created for spying and deception, I thought I put it to much better use. I smirked as I ran my tongue along his lips before kissing him deeply.

The moment we were in our bedroom, he slammed the door shut, and I whispered a spell, locking it. Twisting my hand into his hair, I whispered the spell, staring into his piercing green eyes. A surge of power swirled around me, and I felt Chris tense. Then, I felt the pull from inside, and I pricked Chris' neck, using the drop of blood needed, and suddenly there stood another Chris right next to the original.

"Fuck, that's still crazy," Chris remarked as his double, who I thought I'd refer to as Kris, stood there smirking. The only thing about the spell was that the double couldn't talk.

"Very appealing on the eyes," I replied, gasping when Kris stepped up behind me, his hand twisting in my long hair and kissing my neck sensually from behind.

"Now, let's have some fun," Chris growled huskily.

Chris' hands roamed my body as Kris made quick work of ripping my top off, his hand reaching over to unzip my pants before Chris carried me to the bed. Placing me down, he pulled my pants off. My heart was racing as I stared up at the two sexiest men on the planet. Two pairs of piercing eyes were looking at me as if I was a feast to be devoured. I cupped my large breasts, massaging them sensually and looking at both hunks.

"What are you boys waiting for? Strip."

Both smirked as they reached for their identical zippers and began pulling them down before taking their jeans off, looking so damn hot that my core was already clenching in anticipation. The dampness in my panties increased. Clad in their designer-fitted boxers that supported their huge cocks, I bit my lip, sitting up and pulling Chris' boxers down. Fuck, I could never get enough of him.

"Oh fuck, look how hard you are for me, baby," I whimpered hornily, running my hand around his shaft.

"Then open up. Let me see how much this pretty mouth can take," Chris commanded huskily, tangling his hand into my hair and pressing his tip to my lips. I gasped as Kris bent down and ripped my G-string off.

"I think we can tag team." Chris winked as my core knotted, knowing what was to come.

"Fuck, yes."

I gasped when Kris pushed my thighs apart, burying his face in my pussy just as Chris shoved his cock into my mouth, stretching it as I began sucking him off. Pleasure ripped through me, and the scent of my arousal filled the air. I tangled my hand into Kris's hair, the other on Chris's cock as he thrust into my mouth, fucking me roughly. I moaned against him, my pleasure heightening. Chris was a sex god, and he could ruin me with pleasure. Now, there were two of him, both of whom knew what turned me on, which only made this even deadlier in a sinfully pleasurable way. Every emotion and feeling in my body were heightened, the pleasure sending me into a lust and sex-filled haze.

Fuck, that's it! I moaned through the link.

Kris slammed three fingers into me, his tongue flicking my clit with just the right pleasure that sent me crazy. At the same time, Chris shoved his entire length into my mouth, hitting the back of my throat. Fuck!

I barely managed to relax my throat before I gagged as he throat fucked me harder. I was no longer in charge of anything, the intensity of how he was making me feel driving me crazy. The erotic sounds of me sucking him off mixed with his sexy moans as he neared only tipped me over the edge, making an intense orgasm rush through me. I tried to breathe and move away from Kris, but he didn't let go, pinning me to the bed as he licked up my juices. My entire body shivered from my orgasm. The pleasure was beyond delicious and an addiction that I could never get enough of.

Chris pulled out, stroking his dick a few times, and shot his load over me. I gasped, sticking my tongue out as he pumped his dick until the last drop dripped onto my tongue. He tasted so, so good.

"Fuck, Princess," he growled, pushing me back onto the bed as he straddled my hips, grabbing my breasts as he claimed my lips in a hungry kiss.

Kris was placing soft kisses along my pussy whilst Chris sucked on my nipples. I cried out loudly. Oh, fuck! This was intense. Suddenly, Chris flipped over, lying next to me and sucking on my right nipple. His hand ran down my stomach as Kris dropped onto the other side, giving me the classic smirk I was so used to. He took my left nipple into his mouth, making me moan.

"Softly!" I whimpered. Recently my nipples felt extra sensitive.

"Fuck, you look so fucking good…" Chris murmured, taking a second to look me over. I pulled him close, kissing him passionately as he rubbed my pussy for a moment before he ran his fingers lower and between my ass, pressing against my back entrance. "Let's stretch you out a little bit so you're all ready for us."

My core clenched at the thought, and the moment his finger slipped into my ass, Kris shoved his fingers into my pussy. My eyes flew open, and Chris chuckled, attacking my neck with hot kisses, sucking hard as they both pleasured me. Fuck, it was too much. My eyes fluttered shut as I saw stars, my cries of euphoria getting louder.

"Fuck me now, baby," I whimpered, twisting my hand into Kris's lush blond locks.

"Cannot fucking wait," Chris replied huskily. Slipping his fingers out of me, Kris adjusted his position, resting back against the pillows and lifting me on top of him. My back was pressed to his firm hard chest. "I want to see you filled to the fucking brim."

Chris's eyes darkened as Kris positioned his cock at my back entrance, wrapping one arm around my waist whilst the other squeezed my breasts from behind. I spread my legs wider, licking my fingertip softly before placing it over my clit and moving it in a circular motion, my eyes fixed on Chris. He grabbed the tube of lube from the bottom drawer beside the bed, squeezing some out and running it along his double's dick. I moaned, not holding back how horny I sounded as Kris squeezed into me, making me gasp.

"That's it, baby girl, breathe," Chris commanded, running his hands up and down my thighs.

We'd used toys, but anal wasn't something we did often. Knowing that there were going to be two monster cocks buried in me was already exciting me, despite knowing it was going to hurt a little.

Chris bent down, running his tongue along my pussy once before he positioned himself at my entrance. His eyes ran over my body as Kris carried on playing with my breasts.

"You're made to be worshipped," he murmured before he thrust into me, making me scream in pleasure. Oh, fuck, it felt so good.

"Fuck, Chris!"

I could feel them both buried deep inside of me. They gave me a moment to adjust, and then they began fucking me, drowning me in pain and pleasure. The perfect mix of sin and love. My moans were so loud as I held on to Chris, and they both fucked me relentlessly.

"Fuck, Ri," he growled, his eyes blazing, and to my surprise, I could see his canines.

"Chris, ah!" I cried out.

I was so close! The pleasure was too much. Goddess, I was in heaven. He suddenly pulled me up by the back of my neck, sinking his teeth into me just as my orgasm tore through me, and I felt both men release their load in me. Chris's groan of pleasure made me whimper before he pulled out at the same time as Kris, leaving that pleasant ache behind. I knew it was going to hurt later, but it had been so worth it...

Chris rolled onto the bed next to me, claiming my lips in a rough, passionate kiss as Kris kissed my neck from behind, dizzying me. I whimpered softly as Chris pulled me tightly against his body.

"You can get rid of him now," he whispered with a cocky smirk.

I smiled back, staring into the eyes of my love as I turned and looked at Kris, who wore an identical smirk on his face. He leaned over, wrapping his hand around my neck and kissed my lips passionately before I whispered the spell, and with a small puff, he vanished. I turned back to Chris, who was smirking cockily, running his fingers down the curve of my hips.

"Well, that's something I wouldn't mind doing again. Seeing you taking two dicks... really fucking turned me on," he whispered in my ear, making my heart skip a beat.

"Oh yeah?"

"Yeah."

"Good, because I loved it too," I whispered, locking my arms around his neck before we kissed once more.

I love you, baby.

I love you too, ma ch-

The phone ringing made us both pause. If it was any other tone, we would have ignored it, but it was Rayhan's, and with the current situation, there was no way we could not answer. Chris leaned over, grabbing his phone.

"Yeah?" He answered, his arm still holding me close.

"Sorry to bother you so late at night. Mom just rang. Dante's the target. Can you and Ri come here? I think we could use any extra security possible, just in case something happens," Rayhan's voice explained. Chris frowned slightly; I knew he didn't want to put me in danger, knowing I was pregnant, but I placed my hand on his chest and nodded, giving him a look.

Please just agree, I said through the link.

"We'll be there within the hour," Chris replied after a moment before hanging up. He tossed his phone onto the bed, exhaling sharply, all playfulness vanishing as he sat up.

"Chris."

"You need to prioritise yourself, too, Ri. I can't have what has happened to Del to happen to you," he said quietly, running his hand through his messy blond hair. I got up onto my knees, my legs feeling like jelly, and wrapped my arms around his shoulders from behind.

"It's okay, baby. I can handle this," I whispered, very aware of my nipples grazing against his back.

"Yeah, I'm sure, we all think that, but when shit goes down, we don't even fucking realise where things went wrong. You know some of the reasons witches began hating werewolves? It's because they're always used as collateral damage," he said quietly, unable to keep the bitterness from his voice. My heart clenched. I understood him, I really did, but my family needed me.

"I know, baby, but Uncle wouldn't allow me to -"

"Tell me, Princess, when stuff went wrong, who did Kia call first? Delsanra. Then what happened? She ended up in the state she is. Now that Dante may be in danger, who did Ray call? You. Fuck this. I'm tired of you risking yourself again and again."

"Chris, it's not like that. Ray has a witch mate, too, he understands how you must be feeling. Plus, I'm his sister. Look, we are all risking ourselves, doing the best we can, and I need to do my best too."

"But the witches are always the first line of defence," he responded quietly, removing my arms from around his neck and standing up. A flash of pain rushed through my chest. I hated when he was upset... and I hated it even more when he was upset because of me. "I'm telling Rayhan you're pregnant when we get there," he added quietly before he stormed out of the room, his anger palpable through the bond.

I closed my eyes, sighing heavily. I knew once he made up his mind, there was no changing it...

Responsibility

RAYHAN

I HUNG UP THE PHONE, frowning. We had five kids in the house, plus Delsanra. If anything went down…

I was glad Chris and Ri would be coming soon. It was just a little more security, although our own security was already at the max. Uncle Elijah was here, too. It should be okay, right?

For a second, I realised how Uncle must feel, knowing that everyone's responsibility was on his head. I paced the lounge, running a hand through my hair. I needed to relax. There was no way the Djinn would come here. I had a strong feeling that he couldn't, or, by now, wouldn't he have already done so?

"You know, if you can't take care of Delsanra, I wouldn't mind doing it."

I stopped in my tracks, turning and looking at Dante, who was standing there. His arms were crossed as he smirked smugly in the doorway to the living room.

"Don't worry. I can handle my kitten," I replied, giving him a cocky smirk back.

"Hmm, sure."

"Why are you awake?" I asked, watching as he looked down the hall.

"I want hot chocolate. Shall I make you some?" He asked, surprising me.

"How about I make us both some?" I suggested. He shrugged as I walked past him.

"That's better." His cocky reply came.

This kid. You can love him and still get irritated with him.

Entering the kitchen, he got onto the bar stool. I saw the slight struggle it took him to pull himself up. Although he was fairing way better than Delsanra, who was unable to even sit up by herself, he was still struggling but hiding it the best he could. Just the thought squeezed at my chest.

I glanced around, spotting the hot chocolate machine, and took the milk carton from the fridge before I began looking for the hot chocolate sachets.

"Second drawer to your left," Dante remarked

"You could have spoken earlier."

"Well, it's quite fun to see the Alpha of the Black Storm Pack search a kitchen," came his snarky reply.

"You really are an asshat," I replied, pouring the milk into the machine.

"I'll have mine in one of those glass mugs once it's done," he stated.

I grabbed two mugs before switching the machine on, leaning against the counter as I waited for it to be ready. He was watching the machine before he turned his red eyes on me.

"Can you get me some chocolate? Why aren't you asleep?" He asked, glancing at the pantry.

I crossed the kitchen, grabbing a few bars from the huge stash in the pantry and placed them on the counter in front of him. Opening a Caramel Cadbury bar for myself, I looked over at him.

"Mom called, so sleep went out the window." I shrugged as he picked up a bar of Galaxy chocolate.

"Hmm, what did she say?"

I knew he knew a lot more than he let on, and I wondered if he knew anything more about Mom's trip. A sudden thought came to me, and I tilted my head.

"She found some answers. They're on their way back," I replied, biting a chunk off.

"Oh really? What did she find out?" I smirked.

"You may act like an adult, but you are only eight," I reminded him.

"Going on nine," he countered, staring at his chocolate before placing it flat on the counter. He picked at the corner of the wrapper as if not wanting to rip it open.

"You know more than you let on, too. So, want to share exactly what you know about this Djinn and what he wants?" I suggested lightly. He looked up and smirked,

"We both know what he wants." He shrugged. I frowned slightly; I didn't know exactly how his 'gift' worked.

"Dante, you knew… I know that there must be a reason you don't say what is inside you. Can I ask what that reason is?" I asked quietly, moving away as the machine beeped, signalling that our hot chocolate was ready.

"I just can't say it. I know things… but I can't put them into words…" he muttered quietly, and, for a moment, he looked like the eight-year-old he was. I poured the hot chocolate into two mugs and carried them to the counter, pulling out the stool for myself.

"So, like, it's in your head, but you can't speak it?"

"Yes… I also know that if I speak of everything I know or see, it can affect the balance."

"Who told you that?" I asked. He looked at me as if considering whether he should tell me or not.

"I just know."

"So you can see the future and stuff, right?" I asked, remembering how he knew Kiara was having twins, among several other things.

"I see outcomes. They constantly change. And I don't see everything, just bits." He shrugged, picking up his mug, and for a moment, I wondered how hard that must really be.

"Outcomes… must be rough having to carry all that." He smirked arrogantly.

"Well, I can obviously handle it."

"Yeah, you can." I ruffled his hair, making him frown. "So, this infatuation with *my* mate. What's with that?" He gave me a look as if I was dumb.

"Really, Rayhan? If I like someone, it's because I like them. It doesn't have to mean anything. Besides, she's so pretty, and her eyes are red like mine." I frowned. Yeah… we realised long ago that he didn't see Del in her human form but her demon form. Could I blame the damn kid? "Tell me, are you scared I'll grow up and steal your mate?" He asked smugly.

"No," I growled. He snickered before sipping his hot chocolate. Fucker indeed.

"Have you ever seen your mate?" I asked curiously. He looked at me, raising an eyebrow as he ate his chocolate.

"I can't actually see my own future," he stated so casually as if he was telling me about the weather.

"What?"

"Yes... I've seen Kat's mate... I've seen Sienna's..."

"What?" I narrowed my eyes, but he simply smirked.

"I can't say more, but I'm just telling you that I can't see my own. Maybe I don't have a mate." He shrugged, then looked me over with a sly smirk. "Maybe I'll steal yours."

I knew he was trying to piss me off, and he was almost succeeding, but more than that, the fact that he knew Sienna's disturbed me. She was my little princess. Fuck, I did not want anyone near her. Dammit.

"Uncle said you advised him to take Kiara with him. Why?" He simply looked at me blankly but didn't reply. I guess I had asked enough.

"Your hot chocolate is cold," he smirked before sliding off his stool. "Chris and Raihana are going to be here very soon; they have more news for you."

With that, he walked out of the room, and I glanced down at the chocolate wrapper he had folded neatly into a square. I was sure he was going to have a mate, but I wondered what kind of mate he would be blessed with. Dante was no ordinary Alpha; we all knew that.

I shook my head, glancing at my watch. He wasn't wrong. Chris and Raihana would be there soon.

��‿��

A short while later, Raihana had just gone to put Tatum into bed. Serena, Claire, and Clara were keeping an eye on all the kids, apart from Si, who was with Del.

"What's up, man?" I asked Chris. He had seemed a tad quieter than normal, and I could see from Raihana's neck that they had obviously had fun before coming, so I wasn't sure what his problem was.

"Nothing really," he replied, but I knew him better than that. He and Lola were my best friends, and I knew when either of them was upset or had something on their minds.

"I know you better than that."

"Yeah? Then you should know that having Raihana constantly risking herself is really fucking me over," he said quietly, taking me by surprise.

"I get you. Trust me, I know how it feels, knowing that Delsanra is in the state she is because she was trying to help. It kills... but we love Ri-"

"You love Del, too, and she's still on her deathbed."

"She's not dying." My eyes flashed, my anger flaring up, but he just shook his head.

"No, but she's fucking close. I love Del, I hate seeing her like that. Now with her unable to do more, it's all on Ri, isn't it? Even you called her just in case something happened."

I frowned, looking down at my hands. I did, but I never ever considered putting her in danger. She was my sister. I love her.

"Raihana is -"

"A Rossi, the first Rossi princess, and I am no less than anyone else risking their life for our loved ones. I will do the same as all you men do for us, but I will be careful. Relax, boys." Raihana walked in, her heels ticking against the marble before she straddled Chris, locking her arms around his neck and kissing his lips passionately. Those two never really cared about PDA.

I glanced away, letting them have their moment before Raihana sighed and adjusted herself so she was sitting sideways on his lap, facing me.

"Chris is just concerned because I'm pregnant," she explained airily, placing her hand on her stomach, surprising me.

"Obviously, I'm going to be concerned." Chris placed his hand over hers, kissing her shoulder as I stood up, unable to keep the smile from my face.

"Wow, so I get to be an uncle to another little angel?" I asked, making Raihana smile as she stood up, and I hugged her tightly. Despite how hard times were, this was a ray of happiness. "Wow, no, he totally has a reason to be concerned. You should have told me before I made you guys come all the way over here." I kissed her forehead as she tossed her hair, looking at Chris, who was smirking slightly now.

"See? My family cares for me, too."

"Yeah, how can they not? But it still messes me up."

"Congratulations to you, too," I added to Chris before smiling down at Raihana. "Del is going to be super excited."

"She is. I told her before I came downstairs. Do you think I'd tell you before her?"

"Ouch," I replied, grimacing.

"She's choosing my baby's name, too," she stated before returning to her mate's lap.

"Nice plan," Chris smirked, kissing her neck. The news was still fresh, and it took me a moment to let it actually settle in.

"Wow… you need to be careful then," I said quietly, running my hand through my hair. That was another one off the list. Knowing she was pregnant, there was no way I wanted her to risk herself.

"She does."

"Uncle knows, and he said the same thing, just my baby here still feels I do too much when I don't," Raihana replied, running her finger along Chris' lips.

"You do, and I don't like you getting hurt. I need you safe."

"Always," Raihana replied. I massaged my jaw thoughtfully.

"I know you have reasons to worry, but we've learned from what happened with Del. I can assure you both Uncle and I will not let anything happen to her. Just the way we won't let anything happen to you or anyone else." Dad came to my mind, accompanied by a pang of pain. We had already lost far too many.

"So, you have nothing to worry about," Raihana was saying, kissing him softly.

"I will still worry when it comes to you, ma chérie." They began kissing, and I shook my head, standing up.

"Alright, I'll leave you two to it. I'm off to bed."

They didn't reply, and I headed upstairs. Entering the bedroom, my eyes fell on the slender form of Delsanra, who was lying on the bed with her eyes half-open. When she saw me, a flicker of light returned to them. I smiled at her, closing the door and removing my shirt before I slipped in beside her. Lifting her head gently, I kissed her neck.

"I love you," she whispered.

"I love you more."

Placing my hand on her tiny waist, I inhaled her scent, letting it calm me. On her other side was Sienna, her mouth hanging open as she slept without a care in the world, with Del's hand resting on top of her tiny little belly. My beautiful girls.

"Raihana's pregnant," Del whispered, smiling up at me, making me press my lips to hers.

"Yeah, I wonder if it'll be a girl or boy," I replied, brushing my fingers over her hips.

"Either way, I cannot wait," she replied softly. I hugged her tightly, pulling her against me, and she smiled when I throbbed against her ass.

"And I can't wait for you to get better so I can do a lot more to you than just hold you." I smiled teasingly, kissing her jaw. "We are finally getting answers, and I'm sure Uncle will find something out, too." I just wanted her to be healthy and herself once again.

She nodded, and we fell silent. I was sure Uncle would, and then with that knowledge combined with what Mom learned, we could work on a plan to find this Crimson King and kill him.

I had organised a regime for a special group, with the help of other trusted Alphas, to gather the blood we needed. We currently had the blood of one hundred and two virgins. We still had a way to go, but we had sent some men to go to the human areas of the country and were attaining blood from humans as well. I just hoped we had the six hundred and sixty-six soon because it was high time this Djinn was sent back to hell.

The Price to Rule

ALEJANDRO

W E HAD RETURNED EARLIER today, and to my surprise, it was a fucking full house. Scarlett, Raven, and her pups were all here. It seemed Scarlett hadn't known when Kia and I would be back, so had come to help with the kids.

We were having a meeting later, but Maria had quickly filled us in on what they had learned. Dante was the target. It all made sense from the start. Even Enrique had tried to attack him. I just fucking wished I knew why they wanted him. What exactly did his blood offer them?

The smell of food wafted through the house as dinner was being prepped. Kiara was baking with Scarlett, and even Maria was making some desserts. Everyone had been happy to hear the news of the new pup. Chris seemed a little quieter, but I was sure the concern for his mate and pup would do that to anyone.

Raihana had bought all the kids and women new clothes; the girls were all in glittering dresses that reminded me of disco balls. The women were in equally fucking sparkly dresses as well. I wondered if I should grab a pair of sunglasses. As for the boys, they were in matching shirts, pants, and boots - only Dante was refusing to wear them. He was sitting on the sofa opposite Raihana, who was in a deep pink sequined dress, glaring at the clothes on the sofa next to him.

"I am not matching babies." He scowled across the sitting room, directing it towards Raihana.

The living room in itself looked like a tornado had fucking hit it. There were toys, cups, clothes, as it seemed all the younger pups had changed in here, as well as Raihana's table full of makeup products. It was obvious she had decided to go full-out on dressing everyone up for this small dinner in celebration of her new addition. I wasn't complaining; it was good to see them all enjoying shit, but the makeup and the glitter were fucking too much.

"Oh, zip it. Stop being dramatic, you'll look cute!" Raihana replied to Dante as she applied makeup on Delsanra, who I felt fucking sorry for. Kiara rushed to heal her and Dante upon our return, but it did little to help raise her energy levels. She was getting worse. She lay there with her eyes closed, whilst I had to admit Raihana did a good job of covering those veins that covered her.

Kataleya was sitting against the far wall, holding a teddy bear tight to her chest and staring out at the sky from the window.

"Perfect…" Raihana smiled proudly, finishing applying Delsanra's lipstick. The woman could barely keep her eyes open, and Raihana was using her as a fucking makeup doll. What the fuck was wrong with her?

"I am not wearing these clothes. You wear them," Dante shot at Raihana.

"Dante, listen to your sister," I remarked, wanting the fucking conversation over with.

"No. She's annoying."

"I am not! You'll look so handsome! Look, I even chose a shirt for you to match your eyes! Come on, you're making me sad," she pouted. I glanced at her as she looked at Dante. Yeah, that shit worked on everyone but the fucker.

"A no is a no, or do you want me to answer you in a different language?" Dante remarked arrogantly.

"Oh, don't show off your bilingual skills. I can speak several languages, too," Raihana replied.

"But you still don't understand a no in simple English?" Dante replied, smirking victoriously as Raihana pouted, and he lay down on the sofa, closing his eyes.

"That boy…"

"Is a bit like you," Delsanra said, opening her eyes. Raihana smiled, holding up a small mirror so Delsanra could see what she had done. "Thanks, it's gorgeous." She smiled at her friend.

"You look a tad fucking better," I added, making her smile grow.

"Thanks, King Burrito."

"Daddy, look, I am Maleficent!" Skyla said as she did a twirl in her green dress, which made her eyes look even greener.

And Raihana had put black lipstick on her.

Seriously.

"You fucking do."

"Yes, I just need horns. Now, give me one pound for swearing." She held her hand out, and I frowned.

"Later," I growled, leaving the room, being careful not to step on any of the scattered clothes or toys.

I heard the giggling from the side of the room where Sienna was busy playing with Ahren, Tatum, and the Westwood five. Dante had a fucking point. Why the fuck were they all dressed exactly the same? One sparkly princess with seven bodyguards. That's what that shit looked like.

I shook my head, leaving the room and almost knocking into Rayhan.

"Seriously, this fucking place is a tad too fucking small," I growled, making him smirk.

"Or you are just too big to manoeuvre smoothly."

"Jealous that I'm fucking taller?"

"Not at all," he smirked. He had his hair pulled back, making him look a bit less fucking annoying.

"What's the count now?" I asked, knowing he'd get what I meant.

"Just another twenty. Stuff has slowed, it's hard to find those who fit all the criteria. Although the witches the coven sent to check the blood said fifteen of the previous batch weren't of virgins," he replied quietly, glancing down the hall, but it was just us other than near the far side, but it was only Liam and Chris who were talking to Darien and Serena. We just had to be careful that Kiara didn't hear of this. I hated hiding stuff from her.

"But those who said they were were questioned under Alpha command… unless they didn't know…" I mused, frowning as we exchanged looks. The same thought came to both of us at the same time.

"Yeah, I thought the same thing." Rayhan crossed his arms, a frown on his face.

"They had the bottles labelled with identities, right?" He nodded. "Good, then find the details of those who didn't qualify. Check if there's any sexual abuse or anything involved. For someone to believe they were a virgin but aren't… I want to make sure it's not ignored. Have Nicholson handle it. I need someone who's trustworthy to deal with this."

"Sure. I'll let him know." Rayhan nodded, walking off to make a call just as Kiara stepped out of the kitchen with Raven, both laughing over something.

"I swear it was the funniest thing." Raven smiled.

"It was not funny," Azura added, stepping out of the kitchen from behind them. All three were in the dresses Raihana had gotten, with Kiara's being a blue-green that suited her eyes and Raven's black. The Westwood devil's was a bright blue. "Hey, Al!" She waved.

"Hey, pup."

"I'm not a pup anymore," she stated, tossing her hair.

She was about to say something else when she smiled slyly, spotting Liam. I really didn't give a shit about stuff, but I did feel for the fucker. The girl loved to play pranks on him, and he didn't even realise she had him twisted around her finger. She walked off sneakily, and I looked back into Kiara's gorgeous face. She smiled at me, and I closed the gap between us, pulling her close and kissing her passionately.

The dickhead Elijah coughed loudly, and Kiara pulled away, blushing lightly. I ignored him, my eyes dipping to her breasts. She was so fucking sexy.

"You look fucking fine," I growled huskily, making her let out a breathless laugh, her cheeks only darkening.

"You, too, handsome." She kissed my neck before pulling away.

"Are you two done?" Elijah remarked.

"Not really, but -" Kiara placed her finger to my lips and smiled at her dad.

"Yes, we are."

Before Elijah could reply, Maria and Scarlett came out of the large dining room. They, too, were wearing the same blinged-out dresses in red and silver.

"I'm so happy to hear the news," Scarlett was saying to Maria.

"Another grandchild, although I still have a way to go before I match your eight."

"We are not having more kids, Mom," Rayhan added, walking back over to us and looking at his mother.

"Ya hayati, you never know."

"You never know. They are still young," Scarlett smirked.

"I'm pretty sure," Rayhan replied, smiling at both women.

"Five kids are too much, trust me," Raven said, making Kiara smile.

"You are superwoman. Liam is immune to it or something, but just thinking of five is intense," Rayhan replied.

"I like the house full," Kiara added.

And I like you fucking full with me, I added, making her blush.

Just then, my phone rang, and I pulled it out, frowning down at the number. Janaina. Giving the group a nod and Kiara a tap on the ass, I walked towards the front garden, not wanting anyone to hear the conversation.

"Yeah? What's up?"

"I wanted to let you know that I have created the blade. The question is, have you chosen someone to wield it? Remember, there is only one chance," she said quietly.

I glanced back towards the open front door at Chris and Liam, seeing Liam's sharp eyes watching me. The fucker's hearing was good. I walked around the side of the house for some fucking privacy and stared at the dark cloudy sky.

"You just need to deal with the blade. I'll handle the rest," I replied, taking out a cigarette and lighting it. She sighed heavily, her irritation obvious.

"You know the price."

I did. Her words from that day still rang in my mind. The price to kill an immortal meant death.

"You know you cannot do it yourself. This world still needs you," Janaina admonished. I frowned. I wanted to fucking live and be with my family. It wasn't like I wanted to fucking end all that.

"I know, but it's my fucking job, and I am not going to send someone else to their death," I growled. "You've done your part, I'll do mine."

"There is still so much darkness in the world, King Alejandro. Your son is still a child." *I know that.*

She hung up, and I resisted the urge to throw the phone across the fucking garden. I turned sharply, frowning as I scanned the area. For a moment, I felt as if someone had been there, but I didn't pick anything up. Fuck that shit. Maybe I was just being paranoid.

I stormed inside, trying to hide my irritation, only for Kiara to take hold of my arm, her eyes filled with concern.

"Are you okay?" She whispered.

"Fucking perfect," I replied coldly, kissing her, the frustration within me only rising.

I glanced around before pulling her against me and rounding the corner. I tugged her into the nearest room. I shut the door, drowning out all the sounds from outside as I claimed her lips once more and deepened our kiss, pushing her up against the wall. Her body reacted to me instantly, and she returned my kiss with equal passion.

We broke apart after a few moments, both of us breathing hard. Her eyes were shimmering a dazzling purple, the sparks still dancing along our skin, and I could still feel her against my lips. My dick throbbed against her, and I had to force myself to put some space between us before my semi-hard state became fucking obvious. I didn't think now was the time to fuck her in the bathroom.

"What's wrong?" She asked me. I wanted to tell her, but Dante's words returned to my head, and I knew I couldn't risk it. I cupped her face, pressing my forehead against hers.

"Nothing I can't handle," I said quietly. She looked concerned but nodded.

"If you do need to talk, I'm here." She reached up, kissing me once more. I looked into her blue-rimmed green eyes; I couldn't wait for the day that all this crap was over. "Alejandro... you're scaring me," she murmured, cupping my face.

I was given a second chance once long ago... I didn't think third chances existed. I had lived several years of happiness. My queen was strong enough to live without me. I fucking didn't want it to come to that, but there was no other option. I didn't want to hurt her or leave... ever. But we needed someone strong, powerful, and able to deliver the final attack.

I pulled her into my arms, hugging her tightly. Her heart was thumping, and I wasn't sure if it was her fear or my own that swirled through me. She locked her arms around me just as tightly. I didn't want to do this... but for our family, if I had to make a sacrifice... I would.

"Alejandro..."

"I love you, Amore Mio. Let's get back out there," I replied quietly.

"Everything is going to be okay. As long as we're together, we can rule the world." She smiled, and I couldn't resist giving her a small one back.

Yeah, the only fucking thing was, with great power came great fucking responsibility...

I placed a soft kiss on her knuckles. What fucking killed me most was knowing that my decision would break her.

The Fear Within

KIARA

"So, how far along are you? Any chance it's twins?" Raven asked Raihana.

We were all sitting around the table, eating and chatting. There were a huge variety of dishes; grilled platters, wraps, enchiladas, and much more, spread across the huge table before us.

"Oh, it's definitely one," Raihana replied, kissing Chris.

I smiled as I sat between my twins. Although I didn't remember anything about any of them, in the short time that I had spent with them, I already felt like I was one of them. I mean, I was, but with no memories, it was daunting. I planted a soft kiss on top of my little Maleficent's head and then one on Kataleya, who wore a deep plum sequined dress. She was still holding her teddy bear tightly in one arm and had refused to put it down to eat.

"Kat, want me to break the chicken for you?" I asked quietly, seeing her using just her fork and one-handedly trying to break it. She shook her head, her right arm tightening around her teddy. She was doing it again... refusing to use both her hands. "Okay," I replied softly, caressing her soft sandy locks. I kept my voice low, not wanting to draw too much attention, although obviously, everyone could hear.

Next to Kat was Azura, and then Mom and Dad. Alejandro was opposite me, with Dante next to him. Dante had stopped talking to me lately, and that unnerved me. Even now, when he looked up at me, I felt that rush of anger and fear rush through me. I broke eye contact, wondering what hold the Djinn had on me. Was it possible he was seeing everything through my eyes? Was he getting insight into everything going on around us?

"Amore Mio."

I was pulled from my thoughts by Alejandro calling me. I gave him a small smile before I turned to Skyla, who was adding salad to her plate.

"Want some, dearie? It is good for you, my pretty…" she asked me, giving me a small, sly smirk.

"Sky, that would be the evil witch from Snow White, not Maleficent," Azura decided to input.

"Oh, yeah… I'm a combination of villains!" Skyla decided, poking her fork at Azura. "Be careful, blue-eyed bat! I will have your heart and enjoy the beauty from devouring it!"

"Girls are so damn loud," Dante remarked, sipping his juice just as Renji knocked something over and Jayce pushed him, making the younger one begin to cry.

"Jayce, behave," Raven warned as Liam comforted Renji.

"Renji is baby," Theo added, only for Mom to try to distract him from making matters worse, but Renji had heard and began crying louder.

"I take it back," Dante sighed as Sienna giggled from where she sat next to Maria. She looked pretty in a cream sequin dress, the multi-coloured sequins creating a green-blue shine to it.

Delsanra was sitting back in the armchair that had been placed near the table, and Rayhan was feeding her. The love they had for one another was obvious in their eyes. I smiled as Rayhan raised Delsanra's hand to his lips, kissing her wrist. Even in the hardest of times, he was there for her.

I returned to my food, listening to the talking around me, when I felt a strong, intense rush of anger through me, one that was not mine. My heart skipped a beat, and for a moment, it felt like an out-of-body experience. Everything faded, and when I looked around, I could hear nothing but the raging anger that was consuming me. A flare of pain rushed through me, and my eyes snapped to the knife on the table. What was going on?

Alejandro, I called him through the link, my voice sounding panicked. I could feel my wolf's agitation, and I stood up quickly.

He frowned, standing up instantly, and within seconds he was in front of me. His touch sent a wave of coolness through me, and I smiled smoothly, noticing everyone watching us and not wanting anyone to get worried.

What is it? He asked, his dark eyes piercing into mine.

I just felt emotions that weren't mine, I replied, locking my arms around his waist tightly.

When he was close, those feelings were at bay. I could no longer hear the voice in my head since he had made me his once more, but something told me he still lingered within some part of my mind. Was that why every time Dante and I locked eyes, I felt something? Because the thing inside of me was afraid of him?

If that was so, then why did he want Dante? I wished we knew of a way to kill him; I just hoped Alejandro found the answer. I felt useless as it was.

"Want to go for a walk or something to clear your mind?" He asked quietly, cupping my face.

"Oh, no, I'm fine." I was not going to ruin dinner.

"Alright." He pulled me close, kissing my neck. I bit my lip, stopping myself from moaning loudly. When he pulled away, I felt calmer and took my seat once more.

Much later, Alejandro, Maria, Mom, and the rest of the men were heading out to the packhouse for a meeting. I found it a little strange that they weren't using the home office or that I wasn't invited. Did Alejandro not trust me? I mean, I didn't blame him because I was beginning to get scared of the sudden surges of emotions and feelings that consumed me.

"We won't be too long," he said, coming over to me.

"Nothing important for me to know?" I couldn't help but ask.

"It ain't nothing too important. Enjoy time with the ladies." He jerked his head towards the living room, and I nodded.

His black shirt stretched over his chest and arms, and I tried not to let my gaze linger on his pierced nipples. It wasn't too important… but it was important, I could sense that, and the slight hesitation behind his words.

"Okay…" I said, "I'll keep an eye on the kiddies."

He nodded, kissing me hard. His enticing scent made my heart skip a beat, and when he pulled away, I gave him a warm smile. I wouldn't let on that I knew he didn't trust me, because if he was hiding something, it wasn't because of me but the evil presence that lingered in the corners of my mind. Like a thief in the night, I was unable to pinpoint it unless he showed his emotions.

I watched them walk away. Mom gave me a small smile before I turned and walked back into the living room. The kids were happily playing, and as I watched Raven, I couldn't help but smile at the sight of her with her five little munchkins. I could just picture them as these big alpha males with their tiny, bite-sized mama.

"Carter, baby, stop," Raven said, watching him biting onto the edge of the table.

"How old are they now?" I asked, taking a seat next to Delsanra. I placed my hand on her leg and let my healing pour into her.

"They will be three in a few months," Raven replied, turning as she watched Azura scanning the curtains. "Zuzu…"

"What? I'm not doing anything," Azura replied in a scandalised voice. "I swear."

"No one trusts you," Dante remarked.

"What's not to trust?" She replied, watching him unblinkingly.

"Did you know psychotic killers tend not to blink?" Dante stated.

"I'm no killer, and that isn't true."

"It is."

"Isn't"

"Is."

"Isn't!"

"Guys, stop. Seriously, positive energy!" Raven reprimanded. "Zuzu, you're a big girl, right? Behave, okay?"

"Oh, yes, I forgot that he's my baby nephew." Dante rolled his eyes.

"We both know who acts more childish."

"Okay, smart guy," Raihana added before the argument blew up even more.

"Dante isn't feeling well," Kataleya said softly as she sat down next to her brother. "Be nice to him, please."

She was still holding that teddy tightly and I wondered if she needed extra comfort. I would have gone over, but with Dante right there, something deep within me was telling me to stay away for his safety.

"I'm always nice, Kat." Azura turned around, not sounding very convincing.

"I hope the meeting goes well." Raihana sighed, "I was meant to attend, but they told me I wasn't needed."

"Well, maybe you just need a break, babe," Raven replied.

"I agree. Plus you are pregnant, you need to take it easy," Delsanra reminded her.

"I'm totally fine, I don't need to be bubble-wrapped."

"But Chris would want you all wrapped up," Delsanra replied weakly.

"No, trust me, he'll prefer me unwrap-"

"Kids!" I coughed, making the other women laugh.

"Oopsie," Raven smiled.

"Hey, you're one to talk. We saw Uncle get all handsy," Raihana replied, smirking.

"I'm sure most aren't paying attention…" Raven added, watching the kids suspiciously as I tried not to blush.

"Of course, we aren't," Skyla remarked from where she was building something from Legos. "Oi, Theo! Stop."

"Careful that the kids don't take the Legos, Sky," I said, getting up and sitting down on the floor next to her, brushing a small piece away from Tatum.

"Why do babies put everything in their mouths?" Sky rolled her eyes as she continued to work on her creation.

"Because it's how they explore. I'm sure you did it, too," I replied with a smile, ruffling her dark hair.

"Maybe." She shrugged.

"You know, when everything calms down, we need to take a family holiday abroad," Raihana mused as she stretched, patting her stomach.

"I think that would be a lovely idea," I agreed. "Somewhere with a beach…" Just the image of Alejandro in swimming trunks with water dripping down his body made my stomach flutter and that familiar ache settle into his core once more.

"Oh, I'm all for it! A beach would be amazing," Raihana agreed.

"I can imagine us chasing after the kiddies," Raven said with an amused smile.

"Oh, don't worry, Del and I will keep them in check with our magic. We won't even need any nannies!"

It was something I thought we would all love to do once things were better again. Even though we didn't know when that would be, just discussing something and making plans seemed to lighten the mood considerably. A reminder that times won't always be so dark and trying.

We talked for a while longer, from the plans of a holiday to just general things that they had planned for the coming months, before we finally began putting the kids to bed. Kataleya had sat silently, and even when Delsanra and I tried to talk to her, she gave short replies, clutching her teddy tightly.

We all settled the younger kids to bed, and I kissed all the little kiddies good night, apart from Dante, whom I had just told to get some rest and wished him good night from afar before going to the kitchen. I had a headache coming on, which was kind of weird, and decided to make myself some tea after asking the girls if they wanted any.

Rayhan, Mom and Dad had returned from the meeting, but Alejandro wasn't back yet. I wondered if he had other things to tend to.

I had just poured the hot water into my mug when I heard footsteps behind me. By the scent, I knew who it was before I even turned, spotting Dante going to the fridge. He took the six-pint bottle of milk, and I hurried over, seeing how he was struggling and using both arms to carry the bottle.

"Here, let me get it," I said, but the moment my hand brushed his, a searing pain shot through my arm, and it felt like I had just been burned. I jerked away from him, looking down at my hand, which looked perfectly normal. I felt a sharp pain rip through my head and arm, making me stumble as I clutched my shoulder, my eyes stinging as I tried to breathe. Once the pain became slightly more bearable, I exhaled.

"You should really be careful," Dante remarked, taking the milk to the counter.

"Dante…" I whispered softly. He looked at me, his eyes hard, and I felt my heart squeeze with sadness. Memories or not, he was my son, but the hostility in his eyes hurt. So much….

I remained silent, watching him as he got a glass and poured himself milk. The sound of the milk sploshing into the glass, the thudding of our hearts, it all seemed to intensify. Then, suddenly, I felt an influx of emotions course through me, but they weren't mine. The hatred within me was terrifying, of a level I had never felt. The strong, intense urge to grab the biggest knife I could overcame me, and my blazing purple eyes skimmed the worktops before they fell on the knife block. I walked over to it as if my legs had a mind of their own before reality hit me hard, and I willed myself to stop, grabbing onto the counter to control myself. My heart was pounding as I tried to regain use of my senses. The glaring hatred within me felt so foreign. I had never felt such hate for anyone…

I turned towards Dante, feeling his eyes on me, and, to my surprise, they were soft. The usual calculating look in them was gone.

"Dante, go to bed now," I commanded breathlessly, trying to battle the foreign emotions within me. "Please," I begged.

He drank his milk slowly, his eyes not leaving my face as I fought with everything I had. Just when I felt like I might not be able to do anything more, he put the glass down, and, once again, he looked like just a young boy. He gave me a nod as he walked to the door and paused to look back at me. He gave me a small smile.

"I love you, Mama."

His words shattered something inside of me, and I clamped my hand over my mouth to stifle the sob that threatened to escape. The door shut behind him, and I felt a wave of guilt overcome me.

I had almost hurt him. I needed to stay away. I was a danger to everyone around me.

This Emptiness

ALEJANDRO

"WE'VE FOUND A LOCATION, but we haven't pinpointed it. Last time he fucking knew Kiara was around, but I don't think they were banking on the pup knowing those locations," Darien said as we gathered around my desk. Both of my Deltas were there, as well as Carmen.

"But if the Djinn does try to probe Enrique's mind, there are chances he'll learn of it. Either way, I have a plan," I said, lighting a cigarette.

"What plan?" Maria asked, doing her best not to wrinkle her nose. Got to love how she wasn't able to hide her dislike for things like smoking, no matter how much she tried.

"Kiara…" I said, hating that I was going to resort to this. Not everyone in this room knew what Dante had hinted at me, and as much as I fucking hated it, I trusted everyone in this room and would share the truth with them.

"What about her?" Scarlett asked sharply.

"The Djinn still has a hold on her, and she's feeling emotions that aren't hers," I told them quietly. It fucking hurt, but there was nothing I could fucking do about it. Even the plan I had, I didn't like it, not one fucking bit.

"Really… fuck…" Liam frowned.

"And what exactly is your plan?" Scarlett asked, frowning as she glanced at Elijah.

"I'll make her learn of our plan indirectly, and the Djinn will most like hear it… I'm sure of it. Obviously, it won't be our real plan, but if it comes off that she hears it by accident, the chances are they'll believe it. If played out properly, she'll eat it up, and in turn, the Djinn will, so when we actually carry out our fucking plan, they won't know what fucking hit them."

"Kiara can tell when someone's lying," Elijah added with a frown.

"I know, that's why I'm telling half of you one plan and the other half another plan. Then I'm having two of you have a conversation, and I'll handle the rest," I explained confidently. Rayhan frowned, running his hand through his hair.

"So, if she can hear it all, see it all… then she knows most of what's been going on?" He asked. "Is she safe around the kids?" A flash of irritation rushed through me; I knew he was just fucking worried, but I also knew Kiara was fucking strong. She would not hurt them.

"She's still my fucking mate and she's still the queen. Kiara is not fucking weak," I growled, my eyes flashing.

"I get that," he replied, frowning.

"Rayhan's concern is fair, too," Scarlett said quietly.

"The Luna won't fail us," Drake added. "We will await your plan Alpha, and act accordingly." I nodded. *Yeah, that's fucking more like it.*

"I agree. Luna Kiara is strong, she is the queen for a reason. Let's not forget she is a blessed wolf," Carmen added, crossing her arms.

"What is the cost to kill him anyway?" Darien asked.

"Just that blade, and it's got to be done in one stab," I replied lightly, not wanting to share the actual fucking price. I knew I had people who would try to take that chance in my stead… and I couldn't do that. Not to any one of them. Plus I needed to make sure it gets done. I was the fastest and most powerful…

We talked for a little while longer, and I told half of them to wait outside. I gave Elijah, Scarlett, Liam, and Darien one plan, which was actually the fake one. Then I called the others back in and told them the real plan.

"Dismissed," I said, taking a drag on my cigarette and motioning for them to all leave.

Rayhan nodded, about to walk out. He paused and glanced at Maria, who was holding a book from the shelf behind me.

"You go along. There are a few things I wanted to discuss with Alejandro, ya hayati," she said, giving him a small smile. He nodded, although I knew he was curious as to what we wanted to talk about.

"Run along, kid. It's adult talk," I mocked.

"You know, I'm the same age as Kiara, right? Ah, I guess compared to the old man you are, I must seem like a kid." Smirking, he shut the door before I could reply.

"Fucker," I growled as Maria shut the book and slid it back onto the shelf. "What did you want to discuss?"

"I want to know the actual price of killing a Djinn."

My stomach twisted, caught off guard. Like always, she had that emotionless, perfectly sculpted face that didn't betray any thoughts. Our eyes met, and in that fucking moment, I realised she had been the one in the garden earlier, as quiet as a fucking assassin. Which meant Maria already knew what the price was…

"You already know what it is," I said coldly.

"A life. The wielder will die, correct?" She asked. She walked over to the desk, standing on the opposite side, her hands folded in front of her.

"That's not your concern. I will handle it."

"You will die to save Kiara, Delsanra, and Dante," she stated, her eyes hard.

"Three lives in return for one. It's pretty fair…" I replied emotionlessly.

It was fucking weird, but there was once a time that I didn't care if I died… but now… I wanted to live. For them. For Kiara, for my kids, for my family. I wanted to be part of all the weird family shit we did together. The celebrations, the movie nights, the meals, and time together. I wanted to see Ray and Raihana's kids grow up. I wanted to play that role as their grandfather, to be there for them where I know Rafael would have been… I wanted to show Leo he fucking isn't alone. To bid the kids goodnight, to wake to Kiara's smile every fucking day…

"Fair. Then I will ask you to allow me to do it."

Her words sent a flash of coldness through me. My eyes were blazing red as I looked at her, narrowing them.

"No," I growled, but she didn't even flinch.

"Why not?" She asked icily, folding her arms. Even with her sparkly dress, she meant business. "Do not forget that I am from the Ahmar Qamar pack. We pride ourselves in stealth. Where do you think Rayhan gets it from? I can sneak up on him when others keep him busy," she snapped as if she was talking to a fucking kid.

"I don't care if he got it from you or fucking Santa Claus. I am not letting you fucking sacrifice yourself," I growled, my aura rolling off of me. That made her step back, but even then, she stood her ground defiantly.

"I have far less to lose, Alejandro. Unlike you, my children have grown up, started lives of their own... I am not needed –"

"I don't care if they are ten or fucking fifty, they will always need you. You can't leave them when they have already lost their dad."

"But your children are barely even ten! Kataleya needs you now more than ever... Dante is holding the world upon his shoulders. He will need a father's guidance. That much power in such a young boy, he needs a father to support him, to be there for him, to show him the way and tell him that it's going to be ok–"

"He has Elijah, Liam, and Rayhan. He won't be alone."

"Really, Alejandro? And Kiara? Will you just leave her in this world alone? Will you be so cruel?"

That felt like a fucking gut punch.

Kiara. Life without me... she would feel it as much as I fucking would if I had to live a life without her. I wouldn't even want to live without her...

"I am not trying to be fucking cruel. I have to do this."

"You have the option to be here with her. Can you imagine how hard it will be for her? To be queen until Dante is old enough, to carry on all alone?"

"I know it'll be fucking hard!" I growled, crushing my cigarette in my fist.

"Exactly, and just how it would be hard for her, that is how I find my life without Rafael." I looked up sharply, her poised front cracking and the agony in her eyes fucking killed me.

"Maria... look, it's just –"

"I'm tired, Alejandro... I want to be with him. I'm living my days without my sunshine. I spend the nights without my stars. The emptiness inside, it's only growing. I miss him, and I just want to return to him. Let me do this, Alejandro, for my sake, because I can't carry on like this. I told myself I would never beg anyone for anything. However, I am pleading with everything I have. Please, let me do this."

I looked into her grey eyes that held raw pain, but what she was asking for... to let her sacrifice herself... *How do I accept that?*

Making a Choice

ALEJANDRO

"PLEASE," SHE PLEADED, TAKING a seat on a chair opposite my desk.

"You're asking me to fucking send you to your death," I said quietly. "How the fuck do you expect me to agree to that? I know that it's hard living without your mate, but…" I looked down at my hands, the slight scorch mark on my palm healing over before I took another cigarette out.

"I am asking you to make the smarter choice. Someone who yearns to be by their mate's side and has adult children over someone who is leaving their eight-year-old as Alpha and their mate behind. It's obvious which is the better option," she explained quietly.

"And how will you tell Raihana that her mother is going to sacrifice herself?"

"The very same way you would have had to tell Skyla and Kataleya. The only difference is Raihana is a woman, not a child."

Fuck her logic. Even if it made fucking sense, I am not going to let her do this. I couldn't.

"No, Maria." I took a drag of my cigarette.

"I'm doing this. If you don't agree, then I will take this to Elijah," she replied, her eyes flashing dangerously.

"Don't fucking do that shit. Obviously, he'll fucking side you," I growled coldly.

"Elijah will side with the one for who it makes more sense to do this. I force myself out of bed every morning to carry on. I love you all, but it's hard without half of your soul." She sighed, sitting back in the seat and crossing her legs, a pose that wasn't very Maria, who would usually sit with her legs tucked to the side and hands in her lap. Right then, it was as if I was talking to a boss, not a prim and proper Ms Perfect, but she was a fucking queen after all. Her grey eyes watched me sharply. "From heaven, I will watch over my family, but you have so much left to do. I don't like to set an ultimatum, but we both know that there's more logic in me doing this. So, please, if Rafael and I ever meant anything to you, you will allow me -"

A menacing growl left my lips, my eyes blazing red.

"Do not fucking use that shit on me. You know what Raf meant to me and that I consider you my fucking sister. I am not letting you fuckin-"

"Do not growl at me like an animal!" She snapped, irritation clear in her voice.

Did she actually just call me a fucking animal? We were, but she sure made it sound like a fucking insult. I glared at her, and she simply shook her head as if she was talking to a fucking pup.

"Maria -"

"I am no longer asking your opinion. I am doing this because I want to… I have contemplated suicide several times, Alejandro, but I will not go against my beliefs… that is not what Rafael would have wanted. So let me go in an honourable way. All I want is to return to my mate," she said softly, her eyes glittering with tears, yet she refused to let them fall.

I sat back, letting out a breath. Yeah, I could see her fading with each passing year. She had held on for so long. When you were mated to an Alpha, the bond was even stronger…

"And what about Rayhan and Raihana? How will you tell them?"

"I will talk to Raihana and Delsanra… but Rayhan…"

"He'll fucking blow."

"Yes, so I will leave him a message. I will tell him how. by oath, I made you promise to let me do this and that I did not allow you to tell anyone."

"I ain't lying or any of that shit, especially when he won't fucking forgive me. Besides, we all know I don't follow rules or keep secrets. I already have one nephew wanting to fucking kill -"

"You won't be lying because I am holding you to one. If you loved Rafael, then you will uphold this promise."

A memory from long ago flashed through my mind… when I had told her to answer me if she loved Raf, she was using that shit on me now.

"I ain't promised shit," I growled.

"You will promise me, for our family and for me. This is where my happiness lies. I wish to be released from these shackles…" she persisted, running her fingers lightly over her mate mark. Her eyes looked haunted, and she did look tired.

Fuck it.

Even if I understood she needed this… it still hurt. To agree to her demand wasn't going to be fucking easy. I ran my hand down my face as she stared at me, waiting for me to agree. Her grey eyes filled with sadness and hope, and it fucking messed with me. Why the fuck did Rossi women have a hold on me? I swore there was some shady shit going on there, or I was just getting fucking soft. *Maybe Ri did some voodoo shit or something. Can't put anything past her and Del…*

"Fine. Talk to Ri… and I'm talking to her, too, like I want to make sure she's fucking okay with it." A small smile crossed her lips.

"Thank you. I will," she promised softly.

Our eyes met, and the severity of what I agreed to… *No, this was wrong. She couldn't do this shit. I could tell Rayhan or stop her.* But her next words made my thoughts come to a painful stop.

"Thank you for understanding. I cannot wait to be by his side once more…" she whispered, a single tear escaping her eye.

She looked as if a burden had been lifted from her, The spark of hope in those grey eyes told me just how hard living was for her, and I realised it might be fucking painful for us, but it was something Maria needed. For herself.

I stood up, walked over to the window, and stared at the moon in the night sky. *Raf… we fucking needed you… you left far too fucking fast.*

Was this the right choice?

Her heels sounded on the wooden floors as she made her way over to me, stepping up beside me as she looked at the sky.

"He would be proud of you. So proud," she whispered as if knowing what I was thinking.

I looked down at her, her eyes held so much emotion and I knew even the decision she had made wouldn't be easy for her. Talking to Ri… having to say goodbye to everyone…

"And of you. You carried on after him, standing in as Luna so Del could live her life and get her degree. You remained fucking strong even when

I could see how much fucking pain you were in. You've always been good at hiding your emotions." I looked down at her, and she smiled slightly.

"Of course. I was born to be Rafael's Luna, raised to be a queen, and I will handle things just like he would expect of me," she said proudly, and I smirked.

"Yeah…" A fucking king and queen who deserved every ounce of the praise they were given. There would never be another Rafael or Maria. "I heard you're quite good at being a flirt, too." I smirked, making her smile vanish. Was that a faint blush?

"Whoever said that is —"

"Liam doesn't lie," I mocked. "So I can actually start to believe that you and Raf actually consummated your bond and didn't just adopt Ray and Ri. I swear you come off so fucking stiff at times." She frowned at me, and I snickered. "Even Marcel didn't deny that shit."

"I am going to have a word with Liam. I told him not to say anything."

"This is Liam. The guy's smart, but he's also fucking clueless. I think Kiara got all the tact and brains from that duo." She laughed lightly and shook her head.

"Well, you are a tattle-tale too."

"I fucking am not," I growled. She gave me a look as if saying did I really believe that?

Well… I do kinda like stirring shit up…

"It's rather sad, but men often don't realise women can be more danger-ous than a man. It's a shame for them," she said haughtily, and I knew she was still trying to hide her embarrassment.

"Yeah, especially one of the Rossi Queens."

"Hmm… and this one cannot wait to return to her king." Her voice was so quiet, yet her words were clear. The hope in them was as clear as the moon in the sky. "Don't feel guilty. A king must always make the right decision, even if it's not the easiest, and this is the right one." She placed her hand on my cheek for a moment, giving me a small nod and smile. I looked down at her, then back at the night sky.

"Yeah? Well, it sure isn't fucking easy."

For her happiness…

Will you get angry at me, Raf, for allowing her to do this?

I returned home, the weight of the decision made heavy on my shoulders. Right then, I felt useless. A Djinn from years ago still after this family, or more like waiting for Dante to be born. What powers did he possess? Or the bigger question was, what exactly was Dante?

Something told me he was no ordinary wolf or Lycan. I got that history said no two Lycans are born at once, but with all the shit and power that everyone seemed to have, I didn't think those rules applied any longer. But even as a Lycan, I didn't have that power before I shifted…

Born with red eyes… like how Liam's cerulean eyes were stuck magnetic blue like his wolves once he came into his power. His powers were always brimming to the max, a little like Dante… so what was the little fucker?

I paused outside his bedroom, opening the door silently. I looked inside. He was fast asleep, his breathing steady, and he looked at peace despite the angry veins that covered his skin. Dante Rossi… he looked more like the child he was meant to be when asleep than when awake. I closed the door silently, giving the guard outside his room a nod before I walked down the hall to my bedroom.

I opened the door to see Kiara fast asleep, but what fucking surprised me was that she was still fully dressed, her arms wrapped around herself and a small frown on her forehead. Her breasts practically spilt out of that sexy little dress, and her lush thighs were pressed together, only making me want to go over there and wake her up so I could fuck her. Had something happened?

Pulling off my shirt, I walked over to the bed and sat down. I brushed her long locks off her face, looking over her sexy body. No matter how fucking messed up my head was, she kept me distracted and sane. I wished I could talk to her about this… to ask her her opinion, but I fucking couldn't, and deep down, the doubtful question remained. Was I doing the right thing?

My Own Way

MARCEL

I AWOKE TO A PHONE ringing and frowned. Sitting up, I picked it up. Alejandro?

"Hello?" I answered it, wondering what had happened. A thousand thoughts rushed through my mind.

"Hey, sorry to bother you at this fucking hour," Alejandro's quiet voice answered. Sure, it was past three in the morning, but just from his voice, I could tell he was conflicted.

"It doesn't matter, you called for a reason. Tell me what's wrong?" I asked, standing up and began pacing my bedroom. He sighed heavily, and I heard him take a drag on a cigarette.

"Maria talked to me today… it's about the price of killing a Djinn…" I narrowed my eyes. When I had been there earlier, when we had filled each other in on our trips, he never mentioned a price.

"What price?" I asked sharply.

"Don't fucking growl, I need my ears," he growled back.

"I'm just asking because you never mentioned a damn price," I countered.

"Yeah well… there is a price…"

He filled me in pretty fast. The wielder of the dagger would die, and Maria wanted to be the one to do it. Fucking hell.

"I don't know what the right thing to do is, Marcel. Do I let her do it, knowing she'll die? How does that fucking make sense?" I sighed heavily, running my hand through my hair.

"Look, Al, some of us manage to cope… somehow after our mates die. In my case, Endora severed the bond between my mate and me before she was killed. It's hard to survive without a mate. Even now, when I remember her, that pain… that pain fucking rips me apart inside. Maria has lived for years without Rafael. She needs him, and there is no way for her to carry on without him… I see her far less than you, and every time she's lost a lot of weight and looks even more tired with each passing year. She's already dying, Alejandro. Let her go," I said, sighing.

Maria was a beautiful woman, one I knew many of the Alphas who had lost their mates or simply hadn't found theirs had been interested in, but Maria belonged to Rafael, and it was obvious there was no man on earth who could take his place or ease her pain.

"So, I should allow her to do it? You know she doesn't want me to tell Rayhan."

"Yes, and you have promised her already. Giving her hope and then taking it away is wrong," I said quietly.

"Yeah? You're right… I just, I don't think I'm ready to lose her. It's fucking me up. How do you think her kids are going to take this? That shit is going to be rough."

"Life is never easy, but we do what is ultimately for the better. In this case, between you and Maria, it makes sense for her to do it."

Silence ensued, and I heard him sigh heavily. I didn't envy him. Being king came with so many burdens.

"Yeah. I guess you're right," he said after a moment.

"You are doing great, Alejandro. Sometimes these things are hard. The decisions we make will impact others. If Maria wasn't deteriorating, I would have offered to do it myself, but… Leo isn't ready to become Alpha yet."

I frowned, hearing a twig snap outside, walked over to the open window, and peered out. Silence. Hmm… it was late. Everyone was asleep. I was sure Leo stayed in tonight.

"Yeah, no, Leo needs you. If anyone was to do it, I would… but Maria's as stubborn as her daughter."

"Or her daughter is as stubborn as her," I joked.

"Yeah, either of that shit," Alejandro sighed. I chuckled dryly.

"Get some rest, brother, you need it. Maria knows what she's doing, but if you want a third opinion, talk to Elijah."

"Yeah, I might, I'll see."

He hung up, and I put my phone down, scanning the grounds below. Shaking my head, I closed the window and returned to bed, unable to get rid of the shock of what Alejandro had told me. The price was not small...

I sighed heavily, all traces of sleep gone. I couldn't wait for these dark times to pass...

੭ੳੳੴ

LEO

I stared up at the night sky. There wasn't long before my eighteenth birthday, and I'd shift. I couldn't wait, wanting to come into power. I knew I had it in me. I trained hard and fucking pushed myself every single fucking day to surpass my limits. I could feel the power rippling through me at the brink of release. Power I needed, power I craved...

The world was fucked up, and even until this day, those with power and money got away with shit. Yeah, Alejandro had 'tried' to create an ideal world where packs were allies, but that was all fucking bullshit. He established peace on the surface; there was so much crap going on, on the low... and, of course, the so-called elite could do whatever shit they wanted and get away with it.

Rayhan.

Like always, the mere thought of that bastard sent blistering hatred rushing through me like a fucking white-hot fire. I clenched my fists, trying to calm myself. I would never be able to forget that fucking night... the night he walked into our pack and acted like he was in charge. Without even consulting with Dad, who was the Alpha, he had come in and did whatever shit he wanted. Dad lost face after that, but, of course, he wouldn't let his brother or anyone know that. The pack insulted him, and he just took it. Yeah, he made a fucking mistake by bowing down to Rayhan. Pathetic.

We were and always will be the outcasts, but when I became Alpha, I would break away from the council. I didn't follow any rules, and there was no way I'd ever sit around a table of entitled bastards pretending to give a shit about the fucking country.

I pulled out a cigarette and was about to light it when I heard a phone ring and paused, thinking, who was calling Dad at this hour? After their small exchange, I realised it was Alejandro. I stayed silent, listening to Dad's side of the conversation. I got the gist of the conversation. So there was a price to pay for killing it… and the bastard's mother wanted to do the deed. I felt a tad bad for her and Raihana, if anything, but the fact that Rayhan didn't know… I smirked. Now I hope he'd understand how it felt to have people do shit without asking you.

"… Leo isn't ready to be Alpha."

I froze as anger flared up inside of me. I wasn't ready to be Alpha? I have not lacked in any fucking way. The urge to go up there and ask Dad right then about what the fuck he meant was on my fucking mind but, instead, I stormed off. Lashing out would only make Dad say I was proving his fucking point. I'd talk to him tomorrow.

❧

The following day, Dad and I were in the kitchen. Dad had thrown break-fast together, and I was sitting at the counter, digging into the pile of toast, eggs, bacon, and sausages he had fried up. I was still fucking pissed off with what he had said to Alejandro, and I planned to ask him about it.

"So, Maria's going to sacrifice herself," I declared emotionlessly. Dad fucking reacted, and he almost dropped the pan on his fucking feet.

"You were in the yard last night."

"Yeah, pretty glad I was, considering I learned I'm not fit to become Alpha any fucking time soon," I replied, unable to keep the anger out of my voice.

"Leo, don't get me wrong, you have achieved a lot and are able to defeat all the warriors despite not having shifted, but your anger gets the better of you, and I can't make you Alpha until you work on that." I bent the fork in my anger, tossing it on the counter as I looked at Dad, clenching my jaw.

"Yeah, yet you haven't noticed my anger is only displayed when I'm around that bastard? When do I lose my shit around here?" I growled.

"How about now?" Dad glared at me, his eyes flashing and his aura swirling around him. I scoffed bitterly, sitting back on my stool.

"So, in simpler fucking terms, you're just concerned about my retaliation towards your so-called family." Our eyes met, and I shook my head in disgust. "Well, enjoy it. I hate the fact that I'm even tied to that name. I'm out."

"Leo, sit down. You don't get what this family has done for us -"

"This family hasn't done shit! The crap they act entitled to was your fucking birthright! You are not fucking less than them, and I am fucking done with you acting like it's okay or we are beneath them, but that's the fucking thing here, isn't it? We are treated like that!" I shouted, anger rushing through me, and all I could see was fucking red.

"Leo! That is not how we are treated! They welcomed us home! They helped us despite the things I have done in siding with Endora!" Dad snapped.

"Nah, you're just blinded, and you know what? I once thought you were a brave Alpha, but you're nothing more than a fucking loser, Dad. I'm just glad Mom isn't around to see the fucking dud her mate has become," I said coldly. The flash of hurt that crossed his face was satisfying. "The moment I turn eighteen, the first thing I will do is change my name to Leo Herrmann. It's a fucking insult to be called Rossi."

"*Leo!* Your mother would not approve of you taking her name! She would not want her son to throw aside his lineage -"

"Nah, you just can't take it. You know what? To hell with the fucking Rossis. I'd rather only be tied to her and be known as her son alone. As for the title of Alpha, keep it for now. Sooner or later, it will be mine." I simply smiled coldly. "But, pack or not, I will raise hell single-handed."

With those final words, I turned, giving him the finger, and left the kitchen, slamming the door so hard I heard it splinter. Fuck em all.

There Was Once a Princess

KIARA

THE FOLLOWING DAY, ALEJANDRO looked restless and had been distracted all morning. He had his block up, so whatever was worrying him was obviously something he didn't want to share with me. It did hurt, but I knew he had his reasons… I myself felt so uncertain after what had happened with Dante last night. I wanted to tell Alejandro about it, but I wasn't managing to get him alone for even a moment. Plus, I didn't want him to get too worried; however, I wasn't stupid enough to keep silent about it.

"I'll see you later, Amore Mio." He cupped my face, giving me a deep kiss before he pulled away. I nodded, unable to argue. I had to wait for a few minutes, knowing he was busy.

"I love you," I whispered.

"Love you more." He gave me a sexy smirk, placing another kiss on my lips. His actions made me close my eyes, enjoying the feel of his touch before he walked away.

"Are you okay?" Mom's soft voice came as she placed her hands on my shoulders from behind. She looked at me with concern. Well, I couldn't tell Alejandro, but I could tell Mom, at least.

"Just, something happened last night, and it's unnerving me," I sighed, turning towards her. Mom smiled, brushing my hair off my face.

"Come on, let's go somewhere else," she suggested, and I nodded as she led me through to the back garden. Taking a seat on a bench, Mom turned towards me. She remained silent, waiting for me to start talking.

"Last night, I touched Dante, and it burned… and then I had this terrifying urge to grab a knife," I whispered, my heart pounding at the horrible thoughts and actions that had tempted me. Mom's smile vanished. She frowned, her eyes flashing silver before she placed a hand on my shoulder, giving it a comforting squeeze.

"There is no way you would ever do that. Don't feel bad, Kia, that is not you wanting to do that. We are all here for you, and if it ever feels like it's getting stronger, we are all around you. You will never be alone," she said softly, hugging me tightly. I closed my eyes and nodded, hugging her back. I inhaled her warm, comforting scent. No matter how old we were, we would always need our parents' comfort…

"Mama!" Azura's voice came as she stormed into the garden, hands on her hips.

"Yes, baby?" Mom replied, turning to her. She sighed dramatically and came over to us both, looking at us both before shaking her head.

"Seriously, you two are out here, and me and Sky are trying to get Kataleya to come play with us," she complained.

Mom and I both frowned as worry flitted through me. I didn't like to see her so broken. I may not have my memories, but from the videos I had been watching, she was a happy child. Skyla ran over, too, and nodded in agreement with Azura.

"She's doing it again."

"Doing what?" Mom asked gently, despite the concern on her face.

"Using one hand to do everything. She was buttoning her cardigan, and she was refusing to put her teddy down, and then when I said I'll help her, she refused and was going to cry," Sky explained. Her eyes were full of sadness and worry. I sighed heavily, feeling the pain in my chest growing.

"You girls play. I'll go to Kat, okay?" I said, reaching over and giving both their cheeks a slight pull.

"Owie!" Skyla giggled before smiling and giving me a nod. "Ok, Mama!" The girls ran off, and I stood up.

"Don't worry too much, Kiara. We are here," Mom promised, and I nodded.

She was right. I wasn't alone, and everyone was around. If I felt strange again, I would just call for help or tell someone instantly.

"Thanks, Mom," I replied before I headed inside to find my little Kataleya.

I didn't need to search. As the girls had said, she was in her bedroom, sitting on the bed, clutching the same teddy bear tightly. Her long hair fell down her back, and, although she looked like the cutest little angel sitting there, the sadness in her eyes remained, and it broke my heart. I walked over to her, crouching before the bed, and placed my hands on her tiny knees.

"Hey, my little princess. The weather is so warm outside, why are you sitting here?" I asked gently, cupping her cheek with one hand. Her arm tightened around her teddy, and she shrugged.

"I don't want to go outside," she said, staring down at her lap.

"Why not?" I asked softly. She shook her head, refusing to speak. I stood up and sat next to her on the bed, putting my arm around her.

"So where did you get this teddy from? I'm sure I haven't seen it before." I tried to make conversation.

"Raihana ordered it online for me," she said, brushing her hand over its fur gently.

"Tell me, what's your teddy bear's name?" She remained quiet.

"Shall I name it? Hmm, what is a good name for a teddy bear as cute as this one? Hmm, hmm…"

I looked around. Maria had told me Kat usually preferred to play with her array of pastel-coloured teddies and unicorns. In comparison, this one was a rather interesting and different choice. A quick scan of her bed and the room told me it was far different. Skyla's toys were obvious from her action figures, Disney villain collection, and superhero dolls. Then, there was Kataleya's pile of pretty and fluffy teddies. Her porcelain and baby dolls were a stark contrast to the teddy in her hand.

"What about Coco?" I suggested, looking at its dark brown fur. She shook her head, tightening her hold on it before she moved it and looked down at its face. "No? Okay, what about Brownie?"

"No, his name is Kiké," she said quietly. With sudden realisation, I stared down at the teddy. Hazel eyes and brown fur. Kiké – Enrique…

Goddess, she had named it after him.

I fought back the surge of tears that threatened to spill and scooped her into my arms, hugging her tightly.

"Oh, baby… I love the name," I complimented her lightly, rocking her gently. "He is so cute."

"He is," she whispered, hugging it tightly.

I wished I could turn back time and make all her pain go away, make Enrique's pain go away. I wished I could protect every child on this earth...

"Shall I tell you a story, Kat?" I asked gently, looking down at the top of her head, a head of hair that was the exact same shade as mine. She nodded. I rested my chin on top of her head and gazed out of the window.

"Once upon a time, there was a little boy. He was brave, compassionate, and caring. But then... he was treated horribly until he became cold and angry, but that was only because he was hurting inside. Then, a little princess was kidnapped and kept locked away, and even though he knew he shouldn't, he still took care of her, but in the process, he was punished severely." Her little heart thumped, and I stroked her back as I rocked her gently. "He lost something special, but it wasn't the princess' fault. It was the monster's fault. The very same one who was keeping the princess captive. But you know when the princess and the little boy were saved? He became angry and would say hurtful things to the princess, and she took it to heart." I felt something wet spill onto my arm and hugged her tightly as I continued, letting her cry quietly.

"And even when the time came for the little boy to leave, he refused to listen to the princess... leaving her little heart broken. But fear not, that isn't the end of the story," I said softly, placing another kiss on her head.

"It isn't?" She asked quietly.

"No, because that little princess grew up into a strong, pure-hearted woman, and that little boy grew up into a strong yet cold-hearted knight. They would meet again, and that little princess and the little boy would have their own journey to heal their hearts." I frowned, confusion rippling through me. I didn't know why I had said those words, but they felt so... real. Almost as if I was certain of them. Kataleya looked up at me, hope lighting up her small face.

"They will?"

"Yes," I promised. A small smile crossed my face. I was certain that one day Enrique Escarra and Kataleya Rossi would cross paths again. A glimmer of hope washed across her face. She looked out of the window and nodded.

"Then... I will work on being a strong woman, someone who can help others... not someone who always needs help," she said quietly. I smiled and nodded.

"Yes, always remember you are so much more than you think," I said softly. She nodded, and a small smile crossed her lips. She turned her gaze to the teddy.

"We will meet again, right, Mama?" She asked again as if she needed that certainty.

I nodded, not only because of that feeling I had but because I would make sure they did. One day, I would let Kat go and find him. She didn't get the closure she needed, so all I could do was give her some hope until that day came.

A short while later, Kataleya agreed to go and play with the others. I fixed the bedding and decided I would go and try to bake some brownies or something to keep myself busy. I left the girls' room and was about to go down the stairs when I suddenly looked down the hall. It was currently empty, as the guards were only stationed here during the night in case Dante needed something or if something happened. I walked to my room and, entering it, headed straight to the closet. I frowned as I realised I had no idea what I was doing there.

Fear suddenly rushed through me the moment I grabbed one of the daggers at the back of my wardrobe, daggers that I saw every day yet didn't think anything of. I tried to pull back, but my hands seemed to have a mind of their own. My chest was pounding as I slid the dagger from its leather sheath.

No. What was I doing?

I moved away from the drawer, closing it slowly, the panic within me growing

Alejandro! I needed to tell Alejandro.

I frowned, trying to concentrate on the mind link, when a splitting pain rushed through my head, making my free hand grab my head as I groaned in agony, but even then, my feet continued towards the exit of my room.

Emotions that were not my own flared inside of me; anger, hatred, vengeance.

Please, stop.

I pushed against them, trying to mind-link anyone, but I wasn't able to. *Alejandro...* Could he feel my panic through the bond?

Fear enveloped me, suffocating me. *No... please, no....* I couldn't stop it; it was far too strong.

Terror filled me as I realised where I was headed, my feet dragging me down the hallway without my consent. My grip was tight on the dagger, and my stomach sank as Dante's bedroom came into sight…

Losing All Control

KIARA

*D*ANTE'S ROOM WAS COMING ever closer, and even as I tried to stop myself, I was only succeeding in slowing myself down a little. I looked around in desperation, trying to scream or make some sort of sound.

No! I am Kiara Westwood - no, I am Kiara Rossi, the queen and Luna of this pack. A mother. I won't do this, I can't! I gripped the dagger tightly. *I would rather die than hurt my son!*

The hatred and fury coursing through me were growing stronger with each passing second, and I was beginning to be pushed into a corner of my own mind. My wolf's pain and restlessness mixed with my own.

Not today.

No one was going to take my body from me.

Summoning every ounce of willpower I could, I forced all my concentration into trying to break free. I screamed as I forced my aura to burst through the barrier that seemed to be subduing it. It swirled around me like a storm, a clear purple visible around me as it blasted in all directions. I heard glass shattering nearby, and distant shouts as my body began moving towards Dante's room faster.

I had to stop myself. I was not going to let this happen! Using all my might, I twisted the dagger and plunged it into my chest, making me gasp as pain rushed through me. I fell to the ground, the blade inches from my heart. The smell of blood filled the air as it dripped onto the floor. I let go of the dagger as I bent forward on all fours, trying to regain control.

Why was this happening?

My own resilience, anger, worry, and determination mixed in with anger and resentment that did not belong to me. The emotions burned through me. It felt like my head was being split open as we both fought for control.

Get out of my head!

My only response was splitting pain as my head erupted with agony, and I curled up, groaning as my vision darkened.

"Kia!"

Raven? Stay back...

A flare of hatred rushed through me, and my eyes flashed as she came into view. Her black and pink hair bounced as she ran to my side as fast as she could, crouching down by me. I saw her eyes glaze and knew she was mind-linking as she reached out for me.

"You won't touch me."

Those words didn't belong to me! Goddess!

"Back off!" I found myself spitting.

"Not happening, babe," Raven replied, and in a flash, I was on my back. It was obvious she didn't want to hurt me with the blade still stuck in my chest.

I felt like a puppet stuck in a body I had no control over as I yanked the dagger out and kicked her off me. She blocked as I swung the dagger at her, her eyes meeting mine as she tried to disarm me. She glanced behind me as if hoping for someone to show up.

"Kiara, listen to me!"

I shoved her off as I ran for Dante's room, only for Raven to aim a sharp kick at my hip and yank me back once more.

"Shit, I'm sorry!" She whimpered as her knee connected with my chest, slamming me to the ground. "Kia!"

I glared up at her, grabbing her hair and throwing her off me into the far wall. Her tiny body slid to the ground, but she was on her feet faster than I was expecting, although I wasn't much slower. I ran at her, anger rushing through me. She was in the way of my mission! I raised my dagger, praying she ran, when an arm locked around my neck and another around my waist.

Mom?

"Kia, listen to me," her strong yet soothing voice ordered, her aura swirling around her.

I slammed my elbow into her side and, hooking my ankle around hers, yanked her legs out from under her. Twisting around with more power than I had ever had before, I threw her across the hall. She rolled over, breaking her fall, and her silver eyes blazed as she looked at me. For a moment, she looked like a phoenix, her aura so intense, her red hair falling in front of her face, and the look of determination told me that she was not afraid of anything.

I heard running and turned to see Maria and Raihana appear at the top of the stairs.

"Kiara, take control," Maria encouraged, her eyes blazing as she walked towards me.

"Take another step, and I will kill myself," I hissed.

How did I lose control of myself? I thought things were getting better…

"You won't," Raihana promised before she whispered a spell, and everything went dark. Her magic confused my senses, and no matter which direction I looked, I saw nothing.

The Djinn's irritation rose within me, and I realised Raihana was using my own weakness against me.

"She's injured…" I heard Raven murmur from somewhere in the darkness as I swung the dagger, making sure no one came close. I felt the force within me grow.

"Raihana, leave!" I heard Mom shout as my powers burst from me and illuminated the area. I was thrown to the ground. I wasn't sure who had thrown me as both Maria and Mom were pinning my arms down, and the dagger was torn from my hold by Maria as I struggled against them.

"Kiara," a deep voice called.

Alejandro?

Pain erupted in my chest, and a wave of guilt washed over me. What on earth was I doing?

I looked up into the blazing red eyes of my mate, the festering resentment within me growing. Even when Mom and Maria let go, I found myself pulling away, not wanting his touch. Or more like the Djinn didn't want Alejandro near me.

Bending down, he lifted me by my waist. His eyes skimmed over my bloody chest, concern and fear flashing in his eyes.

"You need… to lock… me away…" I said, struggling to form my words as I pushed him away. I didn't trust myself.

"Amore Mio…" He grabbed my arm and pulled me into his chest. Intense sparks rushed through me, and although the other emotions seemed to dissipate a little, the urge to kill him was still very strong…

I'm a danger to him, to my family, to everyone. Doesn't he see that?

I could see Dad's pained look and Liam's. My guilt grew as he helped Raven to her feet, kissing her as he held her tight. The concern in Maria's eyes, Mom's worry… Raihana…

I had failed them all.

"Alejandro, you need to lock me away. I'm losing my mind," I whispered. His embrace was tight, pinning my arms to my side. My heart thundered as I struggled fruitlessly in his arms.

"I got you."

His words hit me hard, and I stilled. Silent tears trickled down my cheeks, and the pain within my chest hurt far more than the wound that was beginning to soak us both in blood. I closed my eyes, inhaling his scent. I didn't need my memories to tell me that this was my safe place, my home.

"She needs to be checked over, Alejandro," Maria's voice called.

I realised his heart was pounding, and I pressed my lips against the fabric of his shirt, kissing his chest. This was my fault; I worried him…

"Dante… don't let Dante see this," I said, my vision darkening.

"Don't worry, he's being kept occupied," Alejandro replied before lifting me up bridal style. Our eyes met, but I was unable to hold his gaze. I looked away, a wave of sadness washing over me.

I had failed him.

An hour later, I was partially healed. Raihana had tried to heal me, but whatever was controlling me was making it harder for her, so we told her to stop. She was pregnant, and we couldn't risk it. I had fallen unconscious and had caused more damage by exerting myself even when I was heavily injured. I had lost a lot of blood.

A pack doctor had come to check the injury and had bandaged me up. I was in my bedroom with Liam and Raven sitting on the bed whilst Alejandro was pacing the room. He had changed into a clean shirt and was currently smoking a cigarette.

"I'm sorry…" I said, looking at Raven. She was sitting between Liam's thick legs, looking incredibly tiny.

"Don't be! It was like old times, us two having a friendly match!" She replied, making a fist as she smiled cheerily. There was nothing friendly about it.

"I still hurt you," I sighed.

"It wasn't you," Alejandro said coldly as Liam stroked my hair, his other arm tightly around his bite-sized Luna

"Yeah. Don't blame yourself, Kia," Liam added, looking over at Alejandro. "I thought his hold on her had weakened?"

"I thought so, too, but it seems not…" Alejandro said, walking over to the bed. White-hot anger ripped through me, and my eyes flashed, making Alejandro pause as he was about to reach out for me. "Kiara…" He retracted his hand, taking a drag on his cigarette as he moved back.

"Stay away," I said quietly, my heart pounding as I felt the urge to get out of bed and attack him.

"Nothing can fucking keep me away from you," he growled, stubbing the cigarette on the ashtray on the bedside table and sitting down on the bed next to me.

"I don't get how his control has grown…" Liam murmured.

"Delsanra had a theory," Raven replied, falling silent when Alejandro glanced at her. Hatred blazed through me, and I felt my claws extract. "Her aura…" Raven murmured.

"Lock me away, Alejandro, where I can't hurt myself or anyone," I begged. The fear of hurting my loved ones terrified me. I needed to be kept away.

"Kiara -"

"*Alejandro!* Don't you get it? I'm losing my sanity! Do you want me to run away? No, right? Then lock me in the cells so I don't hurt anyone!" I shouted, frustration clear in my voice. I was fighting it, but it was obvious with each passing day that his control over me was growing. Or more like every passing minute.

"We'll give you both a moment," Liam said quietly as he stood up. Raven glanced at me, worry in her uniquely coloured eyes before they both left the room, leaving me alone with Alejandro. His hand threaded into my hair, and he pressed his forehead against mine, sending sparks of pleasure through me.

"We are going to get through this. Keep fighting like the fucking queen you are." I nodded, my heart squeezing.

"I plan to, but I'm scared to hurt anyone," I said quietly.

His gaze dipped to my lips before travelling down to my neck. He frowned thoughtfully before bending down and pulling me up slightly against him. My heart pounded due to his closeness, making tingles spread through me as his scent enveloped me.

"Marking you helped last time…" he murmured more to himself than to me.

I was about to push him away, but for some odd reason my body wasn't fighting him anymore. In fact, it seemed to welcome his closeness. Something was wrong. Very, very wrong.

"Alejandro -" I tried to warn him, feeling the anger and excitement course through me, but instead of listening, he sank his teeth into my neck.

Pain ripped through me, mixed with a river of pleasure, but I couldn't focus on it because what terrified me was the feeling of victory that rushed through me, an emotion that was not my own. Fear filled me, and, using all my energy, I shoved Alejandro off me. My heart was pounding as he looked at me with concern, licking the blood from his lips.

"Relax, Amore Mio, it's going to-" He suddenly tensed, bending over as he began coughing violently.

"Alejandro…"

I felt like a bucket of iced water was poured over me, seeing the blood that dripped through his fingers as he continued to cough. Pain filtered through the bond, and I clamped my hands over my mouth.

"Alejandro!"

"I'm fine…" he said hoarsely. His face was ashy, and I could see the thin layer of sweat that covered his forehead.

"No you're not," I whispered, horrified.

The temptation to plunge my hand into his back was consuming me, but instead, I staggered off the bed, a hand to my chest, putting distance between us. I needed to get help.

He gripped the bed with one hand as another bout of coughing wracked his body and with icy realisation, the truth hit me.

My blood had poisoned him.

Bindings of Silver

ALEJANDRO

I HATED SEEING THE FEAR on her face as she put distance between us, running to the door.

"*Liam!*" She shouted, pulling the door open before turning and rushing to my side. She hesitated, falling to her knees a few feet from me. "Alejandro, baby, are you okay?" She asked, reaching out, then hesitating as Liam and Raven entered.

"I'll get help," Raven murmured, running off.

"Alejandro." Liam was by my side, and although my entire body was fucking burning up and felt like it was being fucking torn apart from inside, I was in my fucking senses.

"Take care of her," I growled, staggering to my feet. "I'm fine, Amore Mio, calm down." I wanted to pull her into my fucking arms, but she was fucking scared of being near me and I did not want to make her even more panicked.

"I'm going to get some antidote." I heard Liam say as he lifted Kiara to her feet, taking her out of the room with him. I could feel my body fighting it, and the urge to shift took over. A menacing growl that I knew filled every corner of the mansion ripped from my throat as I transformed.

"Al!" Darien's voice came.

I turned as he waved two bottles of antidotes. Something told me those fuckers wouldn't work, but I still grabbed them in my huge, clawed hand and downed them.

Nothing.

I still fucking felt like shit.

I'm fine, I growled through the link, sitting on the bed in Lycan form. "Uncle!"

Tell her not to try healing me. This could be the exact same shit as what happened with Delsanra and Dante, I commanded through the haze.

"Raihana, you can't heal him," I heard Darien say as my vision darkened.

She was arguing, but someone took her away. The last thing I saw was Elijah and Scarlett enter, and then everything went black.

❧⚬☙

I opened my eyes groggily. My body was fucking killing me, but it wasn't as bad as it had been earlier. The sun was still out, which meant I hadn't been out for long. I sat up, squinting, and I was about to get out of bed when Scarlett placed her hand on my shoulder.

"I do not want to see you naked ever again. Stay in bed," she almost growled. Seriously?

"Is Elijah's prick that fucking small that seeing my big dick scared you?" I shot back. I heard someone let out a sharp, irritable exhale and turned to see Darien and Elijah there.

"He's perfectly fine if he can run his mouth," Elijah glared. I smirked. He didn't deny that I was bigger than him.

"How long was I out?" I asked, resting back against the cushions and pulling the duvet over my waist. I wasn't planning on shifting; my pants and fitted boxers were indeed gone.

"Just over an hour. How are you feeling?" Darien asked.

"I won't lie and say that I'm not in any pain, but it is better than before. Did you guys give me something or some shit?"

"Something? Try several things... a few enchantments, which didn't include direct magic from Raihana, so don't get angry, every antidote in existence. We even tried Scarlett's blood," Darien replied, frowning at me. I could tell from his pale skin colour that he was shaken.

"What worked?"

"I don't think anything worked. I think your body just fought it," Scarlett answered.

"Where is she?" I asked. I needed to see her.

Silence.

"I asked, where the fuck is Kiara?"

"In the cells. She asked to be put there," Elijah answered quietly. His pain was unmasked, and I didn't give a fuck about Scarlett's trauma of seeing me fucking naked. Getting out of bed, I crossed the room and heard her turn away sharply. I went through to the dressing room and grabbed a pair of sweatpants.

"And you all did just that?" I asked, re-entering the bedroom after grabbing a pair of sneakers. Just that walk was fucking exhausting, but I was not going to let it get to me.

"You should have seen her state, I wouldn't want my daughter locked up if there was another solution," Scarlett said icily, "but she needed this for her own sanity."

Yeah, I still didn't give a shit. I left the room, even when they called me. I needed to see her.

"Al!" Darien caught up with me. "You can barely hold yourself together." I growled, my eyes blazing as I looked at him.

"I am fucking fine," I hissed. "You locked your fucking Luna away."

"Under her command…" he said quietly.

I knew that. But it didn't mean it made it any fucking easier. We left the mansion, and the moment we got to the cells, I started scanning each one.

"She's in the cells on the lower floor," Darien said hesitantly.

"Why?" I asked, trying to control my rage.

"Her orders."

"Stay here," I warned, taking the keys and unlocking the metal barred door.

Entering the cold corridor, I headed down the stone steps to the lower floor, a place that was entirely made of silver and stone. Kiara was standing in the far cell, her arms wrapped around her waist as she stared at the ground. Her scent overpowered the smell of silver, wolfsbane, and dampness. My fucking queen…

"Amore Mio."

"Alejandro! Thank the goddess, you are okay!" She exclaimed, running to the bars and grabbing hold of them, only to flinch before letting go and hiding her hands behind her back.

The emotions that ran through me were far too much to put into words, seeing her in this place… she was the queen, yet here she was in the cells which were reserved for the worst of criminals. I walked towards the bars, glancing at the chains that hung from the floor and ceiling behind her. To my irritation, I saw her feet tied to the chains on the ground. She shouldn't be here. It was making me physically sick, seeing her in this fucking environment.

"Show me your hands," I commanded, my voice holding a dangerous edge. She shook her head.

"I'm fine," she replied stubbornly. Her voice was as sexy and soothing as ever.

"Kiara." Her eyes flashed with hatred, and I knew she was still battling for control.

"Leave," she said, closing her eyes.

"When is it ever that way between us?" I asked quietly, unlocking the cell door. "If one of us pushes the other away, the other doesn't listen." I left the keys in the door, knowing I needed to be careful. Right then, she was stronger than me.

"Alejandro! Stay away!" She growled, backing away from me. I closed the gap between us.

"No. You're mine, Amore Mio, and there is nothing that can fucking keep me from you, not even the Goddess herself. So what's a fucking Djinn gonna do?" I asked arrogantly. Her eyes flashed, but within the purple, I saw orange. Fucker.

She only stopped when her back hit the stone wall behind her, the chains dragging taut from around her ankles. Fucking silver chains… she was wearing jeans, but I knew they would still be affecting her.

"Alejandro, just listen, please, if you love me!"

Her claws were extended. She was about to dig them into her thighs to control herself, but I was not having her self-harming herself again. She had stabbed herself earlier to stop herself. I grabbed her wrists, pinning them to the walls by her head, making her gasp. Her eyes returned to her beautiful blue-green, and I pressed my forehead to hers, relishing the sparks that coursed through me.

"We are going to get through this because, metres or miles apart, we will always be together. Just hold on for a little longer, and I will fucking handle this fucker," I growled, my eyes blazing red.

Her pounding heart calmed, and her eyes shut. A small hint of a smile crossed her face, and I knew that she had lost the battle for now.

"Are you ready to die?" She asked in a cold, quiet tone, opening her eyes. The glint of orange had covered the blue in her eyes, bleeding into the green.

"For my family, if it comes to it, then yeah, I'm ready. The fucking question is, are you ready to be sent back to the fucking pits of hell?" I asked coldly. "Or better yet, for me to destroy you into fucking oblivion."

"It's not easy to get rid of me, let alone kill me."

"Yet you are bound. If you really were as fucking powerful as you act, you would have come here. You would be able to take Dante, but you can't. I'm not sure why, but you aren't as fucking powerful as you like to pretend," I hissed. The urge to rip him apart consumed me, and I couldn't wait for the fucking day we ended him.

I had hit a nerve. A look of pure hatred and evil crossed Kiara's face, an expression I had never seen on her face. Ever. Even when angry, there was no evil within her. *I will fix this. I'll destroy him. Just hold on, beautiful.* Even if she was pushed to the corner of her mind, I would save her from it.

"You don't know what you are talking about."

"Oh, I fucking do, and the fact that you are getting pissed off just means I hit the fucking nail on the head. What the fuck do you want with Dante?" A smirk twisted on her face. She looked at me with contempt but didn't answer.

Well, fine. Two can play this shit. I was not going to let it rile me up.

"The next time we talk… it's going to be face-to-face. Not when you are using my woman to hide behind like the fucking coward you are," I growled threateningly.

"Let's hope I don't kill her down here. After all… I will have no use for her if she's in the cells."

That was it.

"Fuck you."

Her eyes flashed purple. I saw her struggle to take control as the Djinn tried to rip free from my hold, elongating her claws and pulling one hand free. My stomach twisted as I realised he was aiming for her heart. *Not on my fucking watch.*

I growled, slamming her hand back against the wall, my aura rolling off me.

"Tie me," Kiara groaned as she struggled.

The red from her chest injury was beginning to coat her top once again. She wasn't healed as it was. She needed to stay calm. I didn't argue, pulling her to the middle of her room as she struggled against me. It would be a fucking lie if I denied that she was fucking making it hard for me. I could taste blood in my mouth again. I was still weak. I heard Darien enter the cells, but I didn't spare him a glance. I managed to clamp her wrist into the cuffs, slamming them shut as she tried to bite into my wrist once more, the clang echoing through the empty cell.

"I will kill you!" She growled as I pulled the chains tight so her arms were spread wide and there was no risk left of her harming herself.

"I'll look forward to it," I replied, tightening the chains at her ankles so her legs were slightly apart. "No one is hurting what belongs to me."

She struggled, pulling at the chains, and I knew that they would fucking weaken her. Maybe keeping her unconscious might be better. I'd talk to Callum. With those final words, I tore the lower half off her top and took hold of her chin.

"I'm going to put an end to this shit, I fucking promise you, Amore Mio," I said quietly, kissing her plush lips softly. I hoped that, deep inside, she could feel my emotions as I let the barrier down between us. Her eyes softened, and for a moment, she kissed me back before I moved away. "I'm going to tie your mouth in case he tries to get you to bite your tongue off," I said quietly, placing the torn shirt between her plump lips. She nodded slowly as she fought back her tears.

Be brave, my queen.

I tied her mouth, inhaling the scent of her sandy brown hair. The scent of her shampoo mixed with her own intoxicating scent was soothing, and, leaning in, I planted a soft kiss on her forehead.

Keep strong, keep fighting.

She nodded.

I love you, she replied softly.

Love you more than life itself. I caressed her cheek before I stepped away, putting my walls back up.

I was fucking breaking inside, but I wouldn't show her that because no matter what, I would fucking save her.

Turning, I left the cell and locked the door after me. I didn't look back. I wouldn't be able to leave her if I did. I would stay down there by her side if I could… but I needed to lead our army and destroy this bastard. It took every inch of my willpower not to turn and break her out. Seeing her in that state… having to do that to her… it was so fucking painful that I was finding it hard to breathe.

Wait for me, because it's high fucking time I unleashed hell and showed this bastard that no one messes with Alejandro Rossi or his family.

A United Plan

ALEJANDRO

"A L," DARIEN CALLED ME, but it was fucking hard to keep myself together when my woman was fucking chained up down beneath these very pack grounds.

"Call for a meeting in an hour's time. Have the witches on call and wire the Alphas involved. It's time we took this fucker down. What's the count at?"

"Four hundred and thirty-two," Darien replied after checking his phone. I nodded.

"Spread farther out if we fucking need to. No one rests until we have what we need," I ordered coldly before walking away from him, no longer able to control my aura that was swirling around me in waves of darkness.

This fucker has hurt my family repeatedly… but to try to use my own mate against me… the urge to rip him apart piece by fucking piece sounded very enticing.

I was about to go to my office at headquarters, but I didn't think staying in one fucking room for an hour was going to help. So, instead, I decided to go for a walk around the pack instead, and maybe for a run, a pack that had gone from what looked like more of a military camp to a full-out pack with pups and families. A group of young boys in their teens walked past, laughing and talking, not even knowing the severity of life around them, although they went silent upon seeing me.

"Alpha." They lowered their heads, clearly realising I was pissed off.

I frowned, looking at the boy in the middle with piercing brown eyes and a tumble of dirty blond hair. Fred's kid. One I had never mentioned to anyone, although I knew a few might make the link as he looked like the spitting image of him. I had often been tempted to speak to his mother... but I had always decided against it.

"Can I help you, Alpha?" He asked with a warm smile. That was something different from Fred, who had always been quiet and moody.

"No." He gave me a small polite smile and nodded. "None of you has a fag on you, do you?" They exchanged looks, wondering if it was a trick question, before they shook their heads.

"We aren't eighteen yet..." one of them said.

"Yeah? I'm sure you all get up to crap," I said, making a few of them look guilty. Yeah, I fucking thought so.

"But we don't have cigarettes..."

"Sorry."

I nodded, motioning them to go as I walked off, leaving them behind and frowning deeply. Azura was his half-sister, and I was sure the day would come when I would have to share that truth... but for now, I didn't plan on delving into it.

I reached into my pocket, only to frown when I realised they were empty. I needed a cigarette, and there was nowhere I could fucking grab one. I didn't want to ask anyone to bring me a pack either because I wanted to be alone...

Kiara. Chained and fucking alone...

I couldn't have anyone watch her because she could use her command on them. At least the silver in her cuffs cut the mind link from her. Isolating her.

I sighed as I mind-linked Callum and explained the situation to him.

Don't worry, Alpha. I will look into drugging her so she is unconscious and can't harm herself.

Do that.

I cut the link and entered the trees. I removed my sweatpants and shifted. I needed a run to clear my head.

ELIJAH

Scarlett wrapped her arms around my neck from behind, her breasts pressing against my back as she kissed my neck softly.

"Hey…" she whispered. I stroked her arms, sighing heavily. "What's on your mind?"

"You know, with Kiara losing control, Alejandro's plan to leak false information has gone out the window," I said, turning and looking into her beautiful sage-green eyes.

"Don't worry, I'm sure we'll sort this out. The other night he mentioned he wanted one of us to stay here… Elijah, will you stay?" Always a beauty, always strong, and always a fearless Alpha, but I didn't want to risk her…

"Kitten, I don't want you to be out there on the battlefield when I'm here -" She pressed a finger to my lips and shook her head.

"I heal faster… I need to be there. You know we need someone powerful here, too. That's you. To look after the pups and Kiara," she replied, frowning softly. I sighed.

"You really haven't changed. As hot, tight, and stubborn as that first day I realised I was in love with you," I said cockily, enjoying the way her heart skipped a beat.

"And, although you are super possessive… you have always let me do what I needed to. Never treated me as anything lesser."

"We're equal, like you once said, and I have to admit it is probably one of the hottest things you have ever said; I may not have a dick, but -"

"I'm a fucking king." She smiled, finishing the sentence as we thought back to that moment from long ago.

"Yeah, and you were right," I smirked, reaching behind me and pulling her into my arms. I inhaled her scent as I buried my nose in her neck.

"So, will you let me go?" I tilted my head, squeezing her ass as she straddled me.

"You know if anything happens to you -" She placed a finger on my lips and smiled slightly.

"We live together, and we will die together. I know," she whispered.

Yeah, a promise we made… but we both knew that if it came to that, we couldn't abandon Azura. Neither of us had to say it out loud; our eyes spoke what our lips were unable to. If something were to happen, the other would have to live on for her… even if only until she was ready to spread her wings and fly.

She hugged me tightly, her heart racing. I held her just as tight. Scarlett may be an Alpha, heck, a king, but she, too, had her fears and worries, yet she continued to be brave for everyone else.

Earlier, when Kiara had begun to lose herself and was begging to be locked away, it was Scarlett who had given the command to listen to Kiara and lock her up, a decision we all weren't able to make. Her voice had been strong, but I had felt her agony and pain leaking through the bond as she remained in control for those around us.

My phone beeped, and we both moved back, realising it was time for the meeting.

"I love you, sweetheart," I said quietly, giving her my best sexy smirk, one that she fell for back in the day. She rolled her eyes.

"I guess I love you, too." Despite her airy tone, she gripped my face and kissed me passionately, sending off explosions of pleasure through us both…

ALEJANDRO

An hour later, we were still in the middle of the meeting. We had several people on video call, and I had finished outlining the plan. The extra batch of people sent to gather blood from farther out would hopefully speed up the process and get us the needed amount faster.

"There're five groups being made: decoy, defence, infiltration, extra backup force, and, of course, the main group," I said, tapping the tabletop screen where I had a battle plan pulled up. "Elijah, who's staying behind from you two?"

"I am," he replied instantly.

I frowned, but I had a feeling he would be. Scarlett had been adamant that she was going to go to battle when I had mentioned I wanted either or both to stay behind. I gave a curt nod, trying to ignore the pain in my body. Whatever this was, it was fucking draining, but my body was continuing to fight against it.

"Raihana and Elijah, you two are staying here. My two Betas will also be staying behind. That is the defence for the pack," I stated.

"Nicholson, you will take charge of Blood Moon, and Chris, you will handle Black Storm if needed," I said as Rayhan nodded. Although we shouldn't be gone for too long, we needed to make sure everything was in place. I continued explaining everything until I was sure everything was covered.

"Any questions?" I asked.

The screen crackled before another window popped up, and a smirking Leo appeared.

"You really need to work on your online security. That took me max twenty minutes to hack into."

Fucker.

"Yeah, well, not everyone is a fucking computer whizz. What do you want?" I asked, frowning as Marcel's frown deepened.

"Leo. This is not a joke," he growled. I motioned for him to leave it.

"I want in. I heard that we'll be heading out literally right after my birthday, meaning I'll have shifted by then," he smirked. I didn't need anyone to tell me that he was thrilled about his shift, but then again, who wouldn't be?

"And why would you want to come on such a risky mission?" I asked, very aware of all the Alphas on screen and everyone in the room watching us. He shrugged, sitting back and lighting a cigarette.

"You know Dad isn't the toughest guy around. I'm just going to be there to make sure he comes back in one piece," he said, but his eyes were ice cold.

Although his words seemed normal enough, making a few Alphas nod as if understanding his point and smiling at how protective he seemed of his father, I understood the underlying meaning. It was obvious he thought I'd let Marcel die or that I would put him in the line of fire and use him for collateral. That wasn't true; I didn't want anyone to fucking lose their lives, and I would protect Marcel if the need arose.

"I'll let you come, but this is a team battle. Are you sure you will get along with everyone on the team? If you try anything or come in the way -"

"I won't. I'll make sure to steer clear of everyone's way," he cut in, and I nodded, not missing Rayhan's frown from the corner of my eye.

"And stop hacking the fucking system," I growled. He raised an eyebrow.

"I'll give you some tips on how to strengthen this crap if you come out of this battle alive," he said, shrugging, making Maria and Scarlett frown. *This fucker…*

I turned back to the group.

"It is going to be risky. Lives will be lost… but I promise you all I will do my best to make sure they are minimum."

"I understand that, Alpha. I do have a concern, though. Are you sure killing this enemy with just a special blade will be enough?" Jacob, an Alpha from up north, asked. I nodded, trying not to glance at Janaina or Magdalene.

"It's no simple weapon. It will do the job," I said before looking around at everyone. "I have one request; as always, I have given the option to those who want out or do not want to participate. All of you have offered to help, and I'm fucking grateful for it. However, don't force your people. Only those who are willing should come forward."

"I appreciate that, Alpha King, but they are our pack members. They will obey."

"They will, but if their heart isn't in it, then there's no power behind that warrior. A time may come when every man and woman will have to stand in battle whether they like it or not, but right now, we have the power to give them the choice," I said quietly. I saw Leo frown. He probably didn't believe me, but I meant it.

"We are with you, King Alejandro."

One by one, they all followed suit, and the weight of the situation cast a sombre feeling across the room.

"This battle may be personal for you, Alpha Alejandro, but the Queen, Luna Delsanra, and Dante are important to us all. Besides, by letting this thing do as he wishes, he will only harm more and more of our kind. He needs to be stopped anyway," Damon said seriously. I glanced at him and nodded.

It was true. He wanted Dante, and although what exactly he wanted with him was still a mystery, I was certain we'd find out one way or another.

Rayhan's phone rang, and everyone turned their attention to him. He cut the call, looking down at the screen before a small smirk crossed his lips.

Has the blood count risen? I asked through the link. He gave me a nod, and I smirked. Perfect.

The taste of blood filled my mouth once again, but I swallowed it. I needed to remain strong for my people and for my family.

"We got this," Elijah said, and I glanced up sharply. Our eyes met, and I nodded.

Yeah, we fucking did.

Mother to Daughter

MARIA

*F*OUR DAYS HAD PASSED since the meeting, and we were getting ever closer to the blood count, which meant the time to leave would be soon. It had been four days since Kiara had lost control and was being kept unconscious. Seeing her lying there on a bed of silver with chains holding her down was painful.

I had wanted to talk to her before I left, one final time... to ask her to take care of my grandchildren... to take the place of that grandmother figure for them that I would no longer be able to fulfil... but I didn't have the luxury to bid her goodbye.

I stood outside Raihana's bedroom, hesitating. I had told her I had wanted a word, so she was expecting me, but I was feeling a little uncertain. Scared even. I swallowed hard, trying to be strong. How do I tell my daughter that I wasn't coming back?

"Aunty Maria, come in," Chris said, opening the door and flashing me a smirk. I smiled and entered their bedroom, my heart pounding, which made Chris look at me suspiciously "You alright?" He asked

"Of course I am," I replied smoothly, walking over to the travel cot where Tatum was fast asleep. My little prince...

"Mom," Raihana greeted, coming out of the adjoining bathroom in a silk nightgown.

"Could you close the door, please, Chris?" I asked as he was still standing there. He closed it slowly, exchanging looks with Raihana, who came over to me and felt my forehead.

"Your heart's racing, Mom," she murmured, concerned. I sat on the edge of the bed, pulling her down beside me.

"I wanted to talk to you both about something," I started, taking her hands. "Promise me you both will hear me out before saying anything, and what I speak of stays in this room."

"I promise," Raihana said, brushing it off.

"No, Raihana, take an oath on Tatum."

"Mom... you're asking for an oath, what is going on?"

"You won't know until you take the oath," I said pointedly. She rolled her eyes as Chris smirked.

"I take an oath on Ri. You have my word; I won't repeat anything to anyone," he said, placing a hand on his heart.

"I swear on Tatum's life," Raihana said, shaking her head. "Happy?"

"Yes," I said quietly, looking at my son-in-law. *I will need him to be here for Raihana...*

"Mom? Hello? You can tell us; you are acting really weird." She felt my forehead again, looking confused. *Here it goes.*

Taking a deep breath, I closed my eyes for a moment, giving Raihana's hand a gentle squeeze.

"It's about the upcoming battle," I said softly.

"Oh, Mom, I wish you didn't have to go. Don't worry, you will be okay. Uncle Al won't let anything happen to you," Raihana said, smiling at me. I nodded.

"I know he won't, but... there is a price to pay for taking a demon's life," I began, my heart thundering as Raihana's smile vanished, replaced with a frown. "A life. The one who stabs him with the dagger will die."

"Shit! Is Uncle planning –"

"I said, hear me out, ya habibti!" I scolded as Chris stood there, watching me sharply with his piercing eyes.

"Okay, but uncle can't –"

"He was planning to, but the kids are still so young, Kiara is so young, they have their entire life ahead," I explained, and Raihana nodded. "And, well... I want to return to him," I finished softly, and for the first time, I looked into her eyes. She frowned, trying to understand before her eyes widened. Her heart thundered as she stared at me, realisation burning in her brown orbs.

"Fuck," Chris muttered.

Her eyes began filling with tears, and I knew I needed to say what I had to before I couldn't hold myself together any longer.

"Every day that passes feels like a burden upon my soul. Life is… empty." I felt guilty. I was their mother. I was meant to continue going for them. "I'm sorry. I know you must think I'm such a coward for leaving all of you. I truly miss him." She shook her head, her lips trembling as she squeezed my hand tightly. "You and Rayhan have your lives before you, your mates, your children, and I think I can leave you now." I cupped her face as her lip quivered, and, for a moment, it felt like a fifteen-year-old Raihana was before me. "May I return to my mate?" Those were the words that broke the dam on her tears, and she lowered her head.

"You will leave us? What about our little baby? He or she will never get to meet you," she whispered, placing her free hand on her stomach. "My children won't have any grandparents."

"I know, ya habibti, but Alejandro cannot do this or anyone else. It isn't fair. I want to go… and this is my chance. You will never be alone. You will have Alejandro, Kiara, Delsanra, Rayhan -"

"Does Rayhan know?" She asked, brushing her tears away angrily.

"No, and I don't plan to tell him. I am leaving a small video for him and for Kiara," I said softly, brushing her tears away as she shook her head.

"Goddess, there has to be another way!" She cried in frustration.

"Baby," Chris said as she stood up. He pulled her into his arms forcefully. "She said she's tired."

"She can't go!" Raihana snapped, despite the tears running down her cheeks. "No!"

Her loud shout disturbed Tatum. I stood up as he started crying and took him from the cot. My own tears threatened to fall as I hugged him tightly, and I turned away. *I will not show my weakness…*

"Please, Raihana, Living without your mate is like living when your inside is empty."

"And what of us? Don't we make you happy? Come live with us if you feel alone at home! Please, Mom, don't do this!" She sobbed. She came over, grabbing my shoulders as I rocked the child in my arms.

"You all do, but I cannot explain it… tell me, Raihana, can you imagine life without Chris?" I asked quietly. She looked over my shoulder, her eyes filling with pain. "A life where your other half is gone? Waking every day with the absence of his smile, touch, and presence? Everywhere I walk, I see memories that we once shared... I need him, Raihana. Please don't make this harder for me. Let me go."

"Mom..." She hugged me, the little prince between us staring up at us as he watched us curiously. Our foreheads were pressed together, and a few tears escaped me despite my greatest effort, making Tatum giggle as he clapped, staring up at us.

"How did Uncle even agree?" She whispered between her sobs.

"He saw my pain," I replied, taking a deep, shuddering breath. "He didn't want to, but I begged him."

"Rayhan is going to kill," she said, shaking her head.

"And that is why I want you to make sure he sees this video." I reached into the pocket of my skirt and held out a small drive. "Make sure he sees it." She nodded before a fresh wave of tears consumed her.

Chris took Tatum from my arms, and I hugged my child, knowing that these moments were coming to an end and the sheer weight that I would no longer have my children in my arms hit me hard. There was indeed a price for everything...

⚜

I left their room an hour later and made my way to Delsanra's room. Rayhan was gone for the night, and I was going to spend the night watching over her. She was no longer able to get up from bed, and she spent most of the time sleeping. The curse was taking its toll, and we all feared what would happen without Kiara to help ease it a little. Even Raihana's healing spells did nothing to ease her pain.

The Omega, Clara, smiled at me when I entered, holding a sleeping Ahren in her arms.

"Was he not asleep?" I asked quietly.

"He wanted his mother," she replied, looking older than ever. This Djinn was taking its toll on the entire pack.

"Pass him to me and get some rest yourself," I told her with a gentle smile.

"Shall I take Sienna?"

"No, I will have them," I replied, going over to the bed where Sienna was already asleep next to her mother.

"Okay, ma'am. If you need anything, don't hesitate to call," she whispered before leaving the room.

I looked at the child in my arms and, walking over to the bed, I slipped in, placing him down by his sister and laying down next to him.

"I'll miss you all," I whispered.

Was I selfish to leave them? Would Rayhan hate me?

I stroked the children's curls, and I remembered when Rayhan and Raihana were little pups. Rafael would come home late, but he'd always go to kiss them, and if they woke up, he'd just bring them to our room. I'd scold him for ruining their routine. I closed my eyes, letting the tears stream down my cheeks now that I was alone.

I looked over at the second daughter I was blessed with. No matter how hurtful the things I said when I first realised that she was a witch were, she still forgave me. She was the best mate I could ever wish for for Rayhan.

"Mama Mari, what's wrong?" Her weak voice asked. I looked away, wiping my tears. I hadn't realised she had woken up.

"I just… nothing."

"I know it's not nothing. Talk to me," she whispered, her eyelids opening slightly. Our eyes met, and I smiled softly, despite the tears in my eyes.

"I can't have you telling Rayhan," I whispered.

"I… what is it?" She asked, worry crossing her face. I shook my head. I loved her, but… what if she told Rayhan?

"Just know that I love you, and you *are* going to get better soon."

"Thank you." She smiled despite the pain she was in. "I love you, too. You are the mother I always wished to have." I nodded.

"I'm glad. I, too, was blessed by the gods to have gotten another daughter as perfect and strong as you." I reached over and caressed her cheek. She closed her eyes before she opened them again, and this time, they were full of sadness.

"Didn't you say I'll be okay? Why does this sound like a farewell?" She whispered. She tried to smile, and I simply shook my head.

"I'm just having a moment. You will be okay. Absolutely." She nodded, and we fell silent. I wasn't sure if she fell asleep, but just as troubled sleep was overcoming me, I heard her speak,

"Mama Mari… this isn't farewell, is it?"

I didn't have the heart to reply.…

An Awakening

ENRIQUE

"*I* WILL KILL HIM!"

My heart was thumping in fear. I was terrified. I had returned to my pack in Puerto Rico, but when Padre found out I was back, he demanded I be brought back to England because he wanted to see me. I hated this place. It was nothing but a nightmare for me. My entire body hurt, but Father didn't stop. He kept kicking me. Again and again. I wanted to ask him why he didn't come for me. Didn't he love me?

"Tell me, you hijo de puta! *Tell me!*" Father screamed.

Father…

"I don't know anything." I coughed as he kicked me again.

"There is no way he would have let you go without something in return!" He hissed. "Tell me, what did you tell him?"

"Nothing, Padre, I don't know anything to have told him!" I cried out fearfully.

Another kick to the head. I had pleaded for the last hour, yet he didn't believe me. He kept hurting me, and the memory of how I was always in pain returned to me. But why did it feel so much worse?

Will I die?

"You won't speak? You won't tell me why he let you go!"

"Because he isn't a monster!" I shouted.

He fell silent and I felt the unease in the room grow. Through the blood and haze of pain, I looked up at my father. A darkness emanated from him, and it filled the room, filling me with fear and dread.

"Want to see a monster, son?" He hissed. His burned skin looked even worse than normal. His eyes were glowing terrifyingly. Father wasn't well... the thing inside of him was killing him and making him angrier. "Bring his mother."

Mother? No...

"No! Padre, please! I'm sorry. I didn't mean to say that!" I cried out.

"I think this is a lesson you need, son. A few days in his hold, and you think he's better than me?"

"No, Padre, I swear! He isn't better than you! I never said that! I just said he let me go because ~"

He kicked me across the room just as I heard mother enter. *No, Mother, go!*

"Alpha Sebastian…" Mother murmured respectfully, looking at Father. The evil look on Father's face was scaring me. Mother's attention fell on me, and her eyes widened in horror. "Enrique is back!" She cried, breaking away from the two guards who were flanking her and ran towards me.

"No, Madre, run!" I shouted in horror the moment I saw father raise his hand, and before my very eyes, the blazing fire engulfed Mother's body instantly. A shriek of pain left her lips, her eyes widening in horror as they stared at me. Then, Father was behind her, his hand ripping through her chest and tearing her heart out.

"No!"

No. No. No. *This can't be true.* My heart was hurting so much.

The smell of blood and burnt skin filled the room. Mother's lifeless body fell to the ground, and I couldn't stop the tears from falling from my eyes. *Please, don't let this be true.* Was this it? I didn't even get to hug her…

The way she ran to me when she saw me… it meant that she did care for me, but… did her death not affect Father?

"Now *that's* a monster," Father hissed as he came over to me, kicking me in the stomach once more. Maybe I was wrong... maybe I had always been wrong…

No, not maybe. I am wrong; Father is evil. I won't speak. I'll never tell him what I told the Alpha King.

I didn't move. I didn't react as he kept kicking me. I just stared at the burned body of my mother lying a few metres away. All I could do was look at it. I didn't even get to say goodbye.

I closed my eyes, praying to the goddess, if she really existed, to save me. Did she not love us? Why was she letting this happen to us?

"Throw him out!" I heard Father order from somewhere far away.

Was I dying? I was all alone. No one cared for me... maybe it was better if I died, too...

"Take him before I kill him!" He hissed, and I felt a wave of relief wash over me.

Yes, kill me. I want to go to Mother...

He turned and slammed his foot on my head. Searing pain filled my body, and I wondered if this was what death felt like. When your body was in so much pain that you could no longer breathe. Everything was getting darker. I thought I saw Father walking away.

"Stay awake, young master..." someone was whispering

I don't want to... just...please, let me die.

Darkness was calling me, and I welcomed it happily.

MARCEL

Leo's eighteenth birthday was finally here, with only an hour to spare. It was something I wanted to celebrate with our entire pack, but he didn't want that. Even though we were in trying times, it was still a special one.

I was concerned as to why he wanted to come on the mission or why Alejandro would agree. Did he trust Leo to behave? I didn't. I was worried he'd mess something up and it would cause more problems, but when I spoke to Alejandro yesterday, he had said Leo was only concerned about me.

Looking at the boy who sat there, tapping his foot, earphones in and smoking a cigarette, I felt like I was losing the boy who was once full of innocence and hope. Maybe I had lost him years ago... but seeing him sitting there, so grown... I wondered where the time went. His mother would have loved to be here...

"Are you just going to stand there?" He remarked coldly, glancing up at me.

"I want to witness my son's first shift," I replied. He didn't respond to that, and I sighed. "Leo. It's still not too late to celebrate in the morning -"

"With what? A cake and candles? I'm eighteen, Dad, not eight."

"Well, you should do something with your friends at least. Maybe pizza, a movie -"

"Nah, we're going to head down to a strip club tonight," he smirked arrogantly, and I frowned.

"That's not the best choice. Your memorable eighteenth, and you're going to go spend it at a club."

"Oh, for fuck's sake, I've been to one countless times. If you can't tell, people already think I'm older than I look." He shrugged.

"You are at the age where you may find your mate," I reminded him. Just the thought of it made me think that the poor girl would have a lot to deal with.

"I don't think I'll find my mate this early. Hopefully, never." He shrugged, unbothered as he glanced at the time.

"Don't say that. They are a blessing."

"Or a curse."

"Leo, why do you want to go on this mission?" I asked quietly. He frowned and looked at me sharply, all laziness and attitude vanishing.

"I already told you, to watch your fucking back," he growled.

"I don't need a pup to watch out for me." I frowned.

"Actually, you fucking do, especially when we all know they'll throw you to the fucking devil first." He believed that. He truly believed that...

"Leo, do you truly believe that I will be alone out there?"

He stood up, towering slightly over me as he walked towards me, taking out his ear pods.

"You will be. And the most pathetic part is, you don't fucking see it."

"Actually, you don't see the truth." He scoffed, glancing up at the sky.

"Yeah? Well, even if you're a lame Alpha, you're the only family I've got. So, if I have to come to watch your back, then I'm coming. As for the rest, I don't give a fuck."

"Leo -"

"It's time." His voice was an animalistic growl as a huge surge of power wrapped around him, and I almost stepped back.

His eyes glowed a dark steel blue, and he grinned before the snapping of bones filled the air. Then, there before me was a huge, magnificent wolf.

His fur was a light brown, but what awed me was the blue undertones to it, a colour that I had never seen before. His aura was emanating off him in waves, and when he raised his head to the moon, letting off a mighty menacing growl that oozed nothing but pure power and dominance, I realised that before me not only stood a strong Alpha but either a mighty ally or a terrifying threat. However, it was his next words that truly planted the seed of fear within me.

What's wrong, Dad? Scared? His powerful voice came through the link. His deep steely eyes met mine and I was unable to reply.

The boy I had known was gone.

In that moment, I made up my mind. Unless I ended up dead, I would not give him the position of Alpha. Leo had waited for this moment for years, not only because he wanted his wolf but because he craved power, and that very thought terrified me. He was now capable of unleashing hell.

A Revelation Beyond Imagination

ALEJANDRO

"COME BACK, RAYHAN. WE only have a couple dozen to go. You need to be here with Delsanra, even if it's just for a bit," I said quietly through the phone.

"Yeah," his quiet reply came. "I want to, but me coming back slows things down. We need to work as fast as possible."

He'd been fucking strong, even with each passing day. Delsanra hadn't woken up in the last twenty hours and we were all getting fucking worried. Her heart was fading, and time was running out.

Kiara was knocked out in the cells, yet at times I felt the pain and agony through the bond. He was hurting her, trying to awaken her, and it fucking hurt knowing I was causing her pain, too.

"Alright… how long do you think it'll take?" I asked.

"I'm going to say a day at most. I'm getting this fucking done," he replied, his voice dangerously low.

"Got it."

I hung up, dropping into my seat. I was trying to keep my shit together, but the poison was fucking messing me up, too.

Janaina and Elijah were in the room. Everyone was gathering here ready to leave when the time came. Only Leo said he would meet us on the way. He had shifted two nights ago, and Marcel had said he was a powerful wolf. I expected no less from a Rossi. The conversation from the day before yesterday played in my mind. Why had his words made me uneasy?

TWO DAYS AGO

"Congrats on your shift. Your old man said you're a fucking sight."

"Maybe."

"I'm proud of you. I wouldn't have expected anything less from a Rossi." A cold scoff came down the line.

"Oh, yeah? I don't really consider myself one of your kind."

"My kind?"

"Yeah, the kind I hate."

"Leo, I know you hate Rayhan, but try to understand what he did was because his mate –"

"Was tortured under Endora's command, right? Yeah, I know. If you forget, I was there. I remember sneaking her medicine and food when I could. Even if she was a witch, she was just another prisoner... like all of us."

"Then you understand why he did it."

"Rayhan's mate, Rayhan's mate, Rayhan's mate... I'm getting bored of hearing it. What about the mates of those who were forced to hurt her? Those who suffered from the trauma of being spelled to commit crimes, knowing their families would be killed before their eyes yet still begged not to be forced to hurt her? What about when Rayhan beat those victims? Did he not think their innocent mates would also feel the pain? Tell me, King Alejandro, in his revenge he hurt so many innocent people. In fact, two of those who were kept prisoner, their mates were pregnant at the time, and one almost miscarried. But you all don't care, do you? Because it's your fucking Rayhan. Congratulations, Your Royal Highness. You really are the perfect king."

The phone was cut off, leaving me feeling ice cold.

Did I feel uneasy because the facts he stated were something I had never considered? Or because I let it happen? It was true; even Marcel had been under Endora's command to the point that he was a mere puppet like most of them... but had we been right to give Rayhan that power? I had given him those files... data I had promised I'd share with no one...

Had I made a mistake?

Puppets of Endora who had regretted their actions... and above that, their mates suffered...

I ran my hand through my hair.

"It's a shame Delsanra isn't up to this," Janaina sighed.

"What the fuck do you mean?" I asked, glad for a distraction from my thoughts.

"I found out that any kind of demon can kill a Djinn without dying," she stated haughtily.

"Well, we don't fucking have demons walking the fuck around now, do we?" I growled.

Each fucking day closer to ending this shit also meant saying goodbye to Maria, so my mood was getting fucking worse. Elijah frowned as he watched me calculatingly.

"So, Rayhan almost has the entire blood count? At this rate, you can set off in the morning," he said quietly. I nodded.

"Yeah. I think I'll let everyone know," I said, standing up.

Only the most trusted would know of the plans. My warriors were ready to leave at any moment anyway.

"No, you rest. Take it easy. Keep your energy up, and I'll let them know," he said quietly.

"Thanks," I said quietly. He left the room, and Janaina looked at me.

"You know, I came here earlier for a reason," she stated.

"Yeah, I'd hope so because I didn't fucking call you."

"I still truly dislike your attitude," she snapped as I sat down again.

"Yeah, I'm not very likeable. Any other obvious fact you want to share?" She frowned but turned away, crossing her arms.

"I'm here because I know exactly why the Djinn wants Dante. Do you wish to know?"

"You have been here for a few fucking hours, and you are telling me this shit now? What do you want in return?" I asked. A smile curled the corners of her lips, and she nodded.

"This time I do want something. We need funds to expand certain areas of our coven, however, we are not as rich as you."

"You can't just magic yourself into some bank vault or some shit and steal whatever the fuck you need?" I asked, raising an eyebrow as I lit a cigarette. She narrowed her eyes and glared scathingly at me.

"We don't steal," she hissed.

"Fine, I'll give you the fucking funds. Now, why does he want Dante?"

"It's a little ironic actually, but he wants Dante's blood. Your son's blood will give him a solid form to walk the earth in all his power, not just possessing a vessel like he has with his current host."

Blood. What the fuck were we all high on? Some vampire-like shit? It came down to that for both parties then.

"So you're saying he isn't fully here? Yet he's that fucking strong?"

"Not exactly. He is here, but he can't retain his form without a vessel, and since he was summoned by an Escarra, they are his only hosts. However, Dante's birth was foreseen centuries ago…" I frowned. What was it? What powers did Dante hold that the entire fucking world made him a target? "Do you remember what I told you when you first came to me? That the entire world will have their eyes upon him?"

"Yeah, it's why he keeps that amulet on."

"Yes… that amulet is far more powerful than you think. History says it came from Hecate herself."

"Yeah, okay, now tell me, what the fuck is this entire prophecy around Dante?" She frowned.

"So impatient as always. Well, I lied. Not only would the entire world have its eyes upon him, but the eyes of the gods would be on him, too." A wave of uneasiness washed over me. What was he? What power did he hold? "The prophecy regarding Dante was destroyed by Selene to protect him, and those who knew it were to pass it down but were cursed not to speak of it." I frowned. Is that what happened to the man in Italy? We had thought it was the Djinn at work…

"So, then, you telling me -"

"Oh, I'll live because I was given this message to pass on when the time came. I may be a witch, but I am also what you may call a prophetess." She pulled up her hair from the nape of her neck, showing me an intricate symbol that seemed to be glowing. "I was sent to assist and protect Dante's identity. Although I hated werewolves, we cannot choose our purpose. It was why I became a lone witch." My mind was reeling. How far back had she known?

"So you knew this shit years back, but didn't think to tell me?"

"The time was not right. It is now," she said icily. "It is why I purposely crossed paths with Callum, knowing he'd end up in your pack. He was the one who told you about me."

"And as a prophetess, or whatever that shit is, you are still asking for money in return?"

"Don't be so stingy."

"What the fuck is he?" I asked. Something told me he was far more than what we were thinking. She smiled knowingly before she raised an eyebrow.

"You really can't think of anything more powerful than a Lycan? Than a blessed wolf, demon, Djinn, or a bloodline prince? Really, King Alejandro, is the poison tampering with your brain?" I frowned. More powerful than everything we had come across...

"What being is as strong as a fucking god?" I growled, irritated at her roundabout answers. Her smile only grew.

"Just that. Your son is a miracle on earth, one that Selene has fought to place on this earth, for when the time comes, the world will need him. Your son is not only the future king, not just an Alpha, not just a young boy; he is the most powerful being to grace this planet and one that the entire world will bow down to. Your son is a Demi-God, King Alejandro. A real God."

Her words came crashing down on me, and my mind was beyond fucking reeling at the revelation. What. The. Actual. Fuck.

I bet if I was Liam, this would be the part where I would end up passing out, but instead, I sat back in my seat trying to process it all. Dante was...

If I didn't see how serious she was I would have thought this was a joke. He was a fucking Demi-God.

"Well, fuck. I didn't see that coming."

The Day Before

RAYHAN

I HAD RETURNED BACK TO Uncle's pack the day after he had called and told me to come home. I had refused, but I had finally gotten the blood count we needed, plus an extra ten in case some were not viable. I couldn't afford to lose more time; with each passing day, my kitten was getting worse. I couldn't just sit back and wait.

Seeing her state when I entered our bedroom had made my stomach plummet, the fear and worry I was feeling only worsened. She hadn't woken up since last night.

"What was the last thing she said?" I asked Mom quietly as I rocked Sienna.

I ran my other hand through Delsanra's white hair, hair that I loved as much as the woman it belonged to. The sun shone through the window, illuminating her pale skin. If it wasn't for the veins that covered her, it would seem as if she was just asleep.

"She simply said something to me, I'm not sure what time it was," Mom said quietly, trying to keep her face blank, but I could see the emotions and the pain in her eyes. She was trying to remain strong, but it wasn't easy. This entire situation had taken a toll on us all.

"When are we leaving?" I asked Uncle without looking up.

"Tomorrow. Janaina will finish the ritual on the dagger, so it will be ready," he replied coldly. His eyes were on Mom, and I frowned. Was it just me or were those two acting a little tense?

"I'll go check on the girls. Come on, Ahren." Mom picked him up and carried him out of the room, leaving Uncle and me alone in the room with Delsanra.

"What's up with you and Mom?" I asked, glancing up at Uncle.

"Nothing," he answered, running a hand through his hair. "But there's something I want to ask, Rayhan, and I know now's not the fucking time, but... it's been on my mind for a couple of days."

"What is it?"

"Daddy," Sienna chipped in, reaching up and kissing my cheek.

I smiled down at her, her dark grey eyes sparkling. I was glad she was far too young to understand what was happening. I gave her another smile before glancing at Uncle. He sighed, and I could tell whatever it was weighed on his mind.

"It's about the Sangue Pack... I've never asked you the extent of what went down back then. Marcel never said anything either... but the other day, when I rang Leo to congratulate him on his shift, he said something that has been on my mind, and I can't fucking get it out," he said seriously, his dark eyes boring into mine. I frowned, remembering those who had hurt Delsanra and feeling anger flare up inside of me at just the thought.

"What do you want to know?"

"Leo said you punished those who were under Endora's control and were forced to hurt Del-"

"Those who didn't have any remorse, yeah. Those who were forced to do it and regretted it were let off lightly. However, those who didn't seem to care because she was a witch, forced or not, were punished. I still let them live." Delsanra had suffered so much, and that trauma lingered. What I did was nothing in comparison to what they had done to her.

Uncle looked thoughtful, a deep frown on his face.

"There was a group who were kept in prison for a time, from the group that lived I mean, correct?"

"Yeah, I told you that," I replied, sounding colder than I meant to.

The topic got to me, and although I had tried to talk to Leo, the fact that he couldn't bring it up with me directly was beginning to irritate me. Of all times, he found now to be the best time to add stress to Uncle's already heavy workload. Kiara was in the cells, too, and I knew it was probably ripping him apart just as much as my feelings about Delsanra.

"He made a point which made me think. The ones who were beaten, and those who were also kept in prison, bound by silver... the pain they went through... he asked what about their mates? Did you not think that, by punishing those, you were also hurting their innocent counterparts?"

Uncle's voice was quiet, almost as if he didn't want to say the words out loud, and I froze.

No. I hadn't considered that.

I was so consumed by my own pain, by the pain Delsanra had gone through, that I didn't consider anything else. For the first time in the last six years, I questioned if I did the right thing… but still… I couldn't have just let them off…

"I'm not blaming you. Marcel, myself, neither of us said anything either. I'm going to have a fucking word with Marcel, too, because didn't he consider this shit? I wasn't there… we all may have fucked up, but I know shit happens, and what Del went through, we would all kill for our mates. I get that. But once this fucking Djinn is taken care of, I do want you and Leo to have a sit-down. It's high fucking time we talked this shit out. Properly."

I didn't reply for a moment, running my fingers through Sienna's soft curls. She was humming. It reminded me of a cat. I nodded.

"If you can get him in the same room as me, I'm game." Uncle scoffed, giving me a cold smirk.

"I'm still the fucking king. He may have shifted, but I'll put his ass in the right place if need be. He's hurting, and I'm not going to allow this shit to continue. He's always spoken about that night, but it's obviously affected him far more than he lets on. He wasn't like this when the pack was first formed. We both know growing up and always being around Endora would fuck anyone up. We can at least try, one more time."

"Yeah, I know. I'm ready to listen, but I won't forget what happened to my mate either. Those men and women were given a chance at a new life, but we both can't deny that not all of them were innocent."

"The worst were thrown in prison," Uncle replied, crossing his arms.

"Yeah, but there were enough criminals in that pack that remained," I said, frowning.

"Everyone deserves a second chance."

I didn't entirely agree, so I didn't bother replying. To each their own. He came over and slapped my shoulder.

"You're a good man, Rayhan. We just need to get through to Leo as Raf would have wanted us to," he said quietly. I smirked slightly before looking at my sleeping beauty.

"It's good to hear I've gone from kid to man," I replied cockily.

"Man!" Sienna piped in, giggling before planting a kiss on my cheek. Uncle chuckled dryly before taking her from me.

"This one looks like a fucking angel, but I swear she's going to become a little demon," he said, tossing her up into the air and making her giggle.

"That could possibly be literally true, considering her mama's part demon," I replied with a smirk, leaning back on my elbow and kissing Delsanra's lips, enjoying the sparks that coursed through me.

"Hm, that's a fucking good point... witch, demon and werewolf genes, the fuck are these kids mutating into? I'm getting too fucking confused with all the shit I'm hearing lately. Nothing would surprise me. So, there's a chance your pups could be hybrids or tribrids, if that shit even exists," Uncle remarked, tossing her up again and making her shriek in excitement.

"Who knows?" I glanced at them, watching her kiss Uncle's cheek before getting all shy. I smiled, watching them. It impressed me the pups were not scared of him.

I sighed inwardly. Uncle was right... and I knew Delsanra would agree. I needed to put aside my ego and have a conversation with Leo... no matter how hard it was going to be...

"I'll take her down. Get some rest or some shit," Uncle said, placing Sienna on his shoulders and walking to the door, watching her try to grab his dangly earring.

I smirked watching them. He had to crouch down to get through the door. No matter how trying stuff was, there was a lot that we still had that we were grateful for.

❧

Night had fallen. The team had begun to assemble, but some would arrive in the morning. The tension and nerves that were running through the mansion were palpable. Even the kids seemed to notice it, no matter how subtly we acted about it. Uncle's kids knew we were leaving, and I felt bad for them, considering they hadn't seen their mom in a few days either. Kataleya had been terrified that Kiara had been kidnapped. She had gotten so worked up that she had wanted to see Kiara in person, so Uncle had had to explain stuff to her without giving her the full details.

We would be leaving around mid-day tomorrow, hoping to get to the planned location by night. We'd had a meeting earlier on and there would be one final one before we left tomorrow. The final showdown…

I still didn't want Mom to come, but she was adamant about going. Her and Uncle's odd behaviour was beginning to worry me. I wanted to have a final word with her, really wanting her to change her mind about going. Raihana had come to check on Delsanra, as she hadn't awoken.

"Mind watching her for a bit? I just want to go have a word with Mom," I said, standing up. She looked up at me and nodded.

"Sure," she agreed, looking back at Delsanra.

"Thanks."

I left the room and walked down the hall to Mom's room. I knocked lightly, but there was no answer. I opened the door slowly, peering inside. I was about to call her when I saw her sitting on a prayer mat with her legs tucked under her. Her eyes were closed, and her hands were raised in front of her in silent prayer. I hadn't seen her like this in a while. Silent tears streamed down her cheeks, and I knew she was so immersed in whatever she was praying for that she hadn't heard me.

Now wasn't the right time. I'd talk to her in the morning. I was about to close the door when I sensed someone behind me. Before I could even turn, he spoke,

"She's going to sacrifice herself, you know."

A Risky Plan

RAYHAN

I TURNED SHARPLY TO SEE Dante standing there. Reaching over, he quietly shut the door.

"What do you mean she's going to sacrifice herself?" I asked sharply.

He looked down the hallway before motioning for me to follow him. Why did he act like a twenty-year-old rather than his age? This boy... but I was far more worried about what he had just said outside Mom's room. A thousand thoughts crossed my mind as he opened my bedroom door, making Raihana look at us questioningly.

"You can leave," Dante told her, making her frown.

"And what are you doing here?" She asked.

"I came to see Delsanra," he replied haughtily. Walking around the bed, he looked down at her. Side by side, it was clear that the veins on Delsanra's skin were a lot worse. The asshat bent down and placed a kiss on her forehead, making Raihana smirk.

"Ah, the cousins are fighting over a girl," she teased.

"We aren't. She's mine." I said, crossing my arms. I wanted to ask what he meant, but it was obvious he wasn't planning on telling me until Raihana was gone. "You can go." She stood up and stretched.

"Sure. Keep an eye on her..." she said, concern crossing her face.

"I will."

She gave a nod before she left the room. I turned to Dante, who was standing there stroking *my* kitten's hair.

"Oi, stop touching her. What did you mean earlier?" I asked. He raised an eyebrow before crossing his arms.

"I meant that Mama Mari is the one who will deliver the final blow to the Djinn, and she will die doing so."

What? My head was spinning as I stared at him, trying to collect the emotions and thoughts that were storming through my mind.

"I don't get it, what do you mean?" I said, running my hand through my hair. He frowned seriously as he looked down at Delsanra.

"The price of killing a Djinn... the one who uses the virgin blade will die unless they are of the same kind; djinns, devils, and demons are all of the same family. Unless you are one, the wielder will die..." he said quietly.

"Does Uncle know this?" I asked sharply. From what I knew, Uncle was going to go in for the final attack...

"Yes, and so does your mom. She wants to return to Uncle Rafael," he said quietly. His frown was deep, and all traces of cockiness were gone.

Mom was ready to die...

The tension between Uncle and Mom now made sense. For Uncle to agree, Mom must have convinced him somehow...

I knew as the years had passed, her missing Dad and feeling alone had grown. I would see her awake at night, sometimes walking around the mansion gardens. She was always staring off into space, and the amount of time she spent in Dad's favourite spots was unnerving. But had she really come to that point where there was nothing worth living for?

Was I being selfish that it stung to know we weren't enough?

Was I being selfish to want her to live?

Was I wrong for feeling angry that she didn't talk to me about it or about this decision?

I looked at Delsanra lying in the bed. She didn't have the love of her parents, didn't she deserve some more time with Mom?

"Rayhan."

Dante's voice pulled me from my thoughts. I could feel my aura swirling around me, my eyes blazing as that storm within me only continued to grow into something that was getting out of control. Rage began overpowering all sense of logic. How dare they not tell me! Both she and Uncle. I had a right to know.

"Rayhan." Dante glared at me, and I glared back. "Hear me out."

"What more do you want to say?" I growled.

"Well, nothing if you don't want to hear it," he shot back, frowning at me. I exhaled sharply.

"Don't test me, Dante. I am pissed off."

"I know, and I wouldn't have told you if I didn't have a plan," he stated, walking around the bed. He sat on the other side of the bed, leaning against the headboard as if he owned the damn thing but making sure not to disturb Ahren, who was asleep in the centre of the bed. Mom had Sienna for the night.

"What plan?" I asked, narrowing my eyes. He looked up at the ceiling, then sighed.

"You must stop her." I frowned.

"What?" Was he telling me to stop her from going tomorrow?

"You know, if I stop her, we will still lose someone?"

"It isn't her time yet. She can't go."

Although I wanted to ask him what he meant, I knew he wouldn't be able to tell me. From the way he was speaking, it was as if he was telling me the most he could. However, yeah, I agreed entirely that she couldn't go.

"Explain."

"Her time has not yet come. Before I explain further, I need you to promise you will do whatever I ask." I raised an eyebrow.

"You want me to listen to a pup? You might ruin everything; you know this battle is crucial for everyone's sake." He glared at me.

"I am not a pup. I know it is important, but if you promise me that you will do as I say… then I'll promise you…" He turned to look over at Delsanra, and his eyes filled with sadness before he looked back at me. "Then I promise I'll let her go. I will try to get rid of my feelings."

Seriously, was he trying to bargain with my own mate? I crossed my arms, frowning.

"She's my mate, kid."

"I know, but when I grow up, you know I can steal her," he added arrogantly, making me glare at him, but then his eyes softened. "But I'm promising you all I can. Do you think I want to do this? I like her. She's so pretty and kind…" He sounded like a child again with a crush on a pretty girl that he knew he'd never have, but I realised what he was trying to do, to show me that he really needed my help. He was giving up the only thing that would work on me by promising me that he'd back off from Delsanra.

"She is," I said quietly. He nodded, and I felt bad for him. "What do you want me to do?"

"You promise to do whatever I ask?"

I wasn't sure if trusting him blindly was smart, but it was the only option I had right then. If this was the only way to help Mom, then so be it.

"Fine," I promised. He nodded.

"Then call Leo on a withheld number because we will need his help."

"Wait, what? Leo? Seriously, Dante, he won't listen."

"He also likes to break rules. He will agree. I will talk to him. Seriously, you two need to grow up." He frowned, picking up my phone and holding it out to me. I took it reluctantly.

What the hell was he planning? Well, I wouldn't be doing the talking. Leo would hang up before I even managed to say anything. I had his number, but I wasn't sure he had mine because, if he did, he would have it blocked. I dialled the number, making sure my caller ID was hidden, and held the phone out to Dante. He took it, putting it on speaker. Ahren stirred but stayed asleep.

"Who the fuck is this?" Leo's cold voice came. "Get out," he added to someone. I raised my eyebrows when I heard a girl. Fuck boy.

"It's Dante."

"What do you want, kid?"

"I want you to do something that would piss Dad off. Will you help me?"

Silence.

"Depends. I'm not a fucking fool to promise some shit without even knowing what it is."

"Well, it's about the mission tomorrow. The thing is, the one who kills the Djinn-"

"Will die. Yeah, I know, and?"

How did he know that? Did everyone but me know? It didn't help my irritation.

"Then do you know who is going to do it?" Dante asked, watching me.

"Maria," Leo replied. So, everyone did fucking know.

"Yes, but the thing is, she can't die... so we need to make a plan -"

"We?" Leo asked sharply. Damn. Even Dante paused, clearly not having realised what he had just implied.

"Yeah, us cousins…"

Leo was silent.

"I'm not doing this shit," Leo said icily after a moment. "If Rayhan's there, tell him to go suck a dick." Dante scrunched his nose. I was tempted to speak and tell him to watch his damn mouth around a kid, at least.

"Please," Dante said quietly. "I will owe you a favour in return, anything you wish." That seemed to get him thinking, but I wasn't sure if it was a safe thing to promise. I didn't trust Leo…

"Swear it. That when I ask for whatever I do, you will not deny me."

"Fine. When the time comes, and you ask for a favour, I swear by oath that I will honour whatever you ask for. I swear on… Azura." Dante smiled slightly. I frowned. I didn't get it. He and Azura argued a lot, but he would never make a false oath on her life.

"Who?"

"Azura, my sweet but annoying aunt, or whatever you wish to call it. My family has been through much for me to swear on them," Dante said, but I could tell from that sly hint of a smile that he was up to something. I was actually worried for Azura at this point… he never called Azura sweet. What was he up to?

"Fine, whatever, but I will hold you to that. Even if it's years from now, Dante. An Alpha always honours his words."

"I know. So, will you help?"

"Fine."

"Good. It involves Rayhan…"

"Can we somehow have him kill the Djinn and die in the process? I wouldn't mind that." I frowned, but Dante sighed.

"No, because Delsanra needs him," he replied. Wow, was that my worth?

"At least you acknowledge she needs me," I remarked sarcastically. I glared at Dante, who simply smirked.

"You know, if he's out of the picture, you get to keep her," Leo implied.

"That's true…" Dante agreed arrogantly.

"Can you two cut it out?" I growled.

"So the bastard is there," Leo said coldly.

"Yes, because I need you both to do this together. I can't explain it fully, but I really need you both to pay attention," Dante said, closing his eyes.

We both stayed quiet, and I knew whatever Dante was going to ask for would probably impact Leo's final stance on this. I knew that there was no way I could stop Mom, and I was holding on to whatever Dante had planned because, as he said, it was not Mom's time to go yet. I knew it was selfish, but I couldn't lose her.

"Mama Maria or Dad will be carrying the blade… I don't know, but when you see Mama Maria going for the Djinn, I need you both to work together to get the blade from her. Leo, I think it will have to be you because Rayhan won't be able to risk hurting her."

"I don't get why her dying is a problem," Leo added, making my eyes flash.

"Listen to me," Dante said. I could tell he was feeling exhausted already. He may have been acting all right, but he was weak. "You need to pass the dagger to Rayhan by all means necessary… Rayhan, you will need to stop Dad. He's weakened due to the poison, you can take him."

"That's fine, but then what?" I asked. I heard Leo scoff.

"What? Can't you go and kill the djinn yourself?"

"No. The one who will kill the Djinn will be there," Dante said.

"Who?" I asked. It was inevitable that someone was going to die.

"I can't say… but at the last moment, when all hope will feel like it's lost, he will come, and you will know he is the one to do it. Trust your instincts and give him the dagger."

We both fell silent, letting Dante's words sink in. It all sounded fine, but this was messed up on an entirely new level. Not only was I listening to a smart, all-knowing pup, but to work alongside the one man who hated me more than anything… and above that, telling me to give the dagger to someone who I didn't even know by following my instincts? This could go wrong on so many levels…

"You both just need to do exactly as I said, no matter who tries to stop you. Look for the man in black. You must get him the dagger."

"Won't he die?" I asked quietly.

"Or worse yet, what if this bastard misses?" Leo added.

"He won't. Do you both promise?" Dante pushed.

"Fine," I agreed. It was obvious Dante knew what he was going on about, but his promise regarding Del and the way he knew what was happening made me think this plan would work.

"Fine, but I don't care what happens to that bastard who's there with you. I'll give him the fucking dagger, then I'm done," Leo said icily.

"Thank you," Dante replied with a small smile. "Goodbye, Leo."

Leo hung up without saying anything else, and I looked at Dante, who was looking at Delsanra and Ahren.

"Are we doing the right thing?" I asked. "You know messing this up could cost us a lot…"

"I know, but it won't get messed up. I mean, you two won't. You can do it." Our eyes met, and I sighed. I would put my faith in him because I really had no other option…

"Then tomorrow, the day has come," Dante said, leaning back as he began playing with Ahren's hair.

"Yeah…" I replied.

We both stayed silent, the weight of the upcoming battle weighing heavily on our minds. This plan could help save a life or destroy thousands more. It was a double-edged blade, and I was siding with the one that was risking far more, on the words of a powerful child and with my only ally being the one man who hated me more than anything.

How badly could things go wrong?

Goodbyes

ALEJANDRO

THE MEETING WAS OVER. We would be leaving soon. Everything was finally in place. I had given the men of my pack half an hour to say goodbye to their families because, although I would do my best to make sure the losses were minimum... there would still be losses.

"You aren't well, Alpha. Are you sure you should be leading?" Carmen asked quietly as we walked towards the cells. I cast her a cold glare.

"I'm fine. Go do whatever the fuck you need to," I commanded coldly. "I am the fucking king, and I plan to lead my men regardless of my health."

She lowered her head and walked out, leaving me alone to head down to where my queen was bound. Sure, I was in fucking pain, and the bouts of coughing up blood were growing, but I was still fucking strong. My stomach twisted the closer I got to where Kiara was locked up. Taking a deep breath, I unlocked the door and walked down to the end cell.

She lay on a slab of silver, chained to it. She was also hooked up to a machine that was keeping her unconscious via a drip. Her face was pale, and she looked like she had lost some weight. *Fuck, Amore Mio...*

I picked up her slender hand, which was restrained by cuffs, bending down and kissing it softly. The strong sparks danced between us before I placed her hand back down gently. I wouldn't be able to bid her farewell or tell her I got this shit under control because it could alert him.

I love you. I swear we will destroy this fucker and send him back to hell once and for all.

I stroked her hair, frowning deeply. Was I doing the right thing by letting Maria do this? I knew she was adamant, but I really needed to be sure. I didn't like it, not one fucking bit.

Delsanra, Dante, you... I'm going to fix this. Wait for me because I will be back. No one messes with my family and fucking lives. Leaning down, I threaded my fingers through her hair and kissed her lips. *Hold on.* I forced myself back and looked down at her for a final time as if wanting to etch this moment into my mind. I hoped that with his death, her memories would return.

I turned away, not wanting to linger for longer than normal or make the Djinn suspicious if he was somehow awake. I glanced at my watch. I had twenty minutes to meet the kids and get ready.

❧❧❧

I had gotten changed and had just gone to see Del, who was still unconscious, only to find Maria was there, too. She was already dressed and ready for the mission.

"You can still change your mind," I said quietly. She shook her head.

"My mind is made up, and I cannot wait to see him again," she said, smiling at me with a glimmer of hope in her eyes. My heart squeezed, and I nodded. She fucking wanted this...

"Say hi to him for me then," I said quietly. "I hope he's proud. I know I'm not even half the man he was... but I'll carry on trying."

She nodded, her eyes glittering with unshed tears. I quickly bent down, giving Delsanra a kiss on the forehead before leaving the room. I hated fucking goodbyes.

Leo's come, Al, Darien said through the link, making me frown.

I thought the fucker was going to meet us on the way.

He said he couldn't bother waiting. Shall I let him into the mansion?

Yeah, Raven and Raihana are with the kids in the lounge. He won't try anything.

Got it.

I cut the link and headed downstairs myself. Entering the lounge, Dante looked at me as two of the Westwood five sat next to him. He played a game on the tablet while they watched with rapt attention. Raven was carrying Tatum and Sienna as she sang some weird shit to them. Ahren and her other three were playing on the floor. One thing I had to admit was she sure fucking knew how to look after multiple kids.

"Where's Ri?" I asked Raven.

"She went to say goodbye to Chris," Raven said, her eyes filled with concern. I nodded, frowning.

"And Liam?" I asked.

"In the garden, watching the girls." I nodded and turned to Dante.

"I'm leaving soon," I told him.

"I know," he said, looking up at me.

I nodded, crouching down by the Westwood three and Ahren, who were busy playing with blocks. I ruffled their hair for a moment before I stood up. Ahren grabbed onto my leg, staring up at me.

"Bye-bye," he said, with a cute as fuck wave. I smirked.

"Rather impatient to get rid of me, aren't you, pup?" He simply toddled off, so I went over to Dante, sitting on the other side of Theo.

"We shouldn't be too long. Take care of all these fuckers. I don't know if your aunt will be able to cope alone," I said, looking at Raven.

"Oh, I'll manage. Don't worry," Raven replied with a smile just as Elijah entered with Scarlett, who was also ready to leave.

"I'll go meet the girls."

"Yeah, and bring Leo back," Elijah remarked, shaking his head, and I wondered what he meant. I hoped the fucker wasn't being a dick.

Ruffling Dante's hair and earning a frown from him, I stood up. He was going to be okay. He was a goddamn Demi-God. I looked at him, but it was still fucking hard to get my head wrapped around it. He looked at me, the hint of a faint smile crossing his lips.

"Want to say something?"

"Nah, just stay strong," I said quietly. I didn't give a shit if he was a demi-god or not, he was still my pup. He nodded, giving me a smile.

"I will, Dad."

"Scarlett, can you get Rayhan out front? I don't want him and Leo to cross paths. I don't have time to deal with that shit." She nodded, kissing Elijah a final time before she left the room.

"I'll go meet the girls, then I'll be heading out, too," I said, leaving the room.

I reached the open doors, stopping in my tracks. Liam was standing there looking worried. I cocked a brow, stepping out into the sunshine to see Kataleya and Skyla watching Azura, who was sporting a rather red forehead and staring challengingly at Leo, who was sitting on the steps. His legs sprawled out in front of him, and I could sense his aura.

"Again," she said, crossing her arms.

Leo raised an eyebrow, picking up the ball and bouncing it off her head. She didn't even flinch, instead catching the ball and throwing it back at him.

"Again." Fuck, she was doing that weird shit again…

Leo frowned, clearly wondering what the Westwood Devil's angle was.

"You're fucking weird," he said coldly, tossing the ball at her forehead again. Liam looked relieved to see me, whilst Kataleya was clearly worried, and Skyla was obviously enjoying it.

"Again," she said, unblinking as she stared at Leo.

"This kid's fucking psychotic," Leo remarked, glancing at me as he hit her forehead with the ball again.

"Again," Azura said, making Leo frown.

"Nah, I'm bored," he said, tossing the ball to the ground and letting it roll away.

"Cut this shit out," I warned. Azura watched him for a moment before she ran after the rolling ball.

"Leo started it," Skyla chimed in, frowning at him.

"Yeah, once. She's the one who told me to hit her again," Leo shot back, taking his lighter from his pocket. Liam sighed.

"Azura is just…"

"A weirdo," Leo finished, pulling out a cigarette.

"I thought you weren't going to come here?" I asked, crossing my arms as Azura returned with the ball, looking as normal as ever as if she hadn't just had a ball bounced off her forehead several times. She stopped a foot behind him, and, despite her casual expression, I had a feeling she was going to try something.

"I changed my mind; I was bored as fuck waiting around." He shrugged, but just as he was about to light the cigarette, Azura slammed the ball at the back of his head, knocking the cigarette from between his lips.

He growled menacingly, turning as fast as lightning. Kataleya gasped in horror, Liam muttered a swear, and Skyla cackled. As for the devil herself, she simply stared at the glaring man, despite her heart pounding.

"What the fuck was that?" Leo hissed. I was by his side in seconds. Although I knew he wouldn't hurt her, I wasn't going to risk it.

"What the - was what?" She glared back.

Okay, she was obviously really pissed off. The young Alpha wolf's eyes flashed, his powerful aura emanating off him.

"The actual fuck? You psychotic -" Leo started.

"Stupid person!"

"Leo did that to Azura first, Daddy!" Skyla added defensively as Liam scooped his sister up into his arms protectively.

"Put me down!" Azura snapped.

"Come on, Zuzu, calm down," Liam tried to soothe her.

"No! He hit me first!" She shouted.

"But weren't you saying 'again, again'?" Liam tried to calm the struggling girl who was kicking wildly in his arms.

"I don't care! Give me the ball!" She shouted.

Leo stood up, glaring at the screaming girl before I placed my hand on his shoulder firmly.

"She's a kid. Are you seriously going to start a fucking fight? Why the fuck were you using her as a target?" I asked, pulling him back. He shrugged me off roughly, his eyes blazing a steely blue.

"She's a fucking maniac," he growled.

"You're the maniac!" Azura shouted, glaring at him murderously. "Get out of my sight, or I will poke your eyes out and cook them!"

"Azura!" Liam tried to stop her.

"Oh, yeah?" Leo growled.

"Yeah!" Azura taunted. Her bright blue eyes dazzled with anger as she glared at him.

"Oh, for fuck's sake, can you two cut the fuck out? Leo, Liam, let's go!" I growled, bending down next to my own girls. "Sky, why are you enjoying this?" She shrugged, pondering over something thoughtfully.

"I don't know, it was funny. Daddy, can you pay me for every time Leo swears, too?" She asked hopefully. What the fuck was this girl so deprived of that she needed so much money?

"No," I answered, not missing Kataleya's small smile. I pulled them both into my arms and planted a kiss on both of their heads. *They may be weirdos, but they are my weirdos.* "I'm going to head out. We're going to make everything okay again. I want you two to be good girls, alright?"

"Okay, Daddy," Kataleya whispered, fear filling her eyes. I looked into her eyes.

"I promise you, he won't be able to hurt anyone ever again." She nodded before giving me a tight, one-armed hug. That teddy she always carried around was held tightly in her other arm.

"Alright, let's get going," I said, standing up and looking over at the other three.

Liam was still holding onto Azura tightly. She was looking at Leo with distaste, something he was finding amusing.

"I hope you get hurt," she said to Leo.

"Yeah, and I hope you walk off a fucking cliff," he shot back, smoking his cigarette.

"Leo," I threatened. "Let's go."

Marcel was right, his aura was very powerful, and I was curious to see what his wolf's true capacity was.

"Take care of yourself, kid," I told Azura.

I was about to ruffle her hair, but the look of pure rage on her face made me decide I'd rather want to keep my hand intact before her fucking piranha side came out, and she bit it off. I swear that pup was fucking rabid.

"Love you, Zuzu…" I heard Liam say before I glanced back at the twins. Both were watching me, and I gave them a small smile.

Everything would be okay.

❧☙

The team was assembled. Everyone was sombre and serious. They had all bid farewell to their families and mates. I had seen Liam say goodbye to his kids and mate. Scarlett and Elijah… Chris saying goodbye to Raihana and Tatum. Maria met everyone one final time…

The chances of lives being lost were high… but I hoped the losses were minimal.

"For our packs, for our families, for what's fucking right, we will see this mission through. We should get there by nightfall! Remember to stick together and protect your allies! We will come out victorious," I said loudly, knowing that every werewolf and witch present could hear me clearly. A roar of approval rippled through the crowds.

"For victory!"

Everyone followed suit, and I gave a curt nod. They knew their jobs, the rules, and their orders. I knew they would carry them out accordingly.

Darien had the blade, and he would pass it to Maria at the right time. He didn't know that the wielder would die. I had told him that she would be carrying out the final attack, but we had kept the vital points of the mission secret. The Djinn would be expecting me, and I planned to be the decoy. I just hoped Rayhan forgave me for not telling him...

A sharp wind blew through the crowds as I looked into the eyes of the men and women warriors. I kept my emotions hidden, only showing confidence and power. It gave them the courage they needed, and, with it, my own resolve only strengthened. We were going to succeed. One hundred fucking percent.

"Alright. Let's get this shit done," I growled before I shifted and broke into a run, the rest following my lead...

The time to kill this fucker was finally here.

You're Mine

ELIJAH

THE SILENCE THAT FOLLOWED once the rest had left was deafening. The unease I could sense from Raihana and Raven was growing, and even the kids were quieter.

Azura was still in a strop from her little run-in with Leo, frowning as she sat there with her arms folded. She may be a feisty little one, but her stubbornness and the ability to hold grudges topped even Scarlett's. She was staring at the floor, her chest heaving, and her nostrils still flared.

Dante was lying down with his eyes shut, but I knew he was awake. His fists were clenched, and he had a frown on his face. The quintuplets, Ahren, Sienna, and Tatum were playing with Raihana, who was keeping them occupied with magical bubbles that were floating around endlessly.

"How long until they get there?" Raven asked me quietly.

"A few hours more. It's only been about one," I replied, glancing out at the sky. It was late afternoon now.

I didn't blame them. Knowing that Scarlett was out there... I felt frustrated and helpless. But it made sense that I was here. When it came to strength, I was ultimately stronger, and if anything happened here, we would need a strong defence. We had several barriers placed around the pack the moment they'd left, barriers that Magdalene, Raihana, and one other witch had worked on. They were so strong that no one could come in or go out. Janaina had also placed a few more spells so we would know if anyone approached the pack area. The magic was so strong that I could feel it in the air, weighing down on us, and it made me physically sick.

Kataleya was by the window clutching her teddy bear, which she had named after the Escarra pup. Skyla was watching some Disney villain kid's movie, but she was more distracted than focused, stroking the cat she had abducted from somewhere. I was certain it belonged to one of the Delta's kids, but... she was adamant that it was hers.

"How about pizza?" I suggested, trying to lighten the mood.

"Barrier?" Raihana reminded me.

"I know, but we can make it together. What do you girls think?" I suggested to the twins and Azura. Azura frowned deeply.

"I don't want to. When will Mama be back?"

"I'm not sure, but how about we make pizza and we save her a few slices?" I suggested, standing up.

"I don't want to do anything; my life is so hard," Skyla said, dropping onto her stomach. Well, there went that plan.

"You go to Delsanra. I'll mind the kiddies," Raven said to Raihana. She nodded, standing up as Tatum began crying.

"Come here, Tatum," Raven cooed, picking him up.

"Thanks, babe." Raihana smiled at her before she left the room. Ahren hurried after her, and she picked him up. "I'll take him with me."

I looked around, trying to hide the unease inside of me. I couldn't help but wonder which of those men and women I saw earlier would not return. Just like all these kids, many of those who went had families of their own.

"Alright, come on. Enough of this gloominess. Let's do something fun," I said, standing up. Skyla groaned, squeezing the cat and stroking its head before pausing and smiling suddenly.

"I want to sew," she said. Although I knew she was up to something, I nodded. Was it because she probably knew I'd struggle with it?

"Sure," I said, running my fingers through my hair.

"I want to make a rag doll," Azura piped in suddenly, her head jerking up towards me.

"Good luck, Grandad," Dante added, his eyes still half closed. "I'm sure Claire or Clara will have everything you'll need."

"Oh, I can help, too! Let's get sewing!" Raven added excitedly.

"I want to make Kiké a shirt, too. Will you help me, Aunty?" Kataleya asked Raven, her eyes hopeful.

I wasn't sure if it was a good idea, but at least all three were all for it. It would keep their minds off of everything, at least, and that was how we all ended up sitting down and beginning on the three individual projects. *Be safe, Red.*

❧❧

"No, no! This is for my cat!" Skyla scolded Azura, who had just said her 'dress' looked weird.

"It's so cute!" Raven agreed.

My fingertips were throbbing from all the times I had pricked them with needles. I had given up and decided to simply watch. Kataleya had brought the torn fabric she always carried and asked Raven to help stitch it onto a tartan fabric for her teddy's shirt. The effect that kidnapping had on her would stay with her... I knew that much. I also hoped that kid was okay, too, wherever he was.

Claire and Clara had taken the quintuplets to the playroom, and Sienna had fallen asleep. Skyla was making some odd outfit for the cat, and Kataleya was finishing off with her torn fabric. Of all three, she was the best at this. As for my girl, I had no idea what she was making... it looked like a knitted doll. Raven helped her, although she had been the one to choose how she wanted it. The black stitches made it look a little creepy.

"What's that meant to be?" I asked her. She paused and looked up at me with her large blue eyes.

"A voodoo doll," she said seriously, making Raven pause and look at her.

"Of who?" She asked curiously.

"Dante's ugly cousin," she stated.

"Oh? Which quintuplet are you talking about? I was assuming you're the only ugly one in my life," Dante replied haughtily.

"Hey, the Westwoods are not ugly! And I am not ugly, unlike you and your ugly cousin!"

"Us Rossis tend to be very handsome, actually," Dante replied.

"She means Leo," Skyla cackled. "Wait! Do you need, like, a hair of his or something?"

"No, not at all. It'll work anyway," Azura replied. She shoved wool into the body, the half-detached head lolling. I wasn't sure it was going to stay attached at the rough, brutish way she was handling it. "Besides, I found his cigarette that he dropped earlier. You only need something that belongs to them, so this will work."

I frowned as she took out the unused cigarette and pushed it into the body. Were we raising normal kids? I didn't know… I looked between Skyla and Azura, both of whom looked very excited about this voodoo doll. Raven laughed as she took the doll from Azura and began stitching the neck up.

"I'll add the eyes," Azura said, rummaging in the button box and picking out two light blue buttons. "Ah… he has this colour eyes. The evil man will be punished." Dante chuckled.

"You're so weird, Azura."

"Your weirder, Dante," she shot back. "Don't make me make a Dante doll."

"Doll or not… aren't we puppets anyway? Simply being used to play out a bigger game?"

I frowned. That was a pretty deep way to think for a kid, but this was Dante. He simply sighed and turned on his side, watching us.

"See? You talk so weird," Azura replied, brushing his comment off.

"Want to talk about it?" I asked him quietly.

"No. I just… I hope everything goes okay…" He frowned, his eyes full of worry, so I gave him a small smile.

"Don't worry, they'll handle it," I reassured him.

"They'll be fine. Let's just pray Leo gets hurt," Azura added.

"That's not something you should say about an ally, Azura," I reprimanded her lightly. She glared at me as Raven passed a toy to Sienna.

"I don't like him, so I'm going to poke some pins into his body and soak him in spices and vinegar. That will teach him for messing with me."

I was glad she didn't know real black magic because I was certain the rows of voodoo dolls would be endless, with Liam being her main victim. He somehow always said the wrong thing at the wrong time.

"Thank you, Aunty. I really like it," Kataleya said happily, looking down at her teddy, which now wore a tartan green and black shirt. The torn fabric was a neat square on the front, and Raven had stitched 'Kiké' in green on the front patch.

"I'm glad you at least know how to sew," I said to Raven. "That teddy looks great now," I added to Kataleya.

"Thank you, Granddaddy," she said gently. She smiled at me, and I smiled back, standing up.

I think I'll go for a quick round of the mansion. Despite the heavy security, I still needed to be on alert. I was the only one allowed to go see Kiara. The key code had been changed just in case she somehow had someone release her. We needed to be extremely careful. After doing a quick round, I'd go take a look at her, too. I needed to make sure everything was in order around here. Anything could happen, and we needed to stay on guard.

❧☙

SCARLETT

"The spells are all in place," Liam said through the earpiece. "No one can go in or out."

"Got it," I said, looking over at Rayhan, who was frowning deeply.

Liam was leading one of the three teams; they had broken through the Crimson King's defences. The three teams had attacked from all sides, closing in on the enemy's location. We had made sure he was there first, and he had been. We had succeeded in coming without being detected, thanks to the witches.

The other two teams, who had taken the first attack, were headed by Marcel and Alejandro. Leo and Maria were on Marcel's team. As for Rayhan and me, we had a smaller team and were heading a backup squad that was going to join the fight upon the signal. Our job was a little different, but it was vital.

"Are you okay?" I asked Rayhan. He seemed tense and restless. He gave a curt nod.

The sound of menacing howls filled the air and through the earpiece as both sides clashed. Each of the main three teams had five witches on them. Mine had two, and I prayed it gave us the advantage we needed.

"Ready, Scarlett? Rayhan?" Alejandro's low voice asked.

I took a deep breath. This was it. We needed to kill the host before we could kill the Djinn, and that's where I came in. We needed to rip the heart of the host out, resulting in weakening the Djinn. For the Djinn to take a new host, he needed time, and when he was in his true form, right after I killed the Crimson King, that was when Maria would do her part.

Alejandro and I were the ones who would attack the Crimson King. Whoever succeeded in killing him was fine as long as it got done. I just hoped it was me as I healed faster, and we all knew whoever got close would suffer greatly. Rayhan and our squad would watch my back as I went for the Crimson King, making sure I wasn't attacked.

"Ready," Rayhan said, his canines coming out and his eyes blazing green.

Maria… I glanced at Rayhan, wishing he knew the truth. He deserved to know. He looked at me, and, for a second, I thought I saw a flicker of sadness in his eyes.

"Ready," I replied determinedly. My eyes flashed, and I shifted as one with the rest of my team.

We broke through the trees. The huge stone wall that came ever closer suddenly exploded, sending stone and debris flying in all directions, paving the way for us to join the battle. I jumped over the rubble and through the flames, landing lightly.

Havoc surrounded us in every direction. The smell of blood and ash hung in the air. Wolves of all colours fought against the army of similar-coloured wolves, all in shades of auburn and reddish-brown. Each one had orangey-red eyes, and I realised that they were all puppets of the man that stood in the centre. He had his arms raised, a look of pure fury on his melting, burned face. It was obvious that the host was dying. I had a feeling it wouldn't last long.

The Escarra boy must not be near, Magdalene's warning rang in my head.

The Djinn's deal with the Escarra line meant he could take the Escarras' bodies without delay, unlike if it was anyone else. I was glad the boy was all the way in Puerto Rico, not only for his safety but for all our sakes. We just needed to make sure he didn't have the time to change to a new host.

It was obvious he hadn't been expecting us. His eyes blazed with rage, his aura surging as he commanded his army. Flames surrounded him as he slayed our men and women without mercy.

So, this was the Crimson King. This was the man who hurt my family…

Two of the fire wolves lunged at me, but Rayhan knocked them aside, killing one in seconds. The second followed moments later, its blood splattering over my grey fur.

I scanned the crowds and saw that Alejandro had shifted. His Lycan form towered above all the wolves as he let out a vicious growl, engaging in battle with the Crimson King. The Djinn's power was immense, and he was thrown back. His aura wrapped around him protectively as he lunged at the Crimson King once more. He swiped his claws down his chest, injuring him before he was thrown across the ground. His head snapped to me, and I gave the smallest nod.

Be careful, he growled through the link.

I knew what I was doing.

This was it. My moment.

Tensing, I broke into a run, launching myself off the ground, claws raised. It was then that the Crimson King's head snapped upwards, and I found myself staring into a pair of burning orange eyes. Eyes filled with such power and hatred that I felt it deep within me.

"You're mine," he hissed in a voice that was far from human. He raised his hand, and a huge surge of fire roared around us. I bit my lip, feeling it burn away at me. Fuck, I couldn't breathe.

I heard Alejandro growl as he joined, distracting him for a moment. I don't think the Djinn realised that, although I may not be as powerful as my daughter, I had experience and wit on my side. Alejandro engaging him had given me the moment I needed, and I shifted, the momentary change easing the agony in my body as I slammed him to the ground with all my strength, my aura surging around me. My red hair fell in front of my face, my heart beating rapidly. I raised my hand, ready to tear his heart out.

"Wrong. You're mine," I whispered venomously.

It was almost as if we were moving in sync as our claws came out, and we plunged our hands into each other's chests...

A Son's Despair

ALEJANDRO

IT WAS AS IF time had fucking slowed, flames surrounding Scarlett and the fucker. I could see her skin melting away to reveal a raw layer beneath it. I watched as she plunged her hand into his chest fearlessly, but my stomach twisted the moment I saw his clawed hand ripping into her chest, too. He gripped her other arm, crushing the wrist of her hand that was trying to bury itself into his chest. He was clearly unharmed by her attempt. His eyes blazed, and I saw the determination in them, knowing he was ready to kill.

Fuck, no. Not on my fucking watch.

I was by her side in a flash, grabbing hold of the fucker's hand before he managed to rip her heart from her chest. It fucking burned like a bitch to touch him. He was fucking powerful. His eyes were blazing with unspeakable fucking power and his aura swirled around us like a fucking tornado. So, this was the man behind everything.

"Well, well, well… the Lycan King himself still came to battle even when he's so weak…" he hissed venomously.

I'm still fucking stronger than you. But I couldn't say anything in my Lycan form.

Scarlett's face was pale as she gripped his wrist, trying to stop him from wrenching her heart. I held on fucking tight, making sure he didn't penetrate her any further. His fingers were almost completely in her chest, slowly pushing forward. She coughed up blood as I used all my strength. I aimed a kick at him, only for him to block it. It was then that a strong wave of powerful blue fire created a huge force-field between us, instantly easing the heat.

Liam.

I took the chance and sliced the fucker's hand right off with my dagger. *That's for the pup.*

He roared in anger, scooping Scarlett up with the hand still buried in her chest. I jumped away as a huge force shattered Liam's barrier and threw us back. I shielded Scarlett's body as we both hit the ground brutally. My head slammed against the rocky ground, sending spasms of searing pain through me, and I hissed. Fuck, I wasn't up to my normal standards…

I was forced to shift back, feeling blood in my mouth as I rolled over and placed Scarlett on the ground slowly. She coughed up blood, I looked down at her chest to see she was already healing, but that hand was still stuck in her chest. Fuck.

"Don't look!" She growled, despite the fact that she looked like death and couldn't even sit up. I raised an eyebrow. I had seen plenty of naked women. Was she seriously worried about that right now? I was looking at her damn injury.

"Nice piercings," I remarked, unable to stop myself from trying to piss her off. "Hold the fuck still."

As expected, she gave me a cold glare and covered her nips. I frowned, looking down at the burnt, disgusting hand that I needed to remove.

"I'm going to take it out," I told her, impressed that she was still conscious.

She nodded, closing her eyes. I grabbed her shoulder with one hand, holding her down, and placed my knee on her stomach before I yanked the hand from her chest. That was fucking sickening. The smell of blood and burnt flesh filled my nose. She hissed in pain, her eyes blazing as she groaned in agony. Blood splattered everywhere as I tossed it aside. She let out a whimper of pain and rolled over onto her side. I could see she was already healing.

Damn. I think she heals a lot faster than I do.

"Thanks for saving me," she said, sounding a lot more normal again.

"Just don't do that shit again. Stay here until you're ready. We'll go at it again," I added quietly. She nodded.

"Just give me a couple of minutes," she replied hoarsely.

I promised Elijah I'd keep her safe, and I planned to. Standing up, I turned back to the commotion all around us. Wolves in all directions were engaged in battle but the enemy side was relentless and didn't seem to be dying.

I saw Leo's huge wolf. It was almost on par with Rayhan's. He still had a few years to grow, and he wasn't Alpha yet... but I could sense his power radiating off of him as he slayed wolves without hesitation. I could see he was sticking close to Marcel and realised he actually did think I would let him die.

I took a deep breath and mind-linked three of my warriors who were closest, including Carmen, to shield Scarlett until she healed. Rayhan came over, his green eyes blazing and blood dripping from his fur and teeth that were holding some sort of fabric, which he placed around Scarlett's shoulders. Ever the gentleman.

I turned away, knowing she was fine, and looked at the main target once more. *This fucker needs to go down...*

I assessed the carnage, trying to see how we could get close to him and actually do some damage. Wolves clashed with wolves in every direction. I needed the help of the witches. They were fully protected and offered our kind protection, too. I knew that without them, we would probably have had a lot more losses by now.

I glanced towards Maria. She was fighting a few wolves, but she wasn't overly exerting herself, saving herself for the last and final job. Darien wasn't far from her, and I knew he had the dagger, ready to pass it to her when the time came. Four of the Black Storm Pack warriors surrounded her. Those were the ones we'd have to handle when the time came. They had been assigned by Raf to protect his Luna, and, until now, they kept that job.

I turned to the fucker, my eyes blazing with hatred.

"What the fuck do you want? We were willing to pay the debt if you told us what it was," I growled, launching myself at the Crimson King and trying to buy us some time. I knew exactly what the back story was, but something told me the Escarras' revenge was far gone and left behind. All that remained was the Djinn and his hunger for power.

Once again, a blast of fire threw me back. This time, I was ready and jumped aside as the ground trembled. Two witches raised a barrier between us, and his eyes flashed.

"Does the beast's father still not know the answer?"

I shifted back, trying to reserve energy. I didn't miss the knowing smirk on his face. He fucking knew I wasn't at my usual level...

My men were going to begin to tire, unlike his wolves, which were relentless, just like they were the day Kataleya was kidnapped.

"Well, obviously, you're referring to my son. Well, guess what? Whatever the fuck you want, you won't get it because no one touches my pups and gets away with it," I growled, mind-linking one of my men.

Milo, my sword.

"Shame you won't be able to protect anyone," he spat with hatred.

"That's where you're fucking wrong," I growled.

The moment my hand touched the leather-bound long hilt, I smirked. Since I wasn't able to keep my fucking Lycan form, we'd do this the other way. Six feet long and half a foot wide, this bad boy was made to chop fuckers to pieces. The moment it was in my hand, the weight of the adamantium steel was heavy yet perfectly comfortable in my hand. I ran at him, swinging it down. He jumped back, frowning as the blade hit the ground, creating a crack. I smirked coldly. When the magic of two of the strongest witches on the planet helped create this, it was no ordinary weapon – a gift from Del and Ri for my 40th.

"You do not even know what that boy is!" He spat, raising his hand and blocking the sword. Another huge wave of power came my way. One of the witches blocked it as I sliced through the force, trying to get at least one or two hits in.

"I know exactly what he is. He's my son, one you tried to harm!" I growled.

I didn't want anyone to know the truth. I wanted to keep it a secret for as long as possible because if it got out... I didn't even want to fucking know the consequences

"What did you want him for?" I hissed as I swung my sword. I saw Scarlett, Rayhan, and Liam trying to get closer, but the sudden influx of wolves wasn't helping.

"What do you think? Draining his vessel of blood will give me a permanent form on this planet, and then... the world will be mine."

I snarled, "You ain't fucking laying a finger on him." I spun around, feinting a hit, and my sword connected with his shoulder.

"I will! As we speak, I'm getting closer and closer to him!" He shouted manically, not caring about the blood that spurted from his shoulder. A sliver of fear washed through me. Something in his eyes meant more…

Darien! Get someone to find out what's happening back home. Tell Elijah to stay on alert!

A huge wave of power slammed us back. I felt a few more bonds snap at once as my pack members died. Fuck.

I was unable to look away from my target, knowing if I made one wrong move, I'd be dead. He slammed me to the ground, just as the witch who was creating the barrier around me was cut down by the fucker.

"Fuck!" I growled as she crumbled to the floor.

Take Olivina to safety! I commanded through the bond.

Right then, we were one. One team, one side, and I was going to do my best for them all. I shielded her as the fucker raised his hand and sent a huge wave of fire straight towards me. Something about this power was different. Whatever it touched would disintegrate instantly. I grabbed the bleeding witch and rolled over, but immediately another wave followed. I was ready for the impact, raising my sword in defence when I was shoved aside roughly.

Alpha! I turned as Carmen's wolf stood where I was moments earlier, and, right before my eyes, her body became a burnt carcass. I felt the bond break, my heart thudding as the burnt wolf crumbled to the ground. The fire was so powerful that she hadn't even shifted to her human form, burnt and frozen in wolf form. A flare of rage flashed through me to every corner of my body. Carmen, she had been by my side from the fucking start. No matter what, she was always there…

My eyes flashed red, the taste of blood strong in my mouth as I shifted, dropping my weapon and launching myself at the monster. Not caring about the blasts of fire, Liam fell in step next to me. His aura was raging around him like a huge shield, and he focused it towards the Djinn. His eyes blazed as he threw him back with a huge wave of blue fire. The intensity sent waves across the entire grounds. I wondered how he and Kiara would work together in battle. That one would be pretty impressive to watch if ever the time came.

I saw Scarlett run forward, her fur glowing under the setting sun. This was it, our last fucking chance.

Liam was thrown into the air. He shifted mid-throw, landing on his paws and growling at the fucker before he and Rayhan lunged at the so-called fucking Crimson King. I saw Darien move towards Maria from the corner of my eyes. Her guards weren't around… which meant she had managed to get them to leave her.

Fuck. My heart clenched, knowing what was to come. Scarlett and I moved at the same time as I fought the storm of emotions that consumed me.

"You will never defeat me!" This time, the voice held no trace of humanity. It was unearthly. I flinched as it grated into my bones.

Splitting pain filled my head, but I still pushed forward, grabbing my sword and swinging it at him. Scarlett managed to throw him to the ground, the flames around him burning into her. I knew she wouldn't be able to last long, and I was in front of them in a flash.

I heard a witch chanting behind me, knowing she was one of the most powerful ones. Liam's aura surrounding Scarlett was the only thing keeping her alive as she pinned the man down.

"I will never die!" He hissed, a menacing grin crossing his face. "Never."

"That's about to fucking change," I growled. My claws came out, and I plunged my hand into his chest.

"No!"

I froze, my heart thundering as I recognised that voice.

Enrique. Fuck, he shouldn't be here… why is he here?

The monster beneath me smiled victoriously.

Get him out of here! I growled at Liam through the link. The Djinn could take any one of the Escarra blood as his host instantly, thanks to the deal made long ago. Liam was by his side in an instant, picking him up and backing away, but it meant he wouldn't be able to hold the shield around Scarlett for long.

"Please don't kill my padre!" Enrique shouted over Liam's shoulder as I felt an odd wave of power pulsating around the man beneath us.

"Your father is long gone, kid. He's only a monster now!" I shouted back, looking up at him.

Our eyes met, and I realised I should never have let him go. The boy I had set free had been broken, but the battered, bruised boy in front of me was… empty. Something told me he was far past the point of being fixed.

Like the dying sun behind him, all hope seemed to have gone for him. If I killed his father in front of him…

But I had to, for him and for us all.

Through the sweat, blood, and pain, I knew that no matter what, I had to do this. There was no other way.

The odd pulsating was growing stronger. Was he trying to switch hosts?

"Barriers around the boy!" I thundered, trying to plunge my hand into his chest, but he had something around him that was stopping me. Even with the witch's power assisting me, I could feel the fire biting through it. Soon, if this fucking continued, I wouldn't have a fucking hand left.

"He's mine!" The monster beneath me roared.

"No, he fucking isn't. You've destroyed him already!" I hissed.

"Please, don't! My padre needs help!" The boy's distant shouting came. "You said you'd help me!" His cry was heartbreaking, and I knew I'd never forget it…

I'm sorry, kid… I'm fucking sorry.

A menacing growl ripped from my throat, and, using my all, I managed to break through the barrier and tore his heart from his chest. Instantly, one of the witches obliterated it, and both Scarlett and I were thrown back with incredible force as a huge explosion of fire erupted. Above everything, over the roaring of the Djinn, the screams and howls of the fighting wolves… all I heard was the piercing scream of anguish and despair of the young boy who had just lost his father.

A huge surge of fire emitted from the dead body, taking on a fiery form of part-man, part-beast, with blazing eyes, horns, and a tail. He towered far above me, easily measuring over ten feet tall, as his aura threw us all back. The heat was burning our skin, and I looked down at the dead body of what once used to be the Alpha of the Fuego De Ceniza Pack at his feet…

"Keep your distance!" I commanded before darting forward. I may have killed him, but I needed to get his body for the pup.

"Al!" Marcel growled.

Al, get the fuck back! Darien shouted through the link.

I ignored them, but before I could even get to the body, the Djinn stepped on him, instantly turning him to a burned crisp. My heart plummeted, and I jumped back.

"Don't let it touch you! One touch and you're fucking burnt toast!" I growled.

The Djinn let out an unearthly roar, waving his fiery tail. It connected with two wolves, one of his own and one of ours. I felt the snap as I lost yet another man. The Fuego De Ceniza Pack was without an Alpha... but it was obvious that whatever magic was on these wolves meant they were under the Djinn's command. I couldn't command them to step down as a whole because even our side would fall to my command.

Liam was gone, and I was glad. We needed that pup far away.

The witches were trying to contain the Djinn from advancing, but we were failing.

She's ready. Darien's voice came through the link.

My heart thundered, and I looked at Maria, who was far behind the Djinn. Her grey eyes met mine, and I felt the agonising pain of what was to come. I had already lost several... but to know I was going to lose her...

Her hair was hidden beneath a turban-like black scarf, which also covered her face. She was dressed in complete black with her signature look of flared pants, fully covered... only her eyes could be seen. Her long curved swords were held in her hands.

I love you, and I'm going to fucking miss you, I said hoarsely through the link, hoping she heard. If she did, I knew she wouldn't be able to answer.

I saw her eyes sparkle with unshed tears, yet the crinkle on the corner of her eyes told me she was smiling. She was happy. Fuck...

This was it. The time had come.

Letting out a howl of rage, I shifted, ready to keep the fucker occupied so she could do what she needed to.

Forgive me for not being able to keep her happy, Raf.

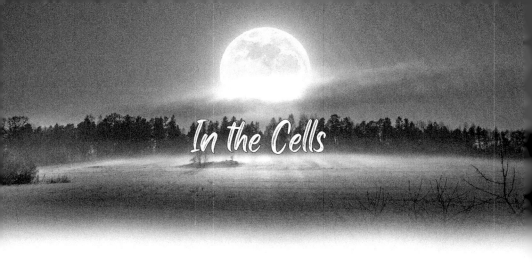

In the Cells

ELIJAH

I HAD JUST DONE THE round of the pack grounds when I felt a searing pain that made me double over.

Scarlett.

Fear enveloped me as the pain blinded me, making several men run to me, but soon it was gone, and I knew she was okay. I hadn't felt the bond snap... fuck...

Unlike the rest of the pack, who was tied to Liam, my mate was the only one bound to me. She needed to be okay. Whatever had happened had been a close call, and although I wanted to get someone to find out, they needed to focus on the battle.

It took me a few moments to regain myself before I entered the Night Walkers' Headquarters to go have a look to see if Kiara was okay. Doctor Callum was waiting for me inside, as he needed to administer the dose to keep her weakened and unconscious. A few guards and others working were carrying on with their jobs, but the tension that hung in the air was obvious. Several gave me a polite nod as I walked past and headed down to the cells. Two of the guards flanked the door, and Doctor Callum was already there, his kit in hand.

"Alpha Elijah."

"Doctor."

He gave a small nod and a forced smile, but it was obvious he didn't like doing this. Neither did I, but there wasn't much we could do but keep her sedated.

I frowned deeply, remembering what Alejandro had said about Dante and what he was. It had been fucking shocking, to say the least, but it made sense. Dante was the only one with such a powerful aura from birth. Even Alpha pups did not hold that. He knew far more than Liam and Kiara's intuition… but the Djinn also knew his truth, and the fact that he wanted him meant he would go to any lengths to get him. We needed to make sure Kiara was kept unconscious no matter what.

I keyed in the code Alejandro had changed specifically so that no one else knew it but me. I stepped inside, shutting the door behind Doctor Callum.

"We just need to keep her unconscious for a while longer. I do hope the king can deal with this threat immediately so I don't have to do this to my Queen," Callum said gravely. It was taking a toll on him; I could see it in his eyes.

"I am sorry that you're the one who has to do this, considering you are a doctor, but it is for Kiara's sake as well," I said quietly as we walked down the steps to the cold dark cells.

There she was, lying on a slab of silver with chains wrapped around her. Her arms and ankles were cuffed. It was almost as if she was simply sleeping. Her heart beat steadily despite the fact that it was weaker than normal.

I unlocked the cell door, and we stepped inside. The sound of the keys chinking echoed in the quietness.

I hated seeing her like this, and I wondered how Alejandro must have felt having to leave his mate beneath the grounds of his pack and go to battle. I had seen the pain in his eyes, but he remained strong, like always.

The stains of dried blood around her wrists made me frown. She must have woken up at some point as the restraints had been pulled at, causing her to bleed.

Callum opened his pack of supplies and began walking forward when I suddenly grabbed his arm, pulling him back.

"Wait."

"Alpha -"

He looked at me, and I shook my head, motioning with my eyes at the restraints. He frowned before following my gaze. His frown vanished as he realised what I was pointing out. Kiara should have been in a state where she couldn't even wake up, let alone fight against her bindings.

'Go,' I mouthed to Callum, taking the syringe from him and stepping closer to the table. I paused, my eyes flashing as I motioned for him to leave. If something happened, I needed to make sure we were locked in. She couldn't get out.

The moment I was within reach, her eyes snapped open, deep orange burning brightly as she shot up and grabbed my neck.

"Lock it!" I growled at Callum, aiming to slam the syringe into Kiara, but she knocked my hand aside, jumping up from the bindings she had already broken. Fuck.

"Not so fast," she hissed, lunging at me, and I felt a sliver of fear rush through me. I couldn't hurt her.

"Kiara."

She smiled coldly, running to the cell door, but I grabbed her by the arm, pulling her back. She lashed out, and we both hit the table she had been lying on. Her claws came out as she bared her teeth at me. My eyes flashed as I pushed her back before grabbing her arm and slamming her against the wall, just as Callum managed to lock the door, leaving me here with Kiara.

"Open it," she commanded, her aura swirling around her. Her claws were digging into my arm.

"Callum, go! Now!" I growled venomously. He frowned, forcing himself away from the keys. I knew his wolf wanted to obey his queen.

"I'll call for help!"

"No. No one from this pack is to come down here," I growled, my eyes fixed on Kiara, who shoved me off and stood up.

Raven, Kiara's awake. I need you to get Raihana to make sure the pack members stay away from the cells. If Kiara commands them to help her, they will not be able to deny her request for the most part.

Shit. Okay, got it. I'll tell Raihana now. Do you need my help?

I don't think she can mind-link. Just make sure no one gets close. I'll deal with Kiara.

Got it!

I cut the link, knowing Raven and Raihana would handle the rest, and I would handle my daughter. She smiled, a smile that was so much like Kiara's that for a moment I wondered if she had any control.

"What's wrong? Scared that now I'm the queen you won't be able to handle me?"

"I'm still your father," I said quietly, my eyes blazing cobalt blue. Although I knew I'd never be able to hurt her, I knew the faster I took her down, the better.

"Game on, Papa," she said mockingly.

At once, we both sprang at the other. Her purple aura mixed with orange, wrapping around her, but it wasn't anywhere near as powerful as usual, and, at that moment, I realised he could never completely control her. Kiara's power came from the light, from the moon itself. Something evil and dark could never control it...

With this theory, I suddenly stilled, something she hadn't expected, but I knew, deep down, my girl was in there. Her eyes flickered as her hand connected with my chest, the impact far less than it should have been. Kiara was still in there.

I smirked and stabbed the syringe into her neck, using her hesitation to help me. Her eyes widened in shock before the orange gave way to the familiar, blue-rimmed green eyes. Eyes that were filled with pain, guilt, and sadness.

"Dad..."

"I'm here, Princess," I said quietly, pulling her into my arms.

"I-it's not safe, I'm not safe…. Leave…" Her body was becoming heavy, and she soon slumped in my arms, unconscious.

"Everything will be okay." I lifted her up, placing her on the silver.

Raven, get Dr Callum to come back down. We need to up her dosage…

I frowned, caressing her hair. How the hell was it possible for her to have broken free of the cuffs…? Her body was bound and kept subdued… where did the Djinn get the energy from? Was he somehow pulling on Alejandro's power through the bond? This was a magic and power beyond my understanding.

I heard footsteps soon after, and Serena and Callum both came hurrying over.

"Alpha, never ask me to do something so risky ever again," he said, looking as if he had aged a few years. I raised an eyebrow.

"Look at these cuffs. She broke through them somehow; she was fully unconscious. How is that even possible?" I mused as Callum administered another round of drugs.

"Is it possible that his hold on her is getting stronger and he's beginning to take over?" Callum murmured. I shook my head.

"He can't possess her unless he is physically here. He did something to attain a hold on her, but he isn't 'in' her, if that makes sense. The elder witches explained that clearly."

"But then how did he wake up?" Serena asked worriedly.

"I don't know. He has to be drawing strength from somewhere," I said quietly. Serena frowned, her eyes thoughtful as she felt Kiara's pulse.

"It's so weak…" She stroked her hair, and I could see she loved her Luna.

"We need new chains," I said quietly.

"I've asked Drake to bring some more chains and cuffs…" Serena replied unhappily. Callum paused before he suddenly looked up sharply.

"I have a hypothesis…but I am uncertain if there is any truth or logic in it…" He seemed hesitant as he looked down at Kiara.

"What is it?" I asked. He seemed to struggle before he bent down, placing his ear against Kiara's stomach.

"You said he needs to be drawing strength from somewhere, my assumption was… well…"

"Spit it out," I growled impatiently.

"I… well, what if the Luna is pregnant? The Djinn may be drawing his strength from the foetus." I looked at him sharply. Kiara was pregnant? I was sure she was done with kids…

Serena's eyes were wide with shock. I simply watched Callum waiting for his verdict. He moved back slowly, his face looking thoughtful.

"I'm not sure… perhaps, Alpha, you can check; your hearing would be better than mine…"

"But if that's true… and we are here binding her in silver…" Serena murmured.

"But the Luna heals. It would make sense. If the Djinn is constantly using an unborn foetus to survive and Kiara is fuelling it with her healing, it's a winning situation for the demon," Callum said quietly.

I didn't reply, pressing my ear to Kiara's stomach and closing my eyes. Trying to focus, I strained my ears. The sound of Kiara's heart, Serena's… Callum's… mine… and there it was. The tiny beat of a fifth heart. I jerked back, looking at Callum in shock.

"Well?" He looked at me with concern.

"I think she is…" I whispered, unable to make anything of the shocking revelation as I tried to process it all.

"Then we need to move her to the hospital. We can place her in one of the secure rooms that were used for rabid wolves or those who had been poisoned by the Wendigos and Manangals years ago," Callum said worriedly. "We need to make sure the poison and silver we have been giving her haven't harmed the baby. Even though she has the gift of healing, we need to be careful." I nodded, fear twisting in my guts.

If Alejandro learned of this, if he realised she had been pregnant all along and something happened to the baby, he would never be able to forgive himself.

"Darien just had one of the backups call to ask if everything is okay here. What do we say?" Serena asked, looking at me for answers.

"Just tell them Kiara woke up, but she's sedated once again, and everything is fine," I said firmly before turning to Callum. "Keep her sedated, up the dosage. I will place guards from the Blood Moon to watch her so she cannot command them like her own pack. As for the baby, get a scan done and make sure it's okay. The most we can do is hope that Alejandro and the rest succeed in tonight's battle quickly and efficiently." The severity of the situation was worsening, and everything was hanging in the balance.

I picked Kiara up and carried her out of the cells, mind-linking my men on what their new orders were. I placed a kiss on my princess' forehead, hating that she was going through so much. Twenty minutes later, Kiara was set up in one of the holding rooms on the secure floor of the hospital with ten of the Blood Moon men on guard. Callum was inside with a sonography machine. He carried out the scan whilst Serena and I waited with bated breath.

"Ah… it's there. It's still very small… I'm assuming she became pregnant not long ago…"

"After she lost her memory," I stated, and Callum nodded.

"It would make sense. Perhaps she was no longer taking her contraception." Well, that was on Alejandro. He should have been more careful. I frowned in concern, looking at the screen.

"And is it healthy?" I asked the question that I knew was on both my and Serena's mind.

"Yes. It's weak, but that's to be expected… she is sedated, however, otherwise it seems well," Callum replied, sounding relieved. A wave of relief washed over me, and I exhaled.

"Thank the goddess…"

But I didn't get to revel in that revelation because Raven mind-linked me, panic and fear in her voice.

Uncle! We need you here! Her voice was distraught, and it made my mind race, thinking of a thousand fucking reasons that could be behind it.

Raven! What is it? I asked, my heart skipping a fucking beat.

It's Delsanra! She's… Raihana can't do anything! Goddess! Nothing is working! She's not breathing! Delsanra's stopped breathing!

Fuck, please, no.

When Hope is Lost

RAYHAN

*T*HIS WAS IT…

I saw Mom and Uncle exchange looks, almost as if Uncle was trying to relay a message. I didn't need to be able to read minds to know what was on his. The emotions in his eyes spoke louder than words ever could. If there was any doubt that maybe Dante was wrong and this wasn't going to happen, it vanished. That exchange said it all.

I saw the pain in Uncle's eyes before he lunged at the Djinn, hatred and anger clear in his eyes as he roared. His aura radiated off of him. The Djinn intercepted him, knocking him back and roaring in an unearthly way, his fiery body illuminating the darkening skies.

"He will not be able to hold that form for too long, but it gives him enough time to find a new host!" Someone shouted.

Time was running out. A clash of attacks was happening in all directions, and I took a moment to try to assess our next move.

"When all hope is lost…"

Right then, we were holding well. When was the right moment? And how was I meant to work with the one guy who hated me the most? I looked over at Leo. His huge wolf was an impressive sight. He was truly an Alpha wolf. His brown fur, that held hints of steely blue, was matted with blood, but it did nothing to dull his power or magnificence. A true beast that matched the Rossis, and deep down, I wondered if Dante was right. Would he really help me? Would he care if Mom was killed?

A shrill, painful roar left the Djinn's mouth, the flames growing higher, and we were all thrown back. Liam had returned, but even his power was doing nothing other than holding off the heat a little. His aura raged around him powerfully as the Djinn lunged at him. Liam ducked, moving aside as he met him mid-attack.

The witches were doing their best, and as I cut down another wolf, I felt the ground tremble beneath me. I cut down two more wolves, wishing they weren't simply his puppets...

Puppets... just like those under Endora...

Uncle's words about some of the Sangue Pack members still played in my mind, and I couldn't forget the little boy's cries of pain. Would he become another Leo? Would he hate us? The situation was different, but...

The smell of blood, burnt flesh, and smoke hung in the air. Soon, all I could see was the black smoke that was making it harder to breathe. The Djinn was not being affected by anything. No matter how many times someone managed to touch him, it did nothing to injure him, but he was, in turn, burning those around him to death or close enough. My stomach twisted as I watched one of the Betas from another pack attack the Djinn, but the moment he made impact, he was burnt entirely.

How the fuck do we get close? Or at least stop those who do manage to get close from dying instantly?

The ground beneath us erupted, throwing us back violently. A sharp rock hit my left flank, and I was tossed to the ground like I didn't weigh a thing. Damn this.

I saw Uncle jump up, his sword raised and his aura visible against the flames, like black waves enveloping his body. So, only Alpha-level wolves were able to get close and not die... that hacked down our numbers vastly, but it was obvious Uncle had clicked on too.

Get your men from Beta rank and below to back off. Everyone is to hold the attacking wolves at bay! Alpha Blood and witches are to step forward! Uncle's voice came through the link. Frowning, I relayed the message to my pack.

Got it, Alpha!

Yes, Alpha!

Seven Alphas, two ex-Lunas, and fifteen more of Alpha blood all stepped forward, along with thirteen witches. Our pack members created a wall around us, fending off the attacking wolves. The witches were at the back, the sound of their chanting only growing louder.

"When all hope feels like it's lost..."

The power around me was immense. It felt as if we had cornered the Djinn as each Alpha-blooded werewolf attacked him, with protective shields created around every werewolf there. What did he mean?

The Djinn was beginning to struggle to block all the attacks. We would win, right? The Djinn's flames and aura were diminishing.

I jumped, swiping my claws across his face. His eyes filled with hatred as he turned his gaze on me. *This is for my kitten.*

With renewed hatred and anger, I attacked again, but with each passing moment, it was becoming increasingly obvious that he wasn't going to die. Every one of us who attacked was being thrown aside like ragdolls. I growled, seeing Chris being slammed to the ground and instantly shifting back to human form. His entire body was covered in blood, and I could see a heavy injury on his shoulder and neck. I growled in anger, running over to him and pulling him to safety. He was injured, but he was alive. I frowned, sensing Raihana's powers around him, and smiled internally. His woman definitely wouldn't send him to battle without backup. Whatever she had done had stopped him from having his head ripped off.

I turned back, hearing a scream as Aunty Red was thrown in the air. Blood sprayed down on us, making me flinch when her human form hit the ground. Blood as red as her hair covered her body. She was someone I would never want to fight in battle; violent, dangerous, and aggressive. Whatever she had done made the Djinn stagger as he tried to regain himself, black smoke coming out of his ribs. His power kept steady, but his rage was directed at Aunty Red. He launched himself towards her, ready to tear her to shreds, but Uncle Al and Marcel attacked him, cutting off his path.

He roared in rage, slamming them both back. Uncle was in human form, and I could tell he was weakening. Despite that, he remained strong, commanding and assessing the situations, always at the heart of the battle

"I will never die!" The Djinn hissed in a voice that was not for this earth. I felt it inside, the shuddering power in it instilling fear in those who heard it.

His gaze was on Uncle before he sank his claws into his shoulders. I felt an odd pulsating that I had felt earlier oozing off of him. Uncle let out a roar of agony that filled the air.

"Do not fight me! Or I will kill all!" He hissed venomously.

With sudden realization, it hit me. He was trying to take him as a host. Fuck!

I saw the flash of silver from the corner of my eyes as Darien handed something to Mom. The dagger.

I looked at Leo, who had just failed at another attempted attack, his eyes blazing with rage. As if sensing me watching him, he turned his attention to me. Our eyes met, and I knew it was time...

From the corner of my eye, I saw the Djinn dig his flaming claws into Uncle's chest, slamming him to the ground.

Leo.

We had to do this.

He gave me the slightest nod before he broke into a run towards Mom, just as Marcel attacked the Djinn, causing Leo to hesitate when he was thrown to the ground again, a bloody mess, but I would let him know I was there. The Djinn turned his gaze upon Marcel. A shrill whistling hiss filled the air, and black smoke emitted from his shoulder.

Marcel had done some damage, and it was obvious that the Djinn wanted him dead. I jumped in the way, growling ferociously. Leo needed to know we wouldn't leave Marcel to die. I saw him glance at his father before he ran towards Mom, who had broken into a run.

Leo... you can do this...

I jumped at the Djinn, but even though he was fighting back with one arm, he was still powerful. I saw Darien get knocked to the ground by an immense wave of power. The Djinn's hold on Uncle remained throughout, the flames beginning to wrap around his body. Even the witch's shield around Uncle was failing. He had managed to kill a few of them as well. A few Alphas had died, too...

Fuck. Time was running out...

I looked at Mom, who was dodging attack after attack. She was fast and lithe. When she jumped, spinning in the sky, she was the perfect example of the Ahmar Qamar fighting style. Her father would have been truly proud.

A flash of brown and blue crossed my vision, and then Leo had his jaw around her waist, knocking her out of the air. I heard her gasp. She hadn't been expecting an attack from one of our own.

"Leo! You fool!" Marcel thundered from where he was staggering to his feet. Mom knocked Leo back, her eyes flashing with rage. She had been close...

"Leo! Don't do this!" She shouted as Leo shifted back.

"I don't fucking follow rules," he growled, grabbing her arm and ripping the weapon from her grip.

"Leo!" Her anger was palpable, but Leo ignored her, holding her in a death grip before he turned to me and threw the dagger. I shifted back. Mom gasped as the Djinn turned, realisation hitting him as he stared at the blade that I'd just caught.

"A Virgin Blade..." The same term that Dante had used... a term I hadn't heard from anyone before Dante...

The fear in the Djinn as he slammed Leo and Mom to the ground before he began advancing towards me was clear. His aura of fire grew as he turned his gaze on me. I wasn't going to make it...

"You... no... it's not... the time is... I have time... I have time..." the Djinn was rambling, his fury growing.

I scanned the area. Aunty Red was down... Chris, Marcel... Uncle... they were alive thanks to the barriers made by Liam and the witches. But aside from Darien, Liam, Mom, Leo, and I, everyone else was out...

"When all hope is lost... look for the man in black..."

But there was no one.

"The time of the werewolves is over. The time of the witches is over... the time for the immortals has arrived..." the Djinn hissed, sparks flying from his mouth as he spat the words out. "No one can kill me. No mere werewolf scum," he hissed.

I would do it. *Fuck the man in black, I'll kill –*

Agony ripped through me, and I felt an excruciating pain tear into me and wrap around my heart. Fear enveloped me as I realised what it was.

Delsanra!

She was dying.

Fuck, no!

"Die, Son of Selene."

"Ray..." Uncle growled, managing to rip free from the Djinn's hold. I didn't know how he was walking... the number of injuries on his body... he looked like death, yet the will in his eyes didn't diminish.

The Djinn let out a mighty roar, raising his arm. Uncle stepped in front of me, shielding me. Even this close to death, he still had the power and strength that came from within. He was a true king, and I knew he was ready to die for me.

Just then, a blinding deep red glow filled the air. It was far darker and deeper than the orangey red of the Djinn. I shielded my eyes, blinded by the intensity and power of the aura that clashed against the Djinn's. It diminished, and there, a few metres away, stood a man. He was lean, tall, and muscular, wearing all black with a black cloak around his shoulders, but what got to me was that his clothing was similar to Mom's; he had his hood up, and a black mask covered his face. His hands were gloved, and the only part of him that was visible was his eyes.

The Djinn hissed, and I could sense his fear.

"You... there's no way you could be here... I chose the right time!"

"You were destined to die by my hand, no matter where or when," he replied quietly. His voice was low and husky, yet it held a melodic hum to it.

Uncle was tense, but I knew what I needed to do. The man held his hand out as if expecting it, and I threw the dagger at him. He caught it without even looking at me just as the Djinn roared, his aura blasting away the barriers. Fear, rage, and desperation were clear in his eyes. We were all blasted back, our bodies beginning to burn with the heat of the fire from the Djinn.

"I have waited too long! You cannot kill me! I hold the fire of hell within me!"

"Your time has come," the masked man said quietly, yet the power that he held seemed to seep through us all. His voice held nothing but calmness, and, in a flash, he was right in front of the Djinn, unbothered by the blazing fire that was radiating off him. I saw a flicker of a black tail from under his cloak, and I smiled slightly.

A demon.

Somehow, Dante knew a demon would come.

He raised the dagger, and a huge wave of power swirled around him, pushing past the flames of the Djinn. The Djinn jumped up in the air, but it didn't deter the demon. He held the dagger firmly, and I felt a sense of deja vu as he pushed off and flipped it in the air like Mom had before he plunged the dagger into the Djinn's chest.

A terrorising scream left the Djinn as a tidal wave of power caused a tsunami. We were all lifted from the ground and thrown back. Nobody was able to withstand it; even trees were ripped from their roots. I shielded my eyes, staring up at the two kinds of Demon in the centre. The man in black held strong, despite the waves of power that rolled off the Djinn.

Through the pain of the breaking bond, my fear, and the ray of hope, I saw the Djinn beginning to blacken and cracks began to appear in him. A final, fierce scream of despair left him as he stared at the night sky, his arms raised in hopelessness.

"I think I fucking hit my head harder than I thought…" I heard Uncle mutter.

I almost smiled. Uncle never lost his ability to comment, but my eyes were on the two before us, watching as the Djinn seemed to explode. Then silence.

I felt the pain that had been crushing me inside vanish, and I knew Delsanra was okay; relief flooded me. The bond was intact.

The mystery man turned towards me. Deep red eyes rimmed with thick black lashes met mine, and an odd wave of familiarity washed over me.

"We won," he murmured, winking at me before a huge flash of deep red light filled the sky. Then he was gone, leaving behind the dagger that had fulfilled its purpose…

Leo was the first to rise. Walking over to the dagger, he picked it up, interest clear in his piercing blue eyes before he smirked like the predator he is.

"Well, that sure was fun."

An Offer

RAIHANA

*M*Y HEART POUNDED WITH fear when Delsanra's heart stopped beating. I jumped up from the bed, chanting a spell, trying to heal her or do anything to bring her heartbeat back. *Goddesses above, help me!*

"Delsanra! You are not leaving me!" I cried out. "I need help!"

Damn her heart. No! No!

Ahren, who had been playing on the bed, froze in panic at my shouting, his eyes pooling with tears.

"Fuck! *I need someone!*" I screamed. Where the hell were the guards?

Hold on, girl… hold on…

"Delsanra!" The door burst open as Raven appeared with Dante, Azura, and the twins. "Teleport her to the hospital!" She told me, scooping Ahren up.

"She's not breathing!" I exclaimed.

"Calm down. She's going to be fine," Dante interrupted, staring at Delsanra. Despite the calm in his voice, his heart was pounding, and his hands were shaking as he approached her. "She's going to be okay… she has to…" he whispered, staring down at her as he took her hand in his.

"Then why are you terrified?" I whispered fearfully before shaking my head and chanting another spell of healing. It couldn't be her time! Not yet!

Raven had run out, and I was sure it was to call a doctor, but it wasn't going to help. Her heart had stopped. I knew it hadn't even been a minute, but it felt like eternity as I did my best, trying to use every spell I could think of.

"Was I wrong?" Dante whispered, his face pale. What was he going on about?

The girls stood silently, with fear in their eyes. Kataleya looked fearful; Skyla was frowning, whilst Azura was scanning the room as if it'd give her an answer.

"We need to shock her awake," she said in a panicked whisper. "Like a lightning bolt, a jolt!"

She was right, we may not have the machinery here, but I could use a spell. I could -

Delsanra's eyes flew open just as Dante gasped, staggering back. A darkness emitted from them, followed by a blinding light, and, before my very eyes, their skin returned to normal. The veins vanished and colour returned to them. The bright light and that surge of power vanished, and I wasn't the only one to sigh in relief. Delsanra shot straight up in bed, her eyes blazing red, looking as beautiful as she did the first time I saw her in her demon form. Dante's eyes seemed to sharpen as he rolled his neck, removing the kinks from it.

"Ri," Delsanra whispered. Her voice was hoarse despite the fact that her pale skin was glowing, and her hair seemed to be full of life.

"Thank the goddesses! I could kiss you right now!" I exclaimed, flinging my arms around her, hugging her tightly. My best friend… Goddess, my best friend was okay!

"That scared me for a moment," Dante muttered, frowning slightly. I looked up at him, wiping my tears.

"Aw, my poor baby! You looked terrified, too. Come here," I said, pulling him into a tight hug.

"Let go of me!" He retorted, trying to pull away. "I wasn't scared."

"Weren't you?" Delsanra asked teasingly before she smiled at the girls who stood there looking relieved.

Two doctors, Uncle El, Raven, and two guards appeared in the doorway.

"Not at all," Dante said, quietly looking at Delsanra before glaring at me. "Let me go, you're squishing me." I raised an eyebrow before letting go of him. It was good to have him back.

"Thank fuck," Uncle El muttered, hugging Raven, who was grinning happily.

"This means they did it, right?" She asked, kissing Ahren's cheek.

"They did it," Uncle El replied with a nod, exhaling in relief.

"Did it!" Ahren repeated before he giggled and hid his face in Raven's shoulder, then jumped up as if just realising Delsanra was awake. "Mama!"

"My baby," Delsanra whispered, her eyes full of emotion as Raven brought him over.

"Sienna's asleep, I'll go get her," she said gently. Delsanra smiled, trying to control her tears before she hugged him tightly, rocking him gently. Dante watched them, and for some reason, he looked... sad and happy at the same time.

"Hey, what's up?" I asked him.

He shook his head, shrugging before he turned and brushed past the guards and left. I frowned, feeling concerned, as Skyla jumped onto the bed.

"We thought you died," Azura stated bluntly.

"We were thinking we had to bury you," Skyla added dramatically.

"We knew you were going to be okay because Daddy promised," Kataleya added, making Delsanra chuckle.

"I missed you girls, too," she replied, ruffling their hair.

"This means it's over," Uncle El said, running his hands through his gorgeous sandy brown locks.

"And it means our mates are okay," I added, feeling my chest feel lighter, but with it, my heart suddenly plummeted. It meant Mom was gone... fuck...

Suddenly, I felt my body become numb and I excused myself from the room before the tears came. I needed to be alone.

"She's alive."

I froze, turning and looking at Dante, who stood there.

"What?" I asked, refusing to cry.

"Mama Mari is alive," he repeated. Confusion hit me and my head spun.

"What... how? She was..."

"It's not her time," he said quietly, looking down. I sighed, placing a hand on my heart.

Was it selfish that I was relieved she was okay? I promised I'd work on something, even if it was by using magic, I would make sure Mom stayed strong...

Dante was glancing at the open bedroom door, and I crouched down in front of him.

"Tell me, my Alpha prince, why are you behaving weirdly? Shouldn't you be in there so when Rayhan comes back you can piss him off and say you were by her side when she woke up?"

"I… I told Rayhan that if he followed the plan… that I'll let Delsanra go. So I can't keep annoying him anymore. I have to stop." I frowned. What? Rayhan knew? Dante knew? Okay, my mind was spinning, but I'd get the deets later. For now, I needed to handle this.

"So let me get this straight, you asked Rayhan to help you save Mom, to save everyone from being sacrificed, and you have to give up crushing on Delsanra? I find your crush really cute! And if Rayhan has an issue, I will handle him! What an ass! Making you do that? What the heck! Let him come back!"

"Ri!" Dante snapped his fingers in front of me, a frown on his cute little handsome face.

"What?" I growled.

"Calm down. Why are women so emotional…? Jeesh… it's fine… I need to behave. Mom and Dad keep telling me to anyway… I need to realise she is Rayhan's." Despite his words, he rolled his eyes, making me chuckle.

"Yes, but you know… even if you aren't going to pursue her, you can still be her friend?" I suggested, wiggling my eyebrows. "No one said you have to avoid her like the plague." Seriously, Rayhan needed a smack. He nodded, smirking slightly.

"That's true."

"See?" I stood up crossing my arms. "Let's go inside." He nodded before pausing.

"Don't tell anyone about this conversation. Or that I admitted that she's…" he warned me, trailing off as he glared at me. I frowned despite the amusement I was feeling inside.

"I'm not a tattle tale. That's your Dad's talent or your Uncle Liam's," I shot back.

"Hmm, maybe, but either way, if you don't tell anyone, then I will tell you about your baby." I narrowed my eyes.

"Oh, you little brat. You know the gender, don't you?"

"Maybe," he replied haughtily. I frowned as he smirked arrogantly. "So it's your choice."

"Fine, I won't tell anyone about our conversation…"

"Good."

He gave me a once-over before walking back into the room. I smiled. Our little Alpha prince was back, and so was my best friend. Now, I just needed Chris back, so we could fuck until we dropped. *I swear, the moment I see my man, I'm not letting him rest.* My smile vanished and I frowned.

I had felt the pain through the bond. I knew he was injured, but he was alive. I was scared of losing him, but I wouldn't admit that. *I'll just scold him for being careless.* My annoying, sexy man...

I almost bumped into Uncle El as I entered the room.

"I'm going to go see Kiara," he said. I smiled and nodded.

"I'm sure she's okay. I'll come with you."

"Me too!" Raven added, then hesitated. "Will you be okay?" She asked Delsanra.

"Of course. Besides, I have Dante here to help if I need him," Delsanra said with a wink at the boy, who was acting so awkwardly that he was making it obvious that something was up. He shrugged, pretending to be unbothered, only making Delsanra more curious.

"I'm here, too," Claire said politely as she had just entered.

"Perfect then," I said as the three of us left the room.

"Can I come to see Mama, too?" Kataleya asked. Uncle El nodded and held his hand out to her.

"Of course you can. Come on."

ALEJANDRO

It was over... the aftermath was horrific, but we were done.

The Fuego De Ceniza wolves instantly seemed to change in colour, taking on hues of different colours. They were mostly of warm colours, but there were changes in them, the biggest being their eye colours and demeanours. From brutal killing machines, they suddenly became wary and alert as they backed away. Their eyes were full of emotions. Our own were tending to the injured and dead, passing around pants and shirts for those who needed them.

"Shift," I commanded coldly, tightening the drawstring on my baggy shorts that were a fucking mess with blood and dirt. They did, and I was fucking surprised that half were still on their feet.

Give them clothes, I commanded through the link.

"Return home. You're free from the curse of the Djinn. He no longer has any power over your Alpha's family," I said coldly. They exchanged looks before one of them stepped forward.

"We apologise for everything... please don't punish us."

"I already said you can go. Liam, bring the pup," I commanded.

He nodded, seemingly mind-linking someone before I heard footsteps and two Blood Moon warriors alongside a witch came, leading the young boy. He stared ahead blankly, and I crouched down before him. Instantly, several wolves from his pack tensed, and a few ran forward. I cast them one last cold glare before looking at the young boy.

"Do you want to come home with me?" I asked quietly, placing my hand on his shoulder.

"My home is in Puerto Rico," he said emotionlessly, not looking me in the eye.

"You can start a new life here. If you want, I would happily take you under my wing. Kiara and I can take care of you. When you're old enough, you can return to Puerto Rico and take your place as Alpha if you so wish. I can make sure you get to visit-"

"No, thank you. You have done enough," he cut in bitterly.

He looked around at the ground that was covered in blood and bodies. I knew no matter what I said, he wouldn't change his mind. I nodded and stood up, looking at the pack members.

"Before you leave, I need to make sure this pack takes care of him. Does he have family in Puerto Rico?" I asked, knowing that many of them had family they hadn't seen in ages. The werewolves split as an older man walked through the middle, his face solemn. In his smart suit, he didn't seem to fit in with the rest of us who were covered in injuries, blood, soot, and sweat. He held a cane in hand.

"I vouch that the young master will be safe. He does have family and a pack that loves him. We were just bound to the devil without a choice. We will forever be indebted to the Lycan King and his army for defeating this monster -"

"We are not indebted. Let's go home," Enrique cut in, his eyes full of anger as he looked at me. "Killing isn't the answer. The Queen Luna said kindness was the answer... but she was wrong, too..."

I frowned as he turned away and walked off through the group of his people, who parted, letting him through and bowing their heads to their future Alpha.

Violence wasn't the answer...

No matter how much we did, there was so much more that needed to change...

The man bowed, passing me his card.

"We will keep in touch so you can rest assured the young master will be safe. Don't take his words to heart, he is just hurting."

"And you don't seem to care that I killed your Alpha," I remarked coldly, taking a bottle of water from a warrior who was offering it to me and gulping it down. Fuck, I was thirsty.

"He was far too gone to save, but I have never seen the young master as healthy as he was after being in your care. That in itself says more to me than anything you say verbally. Thank you for taking care of him and remembering that he is a child. I will look forward to your call."

"Yeah, I will call you soon. If the pup needs anything, I'm here. If you need assistance in returning to Puerto Rico, I am willing to help. I will also want to ask a few questions regarding everything that happened and to the extent of what your people know," I said. I would ask them if they knew about Dante's truth, and if they did, I wanted it kept hidden. "As for the pup, even if it's from the shadows, I plan to help in any way I can," I added quietly.

"Thank you, Alpha King."

"We'll discuss this more when I'm a little rested. You can go, I have your number. I will call," I said. My entire body was aching, but the moment that fucker died, I had a burst of energy that I had been deprived of, thanks to the fucking poison. He bowed his head before mind-linking his men something, and they all backed away, some carrying the dead and injured.

I turned back to my own people. Scarlett, already healed, was bent over Carmen's wolf. She touched Carmen's burnt wolf only for part of her body to crumble. She was burnt to a crisp, which meant we couldn't move her.

"Someone collect the ashes of those we are unable to move," I commanded, emotionlessly walking over to Carmen. I looked down at her, wondering if I ever told her that I did appreciate her and admired her skill? She was a good head warrior; brave, smart and skilled, but now was a tad too fucking late...

I turned away, searching for Maria. I spotted her standing to the side, her long black hair billowing around her, her arms wrapped around her slim frame. Rayhan was trying to talk to her, but she was refusing to listen to him.

"…tell me, not even once?" Rayhan was asking her.

"Not now, ya hayati," she replied. Her voice was bleak, and it fucking killed me. As happy as I was that she was here, hearing her sound so defeated sucked.

"Rayhan, can you call home and make sure everyone's okay?" I asked. He looked at me, hesitating for a moment, but I knew, for his mate, he would agree. Sure enough, he nodded, glancing between Maria and me before running off.

"Was this your plan?" She asked, hurt clear in her eyes as she looked at me accusingly. I sighed.

"No, it fucking wasn't. I don't even know who the fuck that guy was or how the fuck Leo and Rayhan were working together," I said, placing my hands on her shoulders. She didn't respond, staring at the ground, her body tense. "Maria…"

She refused to look at me, her chest heaving as she tried to control her emotions. I sighed, pulling her into my arms and hugging her forcefully. She may have been strong as she tried to pull away, but I was fucking stronger.

"I'm sorry… I know you were looking forward to seeing him, but it wasn't meant to be. Maybe Raf didn't want you to do this," I said quietly, not sure how to explain what had happened.

"I said goodbye… I was ready to meet him, I was so close and then… that chance was pulled away from me," she whispered.

"I know… and call me fucking selfish, but I'm glad you're still here. We all still need you, Mari." She didn't respond, but her body relaxed a bit as I rubbed her back. "You really need to fucking eat," I remarked. "I can feel your bones." She pulled away, giving me a scathing glare.

"I'm perfectly fine as I am."

"He doesn't know any boundaries," Scarlett added, making me smirk arrogantly. "Or how to not speak every damn thing that crosses his mind."

"Still holding a grudge about that comment I made earlier?" I taunted. "Who would have thought we'd have that in common?" Her eyes flashed.

She sure wasn't Elijah, and if Liam didn't step in, I was sure she would have lunged at me.

"Mom, relax. What's wrong?"

"Nothing," she growled as I smirked tauntingly back at her.

Westwood women… I swear, I wouldn't ever admit it out loud, but Kiara was definitely more like Elijah. As for the little crackpot, she was like her mother. It seemed like Liam was the common peacemaker.

My smirk faded away as I looked at Leo, who was smoking a cigarette, just as Rayhan returned, a smile on his face.

"They're all okay, all of them," he said, relief clear in his voice.

"Thank the goddess," Maria murmured, a hand on her heart.

I knew they would be, and I felt even more relaxed knowing my nympho and family were fine. Things were finally going to be okay. Crossing my arms, I turned and looked at my two nephews.

"Do you two fuckers want to explain what the fuck that was that you guys pulled?" I asked coldly.

"Yeah, I want to know, too," Marcel added, frowning coldly.

Leo shrugged. In nothing but his sweatpants, I could see he already had a vast number of tattoos, a lot more than I'd had at eighteen.

"You might want to ask your own fucker first," he replied coldly.

"Dante?"

"Yeah, unless you got another?" Leo shot back cockily.

"He knew what he was doing, obviously. No one died," Rayhan said seriously and quietly, looking back at his mom, sadness and an apology clear in his eyes. "He said it's not your time. I'm sorry."

Silence ensued. One thing was fucking clear; if Dante had said it… it fucking meant something. For him to know what was to happen, and the fact that he knew we'd get help, was fucking intense. The level of his power was worrying. I needed to make sure he was safe until he was ready to protect himself. The fact that he was put on earth meant there was a purpose, and I would be lying to say that didn't fucking worry me.

There's an old saying that the gods test those they love most. If that was the fucking case, I sure didn't want to be loved by them. *What are you planning, Selene? What more do you have in store for us?* Because something told me it wasn't fucking over.

When the time comes, we'll handle it like we always have. For now, we will celebrate our victory and mourn our losses. For every child who had lost a family member tonight, I would make sure their future was funded by myself.

I scanned the area, assessing what was left to do. There wasn't much left. I went over to where a few other pack Alphas were to thank them and let them know that, like always, I wouldn't forget their help. Once I was done, I turned back to my family.

"Let's head home," I said loudly and clearly, before looking up at the sky for a final time.

We had fucking done it. The Djinn was gone, and our family was safe once again.

Moments to Cherish

KIARA

MY MIND FELT FREE despite the sheer weight of everything that had happened. Everything I had forgotten returned to me, new memories and old. I would cherish them all.

Meeting the kids, Delsanra, and, of course, everyone else with my memories back was special. I truly felt like I had missed them. Although they were around, with my memory back, it just felt so much better. I was relieved that Alejandro had managed to convince me because if I had not trusted him or pushed the kids away, I would never have forgiven myself.

Dante, Delsanra, and I had all just showered and gotten dressed, whilst Raven had gone to get us something to eat. We heard that everyone was on their way back, and although the kids were ready for bed, no one was sleepy. The excitement and relief of the battle being won had pumped everyone's adrenaline.

Dad had just said he wanted to have a word with me. I wondered if everything was okay. Eating quickly, I left the room with him, allowing him to lead the way into one of the less-used living rooms.

"Is everything okay?" I asked the moment we were in a room alone. He gave me one of his half-smile, half-smirks before cupping my face and kissing my forehead.

"It is. Everything is," he said quietly before hugging me tightly. "I'm just glad you're alright." I smiled softly, wrapping my arms around his waist.

"I love you, Dad."

"Love you, too, cutie patootie," he said quietly, making my heart thump as I pulled back, unable to stop the huge smile that crossed my face at the mention of my old nickname.

"You haven't called me that since I was a child," I said, trying not to get teary.

"No matter how old you get, you're still my little angel." My eyes filled with tears, and I hugged him again.

"You're right. I always will be, just as you will always be my dad. My first protector," I whispered. He stroked my damp hair.

"Always," he promised softly.

We stayed silent for a moment before I slowly moved back from the warmth of his embrace.

"As much as I loved a trip down memory lane, I'm sure there was something more you wanted to talk to me about, right?" I asked, trying not to worry. He nodded.

"There was, actually. Ready to hear it?" I nodded as he gave me a smile, cupping my face.

"You're pregnant." I stared into his cerulean eyes, letting his words sink in.

"I… what… How?" I placed a hand to my forehead, shocked at the news. This was as unplanned as Dante had been.

"Three kids later, I'm sure you know exactly how," Dad remarked, crossing his arms. I blushed before placing a hand on my stomach, my heart beating as a new wave of emotions rushed through me. Excitement, nervousness, and happiness.

"Are you sure I am?" I whispered.

"The doctor did a scan to confirm it, too. It's still early, though." Dad explained, going on to quickly fill me in on how the Djinn was still able to struggle against my sedated state. He had been drawing on my baby's energy. Just the thought of that made a flash of worry for my child rush through me. Thank the goddess he was gone.

"And Alejandro doesn't know, does he?" I asked softly.

"No, he doesn't. We only found out today. Only the doctor, Serena, Raven, myself, and a few guards who have been given orders not to speak of it know," Dad replied. My heart skipped a beat, and I blushed, remembering how much sex we'd had. Not that we always didn't, but…

I bit my lip, pressing my hand gently on my stomach.

"I can't wait to tell him. He likes me pregnant…" I trailed off, blushing when Dad raised an eyebrow with an amused smirk on his face.

"I'm glad he takes care of you. Back then, I never expected him to be your mate, and when he proved he cared for you, I was content. I didn't think there was anything that would make me approve even more of him. Yet with every passing year, he has shown he is the ideal mate, father, Alpha, and king. My girl deserved the best, and she got it." I smiled, my heart warming at his words.

"I couldn't agree more… he may not be perfect to others, but he's perfect for me." Dad gave a small nod, and I smiled. He may not admit it, but he and Alejandro also had a good bond.

"They're back! They're back! They're here!" I heard Azura's shout, my heart pounding at the return of my king.

"Fuck, thank god," Dad breathed a sigh of relief, and I knew he was as impatient as I was to meet Mom.

He opened the door, letting me step out first. I smoothed the black top I was wearing with black sweatpants, my heart thudding with nerves as if it was the first time I was seeing him. Azura was the first one out the door, running out into the night in her sky-blue pyjamas.

The mansion gardens were lit brightly, something especially in place for me, just like the rest of the pack.

"Mama!" She shouted, jumping up into Mom's arms.

"Baby!" Mom replied, hugging her tightly. I smiled at them, my eyes searching for my king.

"Del?" Rayhan whispered, looking past me, and I realised Delsanra had stepped outside.

She ran past me and straight into his awaiting arms. He lifted her up, spinning her around before kissing her like there was no tomorrow. A perfect couple, one who had been put through so much… *Thank you, Selene, for uniting them once again.* She was crying softly as he stroked her hair, whispering sweet words into her ear and promises that I knew he would always keep.

Dad walked over to Mom, hugging her tightly before he kissed her hard, but I was somehow rooted to my spot. The quintuplets came running out to Liam, and he crouched down as he gathered them all up in his arms, kissing them. Raven paused, giving me a hug, before she ran to Liam.

And that's when I saw him. He towered over the rest as he came into view. He was in a clean pair of grey sweatpants, his god-like body on full display, igniting that pleasure that only he could deep within me. His dark eyes flashed red, glowing as they locked with mine before he walked through the crowd swiftly, and then he was before me. His sexy dark eyes held a thousand emotions. He threaded one hand into my hair, the other cupping my neck and face, making a flurry of sparks course through me. My heart was pounding, and my eyes were fixed on my king.

"I fucking missed you, Amore Mio…"

"I missed you, too, my king," I whispered, cupping his face. I pulled him down, locking my arms around his neck.

His lips met mine in a powerful hungry kiss, one arm snaking around my waist and the other supporting the back of my head as he kissed me so deeply I felt giddy. Sparks, emotions, and pleasure created the perfect magic that only Alejandro could inflict me with. The taste of his mouth… his scent… it was heaven on earth for me. He was my everything. I hugged him tightly as he slipped his tongue into my mouth, and my eyes fluttered shut. I bit back my moan, simply sighing in pleasure. I could feel every inch of his body against mine, every ridge, every muscle…

My Alejandro.

My mate.

My king.

My all.

We broke apart when I gasped for air, and he forced himself back, both of us very aware of the semi-hard-on he was sporting. My eyes dipped down, and I smiled seductively. I loved him in grey sweatpants, and right then…. Goddess…

"Do you remember everything again?" He asked me, concern clear in those eyes as he took hold of my chin and rubbed his thumb along my lips. I flicked it with my tongue, making his eyes flash.

Keep at it, and I will fuck you right here, he warned me through the link. I smiled slightly at the thought, and it made my core knot before I looked up into his eyes again.

"I do. Everything… when you saved my life outside the cinema, the time in the doctor's office… the first time you told me you loved me… when you asked me to marry you…" My heart was thumping. I knew right then everyone was around… but I wanted to tell him. "The time you asked me if I wanted to be a mama? Remember?" He smirked cockily, despite the relief I saw in his eyes.

"Yeah, I fucking do."

"Well, then... tell me, my sexy beast, what do you think of pups?" I asked, trying to hide my smile as I blinked up at him innocently.

He glanced sideways at where Skyla and Kataleya were standing with Mom and Dad. Rayhan had his arm around Dante's shoulders, although most eyes were on us. Ahren, Sienna... Tatum, all were present as Maria hugged and kissed them.

"Pups... yeah, they are weird as fuck, but they're not bad," he said, making me smile.

"Hmm... so... want to be a papa again?" He looked surprised. Something that was pretty rare for Alejandro. I heard Leo scoff,

"A dad at that age? Is his dick still even functioning?"

Okay, so everyone's attention was on us. Alejandro glared at him as Azura looked between us suspiciously.

"Trust me. It works way better than yours ever will."

"Boys! There are children here," Maria scolded.

"And this is why you're needed," Marcel remarked. Maria smiled sadly and gave a small nod, looking down at Sienna in her arms. A few of the others laughed, and I could feel Dad's, Raven's, and Serena's eyes on me. Alejandro looked back at me, raising an eyebrow.

"Didn't you say we were done? Even though you know I like you pregnant," he said, winking at me suggestively.

"Good, because I am pregnant," I said, once again surprising him.

"What?" Dante asked, shocked. I looked between him and his father as a few gasps filled the air, and then silence filled the garden. Okay, no one was expecting that.

"Oh, Goddess, not another Rossi," Azura exclaimed dramatically, placing the back of her hand against her forehead before she fell flat on her back, pretending to faint.

"A baby, Mama?" Kataleya asked, her eyes sparkling.

"Yes, my angel. A little sister or brother." I held my hand out to her, and she came over, hugging me tightly. She placed her hand on my stomach.

"Azura! I got a minion, too! Another one! Now I have Ahren, Sienna, Tatum, and two more babies! I have five, too," Skyla said victoriously. Azura sat up, frowning.

"Oh, yeah…" She wasn't pleased.

"Fuck…" Alejandro said as if it had just sunk in, making me look away from the children and up at him. "You seem okay with it…"

"Of course I am. Even if it wasn't planned."

"Then I'm fucking happy," he said. Bending down, he kissed me again, placing his hand on my stomach. His eyes met mine before he nudged my nose with his, making me smile. He kissed me softly before lifting Kataleya into his arms and placing his other arm around me.

I guess we got a little carried away and didn't think of contraception, huh? He added, through the link.

A little? I think that's an understatement.

Well, at least I get to see my nympho all hot and pregnant again.

You have a kink.

I won't fucking deny it. There's just something different about fucking you when you're pregnant.

I blushed as he smirked, knowing he had won that conversation. Everyone, aside from Leo, came over to congratulate us. I hugged Mom and Maria. I was glad everyone had gotten home safe and sound.

❧☙

It was past midnight, but it was obvious no one wanted to sleep. It was nice to see Leo and Rayhan both in the lounge at the same time, although Leo was in the corner on his phone whilst Rayhan was with Del and his kids. Dante had just come over, staring at my stomach, deep in thought.

"What's up, Dante?" I asked him, wrapping my arm around my brave little boy.

"I never saw it… I always know…" he murmured. I frowned, a sliver of fear rushing through me. Did it mean it wouldn't last or something?

"You don't see your sibling in the future?" I asked, trying to sound normal. He smiled slightly.

"I do now, a little… but I think he was blocking me from knowing…" He frowned, and for a second, he looked angry.

"Maybe, but he's gone now," I said, knowing what he meant. That made him smile confidently.

"He is. He didn't even get to return to hell," he said proudly. Our eyes met, and I planted a kiss on his forehead.

"I am proud of you," I whispered.

He had so much on his shoulders despite how young he was. It hurt at times knowing the burdens he carried. Who knows the extent of what he had to carry yet couldn't share with anyone?

"I'm proud of you, too," he said, making me smile.

"Are you sure you're not in pain?" Azura was asking Leo. "Like, sure sure?" I turned, wondering what that was about, as Raven smiled.

"She made a voodoo doll of him. It's currently in the kitchen, soaking in vinegar and chillies," she whispered as Leo raised an eyebrow, frowning at her.

"No, I'm not. Why the hell do you keep asking me that?" Leo growled.

"Azura, stop annoying him. Come here," Mom said.

"Gosh! It's his time of the month," Azura said, rolling her eyes as she turned away from him.

"What?" Leo growled.

"Liam says Raven is always angry when it's her time of the -" Liam was by Azura's side, clamping a hand on her mouth.

"Why not let her finish that sentence, baby?" Raven suggested sweetly. Her eyes flashed dangerously, making a few of the men in the room snicker.

"Nah, I think she's done," Liam replied, looking down at Azura, who was glaring daggers at him, whilst Leo smirked at Liam's expense.

"You really are unlucky," Rayhan remarked, looking at Liam. Just then, Claire and Clara entered with trays of hot and cold drinks.

"Thank you," I said, smiling. "Come join us. You both have done so much. Thank you." The rest agreed with me, and Mom, Maria, and Raven also thanked them.

"Oh… thank you," Claire said, not refusing me as she took a seat to the side near the children. They were a part of our family and had always been there for us.

I smiled, looking around. Alejandro had his hand on my thigh whilst playing with the younger boys. Kataleya was sitting, hugging her teddy near my feet and smiling happily. She had asked Alejandro about Enrique, and he had told her he was with people who loved him and that he'd be keeping an eye on him, too. Sienna and Tatum had fallen asleep. Serena and Darien were cuddled together, Mom and Dad… Delsanra and Rayhan.

Raihana had her head in Maria's lap with her legs in Chris' lap. Marcel was sitting on the sofa next to Raven as Liam sat back down, hugging her tightly and mind-linking her something which made her blush. Skyla had gone to get something but still wasn't back.

I felt relieved, though. We could relax once more. Everything was okay again. Yes, we had lost some, and that was something that would remain with us and the families of those who had lost their loved ones, but we would try to be there for them the best we could. I was still grateful for everything we had.

"Tada!" Skyla said. We all turned to look at her, and my heart almost skipped a beat. In her arms, she was holding what looked like an alien.

"The fuck..." Alejandro muttered.

It took me a few seconds to realise it was a cat, one that had been shaved, put in a dress, and was wearing a black wig with two plaits. It looked scary.

"This is my minion. Every villain had a minion," she stated.

"That's scary," Liam stated, earning a frown from her.

"Don't judge things and people by their looks, Uncle," she scolded.

"Yeah, Liam," Azura said, truly fascinated by Skyla's horrifying creation.

"Do you guys like it?" Skyla asked, her green eyes glinting.

"Um..." Mom started as Delsanra simply blinked at the cat that had jumped from Skyla's arm and meowed, running to the window. If that wasn't a sign of its trauma, I didn't know what else we needed.

"My question is, how did you remove the hair?" Raven asked. You could tell she had missed spots.

"With an electric shaver," Skyla replied, making Alejandro sigh.

That's some weird shit, he said through the link, massaging his jaw.

"And my question is, where did that cat come from?" I asked, looking around. Was it new?

"I think it belongs to Drake's son," Serena added, making me frown.

"Skyla, did you steal it?"

"No, I just took it," she said, looking guilty.

I raised an eyebrow but decided I would talk to her alone. She would be taking the cat back to its rightful owner, and if they didn't want it anymore, thanks to her horrific transformation, I would make sure it was given to a new home. I thought she had been given a little too much freedom with everything going on, and it was high time I got back into Mom mode and held her accountable for her actions.

"We'll discuss this tomorrow," I said firmly with a small smile. She gulped and nodded, exchanging looks with Azura.

"Oh, dear... it seems like another Rossi's in trouble. What else is new? " Azura remarked, making Leo snicker.

"That kid's on crack."

"Yet you find her amusing," Marcel replied, frowning at him.

"She's entertaining," he replied, shrugging, his eyes fixed on his phone.

"Crazy fuckers all around. So, who's tired?" Alejandro asked, picking up a mug of hot chocolate.

"No one," Azura replied.

"Oh, yeah? Rayhan, tired?"

"No, not really. Why?" He replied, clearly wondering why Alejandro was asking.

"Good, then how about I have a word with you and Leo now," he said, standing up. The room went considerably quieter, and I heard Leo sigh in frustration.

"Really?"

"Yeah, because I know you won't be here in the morning," Alejandro replied, looking at him.

"Fine." He stood up, frowning coldly, his aura radiating off of him.

"Someone's in trouble," Azura sang tauntingly. Leo glared at her before turning his eyes to Dante.

"Now I fucking know why you swore on her. She's fucking psycho," he muttered.

"Leo," Marcel growled in warning. But the youngster simply gave his father the finger before disappearing from the room.

Mom frowned but said nothing as she pulled Azura into her arms, kissing her cheek and smiling at her. No matter how tough Mom acted, I knew she worried about Azura. We all heard that she acted the way she did because she was born by magic. Even though that wasn't true, it was what many thought. I knew it affected Mom, and why wouldn't it? It affected us all. Azura was a child, and it hurt to know she would face a lot of challenges growing up. I just wished people would change their mentality before then.

Rayhan kissed Delsanra, clearly not wanting to leave her, and I didn't blame him. They had suffered the most in many ways.

"Let's get this over with then," he said, running his hand through his hair as he looked at Alejandro.

Alejandro nodded, looking down at me, and I stood up. He wrapped his hand around my neck, kissing me and leaving my lips tingling before he, too, left the room. I knew what they were going to talk about, and I just hoped it went well.

"That one was a long time coming," Dad said, and Marcel nodded in agreement.

"Yeah, they needed to do this."

"I'm still impressed that they worked together," Mom added with a smile.

Dante smirked slightly, and I glanced down at him. I had heard what happened, but he hadn't said much more than what we already knew. My little hero may not have been on the battlefield, but he had still contributed.

Good luck, my king, I told Alejandro through the bond.

Thanks, I might just fucking need it. I smiled at his response, knowing if anyone could get through to the boys, it was Alejandro.

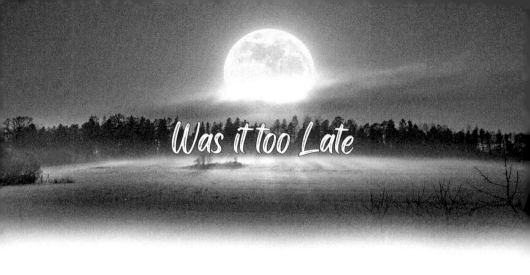

Was it too Late

ALEJANDRO

I SHUT THE DOOR TO my office behind me. Leo was already sitting in one of the chairs, his long legs sprawled out in front of him, hands in his pockets, and his face set in a cold frown. Rayhan walked over to the window, leaned against the wall, and crossed his arms.

As much as I didn't want to do this right after that hell of a battle, knowing there were families who were mourning their losses… knowing that I had a shitload to do in the morning and so much fucking more, I also couldn't let this chance slip away. I knew Leo would be gone before morning came; I knew him enough to know that. The fact that he and Rayhan worked together gave me some hope and that he had stayed in the same place as Rayhan without causing issues for a few hours.

"I ain't got all night," Leo said as I dropped into my office chair. Damn, my body was fucking exhausted.

"Yeah well, I'll get to it. You both know why I've called you here. I want you both to say exactly what you feel, but I want you both to listen whilst the other talks, alright? No fucking interrupting," I commanded, my Alpha command weighing down on them. I saw Leo's eyes flash with irritation.

"Fine," Rayhan said quietly.

"I'm not forcing you to agree. Just give each other a chance," I added quietly, knowing Leo hated any form of command.

I sat back, taking out a cigarette from a packet. I was about to put the box away when, instead, I offered it to my younger nephew. After a moment's hesitation, he took one, and I lit his before lighting my own.

"Want one?" I asked Rayhan, who simply raised an eyebrow.

"No thanks," he said before opening the window next to him. Leo scoffed as he sat back, and I ran my hand through my hair. *Well, here goes...*

"We all know what Delsanra went through at the hands of Endora. I've had this conversation with you, Leo. Do you want me to go over it?"

"Nah, I know. I was there, remember? I witnessed all the shit that went on there," he said coldly, his eyes becoming ice. I frowned and nodded.

"Very well. So you know that she was beaten to within an inch of her life on a daily basis, made to do Endora's biddings, and, if she refused, she was simply beaten further?" I asked quietly.

There were the fucking hunters who had done worse to Delsanra, but Rayhan had hunted and killed them all. We had lost Raf because of that fight. There were also corrupt witches who had helped the hunters... I knew Rayhan hated the hunters with even more vengeance than he had the Sangue Pack, but he had killed all those involved. I sighed heavily.

"There were many who hurt her willingly, many who were commanded to hurt her, blackmailed, or out of fear of being beaten themselves, for survival... and those who were brave enough to refuse were then compelled under magic to hurt her. These rogues were all gathered by Endora, and she built her army by fear and control." I looked between both of them. Both were quiet. "Rayhan did what he felt was right. Seeing what his mate had gone through would fucking affect anyone; we would destroy the world for our mates. The need to protect them is so fucking intense that, until you have a mate, you won't understand that. I'm not saying that it was completely right; I'm just saying when your mate is hurt, you don't see anything but to make it better," I said quietly.

I could feel Leo's anger rising, but he didn't speak, although I knew even with my command he could if he wanted.

"Rayhan, do you want to put your points forward? Do you want to tell Leo exactly what happened when you went to the Sangue pack long ago?" He gave a curt nod before slipping his hands into his pockets.

"I first took the files from you after promising that I wouldn't show them to anyone. You were reluctant to give them to me. I then asked Delsanra which ones had hurt her. She pointed out those that she remembered, and then we went to the Sangue Pack. I had told Marcel which men it was, and so they were already gathered." He sighed, turning to look out at the moon. The pain in his eyes was clear. No matter how much fucking time passed, it was obvious it didn't go away entirely. I glanced at Leo, who was smoking away indifferently, tapping his foot silently as if bored. "Delsanra told me that there were those who had been forced to hurt her and not to do this."

"But you didn't listen," Leo said. Rayhan frowned.

"They couldn't just get away with it. I first separated those who were forced and had felt guilt to step forward, deciding they would get one beating and be let off. I only beat a few of them because Delsanra pleaded with me to let them go, and I did." As I had thought and heard, but still, Leo didn't seem to look surprised, almost as if he knew that. I frowned as Rayhan sighed, "I let them go. That group felt remorse and had been under spells. There was an older man who even talked about some she-wolf who hung with Delsanra when she was mid-mutating to a wendigo or something," he continued. "Then, I sent Delsanra with Liam. After that, the group who were compelled and felt no remorse were -"

"Beaten and bound in silver for a month," Leo cut in.

"Yeah. And the rest who hurt her willingly, I killed." Leo smirked and nodded.

"Yeah…. Anything else?" He asked. Rayhan frowned but looked down.

"Maybe I was too harsh, but there were guards in your pack who had hurt her, too. Those in the upper ranks of the Sangue pack. Should people like that be given a second chance? Rogues are exiled wolves; either they committed crimes or weren't worthy of staying in a pack because of disobedience to begin with. Having ranked wolves who had committed that many crimes? That isn't something that should ever be allowed. "

"And then there are those who were born rogues. Does a child need to suffer for their parent's sins?" Leo asked, sitting forward as he turned and looked at Rayhan. "The thing is, this is the last time I'm going to talk about this because it's obvious you both will never fucking get it. Dad was born a rogue. He knew nothing but what Endora had taught him. Most of those men were born to rogues that Endora gathered. That's the only life we knew. Obey or be killed. Survival – it's the basic instinct all living things have." He licked his lips, exhaling sharply as he stood up. "You mentioning where we came from, that was the fucking last straw, and it shows that you'll never get it. We will always be beneath the elite: you folk." He raised his hands in a mock surrendering gesture.

"Leo -" I began when he shook his head.

"I'm not fucking done," he said quietly, his eyes flashing. There was something different in the way he was talking, and deep down, I worried that if I didn't get through to him tonight, my chance would be gone. I nodded, motioning for him to carry on.

"You know those men that you killed? The ones that hurt her willingly? Do you know they were told to beat a witch, which, if you forget, was the common enemy for us werewolves? Or did you all forget that little detail when you changed your opinion the moment a Rossi had a witch mate and a witch daughter? When it affected the Lycan King's family, of course, he was going to suddenly change sides or consider acceptance." I frowned, as did Rayhan, my stomach twisting. He had a fucking point.

"But that's because we saw the good in them. Del and Ri showed us that not all witches were bad. We were wrong to judge them all as one," I said quietly. He nodded.

"Yeah… but how do you explain that to a man whose own mate was threatened to be killed off if he didn't beat a witch? A monster as we were taught? Obviously, he'll choose to attack a monster who was helping Endora, who was a fucking psychotic bitch."

"And that is why the rogues were given a chance at a fresh start because I don't agree with Rayhan there. They deserved a chance at a new life -" I began.

"Sure, but you took that promise right fucking back when you gave him access to those files! You gave us so much fucking hope that me and the other kids were so fucking excited to live a life like we heard others had. We'd get to go to school, train, watch movies, listen to music, have proper homes, and have fucking fun like normal kids, but everything was taken away the moment you let another Alpha walk into our pack and force our Alpha to submit." The pain in his voice was thick, yet his tone remained hard and angry as he glared at me. His eyes held a haunted look that I had seen on the faces of many back in those caves…

"Leo -"

"I'm not done… Dad never mentioned it, but years after the effect of that massacre, and what Rayhan did was a fucking massacre, it haunted us. When you killed all those men, you killed their mates. You made so many children orphans. Dad is at fault, you are at fault, and, above all, Rayhan is at fault. I don't care about the reasons, the way that was handled was wrong. I watched those killings, those beatings through a fucking vent. I watched how Dad sat in an adjoining room, head in his hands, as his pack members were beaten! You did it all for your mate, yet you took away the mates of many!" Leo continued, his eyes going from me to Rayhan, blazing a steely blue. I could tell it was hard for him to talk about it, and I got it... I had fucked up.

"And you know, from those who were compelled, who had been brave enough to refuse to beat her? Let me give you an example, you know one of them: he had refused to beat her, and Endora ended up killing his daughter. His mate also struggled to carry a fucking pup due to being beaten because he tried to do the right fucking thing. So, when you asked him if he felt remorse, why would he? She was just a witch to him. He was still mourning the loss of his daughter! What did you want him to say? Yeah, I fucking felt bad? And to top it off, his mate, who had suffered beatings, was pregnant when you showed up, was classed as high risk, and she almost died when he was bound in silver for a fucking month by you. You hurt a pregnant woman, almost killed their miracle child." Rayhan was looking down, and I saw the guilt in his eyes.

"Dad could do fucking nothing because he's a fucking coward, one who had just found his family and feared losing you all, but if he was half the fucking man he should have been... he should have protected his pack. Not appeased his so-called family because his real family was meant to be his pack. Blood does not make you family." Leo shook his head and smirked coldly. "And that's why I will never consider you all my real family, because my fucking duty is to my pack, to make sure no one ever abuses them the way you all did. Yeah, you, too, Alpha King Alejandro. You created fucking files on us like we were fucking criminals! Given a chance, sure, that's what it was... but we had thought we were given the chance to a fresh start. Fresh start, yet criminal files? Doesn't fucking sound like a clean, fresh fucking start to me."

"That was for the safety of all packs, Leo," I said quietly.

"Oh yeah? Then tell me, did you have a file on me and Dad?"

I frowned. No. I knew where he was going with this, and I knew he was fucking making fair points.

"No? Surely the rogue king had an entire fucking list of crimes on his back. He should have been on the records. Shit, I forgot, he's a Rossi. You get an entire fucking pass, right? Let's be honest, it's the only reason I can behave like a dick, and none of you does shit, right?" His words were bitter and full of resentfulness.

"I get it. I made a mistake… I didn't think it through. I'm sorry, Leo. I'll admit to it. If I can make up for it, then tell me what you want," Rayhan said quietly, to my surprise, and he meant it. I could see it in his eyes. But even before Leo replied, I realised it wasn't going to be enough. It was too late, and Leo's hatred wasn't going to go away…

"You're sorry… your sorry won't bring back all those lives you destroyed. The Sangue Pack has so many people who suffer from PTSD due to everything we witnessed and suffered, but the mate of an elite was far more important than all those other lives, right? Well, carry on. No fucking sorry, no fucking regret will bring that back, and what fucking gets to me the most is that you all are so far up your own asses that you needed me to fucking lay it out to you, years later, for you to even consider that you lot fucked up?" He tossed the cigarette he had crushed in his hand onto the ashtray, looking at us both with unmasked hatred.

"You're right, and I'll work on this. I'll try to fix things. I get that we -" I tried again.

"It's too late… six fucking years too late. We're doing okay without your help, thanks," he replied coldly, "but I promise you here and now, the moment I become Alpha, the Sangue Pack will not be under this council. Oh, and don't try to treat me like your family, because I don't consider you mine. Touch my pack… and I will fucking destroy you all."

Not waiting for a reply, he turned and walked out.

"Leo! Listen!" I stopped the moment the front door opened. He pulled his jacket off, shifted, picked up his jacket in his mouth and ran off into the night. Rayhan sighed.

"I messed up. I didn't think of it like that… even Delsanra wasn't happy with what happened."

"It's not only your fault. You were, what? Twenty-one? I should have thought… Marcel didn't say anything either… it had been two years didn't he think he could speak up?" I said quietly.

"I'm sorry. I felt it was atonement for the crimes I had committed under her control," Marcel said quietly. "This is on me, too; I wasn't a good Alpha or father."

"Marcel, this has happened now, but when Raf and I fucking accepted you, it meant we accepted you, not for you to just try to keep us happy. None of us is fucking perfect, but that's how shit is. We talk, we discuss, we advise, and we fucking disagree," I said. He nodded, and for a moment, he looked older and tired.

"I know... with time, I realised that..."

"Then promise me from here on that you'll fucking use that brain and speak your damn mind," I said.

He gave me a small smile and nodded, but the mood was heavy as we all stared at the open door. I didn't say anything. Right then, I felt like I had fucking failed. Leo had been suffering more than he let on. You could tell he cared for his pack, for those that had suffered, to the point that he used to defy Endora's commands and sneak Delsanra food. He had a heart that cared, yet he felt inferior...

His remark about leaving the council remained, and I wondered if he truly would follow up on it...

A Summer Day

KIARA

*I*T HAD BEEN A week since the day I got my memories back. Everyone had gone home, and we spent the last few days busy with burials, supporting families who had lost loved ones, and making sure everything was in order once again. Although Alejandro wanted me to rest, I refused. I had just gotten my memory back and I had been enough trouble for everyone, so I just wanted to do what I could. Besides, I was completely fine. The pregnancy was going well so far, and I couldn't even tell I was pregnant. I felt great.

I made Skyla return the kitty, and the poor boy had taken it, bursting into tears at the fact that she had shaved it. I decided she wouldn't be getting any money for the next three months from Alejandro, something he thought I was being really harsh with because we both knew Skyla loved money a bit too much. But she needed to learn that taking things without permission was extremely wrong. It wasn't like she was lacking anything.

Kataleya was getting therapy from Delsanra, and we all agreed she had a long way to go before she would be healed. What happened was something that would stick with her for life.

Alejandro had contacted someone from the Fuego De Ceniza Pack, but the man had been adamant that they needed nothing and that they would take care of Enrique. Alejandro didn't back down, but they were adamant that they wanted nothing to do with us. We were both sure it was from Enrique himself, and if that was the case, it meant he didn't really have a guardian who could guide him. Alejandro decided he would send someone to Puerto Rico to keep an eye on him from the shadows, feeling it was his responsibility to look out for him.

When Leo had left, Alejandro had told me exactly what had happened. I knew Alejandro was disappointed in himself, but even I was at fault. I had been the one to encourage him to give Rayhan the files back then. We were all at fault, but even though Delsanra, Rayhan, and I had offered to apologise to the people of the Sangue Pack, Leo had refused to even hear from any of us. Marcel said Leo had decided to go abroad for further studies. He was worried, but it was obvious Leo needed to get away from us all and just have a break. Maybe it was what he needed.

Maria had a good cry before she left for home, and although she had wanted to go to Raf, it was obviously not her time. She said if this was a sign, she'd try to work hard and carry on. Alejandro had suggested she make herself busy with the pack, and so she had decided to take up the position of the Black Storm head warrior, something she had never ever considered until Al had suggested it, saying she was an incredible warrior and she truly was. I just hoped it kept her occupied, and I promised to call her more often, too. We would be there for her as a family should.

Alejandro and I were going out for lunch today. It was the first peaceful day after a crazy week. The kids were over at Drake's place since they had a kids' party going on, and it gave Alejandro and me a chance to get away.

The weather was warm, and I was wearing a white and pink floral chiffon high-low dress with a string criss-cross back. I was wearing beige heels and carrying a matching bag. I had dressed up after ages, but with everything going on, it wasn't the same. The moment Alejandro had seen me… even now as we walked through the pack grounds, his eyes were stuck on me. I smiled. I guessed getting my nails and hair done had been worth it. I loved how he looked at me like I was the only woman in the world. Knowing he was undressing me with his eyes…

He himself looked incredibly sexy and totally fuckable as usual, wearing a white shirt with his sleeves pushed up and some buttons left open that showed off his chains around his neck, paired with grey pants, shoes, and a pair of shades.

"So where exactly are we going?" I asked. He gave my hand, which was entwined with his, a gentle squeeze.

"You'll find out…" he said, not giving much away.

I leaned in, tilting my head up slightly, and he smirked as he bent down and kissed me deeply. Letting go of my hand, he pulled me tightly against himself, his hand tangling into my curls as he deepened the kiss. I moaned softly, my core throbbing, and when he squeezed my ass, I was unable to hold back the whimper that left my lips.

"Don't worry... today and tonight... you're all fucking mine."

"Willingly," I replied softly, licking my lips. He smirked,

"You always have been fucking willing to spread those legs for me, Amore Mio." I gasped, feinting a mock offended look.

"Oh? It's not like you never get hard for me, just like now..." I whispered seductively, slowly running my hand down his abs. Before I could even stroke his dick, we heard footsteps, and I smoothly stepped back. It was just a few of the pack's teens. I saw Alejandro frown for a fraction of a second before he schooled his face into passiveness once more.

"Afternoon Alpha, Luna," they greeted.

"Hey, boys." I smiled.

"You look beautiful," one of them complimented me before looking at Alejandro furtively.

"Yeah, move along," he growled, making me laugh.

They nodded, chuckling as they ran off. With time, the fear that they had of Alejandro changed. Yes, they feared and respected him. With the passing of years, I had seen how much Alejandro had changed, saw the growth in him and how he continued to strive to do better, to make things better for us all and admit to mistakes. My man was more than a king by name. He was so much more, and every day, he only made me prouder.

"What's on your mind?" I asked, sensing his emotions.

"The boy in the middle... he's... Fred's."

Fred's? It took me a moment before I realised what he had just said, what he meant. My heart thumped, and I looked towards the boys. I knew instantly which one he meant. Atlas... The boy with the dirty blond hair. How had I never noticed it?

I looked at Alejandro, seeing the conflicted look in his eyes.

"Why did you never mention it?" I asked quietly. He sighed; his eyes met mine before glancing around.

"Let's get out of here first."

I nodded as he placed an arm around my waist and led me away...

A short while later, we were down by the river. An entire picnic had been set up for us in the secluded area, with Al smirking as he stated there wouldn't be anyone within miles. It was obvious he had planned for us to do a lot more here than eat, not that I minded…

The sun was warming my skin, and the pleasant gushing of the river felt like a peaceful melody to my ears. We had just opened the picnic basket and were eating as I waited for Alejandro to tell me about Fred's son.

"I don't know why I never mentioned it, it's just… obviously you can tell by his age that he was born whilst Fred was mated to Indigo."

"Yeah, he's not even of age," I said quietly.

"Yeah, but he isn't at fault. I didn't want it to become known to the point of it affecting the pup in any way. The topic of Indigo was sensitive to your parents, and so it just never came up. Fred was a fucking player, and that's what I always thought was going on between them. I never fucking thought that he was actually fucking abusing her as well," he said seriously, drinking some of the cold juice. I nodded. I understood that, and he was right; the child was not at fault.

"I get it… but that means that Azura has a brother," I said softly.

"Yeah. I fucking guess so," he replied. Our eyes met, and I knew that it was something Mom and Dad had a right to know.

"You know we have to tell Mom and Dad. Even Azura has a right to know one day."

"Yeah, I know."

I looked at him, and although I was sitting just a foot away from him, it felt too far. I got up, climbed into his lap, and cupped his face, enjoying the sparks that shot through me.

"Don't blame yourself for what happened to Aunty Indy. It's a little like Raven. We never knew what she was going through. Sometimes we don't know what's happening behind closed doors or behind a smiling face. You have always done your best, Alejandro, and you always will. If you want, I can tell Mom and Dad myself," I said, trying not to react to the way he was running his hands up and down my waist.

"I'm not a fucking wuss, Amore Mio. We'll do that shit together when the time comes." I couldn't help but laugh at that.

"Okay, my sexy beast, as you wish." Our eyes met before I slowly placed a hand on my stomach, and he kissed my neck sensually. His scent made me giddy. "Can you believe we are going to be parents again?" I whispered, still feeling awed.

"To be honest, it's still fucking crazy, but I'm looking forward to it. What do you think the gender is?"

"I don't actually know. I asked Dante, and he simply said it doesn't work like that." I smiled. Alejandro's smirk faltered, and he nodded.

"The fact the Djinn was shielding it from him… from us…"

"Obviously, he knew that if we knew, we would have made sure I was taken care of, but he needed something to fight my body with."

"Using our pup to do it…" His eyes flashed, and I softly kissed him on his mate mark.

"He's gone now, completely. Even Janaina said the only reason he had such a strong hold on me was that I was pregnant. He was drawing strength from the foetus, and I was, in turn, healing the foetus, keeping the Djinn's hold strong," I sighed.

"Yeah, it's how his hold on you strengthened… once you got pregnant, he got an extra hold, one that didn't bind you to me. At least you're both fucking okay…" he said, brushing his hand down my stomach. His eyes softened. "Another little weirdo." I smiled.

"*Our* adorable little weirdo."

"One hundred-fucking percent."

Our eyes met, and we leaned in, our lips meeting in a passionate kiss. This was the contentment and happiness one needed in life, and although I knew the future would hold many more trials as our children grew, facing their own trials and tribulations, we would be there to handle it, to help and guide them. Dante was a demi-god, and that in itself blew my mind away, but even my own senses told me there was a reason for it…

When the time came, we were all here, ready to be by his side to deal with whatever came our way. Together forever. One for all, all for one. United, we would always be strong.

We broke away, eating a little more before Alejandro stood up and began to undress. I bit my lip, enjoying the view of the god before me, the sun shining down off his glorious body.

"Enjoying the show, Amore Mio?"

"Oh, absolutely… do I get a strip dance?" I teased.

"No. If anyone's dancing, it's you with your ass up in my face. Now strip."

I raised my eyebrows as he removed his pants, only keeping his boxers on, and I realised he was about to get into the river. He walked over to the edge and stepped into the water before turning and watching me. I pulled my dress off, tossing it aside sexily, making his eyes flash as he admired my naked breasts. I kicked off my heels before I broke into a run. A few feet from the riverbank, I did a flip, my eyes on Alejandro.

Three... two...

"I got you," Alejandro smirked the moment I landed with my legs on his shoulders. He gripped my ass as I raised my arms as if celebrating my victory.

"Damn, I'm still as agile as I was years ago," I said, tossing my hair over my shoulder.

"I think I should get the credit for that since I'm the one who keeps you so fucking flexible with the intense workouts," he remarked cockily. I raised an eyebrow, looking down at him as I twisted my hand into his hair, loving the way his eyes were on my breasts.

"Oh? Then how about we have another intense workout, Alpha?" I whispered seductively as I slid off his shoulders gracefully and let my legs drop into the water, pressing my bare breasts against him. He hissed in pleasure, his eyes flashing as I ran my hand down his boxers. "Looks like my favourite toy is all ready for me," I whispered, pushing his boxers down.

Biting my lip as I went down onto my knees, the water was to my neck, but I knew the moment I was level to his cock I'd be underwater. I didn't mind. There was just something so fucking hot about lacking oxygen and knowing I'd be at his mercy entirely...

"Always... now, how about you be a good little girl and start playing with your favourite toy," he growled huskily, his hand twisting into my hair. His words alone made me shiver in anticipation.

"With pleasure," I whispered seductively, running my hands along his thick, long cock. Then, I took a deep breath, plunging my head underwater.

I wrapped my lips around his deliciously hard cock, moaning as pleasure consumed me. There was just something so good about throating his dick, I just could never get enough. He was my addiction, one I craved day and night... and I was the only one who had power over my sexy Lycan King. The only one who was able to pleasure him like this and the only one he would ever submit to...

Just as he was my king, I was his queen.

Heat, Passion & Love

ALEJANDRO

THE MOMENT MY NYMPHO dipped into the water and took me in her mouth. Fuck, it was heaven.

Pleasure rushed through me, and I didn't hold back the groan that left my lips. Reaching into the water, I tangled my hand into her hair. The glittering surface of the water distorted her gorgeous figure. My fucking world.

I was fucking glad her memories were back, but above all, the fact that she was fucking safe and herself.

"Fuck," I hissed as she used both hands to pump my dick as she sucked on it, not leaving an inch of it unattended. My eyes flashed, the pressure building, and I began thrusting into her mouth faster. "That's it, Amore Mio," I murmured, knowing that her time underwater was limited. It only fucking added to the pleasure and excitement as I chased my release. I closed my eyes, letting the pleasure consume me and when I was at the edge, I hissed.

I'm coming, I growled through the link.

Come in my mouth, baby. I want to taste you, she replied, tipping me over the edge as I shot my load into her mouth.

Sparks and pleasure rocked my entire fucking body as I slammed my cock into her mouth with a few brutal thrusts, feeling my cock hit her throat as I buried myself to the hilt, sending another fucking wave of euphoria through me. For a few glorious moments, I saw fucking stars. She gagged, for a second, choking on my dick, which gave me a flash of satisfaction. The only thing that would make this moment better was if I could see her fucking clearly.

I tugged her back and up out of the water as she gasped for air. I wrapped my arms around her tightly, pulled her against my chest, and kissed her neck hungrily. I was breathing hard from the pleasure that was still tingling through me, and it gave her time to recover. Her breathing was heavy. Her heart was pounding, but when I looked into those gorgeous glowing purple eyes of hers, I only saw satisfaction, lust, love, and desire.

"You're fucking heaven and sin all in one," I growled huskily before kissing her lips roughly. She instantly locked her legs around my waist as we kissed like it was the first fucking time, but with her, it was. Every moment, every fucking touch, and every fucking kiss was something new and fucking intense.

I love you. I fucking love you, I said through the link, unable to hold back the intensity of my emotions. She broke away from my lips, hers looking plumper than normal.

"I love you, too, now and eternity," she whispered. Her husky, sexy voice sounded so fucking good.

She caressed my face, and her eyes softened before she leaned in, kissing me softly. Our hearts were pounding, and this time when I kissed her, it was slower, painstakingly slow, yet it felt so fucking good. Each caress, each nibble or suck on her plush lips, was fucking perfect. Our sensual kisses created moans from those heavenly lips of hers, and I wouldn't fucking deny that I didn't bother holding back my own fucking sounds of pleasure. Our tongues played with each other's, sucking, stroking, dancing to the same rhythm, one of fucking love and pleasure.

I ran my hand down her naked body, tugging at her thong. She whimpered, grinding her pussy against my abs, and as much as I was hard again wanting to fuck her, I intended to show her just what she meant to me.

I broke away from her lips, kissing her along her jaw and neck and sucking slightly harder yet softer than usual, keeping the beast within me from ravishing her right then. She sighed softly, running her fingers through my hair as I placed kisses over her tits.

"You know you're fucking perfect," I growled, taking one of her nipples in my mouth.

"Fuck!" She whimpered, and I knew they were probably already extra sensitive due to her pregnancy.

When she threw back her head, giving me the perfect fucking view of her tits with her stiff nipples, my self-control snapped. I kissed her hard, carrying her to the edge of the riverbank and placing her on the ground. The branches of a nearby tree hung over us slightly, casting some shade over her soaking body that glistened under the sun. She looked up at me with hooded eyes as I trailed my gaze over her body. The sexiest fucking woman on the fucking planet.

Pinning her wrists to the ground I began kissing her body, from her neck, down over her breasts as she writhed and moaned under me. The scent of her arousal overpowered every other thing around me.

"Oh, fuck, baby, that's it," she whimpered when I sucked on the narrowest part of her waist, leaving a mark. I quickly discarded my boxers, which had been half down until now.

She shivered under me, her back arching as she begged for more. I continued my descent downwards. Reaching her pussy, I ripped off her panties, admiring it. My cock throbbed as I went down on her, making her cry out. I grabbed her hips, flipping us over so my back hit the ground, and she was straddling my face as I lay down, ready to eat her out.

My favourite fucking place to eat.

"Al…" she moaned as I flicked her clit with my tongue, kissing her there. As much as she loved me playing with her clit, there was one thing she liked fucking more…

I slapped her ass, making her gasp as I partially shifted, letting my tongue grow and plunging it into her. She screamed out as I growled at the feel of her tight slick sides around my tongue. Fuck, did she taste heavenly.

"Oh, fuck…" she cried wantonly as she arched her back, placing one hand on the ground next to my waist.

I began tongue fucking her as she met my moves with her own, gyrating her hips against my face. Her pleasure was building, and her cries of pleasure got louder. I gripped her hips, slamming my tongue into her faster and curling it up towards that spot that got to her.

When the first of her screams filled the air, her juices trickled out of her faster. She grabbed onto my hair, groaning erotically with pleasure. It only took a few seconds more for her to come undone, allowing me to lap up her juices, but I wasn't done. As her body shivered and her heart pounded from her orgasm, I flipped her onto the ground so I was on top, running my tongue, which was back to normal, over her soaking pussy. I pushed her legs apart, flicking her clit. She whimpered as she struggled to move away, her lower region feeling more sensitive after her orgasm.

"Alejandro… stop," she moaned.

"Oh, Amore Mio, I'm only fucking starting," I growled, making her eyes flash purple with obvious lust. I smirked as I thrust two fingers into her, making her whimper, using my thumb to rub her clit. "Fuck…" she whimpered.

"I'm not fucking done," I growled, shoving a third finger into her.

She cried out in pleasure as I began fucking her with my fingers roughly. My eyes were fixed on her. Her cheeks were flushed, her wet hair falling in front of her face as she moaned in pleasure.

"Tell me, who do you belong to?" I asked quietly.

"You…" *Yeah, you fucking do.* "Ah!" She screamed the moment I shoved my index finger into her ass.

"Come on, Amore Mio… you've taken a lot more than that up your ass," I smirked arrogantly. My dick was fucking aching for more. She blushed, despite how her body was reacting.

"Fuck, baby, that feels so good…" she whimpered, squeezing her breasts as I kept going.

Her orgasm was nearing. I could feel her juices soaking my fingers. I bent down, kissing her lips roughly before I moved back, speeding up as I watched her body react to my assault on her. She screamed out as her orgasm reached a teetering point, her juices squirting out and spraying over her thighs and my stomach, but I didn't stop. Her release shot through her, and her walls tightened around me. Her entire body arched, eyes fluttering shut as she let out a fucking sexy groan of pure satisfaction. Only when she came down from her orgasm did I slip my fingers out, making her wince.

I climbed on top of her, claiming her lips in a passionate kiss despite the fact she was still struggling to get her breath back. My dick pressed against her stomach. She reached down, running her fingers over it before fondling my balls.

"Fuck me, my love," she whispered, kissing my neck.

I sighed, enjoying her touch before I moved back, positioning myself at her entrance. A wave of water hit our legs from the river behind us as I rammed into her roughly, making her moan loudly before I began fucking her. I lifted her legs onto my shoulders, letting her squeeze her pussy together even tighter. The sound of her moans was fucking music to my ears, and watching her tits bounce with every fucking thrust only made me never want to stop…

"Fuck, Amore Mio," I growled huskily, feeling her walls tighten around me as I did my fucking best to hold out. She nodded, her hand on my chest, her cheeks flushed, and a look of pure pleasure on her face.

"I… almost there… I'm coming…" she gasped.

The moment her orgasm rocked through her body, I let myself go, coating her insides with my seed. After a few rough thrusts, I pulled my cock from her. I let her legs down, and for a moment, I let my weight rest on top of her as we both got our breath back, burying my face in her neck. I moved off her, slipping my arm under her head and pulling her closer as I palmed one of her breasts, kissing her neck.

"That was so good…" she breathed.

"Yeah…"

"So much for getting my hair done." She laughed softly.

"You still looking fucking ravishing, no matter whether your hair looks fucking good enough to yank on or whether it's full of twigs and leaves," I smirked, making her pout as she reached up to touch her hair.

"I don't think I want to see it," she pouted, making me smirk.

"Oh yeah? Well, trust me, you look fucking perfect…"

Our eyes met. In the distance, we could hear birds chirping and the rustle of leaves, but the only sound I could focus on was her heartbeat and our intense emotions running through the bond, emotions that blended together so perfectly that I couldn't make out where mine ended, and hers began.

I looked into those gorgeous eyes of hers before I leaned down and kissed her deeply. The sweet taste of her mouth was so fucking tantalising, and after a moment, I forced myself back, throbbing hard.

"Come on, let's get back in the water," I said, sitting up and tugging her up. We both slipped back into the water, brushing the bits of twigs, dirt, and leaves off us.

"We didn't even finish our food," she said, sounding fucking cute as I picked a leaf from her hair.

"Didn't I fill you up enough? Or do you want me to go a few more rounds?" I asked huskily, making her bite her lip.

"That doesn't sound like a bad idea, but you know tonight we are having movie night with the kiddies. I need to be awake for it," she replied, clearly amused.

"Oh yeah?"

"Yes." She poked her eyes out at me. Smirking, I pulled her into my arms, simply holding her against my chest.

"So, I was thinking. Want to go on a family holiday somewhere?"

"That would be nice. So, like, everyone, right?" I raised an eyebrow.

"Well, I won't fucking lie, I was thinking just us two and the kids." She turned in my arms, wrapping hers around my neck.

"That would also be nice."

"Ri's planning some shit for December time anyway, but I thought before this pup comes along, let's just do something with the kids. Kat's become more fucking closed up, and I think she could do with the fucking calm, and so could I. I love our family, but, you know, sometimes we just need some alone time, too." She smiled.

"I like the idea. We could ask the kids where they would like to go, too," she suggested kissing my chest. I was already fucking aware of her rubbing against my dick, and although I wasn't fucking done with her, I needed to make sure she wasn't entirely spent.

"Sounds like a plan." I kissed her neck as she ran her hands down my back, digging her nails in. "Fuck," I growled. She grabbed my ass, pressing us together entirely.

"That also sounds like a plan," she whispered seductively in my ear.

"And that's why you're my fucking nympho queen," I growled, squeezing her ass before I lifted her up, kissing her again.

She let out a breathless laugh in between kisses before she thrust down onto my dick, making me groan with satisfaction as I looked into my nympho's eyes, and she began riding my cock…

Together

KIARA

"PLEASE, BABY," I PLEADED, looking at Alejandro, who was glaring at the wine-red satin pyjama bottoms I was holding out to him.

"Fuck no," he growled, reminding me of a child refusing to do what they were told.

"Alejandro…" I pouted, putting on my sultriest pleading face.

"No is a no," he said, turning away from me.

I huffed in exaggerated annoyance, rolling my eyes. It was evening, and we had gotten back about two hours ago after having fallen asleep near the lake after a few hours of sex. I could still feel the aftereffect on my body. My core ached, and so did my ass. There was not an inch of my body that Alejandro had left untouched. We returned, showered, and then I arranged the trays for our family night with the goodies I had baked that morning whilst Alejandro had left to collect some things.

I was trying to force Alejandro to wear the matching pyjamas I had ordered. It had been Kataleya's idea for our little movie night, and although she had initially chosen powder blue, I wasn't sure Alejandro or Dante would even have considered them.

"Don't be silly. It was Kat's idea," I tried again, knowing it may have some impact. He frowned, turning back with a pair of sweatpants in his hands.

"I don't wear fucking silk," he growled.

I tilted my head, trying not to burst into laughter at how amusing this was. He stood there in his fitted black boxers, several chains around his neck, and his wet hair brushed back with one strand falling teasingly over his forehead, glaring at the fabric. I stepped closer to him, batting my lashes.

"But I really wanted to see how you look in satin... it has the ability to shape things ever so nicely..." I whispered seductively, letting my gaze fall to the front of his boxers. He raised an eyebrow.

"I don't need fucking satin to look like I have a dick. It's pretty noticeable no matter what I wear," he replied cockily, making me sigh.

"Fine, don't wear them, then. I guess I'll just tell Kataleya that even though we spent an hour trying to choose what colour you'd like, you still don't want to wear them," I said, dropping the bottoms onto the drawer. It was only the bottoms; the top wouldn't have fit him anyway. It had been such a mission even finding anything that would fit him with his height, and this had been the most suitable colour.

"Kia," he growled.

I didn't reply, simply dropping my towel as I slipped on my lace panties with a matching black bra. I heard him mutter a swear as I bent down and slipped on my own wine-red pyjama bottoms before putting the top on. I was about to button it up when Alejandro stepped up behind me and grabbed my breasts from behind, giving them a squeeze.

"You're fucking annoying," he growled, kissing my neck. I tried not to sigh in pleasure as I suppressed a smile and raised an eyebrow. I pulled away and turned towards him.

"How? I just said fine," I said innocently as I buttoned my top up, leaving the top three open, which gave him a very appealing view of my breasts.

"You're playing reverse psychology and shit on me," he growled.

"How? I just said it's fine. I'll tell Kat you didn't want to," I replied innocently as his eyes flashed. My poor sexy, angry, hot king.

"Fine, I'll wear the fucking things," he said, glaring at the pyjama bottoms. If his eyes could destroy things by simply looking at them, those pyjamas would have been a pile of ash. I bit back a laugh and ran my fingers down his muscled arm.

"Satin or not, nothing will make you lose your masculinity. Don't worry," I replied, kissing his shoulder since I couldn't really reach his lips as I was barefoot. He narrowed his eyes before looking at me.

"The things I fucking do for you girls."

"Everything we could ever dream of," I whispered.

"Yeah, I know what you did by playing fucking innocent and emotionally trying to blackmail me. In case you think you won this, I chose to agree," he replied coldly as I left the room, unable to hold back my laughter.

"Of course, my sexy beast." *As long as you listen, I don't mind you thinking you won.*

Smiling, I looked over at the huge bed in my room. We had already arranged the trays of treats on the edge of the bed, consisting of a chocolate and fruit dipping platter, a variety of sweets and baked goodies that included brownies, blondies, red velvet cookies, and cupcakes. On the bedside table was a selection of iced drinks. Dante was already sitting in his matching pyjamas in the centre of the bed whilst browsing through the selection of movies. Kataleya and Skyla weren't here yet, so I decided to go get them.

"Did Dad agree?" He asked, making me smile as I walked to the door. I gave him a small nod, and he smirked.

"Obviously," I whispered.

"I can fucking hear you two," Alejandro called.

I laughed, leaving the bedroom and almost knocking into Skyla, who was standing there with her hair neatly braided after her shower as she held a black kitten with sharp green eyes, a kitten that suited her very well.

"Me and Malevolent are ready." She held it up to my face, showing off the silk ribbon around its neck, making me step back as the kitty hissed.

Alejandro had felt bad for Skyla and apparently had chosen this kitten for her yesterday. He had gotten one of the men to collect it. Skyla had been beyond happy. Although I didn't think she deserved it right then, with everything going on, I thought we all just needed to relax and ease up a little.

"Malevolent. That's a nice name," I smiled.

"Oh, it is. She's very evil, aren't you, my little kitty cat?"

The kitten meowed, and I stepped aside, allowing the duo inside. I walked towards the girls' room just as Kataleya stepped out with Claire. Like always, she held her teddy in her arms. Her hair was braided as well, and she was in her matching pyjamas. I smiled at them both.

"Thank you, Claire."

"Nothing to thank me for, Luna. Would you like me to tuck them into bed later?"

"No, I think we're having a family sleepover today," I said, making Kataleya's eyes light up.

"Really, Mama?"

"Really," I said, taking her hand and leading her back to mine and Alejandro's bedroom. We had all just gotten comfortable on the bed as Dante glared at the kitten, who was purring against Skyla's arm.

"Aww, Malevolent is such a good, bad kitty...." she cooed as Alejandro stepped out of the adjoining room, phone in hand and a frown on his face.

My heart skipped a beat. He could deny it all he wanted, but he looked pretty sexy in those satin pyjama bottoms... even that was an understatement. He looked too good. His tatted body was on full display with his piercings and those drool-worthy abs. I could see the black band of his designer boxers, and every step he took made my attention fall to his package. *Oh, Goddess... I could worship him day and night...*

My mouth felt dry, and I licked my lips, swallowing hard. My core throbbed, and I was about to look away when his eyes snapped to mine, making my heart thump.

Keep eye-fucking me, Amore Mio, and movie night will be over faster than you can say, 'fuck me now'.

I smiled slightly. As much as I'd love that, this movie night was something I was not going to risk.

Noted, my sexy beast, I replied with amusement as Kataleya settled next to me on the bed.

"Not wanting to dig into the treats just yet?" I asked her, as the other two already were. Alejandro sat down on her other side, making the bed dip slightly, and planted a kiss on Kataleya's forehead before leaning over and kissing my lips.

"So, what are we watching?" He asked, leaning back against the headboard and picking up a can of Coca-Cola for himself.

"This movie," I said as Dante went back to the movie we'd had on pause from the start. It was a new kid's movie and one that I was sure we would all enjoy.

"A kid's show," Dante said, dropping onto his stomach. The kitten climbed off Sky, coming toward us and making Kataleya giggle.

"Daddy, I named the kitty Malevolent," Skyla said as she helped herself to some chocolates.

"That's a weird name," Alejandro replied as Kataleya stroked it.

"It isn't. I asked Claire to help me find a name that is similar to Maleficent," Skyla stated, "and this one is purrrrfect!"

"It is."

The movie began. We chatted and joked as we watched it. It felt good to have everything back to normal again.

"So, why didn't you ask if you had a gift since I got Sky the cat?" Alejandro asked Kataleya, who was resting her head on his chest as she watched the movie. She looked up at him curiously.

"Did Daddy get me something, too?" She whispered.

"Yeah… it isn't much, but I thought you'd like it." He leaned over and took something from the top drawer next to the bed as I watched them, smiling. He grabbed a little pale pink box and, opening it, took out a golden locket, making me smile as Kataleya smiled softly.

"For me?" He opened the heart pendant and held it out to her. I could see there were two tiny images already inside.

"Yeah. See? You get to put two pictures in it. I put us in there already. I look weird as fuck, though," he said, making me smile as I watched him. She giggled, taking the necklace.

"No, Daddy, you look very handsome," she said, her smile fading as she looked at the other image. "This…"

Enrique.

"You can remove it when you want, but… you don't need to always carry Kiké around. I thought this shit might be better? Like, when you go to school." Her eyes pooled with tears, and I struggled to keep my own back as she flung her arms around Alejandro's neck, kissing his cheek.

"Thank you, Daddy," she whispered as he wiped her tears away.

I looked away, trying not to get emotional. Whether anyone wanted it or not, Enrique was someone she wouldn't forget for a while, and until she was ready to move on, we would support her in any way possible. Alejandro leaned over, pulling me into his arms, too.

"So not fair. How dare you have a family hug without me, Malevolent, and the red-eyed cockroach?" Sky asked as she launched herself on top of Alejandro. "Oof! Daddy, you knocked the breath from me! Why are you such a rock?"

"You jumped on me, remember?" He reminded her, wrapping his arm around her and kissing her cheek as Malevolent meowed, wanting to escape the family hug. "Oi, roach, wanna join?" Alejandro asked Dante, making Skyla cackle. Dante turned, raising an eyebrow.

"Oh, I didn't realise she was talking about me. I thought Skyla meant you," Dante said haughtily with a small smirk. I smiled as Skyla and Alejandro frowned at him.

"Come over here," I said, holding my arm out to him.

"This is so mushy," Dante muttered, but, even so, he was trying to hide his shy smile.

"Yeah, it's weird as shit," Alejandro agreed despite the small smile on his own lips.

"Well, we are a weird family," Skyla said, not caring that Malevolent was clawing Alejandro's chest.

"Skyla, don't terrify the poor kitten," I said as Dante joined the hug. Kataleya let out a small laugh, holding her necklace to her chest, along with Kiké. I smiled as I hugged them tightly. My perfect family.

My eyes met Alejandro's, and we smiled at one another. This was true happiness, having our children safe and happy by our side.

"I love you all," I said softly as we all moved back.

"Love you, too!" Skyla and Kataleya said in unison.

"Love you, too, Mama," Dante said, looking up at me before he reached over and brushed a strand of my hair back. "I'm sorry for everything you went through."

"It was not your fault," I said softly, my heart thundering as I remembered how I had tried to stab him. There was just no way that I could ever think of doing that.

"You're still the most amazing woman ever," Dante said.

"Until your mate comes along. Then you'll be fucking running after her," Alejandro remarked. Dante frowned.

"If I have a mate," he murmured. It wasn't the first time he had said that.

"I'm sure the Goddess would not leave you without one," I said, caressing his face. He shrugged, smirking.

"It's okay either way. Mates just make you do whatever they want, and men just listen like puppies," he said, slyly glancing at his dad. The girls and I started laughing as Alejandro frowned, displeased.

"Ooo, I need mates! So, I can make them my minions!" Skyla exclaimed.

"Mate," Alejandro corrected her.

"No, no, I need an army!" Skyla stated, making me smile at her innocence and Alejandro's annoyance. Dante bit into a cookie as he turned back to the tv.

"So, tell me what you kids want to be when you're older," Alejandro asked them.

"Easy. An Alpha," Skyla stated.

"Yeah? What else?"

"You know I want to be a villain and take control of the world, too!"

"That's your dream, but what do you want to become? Like a doctor, a teacher…" I helped.

"*Oh*… now I get it. Hmm, I want to be a cop! So, I can beat people up."

"That's not what cops do…" Alejandro remarked.

"But I will."

It was obvious that our wild princess hadn't thought about her future yet. I turned to Kataleya, remembering her wanting to be a teacher.

"What about you, Kat?" I asked softly. She stared down at her lap before she held out the necklace to me.

"Will you put it on me?" I nodded, moving her hair and slipping it around her neck. "I want to be a scientist or doctor, someone who can help all werewolves who get hurt to get better… to find a way to help them all, so they can still live completely normal lives," she whispered, making my heart break for her. Alejandro frowned, and I hugged her tightly.

"That's a beautiful idea," I whispered, kissing her forehead. I held her close for a moment before Alejandro nudged Dante with his knee.

"And you?"

"Me? Who knows…" he said, glancing back at us both.

"Don't be so fucking cryptic." Alejandro frowned. Dante just chuckled.

"I actually don't know what I'll be in case you think I do. You know I can't really see my future."

"Hmm, well, what do you want to be?" Alejandro asked him.

"I want to be strong so I can protect everyone. I want to be fair so I don't do anyone injustice." Alejandro and I exchanged looks as Dante continued, "I want to be wise so I can guard justice, and I want to be the best son so my mama is proud of me," he finished with a cocky smirk, making Alejandro narrow his eyes.

"Aww, I am already so proud of you, baby," I said, so proud of his words.

"Mama's boy," Alejandro growled as Skyla and Kataleya laughed.

"Jealous?" Dante taunted.

"Nah, just fucking know how Rayhan felt," Alejandro muttered, making me shake my head.

Dante smirked. He had told me he was taking a step back from his childish crush and how he would try to stop annoying Rayhan when it came to Delsanra, at least.

"So, didn't Dante and I get a present?" I asked.

"Didn't I give you anything earlier?" Alejandro replied with a cocky smirk making me blush.

"What did you give Mama?" Skyla asked.

"Flowers," I lied quickly.

Flowers? Alejandro remarked mockingly through the link. I poked my eyes out at him warningly, but he just smirked and gave me a wink.

"I got a new scooter," Dante smirked. "The one I wanted a few months ago."

"Perfect," I said, trying to avoid Alejandro's gaze.

The movie soon came to an end. We all got into the bed with the girls on either side of me, Alejandro next to Kataleya, and Dante on his other side. We discussed where to go for a holiday and when we would go. They were all excited, and so was I. Malevolent was asleep at the edge of the bed near Skyla's feet.

The kids soon fell asleep, and Alejandro took my hand, kissing it softly as he looked at me from over Kataleya's head full of hair.

"Thank you," he said quietly.

"Hmm?" I said, closing my eyes as he caressed my jaw, relishing in the sparks.

"Thanks for fucking giving me a life I could never have imagined ever having or hoping for," he said quietly.

My eyes opened, and, even in the dark, I could see his glowing eyes. My heart pounded as I leaned over, smiling when he cupped my face and claimed my lips in a soft kiss.

And thank you for being you. I am the luckiest woman to have you in my life, and our kids are the luckiest to have you as their papa, I whispered through the link as we broke apart. He kissed my forehead, his stubble prickling me slightly, and I smiled softly.

My mate.

"I love you," I whispered.

"Love you fucking more."

We settled back, Alejandro's hand on my stomach as we, too, fell asleep with all our pups by our side…

An Alpha

ALEJANDRO

I LOOKED OVER AT RAYHAN as we stood outside the entrance to the Sangue Pack. His hair was pulled into a bun, and he had a frown on his face.

"This is it," I said quietly. "Sometimes, admitting that we made a mistake takes a lot. For you to want to do this yourself, I'm proud of you, and I'm sure more than me, Rafael would be prouder." He nodded as Kiara placed a hand on his arm.

"We got this, and besides, we're doing this together," she said, giving him a warm smile.

"Don't make me out as a good person. I only regret that others suffered, not what I did to those individuals," he said, looking at the gates. Kiara nodded.

"That is enough in itself," I replied.

"Hm, does Marcel know we're here?" Rayhan asked quietly. I nodded.

"Yeah, someone should be here to escort us inside," I replied, pulling Kiara into my arms.

A few days after my picnic date with Kiara, Rayhan rang to ask if, although Leo refused, it was okay to visit the Sangue Pack. He said he wanted to apologise to those who suffered indirectly from his actions. I was proud that he wanted to do that. We all knew it wouldn't change the past, but at least it would give some sort of closure to those who had suffered.

Marcel soon arrived, and, after meeting us, we all walked through the grounds.

"How are you holding up since he left?" I asked him, referring to Leo. He gave me a small smile.

"It's hard. Even though he gave me a lot of stress, he was always looking out for me. Leo has a good heart, he's just…"

"Hurting," I finished. "He had a point. We all fucked up."

Kiara brushed back a strand of her hair as the wind blew through the trees. She looked as beautiful as ever, with her sandy brown hair pulled back into a braid and a few strands framing her face. She wore a green silk blouse with a black print on it and black trousers. She looked at me, and I pulled her close, kissing her lush lips softly.

Delsanra had wanted to come as well, but Rayhan had told her he'd rather she didn't. I understood his point. After all, this was the pack where her abusers lived. It would still be triggering for her, although I knew she was a strong woman. Besides, she had done nothing wrong, so she didn't need to apologise. Rayhan coming was more than enough.

"What do you plan to do? Are you sure you don't want me to call a meeting?" Marcel asked.

"No, we will see them individually. A *visit*, not a command for a meeting. Right now, we are here to apologise, and summoning them isn't going to help that," I said coldly.

"I agree, and if they don't want to see us, that's okay, too. No one is to be forced," Kiara added, looking at Marcel. He nodded, sighing heavily as we reached the first house.

"I did tell them I'd be stopping by," he said. I nodded as Marcel rang the doorbell. Kiara had wanted to bring gifts, but we had decided against it. We weren't here to display our wealth. To admit we are wrong doesn't make one any less.

"Alpha…" The woman at the door paled the moment she saw Rayhan and me. Her heart was racing as Kiara stepped forward, smiling gracefully.

"May we come in for a few moments? It won't take too long," she said softly.

"Opal, who is it?" A man's voice asked before he came into view.

His eyes snapped to Rayhan, and I realised he was definitely one of the men he had beaten. It took me a moment to pair him to the files, files I had already burned a few days ago. There would be no fucking records on them unless they committed a crime by will. This was the man whose child had been killed when he had refused to beat Delsanra…

The tension was thick. I stepped inside the house, making the woman back away.

"Momma!" A child came running. She was around the twins' age, and she looked at us curiously.

"Go to your room, Ophelia," Opal commanded her, and the girl obeyed.

"Can we have a quick word?" I asked, doing my fucking best to sound calm. I was already trying to suppress my aura entirely.

They nodded as the man wrapped his arm around his mate. I could smell their fear and feel their distrust. It showed they only agreed because they felt they had no choice.

"Please, sit, Alpha King," the woman murmured. We all sat down, and it felt too fucking small in here. The man remained standing as his mate sat down, her heart thundering with fear as she gripped her mate's hand that rested on her shoulder.

"The reason we are here is to apologise," I said quietly.

"I'll take it from here," Rayhan added, looking at the man. "Years ago, I came here, blinded by my pain and rage. My only goal was to hurt all those who had hurt my mate, but without even realising... I did the very same thing that I was punishing others for. I hurt you, but indirectly, I also harmed your mate. A woman who was innocent... you lost a child for refusing to beat the very species you hated. I can't imagine losing a child... I, too, would do anything to protect them, so I'm sorry. It won't take back what I have done, and it won't change the past, but I apologise." He lowered his head to the man, who looked surprised. The woman looked up at her mate, her eyes glittering with unshed tears of surprise.

"It's fine... it's in the past," the man replied curtly. Rayhan shook his head.

"No. Whether it's in the past or present, I still made a mistake." The man smiled slightly and nodded.

"We all did, but we are beings, we are made to make mistakes. It's fine, you need not worry about it. Thank you for your apology."

"Thank you for accepting it. I'm sorry for the loss of your child at the hands of Endora," Rayhan said quietly. Silence fell in the room, but somehow, I fucking knew the small gesture would help the couple in their healing.

"There is always light," Kiara said warmly. Leaning over, she placed a hand on the woman's knee, and I sensed her healing aura flowing into the woman, no doubt, healing whatever internal damage there was. The woman visibly relaxed, and Kiara simply smiled at her.

I think I will start going around to every pack in the country and offer to heal what I can. Although we have always made it clear that everyone is welcome to come to us, it's obvious not everyone does or can.

Sounds like a fucking plan. Proud of you, Amore Mio.

Our eyes met, and she smiled softly at me. She was my fucking life.

We left after a short while, going on to the other houses. There were a few who refused to see us, but that was understandable. Those who had had their mates killed were more hostile, but still, Rayhan did his best. I knew he didn't regret killing those men, but he did feel for those who suffered because of it. Once we were done and seated at Marcel's having some refreshments, I looked across at my brother. It was my fucking turn.

"I also owe the Sangue Pack an apology. I promised you all a fresh start but didn't hold true to my fucking word. Going forward, that's going to change. The files I created on this pack have been destroyed, and, as for those who were orphaned back then, those children will have funds created for them so they can have a good start to life and a good education," I said. Marcel smiled.

"You don't owe us an apology, Alejandro; you have done so much, and we appreciate it. You have given me my share of the Rossi empire, and it is more than enough for me to cater for those orphans, although the number is extremely high."

"And that's why I'm fucking helping, don't fucking argue with me," I growled.

"Alright, I won't. You know this life we have is because you gave us the chance. Going forward, I, too, hope that we can carry on stronger than ever. I'm sure Leo will come around. This action from you, Rayhan, was truly admirable, no matter how hard it was. Our mates mean the world to us, and you only did a mate's duty, yet you were man and Alpha enough to admit the damage it did to others. It's not something easy for us of Alpha blood to admit, but you did it. Humbly and earnestly. You are a son that anyone would be proud of, and I know that Rafael will be proud of you," he said in a voice so similar to Rafael's that it fucking tugged at something inside. Rayhan smiled slightly.

"Thank you," he said quietly.

"Yeah, he fucking would be…" I said as I leaned forward, picking up my cup of tea from the table.

A ray of sunshine fell over my hand, illuminating the room in a warm glow, and I turned towards the window. *I hope you are proud Raf… are you watching over us?*

Kiara placed her hand on my thigh, sending sparks of warmth through me. I turned, smiling at her.

"To bonds of every kind," Marcel said, raising his teacup. Rayhan smirked as he raised his own and we all followed suit, clinking our cups together.

To family, friendship, honesty, loyalty, and to fucking equality.

I downed my cup, giving them a cold smirk as the hot liquid ran down my throat.

Yeah, to better times.

ENRIQUE

I walked through the empty halls of the Escarra mansion, a place that had remained empty for the last few years. The sun shone through the window, and I was able to see the dust particles that hung in the air.

Hugo walked behind me. Over the last few weeks, he had become my shadow. He had been our family butler before Father had refused to allow him to come along to take care of my mother and me when we left Puerto Rico. He was the one who had saved me the day I almost died, the day that Mother was killed.

"The Lycan King wanted to stay in touch with you, no?" I asked coldly.

"He… is only worried for your wellbeing, young master." I frowned. No. No one cared for me.

The memory of him killing my father when I begged him not to remained. Hours before that fight, I had learned of the curse on our family… the deal with the devil and how Father had come to England to find a way to protect me. He only wanted me not to go through what he and our forefathers had.

"From this day forth, you will refer to me as Alpha. Anyone found to be conversing with the Lycan King will be punished," I said, my voice loud and clear as it echoed in the empty halls.

"Youn- Alpha…"

"The passage of the Alpha ceremony will be held tonight. I will officially take my place as the leader of this pack, and I expect everyone to listen. The Escarra name will not be forgotten. I will fix this pack, and… I will need your help, Hugo. I promise to pay you well."

"Young master… I would help you without being offered pay. My duty is to -"

"No. I don't need loyalty to my family, I need you to promise your loyalty to me. To show me that I am your Alpha."

"Y-yes young master," Hugo whispered.

"What did the Lycan King ask you after I was taken away?" I asked, knowing Hugo had spoken to him.

"He asked if you had someone to take care of you," Hugo replied.

"And you also called him," I said, staring at the slate floors. My anger raged within me, clenching my fist tightly around the item in my hand. It was digging painfully into my palm.

"I did… he… he just wants to make sure we are all okay, if you are okay, and if we knew the truth about his son."

"What did you tell him?"

"I told him we do, but we will not utter it to anyone…"

"That's fine. We won't. I don't care for him or his family."

The image of the chica came to mind, and I frowned. An act of kindness which didn't feel wrong… but it… it cost me so much. I looked at my stump. We were in the process of getting a prosthetic made, but it would never be the same…

"Then we will make it clear to the pack as well."

"They know the law. They won't talk about it. I will make it clear that those rules are the same. From this day on, I am Alpha, and we need no one else. No one's help. Nothing."

I need no one.

"Yes of course, Alpha."

"You may go, Hugo. I want to be alone."

"Ah…yes, of course, young mast- I mean, Alpha."

He walked away, and I opened my hand, staring down at the clear quartz crystal necklace that was wrapped with gold metal wire with distaste. I don't know why I didn't just throw it away… I didn't want it. The stupid Lycan had given it to me even when I left it in the bathroom. A flare of anger rushed through me, and I flung it across the centre courtyard, my heart thumping.

"I hate you! It's your fault! It's your fault that everything went wrong!" I shouted, my voice ringing in all directions. "I will never be the Alpha I was meant to be because of you! You took away my life!"

I refused to cry, but the pain was so much. I just prayed to whatever god there was above that I never saw her or her family ever again.

A Treasure

DELSANRA

"SMILE, MAMA MARI," I said, giving her a hug.

"I am smiling," she replied, giving me a small smile.

Of everyone, she had been the only one with mixed feelings about the outcome. She had been so prepared to meet Papa Raf that it was as if it had been stolen from her. But she had kept busy, and I thought it was really helping her. Both Rayhan and I had told her to talk to us when she felt down, and I planned to keep on top of it, too. I would make sure she didn't feel lonely, and I had talked to her about calming sleeping spells for night-time as I knew that was when she felt the loneliest. She had said she would have a think about it.

Her job as the head warrior was something everyone was excited about. The Ahmar Qamar Pack fighting style was one of the best, and the fact that Mama Mari was the last remaining member who was trained in it was something that Rayhan said was something to think about. How she needed to pass it on, and although she had said that she would teach it to her grandchildren, she had also agreed to train the pack. The previous Luna was respected, and everyone worked hard to do their best, and on top of that, they knew that Rayhan wouldn't stand for any disrespect towards his mother. They were all doing well and working hard. Mama Mari said that when Ahren turned three, she would start training him, too, as she had started learning from the age of three herself.

It had been a few weeks since everything had returned to normal. I had grown up being tortured and abused, but the pain that I had felt under that curse… it had been worse than anything I had ever gone through. The fear of not knowing if I'd make it back to my mate and children… that fear I had tried to hide as I tried to stay strong in my weakest state for Rayhan, who had remained strong trying to find the solution that we needed.

Once you had a family, the fear of death was different. You not only lived for yourself but for your family, too. As for Rayhan, he was truly admirable. My perfect yum yum…

Somehow this entire thing had made us even closer, and we didn't want to be apart from one another for long. Rayhan was one of the strongest, smartest, and most caring Alphas, so when he told me that he was going to visit the Sangue Pack, it had made me happy. There were so many who were affected by it all that it really was a noble move from him. That was where he was gone currently, along with Kiara and King Burrito. Rayhan had said he'd be back by nightfall, so hopefully soon. I missed him already.

"Si, come here," I said, holding my arms out to my precious little chocolate chip cookie as she toddled over. Her walking was a lot better now, and she gave me the cutest smile as she came over to me.

"Mommy," she said, holding my face and kissing it.

"Ahren's gotten a little naughtier," Mama Mari said, glancing at Ahren, who was up to no good in the corner. He was currently trying to chip off the paint from the wall.

"Very naughty. I think you all spoiled him," I replied, smiling.

Mama Mari laughed, lightly shaking her head as she got up and moved him away from the wall.

"I'm home," Rayhan's voice called, making my heart skip a beat. I hadn't even sensed him enter!

I stood up, spinning around to see him leaning against the doorframe. His hands were in his pocket, his leather jacket straining on his muscular arms, and his hair was tied back save a few strands that framed his face looked so hot. I ran over to him, flinging my arms around his neck.

"You're home," I whispered before I kissed him. His arms wrapped around me as he pulled me out into the hallway and pushed me up against the wall. "Rayhan…"

"I think this might be a bit much for Mom and the kids," he whispered sexily, cupping my thigh and lifting it. He pressed it against his waist as he pushed himself against me firmly, making me gasp.

His lips met mine in a sensual, erotic kiss. One hand gripped the back of my neck as he slipped his tongue into my mouth. I sighed softly, feeling the electric sparks rush through my body. This was home, in his arms. He let up after a few moments, letting me get the breath I needed.

"I missed you, kitten," he murmured, kissing my neck as his hand ran up my thigh and squeezed my ass before slipping it under my top and grabbing my breast.

"I miss Daddy, too."

We both froze before I pushed Rayhan away, my cheeks flushing, and his hand slipped out from under my top quicker than lightning. We both looked down at Ahren, who giggled.

"Did you now?" Rayhan asked, flashing me a sexy smirk before he lifted him up, making our little boy giggle. I squeezed his chubby cheek before Rayhan leaned over, kissing me just below my ear. "We'll continue that later." I blushed lightly as I looked into those sexy grey eyes.

"Can't wait," I said, biting my lip.

A dose of my sexy yum yum was something I would always look forward to. We entered the living room, and Rayhan walked over to his mother. Crouching down in front of her, he placed Ahren down and took her hands in his.

"How was training today?" He asked, kissing her hands softly.

"Good, I think I have a good regime set up now. How was your trip, ya hayati?" Mama Mari asked, cupping his face.

"It went okay. Better than expected. I hope one day Leo finds it in him to forgive me… one can hope," he said quietly as I sat down on the other sofa, watching the mother and son. I loved their bond, and I hoped it always remained because she needed him as he needed her. Mama Mari nodded.

"Regardless of if he does or not, you did the right thing. I am proud of you."

"Thank you," Rayhan said softly as Mama Mari kissed his forehead.

"Has Raihana messaged or called today?" Mama Mari asked me. I shook my head.

"No, but she will later. She said she and Chris had a few meetings today, but she was definitely going to video-call us."

"Perfect. I heard Dante told her the gender, but she doesn't want to do a gender reveal party this time," Mama Mari said with a smile as Rayhan got up and sat on the sofa beside his mother, and he began playing with Sienna.

"That's shocking for Ri," he replied, too amused, kissing Sienna's cheeks as he picked her up and tickled her.

"She may just be growing out of her partying stage," Mama Mari said with a small laugh.

"I doubt Ri will ever grow out of getting attention and being extra," Rayhan smirked.

"I think she just wants to keep it small this time," I said, defending my friend.

With everything going on, Raihana had told me she just wanted to keep everything simple and small so she could cherish it with family. However, she promised to tell me the gender as today she had an official scan. Although she had complete faith in Dante, she wanted to have the scan to confirm it before she announced it.

"Well, she had a scan today," I added, as Rayhan raised an eyebrow.

"Really? She never said," Mama Mari exclaimed with surprise. I shrugged sheepishly.

"I think it may have been a secret?" Mama Mari let out a small laugh.

"You girls can never keep anything from one another." No, we couldn't.

I smiled as my eyes met Rayhan, who was watching me with such an intense look that my heart felt all fluttery. We had truly come so far, and I wouldn't change anything for the world.

Sienna was tugging on her father's necklaces. Ahren came over to me and sat beside me, playing with a toy. I ran my fingers through his hair, feeling content.

My perfect family.

RAIHANA

I watched Chris sit back as he discussed the new building plans to extend the pack territory. He looked incredibly sexy as he talked to the men. We were in the city, and the businessmen were human.

"Of course, that sounds great, Mr Somers," one of the men said as I ran my hand up Chris's thigh, now that the important part was done.

"Perfect, so what do you think Mrs Somers?" Chris asked me, raising an eyebrow. I smiled slightly, my hand dangerously close to his manhood.

"I think it all sounds great," I replied before I leaned over and kissed his lips softly.

So proud of you.

I really was. There had been a time he'd had to prove how capable he was, and he did it effortlessly. Chris was an excellent Alpha, and when it came to doing the job, he was an entirely different person. Focused, serious, and so damn sexy. I was tempted to see if we could get the conference room to ourselves so I could have him take me right then. He looked at me as if he knew exactly what was going through my mind.

"Well, if that is all, we will take our leave," he said, standing up and giving me his hand. I took it and stood up as the men stood up politely.

"Thank you once again, Mr and Mrs Somers."

Bidding farewell, we left the room and entered the elevator. We were on one of the top floors, and I pressed the button for the ground floor.

"So… what did you have in mind?" Chris smirked suggestively, backing me into a corner.

"In here? There's a camera right behind you…" I whispered.

"Hmm, cover it. I think I have just over a minute to make you come. Challenge accepted," he said, pushing me into the corner. His body shielded me from the camera, which I had misted over just as he pulled my skirt up, slipped his hand into my panties, and his lips met mine…

❧❧❧

He had succeeded in making me come, and we had left that elevator with my legs feeling like jelly but thoroughly satisfied. We spent another twenty minutes getting hot and steamy in the car before we finally returned home.

It was later in the evening. I'd had a scan earlier today, and we were video-calling Mom and them to let them know the gender. I had just put Tatum to bed, and we were in bed. We had already known the gender, thanks to Dante, but it just didn't feel right to tell anyone until we had it confirmed, and it was no surprise to find out he was indeed right.

We sat side by side, with Chris's arms around me, just as Delsanra answered the phone, setting it down on the table so I could see them all.

Rayhan was holding her in his lap whilst Mom sat next to them, looking at the phone with rather well-masked excitement, but even then, her eyes gave it away.

"How are you two?" She asked.

"Great, thanks for asking," Chris replied. "Hope you're doing great yourself." I was so glad she was here… I really needed her. I would always need my mom.

"Well, what is it then?" Delsanra asked, her eyes sparkling with excitement.

"It's a girl," I said as Chris placed a hand on my stomach. I had a bump now.

Delsanra squealed in excitement as she hugged Mom tightly, both women clearly happy as Rayhan smiled.

"That's great news. Congratulations to the both of you," he said, his hands not leaving Delsanra's narrow waist.

"Thanks, and we also had a request," I said, glancing into Chris's green eyes. He gave me a small nod, and I looked at my best friend.

"Anything, we're here for you. Just tell us what it is," Delsanra replied.

"You sure? We might be asking for a hell of a lot," Chris replied with a smirk. She nodded as expected from her.

"Absolutely! I'm ready anytime."

"Within reason, obviously," Rayhan added, brushing her hair back from her shoulder and kissing her shoulder. I smirked as she resisted a sigh, blushing lightly.

"Well, it's a big deal, and it's specifically for Delsanra," I said, leaning forward as the trio looked at us curiously.

"I'm nervous now," Delsanra said curiously.

"You should be. You are being given the duty…" Chris glanced at me, and I smiled as I placed my hand over his that rested on my stomach.

"The duty to name our little princess," I said, trying not to get emotional.

"Oh, bless, that's…" Mom trailed off, her eyes full of emotion, and I blinked my eyes, trying to contain my emotions.

"You became my best friend so easily. Not only did Ray find his mate in you, I found my soul sister. The most terrifying ordeal about this entire thing was thinking I might lose you and that I couldn't do anything to help you," I said, my voice cracking. I took a deep breath, fanning my face. "Goddess! These silly pregnancy hormones." Chris hugged me tightly, kissing my lips.

"It's okay to cry," he whispered. I glanced at the screen where Delsanra was already crying silently as she looked back at me.

"I'm sorry for scaring you. You know, I'm a stubborn one," she whispered. I nodded.

"I know. I'm just crazy and dramatic, you know that," I said, brushing it off, but every one of them knew me better than that.

"You aren't wearing makeup, Ri, if you want to cry, go for it," Rayhan teased lightly. "By the way, I actually forget what you looked like without all that contour and shine."

"Hey, I'm beautiful without makeup!" I glared at him, and he smirked,

"I never said you weren't. You just look years younger without it and maybe a little more innocent."

"She's far from innocent, though," Chris replied with a cocky smirk. That made Rayhan give him a pointed look, but I left them to it, looking at Delsanra, who was deep in thought.

"You can take your time. We have a few months," I reminded her before she smiled, nodding as Mom asked me questions about how the scan went. After a few minutes, Delsanra smiled brightly, snapping her fingers.

"I have a name, but if you don't like it, I don't mind. I can think again."

"Go for it, Kitten," Rayhan murmured as Mom, Chris, and I looked at her.

I was excited, too. I was a fussy person, and giving someone the choice to name my child was a huge deal for me, but this was something I wanted to give to her. It was one of the most precious gifts I could give her. Whatever name she chose, I would keep it because I loved her, and I knew I'd love the name because of that, too.

"Heaven. Heaven Kamaria Somers," she said softly. I glanced at Chris, a smile crossing my face.

"Heaven. It's perfect. I love it. Heaven Kamaria Somers…" My heart skipped a beat. It was perfect.

"Kamaria means moonlight," Delsanra explained. "Do you really like it?"

"I don't like it, I love it, babe. Absolutely! Heaven is a befitting name for my daughter."

"Our daughter," Chris corrected before we all started laughing.

"It's a gorgeous name, and I like how Kamaria contains my name," Mom added, making Delsanra smile.

"And Kamar is literally Qamar, your roots, Mom," Rayhan added.

"That's such a cool coincidence!" Delsanra said, but from the look of happiness on her face as Mom nodded in agreement, obviously happy with the name, I realised she had done it on purpose. Our eyes met, and she gave me a wink.

"I can't wait to meet her," Mom said, smiling as she looked at me.

"Me too," I whispered softly.

I truly was looking forward to it and more so the fact Mom would be here for it all. For a short while, I had thought I was going to lose Mom, but I hadn't. She was right here by our side, and I was working on a spell to make the pain of Dad's loss easier on her. Delsanra was helping, too, and I was sure together, we would come up with something. No matter what.

A Night at the Westwood Mansion

ELIJAH

I PULLED ON SOME SWEATPANTS before running a comb through my hair. The dusting of greys was even more prominent lately. I actually liked the look; it just made me look sexier, and even Red liked it.

Today had been like any other day in the Westwood mansion. Actually, it had been extra hectic since we had a party tomorrow. I had just showered and decided to go find Scarlett. I could hear Raven trying to get the boys settled into their beds; Liam had just gotten back from a pack meeting and was in the kitchen making him and his mate some drinks. He had taken after his mom in that department, and although I wouldn't really admit it, he was a pretty good baker, just like Red and Kiara.

We all kind of retreated to our bedrooms pretty early most days. The days were hectic with the kids and work, but once they were all in bed, we would get some alone time with our partners. There were the occasional two days each week where we would have some adult time and just spend it together.

"I don't go bed." I heard Jayce shout and then a bang. He had thrown something, I knew that much. He and Carter were the most rebellious, with Theo and Ares being mischievous, and little Renji was an innocent soul.

"Everyone is going to go to sleep now," Raven scolded.

I smirked as I walked down the hall to the quintuplets' bedroom. The door was slightly open, and I poked my head in. Renji was the only one in bed. Carter was playing as he sat up on his bed. Theo and Ares were trying to escape as Raven was on the floor between their two beds, making sure they didn't run off, whilst Jayce stood with his arms crossed on the end of his bed, throwing toys. I cleared my throat and all six pairs of eyes turned to me.

"Who isn't listening to their mom?" I asked, putting on a strict expression. Instantly Theo and Ares settled down whilst Carter carried on playing, but Jayce just stood there unhappily.

"Me. I don't want go bed!"

"Jayce, you have to go to bed now, all right? Look, tomorrow you can do whatever you want to. You know tomorrow is Azura's birthday," I said, walking over to him. He frowned at me, and we locked eyes before he turned his back on me and got into bed with a huff.

"No. My birthday, okay?" I smirked crouching down and pulled his duvet over him.

"I'm sure Azura can share." I smiled, ruffling his hair.

"Thanks," Raven said with a grateful smile as she tucked Theo in.

I flashed her a smile, thinking she really was an incredible momma. With everything that had happened, she had never once complained that she was tired or anything. Not only had she been there for this pack but for everyone over at Kiara's pack, too.

"You're really a superwoman," I told her, making her grin.

"Thanks," she replied, grinning.

She and Liam had had a house made for their pups and themselves, but I would miss them the day they left. I knew that time was coming closer because the boys were already getting bigger, and there wasn't as much space here anymore, but I would miss it; the crazy mealtime drama, the hustle and bustle of the kids shouting in the halls in the morning… I knew Liam had said we should move in with them, but this home was something I had built for Scarlett, a place that had far too many memories attached to it.

We heard yelling, and both Raven and I exchanged looks.

Azura.

I stood up quickly as Raven patted Ares, who was startled by the shout. I left the room and closed the door behind me, not wanting them to get rowdy all over again. I headed towards our little wildfire's room.

"Please, Azura," Scarlett was saying. I knocked lightly on the door before entering.

Azura was standing there, dressed in her pyjamas. Her hair was damp, and she currently had her back to Scarlett, who was crouching on the floor and damn, did her ass look mighty fine. I bit my lip, taking in how her yoga pants emphasised her bubble butt, dangerously sexy. It was illegal to look that hot.

Are you going to just check out my ass, or will you actually talk to your daughter? I smirked as I entered the room.

What's happened?

The usual… plus her excitement for tomorrow is sky-high.

I frowned. Azura had her days where she refused to go to bed, although both Scarlett and I had wondered if there was another factor. However, it was clear our little rebel just liked to play up at times. Usually, something would trigger her during the day, and she would then act out by not going to bed in the evening. There were times she got really worked up to the point where we had talked to the doctors. They had said it was nothing to worry about.

"Come on, angel, let's get to bed. It's been a long day today, right? Plus, tomorrow is a special day, you need to be well-rested," I said, crouching down before her. Her eyes saddened as she glanced at her bed.

"But I want to read." Scarlett raised an eyebrow, and I knew Azura had totally diverted from what she had been demanding from Scarlett.

"How about you read for half an hour and then go to sleep? Want me to read you a book?" I suggested.

"No, I'll read it myself," she said, pretending to be very sad.

"No, if you want me to, I can read it to you," I persisted with a smirk. She frowned at me.

"Dad, no is no, I can read myself. I am not a baby," she pouted before running off and scampering into bed. Scarlett smiled faintly, going over to the bed. We both planted a kiss on her forehead.

"Goodnight then," I said as Scarlett tucked her in.

"Night night, baby."

"Night night Mama, night night Daddy," she responded, closing her eyes. I thought she wanted to read a book? This girl really was just a wild one and really dramatic.

"Love you, baby," Scarlett said.

"Love you, too," Azura responded, her eyes snapping wide open as she stared at me unblinking. "I love you, too, even if you are forcing me to go to bed. Punishing me even though it's my birthday... how mean..."

"Love you to the moon," I said, tapping her nose. "Now, don't be dramatic. We want you to sleep so you can enjoy your wild jungle party tomorrow."

"*I. Cannot. Wait!*" She shouted, making me flinch, and she burst out laughing as my ears rang with her unexpected shout.

"Settle down now," Scarlett said, tucking her in again as she pouted before sticking her tongue out at me. I stuck my own out at her, making Scarlett clear her throat and frown at my childishness.

I smirked slightly at Scarlett, who simply shook her head at the two of us as she dimmed the light, and we walked to the door. I glanced around her room. With each passing year, I could see how her choices and preferences changed. Signs that she was growing up and a cold reminder that one day we would have to tell her the truth about her birth.

"You're doing it again," Scarlett murmured, placing her hand on my bare chest and sending off dangerous sparks. My eyes flashed as I looked down at her. The urge to pin her up against the wall right then was really tempting. She closed the door quietly and looked up at me with those sage green eyes that I truly loved.

"Doing what?" I asked, gripping her waist.

"Thinking about it."

"You know we will need to tell her soon," I said quietly. Her eyes shadowed, and she nodded.

"I know... but she's too little... she's too young yet."

"She's going to be nine tomorrow. She's intelligent," I said quietly. She looked down, her chest heaving, and as hard as this was for me, it was going to be harder for her. "It ain't going to change anything," I said quietly. She looked up at me, and I kissed her neck.

"It's not going to be easy either," she whispered.

"When has anything been fucking easy? But we always deal with it, right? Azura is our daughter, no matter what," I said quietly, pulling her against me.

Although Azura knew of Indigo, Scarlett always talked about her and made sure Azura knew about her, she didn't know the truth about her birth. She referred to Indy as Little Mama; it was what Scarlett had made her call her. How she was her little sister who had died a hero. Azura didn't know who her biological parents were or that she wasn't ours technically. I knew before she turned ten, we would need to tell her. She had a right to know, and I didn't want her to feel bitter or resentful later if we left it too late.

Scarlett was about to reply when we heard a door open and shut, then a breathless laugh from Liam.

"Liam!" Raven hissed, giggling, and I heard the sound of a slap. Scarlett and I exchanged looks; Liam was definitely our son.

"Well, how about we get to our own fun," I said seductively, running my hands up her waist before I claimed her lips in a passionate kiss, not waiting for an answer…

LIAM

"Fuck…" I breathed hard as I dropped onto the bed next to Raven.

That had been a hot round of sex. I looked over at Raven. Her tiny body was covered in hickeys, with her breasts and hips stained with red marks left by my touch. She was the sexiest woman I had ever laid my eyes on, and she was mine. I pulled her close, wrapping my arms around her.

"I love you, Liam," she murmured, snuggling even closer. "Goddess, your dick is huge." I raised an eyebrow. That wasn't something I was expecting her to say.

"It's been years since we've been together, love. I would have thought you'd be used to the size by now."

"Yeah, I know. Doesn't mean it's getting any smaller," she smirked, locking her arms around my neck as she pushed me onto my back and straddled my stomach. My breath hitched as she sat above me, wearing nothing but the marks of our lovemaking. Her perky round breasts, curvy hips, and lush thighs…

She ran her hands up my chest before kissing my neck.

"Tomorrow is going to be wild, huh?" I stretched, my gaze dipping to her pussy. That thin strip of hair looked fucking sexy…

"Yes, she wanted a jungle theme party, and we have everything sorted." Raven smiled.

"Thanks for everything you do," I said, pulling her down to kiss her lips and lightly spanking her ass. She smiled as she wriggled against me, making me throb hard.

"This is my family, too. You know she wants everyone to dress as animals or insects." I raised my eyebrow.

"And what are you all going to be? And what is she going to be, dare I ask?" She laughed.

"Well, the birthday girl is going as a bat. She wanted the boys to go as puppies. I'm going as a kitty cat, and Aunty Red is going as a ladybird." A kitty… something told me Raven was going to look damn cute and sexy as hell at the same time.

"And how did Dad and I not know about this?"

"Uncle's going as a pigeon, and you are going as a squirrel. Zuzu's orders."

"A squirrel, really?" She giggled.

"Yes, you and Damon are going as twin squirrels. Don't worry, Robyn found you both some outfits."

"That girl lives to torture me," I groaned. I swore all these women were out to get me at times.

"Because she loves you," she said softly.

"Yeah," I smirked. Either way, I loved my little sister, even if she did torture me.

"So, I'm assuming Artemis and Asher are puppies, too?"

"Yeah, as well as all the other little ones," Raven continued. I watched her, smiling softly, thinking it felt good just to talk about mediocre things without stress and worry in our heads.

"So tell me, does your outfit involve latex?" I asked, grabbing her ass. She raised an eyebrow.

"You'll just have to wait and see. You do know this is a kid's party?" She whispered, brushing her lips lightly against mine.

"Well, we can still have fun," I replied suggestively.

Tingles of pleasure rushed through me before she moved back, lifting herself up slightly. She wrapped her tiny hand around my dick, which was already hard and ready for her, pumping it a few times before she guided it to her entrance and thrust down on it, making me groan as pleasure shot through me. My dick throbbed with her squeezed around me. Life was good.

To a New Future

Three months later...

ALEJANDRO

THE HUM OF CONVERSATION in the room full of men in suits holding glasses of wine only made me want to fucking leave. I pulled at my tie, wanting to fucking toss it aside. If it wasn't for how important this conference was, I wouldn't be here, to begin with. Oh, and the fact that I called for it.

I looked over at Kiara, who was wearing all white and looking fucking fine as she talked to Delsanra. She had a hand resting on her baby bump, a bump that had grown over the last few months. She was glowing; the light that she always seemed to hold showed on her face, and that small smile that I loved so fucking much played on her lips as she talked. Her sandy brown hair was coiled up into an elegant bun on top of her head.

Our pup… we had decided not to find out the gender this time, deciding to keep it a surprise. I knew this was going to be the last, so I made sure I spent as much fucking time by her side as possible, enjoying the fleeting moments and treating her like the fucking queen she was.

"It's almost time, King Alejandro," one of the men who had organised the event said as he bent down next to me.

I gave a curt nod before looking across at Rayhan. He was wearing a suit, his hair back in a bun, but, unlike me, he was at complete ease in this fucking environment, talking business, stocks and investments. How the fuck did Raf and Maria raise the perfect son who was so fucking good at all this shit as well? More so, how the fuck did he get time to do all this boring shit as well as run a pack?

I hated fucking meetings, I hated fucking ties, and I hated being fucking restricted to one damn seat for hours. Fucking businessmen.

It reminded me of school, and I hated school. Why the fuck did we go to school? I learned nothing.

The fucker Rayhan saw me watching and turned, raising one of his brows at me.

"Want to say something?" He asked.

"No," I almost growled, making both Delsanra and Kiara glance at me.

Kiara placed her hand on my thigh, sending a wave of calmness through me, although I thought what would really calm me would be fucking her whilst I used this damn tie to tie her hands up instead.

Rayhan was currently the richest man in the room. It was obvious he held power in the business world, money that funded more than just his pack. The Rossi Empire was vast, and Rayhan held the most shares. The second most wealthy man here was Kenneth Arden... both men were to play an important part in today's event...

I poured another glass of wine, downing it in one go as I frowned, remembering the meeting I'd had with Arden a few weeks ago...

"I'm not here for pleasantries. I'll cut to the chase, Arden. I know what you did to Rafael back at training camp." His face instantly fell as he sat on the leather sofa before he put that mask of indifference back on.

"I see... please understand. I was a teen with issues. What happened... was unforgivable, but let the past be in the past."

"Yeah, but you were never fucking held accountable because the Ardens are one of the richest families in the country, right? Back then, Rafael didn't have much." He seemed to tense but clenched his jaw and nodded curtly.

"There are many accounts of what happened, but I assure you I meant no harm. What you may have heard was not the entire truth." I knew he was probably fucking lying.... but the fact that Raf let it go meant I wasn't here to stir up shit.

"Yeah, maybe fucking so. I have more than one fucking way to get the truth of what happened, to the extent that I can have us revisit that scene from the past, but I'm going to let it go."

I watched him for a reaction, but he remained emotionless. It was obvious that the first comment had taken him off guard, but since then, he was in control. People like him, you needed to be fucking careful of.

"But I think it's high time the Ardens put back into our community. You were fucking eager to create a relationship between us, but no, I'm not here to fucking offer you one of my pups. I'm here to put forward an offer. If you agree, we will be partners in a business venture that will benefit not only our kind but our entire country."

"I'm listening."

"Alejandro, you need to go," Kiara whispered softly, leaning over. She placed a soft kiss on my lips, moving back before I could even deepen it. *I'll make up for that shit later...* "Good luck," she said softly, and I took her hand, kissing it gently.

"Right, let's get this shit done." I stood up. The talking died down as I made my way to the podium at the front, buttoning my suit jacket up.

There were a few guests from witch families and those who held businesses in the human world called from across the city for this meeting. I just needed as many people on board as I could get.

All eyes were on me, and even with my aura reined in, everyone knew who the ultimate Alpha in the room was. I took my place, glancing down at the microphone before looking out at the crowd. Familiar faces, from family to Alphas and Betas from most packs in the country... those who weren't here were getting this live-streamed. This was it, the time to do something as the king of werewolves.

"Thank you for attending and for your patience. I won't take too much of your time, but I request that before you start throwing questions, you hear me the fuck out before putting them forward."

No swearing, remember? Kiara's gentle voice came. Yeah, maybe I shouldn't swear, but I didn't even fucking realise I did it. I glanced over at her and gave her the tiniest of smirks.

"It's been around two decades since I united the packs of the United Kingdom under me, two decades of many trials and many changes. There was a time when each pack held a handful of allies, and the hostility between us was always there. With time, the number of feral rogues has dwindled, the number of killings has lessened, and we are living a better life. However, there have been times that we have been faced with trials. A decade ago, there were monsters that were becoming a threat to our kind, a time that we fought against Endora and those who worked with her, a battle where we lost many; friends, mates, parents, children, and pack members."

I paused for a moment, remembering how many we had lost back then. The hall was silent, the hundreds of people remembering that night. Even if they hadn't been a part of it, or if they had been lucky enough not to lose someone, there was still someone or other they knew who had been affected by it.

"Back then, many of us united to fight that threat, but that time made the hatred towards witches rise, a race that we were fucking enemies with to start with. Yet, let's not forget that my so-called mother was a witch, too. Her blood runs in my veins, no matter how much I fucking hate her. Witches... it was a witch who told us where Endora's attack was to take place. It was only because of her help that we were prepared. A few years passed, and some witches went on to work undercover with the hunters to try to destroy us, however, it was also witches who stood by our side."

I could see the frowns on many faces. The tension in the witch-kind was present as they listened to me. The men frowned deeply, and the women tensed. Some were on edge, as if they might need to use their abilities.

"A few months ago, a mistake made by my ancestors came back for revenge in the form of a devil from hell, and, once again, witches stood by our side. Without them, we may have had many more deaths, but it's a two-way thing. We gave them the security that they could live their lives without the fear of being hunted. There is evil in every race, and there is good. Witches, werewolves, and whatever else is out there. I'm sure there is always going to be more good to outweigh the evil." This was the part that I needed to relay to them. I also hoped, wherever he was, that Leo was watching this.

"I'm not fucking good with words, and I'm not the perfect fucking king. I'm trying, but even then, I've still made mistakes. I'm learning with every passing day to be better. To do better for my people and for all species around us. I want to create a world where we can live in peace and openly. To get rid of the stigma and fear of other species. I want to abolish the Alpha training regime because, in this day and age, are we really only fuck-ing training our sons?" I saw the elder Alphas exchange looks, but before they even tried to protest, I raised my hand, letting my aura roll off me. "Why? Why do only the men get this training when one of the strongest and most incredible Alphas of our time is a female?" I glanced at Scarlett, who looked surprised for a split second before masking it and smiling faintly. "Why are we ranked? Alphas, Betas, Deltas, warriors, Omegas?

From this day forth, I'm abolishing the rank system that has been in place for centuries. No one will be fucking forced to stay in the rank they are born into. If an Omega rank wolf wants to become a warrior, then they can, same with the positions of Beta and Delta. It should go to the most capable in the pack, not by birthright. These are rules that are already held in my pack, but one pack doing this isn't enough." We all knew my pack was different. Darien was of alpha blood himself.

"As for Alphas… Alpha wolves are different; leaders that are needed to look out for their packs. However, I don't want everyone to only consider their firstborn son to be of the position, but the one who is most capable, whether it is a female or male. Our gender shouldn't decide our future."

I glanced at Kiara as she smiled at me proudly. I knew this would really rile everyone up, and I could see the uncertainty spreading through many, yet it was obvious those who felt entitled to the positions were most worried.

"We have two Alphas who were not born to the position, Damon Nicholson and Chris Somers, both of whom have proven far more efficient than many others born from Alpha blood. As time passes, our kind will only grow in number. We need to break away from the age-old rules and start to do what's best for our packs." I took a moment's pause before continuing, "As for those worried about the abolishment of Alpha training, there will still be training. I mean, we can never rule out another threat, who knows what we may have to face in the future? In each huge battle, we have fought alongside witches… so, I have decided, and this is the reason why I have called you all here tonight, to ask for help for the start-up of an academy for our kinds."

All eyes turned on me, and a whisper spread through the crowd, curiosity and interest rippling through them.

"A school for all supernatural species where we co-exist, and I hope someday all traces of hatred toward one another vanishes, even if it takes a few fucking decades. We have to start somewhere. I have already talked to the elders of the coven, who liked the idea of this school. It won't only be for witches, but their male counterparts as well, where they can also learn to fight and train alongside us. There will be the national curriculum, of course, as well as strategy, survival, training, and more. A school where our youth will have the chance to be themselves without having to hide as they currently do in human schools." I took a gulp of water from the glass that stood next to the microphone before scanning the crowds.

"We will start with one academy, and, as time goes on, I am hoping to have at least four by the end of a decade. It will take time to build, get the staff we need, and set it up, however, we have two of our wealthiest Alphas ready to fund the development of these schools; Alpha Kenneth Arden and Alpha Rayhan Rossi. I myself will, of course, be putting in as much as I can. However, today I ask if anyone is willing to provide funding or any help possible. Please, take a read of the brochures that have been prepared and are currently being handed out. They will answer many of your questions and after a thirty-minute break, we will resume and move on to any questions you may have. Thank you."

Everyone began clapping as I walked away from the dais and toward my queen, who stood up as I approached. The look of pride on her face made me feel like I was doing something right. It was going to take time, but I was ready to pave the path to a new future.

No fucking idea how that shit went, but I hope I at least explained something, I said through the link, snaking my arm around her waist and resting my other hand on her stomach as I kissed her softly.

You did amazingly. You explained everything perfectly. I am proud of the vision you wish to create, and I will help in every way I can, she replied, our eyes met, and I kissed her neck. She always did, standing by my side. Always.

Just then, one of the elders of the coven came over, as did Allen, a council member.

"Alpha King Alejandro, that was a pleasant surprise, and might I say it is an honour how you acknowledged our help," the elder from the council said. He was new, and one of the younger ones, but something told me he'd be one of the ones I'd be dealing most with.

"Of course. Credit should be given where due," I said, shaking his offered hand.

"My niece almost died in the battle against the Djinn, yet she told me you moved her to safety. It shows you indeed treat us well. I have some assets and a vast amount of knowledge if the king is interested in having history taught at this school..."

"Why not? It gets kinda tiring having to ask the witches every time I need answers," I joked with a cold smirk, making both men chuckle just as Kenneth came over, nodding to us all before taking Kiara's hand and kissing it.

"You are glowing, Queen Luna."

"Thank you," Kiara replied with a smile, although I was tempted to pull her away from all these damn men. A waiter offered us some drinks, and we all took a glass. "To a new start?" Kiara suggested with a small graceful smile.

"To a new beginning," Allen nodded.

We clinked our glasses before we downed them.

To a better fucking future.

A New Life

ALEJANDRO

"That's it, keep going, Luna. You're almost there," Doctor Linda encouraged.

I ran my hand through my hair. Fuck, I hated this part. I looked down at the hospital bed where Kiara lay, a thin layer of sweat covering her forehead as she held my hand in a tight grip. Her legs were propped up, and she wore a loose button-down dress that reached mid-thigh. Her eyes were shut as she breathed steadily and heavily. Our pup was almost here, but it was giving Kiara a damn hard time. She had been in labour for the last seventy-two hours, and I swore I was going to give this little one a good telling off for putting her through this shit.

Then again, I'm the one who put a pup in her.

"Is the baby here yet?" I heard Azura's voice from the hallway.

"What have I said about patience if you want to wait here? Come on, let's go get something to drink, baby," Scarlett replied. I knew the walls were thick, but even soundproof walls didn't work on my hearing.

Scarlett, Elijah, and Azura had shown up the moment Kiara had gone into labour, but still, there was no sign of baby Rossi, a name everyone had dubbed it since we didn't know the gender.

"You got this, Amore Mio," I said quietly, kissing her forehead. Her gorgeous eyes locked with mine, and she nodded. My brave queen.

"Push for me, Luna," the doctor ordered as Kiara squeezed my hand, obeying. She was strong, barely any sound escaped her, and she hadn't taken any pain relief either.

"Stop."

Kiara breathed heavily, and I breathed with her, guiding her as I pressed my forehead to hers gently.

"You're doing great. Not long now," I said, nodding slowly as I brushed her hair back. It had been braided, but it was no longer as neat as it was yesterday. Strands of her hair stuck to her face, and I gently brushed them back as she rested her head against my chest. Her heart was thundering as I knew another contraction rushed through her.

"Don't fucking focus on the bond," I growled, knowing she was trying to hold the block up so I didn't feel anything. She gave me a weak smile before she let out a gasp of pain as she pushed.

"Another push, come on, Luna, this is it. Our little baby is almost here!" Linda said, relief and excitement in her voice.

"What's your guess?" She whispered before she pushed, biting her lip to stop her scream.

My guess… the movements were unpredictable, and although it was not as wild as Dante had been with the painful kicking, it was still a strong pup. Kiara had said she thought it was a girl, but I had refused to guess. Even now, I had no idea, but either way, I was excited to meet our pup.

"As long as it's healthy, I don't care," I said, kissing her lips softly as she let out a soft scream and pushed with all her might. Her face was scrunched up, but I could tell it was close.

"The heads out. My, that's a lot of hair," Linda said. "Push."

"I am," Kiara replied breathlessly as she focused on the doctor.

My own heart was pounding. The moment to meet our pup was here… I couldn't explain it. No matter if it was the first or third fucking time, it still filled me with nervousness. Would I have a prince or another princess?

Kiara let out a whimper of pain, and I crouched down by the bed, caressing her forehead and holding her hand that gripped mine to my chest.

"You got this, Amore Mio. Our pup's almost here… you are a fucking queen, and you're doing incredibly," I murmured, wishing I could take her pain from her.

Two pushes later, her eyes flashed purple, and she let out a gasp as our pup's cry filled the room. My heart thundered as I looked into Kiara's gorgeous eyes before turning to the doctor.

"Congratulations, Alpha, Luna. It's a beautiful baby girl." I closed my eyes, a strong surge of happiness filling me as Kiara let out a weak laugh.

"A girl. I was right," she murmured as I kissed her shoulder, standing up and hugging her tightly.

"Fuck, you did it. You're fucking incredible," I murmured before moving back as Linda passed our princess to Kiara, who pulled open a few buttons of her dress and rested our pup against her chest. "Thank fuck that's over," I said, kissing Kiara's forehead before turning my attention to our little pup.

A head full of dark hair greeted me before she turned her head up and stared at her mama. A cute button nose, plump lips, and big innocent eyes.

"Fuck, I don't think I can tell her off for causing you so much pain…" I muttered, making Kiara giggle before she kissed our pup once more.

"Of course not. Look at that face, she looks like you!"

She fucking didn't. She was too damn cute.

It's a girl, I said through the link to Elijah and Darien, knowing they'd pass the message on to all our family and to the pack. Linda cut the cord before she looked between us.

"Excuse me. I will give you both a little while," she said, leaving us alone with our pup, unable to hide the smile on her face. The entire pack would party in celebration of the birth of our new pup.

Kiara scooted over a little, and I sat down next to her, wrapping my arm around her as I half lay next to her.

"Have you told anyone?" I nodded.

"Yeah, think everyone's been on edge waiting for this news. I'm fucking proud of you, Amore Mio." She looked up at me, kissing me softly.

"Thank you… for giving me this little angel," she whispered.

"Well… it was fun to make her." I shrugged, making Kiara laugh. "So… name? You said if it was a boy, I got to name him, and if it was a girl, you got to name her. Wait, did Dante tell you it was going to be a girl?"

"No, I didn't ask him." She smiled. "But I have a name. If you trust me, I would like to keep it for her."

"I fucking trust you with everything, go for it. You carried her and went through the pain of birthing her, you deserve to fucking name her," I said, kissing my pup's head.

She wriggled as Kiara adjusted her so she could latch her onto her breast. I almost fucking pouted. Our pup looked up at me as she began sucking on Kiara's nipple. I hated sharing… and those fuckers knew exactly how it irked me. Look how she was looking at me with those innocent eyes of hers…

"Al, you're frowning at her. She'll get scared," Kiara scolded lightly.

"She's a damn Rossi, she won't," I smirked, bending down and kissing her chubby cheek. "So, what's her name?"

"Alessandra Rossi."

My heart skipped a beat as I looked at Kiara in surprise. She smiled softly, giving me a small nod, knowing I had clicked on. A derivation of my name...

"And it couldn't be more fitting because she looks just like her namesake," she said softly.

I looked down at our pup, unable to say anything. The emotions were fucking making me go blank. *Fuck, I think her emotions were seeping through the bond 'cause I don't get this emotional, right?* Yeah, they were hers. I ain't that fucking soft.

"Do you like it?" She asked, making me look at her, trying to make sense of the influx of emotions that consumed me.

"Yeah, it's... do I really deserve to have a pup named after me?" I asked quietly. Her eyes glittered with tears as her smile faded away.

"Shit, don't cry. Fuck, I didn't mean to make you cry," I said, brushing the first of her tears away.

"Then don't ever ask do you deserve it or not. She is lucky to be named after a true king in all aspects and even luckier to have you as her father," she said. "I love you, Alejandro, and please, never ever think you don't deserve anything. You are one of the most incredible beings I know."

"Yeah, well, thanks to you. I won't, okay?" I promised, wrapping my arm around her shoulder tighter. She rested her head against my chest, and I ran my fingers through our pup's hair with my other hand.

"I can't believe she's here," Kiara whispered softly.

"Yeah? She was a few days late, though."

"I know, but it's still a miracle."

It was. There was just something inexplicable about witnessing our pup come into this world. Seeing the miracle that Kiara was a part of...

"Yeah, it is. How are you feeling?"

"Tired..." she whispered, smiling up at me.

She must be. She had been at this on and off, but the last few days had been killer, not to mention her seventy-two-hour labour had been really fucking draining for her.

"Sleep. I'll take her to meet the rest."

"I want to shower first, but I am exhausted," she said, wrapping a shawl around Alessandra, who had fallen asleep already, a dribble of milk at the corner of her mouth. "She needs burping," Kiara murmured as she passed her to me, and I mind-linked the doctor to come back.

"I'll deal with her. Come on, little one, let's meet the rest of the fuckers."

The moment the door opened and Linda stepped inside, I walked past her and looked at the crowd that awaited us. Kiara's parents, Maria, Delsanra, Rayhan, and my three pups.

"Can I see her?" Dante asked quickly. I smirked as I lowered her to her siblings. Kataleya and Skyla rushed forward as well, excitement clear on their faces.

"Oh, she's so cute," Kataleya exclaimed, kissing her cheek tenderly.

"She's my minion," Skyla breathed in awe.

"She's perfect," Dante said as Azura came over and nodded her agreement, kissing her feet.

"I have such a beautiful niece," she said, sounding way fucking older than she was. "You made a cute baby, Alejandro, well done!" Her words made everyone laugh, and I smirked at her.

"Thanks, kid. "Here you go," I said, holding her out to Elijah with a smirk. "Another granddaughter for you."

Before he could even take her, Scarlett stepped forward, quickly taking her from me as Elijah smiled, looking down at her.

"She's beautiful. Have you got a name yet?" Scarlett asked, kissing the baby as Delsanra and Maria gathered around her.

"Alessandra," I said gruffly. As expected, all eyes turned on me, and I glared back. "I didn't choose it, Kiara did."

"It's perfect," Maria said softly.

"I like it too!" Azura added. I smirked, ruffling her hair as she kissed Alessandra's hand. "I'm your aunty, and us A girls stick together, okay?"

"Raihana's on her way," Rayhan smirked as I heard the sound of heels.

"I want to see my baby cousin!" She said with excitement, holding her own baby, who was six weeks old, in her arms.

Maria took Heaven from her as Raihana scooped Alessandra away from Scarlett. Everyone began gushing over her again, and I glanced over at Heaven, who was eating her hand contently. She was a cutie with light brown hair and brown eyes. I glanced back at the open door, wanting to see my queen again.

"She's not wearing a nappy. I'll clean her up myself once they weigh her and do the checks," Scarlett was saying.

"Raven and Liam are on the way, too," Rayhan added. I zoned them out, simply watching them all talk and chatter.

Kataleya was improving a little. Although she still wore the necklace at all times, she carried her teddy less. She still tried doing everything with one hand. Delsanra was working with her, but it was going to take time... I glanced back at the door to the room as Scarlett stepped forward.

"How is she?"

"Tired but good. She went to shower," I told her with a jerk of my head. Scarlett nodded, and I realised she needed to see her daughter, so when I heard Kiara emerge, I motioned for her to go in. "She's out. Go." She gave me a grateful smile as she hurried inside.

"Kiara, congratulations, my baby!"

"Mom..."

"She's beautiful... I'm so proud of you..."

I leaned against the wall, giving them some space as Elijah stepped up, leaning against the wall next to me.

"Still feels surreal right?"

"Yeah. Can't believe I'm a dad of four now." I crossed my arms, looking at my little one in Rayhan's arms as Delsanra whispered something in baby talk to her.

"Yeah, you fucking beat me. Now don't go making my daughter go through that again. Besides, you ain't fucking young anymore," he said cockily, and I smirked.

"Do you really want me to answer that?" I asked cockily.

"No," Elijah replied, and although we didn't bother turning, I could feel two pairs of eyes watching us, my own green-eyed Lucifer incarnate and the Westwood devil.

"Good," I remarked, about to reach for a cigarette before I decided against it.

After a few more minutes, I knocked, and Kiara told us to enter. The kids ran in first, hugging her. Linda had gotten the room cleaned up, and the sheets changed.

"Mama, are you okay?" Kataleya asked softly.

"I'm perfectly fine, my baby," Kiara responded, kissing and hugging them all.

I heard Delsanra whisper a spell before she hugged Kiara, and I knew she was healing her. One by one, they congratulated her. I gave them space, although all I wanted was to hold my queen in my fucking arms. I watched as Elijah stroked her hair.

It made me think that one day, my girls would have their own mates… how was I going to deal with that shit? Whoever my girls were mated to, they better treat them right, or I fucking swear, I'd destroy them.

❧❦❧

An hour had passed, and although Kiara had wanted to rest, everyone was too excited. Finally, Scarlett had to firmly get everyone to leave, telling Kiara, who had just finished feeding Alessandra, to get some rest. It was finally just the three of us in the dimly lit room.

"I'm sorry you didn't get to rest," I said quietly. Kiara yawned as she stretched, making her shirt strain against her breasts.

"It's fine, Delsanra healed me, so I feel so much better," she said, yawning again.

"But you need sleep. You've not slept properly in three days." She nodded before scooting over on the bed.

"Then come hold me so I can sleep. I've missed having you pressed against me fully."

I smirked. I fucking missed that, too, although I had enough fun either way. I slid into the sheets beside her and lifted her head onto my arm as I pulled her close.

"I love you, Amore Mio."

"I love you too, my love." As much as I could fucking talk to her forever, I needed her to get some rest.

"Sleep," I said huskily as I claimed her lips in a deep kiss.

"Mm," she agreed, her eyes fluttering shut as she kissed me softly before snuggling firmly against me. Although I knew I'd have a fucking hard-on despite the lack of sleep, I was just glad the labour was over and our little princess was by our side…

Welcome to the family, little one.

Epilogue

KIARA

JUST OVER ONE YEAR LATER...

*I*T WAS NEW YEAR'S Eve, and we had all been invited to the Blood Moon Pack this year. Maria, Del, Ri, and everyone was here. This year, although we were having a huge party with the two packs tomorrow, today was just a smaller group which included the Beta and Delta families of the Blood Moon and the Blue Moon. Del, Ri, Raven, Robyn, Taylor, and I were in the kitchen at Mom's. Dinner had been prepared by Mom, Aunty Monica, and Maria, so the six of us were responsible for the desserts.

We'd had a late lunch, and the kids had had an early dinner before they had taken naps as the older ones wanted to stay awake for the fireworks. As for Asher, Sienna, Alessandra, and Heaven, they would be put to bed before midnight, with Raihana saying magic would keep their rooms totally soundproof from the sound of fireworks.

"Daddy, can I have another cookie?" Chase, Taylor and Zack's three-year-old son, asked.

"Not now, okay? Aunty Raven says no," Taylor responded, making Raven narrow her eyes at him.

"I never said that! Here you go!" She took one as Taylor pouted at her before Chase chuckled and ran off.

"That was his fourth cookie," Robyn said with a small smile.

"Exactly." Taylor nodded, crossing his arms as Raven looked at him sheepishly.

"Well... I can't say no to kids, you know that!" She said as she cleared the sides.

Raven wasn't much of a cook, so she was given the task of preparing the trays. Raihana was making the mocktails, although her magic was doing the job as she sat there waving her hands and breastfeeding Heaven.

"Well, it's New Year's. Besides, you can never have enough cookies," Delsanra said, biting into one herself.

"Coming from a true foodie." I laughed. Raihana sighed and nodded.

"Yes, although I feel recently I gain weight faster," she said with a small smile on her face, watching Heaven, who was drifting off.

"I don't see it," I said, shaking my head, and the others agreed.

"How is she during the nights?" Raven asked her.

"She's not too bad, but Chris is a sweetheart. He really helps out as I breastfeed her, so I want her in my room. I have, like, an adjoining room to mine. Chris is an expert at burping her and settling her in again," she replied with a smile.

"He sounds like a sweetie," Taylor said.

"I think all our mates really are," I said, smiling as I looked around at the others.

"I agree. Let's list our top favourite thing about our mates, and I don't just mean what they might be packing." Taylor winked at Raven. I didn't get the inside joke, but when she blushed and giggled, I had a feeling I didn't want to know if it involved my brother!

"He treats me like a queen," Raihana replied with a toss of her head.

"A queen that you are," I added teasingly, putting mini-Oreos into the Oreo cheesecake shots.

"Of course, I am a Rossi by blood. Royalty is in my genes," she said airily, making us all laugh.

"Rayhan... I don't know how to choose just one thing, but he never gave up on me even when I had given up on myself. He's the truest and sexiest man I have ever met. Not only that, but he's an incredible son, too." Delsanra smiled, a faint blush on her cheeks.

"He is. I think Rayhan definitely gets the award for being the most charming Alpha around," Raven agreed. "Robyn, your turn."

"Damon's kindness. He always puts others before him, and he has a heart of gold." I nodded. I agreed with that one, too.

"It's true, Damon always gives and never expects anything in return," Raven agreed, sprinkling chocolate over the trifles.

"Oh, I'm sure he expects enough in return, right Robyn?" Raihana smirked, startling Robyn a little, but even with her chocolate skin tone, I saw the slight blush on her cheeks.

"Aww, someone's blushing," I teased as Delsanra and Taylor whistled.

"I'm not," Robyn denied, making me chuckle.

"My turn! Liam, I love the way he's so pure. He's always so patient and caring. Honestly, you may not see it, but he's always worrying for others. He always thinks about his family and makes time for everyone," Raven stated with a smile. I nodded. It was true, Liam did do what he could for us all.

"For me, it's what an amazing dad Zack is to Chase, and on top of that, what an incredible mate he is to me, someone I can always rely on," Taylor added, smiling faintly.

"Aww," Raven said, hugging him. "You're getting emotional."

"I'm not," Taylor said, hugging her back. "So, what about our queen's mate?"

My mate, my king, my Alejandro...

"His heart. Alejandro always cares for others, and he never expects credit for it. He doesn't even see how much he does or how much he cares. He does everything from the heart. He's perfect," I said softly, my heart skipping a beat at the thought of him.

"That's sweet. You two are an amazing couple," Robyn said with a small smile as the rest nodded their agreement.

"A very hot couple, too," Taylor added, making me smile slightly.

"I guess so."

"Mama?" I turned, seeing Kataleya standing in the doorway.

One year on, her heart wasn't healed, but her smile had returned to her face. My angel was over seven now, and although it broke my heart to see her still using one hand when she thought no one was watching, I just prayed that with time she would heal. She still wore the locket Alejandro had gotten for her, but Kiké was the one she hugged while sleeping at night.

"Yes, my darling?" I asked as I motioned her to come in.

The worktops were covered in trays of baked goodies and mini dessert shots. Raven had asked why they were so small considering how much everyone ate, but visually appealing food was needed, right?

"Can I get some milk for me and the girls?" She asked. I planted my hands on my hips.

"Did Azura or Skyla send you?" She looked at her shoes before glancing at the hallway door.

"Skyla did," she admitted after a moment.

"Tell her she can come have some in the kitchen. Azura, too." She nodded before running off. I went to the fridge to get the milk out.

Azura... Mom and Dad had told her the truth about her birth a few weeks ago, and she didn't seem bothered. In fact, she had asked why it was necessary to tell her when she was still their favourite daughter either way. Mom was worried about her reaction, saying she feared she'd keep stuff inside. Although she didn't say it out loud, I knew she meant like Aunty Indy keeping her troubles inside. Mom had made it clear to her that if she ever wanted to know more or had questions, she and Dad were there to explain and answer them for her. However, Azura didn't change, being the same firework as always. Mom had nothing to worry about because Azura loved her greatly. She was Liam's and my baby sister, Dad's and Mom's daughter, and nothing would change that.

Alejandro had told Mom and Dad about Atlas as well, and although Dad didn't think it was important for them to ever know of each other, Mom said that it wasn't his or her choice to make but Azura's. In a few years, they'd tell her about him, too, not wanting to overburden her right now.

"What's on your mind?" A deep voice came as a strong pair of arms locked around my waist, sending off a storm of sparks through me.

"Oi, no men in the kitchen!" Raven ordered. "It's too crowded in here!" Alejandro cocked a brow before glancing at Taylor, who simply smiled sweetly.

"I'm helping," he said.

"I think Raven meant no useless men," Delsanra added. "Sorry, King Burrito." I smiled as I kissed his lips.

"Missing you," I murmured.

"Same... how long are you going to be fucking stuck in here? The kids are driving me fucking nuts." I laughed. The men had been given the job of entertaining the kids, although the older kids were entertaining themselves.

"Are my nephews annoying you?" I teased.

Liam's boys were a handful, and the older they got, the rowdier they became. They were nearly four now, and, Goddess, they had the energy to channel a hundred adults. Renji was gentler, and Ares was pretty lazy at times, but they were still hyper.

"Very much. Guess they take after their mother," Alejandro replied, casting Raven a withering glare, one that she returned with equal passion. I shook my head as Robyn hid her smile.

"Where's Alessandra?" I asked. Alejandro, who was a little distracted by my breasts, staring utterly shamelessly at them, looked up at me.

"With Scarlett," he said with a cold smirk.

I smiled at our little Alessandra. She was the double of Al, no matter what he said. Everyone saw it but him. She was the little baby everyone spoilt. She was also Dante's favourite sister, something he didn't mind reminding everyone of, especially when Skyla annoyed him, although he said Kataleya was a close second. He and Skyla clashed a lot, with them both having strong personalities. However, Skyla pushed him to his limits often. The older she got, the more her personality came out, and she was the most aggressive of my children. Dad said she was a little Alpha female in the making.

The trio, plus Malevolent, who was Skyla's shadow, entered just as Alejandro left the kitchen reluctantly.

"Who called?" Azura asked as she lowered the shades she was wearing, holding a candy stick as a cigarette in her mouth.

"And who do we have here?" Raven asked, leaning over the counter.

"We are the Devil's Angels, now, who summoned us?" Azura asked, tossing her hair as Skyla put on her best frown as she crossed her arms. Kataleya, who looked like anything but a devil's angel, blinked as she stared at the other two.

"Well, I heard certain angels wanted milk?" I asked.

"Oh, yes." Azura flicked her hair as she took a puff on her fake cigarette, making the rest of us shake our heads. Just that morning, they were pop singers. The trio sauntered over to the table, and I took the glasses of milk over to them.

"Thanks, Kiara," Azura said, giving me a small smile before she slipped her glasses down and crossed her legs as Delsanra placed a cookie in front of each of them. "Thank you, miss." I resisted a chuckle. She was ten now, but she looked so much older. She was Mom's height already, and I was sure soon she'd pass me, too.

"Okay, the trifles are done," Taylor announced, turning and giving us a smile.

"And so is everything else," Delsanra said as she munched on another cookie. "Can we go to our mates now? I miss my yum yum."

"Dare I ask what exactly you miss?" Raihana asked with a suggestive smirk. Delsanra blushed lightly before she waved her hand.

"Hey, I haven't seen him for a few hours," she pouted.

"Hmm, or his -" Taylor was cut off by Robyn placing her hand over his mouth as Raihana burst out laughing.

"You're my type of friend Tay." She winked at him, and he blew her a kiss.

"Kids are present," Robyn reminded Taylor, making Raven giggle.

"I think we are all done. Our witch team can keep the temperatures for each dessert just right. Let's go get ready for the night," I said, running my hand through my hair.

"Already done," Delsanra said with a flick of her finger, and I felt the temperature behind me drop around the trays of mini cheesecake shots.

"My favourite part! Getting dolled up," Raihana said, standing up as she carried the sleeping Heaven in her arms.

"Of course it is," Delsanra responded.

"Okay, let's say we have an hour to shower and spend some time with our sexy men before we meet up again?" I suggested. Although we all had our own accommodations, with some at the packhouse, we were all getting ready here.

"Sexy men. Yuck, there's nothing sexy about all of those gorillas who just growl every time they're angry," Azura snickered as she sucked on her straw, slurping the milk up loudly before she did a mock growl, making Skyla cackle and almost fall out of her seat.

"I'm an Alpha! Growl growl," she said mockingly before she and Azura high-fived one another.

"Daddy and Granddaddy aren't yuck," Kataleya said, looking saddened. "No one is yucky... and Rayhan is never dirty either..."

"Rayhan isn't yuck. He has nice hair," Skyla added. "I think long hair is nice." I raised my eyebrow. Were they really discussing men?

"Well, when you all find your own mates, I'm sure you won't be calling them yucky. Well, if they're men anyway," Angela said, coming into the kitchen.

"Yeah, yeah, but even if they're our mates, they will still be gross men," Azura replied. Kataleya seemed lost in thought again, but the small smile on her face made me relax.

I left the kitchen, spotting Marcel talking to Channing, Damon's mom's mate, and Rick, who was Robyn's brother. The entire house was alive with hustle and bustle, and to my surprise, Damon and Alejandro were talking, but before I could even say it was a miracle, I realised Asher was standing there, looking sad, whilst Alejandro was holding Alessandra rather protectively.

"I don't trust him," he was saying to Damon, who looked thoroughly amused.

"He's just a two-year-old pup," he said, "ain't you, kiddo?"

"What's happening here?" I asked, taking Alessandra, who was beginning to look rather upset in her father's arms.

"He was kissing her," Alejandro growled, making Asher's eyes begin to glitter with tears. I frowned, glaring at Alejandro.

"He's a child, let them kiss if they want," I scolded, placing Alessandra back on the floor. Damon chuckled as Alejandro turned his glare on him.

"That's what I said. He's just doting on her," Maria said as Asher wrapped his arms around Alessandra, and, to my utter amusement, planted a chaste kiss on her lips, making her go all shy.

"I like baby," Asher said cutely.

"This shit ain't happening," Alejandro growled, taking our daughter and walking off. "I don't trust Nicholson men."

"And I don't trust Rossi men!" Azura shouted after him as she came out of the kitchen and picked Asher up. "Mean Rossi men."

"Hey, what did I do to you?" Rayhan asked as he came in from outside with Liam, a small smirk on his face as he looked at Azura.

"You are the only Rossi man that I actually don't mind," Azura said, giving him a wink before she walked off with Asher.

"Ouch, that hurt," Marcel joked, placing a hand on his chest and making a few of us chuckle.

"What did we just miss?" Liam asked, wrapping his arms around Raven and kissing her neck.

"You don't want to know, babe," she responded as he lifted her up to kiss her lips.

I smiled as I shook my head, watching as Delsanra and Robyn went to their respective mates. Damon pulled Robyn against him and kissed her softly as Rayhan kissed Delsanra's hand before pulling her close and claiming her lips in a passionate kiss. Yes, every couple was perfect. I glanced back at Taylor and Raihana.

"No, really, what did I miss?" Taylor asked, having stepped out of the kitchen too late to see what had happened.

"Not much. Just a Rossi behaving in a very typical Rossi way," I said with a small laugh as I decided to go after my stubborn protective mate...

⁂

SCARLETT

I looked in the mirror, applying my trademark red lipstick. Years had passed but some things never changed, like my love for the colour red. I was wearing a sequined black dress that reached the ground, the sequins bleeding into a deep red from the knee downwards. There was also a thigh-high slit on the left. I had my hair sleekly straightened and I had just finished applying my lipstick when Elijah stepped out of the bathroom, already dressed in wine-red pants and jacket, with a black shirt underneath it. His hair was styled sexily, letting his natural waves fall over his forehead, his sandy brown hair now sprinkled with a dusting of silver.

He licked his lips as he looked me over his eyes flashing cobalt blue and his tongue piercing caught the light. Goddess, he still made my core throb, just like he always did. I could never resist that man. I bit my lip as I smoothed the fabric of my dress, slowly watching as he closed the gap between us, gripping my waist.

"So, how do I look?" I asked sexily.

Nearly three decades on, he still looked at me like I was the only one in his world. When he looked at me, it was as if time itself paused, as if it was just the two of us in that moment. His response was to bend me backwards and kiss me passionately, making my body combust with fireworks.

"You look fucking divine, kitten," he said huskily, grabbing my ass as we broke apart. I smiled, staring up into his eye.

"You look pretty sexy yourself," I replied, running my hand down his chest as he slowly pulled me upright.

Our eyes met, and, tiptoeing, I kissed his neck before resting my head against his chest. No matter what life threw our way, we would always face it together.

"Well let's get down there, the food all smells great, although nothing beats how good you smell right now. I'll be saving my favourite dessert for last," he said, squeezing my ass once again as we left our room.

"Can't wait, baby," I replied, just as Azura came running up the stairs. I had done her hair before I had gone to get ready myself.

She looked stunning in a black sequined dress with a touch of eyeliner and gloss - which Elijah had been really unsure about. Whether he liked it or not, our baby girl was getting older.

"You're here! Wow, you both look so good!" She complimented. "Can you call Kiara, too? It's only you guys left to come now!" Not waiting for a reply, she ran back down the stairs.

"She's got energy at all times of the day," Elijah said, shaking his head.

"I think it's a family thing," I said with a smile as I reached up and kissed him before I turned, looking down the hallway. "Kiara, hurry up! We're all waiting for you guys!"

"Kk, Mom, coming!" Kiara called, and I paused, glancing back down the hall. A wave of nostalgia washed over me. I smiled faintly, shaking my head as I carried on down the stairs with my man by my side…

ELIJAH

The garden was already decorated with fairy lights and some balloons. The décor was in deep midnight blue and silver. The tables were all covered in midnight blue cloths with silver confetti decorating them. The buffet table was to the right, with a few tables set up for when we ate. On the opposite side was the dessert table, which had a variety of desserts as well as a chocolate fountain. A shimmering blue cloud hung over it, and, when the kids approached, they were covered with puffs of silver confetti, making them giggle, courtesy of Raihana, I was sure.

The quintuplets, Tatum, and Ahren kept going near the dessert table, getting excited as they tried to avoid the glitter. Artemis was sitting at the kids' table eating chicken. That one loved her food. Despite the fact that it was nearly midnight, those kids were as fresh as if it was morning. Dante was leaning against a tree and staring at the sky whilst Azura and Skyla were already dancing to the music. Kataleya was playing with Chase as Maria watched them.

Rayhan and Delsanra were in the corner, with Rayhan leaning over her as she leaned back against a tree. I glanced towards Scarlett, who came over to me with two glasses of mocktails. Her hips swayed sensually, her dress hugging her perfect curves as she walked toward me.

"Queen of hearts," she said, holding the red drink out to me.

"Hmm, she's right before me," I replied flirtatiously, snaking my free arm around her as I pulled her close, crushing her breasts against me. Her intoxicating floral scent invaded my senses as I kissed her lips softly. "The personification of temptation and sin itself," I whispered huskily in her ear as I kissed her there sensually. Her heart raced, her breath hitching. Years on, and I still had that effect on her.

"And what exactly are you? Tell me, my forbidden Alpha." She winked, and I smirked.

I sometimes forgot the fact that she was my stepsister, but like I'd said a thousand fucking times, I didn't care if she was forbidden to me or whether she was my fated mate. As long as I had her in my life, I needed nothing else.

"Well, like they say, life in forbidden sin is best."

I bent her over backwards, making her gasp as she tried to balance her drink while I kissed her like it was the last fucking time. Someone let off some fireworks, a whistle, and I thought I heard someone saying, 'Go get it, Uncle El!' but I wasn't sure who it was because I was far too lost in my kitten…

RAVEN

I whistled loudly the moment Uncle El kissed Aunty Red, looking so damn fine. I saw Raihana snap a picture of them as she let off a firework. She looked incredible as well in a sexy metallic gold dress; like always, she stood out from the crowd!

"Check Uncle getting it on," I giggled, leaning back against my mate.

Everyone was here. Aunty A and Cassandra were sitting off to the side, looking all loved up. Damon and Robyn were having a moment in the shadows of the trees. Aunty M and Channing were playing with Artemis and Asher. Al had said he needed a restraining order on the poor kid, just because he was such a gentleman! But I guess kissing the king's daughters was not a good idea. I giggled at the thought.

Taylor and Zack were having drinks as they talked to Rick and his mate.

Al and Kiara had just come out. I smiled, watching them go over to Marcel and Maria whilst Kataleya joined them. The entire atmosphere was one of perfection. Life really was good.

I snuggled against Liam, loving when he groaned slightly as I rubbed against his manhood. I was wearing a black, corset lace net dress with a slit down from my right hip with matching gloves and black heels. My purple dark-to-light ombre hair was curled and left open. Liam looked handsome in a dark purple shirt with black pants.

"Oh yeah? If you want to bail on this early, I really don't mind."

"I'm sure you would love that, but didn't we just have a little fun?" I whispered as he kissed my neck, running his hand down my stomach. We had ended up in the shower together, and, well, one thing led to another…

"It's never enough when it involves you," he whispered, tightening his arms around my waist just as Jayce shouted,

"You loser!" to Carter, who was already looking angry. They all looked cute in black pants and different coloured shirts.

"Shut up!"

"Jayce, Carter, language," Liam warned.

I shook my head, watching our boys. It was shocking how fast they were growing. They wore clothes a few years up from their age, but I guessed that was to be expected with Alpha babies. If I was somewhat expecting one of them to take after me in terms of height or size, I was very wrong. My perfect five.

There was a time I thought I'd never belong anywhere, that I'd never truly have a family to call my own. But I was wrong. Not only did I get an uncle and an aunty who were like true parents to me, but I also found so much more. I was given my childhood love, my first love, as my mate. I couldn't be luckier…

"I love you," I whispered.

"Love you too, bite-size," he replied before he kissed me once more…

⁂

LIAM

We broke apart, and I looked down at her, running my hands up her slender gloved arms.

I like these gloves… I murmured through the bond.

So do I, she said, caressing my face.

"Mommy, look!" Ares exclaimed, holding out a cake pop to Raven. "Do you want some?"

"Aw, yes please!" Raven replied, moving away from me and bending down before our son. In a few years, she'd be this tiny doll with her five bodyguards. She took a bite of the cake pop before kissing Ares' cheek.

"Oh, Mommy, careful." He lifted her dress from the floor. "Your dress is getting dirty."

"Thank you, baby." She smiled and stood up as he ran off to the dessert table again, being doused in a puff of silver confetti.

"These boys are going to grow up and protect you, no matter what. Five bodyguards."

"Make it six. I have you, too, remember?" She reminded me, turning in my arms. I winked at her, bending down, and wrapped my arms around her thighs before I lifted her up. She smiled, locking her arms around my neck as I looked up at her, kissing her chest.

"You'll always have me and everyone else. You lived your life caged between expectations and your dreams, torn between what you wanted and what was expected of you, but you're a free bite-sized bird now with a family that loves you immensely. I'm lucky to get to call you mine. This pack is lucky to have you as their Luna, and heck, our sons are the luckiest to have you as their mother. You are my every dream and so much more, love," I said quietly, looking into her unique eyes.

She smiled softly. Her emotions were clear in her eyes, and just as we were about to kiss, we felt several pairs of eyes on us. I didn't need to turn to know they belonged to our pups as I claimed her lips in a deep passionate kiss, pouring everything I had into it…

❧ ❦ ❧

DAMON

"Hey, easy there, Art!" I said, catching hold of our princess. She turned to me, her hair bouncing.

"I'm fine, Dad, don't worry!" She tugged free and was about to run off when she stopped and pouted, "I love you." I chuckled.

"No kiss?"

She ran back to me, wrapping her arms around my neck and kissing my cheek quickly before she ran off.

"You can't catch me, boys!" She challenged before she darted off in the opposite direction.

"She's going to be a fast one," Robyn said with a small smile.

"Hmm, yeah, and a crazy fast runner," I agreed, looking down at her. I pulled her close, thinking she looked so damn good in her brown chiffon mini dress with sequins over the chest area and scattered over the skirt of it.

"Definitely," she said, running her hand down my chest.

I smiled softly, pulling her into a tight hug, I'd always be grateful for having Robyn. She was the queen I couldn't do without. I didn't deserve her, but she had been willing to love me and have me. There we were, happy and content with our little family. She looked up and I leaned down to kiss her, just as Liam and Raven came over.

"Here's to another year," Liam said, passing us both a glass after I moved back from her.

"To another year," I said with a small smirk.

Years ago, we had hit a rough patch in our friendship, but it felt like decades ago. Things were completely fine between us now. We were still the best of friends, brothers, even closer than ever, and we shared everything. Everything but mates.

I chuckled at my own joke, making the three look at me questioningly.

"It's nothing. To our women," I said to Liam, raising my glass.

"To our birdies," he said, clinking our glasses, making me laugh as Robyn narrowed her eyes at him and Raven giggled.

"Liam's still putting his foot in it, I presume?" Zack said as he and Taylor came over. Raven nodded as Liam looked lost as to what he had done.

"Yes," Robyn said pointedly.

"You don't look like a bird," I reassured her.

"I know," she replied.

"Typical Liam," Taylor replied cheekily, shaking his head with a small smile.

"I swear I have no idea what was so wrong about that," Liam said as Raven patted his arm, trying not to laugh at his expression.

Yep, things have never been better.

RAYHAN

"Let me take pictures with my girl!" Raihana said, forcing me to move away from Delsanra, who I'd had up against a tree.

I raised an eyebrow, but she didn't wait for permission, pulling my kitten away with her. She was in a metallic gold dress herself, whilst Del looked fucking fine in a powder blue strapless mini dress with a dipping neckline. The dress was like a fitted ribbed corset that was cut in a V, showing off her thighs, with a bling border and dangly strings of silver gems around the entire hem of it that glittered and swayed with every move she made. Her hair was up in a messy, sexy bun, and even now, as she talked to Raihana, she was the epitome of temptation and beauty.

"I don't know if I should be jealous of Delsanra or smug at the fact you're suffering with me," Chris remarked, coming over. He was wearing a black and gold shirt with white pants.

"Don't you get bored wearing what she tells you?" I mocked, ignoring his taunt. He looked a little gutted.

"She said it's my choice, as she has Tatum and Heaven to match with now," he said, making me smirk.

"You know she said that just to make sure you want to match. Raihana wouldn't sacrifice her aesthetically perfect images, but she's smart enough to put it back on you if you ever said you didn't want to by saying she doesn't care," I remarked.

"Well, it's not like your mate gets much say in her outfits. Ri always chooses hers, too." I nodded, looking at them as they pouted for the picture, arms wrapped around one another.

"Well, Delsanra doesn't mind," I said, running my hand through my hair.

I was wearing a printed stone-coloured shirt with my sleeves pushed up, half tucked into my cropped cream pants, which were paired with brown shoes, a belt, and beaded jewellery. Ahren tied in with us, with his pants the same colour as mine and a blue shirt like Del's dress. Who was I kidding? I guess even she liked to coordinate us.

"One more," Raihana was saying, adjusting Delsanra's hair. "Demon mode, girl, come on, let's see that sexiness."

Fuck.

I watched her shift, her lips becoming plumped, her entire body turning ten fucking times hotter, if that was even possible, and felt myself harden in my pants. I looked away. She knew I couldn't resist her when she shifted…

I heard her laugh, and I knew it was because she knew the effect that she had on me. I glanced back at her, my eyes meeting her red ones. There was a time when I feared she'd never recover from her trauma, and although there were still times her demons returned to haunt her, she was doing better than I could have ever hoped for.

Not only was she a survivor, but she was helping so many others with their traumas as well. She travelled around to other packs, helping where she could and encouraging each pack to have a councillor. I think people forgot that despite being werewolves, we were human, too. Battles, death, and trauma left lasting effects.

Times were changing, and I was happy to see the growth in our kind, seeing Delsanra welcomed into packs. Sure, there were still those who disliked witches, even if they tried to hide it, but still, things were getting better. As they said, Rome was not built overnight. All things took time…

DELSANRA

"Oi, photogenic boy, come here!" Raihana called to Dante, who raised an eyebrow.

"No thanks," he replied.

"Please?" I asked, making him roll his eyes. He may act like he didn't have a soft spot for me, but he still did.

It had been months since we had that conversation, and I was glad to see that the small crush he had on me was fading away. His words were still in my mind,

"It's time I let you go. I know you are Rayhan's mate, and you always will be. I promised him that I would stop pursuing you. Let's be friends?"

He had been nine at the time, but he had acted so much older. Dante was older than his age in many ways, yet his little crush on me had been one of the most innocent and childish things he had. He seemed to have matured even more since. We still had our bond, one that had become even stronger.

He sauntered over, shoving his hands into his pockets as he posed for the picture.

"Oh, look... I'm taller than you now," he smirked as I looked down at my heels, not missing how he smirked at Rayhan.

"Well, something tells me you will be taller than your dad, who is huge as it is," Raihana said as Dante put his arms around us, posing for the picture. I could feel Rayhan watching us and, glancing over at him, flashed him a smile. I guess his trying to annoy him wouldn't go away completely!

"Uncle, picture!" Raihana shouted as Dante and I took the chance to sneak away.

Rayhan had gone over to Ahren and was helping him unwrap a lollipop. I smiled as I ruffled Ahren's hair. He ran off, and I locked my arms around Rayhan's neck.

"With those poses and this dress, I think you could put on one hell of a show tonight," he said, gripping my hips as his nose brushed mine. My heart pounded as I stared up at him slightly coyly, despite the seductive smile on my lips.

"I think I can do that," I whispered before our lips met in a sizzling kiss.

I had nothing, and then he gave me everything. He moved the world for me. He was my king, my god, my destined Alpha, one who would always be mine…

RAIHANA

I had just taken countless pictures of all the kids. Only the youngest four weren't there, but I had gotten lots of pictures of them earlier. I looked up at the moon and slipped my phone into my purse. It was almost time… another hour left until the beginning of a new year…

A strong pair of arms wrapped around me, and I smiled, leaning into Chris' arms as he passed me a glass.

"So, any New Year's resolutions?" He asked, sipping his wine.

"None at all, but I have a wish," I said, looking up at my handsome mate.

"Yeah? What exactly would that be, princess, considering you have the world your feet?" I smiled.

"Of course I do, but the best part is I have you. My wish is for everything to always remain like this. Peaceful, happy, and perfect."

"Aiy to that." He raised his drink before kissing my neck as he admired me. "And to love, to us, and to lots of sex." I smirked.

"Oh, absolutely," I replied, raising my own glass. We clinked them before taking a sip.

Life was perfect. Even if everyone we loved wasn't still here, they would never be forgotten.

Chris kissed me, and I let myself melt into his touch, feeling the sparks storm through me welcomingly.

Wait! I needed to take a selfie of this moment!

MARIA

I smiled as Alejandro gave me a tight hug.

"I like your dress, Mama Mari," Kataleya said, stroking the skirt of my dress. I was wearing an Arabian kaftan today. It was a duck egg colour with gold patterns on it.

"Thank you, darling." I smiled at her. "Nowhere near as beautiful as yours."

"Thank you! Mama chose it," she said as Marcel chuckled.

"I think everyone looks amazing tonight," he added, crossing his arms.

"Yes, I agree." Kiara nodded before staring up at the sky.

I turned my own gaze to the moon, my chest squeezing, but I smiled gracefully, excusing myself. Although the girls had helped me, and I was able to sleep at night... the pain lingered. Nothing they did could take away the pain of Rafael's loss. No matter how much time passed. I placed a hand on my chest, wondering if those who had passed were really looking down upon us. I didn't want to lose hope as I stared at the moon.

I will always need you... your dove will always need you...

I closed my eyes, letting a wave of calmness wash over me, and opened them as a single tear trickled down my cheek.

There were people you learned to live without, but Rafael was someone we would never forget. Not only me but everyone. He truly had been one of a kind...

※◎◎◎※

ALEJANDRO

We had eaten, drank, and there wasn't long now until the new year. The kids were getting impatient, asking every few minutes. I looked at my nympho. She looked fucking perfect in a silver blinged-out dress with a sweetheart neckline. If Ri was the fucking sun tonight, Kiara was the moon.

"Like this?" She was asking Azura. Azura nodded as she, Kiara, and the twins danced.

"Kiara's got moves," Azura said as she did a back flip, spinning around and almost knocking into Marcel.

"Easy there," he chuckled as she gave him an apologetic grin.

"Sorry, Mr!" She said before running back over to Kiara, who clapped.

"That was one incredible backflip!"

"What can I say? I'm Azura Westwood, queen of crazy," she said with a toss of her hair. I smirked. At least she fucking knew that.

With each passing year, I saw Indigo more and more in her, but she was different. If Indigo had been a spark, Azura was an entire fucking firework. Something told me she was going to be a force to reckon with when she was older.

I tried not to stare at Kiara's thighs as she danced, but, fuck, that was a mission. No matter what she was wearing, I wanted to fucking bend her over and fuck her senseless.

Marcel came over and smiled slightly as I took a drag on my cigarette.

"She is going to be a strong one, her and your little one." I knew he meant Skyla.

"Yeah, they're fucking crazy." He chuckled, nodding.

"Back then, when I witnessed Ms Amelia perform the spell... I had a feeling it would cost her her life. I had seen enough magic to know that... but she did the right thing. We need more people with that much life in them in this world." He looked at Azura with a small smile on his face.

"Yeah, I fucking agree," I said, drinking my wine. "Has he called or said if he'll be back soon?" I didn't need to say a name for him to know who I meant. He sighed heavily and shook his head.

"I'd be lucky to get a call every other month," he said gravely. "I feel as if I'm losing him. I told him to let his anger go, and, well, he's let it go to a point where it's like I'm talking to a wall. He just... I don't know."

I frowned. Yeah, Leo hadn't been taking my calls either for months now, but I didn't want to tell Marcel that.

"I haven't talked to him in a while either..."

The last time was when he had said he wondered if ex-rogues would be treated well in this school that I was building, saying he doubted anything I did would bridge the difference between the ranks and status of our kind.

The first school was almost completed, and there would be a certain number of children from all packs who would attend. I wanted it to be fair and hoped that we could get started on the second school soon enough.

"Well, tonight is not a time to worry about him. Let's enjoy the evening. It's almost time," he said, glancing at his watch. I nodded as he walked off, and Kiara came over to me.

"Everything okay?" She asked softly, placing her hand on my chest before kissing me softly.

"Yeah, perfectly. We still got some time. Let's go for a walk." She nodded, and I took her hand.

In the darkness, I was her guidance. The confidence in how she walked into the darkness, one would fucking think she could see, but it was her trust in me, knowing I wouldn't let her fall. A long fucking time ago, I feared she'd drown in my darkness, but instead, she fucking walked into my life and lit it ablaze with light. She would always be my fucking light. She turned and smiled up at me as the music faded slightly. We walked slowly, hand in hand, further away.

"I'm glad we came here this year. It's a nice change," she said with a smile gracing her hot pink lips, the same shade or very similar to what she had worn at that mating ball years ago. I kissed her shoulder softly.

"Yeah, it's nice not having to head the entire shit and be the fucking host," I remarked, making her laugh.

"You are always perfectly hospitable, my love," she said, amused, and rested her head on my shoulder as she looked through the tree branches at the sky. "Can you see the stars?" I glanced up at the night sky. Despite the clouds, I could see the twinkling stars shine through.

"Yeah. It's not too cloudy tonight."

"Hmm, that's good. I'm sure it looks beautiful," she said, softly staring at the moon.

I smiled slightly. If I could, I'd give my sight to her. She never let on or ever felt like she wished she could see in the dark. She was always just grateful for everything.

"Nowhere near as fucking beautiful as you," I replied quietly. "You ain't missing out. They don't fucking hold anything to you." She stopped and turned towards me, raising our entwined hands to her lips and kissing my knuckles softly.

"I know I'm not missing out because I have you," she whispered softly, looking up into my glowing eyes.

KIARA

He scoffed, smirking,

"You're the light, Amore Mio, not me."

"You are wrong because the way I see you is no less. You are my light in every darkness. You are my sun and my moon combined, the guidance through my life. My support in the darkest of hours and my beacon of hope when all feels lost," I said softly as I caressed his jaw, his stubble prickling my fingertips. He wrapped his arms around me and pulled me close.

"I won't fucking argue with you tonight because as long as you alone think that, it's enough for me," he replied softly, staring into my eyes, his glowing ones holding a thousand emotions. I smiled.

"I'm not the only one. Our children adore you. All the children do. You are so good towards everyone."

"That's your doing, I got soft and shit."

I laughed as he buried his nose in my neck, inhaling deeply just as I heard someone shouting that it was almost time.

"Come on, let's head back," he said, slipping his hand around my waist and leading me back the way we had come.

"I have to admit you aren't wrong there, but you have come so far. Been at the front of every battle, leading our people and giving them hope," I said softly. He really was perfect.

We fell into a serene silence as we walked out from the trees, and once again, I could see. Looking around, I saw Dante hug the twins, pointing to the sky as they prepared to let off the first of the fireworks.

We had been through a lot in life, but in the end, we prospered and came out victorious despite every challenge that was created to destroy us. Bonds, unity, trust, and love were our strengths; it was these values and strengths that helped conquer all, values we would teach our children.

"These pups are our future," he said quietly, almost as if he knew what was on my mind. I nodded, tilting my head up to look at him.

"Our legacies," I whispered softly as I reached up and cupped the back of his neck just as the countdown began.

"Three... two..."

But he only had eyes for me, his queen.

"I love you, my king," I said softly.

"Love you fucking more," he replied huskily as the fireworks exploded above us, illuminating the night sky just as his lips met mine in an explosion far more intense than a thousand fireworks.

Until the fucking end of time.

THE END

The Alpha Series may be over, but it is definitely not the end of this journey... Alpha Leo and the Heart of Fire, the first book in the spin-off series will be coming to Kindle and Print soon. Sneak Peak below!

Alpha Leo
and the
Heart of Fire

AZURA

I STARE AT THE GUN, trying to think of how I got here… but I don't know when I fell into this toxic relationship. I'm not someone who needs sympathy. I've never been one who can't sleep at night because of my demons. I'm always carefree, unbothered, and wild. I love to have fun and crush on the good-looking boys in my class or whatever hot Alpha crosses my path. But now… I find myself tossing and turning, trying to push away the nightmares my so-called boyfriend has pulled me into.

"Please, come on, let's forget this." I try to shrug it off, wrapping my arms around his neck and hoping he listens. His scent fills my nose, mixed with the smell of cigarettes and drugs. His hands stroke my waist, and I try to remember the man I fell in love with. Where has he gone?

"Forget what? Oh, yeah, forget what he called you? Let me rephrase that, little pet. You don't want to be an outcast, do you? The outsider… the odd one out… the freak?" His tone is a cold sneer as his eyes burn into mine.

Freak.

My heart thumps as I stare at the bloody wolf on the ground.

I'm not a freak. I am Azura Rayne Westwood, daughter of the previous Alpha of the Blood Moon Pack. Even though I'm a child born in a way that played with the very laws of nature, I'm not a freak.

I should be dead, but I'm not.

"Freak. Freak. Freak," his men begin to chant, only making the anger rise within me. He smirks, knowing it's getting to me, making me yank away from his hold. My heart thumps violently as I snatch the weapon from his hand.

I remember when I was a child, I didn't understand why I was disliked. Occasionally there were kids in the pack whispering behind my back, but they didn't dare to do anything to me because I am the daughter of their Alpha. Plus, I was not someone to mess with. I always made anyone who tried to hurt me or those I loved suffer.

However, there is one name that never left me - The Freak.

"Do it."

I look at my boyfriend. He knows I hate that term, but he still uses it. It's my fault. I'm the one who was blind enough to tell him my darkest secrets.

"Fine." I spit as I turn, pretending to do his bidding and raise the gun. What should I do?

"Shoot him, baby." His quiet voice, laced with a deadly warning, comes from right behind me.

My hand shakes as I stare at the whimpering wolf on the floor. His breathing is so shallow...

No amount of logic makes this okay. I am not going to do this, but the urge to turn around and shoot my so-called boyfriend instead tempts me.

I lower my weapon, the laughter fading as a tense silence falls at my act of disobedience.

"I'm not going -"

I gasp when something knocks into me from behind, making me accidentally pull the trigger. The body on the ground shivers before it stills.

"No!" I scream, dropping the gun, as I run to the wolf's side. No, no, no!

Laughter follows me as I look at the wolf before me. I can't feel his heartbeat, but he doesn't even shift to his human form. Whatever those bullets contain is deadly. It is so fast that he couldn't even shift back.

"Why, Judah?" I scream.

Silence falls as I glare at the man who stands there, his cold eyes on me. Although he says nothing, the anger in his eyes makes my blood run cold. He hates to be disrespected.

"You do not talk to me like that," he whispers menacingly as he strides over to me. Grabbing a fistful of the wolf's bloody fur, he lifts his body from the ground in one sweep. "You did this." With those words, he throws the heavy body of the dead wolf on top of me, the weight crushing my legs. "Do you feel sorry for him? Here, take care of him!" He snarls as I glare back at him. My anger rises as I try to push the body of the wolf off me. "Who said you can get up, my pet?"

"This is not a joke! I'm done with you and your sick ways," I spit resentfully. He's no different from all of the others. In fact, he's worse. His eyes darken, and he grabs a fistful of my hair.

"Oh, we aren't done until I say we are," he snarls menacingly.

"You don't own me, and I am not your pet!" I hiss, glaring at him in defiance.

He simply laughs loudly as if my childish words amuse him, but I know better. He is beyond angry; I have just disrespected him in front of his men. He won't forgive that.

"Yeah, I will. I'm done with you," I spit, my heart pounding with rage.

He tugs my head back violently, and, using the hand that he had grabbed the wolf with, he rubs the blood over my face before shoving me roughly onto the ground.

"I think it's time I show you exactly whom you belong to," he spits as he hits me across the face, making my vision darken...

ALEJANDRO

KIARA

Danté

Skyla

Kataleya

OTHER WORKS

THE ALPHA SERIES
Book 1 – Her Forbidden Alpha
Book 2 – Her Cold-Hearted Alpha
Book 3 – Her Destined Alpha
Book 4 – Caged between the Beta & Alpha
Book 5 – King Alejandro: The Return of Her Cold-Hearted Alpha

THE ROSSI LEGACIES (SPIN-OFF SERIES TO THE ALPHA SERIES)
Book 1 – Alpha Leo and the Heart of Fire
Book 2 - Leo Rossi: The Rise of a True Alpha
Book 3 – The Lycan Princess and the Temptation of Sin
Book 4 – Skyla Rossi: A Game of Deception and Lies

THE UNTOLD TALES OF THE ALPHA AND LEGACIES SERIES
A collection of short novellas.
Book 1 – Beautiful Bond
Book 2 – Precious Bond

MAGIC OF KAELADIA SERIES
Book 1 – My Alpha's Betrayal: Burning in the Flames of his Vengeance
Book 2 – My Alpha's Retribution: Rising from the Ashes of his Vengeance

OBSESSION SERIES
His Dark Obsession
His Fated Obsession

STANDALONES
His Caged Princess
Mr. CEO, Please Marry My Mommy

THE RUTHLESS KING'S TRILOGY
Book 1 – The Alpha King's Possession
Book 2 – The Dragon King's Seduction (Coming 2023)
Book 3 – The Fae King's Redemption (Coming 2024)

SOCIAL MEDIA PLATFORMS

Instagram: Author.Muse
Facebook: Author Muse

AUTHORS SUPPORTING AUTHORS

Jessica Hall – Sinful Mates (Kindle)
Cassandra M – Beneath Her Darkness: The Alpha's Little Demon (Good-Novel App)

Printed in Great Britain
by Amazon

39581251R00334